MATILDA'S STORY

A Biographical Novel

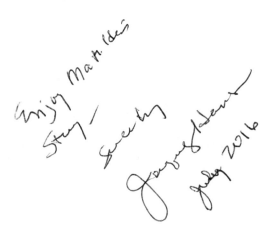

MATILDA'S STORY

A Biographical Novel

by Jacquelyn Hanson

Glenhaven Press   Modesto — 1997

MATILDA'S STORY
A Biographical Novel

by Jacquelyn Hanson

Published by:

GLENHAVEN PRESS
24871 Pylos Way
Mission Viejo, CA 92691

First Edition

First Printing — August, 1997

2   3   4   5

Publisher's Cataloging in Publication Data
Hanson, Jacquelyn,
Matilda's Story — A Biographical Novel

Bibliography: p.

1. Biographical novel based on the life of Matilda Randolph.
2. Frontier life, Local History—Illinois, Kansas, California. 3.
Wars—Bleeding Kansas, Civil. 4. Gold rush, Wagon trains—
Oregon-California Trail. 5. Genealogy—Gardner and Elizabeth
Ann Randolph and descendants.

Library of Congress Catalog Card Number: 97-73356
                    Hardcover   ISBN   0-9637265-3-6
                    Paperback   ISBN   0-9637265-4-4

Typeset with PTI LaTeX
Font: ITC Souvenir Light
Cover Art by Studio II

Dedication

This book is dedicated to the memory of my mother, Ruth Partridge Shellenbarger, whose diligent research and careful preservation of the family history made "Matilda's Story" possible.

Note from the Author

Matilda's Story is a biographical novel, for I have used some fictional episodes and a few fictional characters to bring the story to life. But the essential story is true. Fictional episodes are based on true life personal accounts. For historical background, I have used early local histories, personal diaries, property tax records, census reports, voter records, early newspaper accounts and the like.

Matilda's Story covers thirty years in the life of my great-grandmother, Matilda Randolph, following her as she grows to maturity during a very tumultuous time in American history. It is history as seen through the eyes of one young woman as she struggled to survive and make a better life for her children.

I have received invaluable assistance from the historical societies in Bloomington, Illinois, Manhattan, Kansas, Lovelock, Nevada, and Galt, Sacramento, and Placerville, California. The Oregon-California Trail Association, especially Tom Mahach, proved an excellent source for information on the trail.

I am almost afraid to start naming individuals, for there are so many I fear I will inadvertently omit someone. I must, however, thank my brother, Ed Shellenbarger, who accompanied me on the long trek to follow Matilda's trail from Illinois to Sacramento.

In Kansas, I am indebted to Wally Johnson, Mrs. R.W. Jacks, the late Hooker Boles, and Fossey Rayburn, a descendant of Henry Shellenbaum.

Franklin Dyer and Ruth Green, descendants of Sam Dyer, provided me with the memoirs of Sarah Dyer and other invaluable information on the Dyers.

Phil and Barbara Hale provided me with local knowledge and expertise on the history of Salt Lake City, and Barbara was my technical expert on Mormonism.

Madelyn Valensin, who helped preserve much early Hicksville history, has been a great help. My fellow members of the

Saddleback Writers Guild patiently critiqued the manuscript, page after page, with never a complaint. Shelba Robison, my writing instructor at Saddleback College, taught me the basics and encouraged me to follow my dream of seeing *Matilda's Story* in print.

And I must also thank my two sons, Mark and Jayson, for their often uncomprehending but never failing support.

Jacquelyn Hanson

Mission Viejo, August 1997

Matilda's Story
Prologue

Early in January of 1822, accompanied by his wife, Betsy Ann, and toddlers Britt and Temperance, Gardner Randolph arrived at an Indian campground on the banks of the Kickapoo River. The cart, pulled by Gardner's favorite pie-bald mare, contained their household goods. They had left the swampy land surrounding the Sangamon River because Gardner wished to protect his family from the constant threat of malaria, declaring he was "going north until I get stuck in a snow bank or freeze my nose!".

The wagon with them, pulled by two wild-eyed steers, carried Betsy Ann's sister Delilah and her husband, James Burleson.

Gardner, always at ease with Indians, made his new home among the wigwams of the Kickapoo. He built an open-faced camp, three walls open to the south. The fire formed the fourth wall and Randolph's Grove, the first white settlement in what would become McLean County, Illinois, was an accomplished fact.

The little community thrived. The Hendrix and Dawson families arrived the following May and settled a few miles to the north in what would become the city of Bloomington. In December of 1822, Gardner and Betsy Ann's second son, William, became the first white child born in the area. Their Kickapoo neighbors proved very friendly. In fact, they often spent the night in front of the Randolph fire. Since they made it a practice to enter without knocking, the youngest Randolph greeted the world in a brand new twelve foot square cabin with a solid door that boasted a bar to prevent visitors from entering unexpectedly.

In 1823, Betsy Ann's family joined them. Her father had died of malaria about the time Gardner built his first camp on the Kickapoo River, but her mother, Sarah Boydston Stringfield, her sister Fanny, and her brothers A.M. and Sevier decided they, too, had tired of battling the swamps of the Sangamon.

As the community grew, so did the Randolph family. Sarah followed William, in 1824. Thomas joined them in 1826, Samuel in 1828, and Alfred in 1830.

In 1825, in response to the increasing size of his family, Gardner built a spacious two room-cabin. He borrowed a whip saw from Springfield and made real boards for the doors and windows. He also added a sturdy table, a cupboard, and a free-standing bed, all rare luxuries in frontier homes. The original cabin thereafter served as a smokehouse.

After the winter of the 'Deep Snow' in 1830-1831, the Blackhawk Wars broke out with the Sauk and Fox tribes. John Sevier Randolph was born in 1832, during the unrest. After the war, the State of Illinois confiscated all of the Indian land in the state, driving out even the friendly and peaceful Kickapoo, Delaware, Pottawatamie, and Winnebago Indians.

In 1831, the City of Bloomington was founded, and made the county seat of the newly formed McLean County. Gardner became active in local politics, as a member of the Grand Jury and as a road commissioner for two districts. By the time of Caroline Randolph's birth in 1834, the rush to settle central Illinois was on.

On July 21, 1836, during the hottest summer any of the residents of the little community of Randolph's Grove could remember, Matilda Virginia Randolph was born. Matilda, of course, did not remember her birth. Her first memory, the one that never left her, was the birth of her brother Sinclair. And so, during the winter of 1839, *Matilda's Story* began.

Matilda's Story

BOOK I   ILLINOIS
1839 to 1854

BOOK II   KANSAS
1854 to 1864

BOOK III   THE TRAIL
May to September 1864

BOOK IV   CALIFORNIA
1864 to 1867

Chapter 1

1839-1843

"He's so little!" Matilda's breath formed misty clouds in the cold air on the frigid January day of Sinclair's birth. The icy wind howled down across the northern plains, driving a blinding wall of white against the log walls of the Randolph cabin. Snow piled against the window blocked what little light crept around the boards nailed on the outside to protect the oiled paper.

Matilda's sister Sarah had ushered in the wide-eyed little girl to see the new baby brother asleep beside their mother. Very little of the heat from the fireplace in the main room penetrated the tiny cubicle where Betsy Ann Randolph lay.

The big, free-standing bed took up most of the space. The commode, a pitcher and tin basin on the top shelf, the chamber pot below, stood in one corner. A battered trunk occupied another corner. The small tallow candle that flickered in its holder on top of the trunk only slightly dispelled the gloom.

But Matilda paid no attention to the room. Her eyes fastened on the tiny bundle in her mother's arms. She fondled the damp thatch of blond hair on the baby's head, and marveled at the miniature fingers and toes, briefly unbundled for her inspection. The infant's tiny hand wrapped around her thumb, forming a bond between brother and sister that would last a lifetime.

Displaced from her parents' bed by Sinclair's arrival, Matilda joined her sisters Caroline and Sarah in the fold-down bed in the main room. Alf and John slept in the loft above their heads, while Will, Tom, and Sam stretched out on the floor in front of the huge, stone fireplace, lying on home-cured deerskin rugs, snuggled under warm quilts.

The long winter evenings shared with her sisters in the big bed became some of Matilda's fondest memories. Sarah always told scary stories, making them gasp and squeal until their father demanded silence. Then the giggles would die down to a quiet broken only by the howling of the wind and the crackling of the fire.

Matilda's favorite tales were those her sister Temperance related of experiences with the Indians. The Indians had been gone since before Matilda's birth, driven away after the Blackhawk Wars, but Temperance and Will remembered them very well.

When Matilda was two, Temperance had married Josh Tovrea, the same year her brother Britt married Sarah Evans. A month after Matilda's fifth birthday, Temperance came and stayed a week to help Betsy Ann after the birth of their baby sister, Minerva. Each night, as soon as their father snuffed the candles, Matilda and Caroline begged Temperance to tell stories of when the Indians lived nearby.

Temperance always obliged. She loved to talk about the Kickapoo and Delaware Indians she remembered so well. She told them how Old Machina, the Kickapoo chief, would carry her and stroke her hair.

"He called it the color of the sun," she said. "You'd never know to look at it now, but my hair used to be very fair." Temperance held one of the dark tresses up to the moonlight streaming through the doorway. The door and the windows were open to capture as much as possible of the night breeze. "He fought with the British against the settlers in 1812 and I guess they never paid him what they promised. That's what he claimed, anyway. He swore he would never fight again, for anyone. He kept his word and stayed out of the Blackhawk Wars. He was a wonderful old man. Everyone missed him after he joined his ancestors."

Then she laughed. "It made Mother furious whenever the Kickapoo stole a pig or a chicken, but they never saw anything wrong with it. It was all done in the spirit of neighborliness."

"Pa didn't get mad?" Matilda still stood in awe of her father.

"Pa never cared. Mother always said it was his Indian blood." Temperance chuckled. "I don't think Mother half believes the story that he's a descendant of Pocahontas, but he swears it's true. Claims that crazy John Randolph of Roanoke was a cousin of his."

"But Pocahontas lived hundreds of years ago," Alf contributed, leaning so far out over the edge of the loft Matilda feared he would tumble down on top of them. Eleven-year-old Alf, the studious one, read every book he could find and often cited quotations to impress his siblings with his wisdom. As usual, they ignored him.

Will added, "And old Mrs. Templeton complained all the time because the Indian children ran around naked when they played with us." His voice dropped to a whisper. "She thought it was scandalous."

Temperance giggled. "Even more so when Pa told her," she dropped her voice and mimicked, " 'It's just their way, and in this heat, I think they have the right of it.' Mother said she thought Mrs. T. would have an attack of apoplexy."

That sent them all into gales of laughter and a roar from their father demanding silence ended the story telling for the evening.

The following night, when begged to tell another Indian tale, Temperance thought for a moment, then shook with laughter. Everyone lay on top of the quilts. No one could sleep in the stifling heat of the cabin.

"I've told you how a dozen or more often slept on the floor in front of the fireplace," she said when she caught her breath. Her voice dropped to a stage whisper. "Will! Remember the night Pa stepped on one?"

"I'll say. How could I forget?"

"Tell us, tell us!" a chorus of voices demanded.

"I can't remember which tribe." Temperance frowned in concentration. "Tom was just a baby. Probably Kickapoo." She brushed the dark hair back from her forehead. "Anyway, we were still in the first cabin, so there wasn't much room."

Taking a deep breath, she continued. "Pa never liked to use the chamber pot unless snow blocked the path, so he had to make a trip to the outhouse in the middle of the night." She paused. Her audience remained silent. "He had to step over the Indians to get to the door. I guess he tried to step over two at once."

Tom laughed out loud.

"Shh!" A chorus of whispers shushed him.

"You'll wake up Pa," Sarah said in a fierce whisper.

"Anyway," Temperance continued, "he wound up stepping on one. The one he stepped on kind of rolled under his feet, and Pa fell on top of them all. The one the candle landed on yelped when the hot tallow hit him, and they all started yelling at once. That woke up everyone."

"All the shouting scared you, Tom," Will put in, "and you started to scream at the top of your lungs. Mother hopped off the bed in her nightgown and hollered at everyone to be quiet. She was mad at them all for waking up Tom." Will tried in vain to choke back his laughter. "Mother's patience with the Indians never went as far as Pa's. She threatened to take the broom to all of them, including Pa, if they didn't stop yelling, and ...." He looked up and stopped mid-sentence. All eyes followed his in the instant silence.

In the doorway stood Gardner Randolph, an impressive

figure in spite of the bare ankles below the nightshirt. The flickery light from the tallow candle glowed around him, the shadows making eerie patterns on his face.

Gardner looked from one silent face to the other, then burst into laughter.

Behind him, Betsy Ann's voice spoke. "For Heaven's sake, Gardner, hush! You'll wake the babe."

After the story-telling sessions, they drifted off to sleep, one after the other. Matilda liked to lie awake and watch the fire, fascinated by the patterns the red and gold flames formed as they crept around the logs. As long as she could remember, she fell asleep long after everyone else. Many times during those early years she regretted the Indians had been driven away. She wished she could have known them.

As Matilda grew older, the red curls darkened to a light brown with red highlights. One day in the summer of 1842, the week before she turned six, she went blackberry picking along the river with her older siblings. Not a breath of wind stirred the leaves on the trees in the humid air of the hot July day. Masses of the plump, juicy berries hung from the bushes, and Matilda eagerly filled her little basket.

Her brother Will, assigned to watch the younger children, flopped down in the shade of a hickory tree by the river-bank. "It's too hot," he complained. "Call me when your baskets are full." Seeking relief from the oppressive heat, he opened the front of his shirt to catch the slight breeze wafting off the river.

"Will," Matilda gasped, pointing to the heavy scar that stretched from one side of his abdomen to the other. "What's that black line?" She dropped to her knees beside him and gave the scar a tentative poke. "Can't you wash it off?"

He laughed. "You'll have to ask Temperance. She tells the story better than anyone." He refused to say any more in spite of her entreaties, so Matilda returned to her berry picking, forcing herself to contain her curiosity until Temperance returned.

Temperance had borne her first child the previous week, so a month passed before her sister arrived for another visit. Matilda immediately posed her question about Will's scar.

"Yes, that is quite a tale," Temperance smiled. "Let me get Sarah to sleep first."

"Now, Matilda," Betsy Ann said, a worried frown creasing her brow, "you let your sister catch her breath. She looks plumb tuckered out from the trip over here."

"It's not just the trip, Mother," Temperance sighed. "I seem to have trouble getting my strength back. And it's the worry, too. We lost money when the Illinois State Bank collapsed. Josh's mother has a letter at the Post Office from her sister in Ohio and she can't even come up with the eighteen cents she needs to get it out."

Betsy Ann shook her head. "I know. Had to pay a whole quarter for a letter Delilah sent me from down in Texas. But I paid, as I was real anxious to read it, Jim being a Texas Ranger and all. Some sort of trouble's brewing down there. All those Americans that got their independence from Mexico back in '36 want Texas to apply for statehood."

"So what's the matter with that?"

"Mexico has never recognized Texas as an independent country. Says it's just a rebellious province of Mexico. Say they'll declare war on the United States if Congress admits Texas to the Union." Betsy Ann grinned. "Delilah explained it all, in page after page. That's why I had to pay so much for the letter."

"Let Mexico have it," Temperance laughed. "From what I understand, it's a just a whole lot of rattlesnakes and sagebrush. Certainly not worth having a war over." She dismissed Texas with a casual wave of her hand and returned to the bank failure. "The Funks are going to come out all right. I hear Uncle Isaac bought a whole lot of land the bank took back from folks as couldn't pay their mortgage. So many folks have left he got the land for thirty-seven and a half cents on the dollar."

"Isaac learned not to trust 'em after the United States Bank suspended payments back in the spring of '37," Betsy Ann said. "He couldn't get his money out for the longest time. Now he hoards it in little sacks all around the house. Fanny says Jesse's always teasing him, telling him he's forgotten where he put half of it."

Temperance chuckled. "If a thief got in, he probably couldn't find it either."

"Gardner has never trusted banks or bankers," Betsy Ann added, "so we didn't really lose any cash money. But a lot of folks did, so it's been tough for everyone. Had to take the wheat clear to Chicago to sell it, then didn't get anywhere's near a decent price for it. Sevier says a lot of folks didn't even get enough to pay for the trip. Prices were almost as bad as in '33 when we only got ten cents a bushel for corn." She smiled. "But '33 wasn't all bad, in spite of only gettin' a dollar and a quarter per hundred for hogs. That was the year we got our own Post Office here in Randolph's Grove and didn't have to go to Bloomington for mail any more."

Matilda had no interest in Post Offices or banks or how rich her Uncle Isaac was going to be. She wanted to know about Will's scar. But she knew better than to interrupt. She waited with all the patience she could muster while Temperance nursed one-month-old Sarah, then tucked her into the tiny cradle and rocked it until the infant drifted off to sleep.

"Now," she turned to Matilda, "let's sit out under a tree where it's cooler." Temperance still looked tired. Her face did not have its usual color, and her eyes lacked the sparkle Matilda remembered.

Caroline joined them, as did Matilda's best friend

Agatha Templeton. All of the children loved Temperance's stories, and the three little girls settled down on the soft grass to listen. They sucked on pieces of rock candy, their faces already showing signs of the sticky confection.

Temperance paused, her eyes, with a faraway look, fixed on a spot over Matilda's head. The sunlight through the trees patterned her face. Their brother Tom plowed between the rows of corn in a nearby field and the creak of the harness harmonized with the twitter of birds in the trees.

"Happened just after Blackhawk started creating problems, when Will was about nine," Temperance began. "Everyone was a little on edge during that time anyway. I remember Mr. Orendorff sent Pa and one of the Dawsons, John, I think, as a delegation to both the Delaware and the Kickapoo. Pa always got along so well with the Indians that Mr. Orendorff felt they would confide in him. The chiefs all assured Pa they had no plans to go on the warpath in defense of the Sauks and Foxes, but folks still feared there might be trouble. All the Indians admired Blackhawk, but I guess they didn't want the soldiers after them.

"Pa had sent Britt to start mowin' the hay. Mother and I were making bread and had flour all over our hands. Just as I picked up Mother's favorite big wooden bowl to set the dough in for risin', Tom busted in cryin', 'Mama, Mama, come quick. Britt hit Will with the scythe!'

"I dropped the bowl. You should'a heard the noise when it hit the floor. Split right in two, it did." Temperance paused in her recital for a moment. Her listeners did not move. "I thought, it's killed him. It *has* to have killed him. Pa always kept that huge blade honed razor sharp. But the neighbors always said you can't kill a Randolph. I guess they were right.

"Mother gathered her skirts and headed for the door on a run, me right behind her. Sarah just sat at the table gaping. I hollered back at her to take care o' Sam and Alf. Alf was just a baby, barely walking. We ran after Tom, back towards the field.

"We met them coming to meet us. Will walked real slow, holding his middle, with Britt helping him. When we got closer, we could see Will's insides bulging around their hands, with blood running down his front. Scared me to death. I'd never seen so much blood. Mother, of course, took charge at once and made Will lie down. She covered that awful wound with a cloth and bound it up tight to keep his insides in." Temperance shuddered at the memory. "And to stop the blood. I started to cry. Mother just told me to stop blubbering and get back and tend the little ones. Scared them out of their wits, all of us runnin' out on 'em like that.

"When I turned and started back to the house, she yelled after me, 'And clear up the mess where you dropped that bowl!' " Temperance shook her head. "Imagine her thinking of that broken bowl! Anyways, they got Will back to the house by making a cradle of their arms. When Mother took the bandage off, we saw how bad it was." She closed her eyes for a moment and took a deep breath. "The cut slashed all the way across Will's middle. I'd seen pigs and chickens butchered. I knew what insides looked like.

"Once a neighbor man shot himself in the stomach. Everyone said he died because the bullet tore a hole through his insides. I knew if the scythe cut Will's insides, he would die for sure. Mother started issuing orders. She sent me for fresh water, and Tom for her darning basket. Since Sarah just stood there bawling, she told her to run over to Aunt Delilah's so's someone could go get Pa."

Temperance smiled at Matilda. "You never got to meet your Aunt Delilah. She and Uncle Jim moved back to 'Bama in '35. Got tired of both farming and snow. Uncle Jim joined the Texas Rangers and they went into Texas. He fought with the Rangers in the Texas war for independence from Mexico in '36. Anyway," she continued with her story,

"Mother told Britt to find a stick of wood, whittle one end clean, then hold it in the fire to char. All the time Britt kept babbling, 'He came from nowhere, Mother. I didn't see him or hear him. He will be all right, won't he?' He just kept going on and on. 'Tell me you can fix him, Mother. Please tell me you can fix him.'

"Of course, he felt terrible for nearly killing Will, but I just wanted him to shut up. Mother had her face set with that look she gets.

"Lucky thing Will had fainted. Mother washed the wound and eased the whole mass back inside him. I just stood there shaking, holding the basin of water. After she finished washing, she took Britt's stick of wood and applied the hot, sooty end to the edges of the skin. That's why the scar is so black. From the soot." She laughed softly at the expressions on the young faces before her. "First she sewed the muscle, then she pulled the sides of the skin together and sewed him up with her favorite darning needle and home-spun cotton thread. Even though Will stayed unconscious, he jerked whenever she poked that big needle through the edges of his skin." Temperance shivered. "I can still hear that sound, a kind of a popping noise. Felt it every time she pushed the needle through.

"It took a long time, 'cause the cut went clear across his middle. It's a wonder Britt didn't cut him in two. Mother said it was lucky Will wore his jacket that morning. That tough homespun took a lot of the blow. Had he been wearin' just a shirt . . . ." Temperance shook her head. "Anyway, when she finally finished, she washed off the blood and put on a bandage of clean linsey cloth. Pa arrived home about then, and says, 'Dear Betsy, ever the doctor. Thank the good Lord you knew what to do.'

"Mother told him the bowel didn't look to be cut, but Will could still die if the soot didn't keep the wound from festering." Temperance paused to catch her breath, then laughed. "Pa asked Mother if she wanted him to send to Springfield for Dr. Todd. He was the closest doctor in those days. Dr. Karr didn't come to Bloomington until '35. Mother, as firm a follower of Samuel Thomson then as now, told him absolutely not. She says all doctors ever do is purge and bleed, which would only make Will weaker. Her opinion of doctors has never changed.

"Pa just smiled and said, 'As you wish, my dear. We will leave it in God's hands.' That scared me more than the wound, so I said, 'I'll make him well. Tell me what to do.' She told me we had to keep him quiet so he didn't start bleeding inside. Then she ordered everyone to get back to work.

"When Will woke up, Mother fixed him some chamomile tea laced with catnip for the pain. She also gave him some of that vile Number Six concoction she makes so he would sweat real good. 'Get him to take as much water as you can, Temperance,' Mother told me. 'He's lost a lot of blood.' The next morning, we started the hot comfrey poultices." Temperance laughed. "You know Mother and her comfrey poultices. We put them on the wound three times every day.

"Fever set in the third day. Went right out of his head, he did. Kept trying to get out of bed, sayin' he had to get water for Mother. She'd sent him for water just before he got hurt, and I guess it was on his mind. In fact, he wasn't supposed to be in the field at all. Only way we could keep him quiet was to give him more catnip. That seemed to ease him." Temperance shifted her legs under her. "Foot's going to sleep," she grimaced. "You've kept me here talking too long."

"Didn't the wound fester?" Matilda asked, wanting to know more, concerned that Temperance showed signs of having finished her story.

"Fortunately, no. It looked terrible to me, all red and puffy, but Mother kept sayin' it was healing fine. I spent hours putting cool cloths on his head for the fever, and urging him to drink water and fruit juices and more of the chamomile tea. I even got so's I could make the comfrey poultices by myself, steeping the fresh leaves in boiling water and soaking the cloth."

She rose to her feet. "I just hope he appreciated it," she said with a wicked chuckle. "I think he forgot pretty fast, for just a few months later he told Billy Dawson I was sweet on him, when I really detested him. I had Billy hanging around for weeks until I finally convinced him it was just Will's idea of a joke and a bad one at that."

The first snow of the following winter, the season of 1842 to 1843, fell on November 10, a month earlier than usual.

"Going to be a long winter," Tom grumbled, to no one in particular, brushing the snow off his jacket as he entered the cabin. He dumped the armload of chopped wood he carried beside the fireplace. "Hope we've got enough wood to last."

"Got plenty of stores," Betsy Ann replied, displaying her usual serenity. "Been through long winters before."

Matilda smiled. To the younger children, winter meant a break from chores and long evenings filled with stories. She gave no thought to such things as running out of wood or food supplies.

In March, the thaw started, and it looked like winter would finally break its hold on the land. Gardner, with the help of Sam and Tom, began preparations to plant as soon as the ground dried enough to plow.

"At least it never got as deep as the winter of the deep snow," Betsy Ann commented.

"When was that?" Alf asked.

"Winter of '30 to '31," Will replied. "Right after you were born."

"The winter Pa spent in bed with the fever," Sarah added.

"Yes," Betsy Ann said, "and John Moore, bless his heart, came over and pounded hominy for us all winter. Had just got here to Randolph's Grove from over Ohio way. Don't know what I'd 'a done without him, me with a batch of young-uns like I had. Britt was only twelve."

"How deep did it get?" Matilda asked, her eyes wide.

"Seen the trees cut off fifteen feet above the ground?" Sam laughed. "That's how deep."

"And remember the freeze in December that started it off?" Sarah shivered. "It froze so fast the chickens had their feet frozen to the ground."

"Go on!" Matilda scoffed. "That can't be so."

"Oh, yes, it can," Will said. "I remember watching the wind blow the water into ripples that froze solid. Went from mild to below zero in no time at all. Two hours later, the creek had ice thick enough to hold a man's weight." He chuckled. "And Uncle Sevier and Jesse Funk got caught driving hogs to Galena. Uncle Jim was with 'em, too, if I remember right. Like to never made it."

"Well, I, for one, am glad to see winter over," Sarah declared. "November through March is long enough."

But winter had not yet run its course. On the morning of April 20, Matilda looked out to see white flakes once more drifting to the ground. As a result, no one could plant until almost the end of May. They planted the wheat first, then the corn. Fortunately, the weather subsequently turned benign, and even though the corn did not get planted until June, it grew prodigiously.

When Betsy Ann commented on the phenomena, Gardner replied, "God sent the snow, so He knew He had to make the corn grow faster."

That ended the discussion. Tom shook his head. "Well, I sure hope God lets this stand as the record for the longest winter in the history of McLean County."

Chapter 2

Summer, 1843

*T*HE SUMMER of 1843, shortly after Matilda's seventh birthday, death touched her directly for the first time. When Mary Templeton arrived with her medical bag, the children knew a new arrival would be joining the family. Gardner hustled them out of the house and they huddled under the apple tree to speculate on whether the new baby would be a boy or a girl.

"We really need another girl," Matilda announced to Sinclair. "Already too many boys in this family."

"No more girls," Sinclair responded. "I want a boy. John and Tom are too old. They won't play with me."

"Hush," their father's voice silenced them. "Be satisfied with a healthy babe, boy or girl."

The door opened and Mary Templeton gestured to Gardner. Something in her face made Matilda's heart miss a beat. No one moved until Gardner reappeared. At the sight of his solemn face, Matilda's eyes widened and her heart pounded in her chest. Mother, she thought. Something has happened to Mother. Fear surged through her as she recalled other children whose mothers had died in childbirth.

"I am sorry to tell you your baby brother did not live," he said, his voice solemn, "but your mother will recover."

Matilda inhaled deeply, not realizing until then she had been holding her breath. At the time, her only thoughts were for her mother, but the next day, when she saw baby Andrew's still, white face in the tiny coffin, she felt a sense of loss she did not quite understand. A deep sadness filled her as she watched her father and brother Britt solemnly lower the little box into the grave and she wept.

The day after Andrew's funeral, the normal routine resumed. Gardner Randolph butchered a pig to replenish their stores. While he and Tom cut the meat for hams and bacon, Caroline and Matilda sliced chunks of fat from the hide to toss into the big cast-iron rendering kettle that stood on its three legs over a small fire. John stood beside this kettle, constantly stirring it with a long stick to keep the fat from burning as it slowly yielded its yellow liquid.

"Why does the fat turn yellow when it melts?" Matilda asked John.

John, his face shiny with sweat from the sweltering day and the heat of the fire, looked up and frowned at her. "What a dumb question! It just does, that's all. Who cares?"

Matilda knew John had planned to spend the day fishing with two friends. Since he had to stir the rendering kettle instead, a job he detested on the best of days, she ignored the surliness of his reply. "I just wondered, because it gets white again when it hardens," she said in a meek voice. "Ow!" she yelped as she cut her finger testing the sharpness of the knife.

"Watch what you're doing instead of asking so many questions and you won't cut yourself," said Caroline.

Matilda sucked the cut finger and glared at her sister. Matilda had begged to help, assuring her mother she really was old enough. She regretted her impulsive request, but refused to admit it, especially to Caroline who had said Matilda was too young. In spite of setting up the work table under the shade of a huge spreading oak tree, the heat of the day turned Matilda's face red. Her dress clung to her and rivulets of sweat ran down her back. The mound of fat that remained waiting to be cut into half-inch squares to feed the rendering pot never seemed to get any smaller.

She checked her finger. The bleeding from the small cut had stopped.

In silence, she resumed the tiresome chore of slicing the greasy chunks, whisking away big blue-bellied flies that gathered, along with an occasional wasp. It always amazed Matilda how the flies appeared so quickly and in such hordes. She wondered how the flies always knew when they butchered an animal, but she refrained from asking. She knew her frequent questions irritated her siblings, especially when they were already in a bad mood.

Matilda straightened up from the cutting board and rubbed her aching back, relishing the slight relief from the gentle breeze that caressed her overheated forehead. As she did, she saw a buggy coming down the lane towards the cabin, the horse's hooves stirring up clouds of dust.

"Look, Carrie," she said. "It's Aunt Amelia and Uncle A.M. Wonder what brings them out on such a hot day?"

Caroline followed Matilda's line of sight as the buggy drew closer. "Looks like Aunt Amelia's carrying a baby," she commented.

"Doesn't concern you two," John growled. "Keep carving or we'll never get this wretched stuff finished."

With a sigh, Matilda contained her curiosity and returned to cutting the slimy chunks. John grumbled under his breath as he used the horsehair sieve to skim off the rendered cracklings floating on top of the liquid fat. He piled the golden morsels in a wooden bowl that sat on a block near the fire.

Tom walked up and sampled a handful of the crisp cracklings. "Cheer up," he told John with a grin. "Be glad you don't have to make the head cheese."

Caroline laughed. "Mother says Sarah gets to do that this time. Says she needs the practice."

"I'll probably get stuck making the sausage casings, though," John complained. Matilda knew everyone tried to avoid the job of cleaning the intestines to make the sausage casings.

"Pa hears you griping you'll get the job for sure," Tom warned. He looked over the pile on the table and brushed away some of the most persistent flies. "That hog sure was fat. We'll get a lot of soap 'n' candles out of this lot."

He changed the subject. "You see Aunt Amelia carrying a baby into the house? Wonder if it's the Crose baby. Pa said the babe's mother's ailin' and Aunt Amelia's been helping her." He fanned his overheated face with his battered hat and pulled his knife from his pocket to help Caroline and Matilda finish cutting the slabs of suet. "Guess we'll find out soon enough."

An hour later, Matilda sighed with relief as she dumped the last of the slimy white material into John's pot, now nearly filled with amber liquid.

John wiped his forehead with his big, red handkerchief and grinned down at her. "Almost there, little sister," he said. "How'd you like your first experience at rendering fat? Bet you thought we'd never finish."

"Come on, 'Tilda," Caroline urged, ignoring John's comments. "Let's go and find out why Uncle A.M. is here." She headed towards the house. Matilda wiped her greasy hands on her apron and hurried after her sister.

As Matilda and Caroline entered the cabin, they saw their mother seated in her favorite rocking chair, nursing an infant. Betsy Ann greeted them with a tender smile.

"Come in, girls, and meet your cousin Weldon," she said softly. "His mother died this morning and he's going to live with us."

Matilda looked into her mother's eyes. The pain of the last few days had left, replaced by Betsy Ann's usual serenity. In spite of Matilda's young age, she realized that, in her mother's mind, the lost baby had been replaced.

Chapter 3

1844 to 1845

THE FOLLOWING SPRING, the rains began in May and continued almost daily until the end of August.

"Summer of '44 is going to be long remembered," Gardner grumbled as he sloshed into the house one hot, muggy day in July. "Hard to tell where the creeks begin and the land ends. Some places the creeks grow together and make one."

"Corn's ruined, Pa," Tom stated, sadly shaking his head. "Was gonna be a fine crop, too."

Gardner sighed. "God must have a reason for this," he opined, his voice solemn in his acceptance of whatever he thought God ordained. He hung his sodden hat on its peg and strode into the bedroom.

"Well, it better be good," Tom muttered, careful his father did not hear. Matilda, shocked by his irreverence, glanced at her mother. Betsy Ann gave no indication that she overheard Tom's comment, but something in her expression told Matilda she agreed.

For Matilda's ninth birthday, in July of 1845, her friend Agatha wove strands of grass into a small circlet and solemnly slipped it over Matilda's finger.

"We'll be friends forever," Agatha vowed.

Matilda giggled and admired the ring. "It'll just dry up and fall apart."

"No," Agatha assured her. "I made it the way Aunt Minnie taught my mother. See the tight weaving? It'll last forever."

Touched by the evidence of Agatha's loyalty, Matilda vowed, "I promise to wear it as long as I live."

Shortly after Matilda's birthday, Temperance arrived for a visit. Matilda and Agatha, helping the older boys pick blackberries from the abundance of vines growing along the banks of the Kickapoo River, saw her arrive and waved in greeting.

"Over here, Temperance," Matilda called.

Leading three-year-old Sarah by the hand, Temperance walked down to the riverbank. Glad for the chance to rest, Agatha and Matilda ran to greet them. Matilda always enjoyed Temperance's visits. Sarah had grown into a beautiful little girl, with her father's red hair and her mother's hazel eyes. Temperance still looked tired, but she seated herself in the shade of the tree, smiling at the eagerness on Matilda's face as she tenderly took Sarah's hand.

Agatha lay down on the grass while Matilda fashioned a necklace for Sarah from the flowers growing along the bank. Sarah, trying to help, kept breaking the links.

"Temperance," Matilda commented to her sister, "it's so nice here. Why did the Indians leave?" In her mind, she saw the squaws, babies strapped on their backs, picking blackberries and putting them in their colorful, woven baskets. She had seen some of the baskets. Their father kept one, a gift from the old Delaware squaw everyone had called Aunt Minnie, in a place of honor on the top shelf of the prized cupboard.

Temperance brushed back a stray lock of her long, dark hair then handed Sarah a cloth ball. She looked at Matilda and Agatha for a few moments. "They didn't want to leave," she finally said. "The soldiers drove them off."

"Drove them off? Why?" She thought of Temperance's stories of the Indians. "Because of the pigs and chickens they stole?"

Temperance shook her head, absently tossing the cloth ball back to Sarah, who cried in delight as she caught it. "No, not because of that." She hesitated, then shrugged her shoulders. "It upset Pa for a long time. He considered the Indians his friends."

In the momentary silence, a lone bird warbled in the tree above their heads. Temperance pulled a blade of grass and tore it into little pieces. "So many settlers came." She paused and took a deep breath. "They cleared the land and destroyed the hunting grounds."

Sarah interrupted, tugging on Matilda's hand. "Come on, Aunt 'Tilda. Wanna pick blackberries."

"Not now, Sarah," Matilda hushed the child. "Let's listen to your mother's story."

Temperance smiled with tears in her eyes. "Pa said maybe so many people coming finally drove even the gentle Kickapoo to the end of their patience." She slowly shook her head, her eyes troubled. "During the Blackhawk Wars, some Indians attacked a couple of settlers. The Kickapoo insisted the Sauk Indians did it. Both the Sauks and the Foxes were on the warpath at that time, so it could have been either one. We'll never know for sure."

Matilda's eyes widened in horror. "You mean they scalped people?"

"I doubt they scalped them, if it was the Kickapoo. From what I remember of Old Machina it seems unlikely. He had sworn never to fight the white man again." She sighed. "Anyway, the soldiers decided the safest way would be to chase them all away. The year after the Blackhawk Wars, the State of Illinois claimed all of the Indian land. The Winnebago went to Canada. I heard most of the Pottawatamie and the Delaware moved to the Kansas Territory. I don't know what ever happened to the Kickapoo. Probably some went to Kansas. They say some even went as far as Mexico."

The creek bubbled over the rocks, loud in the silence

that followed. Matilda savored the fragrance of fresh mown hay wafting over them. A shaft of sunlight penetrated the canopy of leaves and played over her hair, catching its red highlights. Consciously aware of the beauty that surrounded her, she grieved for the poor Indians who lost such a lovely place.

Will's voice interrupted her reverie. "Hey, lazybones! We'll never get these blackberries picked if you two lay about gossiping all afternoon."

Temperance pulled herself together. She stood up and took Sarah's hand. "Back to work, you two. I'll see you later at the house."

Sarah pulled away from her mother. "Wanna pick blackberries," she announced.

Matilda took the small hand in hers. "Go on, Temperance. Aggie and I will take good care of Sarah."

But Temperance's story bothered Matilda. She thought about it all the next day as she diligently stirred the blackberry jam that simmered in one of the two big fireplace cauldrons hanging on their trammels. The aroma filled the room and mingled with the smell of venison stew bubbling in the other pot. Wild onions added their piquant touch to the air. The never empty tea kettle hung in its place between the two big pots.

Matilda took her responsibility for the blackberry jam seriously, scowling so hard in concentration that the tip of her tongue protruded from one side of her mouth. The heat from the fire, combined with the muggy summer heat, made her hair hang in damp ringlets.

Betsy Ann entered the room and checked the jam. "Good job, Matilda. Looks done." She swung the pot out of the flame.

Matilda almost told her mother her thoughts about the Indians, but Betsy Ann bustled away to the next chore.

Matilda still did not understand. The circuit preacher always said if she was good, life would be good; that God loved all His children and cared for them. Didn't God love the Indians too? If so, why had He allowed the soldiers to drive them away? She knew the stories Temperance related were true, so the Indians had been everything Reverend Cartwright said they should be. Somehow, it just did not seem fair.

"Tom! Will!" Gardner's voice echoed. Wondering what her father wanted, Matilda paused as she stirred the chicken feathers boiling in the big cauldron on the outdoor fire.

"Yes, Pa," Tom and Will chorused back. Their father's voice brought instant obedience, as always.

"Get your horses and tell everyone Reverend Cartwright will be here this Sunday."

Matilda glanced at her mother. Betsy Ann stood hanging bags of the boiled feathers on the line to dry, her face carefully averted. Matilda smiled to herself, catching the expression on her mother's face. Betsy Ann's father, John Stringfield, had converted Gardner Randolph to Methodism, but Betsy Ann, while a Methodist herself, remained far too pragmatic to take any religion too seriously. No one, of course, ever said so to their father.

Whenever the circuit preacher came around, the meeting would always be held at the Randolph residence. Matilda had overheard her mother tell Sarah how she felt the other neighbors should be so honored once in a while.

Dispatched to the storage shed to fetch dried apples for the pies, Matilda asked Sarah, "Why does the preacher come here all the time, making all the extra work for Mother?"

Sarah grinned. "Mother says Pa, being such a good Methodist, doesn't drink whiskey or smoke or chew that vile tobacco. So she puts up with the preacher."

Matilda made up her mind to ask the Reverend Cartwright why God had let the soldiers drive the Indians away and why He allowed the settlers to take their land. After the meeting, she caught him alone for a few moments and posed her question.

"Why, my child," responded the Reverend, "they weren't using it as God intended." He patted her head. "They just roamed around hunting deer and picking blackberries."

Matilda gritted her teeth and endured the indignity in silence. She already knew the Reverend's answer would be meaningless.

"Besides," he went on, "they didn't own the land. It belonged to the United States Government. The government rightly gave it to the settlers to build homes and farms."

Matilda started to protest, but he continued. "And they were not only heathen, child, they were savages. Why," he looked shocked, "they didn't even wear proper clothing!" He again patted her head and she resisted the impulse to kick his shins. "The soldiers did the right thing, my dear. Don't fret your pretty little head about it."

Convinced in his own mind he had settled the issue, the pompous preacher strolled off to speak to Gardner about the schedule for the next camp meeting.

Matilda stood alone, biting back the words on the tip of her tongue. She mutely screamed after him, you just preached for an hour on justice and kindness and loving your fellow man. Do you ever listen to what you say?

Knowing how her father would react if she showed disrespect to the preacher, she said nothing.

The following Sunday afternoon, as she and Agatha again sat under their favorite tree, Matilda told Aggie what the Reverend Cartwright had said.

Agatha just shrugged her shoulders. "There's nothing we can do about it," she replied. "The Indians are gone and won't be back. We might as well use the land."

Matilda sighed. The casual acceptance of such unfair-
ness upset her. She took comfort in the knowledge that it
also bothered her father. Somehow that made the tragic
story easier to bear. She told herself not to think about it.
Aggie was right. Nothing could be done.

Though the summer chores kept them busy, she and
Agatha spent all their free time together. They played hide
and seek among the trees that lined the creek bed, or climbed high among their branches, pretending they scaled the
masts of the ships pictured in their schoolbooks. Sometimes
they would just lie on the grass, soak in the warm sunshine,
and exchange secret dreams. After summer ended, they
attended school together, their desks side by side. Matilda
wore Agatha's ring all the time.

Then one Saturday morning in November, the day after
the first autumn storm sprinkled a light layer of snow over
the ground, young Alec Templeton, Agatha's brother, galloped up to the Randolph cabin, riding hard. The horse's
hooves tore up little divots of snow from the underlying
earth, his breath making clouds of steam in the cold air.

"Miz Randolph, Miz Randolph," Alec cried, leaping from
the horse's back. "Come quick. It's . . . ." His voice broke.
"It's Aggie," he whispered. "She's took bad sick and Ma
can't break the fever." He turned away, his shoulders heav-
ing, and buried his face in the horse's neck.

Matilda's heart thudded against her ribs. She felt the
blood drain from her face, and the voices around her
seemed to come from far away. Aggie had not been in
school yesterday, but she had been well the day before.
Could she be that sick so fast?

"Tom, please saddle my horse," Betsy Ann ordered, and
ran for her bag of medicinal herbs. Tom hurried to obey.

"Can I come, Mother?" Matilda begged. "Aggie is my
best friend."

Betsy Ann hesitated, then looked into Matilda's pleading eyes and weakened. "Very well," she said at last, drawing a deep breath. "Come along."

Tom led out his mother's gentle, old dappled mare and assisted Betsy Ann into the saddle. When he turned to Matilda, he looked into her tragic eyes and read the torment there. Hugging her for a moment, he kissed her on the forehead before hoisting her up behind her mother.

"God go with you, little sister," he murmured brokenly as the procession left the yard.

That night, back home after watching her mother draw the sheet over Agatha's still, white face, Matilda sobbed her anger and grief into the pillow.

Caroline tried to comfort her. "Pa says these things are God's will," she told her sister. "He says sometimes God takes back his children, like he did our baby brother Andrew."

Matilda pounded the pillow with her fists. "Then I hate Him. I *hate* Him! He's cruel to take my best friend. How could He take her away from me? I've been good, haven't I?" Her voice broke and she whispered. "She swore she'd be my best friend forever. How could she leave me?"

Caroline, unable to find words of solace, held her stricken sister in her arms until the racking sobs subsided into exhausted sleep.

Her face set, Matilda stood dry-eyed through Agatha's funeral. When the family returned home after the services, Matilda walked slowly to the tree where she and Aggie had spent so many hours and shared so many secrets. Brushing away the light dusting of snow, she took a stick and dug a small hole. Removing the woven ring from her finger, she buried it among the roots of the tree.

She stood motionless for a long time, alone under the

tree beside the buried ring, her breath making clouds of steam in the cold air. Her mind reverted to the conversations she and Aggie had exchanged over the tragedy of the Kickapoo Indians. Aggie was right, she thought. There are some things we can do nothing to alter. Some things must just be accepted. Throwing back her shoulders, she defied the world to defeat her.

She never mentioned Agatha's name again.

Chapter 4

1845 to 1850

ONE MONTH almost to the day after Agatha's death, the Williams family arrived in Randolph's Grove. Matilda never forgot her first glimpse of Sarah Williams, huddled on the front seat of the shabby wagon between her parents, bundled against the cold with only her eyes visible above the worn muffler wrapped around her face. When Matilda saw the large green eyes, she felt a pang of jealousy, thinking of her drab, ordinary blue ones.

Sarah's two brothers, almost grown, walked beside the wagon. One led a splay-footed horse with a gray coat already showing white around the muzzle. The younger boy drove a brindle cow whose ribs protruded through the shaggy hide. A half-grown calf trotted by her side. The boys were barefoot in spite of the light spattering of snow on the ground. Their threadbare clothing, though clean, showed years of wear.

"Howdy!" The man clambered stiffly down from the high wagon seat and extended his hand to Gardner. "Name's Jim Williams. This here's my wife Lizzie and daughter Sarah. Boys're Hank and Jim, Junior. Folks tell me you know all the places around here where a man can stake a claim."

Gardner grinned and shook hands. "Yep, I 'spect I do," he responded. "Mighty good bottom land, grows good corn. Plenty of natural grass, good cattle feed. Lot of nut trees, make a lot of mast for the hogs." He turned to the nearest son. "Tom, bring my horse around and we'll help Jim here find a place as suits him." He assisted Mrs. Williams down from the wagon seat. "You and Sarah come in and have a cup of tea and a bite to eat, Miz' Williams. You look plumb froze. You folks can stay here with us until we get you a cabin built."

So the Williams family spent a week with the Randolphs, as had so many families before them. Gardner Randolph's reputation for hospitality had spread far and wide. Too far and too wide, Matilda once heard her mother remark dryly to her sister, Matilda's Aunt Fanny.

When the family returned from the Williams cabin-raising a week later, Gardner remarked to Betsy Ann, "Jim Williams has the look of a man who is always a dollar short."

Sarah seemed to like Matilda's company, and they spent a great deal of time together. As they grew closer and closer, Matilda did not consciously realize Sarah filled the hole left in her life by the loss of Agatha, but she knew they enjoyed being together. As Matilda found herself and Sarah becoming inseparable, she drew back a little, some instinct warning her not to put herself in a position of being hurt again, but Sarah's dynamic personality and energetic enthusiasm for life overcame Matilda's qualms.

One day, about six weeks after the Williams family's arrival, Sarah greeted Matilda when she and her siblings arrived home from the one-room log school. The citizens of Randolph's Grove built the school house, a source of pride to the whole community, in 1828. Matilda asked Sarah why she did not attend school with the other children.

"Pa wants me to go to school, but I'm afraid," Sarah confided.

"Afraid? Why?" Fear seemed so foreign to the Sarah she had come to know. Sarah rode her horse by herself, and always climbed the tallest trees. She even once talked back to the circuit preacher, something Matilda would never dare to do, no matter how tempted. Matilda's parents insisted all of the Randolph children attend school until the eighth grade. Alf even talked of going to the new university at Springfield, and the Methodist Church planned to start a university in nearby Bloomington.

"At my last school, the teacher whipped me when I didn't have a lesson right."

"Whipped you!" Matilda gasped. "I thought teachers only whipped boys."

"Well, this one whipped girls, too. Pa wouldn't let me go back, so I'm terribly ignorant." She looked abashed. "If I go to school here, as Pa wants, I'd have to sit with the babies." She set her jaw. "I won't do that."

"I'll teach you," Matilda announced boldly. "I've got a reader and a speller and a 'rithmetic book. Then we can go to school together."

So every Saturday after that, no matter what the weather, Sarah rode over to the Randolph farm on patient old Buck for lessons from Matilda. After the Saturday sessions, Sarah often spent the night in the big bed in the main room with Matilda, Caroline, and Minerva. They shared long talks and companionable silences watching the fire while the winter wind howled outside. Gradually the ache from Agatha's death grew easier for Matilda to bear.

Spring came early the following year. By March, the snow had melted. In the fields, lush green grass grew rapidly. Flowers painted the tips of the plants with color. The scent of newly-mown grass and the perfume of flowers filled the air.

The early morning sun reached through the east window and touched the golden hair of sleeping five-year-old Minerva. Matilda sat up with a yawn and dressed quickly in the chilly air, donning as many of her clothes as possible under the warm quilts. Shoving her feet into her boots, she poked the still sleeping Sinclair in the ribs. "Get up, lazybones," she hissed. "You have to help me feed the chickens."

"Go away," he muttered, rolling over and closing his eyes again.

Gardner entered the room in time to hear the exchange. "Sinclair," he said sternly.

His father's firm voice had the desired effect. Sinclair groaned and sat up, reaching for his pants.

Gardner tossed a few more chunks of wood into the fireplace, stirring the fire to life once more. "Tom," he instructed, "this is your morning to empty the chamber pot."

Tom grumbled under his breath, but he did not argue. Gardner never lifted a hand against the girls, but disobedience from one of the boys brought swift retribution. Tom picked up the container by its bail, using his other hand to hold the lid securely in place. He turned his face away from the smelly pail and wrinkled his nose. No one liked the job of dumping the contents of the chamber pot into the outhouse pit, but Tom complained the most.

Matilda, with Sinclair trailing sleepily behind her, made her usual morning visit to the chicken coop. On the way, she scooped some corn from a wooden bin in the storage shed attached to the side of the house. She poked the grain with a stick before reaching in with her hand, a practice she developed after the morning she dislodged a large rat.

As she fed the chickens, she told Sinclair, "It's a good thing we'll be able to let them loose to scratch for their own breakfast pretty soon. The corn's getting low."

"Then they'll hide the eggs again, and we'll have to look all over for 'em," Sinclair muttered.

A dozen hens greeted them noisily. Matilda spoke above the cacophony. "I don't see the old red one." She searched the perimeter of the pen and found a hole scratched in the soft dirt under one of the boards. Shaking her head, she said, "Looks like that wily hen managed to get out. She must be setting. The old biddy's been acting broody the last few days. Find a board to plug this hole before any more decide to follow her. We'll catch her after breakfast."

Matilda refilled the water pan from the heavy wooden bucket standing by the gate. "There, chickies, now you can get a drink." She shivered, her breath making clouds of steam in the cold air. The snow had gone, but the mornings remained icy. "Come on, Sinclair. Let's get the eggs and get back where it's warmer."

When they returned to the house, carrying the eight brown eggs they had coaxed out from under the hens, the fire had chased away much of the morning chill. The aroma of freshly ground coffee filled the room. Sam entered the house shortly after Matilda and Sinclair, carrying a pail of frothy milk.

Matilda put the eggs in their basket on the table, then turned to help her mother and sisters Caroline and Sarah prepare breakfast. Matilda would be ten in July. With Sarah's wedding scheduled for October, Betsy Ann announced the time had come for Matilda to take her place helping with the cooking chores. Matilda's job was watching the johnny cake bake in the Dutch oven. Everyone liked johnny cake, especially with some of Betsy Ann's delicious homemade maple syrup and fresh butter.

Keeping the cornbread from burning required her full attention. She pulled embers from the fireplace and carefully piled them around the Dutch oven standing in its customary place on the hearth. She had to keep the heat evenly distributed. Otherwise, one half of the johnny cake would be burned, the other half only partly baked. This had been Caroline's task until Matilda inherited it. She soon learned why Caroline had gladly passed the job over to her. Already one of the embers had burned a hole in her new calico pinafore. She had to kneel by the fireplace, scorching her hands and face . . . .

"'Tilda, stop day dreaming." Caroline's voice cut through her reverie. "You'll burn the johnny cake again."

Matilda yanked the Dutch oven from the pile of embers in the nick of time to save the corn bread.

Her mother fried slice after slice of thick bacon, pouring the accumulated fat into a bucket of cold water by the fireplace. The pure fat rose to the top, to be saved for making candles and soap. Every day Betsy Ann or Sarah skimmed off the tallow, stored it in a covered keg standing in the shed beside the house, and refilled the bucket with fresh water.

I'll probably get that job too, Matilda grumbled to herself. She dared not say it aloud. She watched her mother pour out the grease from yet another pan of bacon. When the hot fat hit the water, it sputtered and hissed, and a cloud of steam arose.

Breakfast over, the men and older boys prepared for the day's work. Gardner stood at the head of the table giving orders. Matilda thought her father the handsomest man in the world. Taller than most men, he always kept his slender face clean shaven. She never remembered him growing a beard. At fifty, his neatly trimmed hair showed a touch of gray in the dark strands. Above the high cheek bones, the intense hazel eyes circled the group. His quiet air of authority filled the room. She felt her chest would burst with pride.

"Tom," Gardner's resonant voice rang out, "if you get the grass cut in that last field today, we can get it plowed by the end of next week. Snow melting early gave us a good start. Looks like we'll get in some extra corn this year."

Gardner then spoke to Alf. "The weather's warm enough to plant the sweet corn in the garden. There's enough seed for a good crop."

He turned to John. "Get your mother another bucket of water from the well before you head out to give Tom a hand, John. I have a meeting at the commissioner's office. Probably be gone all day." He waved his hand. "Sam, get a count of how many shoats we'll have for the drive to Galena. Your Uncle A.M. wants to leave next week and needs to know."

John yanked on Matilda's braids as he passed her. "Whoa, horsie," he laughed, then ducked out the door, dodging the dishrag she threw at him.

Matilda retrieved the rag and returned to her dish washing. "Why do I have to wear braids?" she mourned. "The boys always think they have to pull 'em."

"Because otherwise those curls fly all over the place," Betsy Ann replied. "I swear, each strand has a mind of its own."

"When you're older," Caroline replied with a superior air, "you can wear it any way you like." She was two years older than Matilda, and often pointed out that fact. She patted her smooth, dark hair tied back in a neat bun at the nape of her neck with a bright yellow ribbon.

"Don't be so snooty, just because . . . ."

"Matilda!"

At the warning from her mother, Matilda suppressed the remainder of the sharp retort on her lips. John returned with the bucket of water. In his free hand he carried a small bunch of wild flowers. Handing them to Matilda, he smiled down on her and gently tucked one of the errant red-gold curls back into place. With uncharacteristic tenderness, he patted her cheek, said, "No hard feelings, little sister?" and ran out.

Matilda stared after him, the small posy of flowers in her hand. He usually either ignored her or teased her. Shaking her head, she decided she would never understand brothers. Putting the flowers in a glass jar on the table, she returned to her dish washing.

Sarah Williams, riding the faithful Buck, arrived midmorning while Matilda and Caroline scoured the ham barrel. Their father planned to butcher another hog on Monday. Since Gardner allowed no one to work on Sunday, considering it sinful to work on the Sabbath, they had to finish the barrel before the day ended. Ignoring Caroline's complaints, Matilda happily abandoned the cask cleaning and dried her hands.

Sarah had turned ten in March. Her sleek, black hair and sparkling emerald eyes foretold the beauty she would become. Matilda felt a twinge of the envy she had experienced when she saw Sarah for the first time, but Sarah wore her beauty unconsciously, and never put on airs.

"Hello, Buck," Matilda greeted the old horse this morning as she did every Saturday, patting his soft muzzle. He rubbed his nose against her and she laughed, knowing he wanted his lump of maple sugar. She ran to the casket in the shed. Its four legs stood in small buckets of sticky tar to keep the ants from reaching the sugar.

Sarah had been impressed by the buckets of tar. "So that's why you never have ants," she marveled. " Ma makes sugar, but it always gets full of ants."

Matilda twisted her mouth into a grin. "Pa says no ant could ever cross that Stygian pool."

"What's a Stygian pool?"

Matilda shrugged her shoulders. "I don't know. Something to do with the ancient Greeks." She recalled the conversation with a smile as she offered Buck the morsel of sugar and stroked his nose.

"Poor old Buck," Sarah sighed. "His teeth are worn down almost to his gums. Pa says we should put him out of his misery. I have to cut grass for him, to save what's left of his teeth, but he's worth the extra work." She planted her fists on her hips. "Nobody's going to shoot Buck."

"I don't blame you," Matilda agreed. "If I ever get my own horse, I'd never let anyone shoot him either."

Sarah smiled and hugged Buck's neck with affection, then turned back to Matilda. "Come on. If I'm going to catch up with you so we can be together next term, we've got a lot of work to do."

Matilda found Sarah a very able pupil. She felt confident the girl would be able to attend school with her in the fall. Matilda also suspected Sarah had learned a lot more in her previous school than she let on.

Gardner came in as Sarah and Matilda struggled over a worn copy of *Dabold's Simple Arithmetic* that had long since lost its cover. "Sarah," he frowned, "your pa hasn't started to plant yet. Should take advantage of the early season. Won't get all his fields in if he doesn't get started."

"Oh," Sarah replied with a casual wave of her hand, "he had to fix the plow."

With a flash of insight, Matilda suddenly remembered many things. The worn, haunted look on Mrs. Williams' face. The threadbare look of their clothes. The ever ready excuses for why crops didn't get planted, or fences mended. The whiff of alcohol on Jim Williams' breath when he started bragging about Sarah.

Matilda sighed and returned to the book in front of her. "Come on, Sarah, these numbers aren't that hard. Just try and . . . ."

Her father's voice, as he spoke to her mother from the doorway, suddenly penetrated Matilda's consciousness. "Betsy, I see smoke rising. Got to be a bad fire. Looks to be down by Funk's place."

The book fell to the floor as Matilda and Sarah scrambled to their feet and rushed to the door. They stood beside Gardner, staring at the plume of brown and black smoke roiling up toward the cloudless blue sky.

"Oh, no," Sarah whispered. Matilda saw the color drain from her cheeks, the green eyes looming even larger in her ashen face. The light scattering of freckles across the pert nose stood out against her pale skin. "It's our place."

"You can't know that, Sarah," Betsy Ann reassured her.

"It's a long ways. Could be any of several of your neighbors."

"No, it's ours. Before I left, my brothers built a fire under the kettle to scald a pig. I told them not to build it upwind of the barn but they wouldn't listen." Sarah's eyes narrowed and she mimicked, "'Girls don't know anything about building fires.'" Then she spat, "I know wind can carry a spark into dry hay."

She ran for Buck and jumped on his back. "Come on, Buck. We have to get home before everything burns up." The bitterness in Sarah's voice told Matilda tragedy had touched Sarah's life before.

As Sarah prodded the old horse down the lane, the smoke loomed higher in an ever larger mass. Gardner turned to the only son present. "We'd better go and help, Tom. Get the buckets and sacks. I'll hitch Big Red to the cart."

Matilda, determined to go as well, followed her father and climbed up on the seat beside him. Gardner said nothing.

Gardner, Tom, and Matilda arrived at the Williams homestead to find the barn totally engulfed. Tongues of red and orange flame curled around the plank siding while billows of dark smoke rolled out of the piles of hay stacked inside. The acrid smell of smoke surrounded them.

The whole area bustled with activity. A bucket brigade led from the well to the barn, but the buckets of water barely touched the raging flames. Gardner and Tom hastened to unload their buckets to add to the line.

"The house, the house!" Gardner raised his voice to be heard above the raucous noise of shouting men, clanking buckets and crackling flames. "Told Williams he built the barn too close to the house, the dang idjit," Gardner muttered to Tom. "Lazy fool wanted it close so's he wouldn't have to walk so far." He raised his voice again. "Get a line going to the house! Wet down that roof before a spark gets it. You can't save the barn now. Let it go."

As he spoke, a chunk of blazing shingle from the barn rose through the air and landed on the roof of the cabin. The roof, covered with tar for waterproofing, burst into flame. The men in the bucket brigade scrambled to re-form the line with the house as a target, but were too late to be effective. In moments, flames engulfed the small building. The roar of the fire, combined with the noise of the barn collapsing on itself, created a din that drowned Gardner's voice.

Sarah stood beside Matilda, calm and dry-eyed, a bundle in her arms. "Can I put my things in your cart, 'Tilda? The last time those fool brothers of mine set the house on fire, I lost everything. They weren't going to do it to me again." She smiled in triumph. "I always keep my valuable things, like my books, my new hairbrush and my doll in this satchel, along with the necklace my grandmother gave me. That's so I could get it all out quick."

Matilda looked over at Mrs. Williams, who stood empty handed, wailing at the loss of her possessions. Matilda smiled at Sarah's foresight. Jim Williams might have been born a loser, as Gardner often told Betsy Ann, but Matilda could not see the world defeating Sarah.

In August of 1846, Matilda's brother Will married seventeen-year-old Mary Cottrell, a sparkling, brown-eyed beauty everyone called Polly, at her request. "For," she said with a laugh, "half the girls I know are named Mary or Sarah." Matilda loved her at once.

The following October, Matilda's sister Sarah married Albert Welch, the son of a successful grocer in Bloomington, and they bought a small farm in Randolph's Grove, not far from the Randolph home. With the two weddings, the number of persons in the Randolph household shrank to ten.

Gardner Randolph's prediction that Jim Williams was no farmer proved correct. The following year, in the summer of 1847, after another unsuccessful year of attempting to grow a crop, and another year of living off the largesse of his neighbors, he sold his farm. With the proceeds, he purchased a small ferry crossing on the Mississippi River on the Illinois-Missouri border, upriver from Hannibal, and the family moved. Matilda and Sarah parted with tears and fervent promises to write often.

Time passed slowly after that. Sarah did write, and even came to visit Matilda in the summer of 1849. A very memorable visit, as Matilda recalled, remembering some of their escapades with a smile. Other than that brief interlude, life drifted slowly on. Day followed day in a monotonous routine Matilda felt would go on forever. She thought about it often, sitting under the tree where she and Agatha had shared their dreams. She knew she would grow up, marry, and raise her children here in Randolph's Grove, just like her older siblings, never seeing the world outside. She heard reports of a worker finding gold way out in California, for all of the men talked about it. Some had already gone west to check for themselves. Matilda thought it sounded exciting, but never dreamed it would affect her.

Until one warm spring day in April of 1850.

Chapter 5

Spring of 1850

"MA, PA!" Alf's blue eyes sparkled as he burst into the house that fateful April morning. "I've decided to go to the gold fields in California."

Matilda, then just three months short of her fourteenth birthday, looked up from her wool carding. The carder, bits of wool clinging to the tiny teeth, fell from her nerveless fingers. The sharp metal edge left a nick in the wood when it struck the floor. The dull thud echoed in the stunned silence that greeted Alf's announcement.

For a moment, the only sound in the room was the crackling of wood burning in the fireplace. Even chatterbox Minerva stood mute, her mouth agape. The aroma of the apple pie baking in the Dutch oven seemed stronger in the sudden stillness.

Matilda felt a flare of excitement mixed with envy. She stifled the impulse to beg to accompany him, knowing it useless to ask. Girls never got to do anything exciting.

"But, Son," Betsy Ann began, then her voice failed. Never before had Matilda seen her usually unshakable mother at a loss for words.

Sinclair jumped up, his face showing his excitement. "Can I go, can I go?"

A babble of voices broke out. Gardner held up his hand for silence.

"It's so far, Son," he said. "And how do you know all these stories of gold lying all over the place are true? You know how these tales grow once they get started."

"Been talking to Ben Adams' brother Jeremiah. You remember him. He's been guiding wagon trains across to

Oregon and California since '46. He buys beaver skins and stuff from the Indians on the way back then sells them in Chicago. He's wintered here with Ben."

Gardner's grunt of assent told Matilda the recognition was not all favorable.

"He's getting ready to go back. Says he can get us on as outriders. I won't have to use any of the money I made this spring working for Uncle Jesse. I can save it to keep me in California until I find some gold."

Alf paused and gave his father an anxious look before hurrying on. "Jeremiah swears the tales of gold are true. He saw it last summer. Says the miners bring little bags of gold dust into General Sutter's store on the Sacramento River. Colonel Mason's report to President Polk last year was right. All the newspapers are full of it. Joe and Alec believe it. So does Will Hendrix. They want to go too. Will says a whole bunch from Bloomington went last year, and more are going this year."

He looked from one quiet face to the next and rushed on. "We'll go over to Pekin and catch the boat down the river to St. Louis, then up the Missouri to St. Joseph. Jeremiah says we can get all the supplies we need in St. Joseph." His voice excited, he continued. "But we have to leave right away. The wagons start across in the spring as soon as the new grass sprouts on the prairie. That's so they can get across the mountains before winter." He paused for breath. Not an eyelash flickered. "If the snows start, they can't get the wagons through. Jeremiah says the mountains are tremendous."

His audience made no response, so he added, "Twice as high as the mountains back east."

"Twice as high as the Smokies?" Gardner said, finding his voice at last. He shook his head slowly from side to side in disbelief. "That'd be mighty high, Son. Are you sure he wasn't just making up some tall tales? You know his fondness for strong drink."

"No, honest. Jeremiah's been there and swears it's true. Some of the mountains are so high the snow never leaves 'em." Alf paced about in the small floor space available. "In California, where the gold is, there's very little snow, even in winter. And men are getting rich every day."

Matilda felt her excitement grow. She looked across at Sam and saw his face alight. If Alf goes, she thought, I'll bet Sam goes too.

"Why didn't Jeremiah stay there and get some gold himself?" Sam wanted to know.

Alf grinned. "Says it's hard work, sittin' out in the hot sun digging through the gravel, with your feet freezing in cold water." He chuckled. "Jeremiah's not too fond of hard work. But the idea doesn't bother me, if I can get some free gold."

Betsy Ann found her voice. "But, Son, you'll be so far away. We may never see you again. And what about the danger? I've heard of whole wagon trains wiped out by the cholera. And they say the Indians out there are fierce and war-like."

"Jeremiah says the trains always get through. And since the war with Mexico, there are outposts all along the way." He hugged her. "Really, Mother, it's not that dangerous. Lots of men have already gone. Why, they say last year alone almost a hundred thousand went."

"They prob'ly already got all the gold," Sinclair muttered darkly.

Gardner ignored Sinclair and spoke to Alf. "And what about your plans to go to the University?" he asked.

Alf hesitated. Matilda saw the conflict in his face.

"I've thought of that, Pa. If I get enough gold, I can come back and go to the University. I'd have plenty of money." He grinned and glanced at his mother. "I could maybe even study doctoring."

Betsy Ann's snort of disgust brought a smile to Gardner's face. He looked at Alf for a long moment, then took a deep breath. "Very well, Son, if you're really sure it's what you want."

Betsy Ann looked at her husband in astonishment. Matilda knew from the other faces that Gardner's agreement surprised them as well.

Gardner laughed. "After all, Mother, the boy *is* twenty years old. If this is what he wants, we should give him our blessing." He grinned and tugged on his ear. "Remember, I was only eighteen when I fought with Major Peacock at Horseshoe Bend."

"Yes," she replied, with some asperity, "and I also remember the many times you've told the story of the bullet that put sixteen holes in your shirt." Matilda knew he also usually failed to tell his audience the shirt had been in his knapsack at the time.

Alf, astonished at the ease with which his father agreed, stammered, "Thanks, Pa." He looked around at all the eyes upon him, his face beaming. "Jeremiah wants to leave in two weeks."

"So soon?" Betsy Ann frowned.

Alf hugged her again. "Don't fret, Mother," he said. "I'll be fine. I'll write every chance I get. I promise."

The next two weeks passed in a flurry of preparations and farewells. Since they traveled on horseback and had to carry everything in saddlepacks, they could not possibly take all of the many gifts plied upon them by friends and neighbors. Sam, to no one's surprise, decided to join them. Betsy Ann filled their medical supply bags, discarding the calomel purgative and irritant for blistering from old Mrs. Barnes and the bleeding stylus from Alec's grandmother.

Jeremiah put his foot down at the fancy wooden cradle for washing gold offered by another neighbor. "Just what you can carry easy on a horse, Son," he told Alf, in a voice that left no room for argument. "The trail is littered with all them gimcracks the miners start out with. They overload their wagons and hafta dump half of it to get over the mountains."

Matilda presented each with a warm quilt she and Minerva had made. Temperance rode over with several shirts of homespun wool. Little by little, the saddlepacks filled to overflowing.

Gardner took Alf aside and handed him the hunting knife Gardner had carried since his youth.

Speechless at the gift of the knife he knew his father treasured, Alf could only gasp, "Gee, Pa. Thanks!"

At last the moment for departure arrived. Having packed and repacked the bags what seemed like twenty times, Alf secretly told Matilda he would be glad to finally get under way. Alec, under pressure from his family and Joe's blue-eyed, pert-nosed sister Margaret, decided, with obvious reluctance, not to accompany them. He stood and watched the farewells, envy written plainly on his face. Matilda caught the triumph in Margaret's eyes and felt a twinge of scorn for Alec.

Britt, after much discussion, decided to join his brothers on their trek. "I'll keep an eye on Sam and Alf for you, Mother," Britt assured Betsy Ann with a twinkle in his eye.

All of Randolph's Grove turned out to see them off. Matilda, looking at the crowd, caught glimpses of envy in more than one face. I'll bet more go, she thought. I wish I was a man. I'd go in a minute.

Britt stood a little to the side of the group as he assured a tearful Sarah he would return in two years. "Just give me one full season," he said, "then I'll come home. I've made all the arrangements with Jesse to tend to the farm. And Tom will stay at the house to help with the chores."

He turned to six-year-old Willie and four-year-old Gardner. "Boys," he told them, "I'm counting on you to help your mother take care of your sister and the baby." He solemnly shook hands with both of them. "If I strike it rich, I'll buy you each a pony for your very own."

Betsy Ann, dry-eyed, kissed Sam and Alf. "Good-bye, boys," she smiled from one to the other. "Be very careful. Remember what I told you about cholera, and fevers and snake bite and . . . ."

"Please, Mother," Alf broke in. "We will, we will." He kissed her to silence her and turned to Matilda while Sam embraced his mother.

Matilda, so excited she could not stand still, hugged Alf's neck. "You're so lucky. Find me a big gold nugget. Write, all of you. I want to know everything about your trip and about California." She gave no thought to danger. Having grown up on stories of the gentle, friendly Kickapoo and Delaware, she had no concept of a war-like Indian.

Alf laughed and returned her embrace with enthusiasm. They had been co-conspirators from the start since only Matilda had eagerly backed his decision to go. "I'll write. I can't promise the nugget."

Sam grinned. "I'll let Alf do the honors. He's the hand for writing." He swept the weeping Minerva up in his arms and hugged her. "Be a good girl, Baby Sister." He kissed her wet cheek and gently set her back on her feet.

While Sinclair sulked at being left behind, Alf bid farewell to the rest of his siblings and turned to his father.

Gardner shook his hand. Their eyes met for a long moment, then Alf threw himself in his father's arms. Gardner awkwardly patted him on the back.

"Good journey, Son. God be with you. It's good to follow your dreams."

Quickly, but not before Matilda saw the tears spring into his eyes, Alf turned and mounted his horse beside Britt and

Sam. Will Hendrix followed. Jeremiah, leading the two pack horses, had started down the road, grumbling at the delay. He had no patience with all the fuss. After all, he had made the trip four times already. It had taken some persuasion to get him to agree to the extra horses. He had always traveled with just what he could carry in his one saddlepack.

"Never get there if we don't get started," he shouted back over his shoulder.

"Come on, Joe," Alf called, spurring his horse.

Joe gently removed himself from Mrs. Dawson's clinging grasp, hugged his father and hastened to his horse.

Matilda looked at her father. The tears Gardner had controlled so carefully slid down his cheeks as he watched three of his sons ride away from him. Betsy Ann's eyes remained dry. Matilda, torn between a sense of loss and jealousy at being left behind, watched the horses until they disappeared from sight.

On the last day of May, Tom arrived home where the family had gathered for the noon meal waving a packet from Alf. In his letter, Alf announced they had finished outfitting and would leave St. Joseph in the morning.

> "From now on, there is no certain mail service until I get to Sacramento City. I will write before if I can, but try not to worry. We are well equipped and well manned. Most of the wagons are prairie schooner types. They really do look like big boats. Some are just simple carts with a canvas cover. We bought a cart for the five of us, a small one, for fifteen dollars. It's enough to carry our supplies, and we can take turns driving it.
>
> "I haven't counted the wagons, but I do know there are over fifty, so you can see we are a good sized party. Jeremiah also says we will probably catch up with more along the trail. He said last year some

bunches got up to a hundred wagons in them, with
so many folks heading for the gold fields.

"Most of the wagons use oxen instead of mules.
Jeremiah grumbled, because he says with mules we
could make up to twenty miles a day while the best
oxen can do is about fifteen."

"Don't blame 'em," Gardner muttered. "Mule's the most
bull-headed critter God ever made." Tom ignored the comment and continued.

"Some of our fellow travelers are lawyers and
bankers. We can tell by their dress they are men of
means. Sam says they probably have good reasons
for leaving the States, but I think they just want to get
some of that free gold. Others are poor farmers with
families. Some of them plan to go to Oregon. We
also have an assortment of ne'er-do-wells, but most
are young men just like us, eager for a shot at getting
some easy gold.

"We are all in great spirits. Britt is writing to Sarah,
of course, and Joe is writing his parents. Joe says he
doesn't write very well, so please share my letter with
them. He envies me my ability to read and write.
You were right, Pa, to insist we all learn, even over
our objections."

Tom looked up and all eyes turned to eleven-year-old
Sinclair, who wriggled uncomfortably in his seat.

"Okay, okay," he muttered, ignoring the smug smile on
the face of nine-year-old Minerva, who already read and
wrote well.

The letter closed with affection from all of them, then the
postscript added, "Also, I hear it can take up to two months
for letters to get back east from Sacramento City, so don't
worry." The last two words were underlined several times.

Betsy Ann counted on her fingers. "December." She set
her jaw.

Chapter 6

Summer of 1850

AFTER THE letter from Alf, everyone talked only of
California and easy gold. Several other young men gathered their belongings and followed, hoping to catch one of
the last wagon trains of the summer.

Matilda soon tired of the whole subject. Jealous she
could not go too, she tried to think of a way to avoid hearing
about it all the time.

Then one hot and sultry June morning, a letter arrived
from her friend Sarah Williams. The vision of Sarah's
sparkling green eyes rose in Matilda's mind as she read:

> "I've persuaded Pa to offer John a summer job
> on the ferry. We really do need extra help, with all
> the summer traffic."

Matilda wondered if Mr. Williams really needed the help
or if he had just caved in to Sarah as usual.

> "Anyway, he's writing to ask if John can come. If
> your father agrees, you can come with him and spend
> the summer with me. I can hardly wait."

The accompanying letter from Mr. Williams persuaded
Gardner to let them go.

"After all, Pa," Matilda reasoned. "We can take the
steamer from Pekin. Mr. Williams says we'll have to change
in St. Louis, but we won't have to spend the night there."

She knew her father would never allow them to spend the night in St. Louis. He considered it a wicked city. "We can get right on the boat up the Mississippi and Mr. Williams will meet us in Hannibal." Matilda watched her father anxiously. "We'll be very careful," she promised.

Gardner agreed, with some reluctance, and muttered a comment about Sarah and Matilda and the orange tom cat. Startled, Matilda wondered what the man knew. Sarah had managed to convince Betsy Ann that Sinclair had been the one responsible for stranding the cat on the roof of the cabin. Sarah had wanted to see if the cat would land on its feet when it jumped. Instead, the cat stood at the edge of the roof and yowled until Tom got the ladder and rescued it.

"But, Pa," she said "we were children then." They had actually been thirteen, but from her lofty vantage point of fourteen (in three weeks), she considered all thirteen-year-olds mere infants.

The next morning, as the sun cleared the tops of the trees, John snapped the reins and the horse started forward. Tom rode beside them to bring the buggy back from the boat landing.

Matilda, seated beside John in the buggy, blew a kiss to the pouting Minerva, who plainly did not plan to forgive her sister for refusing to take her along. Unrepentant, Matilda waved her farewells to the rest of the family.

A week after their arrival at the Williams homestead, Sarah hustled Matilda out of sight around the corner of the house. The lively green eyes sparkled with the mischievous look Matilda recognized at once.

"Sarah Jane Williams, what are you up to now?" Matilda remembered Sarah's ability to get into one prank after another very well. She greeted this latest attempt with suspicion.

"Shh! They'll hear you," Sarah whispered. "I've got an idea." Her long, black hair swished across her shoulders as she swung her head to be sure no one had followed them.

"Your last idea got me stuck in the house for a whole week." On Sarah's last visit, they had snatched the big boys' pants while they were swimming. How was Matilda to know her father had decided to join them? Was it her fault Sam and Tom were as big as their father? All the pants looked the same. Gardner did not believe Matilda's protests that she had not known of his presence in the river.

"You won't get in trouble this time," Sarah reassured her. "No one will ever find out."

"That's what you said last time." But Matilda knew she would give in. Sarah always had such exciting ideas. "Okay, okay. What is it?"

"I hear there's going to be a slave auction over at Keeneville, just across the river in Missouri. A traveling slaver had a whole wagon load." Sarah's eyes shone. "I've never seen a slave auction and neither have you. This is our chance. We can ride over on Buck."

"He's so old he might not make it that far." He had been almost toothless when Matilda and Sarah met. Sarah still faithfully cut a pile of grass for him every day.

Sarah ignored Matilda's remark. "We'll take a basket," she said, "and tell my folks we're going on a picnic. There's a great spot on the Missouri side not far from the ferry crossing."

"They'll never let us go alone."

"We'll take John. He's man grown and he'll do it for you. I'll get Tom to help Josh with the ferry while we're gone." Tom, the Williams' hired man, was as besotted with Sarah as Jim Williams. Typically, Sarah did not hesitate to use it to her advantage.

Matilda thought for a moment. John would do anything she asked. She knew their father approved of slavery, but did not feel it right to break up families and violently disapproved of slave auctions. This could get them into real trouble. They might be a long way from Randolph's Grove, but Pa had a way of hearing things.

But Sarah won, as always, and the next morning found the three of them on their way to Keeneville crowded into the Williams' buggy. Matilda felt a twinge of guilt when Mr. Williams offered them the use of the buggy, but Sarah, in very Sarah-like fashion, blithely accepted it. Torn between her conscience and her loyalty to Sarah, Matilda said nothing. John just grinned.

The ferry always made Matilda nervous. If only it was a little bigger, she thought. Designed for light traffic, it consisted of a platform barely big enough for a horse and wagon. Really only a large raft, it was constructed of small logs with rough-hewn scantlings nailed across the logs to create a platform. Two small poles on the sides made guard rails of a sort, but not high ones. Matilda feared the whole contraption could upset at any time.

The swift water of the river swirled by the platform just inches below them. Sometimes rivulets slid over the wooden planks as Josh, the big Negro manning the pole, pushed them across. The smell of the water-soaked wood filled her nostrils.

As she watched, Josh's muscles bulged with the strain of the powerful shove needed to cross the deepest point in the river. In the channel, he could not touch bottom with the pole. The heavy rope that held the raft in place strained against the huge iron rings that held it as the current tried to swing the ferry down river.

What would happen if one of the posts holding the ropes on the bank gave away? Matilda shuddered. Old Buck shared her apprehension, snorting nervously and stomping his feet. John stood by the horse's head and comforted him with a practiced hand.

Matilda would have preferred to get out of the buggy for the crossing. Sitting in the swaying vehicle made her giddy, and she had visions of it tipping over into the river. She did not voice her fears to Sarah, knowing Sarah would scoff. Instead, she sat still as stone, gripping her hands so hard in her lap the knuckles turned white. She tried not to look at the muddy water, closing her ears to the sounds of the rushing river.

When they finally arrived at Keeneville, they found a platform of rough cut boards constructed in the town square. The smell of the wood mingled with the odor of sweaty bodies. As long as she lived, the smell of freshly cut timber reminded Matilda of her trip to the slave auction.

A number of Negroes milled about in a nearby pen of rough logs, sweating profusely in the sticky heat. Many of the men wore no shirts, and sweat glistened on their powerful backs. Most were shoeless, and, judging from their feet, had very seldom worn shoes. The women wore simple cotton dresses which clung to their bodies. A few wore their hair in braids, but most were close cropped. Some had to be couples, the way they clung to each other. There were even children.

A water barrel stood in one corner of the pen, with a dirty cup hooked over the side. The dust had turned to mud around the barrel where the restless Negroes had stepped over and over in the spilled water.

At first, Matilda could not think what seemed so strange about them, then it struck her. All of them, even the children, wore solemn faces. Where were the smiles, the easy laughter, the songs that sprang so readily to the lips of the Negroes she knew, like Josh? She knew Josh was a free man. Did freedom make that much difference?

Matilda began to feel uneasy, but Sarah was enjoying herself. "Come on," she whispered, tugging on Matilda's arm. "Let's get closer."

They approached the pen, dodging through buyers trying to get a closer look at the merchandise. Matilda wriggled her way through the crowd. Reaching one side of the enclosure, she stooped to look through the logs and found herself face to face with a boy of eight or nine. He clung to the hand of the woman beside him, tears staining his cheeks. Matilda met his eyes and saw the fear in them.

Suddenly, it was no longer a frolic. She remembered some of the horrible tales she had heard about slavery. The stories had meant nothing to her until she looked into the child's frightened eyes. She realized he would soon be torn from his mother and sold to an unknown buyer who might or might not be kind. At best, he would probably never see his mother again.

Guilt washed over her. Digging into the simple homespun reticule that hung from her wrist, Matilda found a piece of rock candy and handed it to him. He hesitated, then reached out his hand, a faint smile breaking through his tears. She returned his smile, a little shakily.

Then the heat and the smells became too much to bear. She had to get away. A wave of nausea swept over her. Dizzy, she backed out of the crowd and ran, back to the shelter of John's arm.

"John," she gasped. "There are frightened children in there. They . . ."

"Shh." John put his finger to her lips. "They're starting the auction."

A large number of buyers surrounded the platform. Matilda looked around, half afraid she might see someone she knew. With a flash of panic, she thought of her father's reaction if someone reported seeing them. Fortunately, the men were all strangers.

The auctioneer began with a tall, muscular young man. A slender woman clung to him, weeping. The assistant shoved her roughly back into the pen.

"All right, gentlemen, what am I bid for this fine young buck? Strong and healthy he is. Let's start the bidding at five hundred dollars."

The auctioneer continued with Negro after Negro. Matilda stared, horrified, watching children pulled from their mothers and tearful couples separated. She saw the little boy she had given the sweet torn sobbing from the grip of his mother.

"This is terrible," she murmured to John, tears burning her eyes. He nodded in understanding. "How can they do such things?" she demanded in a fierce whisper.

"Shh," John murmured in her ear. "There's only one left."

Matilda looked up and gasped. The last slave on the block, a girl about her own age, appeared white.

The auctioneer bragged. "See how beautiful she is, gentlemen? Seventeen years old and only one-eighth Negro blood." He leered at her. "And she's an excellent servant. Open your mouth, my dear, and show them what good teeth you have."

Matilda watched, aghast, as the girl obeyed. The bidding began in earnest. Matilda looked over at Sarah's pale face. When she heard a man shout "Two thousand five hundred dollars!" in triumph, Matilda turned and ran. Sarah and John followed at her heels.

Back at the buggy, Matilda threw her arms around Buck's neck and wept against the patient old horse's soft skin. A hand touched her shoulder. Looking up into John's worried eyes, she felt anger burn away her tears.

"How can they do this, John? How? Every one of those men claims to be a Christian, yet they can separate families without a second thought. And the girl!" She turned to

Sarah. "Sarah, that girl was as white as we are." Matilda's indignation made her short of breath. "I've never seen anything so horrible in my whole life."

"Hush, 'Tilda." John tried to quiet her. "If the auctioneer hears, he may file a complaint against you."

Visions of her father having to get her out of jail had the desired effect. Matilda fell silent. She stared after a wagon driving by with three newly purchased slaves huddled in the back. When the wagon turned the corner and vanished from sight, she turned to her brother.

"Let's get out of here, John. I never want to come back to a state where they allow such things to be done. I'm glad Illinois won't let people sell slaves. I never want to see another slave auction as long as I live."

Chapter 7

Summer of 1850

Two weeks later, Matilda curled up in her favorite spot under the apple tree with the latest letter from Alf. She and John arrived home from their visit with Sarah Williams to learn of its arrival. She still wore her travel-stained clothes, and badly needed a bath to wash off the dust and sweat from the ride back from Pekin, but in her eagerness to learn about her brothers' adventures, she ignored the dirt.

She stared for a moment at the outside of the weathered packet. To think the letter she held in her hands actually came from a far away, and, to her mind, a mysterious and exotic place! She closed her eyes, the sheaf of papers in her hand, and tried to visualize the scene. Finally, laughing at herself for her fantasies, she unfolded the letter. Matilda pictured Alf writing the words she read:

> "We arrived at Fort Kearney here in the Kansas-Nebraska Territory yesterday on May 15. As I told you in my letter from St. Joseph's, I got on as an outrider for the bunch that hired Jeremiah for a guide. Joe got himself a job cooking for a man who didn't want to cook for himself. Sam, Britt, and Will Hendrix are driving our cart.
>
> "We opted for oxen instead of mules because they are a lot cheaper, (two hundred dollars a pair as opposed to six hundred a pair for mules). Lots of folks choose oxen because they are easier to handle. Others say they're the best because if you get short of meat, you can eat them. Some logic. Guess they

never thought about what would pull the wagons if they ate the oxen.

"Jeremiah says he knows of folks who've had to eat their mules, too, so if you're planning to eat your animals, it's cheaper to buy oxen.

"We left the Missouri River at St. Joseph and headed across the prairie, A lot of wagons outfit at Independence, but by taking the river up to St. Joseph, it's not so crowded and things cost a little less. The trail from St. Joseph intersects the Platte River trail here at Fort Kearney.

"At a small lodge about a mile outside of St. Joseph, we had our first experience with frontier justice. One of the men woke up to find he had been robbed. The other lodgers ran down the suspect, but they almost didn't find the money. The robber had hidden it in his slab of bacon.

"They didn't know what to do with the culprit since there was no jail, so they gave him fifty lashes on his bare back. He swore never to steal again. The sight of the blood running down his back horrified me.

"The trip from St. Joseph to Fort Kearney took eighteen days. We had good grass for the cattle. Unfortunately, we had to cross the Big Blue River at flood stage. The flood made it too deep to ford, so we made a ferry out of a wagon bed. When it came my turn to ride this makeshift raft across, it upset and I almost drowned. Lucky for me a couple of other riders pulled me out in time. I swear I swallowed half the river. Sam told me I looked like a drowned rat. I know I sure felt like one.

"Fort Kearney is a bustling place, I'll tell you. It's located on the south bank of the Platte, just where Grand Island makes a narrow branch of the river. Must be eighty or ninety soldiers stationed here to protect travelers. They do have a Post Office, so I can mail this letter.

"They used to call this Fort Childs, after a Thomas Childs. Some say he was a brigadier general, some say a major. Who knows? Anyway, after the war with Mexico, they had a new hero and changed the name to Kearney. Only goes to show how fleeting fame can be.

"The buildings are sod and adobe, and the soldiers tell me that during wet weather the rain soaks through the sod and muddy water drips down on anyone underneath. I hear the army bought the land from the Pawnees for two thousand dollars in trade goods. Hard to say who got the best of that bargain."

Matilda looked up from the letter and stared across the fields of corn, tall and lush. A bank of clouds gathering on the horizon warned her of an approaching rainstorm. The old envy she felt when her brothers left surged through her again as she thought of their exciting trek.

"Matilda," her mother's voice interrupted. "You finished with that letter yet? I sure could use your help to get this flax pounded."

Folding the letter, Matilda rose to her feet. She would re-read it later, when she could savor every word. She sighed in resignation. Back to the old, dull routine.

"Yes, Mother. Just let me change clothes and wash the dust off my face. I'll be right with you."

The next letter from the wayfarers arrived at the Randolph's Grove Post Office on a hot, muggy August day. The family gathered so Tom could read it. Matilda's mind never left her brothers for long, for as summer progressed, she became acutely aware of the approaching winter. She thought often of tales of unlucky travelers trapped by the

snows. The story of the Donners' misfortune ranged across
the length and breadth of the state, losing nothing in the re-
telling. Each letter put Alf and Sam and Britt closer to the
Sacramento Valley and safety.

> "We reached Ash Hollow last night. They have
> a Post Office of sorts, so I will write a brief note and
> hope you receive it. It took us twelve days to get
> here, so by my reckoning it should be the second of
> June. Travel has been easy, so we're making good
> time. The hot weather is just starting. We have had
> frequent rain storms, with thunder and lightning, but
> nothing serious.
> "The buffalo begin just west of Fort Kearney. We've
> started using buffalo chips for our fires, because wood
> is scarce. Buffalo cover the prairie in massive num-
> bers. You have to see them to believe it.
> "We saw some Indians on a buffalo hunt. There
> must have been a thousand buffalo and over a hun-
> dred Sioux armed with bows and arrows chasing
> them. Four or five Indians ride up to a fat cow and
> shoot arrows into her until she drops dead. The Sioux
> are right skillful with a bow, let me tell you. I was sure
> impressed. I watched one brave get off at least seven
> arrows before the first one reached its mark.
> "Lucky for us the stampede passed a safe distance
> from our camp or we would have been trampled. I
> got to shoot my first buffalo, a big old bull. I thought
> I shot him in a vital spot, but he got up and charged
> me. I ran for my life, but tripped on a buffalo chip
> and fell headlong into a stand of prickly pear."

"What's a prickly pear?" Minerva demanded as laughter
rocked the room.

"We'll tell you later, Honey," Tom hushed her. Struggling
to stifle his own laughter, he continued.

"I thought I was killed until I heard Sam and Joe laughing their heads off. Seems the bull had fallen some thirty or forty steps behind me. That was my first real introduction to prickly pear. It grows all over the prairie. The Indians eat the leaves and make a sweet from the fruit. How they eat around those thorns is more than I can figure. I still carry some with me. I give any I see a healthy respect.

"We dried slabs of buffalo meat in the sun to carry with us. It's a little stringy, but the flavor is great, especially in a stew with a few beans."

Gardner looked at Betsy Ann and grinned. "I'll bet they would appreciate some of your good cooking. I told you it would be good for the boys to be on their own for a while."

"The trail left the south fork of the Platte and crossed high prairie for about sixteen miles, then came down a real steep hill and into Ash Hollow. We eased the wagons down with ropes, a dozen men on each, to keep the wagons from going too fast and crashing at the bottom. This was the steepest hill I have ever seen. But from the top, I looked west and saw the peaks of mountains off in the distance. I can't help but feel this is just the beginning.

"A beautiful spring comes out of the base of the cliff, with the first really good water we've had since we left home. Cattle from previous trains have eaten the grass down to the ground, but ash trees and dwarf cedars abound. We had a real wood fire to cook over last night.

"I found the grave marker for a young woman near our camp. It reads 'Rachel E. Pattison, Aged 18, June 19, '49.' To die so young! We have seen other graves along the way, of course, but for some reason, this one bothered me. I asked about it at the Post Office. Seems she was a bride of only three months. She took the cholera in the morning and died of it by nightfall. Cholera scares me.

"We follow the North Platte from now on, and I hear we will have good grass and water for a while, but no wood. We will spend two days here, and plan to enjoy a real wood fire as long as possible."

The next letter arrived two weeks later, posted from Fort Laramie.

"I probably won't be able to send any more letters until we get to California. Everyone tells me this is the last reliable Post Office, since we are not going through the City of the Saints on the Great Salt Lake. It took us twelve days to get here from Ash Hollow, and is now the sixteenth of July.

"We are climbing steadily higher. It gets blazing hot during the day, but really cold at night.

"Our luck ran out just before we got to Fort Laramie. Cholera broke out and three of our party died, including one little boy of about six, which was real sad. I couldn't help thinking about poor Rachel Pattison. Jeremiah said the cholera was worse on the trail last year, but this was the worst I ever want to see. Joe took it, but I remembered everything you told me, Mother. I treated him with laudanum and elderberry tea and comfrey tea, just like you said. Lucky you made us bring all that stuff."

Betsy Ann shot an 'I told you so' look at Gardner, which he ignored.

"Sam and Britt and I took turns taking care of him and he is recovering. He is still weak, though, and has had to ride in the cart. He complains because it's so bumpy, says he'd rather be riding his horse, so I guess he's feeling better. The army doctor here at Fort Laramie says he's doing fine. Just needs rest and a lot of elderberry tea."

"So Mrs. Dawson nearly lost Joe after all," Betsy Ann commented. "She's been so worried."

"This fort, like Fort Kearney, is made of the sun dried clay bricks, but is a very imposing establishment. Two blockhouses and the walls form a huge rectangle. Walls must be eleven or twelve feet high. Inside are at least a dozen buildings. Luckily one is a blacksmith, for my horse threw a shoe just the day before. They have a sutler's store, but the prices are real high. Mostly, we trade between ourselves. You can get some real bargains, especially from some who have overloaded. We got three more slabs of bacon for almost nothing.

"Five hundred Sioux warriors are here at the Fort after a battle with the Pawnees. They are covered with war paint and have Pawnee scalps with them. I was scared, but the men here at the Fort say not to worry. I sure hope they're right.

"We'll be leaving here tomorrow, and should be in Sacramento by the end of September or the first week of October. Don't worry about us. We are seasoned travelers now."

Weldon burst through the open doorway, and gasped, "Papa Gardner, Papa Gardner! Mr. Stewart's pigs are in our corn again." He collapsed in a heap, as though his little legs could no longer hold him after the exertion of running from the field.

His words cleared the room of males. Caroline turned to Matilda. "Alf may have to dodge buffalo and prickly pear and hostile Indians, but at least he doesn't have to chase Mr. Stewart's pigs out of the cornfield anymore."

Matilda smiled. "From what I recall, I'm sure he'd rather face a hostile Indian any day."

Chapter 8

September of 1850

ONE HOT September afternoon at the end of summer, Matilda took a short cut across the fields coming back from a visit with Temperance. Dry grass crackled beneath her feet. She tried to remember the last time it had rained. Several weeks before, at least, and each day the brassy heat sucked more of the moisture out of every blade of grass. Grasshoppers leaped out of her path, with little clicking sounds. A meadowlark warbled, a dove cooed. If only it wasn't so hot! She should have ridden the horse. Her face flushed in spite of the shade from her sunbonnet. Waves of heat shimmered across the field.

As she reached the road, a horse approached, walking slowly in the stifling heat. She recognized the rider as Asahel Gridley.

He hailed her. "Matilda? It is Matilda, isn't it? Thought it was you. My, you're a grown up young lady now. Let me give you a ride. I'm on my way to see your father, so you won't be putting me out any."

"Thank you, Colonel Gridley," she panted. "I never realized it would be so hot to walk. I usually ride over to my sister's." She put her left foot in the stirrup and accepted his hand so he could lift her up to a seat behind him.

"Hold tight." He urged the horse into motion again.

During the ride to the Randolph residence, Matilda clung to his waist. Sweat had soaked through the shirt on his back. The masculine odor vaguely disturbed her, in a way she could not understand. Sweat trickled down her own face and ran in little rivulets down her back. She wondered why

Colonel Gridley wanted to see her father. He and her father had served on the road commission together several years before. Rumors had circulated among the community that Gridley planned to run for State Senate this fall. Maybe he wanted to ask for Gardner's support.

"Ase, my old friend, it's been a long time," Gardner greeted them as they rode into the yard. "Thanks for giving 'Tilda here a ride." He assisted Matilda to alight. "Set a spell and cool off."

"I come to see you, Gardner." Gridley dismounted, took off his hat, and wiped his sweaty forehead with a big red handkerchief that looked like it had performed that particular function many, many times. He greeted Betsy Ann, accepted the cool drink of water she offered, and seated himself on the rough bench in the shade of the apple tree.

"As you know," he began, "I'm runnin' for State Senate this December." He paused.

I knew it, Matilda thought. He wants Pa to back him. He knows everyone in Randolph's Grove listens to Pa. Gardner said nothing.

"Alton and Sangamon Rail has got the charter to open a road from LaSalle down to Bloomington," he continued. "There's talk of running it east of Bloomington four or five miles. Business goes where the railroad goes, so we want it to come through Bloomington."

Gardner still remained silent. Matilda recognized that silence and struggled not to laugh. She had seen her father use that technique before. He was going to make Colonel Gridley come out and say exactly what he wanted.

"Then they'll want to extend the line south to Decatur, through Randolph's Grove." The words came in a rush, as though he knew what Gardner's reaction would be. Matilda's father had never made any secret of his opinion of railroads.

"Not through my land," Gardner announced firmly. "Not

going to have one of those noisy, smelly things scaring my horses and killing my pigs."

"Now, Gardner," Colonel Gridley pleaded, "you know they're good for the country. Makes everyone's land more valuable . . . ."

"What's the good of it being worth more unless a man plans to sell it?" Gardner interrupted. "Only makes the taxes go higher. Will Thomas wants to raise the tax rate and he hasn't even been elected assessor yet. Says we have to raise taxes to pay for the new Court House. Shouldn't 'a built it if they couldn't pay for it. One you built back in '32 only cost $339 and worked just fine. Pure foolishness to pay Munsell $6000 for a new one only four years later. And on a twenty year bond at that! Imagine paying eight per cent interest on a twenty year bond for a court house they never needed in the first place. Going to get so's a man will have to sell his land to pay the taxes."

"Railroad'll bring more folks, more settlers. Make our towns grow, make 'em more prosperous. Already been more folks moving into Bloomington since they started talking about opening the road down from LaSalle."

"Yes," came the tart response from Gardner, "and not all will be the kind of folks we want. Railroad always brings more drifters in. And houses in the towns that have trains get all covered with soot." He took a deep breath. "Smell this air. You really want to fill it with the black smoke those trains belch out?"

Betsy Ann nodded in agreement. "Bad for the lungs," she asserted.

Colonel Gridley tried another tack. "Goods'll be cheaper, and supplies we order will get here faster. Imagine ordering a new plow in Springfield one day and getting it the next!"

Gardner remained silent, his jaw set.

"And the mail. Think how fast we'll get mail in. We'll get the news from the rest of the country in half the time."

"Pa! Pa!" Sinclair ran up, out of breath. "Fire! Prairie fire, up towards Bloomington."

Everyone ran to the other side of the house to see. A large plume of smoke billowed to the north of them.

"Still a ways from here." Gardner leaped into action. "Betsy, you and the girls stay alert. Get the roof wet down. If it gets past us, set the stock loose and get across the creek. Sinclair, you're 'most a man now." Eleven-year-old Sinclair's chest swelled with pride at his father's words. "Stay here and take care of the women and Weldon."

Tom arrived driving the cart, buckets and sacks already loaded. "Saw the smoke from Britt's place," he said. "John's on his way. I just swung by to get you."

"We'll continue our discussion later, Ase." Gardner climbed up beside Tom, his voice grim. "That's something else the railroad brings. Prairie fires." He spoke to Tom. "Let's go."

Matilda stood watching as the cart rattled down the lane, Asahel Gridley following them on his horse. The smoke, clearly visible by then, rose even higher. The acrid scent wafted over her, filling her nostrils. She felt a momentary panic. The wind blew straight down on them, driving the fire before it. What if the men were unsuccessful in stopping it?

Minerva brought her out of her trance. "Come on, 'Tilda," she urged. "Sinclair's already up on the roof waiting for us to pass buckets of water to him. Carrie's too busy putting her stuff in the big basket."

"Of course." Matilda shook off her paralysis. "Let's get to work."

They labored for half an hour, soaking the roof until water dripped over the edges. By then the smoke made it hard to breathe. A whinny from the barn reminded Matilda of the horses. John, astride Ginger, appeared before them, seeming almost to materialize out of the smoke.

"Pa sent me back to help you," he said, his voice hoarse. "They've got a back fire going and it should hold." Tears streamed down his cheeks from red-rimmed eyes. "But we've got to get the stock out just in case. 'Tilda, take the cow. Sinclair, open the pig pen and turn 'em loose. They'll have to fend for themselves. Come on, let's get across the river before this smoke gets us."

Matilda waded across the river, the placid cow plodding along beside her. The smoke was less dense here, and she could breath a little easier. John followed with the horses, who snorted nervously at the smell of smoke. Betsy Ann herded Weldon, Minerva, and Sinclair ahead of her. She carried her spinning wheel. Minerva held her doll by one leg and cradled the old red rooster in her arms.

Sinclair held a baby pig under each arm, and Weldon struggled with a third. The sow grunted along behind them, squealing as she plunged into the water. "Babies were too small to turn loose," panted Sinclair. "Carrie's got the rest of them in the basket." At the end of the little procession, the weeping Caroline wrestled with the heavy basket.

Matilda looked around the little group gathered on the sandbar across the river from the cabin. She thought of Sarah Williams, remembered the day her home burned, and tried to be as brave as Sarah had been. After all, they were safe. All they could lose would be some material possessions. She thought of her new calico pinafore with a pang. The Kickapoo bubbled and gurgled serenely along. The horses settled down and took turns drinking from the cool river. The old sow, once she had all of her brood together again, lay on her side emitting an occasional contented grunt while the piglets squealed and jockeyed for position to feed. Minerva silently petted and soothed the rooster in her arms, her eyes large in her pale, tear-stained face.

Only Caroline continued to weep, wailing over the an-

ticipated loss of the house and mourning various possessions she had been forced to leave behind when Betsy Ann
commandeered the basket for the piglets. Finally Betsy Ann
turned to her.

"Land sakes, child, spare us your tears. They'll either
stop the fire or they won't, and your blubbering isn't going
to change anything."

"Cheer up, Carrie," John soothed. "Look. The smoke
is easing up. I'm sure they'll get it out in time."

The fire did not reach the Randolph residence. Gardner
and Tom returned with the cart an hour later and helped
re-install the horses and cow in the barn, the baby pigs and
their mother in the sty. Minerva, Sinclair, and Weldon were
dispatched to round up the strayed pigs.

Asahel Gridley followed Gardner back and helped re-
store the Randolph property to order. A layer of soot covered everything. The smell of smoke permeated the house
and their clothes. Matilda, extremely conscious of her wet,
bedraggled skirt, looked around and saw everyone else was
dirty and sweaty too.

Gardner looked at his old friend with skepticism. "Two
and a half miles of prairie burned, Ase, and there'll be more
fires, once you get your ding-danged trains. Trains always
start fires."

"I admit there are some problems . . . ." Gridley began.

"Problems? Tell that to the three families as got burned
out of everything."

Asahel Gridley gave up. He shook his head. "I'm sorry
I don't have your support, Gardner, but if I get elected to
the State Senate this December I plan to push to get that
line through Bloomington. Congress is allowing the railroad
to buy right-of-way where they choose to put the line. In
fact, they've suspended proving up on unclaimed land until
Alton & Sangamon decides what part they want. And the

most direct route from Bloomington to Decatur is through Randolph's Grove." He mounted his horse and rode off.

"Stubborn old coot," Gardner shouted. He shook his fist at the departing horseman. "Curses on any law that gives railroad men the right to cross a man's land without his permission. Man should be the only one to say what happens on his property." He stomped off towards the barn, still muttering deprecations against all railroads and railroad men.

Betsy Ann commented to Matilda, "He's going to give himself an attack of apoplexy if he doesn't calm down. Good Heavens, they've been talking about this railroad for years and nothing's been done."

"But what will happen if it does go through?" Matilda asked. "Will we have to move?" The idea both excited and frightened her. She thought of her brothers on their trek to California.

Her mother shook her head with a sigh. "I hope not. I'm getting too old to start over again. Did enough of that when I was young." She turned toward the house. "You'd better get out of those wet clothes before you take a chill."

Matilda stood and looked towards the now fading cloud of smoke, across the undulating line of prairie, with the fields of wheat and corn alternating with open grassland. In her mind, she saw a ribbon of metal crossing those fields, and black smoke puffing from the smoke stack of an engine chugging its way south from Bloomington. No, Pa, she thought. Progress will not be stopped, no matter how much you protest.

On December 2, 1850, Asahel Gridley won the election for State Senate. He rode off to Springfield, determined to bring the railroad from LaSalle through Bloomington, then south to Decatur through Randolph's Grove.

But that news was dwarfed by more personal news from

much farther away.

Chapter 9

January of 1851

"'*Tilda, 'Tilda,* come quick, come quick!" Eleven-year-old Minerva hopped up and down in excitement, completely forgetting her new-found dignity as a maturing young lady.

Matilda looked up from the strips of venison she carefully hung on the drying racks in the smokehouse. The snows between Christmas and New Year's drove the deer closer to the settlements and her father had shot two. "For Heaven's sake, what's happened? And close the door. That wind is cold."

"Another letter from Alf! They're in California at last." Minerva's blue eyes sparkled as she tugged at Matilda's apron. "Tom just rode over from Britt's place with it. Britt sent a letter to Sarah, too. Come on! Pa won't let Tom read it until everyone is home." Minerva grabbed at the strips of meat to help Matilda finish. They rapidly emptied the pan and headed for the house. Matilda wiped her hands on her apron as she ran, completely forgetting the blood would stain the linen she worked so hard to keep snowy white.

Sinclair had been dispatched to bring his older brothers. Gardner, his eyes gleaming, held the precious letter in his hand.

Betsy Ann was in mid-sentence when Matilda and Minerva entered. ". . . so worried. It's such a relief to know they arrived safe. I know Joe's mother has been beside herself." She fell silent as the last arrivals filed into the house and settled to hear the long awaited letter.

Gardner stood beside the fireplace and solemnly opened the thick packet. The cover plainly showed the marks of the distance it had traveled. He unfolded it and handed it to Tom, then took his seat in his favorite chair, the only one in the house with arms.

Matilda glanced around the room. She and Minerva pulled the bed down from its storage place against the wall and sprawled on it. Betsy Ann sat near Gardner in her rocking chair. Sinclair sat at the table with Caroline. Will leaned against the wall by the door. Will's wife Polly sat near him in the other rocker, holding three-week-old Michael. Will, Jr. stood beside her, clinging to her sleeve. Though just two years old, he seemed to sense the excitement in the room. John sat cross-legged on the floor, his back supported by the edge of the bed.

Not a sound came from the listeners as they waited for Tom to begin. "October 3," he read, "October? This is January. It took this letter three months to get here? And here I thought he was just too lazy to write."

"Dear, Mother, Pa, and Everyone,"

"We arrived last week. It took us 104 days to go from Fort Kearney to Placerville. The trip over the Sierras was the best part of the whole journey. This is beautiful country. It's pretty dry now because they don't get any rain between May and November, which seems strange, then the rains start again. But as soon as I looked down into the Sacramento Valley, I knew all the stories they told about it were true.

"Joe rode in the cart for another week out of Laramie before he felt well enough to ride. Then as we approached South Pass, what began as two small blisters on my arm got so bad my whole arm swelled up."

"Erysipelas," Betsy Ann exclaimed. "He had erysipelas. I told them to treat it with lobelia poultices. Did he treat it with lobelia? I sent some lobelia with them."

"Hush, Mother," Gardner soothed her. "They probably forgot. You told them more in those last two weeks than they could possibly remember." He reached over and patted her hand. "At least they remembered how to treat cholera."

"I just knew I was going to die, but a Mormon lady from a train on its way to the Great Salt Lake came by and saved me. She lanced the two blisters and gave me some pills, then sat by me all night putting on poultices of bread and milk. By morning, I had improved considerably and she told me I would soon be well. I know a lot of people don't like the Mormons, but this lady really was a Saint. She wouldn't even let me pay her. I am sure I owe her my life."

"I'll say he does," Betsy Ann interjected. "He should have used the lobelia poultices like I told him. Erysipelas is very dangerous."

"After we crossed South Pass, we took Sublette's cut-off, detouring around the City of the Saints. They say it's a shorter route, but we had to cross the Little Colorado Desert. Some say we went thirty-five miles without water, others say fifty, but it felt like a hundred and fifty. We went up through Soda Springs and over to Fort Hall, then down across the Goose Mountains into the valley of the Humboldt. Soda Springs was a very interesting place, but crossing the alkali desert between the Humboldt and Carson Sinks was the worst part of the journey.

"The sinks are really strange. The river just flows along, then gradually disappears into the desert. I had never seen anything like it before. The wheels sank in the alkali and we never had enough water. Many immigrants last year took bad advice trying to avoid the desert and wound up worse off on the Lassen cut-off.

"The trail is littered with bones from animals who died. So many cattle died folks had to abandon wagons and throw away gear to lighten their loads. Broke my heart to watch the poor faithful creatures struggle through the thick sand. The dust blew every day, making everything gritty.

"Along the Humboldt was only place we had problems with Indians. The Utes stole cattle every chance they got. We had to keep guard on our stock all night. Sometimes, if they couldn't steal them, they would shoot them with arrows so they had to be left behind. One trick they used was a brave disguised himself in an elk hide and snuck in among the cattle and horses. When he got to the middle, he started to yell. That scattered horses and men alike. Then the other Indians joined him to help run off the animals. We lost several horses in that raid, as did many of the others.

"We had one tragic accident. One of the men shot himself when he pulled his gun out of the wagon by the barrel. Many of these folks have no notion how to handle guns. I couldn't believe any man would do such a foolish thing. He left his wife and three little ones. Fortunately, his two brothers and their families traveled with him, so the widow and children had kin to care for them.

"We gave the poor fool a Christian burial. Some of the trains won't take the time, but our wagon master is a good man. We had a regular funeral procession. All of us put on clean clothes, which was no small achievement. Some put on uniforms they had tucked away in a trunk. One man had a fiddle and Jeremiah dug out his mouth harp. They played *The Old Rugged Cross* while we all marched to the grave.

"An old man from another wagon train said he was a preacher and read the service. (Someone said later he was a fake, but he made the family happy.)

We had to disguise the grave, though, by running over it with the wagons. The Indians dig up bodies and mutilate them. You were right, Mother, not all Indians are like the Kickapoo.

"When we got to Placerville, Joe decided he had seen all the wilderness he cared to. He left us and went on to Sacramento City. He got himself a job working at one of the stores. There's lots of jobs to be had. I trust he's written his folks, but since he's not much of a hand for writing, please tell them he's doing fine."

"I know they haven't heard from him, Pa," Tom paused in his reading to say. "I saw Jim Dawson yesterday and he asked me if we'd gotten any word yet. The last they heard was Joe's short note from Fort Laramie. They're real worried, because Joe was still sick from the cholera. I'll ride over this afternoon and tell them."

"Good idea, Son. I know they're anxious," Gardner said.

Tom returned to the letter.

"Sam, Britt, and I got some supplies and a couple of mules and headed out to get us some gold. Since then, we've been working in the diggings outside of Placerville. Place was called Dry Diggings because water was so scarce, then the vigilance committee hung three robbers, so everyone changed the name to Hangtown. Last February, the State Legislature decided Placerville had more dignity, so the name got changed again. I must say I do like Placerville better.

"We've made a great friend. We were feeling lonesome, kind of homesick and missing everyone, when one of the miners yelled, 'Hey, Alf, come meet Alfred.' We hit it off real good and he invited us to join him on his claim. It's a pretty good one. Some

days we get up to several ounces between us. Sorry,
'Tilda, no big nuggets yet, but I keep looking.

"Our new partner's last name is Wheelock. He's
from Vermont, and is twenty years old. He's well educated and well read. He even brought a couple of
books with him, all the way from Vermont. You'd
like him, Pa. He talks like a professor. He came to
California across the Isthmus of Panama. From Chagres, on the Atlantic, he took a canoe up the Chagres
River to Gorgona, then rode a mule to Panama City
on the Pacific side. You should hear him talk about
that trip."

Matilda thought this Mr. Wheelock sounded like a very
interesting young man. She shook her head at her foolishness. Not likely she'd ever get to meet him. She returned
her attention to Tom's words.

"...trouble getting passage from Panama City,
since the steamship companies back east sell a lot
more tickets than they have space for. They also have
trouble with crews deserting for the gold fields. But
Alfred is a resourceful fellow. He finally got a berth
(actually just a space on the deck) on the Capitol out
of Boston, and made it to San Francisco in July of
'49. From there he took a sailboat up the river to
Sacramento City. The stories he can tell!

"We came down to Sacramento City from the
diggings to get this letter on the steamer to San Francisco. I was real curious to see the city, and wanted
to see how Joe fared. Sam and Britt stayed on at our
claim to protect it from claim jumpers. Lot of problems with claim jumpers, especially desperadoes from
Texas and Missouri.

"Mail service from Placerville is unreliable, and I
knew you would be anxious to hear from us. I could

not be sure you received my other letters. We also wanted to get some supplies.

"Everything is expensive. Would you believe fifty cents for a loaf of bread and a dollar for a quart of milk? Saleratus is three dollars a pound."

Betsy Ann gasped. "Three dollars!"

Matilda understood her mother's surprise. They used the rising soda for so many things. Three dollars a pound seemed terribly expensive.

"Pickles are impossible to find. Anyone with any to sell can get whatever price he asks."

Tom grinned at his mother. "Too bad we can't ship them some of yours, Mother. They wouldn't have to look for gold."

Everyone laughed. The quantity of pickles from last year's harvest remained a family joke. They had been giving away pickles to every neighbor who would accept any.

He silently read the next paragraph and shook his head. "What is it? Read it!" demanded his audience.

Tom cleared his throat disapprovingly, an action Matilda immediately recognized as an imitation of their father. That raised her curiosity even more.

"While we were in Sacramento City, someone told us about a fight scheduled between a bear and a bull over at Brighton, a community south and east of Sacramento City. I know it was not a good way to spend the Sabbath, Pa, but we were real curious. The bears out here are powerful (they call them grizzlies), but the bulls are pretty tough too.

"There must have been two thousand men come to see the fight. A few of them had shinnied up a tree to get a better view. Alfred and I decided to join them. As it turned out, we almost made a serious mistake.

"They chained and roped the bull's front foot to one of the bear's hind legs while the bear was still in his cage, then they let him out. He promptly fastened his teeth in the bull's side. The man beside me in the tree shouted to his partner, 'Pay up. I tol' you that there bull would be nowhar in a b'ar fight.'

"Well, he was wrong. The bull swung his huge head around, got his horns under the bear and heaved, breaking both the chain and the rope. When the bear landed, he shook his head a couple of times and headed for the nearest hiding place. He crawled under a big building and stayed there. The vaqueros struggled and used a lot of Spanish swear words trying to get him out, but he wasn't having any part of it.

"Mr. Price, the organizer, tried to persuade everyone the fight was over and to go home. But many of the men felt they had been cheated, having paid a dollar to see the fight. When a call went up to lynch him, Mr. Price hastily assured the crowd another bear would be found.

"The second bear attached himself to the bull's jaw and hung on for dear life. The bull stood for a moment, as though thinking it over, then gave a mighty heave of that powerful neck and tossed the bear so far the rope and chain broke again.

"Scrambling to his feet, this bear headed for the nearest tree. You never saw such a commotion. Horses and men both tried to get out of the way. One horse knocked another down and both riders scampered on all fours to get away. Men were tripping and shoving and falling all over each other.

"Alfred and I started to laugh at all the confusion until we saw the bear headed for our tree. The grizzled miner beside me shouted, 'Look out! Here comes the ba'r.' We watched in horror, with no idea what to do or where to go. Fortunately, the vaqueros got the bear to change course at the last minute and he picked another tree.

"I opened my eyes and found myself with both arms and both legs wrapped around a limb, with Alfred laughing at me. I guess I looked a sight, my shirt torn, my arm scratched, and my face white. I even lost my hat. I recovered it later, but not until it had been stepped on several times."

The listeners howled with laughter.

"I'm sure glad the bear picked another tree, for he climbed thirty to forty feet in a matter of seconds. They finally got a rope on the critter and got him out of the tree. Those vaqueros made a circle of a hundred horses to keep him in, but this bear didn't want any more to do with the bull than the first one. He refused to go near him. The bull lunged at the bear and the bear kept dodging until the bull got tired of the whole thing and just quit.

"Mr. Price declared the bull the winner, the old miner in the tree with us paid his gloating partner, and we clambered down from our perch to discover I had also torn my new pants. I have to admit the experience had its rewards, but I don't believe I will bother attending any more such spectacles."

"Good," Gardner commented. "I'm sure glad he learned his lesson. I hope he remembers it."

"I hope this reaches you in good time. Everyone is talking about an overland mail route, since California will soon be a state. We heard Governor Burnett speak just yesterday. They do have a Post Office in Sacramento City, so you can send mail general delivery and hopefully I will get it. The service is not very good. If they can find the letter in the piles of mail they receive, I will get it when we come down for supplies.

"Pa, you will be pleased to hear there is a Methodist-Episcopal church in Sacramento City. The Reverend Pollack founded it last April. They say he planned and built it all by himself. I promised to attend services anytime we can get down from the diggings on a Sunday."

Gardner smiled at Betsy Ann. "There, Mother. I told you the trip would not spoil the boy."

"Mail goes from here to Panama City, on one of Mr. Aspinwall's sidewheel steamers, then across the Isthmus to Chagres, where Mr. Vanderbilt's steamer picks it up and takes it to New York. You should get this letter in two months if all goes well. They started sending mail overland by stage last July, by way of Salt Lake City, but I hear it goes faster by water. I'll send the next letter overland to see."

"Two months? Would you believe almost three?" said Betsy Ann.

Tom looked up. "He closes with love to everyone, then adds a postscript that California voted to join the Union as a free state."

"I suspect the reason is more because no one wants anyone to bring slaves into the diggings than for any feelings for the slaves themselves. It's sort of an unwritten law that any man is welcome to whatever gold he finds, but using slaves and hired help is cheating. A Missouri man with a claim near us brought two slaves to do his work, but they got a taste of freedom and took off, along with the man's two oxen. Guess they figured the oxen deserved to be free too.

"He got one Negro back, because the Fugitive Slave Act pays the federal commissioner ten dollars if he finds for the owner, and only five if he finds for the slave. Needless to say, the commissioner usually finds for the owner. The man whipped the slave for running away and brought him back. Three days later he ran away again. So the man was out the slave and the money he borrowed to get him back. We sometimes wonder how the fellow lives, for he's too lazy to do his own work, too proud to beg, and too cowardly to steal."

With a chuckle, Tom handed the letter back to his father. Gardner folded it up and muttered, half to himself, "This slavery business is going to cause problems yet. People like that Missouri man give these abolitionists more fuel for their fires. Never a problem with slaves long as a man treats 'em right, and takes good care of 'em."

A moment of silence followed the final sentence, then a babble of voices broke out as they all tried to talk at once. Gardner's voice rose above the din.

"Tom," he ordered, "ride over to the Dawson's. Tell 'em we heard from Alf and that Joe is well. And," he added as Tom headed for the door, "swing around and tell Temperance. She'll want to come by and read about her brothers' adventures."

Betsy Ann clasped the letter to her breast. Matilda knew her mother would read and re-read those words.

Matilda sighed. Her brothers were so lucky, she thought. They got to see all those interesting places and do all those exciting things. California. Even the name sounded romantic.

She sighed again. Did she get to do exciting things and go to exotic places? No. She got to hang strips of meat in the smokehouse.

Chapter 10

January to March, 1851

MATILDA CHEWED the end of the quill pen in her hand and stared out of the window at the snow encrusted trees. Her eyes returned to the paper before her and she wrote:

"Dear Alf,

"Christmas seemed strange. Mother said this was the very first time we haven't all been together. It took your letter almost three months to get here. Even Mother had begun to worry.

"Your new friend Alfred sounds very nice. I wish I could meet him. I'm so glad we can finally send letters to you."

The light from the slanting winter sun shining through the window cast a ray through the bottle of ink on the table. She smiled with pride. This bottle represented her first attempt at making ink. Her mother taught her, saying if she wanted to write, she should learn how to make her own pens and ink.

"Now, Matilda," Betsy Ann had said, "you can't hurry ink any more than you can candles." Her mother often chided her for her impatience. Matilda winced at the reminder of her first candles. Eager to see the results, she had taken them from the mold too soon, only to watch the tall and lovely tapers slowly sag to ungainly lumps of tallow.

So when she made the ink, she soaked the logwood chips for the prescribed twelve hours, and simmered the liquid slowly until Betsy Ann pronounced it perfect. When the ink cooled, she poured it into bottles. Before sealing the bottles with their glass stoppers, she carefully measured in twenty grains of yellow chromate from the drugstore in Bloomington as a preservative, making a far superior ink to the pokeberry juice they had used for years.

The results were perfect. The sun shining through the bottle showed not a speck of sediment floating in the ink. She admired her handiwork for several seconds before continuing her letter.

"Mr. and Mrs. Dawson were happy to hear Joe is well. His bout with cholera frightened them. Please get Joe to write to them himself, even just a note. Mrs. Dawson is terrified you are not telling her how he really is doing. She won't rest until she hears from Joe direct."

Matilda's thoughts drifted to the excitement of seeing far away lands. She wondered if she would ever get to go to an exotic place like California. She would love to see a real gold nugget. And the mountains! Having spent her whole life on the flat plains of Illinois, she could not imagine anything like the mountains Alf described. She wished she could have seen the fight between the bear and the bull. The vaqueros Alf described sounded so romantic. Her heart beat a little faster at the thought. She could see them mounted on their magnificent horses, silver shining from their saddles . . . .

Betsy Ann looked up from the pie dough she rolled out on the other end of the table. "If you'd spend as much time writing as you did day dreaming, you'd have that letter finished by now."

Matilda flushed, hoping her all too observant mother hadn't guessed her thoughts. She quickly returned to her letter. She did have to finish. John planned to take the packet to the Post Office tomorrow and she wanted her letter included.

"Pa is talking about moving. The railroad wants to build their line from LaSalle to Decatur. Asahel Gridley got himself elected to the State Senate and is in Springfield right now working to get them to route it through Bloomington. I heard even Stephen Douglas gave a couple of speeches in Congress promoting it. If they do run the line down to Decatur, it will cut right across our property. Pa is livid. He hates railroads anyway, and he feels his old friend has betrayed him. Mother tries to calm him, but he'll have no part of it. She's afraid he really will decide to move."

She looked around the kitchen, recently added to the house. The two new windows held precious panes of glass, far superior to the oiled paper they used for years. The sun shining through the tiny bubble in the center of the pane cast a small prism of color on the table. She smiled. Many homes still used oiled paper for their windows because of the high cost of glass.

"There has been talk of taking the Kansas Territory away from the Indians and opening it for settlement. Poor Mother. She likes having close neighbors, but Pa keeps grumbling about not having enough room to breathe.

"All this slavery business upsets him. More and more abolitionists have moved in. Thank goodness Illinois is a free state. There'd be no living with Pa otherwise. He says it sure was handy, President Taylor dying sudden like that so Mr. Clay could get that dreadful Fugitive Slave Act passed. Mother tries to hush him whenever he gets started.

"I know Pa thinks the South has the right to keep slaves, but I think slavery is wrong."

She underlined the word 'wrong' three times for emphasis, then related the details of her visit to the Williams family and of the clandestine trip to the slave auction in Keeneville. "Don't let on to Pa," she cautioned, "but I, for one was very glad to hear California joined the Union as a free state."

She also described her experiences with the ferry, knowing Alf would laugh. He often teased her about her fear of water. She, alone of all the siblings, had never learned to swim.

> "Mr. Williams is doing very well now. His ferry gets a lot of business since the stage line started crossing the river there. He is even talking of building a larger ferry. Hank and Jim, Jr. see the ferry stays on schedule and Sarah tends to collecting the money. Her father says it's no job for a slip of a girl, but she says if she didn't do it, her father would take a drink of whiskey from one of his passengers and forget to collect half of the money due them."

Sarah had added that if she were Matilda, she would have gone to California with Alf and his brothers. Matilda had no doubt Sarah meant it.

She paused. Rubbing her aching hand, she peered at the worn nib of the pen and decided to make a new one. It would give her hand a chance to rest. While Betsy Ann put the pie in the Dutch oven and pulled hot coals around it so the pie would bake evenly, Matilda pulled one of the prepared quills out of a jar on the table. As she carved, she wrinkled her nose at the memory of the smell when her mother baked the batch of boiled feathers to harden them. Baking them had made the whole house reek of the feathers for days afterward.

While she cut, she thought of what she had written. Would their father really decide to move? If he did, could they take Mother's precious cupboard? She could not see Betsy Ann giving it up. And the new Franklin stove. It was so handy. Sometimes in hot weather, a small fire in the stove was enough to cook a pot of stew and they didn't need to build a fire in the fireplace.

The pen finished, she returned to her letter.

> "Alec is married now. He and Margaret Dawson got married last summer right after you left. Margaret had a beautiful gown. Carrie was her maid of honor, so Mrs. Dawson took them on the stage to Springfield to buy the material. Mrs. Dawson said no store in Bloomington had anything nice enough, even though Mr. Orendorff had some lovely satin.
>
> "Anyway, they went to Springfield and stayed overnight at the Globe Hotel. I wanted to go, but they wouldn't take me. But they didn't sleep all night because the bell on top of the hotel kept ringing and waking them up. Served them right.
>
> "I got to be one of the bridesmaids. At the reception, one of Alec's friends scandalized Pa by putting whiskey in the punch. Several of the younger boys got drunk, including Sinclair. It made him so sick he couldn't get out of bed the next morning. I teased him as he lay groaning on the bed.
>
> "I think Sinclair managed to convince Pa the boys didn't know the punch had whiskey in it, but I heard them laughing about it, so they knew. Sinclair certainly learned his lesson."

The aroma of baking pie filled the room. She stopped to savor the fragrance, thinking of all the time she spent last fall cutting up apples and stringing them to dry. Just the smell of those pies made all the needle pricks in her fingers worth while.

> "Anyway, Alec and Margaret have a cabin in one corner of the Templeton farm. At least fifty people came to their cabin raising. They are so in love they

walk around holding hands. Sinclair says it's disgusting, but I think it's wonderful.

"Will and Polly have another little boy, born last December. His name is Michael. Will, Jr. is jealous. They have to watch him or he hits the baby. Polly is horrified, but Mother tells her it's not unusual. Polly always makes such a fuss over things. Mother says she had the same problem with Britt when Temperance was born, although she says if you tell Britt, he will deny it.

"Mother is worried about Temperance. That cough she had last winter didn't clear up during the summer, and now she coughs up specks of blood. Mother fears she may have consumption."

Tears stung Matilda's eyes. Surely God wouldn't take Temperance away from them, would He? She stared out the window, forcing her thoughts away from her concern for her sister, trying to think of any other news items that might interest her brothers.

"With Britt gone, Sarah is boarding the new school teacher and she has set her cap for Tom, but Pa says she doesn't have a chance. He says Tom's not the marrying kind.

"Do write and tell us more about California. It sounds so exciting."

She paused, fighting the envy she felt. If she had been a man .... She didn't even dare tell him she found the fight between the bull and bear exciting. Her mother said young ladies should not be interested in such things. Young ladies weren't supposed to be interested in anything exciting. It wasn't fair. "I wish I could see your claim," she finally wrote. At least that was a safe subject.

"Are you getting rich? We hear stories of fabulous gold nuggets being found every day, but others say a man can make as much as a day laborer as he can digging. We don't know which side to believe."

She signed her name, then added a postscript:

"Do you have a sweetheart yet?"

Her mother re-entered the room. "Have you finished your letter? If you can talk those chickens out of two more eggs, I'll make johnny cake for supper."

Alf's next letter arrived near the end of March. Winter had loosened its grip on the land, and melting snow turned the fields to mud. The hard packed dirt of the roads stayed firm beneath a several inch deep layer of mud, so horses had to pick their way with great care. Buggies constantly slid off into deeper mud on the sides. John kept Big Red harnessed and ready to pull out any hapless soul who became entrapped in the mud.

"Almost skidded off the road bringing this letter over from Britt and Sarah's place," Tom grinned. "Better be worth it. Sarah says Britt's already talking about coming home. Guess he misses her."

Matilda wanted to take the letter over to share with her sister Sarah as soon as Tom finished reading it, but her father refused.

"Too dangerous," he told her. "What if the horse slips? Wait until tomorrow. Another day of sun should dry the roads enough to travel, long's you keep an eye on the muddy spots."

So early the next afternoon, in bright sunshine, Matilda saddled gentle Old Alice and headed for her sister's home, the precious letter tucked securely down the front of her dress.

Sarah, delighted, greeted her sister with a hug. "How sweet of you to ride over to share Alf's letter with me. Come in, come in." She ushered Matilda into the cabin. "I don't

get out much now that I can't ride again." Sarah expected
her third child in June. "I've told Albert we'll have to get
a buggy when this baby comes. Three is just too many to
manage on a horse."

In the five years she had been married, Sarah had turned
the little cabin into a cozy home. True, the cabin had only
two rooms, but Albert had bought Sarah a little Franklin
stove, and made a small table. Sarah embroidered the
flowered mat that adorned it. In one corner stood the tiny
wooden cradle Albert had made for the first child, newly
scrubbed and sanded in anticipation of the newest baby.

Steep stairs led to the loft they used for storage. That
would become the sleeping area for the children as soon as
they were old enough. The door to the left opened onto
the small bedroom. Through the open portal, Matilda saw
the bed, adorned by the brightly colored quilt she and Caroline had tied for Sarah's marriage. Matilda smiled to herself. She and Caroline had been only ten and twelve at the
time, and the quilt showed some ragged stitching, but Sarah
seemed to treasure it. Sarah's two children, Lawson, three,
and Elizabeth, one, napped on the big bed, surrounded by
pillows.

Sarah smiled. "Since the children are asleep, let's share
a nice cup of tea over Alf's letter. Tell me what he had to
say."

Matilda seated herself on the sofa as Sarah bustled about.
She set the teakettle on the stove to boil and took the towel
off the teapot and cups where they stood on the sideboard.

"They had a cholera epidemic in Sacramento City."

"No!" Sarah gasped. "None of them took it, did they?"

"No, fortunately they were all at their claim in the hills.
Alf found out about it after it was over." She paused. "The
cholera came on the steamer *Abby Baker* that arrived in
Sacramento in October. He says the boat carried a bunch of
miners from New York, and a cholera epidemic got started

in New York by immigrants from Europe. The same boat brought them the news that California had been admitted to the Union." She shook her head. "Good news and bad news together. Funny how the cholera travels that way. Why do you suppose it does that?"

Sarah only shrugged and said, "Who knows?" as she set the tea service on the table.

Matilda took a sip of tea from the delicate china cup, one of a pair the Funk's had given Sarah as a wedding present. Those two cups were saved for use on very special occasions. Evidently Sarah felt a letter from Alf rated the special cups.

"Joe told Alf and Alfred - that's Alfred Wheelock, Alf's partner - all about it. Remember Joe went on to Sacramento City while Alf and Sam and Britt stayed in Placerville to look for gold."

Matilda paused to take another bite of cookie. "Joe told them he found an old man lying on the levee almost dead of cholera. His sons had abandoned him to die while they went off to the gold fields. Can you imagine such a thing?"

Sarah shook her head. "I can't see any of our brothers doing that."

"Absolutely not," Matilda said. "What a dreadful thing to do! The poor old man." Then she shuddered. "And what a horrible disease. Alf said they walked through the cemetery and counted eight hundred new graves. Goodness knows how many were from the cholera. I guess the newspapers tried to hide how many were dying to keep the panic down."

Sarah replenished the plate of cookies and sat down again. She shook her head. "And probably many of them young men like our Alf, with their heads full of dreams of finding gold. Or worse, men like Britt who've left families back here, and maybe no one even letting their folks know."

"Probably," Matilda agreed. "Anyway, on the bright side, he says their claim continues to produce several ounces of gold a day." She shrugged. "I guess that's enough to keep them going, although from the prices he says they have to pay for everything, it must take a lot just to live."

"Do you think he'll ever come back? What about his plans to go to the University?"

Matilda shook her head "I doubt he ever thinks of coming back, not the way he raves about California." She picked up the letter. "Britt's talking about coming back, though. He says the gold that's easy to get has been cleaned out." Matilda smiled. "I suspect he misses Sarah and the children. He did promise Sarah he'd come back in two years."

Matilda shuffled through the sheaf of papers. "Let me read you one part, then you can read the rest yourself."

Carefully setting down the teacup, she located the page she sought. Tucking an errant curl back into place, she read,

> "Our claim did rather well this past month, so when I saw a nice featherbed for sale, I decided to buy it. Alfred laughed at me and called me a sissy, but it looked real comfortable.
>
> "Ever practical, he wanted to know how I planned to get it home, since our mule is half wild and real touchy. I decided to blindfold the brute until I got the featherbed tied on, thinking maybe then he wouldn't notice."

"Imagine Alf on a mule!" Sarah commented.

"I guess they're real popular in the diggings," Matilda responded, proudly using the new word 'diggings'. After taking a sip of tea, she read,

> "But when I took the blindfold off, the mule looked back at my featherbed and started to buck. He jerked me off my feet and threw me flat on my back, nearly breaking my neck. The stubborn critter kept bucking until he got one hind foot in the featherbed. In no

time we had a regular snowstorm of feathers flying around us. Alfred just sat on the ground holding his sides and laughing until he choked. Big help he was."

"I think I like this Mr. Wheelock," Sarah said, laughing.

Matilda giggled. "Me, too. He sounds like a lot of fun. Anyway, Alf goes on to say 'So much for my nice featherbed. The moral of the story: Never pack a featherbed on a wild mule.' "

"Can't you just see all those feathers flying around?" Sarah controlled her laughter with an effort.

"At least he was philosophical about it," Matilda said. "He said it probably would have been too warm to use anyway. His partner says they get a little snow in the diggings, but it melts right away."

"Imagine winter with no snow," Sarah sighed wistfully. "I never imagined there were such places except in far off heathen lands."

"You should have seen Mother's face when Pa said," here she lowered her voice to mimic her father and quoted, "'Sounds like real interesting country out there.' You know Mother's scared to death he'll take a notion to go traipsing out there himself, what with him always complaining about so many people moving in around here." She rose to fill her teacup, emptying the pot. "Especially if the rail line gets built across our land."

"Is he really thinking of moving to California or is he still talking about Kansas?"

"He didn't say. He just paused long enough to worry Mother, then told everyone to get back to work." She handed the letter to Sarah. "Here. Read it yourself while I make us some more tea. I loved the part about the new preacher wanting to get rich in gold instead of souls."

While Sarah read, Matilda made another pot of tea. The fire in the little stove crackled. A slight, pleasant smell of wood smoke permeated the room. The stove put out just enough heat to keep the whole cabin comfortably warm. The oiled paper in the windows, while letting in light, did not allow Matilda to see out. She thought how much nicer glass windows were. Being able to see out always made the room seem bigger.

A murmur from Sarah interrupted her. "Good heavens! They even had a fire during the cholera epidemic."

"Yes. Four hotels and a couple of stores, as I recall. I'd say that was quite a fire." Matilda brought back the refilled cups and handed one to Sarah. "Isn't it lucky they had a modern fire engine?"

"Sacramento City sounds like an enterprising little place," Sarah agreed, absently taking the cup in one hand while she read. Silence filled the room once more. Matilda sipped her tea.

When Sarah finished, she glanced over at Matilda. "What a shame that nice Mr. Pollack had to leave the church. I hope he didn't really die of consumption after he got home to Alabama."

"Me, too." Matilda reached for another cookie. She caught the flash of worry that crossed Sarah's face. "What is it?" she asked.

Sarah recovered quickly. "Oh, nothing. Just thinking of Temperance. She seemed so frail the last time I saw her. That cough just doesn't go away."

Matilda started. "You don't really think Temperance has consumption, do you? If she does, she might die!"

Sarah hastened to reassure her sister. "It's probably just a bad chest cold. She'll be fine, come summer."

Chapter 11

Spring of 1851 to Spring of 1852

BUT TEMPERANCE'S cough did not improve, and she grew weaker. Betsy Ann treated her with comfrey and elecampane root teas, but nothing helped.

"Temperance," she finally told her oldest daughter, "you must get more rest."

Temperance replied, with a wan smile, "I know, Mother, I know. Sarah's taking care of Henry for me." Henry, an active, healthy three year old, was into everything. The effort of speaking brought on another coughing spell.

When the spasm passed, Temperance's mother wiped away the trickle of blood that dribbled from the corner of the sick woman's mouth and coursed down her chin.

"It's too much for Sarah," Betsy Ann said, shaking her head. "She's only nine. You need comfrey leaf poultices to your chest three times a day. The root tea is not enough."

So Matilda moved into the little cabin to care for Temperance and her family. By the third week in May, Temperance could barely raise her head from the pillow. Her cheeks glowed with fever through translucent skin drawn tautly across the prominent bones. Coughing spells came more often and lasted longer.

The bloody sputum frightened Matilda, but she dutifully applied the hot comfrey poultices to Temperance's chest and urged her to drink the comfrey and elecampane teas. A neighbor had urged the use of the new medicine and cold water applications marketed by Dr. Cyrenius Wakefield in Bloomington for congestive fever and chills. Betsy Ann, with her usual scorn for the medical community, preferred her tried and true remedies.

"Might help a bit with the ague," she had declared when the neighbor spoke to her, "but won't do a thing for the consumption." After the neighbor left, she opined that in her view, Dr. Wakefield was a quack, only out to make money from the gullible members of the community.

"Please, Temperance, try to eat," Matilda begged one day in early June. "The weather is so nice. We have to get you strong enough to go outside. Maybe the sun can help dry your lungs."

Matilda also remembered the argument between her mother and Dr. Karr. Dr. Karr said Temperance needed to stay indoors with the windows shut, but Betsy Ann, in strong agreement with Samuel Thomson, considered fresh air much better. At least, Matilda thought with a smile, in spite of their frequent disagreements, Betsy Ann did not consider Dr. Karr a quack like Dr. Wakefield.

Temperance attempted a smile and allowed Matilda to help her raise her head. She made a feeble effort to swallow the beef broth Matilda offered, but finally pushed the spoon away.

"'Tilda," she whispered, then paused, exhausted. She rallied her strength and continued, "You've always been my favorite. I . . . wanted you . . . to know . . . " Her head fell back and her eyes closed.

"Temperance!" Frightened, Matilda frantically felt for a heartbeat. Yes, Temperance still lived. Matilda lowered the frail frame back on the bed and stood up. She could not help comparing the fragile body on the bed with the lively, robust sister she remembered telling the wonderful stories of the Kickapoo Indians. Tears filled her eyes and slid down her cheeks. She wiped them away, afraid sharp-eyed little Sarah would notice. Voices from the next room floated through the door. Sarah, bless her, read to Henry to keep him occupied.

Suddenly, Matilda had to get out, away from the smell of impending death. She almost ran out the door into the open air. The sun dipped in the west in the long summer twilight. As she stared across the field of growing corn, she saw Josh coming towards the cabin.

The look on her face told him Temperance had grown worse. Silently, he took Matilda in his arms, resting his cheek on her hair while she wept, the coarse homespun of his jacket rough against her cheek.

"In the morning I'd better ride for the rest of the family," he murmured.

"Yes," Matilda whispered. She could not bring herself to say out loud they would be coming to say good-bye.

The next morning, Temperance seemed to rally a little. She opened her eyes when Matilda applied the comfrey poultice to her chest and tried to smile. Matilda, hope buoying in her heart, propped her sister up on the pillows and asked, "Do you think you can swallow a little soup?"

The sick woman's arms suddenly flailed out, and a wild look came into her eyes. With one hand, she clutched Matilda's arm with such unusual strength the girl winced in pain. With the other, Temperence clutched her chest and her eyes fixed on a point across the room. Instinct told Matilda her sister was no longer aware of her presence.

"No," Temperance gasped, "not . . . not yet . . . not ready . . . ." A spasm of coughing racked the emaciated body and bright red blood poured from her parted lips.

Horrified, Matilda screamed for Josh. Between them, they leaned Temperance forward as the blood drained from her mouth. The frail body shuddered and was still.

Matilda's eyes met Josh's. The stream of blood dwindled to a trickle. Josh gathered the lifeless body of his wife in his arms and clasped her to his breast, his eyes dark with pain.

Matilda turned to the two frightened children who stood at the end of the bed.

Many graves had been added to Stewart Cemetery since young Sattlefield's burial in 1825. They buried Temperance next to her baby brother Andrew, just east of Britt and Sarah's daughter Minerva.

"Makes two of my children buried here now," Betsy Ann remarked, tears almost breaking through her reserve. "Should be grateful, though. Many's the woman as has buried more."

Matilda wept throughout the whole ceremony, only half hearing what Uncle James had to say. The Reverend Stringfield came from Kentucky to conduct the services. Betsy Ann insisted he be the one, so Tom had ridden for him as soon as it became apparent Temperance would not recover from her illness.

After the skies threatened rain all morning, the afternoon sun broke through and shone brightly down on the little group gathered by the graveside. Matilda wondered how she could feel so cold with the weather so warm. The cold reached her heart as she remembered so many things about her sister, the stories she had told, the happy times they spent together.

Matilda's heart ached as she realized she would never again hear Temperance's quick laughter, or see her toss her long black hair over her shoulder as the hazel eyes sparkled with humor. She felt her father's arms encircle her and she wept against his chest.

After Temperance's funeral, the neighborhood moved en masse to the Randolph residence. Temperance had been well liked, and the Tovrea clan was a large one, so many people gathered about the outdoor tables holding the many dishes contributed for the post-funeral feasting.

As the afternoon drifted into evening and people began to disperse, Betsy Ann beckoned to Matilda.

"Find Carrie and get started washing up," she directed. She added gently, "Be good for you to keep busy. Keep your mind off Temperance."

Matilda nodded, not trusting herself to speak, and started her search for Caroline. She found Minerva sitting under the apple tree looking forlorn. "Min," she asked. "have you seen Carrie?"

Minerva motioned towards the barn. "Saw her headed that way a while back."

"Go start cleaning up. I'll fetch her to help us." Matilda hurried towards the barn, thinking Caroline probably had sought refuge there to grieve for Temperance in private.

As Matilda swung the barn door open, the mingled smells of musty hay and horse manure greeted her. She wrinkled her nose and almost called aloud for Caroline when the soft murmur of voices, one masculine and one feminine, stopped her in her tracks. Her sister's voice she recognized at once. She listened for a moment, then recognized the second. Tommy Evans.

What were Caroline and Tommy doing in the barn? Her heart lurched as a scene from the Christmas party at Stewart's popped unbidden into her memory. Since John Stewart's wife Jane, as well as Britt's wife Sarah, were Tommy's sisters, Tommy and his family had been present. Matilda had dismissed the incident at the time, crediting an overactive imagination. Thinking back, the look she caught between Tommy and Caroline as they shared a private moment grew in significance.

Not daring to interrupt, afraid to move lest she be heard, Matilda stood rooted to the spot, her mind in a turmoil. What would happen if anyone found out? After all, Tommy had a wife and two little boys. And he was old. At least ten years older than seventeen-year-old Caroline.

"I'd better get back. Susan can't stay up long. She gets too weak, and will be wondering where I am." Tommy's voice floated back to Matilda.

"How much longer will we have to wait?"   Caroline sounded wistful.

"Shh," Tommy hushed her. Their voices lowered and Matilda could no longer distinguish the words. She sank against a pile of hay, feeling prickles as the coarser stems poked her arms and legs. She heard footsteps approaching and shrank farther back into the hay. Tommy walked past. If he saw her, he gave no sign. He looked both ways at the door and disappeared from sight.

When Caroline followed him, Matilda stepped out of her hiding place.

"'Tilda," Caroline gasped. "What . . . why . . . ? How long have you been here?"

"Long enough," Matilda replied, her jaw set. "Carrie! What are you thinking of? He's a married man!" Matilda's voice echoed her shock and horror.

Caroline shrugged. "Everyone knows Susan is going to die soon. She has the consumption, just like Temperance."

"But . . . but if anyone finds out you and Tommy are . . . are . . . ," Matilda stammered, unable to say aloud what she thought. "They'll say you willed her to die!"

"That's nonsense," Caroline snapped. "No one can will anyone to die. Besides, how's anyone going to find out?"

"I found out," Matilda told her. "Suppose Pa had come into the barn instead of me? Or worse yet," her eyes widened, "Uncle James? What would he have done?"

Matilda did not address herself to deaf ears. Caroline shuddered. To James Stringfield, a strict Methodist, sin was sin. There were no gray areas. Caroline cast an anxious glance at her sister. "You're not going to tell on me, are you?" She searched Matilda's face, then her reserve crumbled and she burst into tears. "I love him so much!"

Matilda gathered Caroline in her arms and tried to comfort her. While she had never been in love, Matilda had recently read *The Scarlet Letter*, Mr. Hawthorne's new book. A clandestine copy had been smuggled into the barn and kept hidden under a pile of hay. The vision of her poor sister in the place of the fictional Hester made her suddenly sympathetic to Caroline's plight.

"Of course I won't tell anyone," she murmured. "What kind of a sister do you think I am? Come on, we've got to get started on the dishes before Mother sends Minerva after us."

The following April, Gardner Randolph watched another son leave him for the fabled land of California. Betsy Ann's brother, Sevier Stringfield, made the decision to head west and Will Randolph decided to accompany him.

"Too many people around here," Will declared. "Land's getting too expensive, now the railroad's gonna go through, and taxes are too high. Sam's looking to buy himself a place out there, and from what his last letter says, a man can buy good land pretty cheap. Land not all cut up with railroads."

To Gardner Randolph, that was a tender subject. The Alton and Sangamon Railroad, recently renamed Illinois Central, had, with Asahel Gridley's influence, announced their preference for the route cutting the Randolph property in half. Plans were underway to start its construction, although Gardner and some other farmers along the proposed route still attended hearings in opposition.

"I hear Congress plans to open the Kansas-Nebraska Territory for settlement," Gardner said. "If Douglas gets his way, the territories will be able to decide whether to be slave or free. If we could settle there, get enough votes, we could make Kansas a slave state. Have ourselves a real plantation, just like my cousins in Virginia."

"Not me." Will shook his head firmly. "I don't hold with

slavery. I know you think it's all right, long's a man treats his slaves good. But too many don't. If it was a fair system, wouldn't be so many trying so hard to get away."

"You've been listening to those Hicksites again," Gardner accused with a scowl. "You know how they exaggerate stories, make up tales to make slave owners look bad."

"No, Pa, I've heard Will Riggs talk about what he saw in South Carolina. I don't think any man has a right to whip another like an ox, no matter what color his skin is."

They had disagreed about this often, so Betsy Ann interceded. "Don't you two start again." She changed the subject. "Will, does Polly agree? Aren't your youngsters pretty small for such a trek?"

"No smaller than Britt and Temperance were when you and Pa came north from the Sangamon," Will answered. "Didn't stop you. I've written to Sam, told him to speak for a place for me long side of his." He grinned suddenly. "Besides, all this talk about California has given me a real itch to see it. My feeling is one day we'll all be there."

So, on the twelfth of April, 1852, Matilda stood with her parents and remaining brothers and sisters and watched her Uncle Sevier and brother Will whip the oxen into action. The wheels creaked as the wagons began their long trek to California.

"Good-bye, Gramma and Grampa. Good-bye, Aunt 'Tilda," cried four year old Will, Jr. from the back of the last wagon. "I'll miss you."

Matilda stood and waved until the small caravan disappeared from sight around the bend in the road. Was Will right? Would they all eventually join Alf and Sam in California? She shook her head. Not likely.

With a sigh, she turned and walked slowly back toward the house.

Chapter 12

Summer of 1852

"*Mother! 'Tilda! Carrie!*" Sinclair's voice reached their ears before they saw him.

Matilda, startled, poked herself with her needle. Sucking the injured finger, she glared at her brother. "For heaven's sake, what is it? You scared me half to death."

"Britt's coming back." Sinclair reached the porch and collapsed, panting for breath. "Sarah just got a letter he wrote from Sacramento. Greenberry Larison from over Waynesville way is coming back with him. They're takin' a steamboat to San Francisco where they'll catch one of the Pacific Mail Steamships to Panama." He chuckled. "Then they have to go by mule across to where the railroad to Aspinwall starts."

"Haven't they got that railroad across yet?" Betsy Ann interposed.

"I guess it's only as far as a place he calls Bahio Soldado or some such name. From Aspinwall, the new city the Rail Road Company built on the Atlantic side, they catch a steamer to New York. From there, they can get a train to Erie and come by river to Pekin. Should be here in a week or two."

"Oh, Sinclair, that's wonderful!" Matilda exclaimed.

Betsy Ann grunted. "Well, he said he'd come back in two years. Shame he missed seeing Will and Polly. Bet he didn't say he's comin' back rich. Knew those stories of all that gold lying around was just so much talk."

"He says he's bringing some gold with him," Sinclair said. "Didn't say how much." He shook his head. "Sarah

just sits there and cries. She says it's 'cause she's so glad
he's coming back." He snorted in disgust. "She sure has a
funny way of showing it."

Two weeks and one day later, on the seventh of May,
1852, just as the sun sank into a bank of clouds to the west,
Britt rode up to the cabin. Matilda, Minerva at her heels,
raced to greet him. Soon the entire family surrounded him.

"Whoa," he laughed. "I haven't seen Sarah and the
youngsters yet. Follow me over. I'll talk to everyone at
once."

Two hours later, the clan had gathered in Britt and Sarah's
small cabin. As Betsy Ann and Sarah bustled about preparing supper, everyone else clustered around Britt, plying him
with questions.

"Did you really come back by boat?"

"What was Panama like? Like Alfred told Alf?"

"How long did it take?"

"Did you bring a nugget?" This from Matilda.

"Is the country as good for farming as Sam says?" Gardner wanted to know.

"Did you get in any Indian fights?" Sinclair had no interest in farming.

"One at a time, one at a time," Britt grinned. "The country is everything Sam and Alf told you. Good farm land,
good weather, beautiful mountains, even a bustling modern city nearby." He hugged his sons. "Only Sarah and the
children could bring me back. Had I been single like Sam
and Alf, I'd have stayed.

"But the gold for easy picking is about gone. So many
men fight for each speck of land that it's not worth it anymore. Miners can make a living, but that's about all. And
believe me, it's hard work." He drew a small cloth sack out
of his pack and handed it to Matilda.

She gave a startled gasp. "It's so heavy!" She squeezed

the bag. "But it feels like sand. Is it really gold?"

"Yes," Britt assured her, "it's really gold." He turned to Sarah. "Hand me one of those tin plates, Honey." When she complied, he put the plate on the table and poured the contents of the pouch into it.

Everyone had to run their fingers through it. Matilda, fascinated, let a trickle fall from her hand. The tiny flakes caught the light from the tallow candle on the table. Envy shot through her. How lucky her brothers had been to see such a fascinating country!

"I guess," Britt began, "Alf told you all about the trip in his letters. It took us 104 days to cross the plains from Fort Kearney to Sacramento. We actually enjoyed it, especially Alf. And almost everyone can tell some tale about a buffalo encounter. Green Larison told me he had an experience similar to Alf's with his first buffalo.

"While we were on the Sweetwater, I climbed to the top of Devil's Gate. Sam and I wanted to see where Fremont made his sign, near the top. The ledge is almost perpendicular, about 200 feet high. The water has cut a channel right through the middle of the blackest rock I've ever seen. I almost didn't make it to the top, though. I had to pull myself up the last bit by holding on to some bushes. Sam made it up ahead of me and stood there laughing at me while I struggled."

He chuckled. "Alf told us we were crazy. He waited at the bottom and almost got hit by a boot. Young Will Hodge had to take off his boots to make it to the top. He threw them up ahead of him and the one that almost hit Alf fell down. Will threw the second one away, thinking the first one lost. You should have seen his face when he saw Alf carrying his boot back to camp."

"Alf mentioned some Indian trouble," Gardner commented. "I take it you had no serious problem?"

"Beyond losing some stock to the Utes, no." Britt shook

his head. "We did see a lot of Digger Indians. I guess they're called that because they live in holes dug in the ground. The Diggers have an interesting way of hunting. They build two brush fences, each a half a mile long, laying them out so they converge to a narrow gap. Then they get a big bunch of Indians to chase the game between these fences. A small party of the best hunters waits to kill the game with bows and arrows as it comes through the gap."

"I bet they don't do that with buffalo," Sinclair said.

"No, they live past the range of the buffalo. Mostly they get rabbits and antelopes. The rabbits are big ones, with ears like a jackass. In fact, they call them jackass rabbits because of their ears. The antelope is a small one, real clever and real fast." He grinned. "And real tasty. We shot one every chance we got, which wasn't often enough. They were just too fast.

"Uncle James would have been shocked beyond words at these Indians," Britt added with a laugh. "The Diggers were as innocent of clothing as Adam and Eve before the fall. It gets real cold at night up there, too, even in July and August. They just curl up close to their fire. Can't imagine how they survive the winter."

"I take it you didn't find as much gold as you expected," Gardner remarked, running his fingers through the little pile of gold on the tin plate.

Britt shook his head. "By the time we got there, most of the good claims were taken. If we hadn't met young Wheelock, we wouldn't have done as well as we did. And we got there just in time for the drought of the winter of '50 - '51." He chuckled. "Lucky us. They had floods the winter before. We piled up great heaps of earth, ready to wash, but the rains never came. Lots of miners went broke. Green told me he lost about twelve hundred dollars that first winter. We managed to hang on until the rains finally came last fall. Green got enough then to come home, and so did I.

Alf and Alfred are still sticking it out on the claim, hoping to get more. Sam used his share to buy some land just south of Sacramento City, near a place called Hicksville. It's right off the Upper Stockton Road, just past where old man Hicks has a toll bridge across the Cosumnes river."

"Will wrote to Sam," Tom said, "and asked him to speak for some land close by for himself and Polly."

Britt frowned and shook his head. "The land Sam bought is in a Mexican land grant called San Jon de Los Mokelumnes. They got some dispute goin' over who has the right to sell it."

"What's a land grant?" Gardner wanted to know.

"The Mexican government wanted to get settlers for California, so they gave out grants of ten thousand acres of land to any citizen who asked for one. In 1844, Governor Micheltorena granted all the land between the Cosumnes and Mokelumne Rivers, just south of Sacramento City, to Anastacio Chabolla. Chabolla's wife sold five thousand acres of it to an American named Weber, I guess thinking she was entitled. Chabolla got mad and said she had no right to sell any of it. Then Chabolla died and now his heirs are all arguing over who gets what. Sounds like trouble brewing to me."

Betsy Ann furrowed her brow. "You think Sam might lose his land?"

Britt shrugged. "Hard to say. Some are saying since the Mexican government granted the land the claims don't hold, now that California belongs to the United States. The Land Act of 1851 that Senator Gwin pushed through, over Fremont's objections, opens the door for all kinds of claims against Mexican property. All depends on how it works out. Judges tend to favor Americans over native Californians, so maybe he won't lose it. Hope not. He's sure got a right pretty piece of land. Ought to grow a fine crop of wheat or corn. Doesn't rain all summer, but the water is so close to the surface in the swampy areas between the rivers that crops do just fine." He stopped to take a big bite of corn bread, then chuckled. "Sure have missed your johnny cake, Honey," he said to Sarah.

"Did Sam get Will's letter before you left, saying they were coming out?"

"Yep, and was right happy to hear it. Sam thinks we should all come. Says California's the place to be. There's trouble brewing over this slavery business, and he's glad to have two thousand miles of desert between him and the squabblers."

"From what I hear, the country out there isn't all that peaceful," Gardner said with a scowl. The slavery issue was a sore point with him.

Britt shrugged. "Green says he came back because the country is so lawless, but that's changing fast. Still some problems in the hills. San Francisco's had a lot of trouble, especially with the Sidney Ducks, from Australia. But it's real peaceful around Sam's place."

"How'd Green Larison like the country?" Betsy Ann inquired. "Did he come back for his family, or is he planning to stay?"

Britt laughed. "He liked the climate and the country. He'd 'a' been glad to stay except for some folks who make their own laws. He had one real bad experience. He sold his mule to a man named Baker for seventy dollars. Baker got swindled out of it by another miner who claimed it had been stolen from him. That's a pretty common trick. Unless a man has friends to back him up, they get away with it. So Baker came back to Green. Accused him of selling a stolen mule and demanded his money back. Green was pretty disgusted, but with no law to turn to, he lost his money and the mule."

By then, the candles burned low in their holders, so Britt declared the questions at an end. "I've had a long day," he told them. "And you've talked me hoarse. Look, the candles are about gone. To bed, everyone."

Matilda, too excited by Britt's narrative to fall asleep at once, lay awake long after the little cabin was quiet except for her father's gentle snoring. She finally rose from her quilt on the floor and found her way to the table. Moonlight flooded through the window, illuminating the little pile of gold still lying on the tin plate. She sat for a long time, sifting the golden flakes through her fingers, admiring the glint of color as the rays of light from the moon caught the tiny particles of gold.

Some day, she promised herself. Some day.

Chapter 13

1852 to 1853

THE NEXT MORNING, the family visited the cemetery so Britt could pay his respects to Temperance.

"She was my best friend," he said softly. His hat in his hand, he knelt and swept away the few leaves and scattered grass accumulated there. He ran his hand over the marble slab.

Matilda watched with tears in her eyes. She knew how hard this was for him. He and Temperance, with only two years difference in their ages, had been very close.

"We got the stone from Halderman Brothers' new store in Bloomington," Gardner said. His gruff voice showed he, too, was near tears. "They opened up there just a few months before ... before ...." He stopped.

"It's a right nice stone, Pa," Britt said.

The small group stood silently by Temperance's grave for a few moments more. Britt placed a small jar with a handful of wildflowers by the headstone with great care and rose. Then, one arm around his wife, they turned to the grave of the baby daughter they had buried back in 1844.

"Our Minerva and little Andrew have company now," Sarah murmured, her head on Brett's shoulder.

The procession walked back down the hill towards the Randolph residence. "One more thing you should know," Matilda told Britt as they strolled along. "Josh plans to re-marry. He and John Moore's daughter Julia have set a wedding date for July, soon's it's been a year."

Britt shrugged. "Can't fault him. Hard for a man to live alone, especially with young ones to tend to."

Matilda sighed. She supposed he was right, but, remembering the sight of the stricken Josh when Temperance died, it seemed to her he could have grieved a little longer. There must be more to this love business than she understood.

Later that summer, after spending the morning picking blackberries from the bushes that lined the Kickapoo River, Minerva and Matilda strolled homeward, enjoying the cool breeze after days of stifling heat. As they neared the house, they saw their father stalk from the barn scowling and shouting, "Betsy! Betsy!"

Betsy Ann appeared in the doorway, wiping flour from her hands with a dish towel. "For heaven's sake, Gardner, what's wrong?"

"It's all these newcomers. I told you we had problems when I saw the plug hat on the circuit rider. These people aren't farmers. They're storekeepers and lawyers and politicians."

"Land sakes, come in and cool down. You'll have an attack of apoplexy." Betsy Ann pulled him through the door. Stunned, Minerva and Matilda followed. What had happened?

Gardner flung his hat into the corner of the room and paced the floor. "Illinois Central decided to use the route Ase wants, through Bloomington. 'Senator Gridley has convinced us it's the most practical'," he said, mimicking the high-pitched voice of the railroad attorney. "The most practical for them," he stormed, "but it cuts our land in half."

Matilda had never seen her father so angry. The last few years had changed him. He never used to get so upset. She looked at him closely, dismayed to see signs of aging. She had always thought of him as ageless. The hairline of his dark hair, now almost gray, had begun to recede.

Not wanting to hear more, she walked back outside. The murmur of voices came to her though the open door, her father's upset, her mother's soothing. Did this mean they would really move? But to where? Her heart rose. Perhaps now they would go to California, as Alf and Sam kept urging them to do.

But time passed. In June, Illinois Central broke the first ground for their tracks, starting in front of William Flagg's home on the northeast side of Bloomington. By the end of summer, the line ran a few hundred yards east of the Randolph cabin. Betsy Ann, in view of Gardner's distrust of banks, stored the money the railroad paid for the land in an old leather haversack she kept under the bed. Gardner said nothing more about moving.

In the fall, with a grand ceremony shunned by Gardner Randolph, the first train lumbered out of Bloomington en route to Decatur over the new tracks. From then on, every morning, the great black monster steamed and snorted its way past the Randolph residence, between the corn fields. At first the trains terrified the horses, but, as time went on, they, too, became accustomed to the noise and ignored it. Life returned to normal.

The following summer, romance entered Matilda's life for the first time. She and a neighbor, Curtis Stewart, began exchanging smiles whenever their paths happened to cross. The fact that Matilda had long admired him made his acknowledgment of her presence all the more exciting. He finally asked Gardner's permission to take her to the Fourth of July picnic in his new buggy.

Gardner, his eyes twinkling, pretended reluctance for a few minutes, then gave his consent. Matilda knew her father held the Stewarts, one of the wealthier families in Randolph's Grove, in very high regard and was secretly pleased that Curtis showed an interest in Matilda.

Matilda, excited to have her first real beau, prepared her

box lunch with care. She fried a young chicken, seasoning it carefully with sage and wild onion as her mother had taught her. Of course, she had to talk Tom into chopping off its head. Her brothers teased her and Betsy Ann ridiculed her squeamishness, but she had never managed to persuade herself to chop the head off a chicken.

She made a small fresh peach pie with fruit from the tree in the yard and a small apple pie from the store of dried apples. She boiled two ears of fresh sweet corn from the garden and searched her hope chest for two finely embroidered linen napkins. Proud of her box, she gave a finishing touch to the bow on the top.

When her box came up for auction, she gave Curtis her private signal. But Tom and John saw her action and bid higher and higher. Poor Curtis tried to outbid them, but to no avail.

Matilda stomped up to Tom. "How dare you!" She gritted her teeth to keep her voice down. "You know that's my box and you should have let Curtis buy it." She grabbed for the gaily wrapped parcel.

Laughing, Tom held the box above her head, his six foot height making it easy for him to keep it out of her reach. "Whoa, little sister. John and I were just joshing Curt."

John approached accompanied by the abashed Curtis. Tom, with an elaborate bow, handed over the disputed box. "Sir Curtis," he proclaimed, "I hereby present to you the offering of the fair damsel, Matilda." He and John, chuckling at the success of their joke, strode off together.

"Brothers!" Matilda's eyes flashed. She stamped her foot and two spots of bright red appeared in her cheeks.

Curtis laughed. "They were just joking, but the joke's on them." With a smile, he tucked her hand through his arm. "They paid for our lunch, so I have the money I saved to use for the games."

Matilda looked at him with surprise. "You're right," she

said. "Those two clowns outsmarted themselves." She
squeezed his arm and joined his laughter. "I see a lovely
spot under that apple tree. Let's grab it before someone
else does."

Matilda could not remember a more exciting afternoon.
She clung to Curtis' arm, proud to show the envious neighborhood girls that Curtis Stewart, Randolph's Grove's most
eligible bachelor, had chosen her, Matilda Randolph. Her
eyes shone as she watched him win rag dolls and hot pads
and bags of rock candy. Skilled equally in darts or ring toss,
he seemed unbeatable. His green eyes sparkling, his dark
hair clinging to the film of sweat on his forehead, he led her
from one booth to the next.

When the day ended, far too soon, Curtis drove her
home and helped her down. "Thank you for a lovely day,
Matilda." He touched his hat with a little bow, climbed back
into the buggy, and drove off.

She watched him disappear from view, her heart flutter-
ing. I'm in love, she thought dreamily. She drifted into the
house. Her mother's voice intruded on her reverie. "You'd
better get your head out of the clouds and watch where
you're going, young lady, or you'll trip over something."

Two weeks later, on her seventeenth birthday, Curtis was
included in the celebration as a family member. Matilda
began thinking of wedding plans.

Then, the first week in August, her world shattered. As
she walked back from the hen-house with her basket full of
eggs, she saw her father striding towards the house, calling,
"Betsy! Betsy! It's done!"

Done? What's done? Matilda felt her heart lurch.

"Houser has made a fair offer for our land," he announced in triumph as Betsy Ann appeared in the doorway. "Says he doesn't mind the railroad, says he thinks it

makes the land even more valuable. And land prices have been going up since that blasted railroad went through."

Excitement washed over Matilda. Did this really mean they would move?

Gardner continued and she returned her attention to his words. ". . . don't have to stay here and smell these wretched trains any longer. We'll go as soon as the Kansas Territory is opened for settlement."

Matilda knew Congress debated the Kansas-Nebraska Act. Was it settled already? She could not help thinking about the poor Indians who lived there. She knew the Act was supposed to protect their property rights, but she also knew how often Indian rights were ignored by newcomers. Would they be pushed off their land like the Delaware and Kickapoo had been? Probably. She sighed in sympathy.

Then her thoughts flew to Curtis.

Curtis looked stunned when Matilda told him. "Moving? You mean . . . leaving? But, 'Tilda . . . ." His voice failed him.

"Maybe you can come, too," Matilda suggested. "Kansas will be brand new and wide open. There should be lots of land available there."

"Oh, no," he shook his head. He looked down at the hat he turned around and around in his hands, then said shyly, "I've already spoken for a parcel of land for us. We'll have eighty acres, just a couple of miles north of here."

As he talked on, outlining his plans for their future, Matilda's uneasiness increased. She tried to understand. After all, his whole family lived here, and the Stewart name was highly respected. She could see why he would prefer not to go where he would be a complete stranger. At least she told herself she could understand it. But would this mean she was destined to stay in Randolph's Grove forever? Would she never see California? Of course, Kansas was not California, but . . . .

Her love for Curtis pulled her the other way. She watched his face light up as he outlined his plans for their future. She tried to see her life as the wife of a Stewart. She could think of several girls who would certainly envy her the position. But somehow . . . .

"Oh, 'Tilda," Curtis concluded, his face shining as he seized her hands in a tight grip. "Won't it be wonderful?"

Startled, she looked at him, suddenly realizing he had been talking all this time and she had not heard a single word.

"Oh," she murmured, "Yes, yes. That will be wonderful."

Carried away with the emotion of the moment, he swept her into his arms and kissed her lips for the first time. Previous kisses had been chaste pecks on her cheek, usually with a family member present. This time, they were alone and he held her tightly as his mouth pressed against hers.

The surge of feeling that swept through her made her heart pound. Her skin tingled. As her knees grew weak, she realized there existed a world of the emotions of which she, until now, had been totally ignorant. She felt a flash of understanding for her sister Caroline's behavior with Tommy.

Sinclair's snort of disgust brought her back to reality. Matilda pushed herself out of Curtis' arms. Blushing, she ran into the house and slammed the door.

But the feeling remained. Whenever she remembered the incident, she felt Curtis' lips on hers, felt his arms around her. How could she leave him?

She would talk to Caroline. Caroline knew about love. After all, she loved Tommy enough to refuse all other suitors. Without telling them why, of course. Only Matilda knew Caroline's reason for turning down every offer she received from other young men in the neighborhood. In fact, Curtis' first interest in one of the Randolph girls had been Caroline, over a year ago.

When he still regarded me as a child, Matilda thought with a little smile. Everyone wondered why Caroline had turned down such a handsome and eligible suitor as Curtis Stewart. Only Matilda knew and she honored her pledge to keep Caroline's secret, no matter how tempting it had been to reveal her knowledge. Especially when the other girls chattered in speculation about Caroline and Curtis.

On the morning of August 6, 1853, as Matilda washed clothes outside in the big tub under the sycamore tree, Tommy Evans rode up. He dismounted and their eyes met. His were red-rimmed and Matilda knew what had happened.

"Susan," she said.

He nodded. "Last night." He took a deep breath. "Just wanted you folks to know. Services will be tomorrow afternoon at Stewart Cemetery. Please tell ... everyone." He looked around.

"Carrie's not here," Matilda replied, "but I'll tell her." She smiled faintly at the startled look on his face.

He read the knowledge in her eyes. "How long have you known?"

"Since Temperance's funeral," she replied. "I caught you in the barn."

"Two years? You've known for two years? And you've never ... I mean ...." He stopped.

She smiled. "No," she said in a low voice, "I've never told anyone. I promised Carrie her secret would be safe with me. But you're going to have to be extra careful now."

"I know." He stared off across the fields for several moments, his face taut with pain. The train, on its daily morning trip from Bloomington south towards Decatur intruded on the silence, drowning the sounds of chickens clucking and grasshoppers chirping.

Tommy swung back to face her. "I ... it's hard to explain. Susan was so ill for so long." He shook his head. "I do ... "

he caught himself, "I did love her." His voice quavered and he took a deep breath. "I never meant to fall in love with Caroline."

"I know," Matilda assured him. "You stayed by Susan and cared for her during her illness. That's what's important."

"Thank you," he choked, "for understanding." To Matilda's astonishment, he clasped her in his arms with a sob. She returned his embrace, awkwardly patting him on the back. Just as suddenly, he released her. Without a word, he mounted his horse and rode away. Matilda stood and stared after him for a long time, her heart aching with sympathy. In a way she could never have explained, she understood his pain.

The following evening, the family returned home from the Stewart residence where the post-funeral gathering had been held. During the services, Tommy stood beside Susan's grave, his face inscrutable. Five-year-old Ely clung to his coat. Seven-year-old John stood bravely beside his father, his eyes bright with unshed tears. Tommy and Caroline had not spoken a word, nor, as far as Matilda could tell, even glanced at each other. Matilda hoped the secret remained safe. In six months, Tommy could properly ask Gardner for permission to call on Caroline. She knew her father would agree, for not only was Tommy Britt's brother-in-law, Tommy and Sarah's father, Owen Evans, had been a close friend. Gardner and Britt had witnessed Owen Evans' will at his death back in '45.

Poor Susan. To die so young. Matilda knew she was only twenty-three, and had been so sick the last two years she could not even leave the house. Strange, she thought. Consumption killed Temperance so quickly, yet poor Susan, who never recovered her strength after Ely's birth, just gradually grew weaker and weaker. Matilda fervently hoped Susan never knew Tommy had found another love before she died.

Caroline and Matilda followed Betsy Ann into the house. When the three of them were alone, Betsy Ann said to Caroline, "You and Tommy better be careful. Don't let your father get wind of what's been going on between you two."

Caroline and Matilda both gasped in shock. Matilda thought, I should have known Mother would know. She always knows.

Betsy Ann had nothing to add. "Get the candles lighted," she said. "Be dark soon."

Chapter 14

Summer of 1854

PREPARATIONS FOR MOVING progressed. One morning in July Matilda and her mother were alone as they prepared a new batch of candles. Minerva had accompanied her father on a shopping trip to Bloomington and Caroline had stopped over at Britt's. Caroline spent a lot of time with Britt and Sarah. Matilda often wondered if Sarah knew her brother and Caroline were in love, but never dared ask.

Matilda decided to discuss her indecision regarding marriage to Curtis with her mother. Threading an oil-soaked wick through each mold in the block, she tried to keep her voice casual as she said, "Curtis wants me to marry him and stay in Randolph's Grove. He's spoken for eighty acres of land just north of the home place, up towards Bloomington."

Betsy Ann's nod showed the information did not surprise her. "Use a square knot over the holding stick. That's a granny." She stirred the kettle in silence for a moment. Matilda waited. "Matilda, you'll be eighteen next summer. You're a grown woman. That's a decision you'll have to make for yourself. Just remember, once you make it, no more daydreaming over Alf's letters from California."

Matilda started and dropped one of the wicks. How does Mother know I'm so interested in California? she thought, as she fished for the escaped wick. She had never told anyone how she envied her brothers, and how often she wished she could have gone with them. Probably the same way Betsy Ann always knew everything.

Her mother said no more. She picked up the kettle. "Tallow's ready. Got those wicks tied good?"

Matilda had written to Sarah Williams, knowing full well what Sarah would say. The beautiful Sarah brushed off beaus left and right, firmly refusing to marry any of them. She said after seeing what her mother went through, she knew all she wanted to know about husbands.

Sarah did not disappoint her. When the response came back, Matilda laughed as she read, "For Heaven's sake, 'Tilda. There are men everywhere. If you really want to get married, you'll meet another one in Kansas." Still laughing as she folded up the letter, Matilda pictured Sarah writing just those words.

So what should I do, she thought, a little frantic now that moving day approached. Which shall it be? Curtis or Kansas?

Curtis, of course, begged her to stay with him. "Please, 'Tilda. You are the only girl I have ever loved. You know I can give you a comfortable life. We won't be rich, but . . . "

He spoke on. She only half heard his words. If she married him, her life would be secure, serene, peaceful. Was that what she wanted out of life? He loved her, that she knew for sure. Would that be enough? Did she love him? If she really loved him, why did she have so many doubts? Did she love him or did she love the idea of marrying a Stewart?

Her whole body tingled at the thought of the passionate kisses they had shared. She blushed at the intensity of feeling he had aroused in her on several occasions when they had managed to be alone for a brief time. Did those feelings mean she was in love? And could she give that up? Then she remembered all her dreams of going to new places, of seeing exciting things, of meeting new people. And Kansas? What would she find there? Maybe nothing.

But then the other side of her spoke. If you never go, you'll never know.

"I can't decide now, Curtis," she finally said. "You'll have to give me more time."

The previous February, six months almost to the day after Susan's death, Tommy Evans had appeared at the Randolph door to formally ask Gardner's permission to court Caroline. Gardner, oblivious to the sparkle in Caroline's eyes, said, "Well, you're welcome to try. Never seen such a fussy female. She's turned down every other young man to come around."

Matilda scurried out the door, fearful she would not be able to keep her face from betraying her knowledge. In the barn, she buried her face in Big Red's broad shoulder and laughed until the tears ran down her cheeks. "How," she asked the patient old horse, "can Pa be so wise in so many ways, yet be completely blind as to what's in front of him?"

Big Red only snorted.

Tommy became a frequent caller. A wedding date was set for August 22, the proper year after Susan's death.

On the morning of Caroline's wedding, Matilda helped her sister don the lovely satin wedding dress. They had spent hours sewing on the tiny beads around the neckline. The glow on Caroline's face made Matilda wonder if what she felt for Curtis was the same as Caroline's love for Tommy. She never noticed such a glow on her own face. And Caroline had felt this way about Tommy for over two years. Even the thrill Curtis' kisses aroused in her had waned with time. But yet . . . .

"'Tilda," Caroline's soft voice interrupted Matilda's thoughts, "you know how grateful I am to you for keeping our secret all this time."

Matilda smiled. "What kind of a sister would I be if I

didn't? What I can't understand is how Mother knew. She seems to know everything."

Caroline laughed. "Britt says it's instinct. She always knows. She always has. When he and Temperance were little, they could never get away with anything." She struggled with a button on her sleeve. "Help me with this thing. Pa, now, he never notices anything."

"Carrie," Matilda began, then hesitated, concentrating on the recalcitrant button.

"Yes?" Caroline prompted when Matilda showed no signs of continuing. "Something bothering you?"

"It's Curt," Matilda said. "He wants me to marry him. You're happy to stay here with Tommy. Why don't I feel the same way about Curt?"

"If Curtis wanted to go to California, you'd marry him in a minute, wouldn't you?"

Matilda started. She had not thought about it like that before.

"You're not in love with Curtis, 'Tilda my sweet. If you marry Curtis, you won't get to go anywhere, because he plans to spend his whole life right here in Randolph's Grove." She smiled at her sister. "You're not like me. All I've ever wanted is a home with Tommy and a family. You want more. You always have."

"How do you know?" Matilda asked.

Caroline laughed. "Because it's written all over your face whenever a letter from Alf comes. Anyone can see it. You'd have gone with Alf and Sam in a minute if they'd invited you."

Matilda frowned as she carefully adjusted the veil over Caroline's face. Is that the problem, she thought? Is Caroline right? Curtis' face flashed through her mind: the tenderness in his eyes, with the love he felt for her so plain. The same look of love she saw in Tommy's eyes when he looked at Caroline. She would be a fool to give that up, especially combined with the wealth and respect of the Stewart name. She sighed. Plans were underway to leave for Kansas soon. The wheat harvest had finished the previous week, a bumper crop for the third year in a row. Gardner only waited for the creeks south of the Sangamon to go down to make the crossings easier. She had to decide.

She dismissed Curtis from her mind. Today was Caroline's day. She walked around her sister, adjusting a fold here, a pleat there, and pronounced her perfect.

"You and Tommy have waited for so long," Matilda smiled. "You deserve your happiness." She started at the sudden flash of pain in Caroline's eyes. "What is it?" she asked. "What's the matter?"

"Tommy has a cough that doesn't go away, just like Susan and Temperance," Caroline said in a worried voice. "I'm afraid . . . ." Her voice trailed off.

"Oh, no!" Matilda gasped. "You don't think Tommy has consumption, do you?"

Tears filled Caroline's eyes. "I don't know. I pray not, but it worries me."

Matilda's heart sank. After waiting for so long, would Carrie's happiness be snatched from her so soon? Would this be God's way of punishing them for falling in love before Susan died? She remembered some of the sermons of Uncle James on the subject of sin. Was he right? She hoped not. Surely God could never be so cruel.

She hugged Caroline close. She could think of nothing to say.

The day after Caroline and Tommy's wedding, and one week before the date set for the family's departure for Kansas, Matilda still had not decided. The sale of the farm to Mr. Houser had been completed. Over the winter, the men built three prairie schooners, as the big Tennessee wagons were called, for the trip to Kansas. Britt, Sarah, and their four children would accompany them. Tom and John eagerly anticipated the move. Sarah, of course, would stay in Bloomington where Albert worked in his father's grocery store. Caroline and Tommy planned to live in Tommy's home near Lexington, thirty miles northeast of Randolph's Grove. The younger children, Sinclair, Minerva and Weldon would go with their parents.

Betsy Ann remained firm in her refusal to leave her most precious possessions, and space in the wagons was reserved for her Franklin stove and her cupboard. She spent her days packing household goods and her vital stores of herbs and medical supplies. She personally directed Sinclair and John as they transplanted three peach trees and two apple trees into a washtub.

"Only one way to be sure and have fruit to dry, that's to raise it yourself," she announced.

She also insisted on bringing Clementine, her prized cow, named after a girl in a song Alf had sent them from the gold fields. "We're not going without milk and butter. We've done that before." Gardner laughed, and Matilda knew her mother referred to an incident before Matilda's birth. Her father had cut wood for a week in trade for a cow only to have the ungrateful beast die a week later. Gardner had been so disgusted with cows that several years passed before Betsy Ann could persuade him to get another one.

One of the wagons carried the farm implements. The sugar casket, the ham barrel, bags of flour and corn meal, the list went on. Moving involved an astonishing amount of work.

Gardner hugged Betsy Ann and laughed. "Got a lot more now than when we moved here. Remember?"

"Very well," Betsy Ann replied, with some asperity, "and we are not going back to that!" She said it with such emphasis that Gardner laughed again. Then she added, with her usual philosophy, "But it is good to move once in a while.

Gets rid of all the accumulated junk." She gave Matilda a significant look. "Very well, young lady. Do you want your boxes put in the wagon or sent over to Sarah's?"

Memories of Curtis' kisses and caresses flooded though Matilda again. Her body tingled. She longed to feel his arms around her, to experience the rapture of his lips on hers. Her heart pounded. The thought of the days ahead without him created an aching emptiness. How could she leave him?

She looked at the loaded wagons and thought of the new worlds awaiting her. A surge of excitement drove thoughts of Curtis away for a moment.

She knew her mother watched her closely. Britt picked up the first of her boxes and waited for her answer. Dear God, she begged, help me. Which will it be? Curtis or Kansas?

She could wait no longer. The time had come to decide.

BOOK TWO: KANSAS

1854-1864

Chapter 15

August of 1854

AS THE FIRST SLIVER OF SUN appeared on the horizon, Britt called out, "Move 'em! Never get to Kansas lying abed."

Matilda opened her eyes, blinking for a moment at a fading dream, and nudged Minerva, still sound asleep beside her.

"Come on, lazybones," she urged her protesting sister. "We have to get going." Matilda scrambled into her clothes and crawled out of the tent.

Her mother squatted by the campfire preparing breakfast. The makeshift kitchen, two crotched poles driven in the ground to support the truncheon on which the kettles hung suspended, had a half wall of stones on the north side to protect the fire from the wind.

Amazed at the appetite she had on the trail, Matilda hurried to where breakfast awaited. Never before had ham and bacon tasted so good. The tantalizing aroma of coffee rose from the pot hanging over the fire and mingled with the smell of johnny-cake baking in the Dutch oven. Any of the cornbread not eaten for breakfast would be carefully wrapped in paper to eat at the mid-day rest period. That morning, stewing dried apples bubbled in a kettle beside the coffee pot.

"Sure will be glad to get settled again," Betsy Ann remarked as she filled Matilda's cup with steaming coffee. "Gettin' too old to camp out. Got the rheumatics in my knees and this squattin' is hard on 'em."

Sinclair milked the cow each morning before breakfast, and the full pail of fresh milk stood on a block of wood beside the tin plate of cooked ham. Matilda spooned some of the frothy milk into her coffee cup, glad they had brought the cow. Clementine's rich milk always made the coffee taste so good. She sat down on the wagon tongue to eat, balancing the plate on her lap, the coffee cup beside her.

A moment later, Minerva ran up, buttoning her calico pinafore, her boots still unhooked. "Mother," she asked, "can I take my breakfast over and eat it with Becky?"

"If you want." With a shrug, Betsy Ann handed Minerva a tin plate filled with some of the stewed apples, piled a huge slab of cornbread on top, then added a slice of ham.

"Min," Matilda interrupted. "I haven't brushed your hair yet."

"Oh, Mrs. Sanders will do it," Minerva replied, dipping a cup of milk out of the pail. "She likes to do it. Says it makes her feel she has two girls now." Minerva hurried off, trying to walk fast without spilling her plate or the full cup of milk. Her unlaced boots flapped.

Betsy Ann turned to Matilda and commented, "I'm glad Minerva has found a friend her own age." Betsy Ann shook her head. "But Mrs. Sanders dotes on that girl too much."

The Sanders family had joined them when they crossed the Illinois River several days before. Their only child, Becky, a beautiful little girl, had just turned thirteen, the same age as Minerva. With no other girls their age in the group, Minerva and Becky quickly became inseparable.

While the women cooked and tended to the younger children, the men and older boys knocked down the camp and repacked the wagons for the day's drive.

They had left Randolph's Grove on the twenty-ninth of August and Matilda, after much agonizing, had decided to move with the family. The stricken Curtis followed for several days, riding beside the wagon, and tried to persuade

Matilda to return and marry him. She felt a twinge of guilt when the excitement of all the new places and new experiences pushed him so quickly from her mind.

Guess I couldn't have loved him too much, she thought with a wry smile, though she still tingled whenever she remembered the feelings his embraces aroused in her. Other than that, she remembered little about him. Maybe I was more in love with the Stewart image than with Curtis Stewart, she thought. Thinking back, she found him a little stiff, even a trifle dull.

Crossing Illinois, they followed the stage road, and the previous day had covered about twenty miles. Coarse grass grew in abundance on both sides of the road, packed hard from the pounding of thousands of iron-shod hooves. The marshy creeks they crossed became more numerous. They would soon reach the ferry at Hannibal where the trail crossed the Mississippi River into Missouri.

Betsy Ann firmly refused to allow them to camp near any of the creeks between Springfield and Hannibal.

"The miasma brings on the ague. That's what killed my father," she announced. "Fill the barrels at the creek and we'll camp a mile farther on, on high ground."

The flies and mosquitoes that swarmed over the area by the creeks made the others happy to comply. High ground made camping much more comfortable, for the breeze blew away the worst of the bugs.

They camped for an entire day outside of Springfield while Gardner bought one of John Deere's new plows, with a steel mold board.

"Hear the Kansas sod is even tougher than the Sangamon," Gardner said as Betsy Ann demurred at the expense. "Good way to use some of the money we got from the railroad."

Here they also met George, an earnest young man from Springfield. "Just George," he grinned when queried about his surname. "Ain't got no other name. Never knew my folks." He offered his services as a scout in return for food along the way.

"Been through the Kansas Territory four times with wagon trains, Mr. Randolph. Got my eye on a pretty little spot on the Big Blue. Decided as soon as they opened her up for settlin' I'd stake me a claim there." He winked at Matilda. "Gonna try and get myself a wife, settle down, raise a family." Matilda blushed and dropped her eyes.

"Yes, sir, Mr. Randolph," he continued, "you could do a lot worse. Some o' Kansas ain't got a whole lot goin' fer it, but along the Big Blue . . . ." He paused for a moment, his eyes drifting off to the horizon. Then he spoke a little faster, as if to make up for the time lost in the pause. "Good water. Big Blue runs all year, don't dry up like a lot of the smaller creeks do. And trees! Lotsa trees. Walnut, oak, hickory. And berries! Gooseberries, blackberries, raspberries. Even wild strawberries."

Gardner started to speak, but George rambled on. "And antelope and prairie chickens and wild turkey to put meat on the table all year long. Buffalo cross a little to the west, sometimes even come right up to the Big Blue herself. Why . . . ."

Gardner held up his hand and laughed. "Enough, George. You've convinced me. Please, join us."

Britt, having crossed already in 1850, automatically became the leader. The trip had been a pleasant one. The weather stayed dry, not too warm, and lush grass on both sides of the stage road provided plenty of fodder for the cattle and horses.

Finally, as the sun sank towards the horizon, they reached the ferry crossing at Hannibal. It had taken them a little over eight days to cover the distance from Randolph's Grove to Hannibal, approximately 130 miles, averaging nearly twenty miles a day. According to Britt, they made good time.

Matilda noted with dismay that at least twenty wagons waited at the ferry to cross ahead of them. Gardner shook his head as the men conferred. "Might as well camp," he commented to Betsy Ann. "No way we'll get across before dark."

Britt agreed, with a nod. "We'll cross in the morning." He turned and strode towards the ferry. "I'll make sure we don't lose our place in line."

After supper, in the long, summer twilight, Matilda stood on a little rise just outside of the camp and watched the ferry taking wagons across. She thought of her experiences the summer she had visited Sarah Williams four years earlier, riding on Sarah's father's ferry. She wished she could see Sarah, but knew it to be impossible.

She did write to her, though. The letter, already sealed, would be mailed when they passed though Hannibal. In the letter, she told Sarah she had taken her advice and left Curtis behind in Randolph's Grove. She could hear Sarah's "Good for you!" ringing in her ears. She smiled, thinking of Sarah and all the good times they had shared. Her father still referred to some of their escapades. She hoped fate would bring them together again someday.

Being this close to Missouri also brought back the emotions Matilda felt when she and Sarah went to the slave auction. She wondered how she could cope with her feelings if her father really did succeed in getting Kansas admitted as a slave state.

This ferry looked much more reliable than the one Mr. Williams operated on the river by Keeneville. Six big Indian-style dugout canoes formed the base, with split logs fastened across the canoes for the platform. Huge iron rings held the thick ropes that guided the ferry across. These guide ropes kept the current from washing the ferry down the river. The heavy platform, designed to take large wagons, looked quite solid. Matilda's apprehension lessened a little. At least it boasted sturdy rails that stood four feet high on the sides.

She noticed they had cleverly angled the crossing so that the river's natural flow helped propel the heavy load across. The mules could barely pull the empty ferry back against the rushing water. She wondered what would happen if a wagon wanted to come back. The set-up seemed designed specifically for westward bound traffic.

But it could only take one wagon at a time, and the heavy current strained at the ropes. If a rope broke or a ring came loose .... Her old fears of water resurfaced. The skill of the ferrymen reassured her a little as she watched the mules pull across one wagon after another. Don't be childish, she scolded herself. After all, these men take wagons across all day long. Surely they can cross safely one more time.

Her mother's voice broke into her reverie. "Well, young lady, you gonna help me with the dishes or not?"

With a guilty start, Matilda hurried back and gathered an armload of the dishes her brothers had left piled beside the campfire.

Her mother lifted the kettle of hot water from the fire and smiled at her. "Don't be afraid, Matilda. This ferry is really quite safe."

Matilda laughed at her mother's perspicacity. "Am I that obvious?"

Just as Matilda dried the last cup, Minerva ran up displaying a large sugar cookie. "Look, Mother," she cried, waving the morsel. "Mrs. Sanders is baking cookies. And Becky wants me to spend the night with her."

Matilda smiled. If she knew thirteen-year-old girls, they would talk and giggle all night and be exhausted in the morning.

"Roll 'em! Our turn will be up in about an hour." Britt's voice echoed across the camp as Betsy Ann and Matilda finished tucking the last plate in the box.

"Good timing." Gardner tied the box in place and tucked in the last rope. "Where's Minerva?"

Betsy Ann pointed at the frantic activity around the Sanders' wagon and they all laughed. True to Matilda's prediction, Becky's tent had been the last one taken down and a very sleepy-eyed Minerva joined the family when Gardner climbed up to start the horses moving.

"Oh, 'Tilda," the excited Minerva whispered. "Mrs. Sanders is going to make rock candy tonight. Becky asked her to and she agreed."

Matilda laughed to herself at Minerva's enthusiasm. Somehow, thinking of the difficulties involved in the project, she could not see their ever practical mother agreeing to such a request. She did not tell Minerva that. She just smiled and said, "I'm glad you and Becky are becoming such good friends."

When their turn on the ferry came, Gardner skillfully guided Big Red and Old Blue onto the platform. Tom and John stood by the horses' heads to keep them calm. Sinclair led Clementine and her calf aboard and tied their halters to the back of the wagon. He stood by them in case they became frightened.

Usually unyoked cattle and horses were forced to swim, tied to the end of the ferry platform, but Betsy Ann firmly refused to make Clementine endure such a crossing.

"Why, if she gets upset, she might hurt herself," she proclaimed. "Won't hurt a thing for her to ride behind the wagon on the ferry. Plenty of room."

As the platform started to move, the horses stamped their feet and snorted. Clementine remained as stoic as ever, but her calf bleated nervously and tried to pull away from Sinclair's grasp. Matilda felt her heart beat faster. Minerva said nothing, but clung to Matilda's hand as the mules on the opposite bank strained to pull the whole mass across the river.

Matilda's fears again threatened to overcome her. The water rushing past filled her with apprehension. She smelled the damp mustiness of the water, felt the cold metal of the rail she clung to, sensed the vibration of the boards beneath her feet. Her breaths became shorter as she closed her eyes and tried to shut her ears to the sound of the rapidly moving current.

Sooner than she dared hope, Matilda felt a jerk as the horses moved the wagon forward, off the raft. She opened her eyes to see John grinning up at her.

"Welcome to Missouri, little sister."

Shortly after the wagons reached the outskirts of Hannibal, they passed three men on horseback driving more than a dozen slaves. One of the riders had a whip which he cracked across the back of the last man in the line to hurry them along. Matilda immediately remembered her trip to the slave auction with Sarah four years before and shuddered. Sympathy for the slaves swept over her and she felt a rush of indignation at seeing the poor men driven like cattle.

Her face must have revealed her thoughts, for John looked solemn and nodded in agreement. "Probably runaways," he said. "The owners pay men like those three to bring 'em back. Pa agrees that kind of treatment shouldn't be allowed, but as long as the law condones it, there's gonna be some as will act that way."

While Matilda watched the entourage pass, one of the Negroes suddenly broke away and ran towards a grove of trees. Two of the men rode after him. Just as it seemed he would reach the safety of the trees and escape, one of the pursuers raised his rifle and fired.

The bullet struck the unfortunate slave in the back. Matilda watched in horror as he fell forward without a cry. His body jerked a couple of times, then lay still. Without another glance at the dead man, the slaver replaced the rifle in his saddle boot and rode back to where the remainder cowered together in terror.

"Don't nobody else get notions." He waved the whip menacingly towards the huddled mass of men. Prodded into activity, they moved forward at a brisk pace.

By the time the Randolph wagons reached the edge of the woods where the body lay, the horsemen and the slaves were well ahead of them. Two crows had settled on the ground beside the corpse.

Gardner, in the lead wagon, pulled the horses to a halt and climbed down. "Slave or not," he growled, "it's un-Christian to leave a man unburied." He shook his head and continued to grumble. "This is the kind of thing gives that Stowe woman and the Faneuil Hall bunch more fuel for their fire."

Without a word, Britt and Tom pulled shovels from the backs of the wagons and followed their father. John, walking to join them, saw the tears coursing down Matilda's cheeks. He took her in his arms and held her for a moment.

"Yes, little sister," he murmured against her hair. "Welcome to Missouri."

Chapter 16

August to September, 1854

ON THE MORNING of September 7, they reached St. Joseph, on the Missouri River. The day dawned clear and hot as the summer heat persisted. By nine in the morning Matilda's dress clung to her body and sweat beaded her forehead.

They had spent ten days crossing the remainder of the state of Missouri with no further incident. Farms dotted the landscape, some with very nice homes. She saw many slaves working in the fields, usually with a white overseer, but not always. Sometimes the overseer was another slave.

As she rode along on the seat of the swaying wagon watching the slaves at work, Matilda had difficulty keeping the killing she had witnessed outside of Hannibal from her mind. As she relived the scene over and over, the man fell in slow motion. She heard again and again the crack of the rifle frightening the birds into silence, the whine of the bullet loud in the sudden hush. She shuddered as she remembered the crows settling beside the poor man's body, glad her father had stopped to bury him. Had the Negro a wife or children? Would they never know what became of him, or where he was buried?

Her horror at the callousness shown by the slaver never diminished. How could any man so casually shoot down another and just leave him for the crows?

Another question frequently came to her mind. How could her father, a kind, gentle, deeply religious man, so openly appalled at the slaver's actions, defend slavery? Matilda remembered the many arguments between her father and her brother Will on the subject. If her father disliked so many aspects of slavery, why not favor abolishing it?

She thought of the other side of the argument. Was her father right when he said the Negroes could not take care of themselves? She thought of Josh working at the Williams ferry. He seemed quite capable. She sighed and shook her head. They would be in Kansas soon, and hopefully she would not be required to witness any more such spectacles.

St. Joseph, in the ten years since the opening of the Oregon Trail, especially since the discovery of gold in California, had grown from a sleepy little river village into a boom town. It seemed to Matilda that everyone in town had something to sell. Wagons, mules, barrels of flour, Indian blankets, dried buffalo meat, even medical nostrums. All tried to sell their wares to the passing settlers. She learned many westward bound settlers came by river to St. Joseph or Kansas City and bought supplies for the trail there.

"Guess it makes sense," Matilda commented to Minerva and Becky as they strolled along the dusty pathways looking in store windows. "Why carry it all the way when river travel is so cheap?"

"Then how could Pa have brought his favorite chair?" Minerva responded, with such perfect logic that Matilda had to smile.

They stopped in front of the general store and peeked in. "Look at the peppermint candy," gasped Becky to Minerva, pointing to the row of glass jars gleaming on the counter. "Let's go back and get a penny from my father."

Matilda laughed as the two girls ran off, hand in hand. She turned to John, who escorted her. "Bet she'd never get a penny for candy from *our* father."

John chuckled his agreement. "And if you'll look at the prices they want here, you'll see why we stopped in Springfield."

On Monday, the tenth of September, they took another ferry, this time across the Missouri River and entered Kansas at last. The unbroken prairie spread out before them like a vast green ocean. Trees dotted the undulating landscape. Distant objects seemed suspended in air, like reflections in a mirror. Matilda wondered what caused the strange double visions, and posed the question to George, who strolled beside her.

"They call them 'mirages', Miss Matilda," George explained. "I've noticed 'em each time I been here." He shook his head. "I dunno what causes 'em. Peculiar, ain't they?"

Matilda agreed. The strange images fascinated her.

On their third day out of St. Joseph's, they encountered their first Kansas rainstorm. Matilda, with Minerva and Becky in tow, had walked ahead of the train out of the dust from the dozens of hooves to watch the strange mirages. Clouds suddenly massed to the west. Thunder and lightning raged, terrifying the horses and driving Matilda and the girls for cover. As huge rain drops pelted the canvas above their heads, they cowered behind the seat of the wagon.

"Wow," Minerva gasped, "This is scary."

As they watched the lightning, Becky announced boldly, "I think it's beautiful."

Matilda laughed as a bolt of lightning streaked the sky close by and all three of them ducked as the ensuing thunderclap seemed to burst right on top of the wagon.

Tom and John stood in the rain by the horses' heads. "Easy, Big Red," Tom soothed, rain dripping from his hat and down into his beard. He patted the horse's neck in reassurance. "I'm right here."

Big Red wanted to run, anywhere, to get away from the thunder and lightning. Matilda could see the huge muscles bunched to spring. She felt a moment of panic. If the horses bolted away from Tom and John, what would happen to

her and the girls? Maybe they should get out and take their
chances with the rain. When Big Red calmed, Matilda let
out a long, tremulous sigh of relief, not realizing until then
she had been holding her breath.

She heard the hogs squealing in panic and George's
curses as he and the oldest boys ran after them. She laughed
softly. Apparently Gardner had not yet converted George
to Methodism.

Fortunately, the storm passed as quickly as it came. With
a sigh of relief, Matilda clambered back out over the wagon
seat. Climbing down, she stepped ankle deep in a puddle
of muddy water.

"Drat!" she exclaimed as she felt the water seep through
her boot and soak her stocking. Muddy water splashed up
on her skirt.

"Matilda," her father's voice sternly admonished her for
the expletive. Minerva giggled.

Matilda said no more. She ruefully surveyed the splashes
of mud on the dress she had put on clean that morning.
It was the only one left that had been ironed. The other
two, made of plain linsey, had been washed and re-washed.
Tired of those two, she had decided to wear her one calico.
She sighed, wishing she had continued to save it.

But the storm had not finished with them. After rounding
up the scattered hogs and calming the animals, they headed
for the next rise. Britt, in the lead wagon, gave the call to
halt as he crested the hill. Tom rode forward to see what
had happened.

"What's the matter," Matilda asked when Tom came back
to report.

"Little creek is now a big creek," he grinned. "Came
up fast, so it should go down fast. Britt thinks we can ford
it pretty easy once it goes down a little. Doesn't seem too
deep."

They did ford the creek, but not easily. The heavy wagons bogged in the muddy bottom. Matilda, Minerva, and Becky stood on the top of the rise and watched the men add extra teams to get the wagons across. One of the wagons lurched, nearly throwing Tom into the swirling water. Matilda gasped in fright while she watched the wagon slowly right itself as the straining horses, sweating in the sticky heat, pulled it up the far embankment.

"Min," Matilda announced, "I'm not riding in one of those wagons. John," she called, "Come here. I want you."

The grinning John agreed to her request, and, one by one, ferried the girls across on his horse. The water reached the horse's belly at the deepest part and Matilda had to pull up her feet to keep her boots from getting wet. Wetter, she thought grimly. She stared, hypnotized, at the water raging by the horse's legs and clung to John's waist.

John, aware of her fear of water and the only brother who seemed to understand it, patted her hand in reassurance. "Don't worry, Sis. Ginger'll get us through okay."

Ginger whickered and Matilda gave a shaky little laugh. When John helped her down on the other side, she heaved a sigh of relief as she joined Minerva and Becky.

When all the wagons had crossed, they made camp, everyone feeling they had traveled enough for one day.

"'Tilda," Minerva asked in a quavery voice. "Do they have storms like that here often?"

Matilda gave a short, shaky, laugh. "How would I know? I've never been to Kansas before either. We'll have to ask George."

The gentle, rolling hills were deceptive. They quickly learned that many of these dips contained similar steep ravines cut by previous storms. George called these ravines gulches, and rode well ahead of the train to try and steer the wagons safely around the worst ones. The detours added to the distance, but there was no other way.

Along the creek beds grew a profusion of trees. Matilda had seen chestnuts, hickory, and sweet walnut. Spreading oaks were common. Wild grape vines and wild roses climbed the trees, forming canopies between them. One tree she did not recognize, and asked George what kind of trees they were.

"Why, them's cottonwoods, Miss Matilda." He grinned at her, open admiration in his eyes. "Eastern Kansas is full of cottonwoods. Pretty, ain't they? And you think it's pretty now, you wait 'til spring. Wild flowers cover these here prairies. Makes a man think he's in heaven."

She murmured in agreement, and walked on. Matilda found she preferred walking to riding in the wagon. The many wagons that crossed before them had left deep ruts. Cutting across the open prairie was just as bad. The rough terrain made riding on the hard wooden bench miserable. After a week of being bruised and jostled, she took to walking instead. Minerva and Becky often joined her.

Matilda enjoyed having the two young girls walk with her. She showed them the different plants, pointing out comfrey, lobelia, horehound, and other herbs their mother gathered for medicine.

She smiled, watching them run along, hand in hand. They could be sisters. Becky had blond hair like Minerva, though Becky's formed soft curls ringing her face while Minerva's hung straight down her back, tied with a blue ribbon that matched her eyes.

Becky was the definite leader of the two. Minerva, with a large family of brothers and sisters, had learned at an early age that the world did not revolve around her wishes. Becky, an only child, and doted upon by her parents, had learned a coy smile and a tilt of her pert chin would get her anything she wished. Matilda smiled at the memory of Mrs. Sanders making rock candy over the campfire because, as Betsy Ann had snorted, "the little minx asked her to!"

But Becky never seemed overbearing with her wishes. She almost unconsciously made everyone want to do things for her. Matilda had found herself, along with everyone else, almost immediately enchanted by the charming smile and wide, innocent blue eyes.

The growing friendship between Becky and Minerva reminded Matilda of the bond she had enjoyed with Agatha Templeton. A sharp pang of loss hit her, even though it had been ... she pondered. She had been nine the fall Aggie died. Could it be nine years already? Yes. Matilda had turned eighteen in July.

Sometimes, when walking along in the grass, Matilda noticed how many grasshoppers jumped away in every direction. One evening, as the men set up camp, they walked through a particularly thick batch.

"I'll bet the chickens would like to get after these," Matilda commented to Minerva.

George overheard her. "Yep," he chuckled. "Make good chicken feed, they do. But sometimes gets to be too much of a good thing. I heard they almost wiped out the colony at the Great Salt Lake. Was eatin' all the crops until the seagulls come and ate the grasshoppers."

After he strode off, Matilda paid more attention. She watched one of the voracious little creatures nibble on a stalk of grass. As she saw the devoured segment grow larger by the moment, she realized what thousands of them could do to a field of cropland. She shuddered. Could such an innocuous appearing insect do so much damage? Apparently so. She shook off her apprehension. "Come on, girls," she said to Minerva and Becky. "Let's catch some and give the chickens a treat."

While the two girls fed the collection of grasshoppers to the chickens, Matilda helped her mother with supper. She lifted the full coffee pot to hang it on the truncheon over the fire.

As she did, a scream cut through the noise of the bustling camp.

Chapter 17

September of 1854

STARTLED, Matilda dropped the coffee pot, the spilled water making a dark stain on the dry ground.

"That's Minerva," Betsy Ann gasped. She dumped her armload of tin plates beside the campfire and ran in the direction of the sound. Matilda followed at her heels.

Others reached the scene before them, and Betsy Ann elbowed a pathway through. Minerva continued to scream, and Matilda saw why.

Becky's body lay crumpled on the grass, the mark of a horse's hoof imprinted on her forehead. Horrified, Matilda stared at the trickle of blood streaking the white skin, matting the blond curls. The open blue eyes, blank and unseeing, stared into the distance. Betsy Ann knelt beside the still form, seeking signs of life. Matilda clasped Minerva to her breast and turned her away from the tragic sight.

Becky's mother arrived in time to see Betsy Ann shake her head and try to close the staring eyes. With a thin, wailing cry, Mrs. Sanders fell sobbing across the lifeless body of her only child.

Matilda led Minerva back to their wagon, away from the crowd gathered around Becky's body. It took some time to calm Minerva enough for her to explain what happened.

"We were walking by the horses," she said, "and I told Becky not to get too close." Minerva gulped a couple of times and emitted a long, shuddering sigh.

"Go on," Matilda urged in a soft voice.

"Then Becky said .... she said, 'I'm not afraid of the horses and ... '" Minerva covered her face, trying to control her voice. "She . . . she took her bonnet and slapped one of the horses on the rump." Minerva stopped, squeezing her eyes shut, as if to drive the vision from her mind.

Matilda patted her sister's hand in comfort. The rest of the story needed no telling. The mark of the hoof on Becky's forehead said plainly what had occurred.

"I didn't see the horse move, it happened so quick," Minerva gasped between sobs. "Then . . . then . . . Becky was lying on the ground. She never moved." Minerva began to weep again. "It's my fault. I let her think I thought she was afraid. If I hadn't . . . ."

"No, Darling," Matilda interrupted, "it was not your fault. Don't ever think it was your fault." She held Minerva closer.

The simple burial ceremony the next morning cast a pall over the whole group. With no minister among them, Gardner read the Twenty-Third Psalm from the family Bible, and tried to ease the pain of Becky's stricken parents.

"Lord," he intoned, "we know not why You have taken this child from our midst, but we take comfort in knowing she is with You in Heaven."

Matilda remembered the resentment she had felt when God took Aggie, and when He took her sister Temperance. The same emotion flashed through her again. She felt guilty, knowing she had no right to question God, but could not help thinking Mr. and Mrs. Sanders must feel the same way, losing their only child. As she thought of Becky, so young, so pretty, so full of life, she felt the depth of the senseless tragedy even more. She had trouble accepting her father's insistence that such deaths were God's will.

Minerva clasped Matilda's hand so tightly Matilda feared the bones would break. Her heart ached for her little sister. She thought how easily it could have been Minerva the horse struck and shuddered.

As soon as the service for Becky ended, the wagons continued westward. The Sanders' tragedy at losing their daughter, while deeply felt, had to take second place to the need to get homes built before winter set in.

As the wagons creaked by, Matilda and Minerva stood in silence beside the fresh mound of earth with its crude wooden cross. John cut the marker from a nearby oak tree, and shaped it with the froe. Tom had burned the inscription on the rough hewn slab with a hot iron. The simple marker read, "Rebecca Sanders, 1841 - 1854."

Matilda stood with her arm across Minerva's shoulders. "Come," she said at last, gently turning Minerva from the graveside. "We must stay with the wagons." She looked up and saw John and Tom mounted on their horses, waiting for them. She felt a flash of gratitude. How thoughtful of them to give Minerva these last moments with Becky.

Becky's parents turned their wagon eastward as soon as the ceremony ended. Matilda never saw nor heard from them again.

Three days later, as Matilda and her mother prepared supper, they heard George cry, "Buffalo! Buffalo! Quick! Get the women and young'uns into the wagons."

Frightened , Matilda looked up to see the men gathering the stock, herding the animals into the center of the loose circle of wagons. John appeared beside her like magic.

"'Tilda, Min, hurry! Into the wagon. Leave the supper." He jumped from his horse. Gathering Minerva into his arms, he dumped her unceremoniously into the wagon, then turned to help Betsy Ann. Matilda did not wait to be tossed inside like Minerva. She scurried to the wagon and climbed in.

"What's happening, John?" she cried. The ground rumbled with a distant thunder. She felt the vibrations through the wheels of the wagon. The whole wagon shook as the ground trembled.

"It's a herd of buffalo," John replied. The crack of rifles

added to the cacophony of shouting men, bellowing cattle, squealing hogs, and bleating sheep. "We're trying to turn them."

Her eyes met his. "And if you can't?"

"We will," he said. "We have to." He remounted and rode away.

Not very reassured, Matilda held Minerva as the two girls huddled behind the seat and watched the vast ocean of pounding hoofs and shaggy heads approach the small group of wagons huddled helplessly in their path. Her heart raced. Fortunately, in response to the shooting and shouting, the herd divided and went around them on both sides, the wagons forming an island in the sea of clashing horns and gleaming eyes. The sun sank in the west and still the animals rumbled by.

"How many are there?" Minerva stared, transfixed at the undulating field of brown hides thundering past the wagon.

"Thousands and thousands. Have to be," Matilda replied, trying to keep her voice from shaking to comfort her sister. "Lucky for us the men managed to divide the herd before they reached us."

Matilda dropped off to sleep. She awoke, stiff from her cramped position, in the rosy light that heralds the coming of dawn. The rumbling had stopped. She wondered how long it had continued after she fell asleep. Minerva, huddled in the crook of Matilda's arm, slept on. When Matilda shifted to relieve her numbed arm, the movement awoke Minerva. She sat up quickly, and looked at Matilda with frightened eyes.

Matilda smiled to reassure the girl. "It's over, Min. The buffalo have gone."

Chapter 18

October of 1854

BY THE TIME they had been on their trek for over a month, Matilda looked forward to a roof over her head again, and a bed to sleep on. George assured them the Big Blue was "just a piece" farther on.

Finally, near the end of September, they crested a rise and looked across the Big Blue River. Gardner pulled his horse to a halt and shook his head. "Can't cross here," he stated. "Banks're too steep for the wagons."

George reassured him. "No need. Just wanted you to see the spot I've picked out for you. See that pretty creek coming down the other side?"

Matilda sighed with relief. She and Minerva had gone to look at the river, and, while the river did not seem deep, the swift current frightened them. "I'm glad," she whispered to Minerva.

"Me, too," Minerva whispered back, rolling her eyes skyward.

"Government runs a ferry down the river a piece, place called Juniata," George announced. "If we camp here tonight, we can head for the crossing in the morning." He and Gardner strode off together, with George saying, "Come here, Gardner, to the top of this here bluff and you'll see ... " They drifted out of Matilda's hearing.

Betsy Ann watched them leave, then turned to Matilda and Minerva. "In that case, I see no reason why we can't have a real pie for supper. Sinclair," she ordered, "chop some of that firewood and get us a fire going. Minerva, get me a packet of apples." She scooped the proper handfuls of flour into her tin mixing bowl then said to her grandson, "Willy, clear the grass off that level spot so's we don't start a prairie fire."

Everyone scurried to obey, and within twenty minutes, a pile of glowing embers once more surrounded Betsy Ann's old Dutch oven.

The group gathered, savoring the aroma of the baking pie. Gardner returned, a broad grin on his weathered face. George sauntered beside him, looking proud of himself.

"Land across the river is perfect," Gardner announced, "just like George said. In fact, the stream coming into the river is so pretty I'm going to call it Fancy Creek. In the morning, we'll head for that ferry at Juniata and come back up the other side."

A cheer went up from his listeners as he seized Betsy Ann around her ample waist and kissed her soundly, his intense, dark eyes glowing. "Welcome to your new home, my dear."

The next morning, they broke camp and followed the river south. Matilda calculated the date and decided it must be the first of October. Leaves on the trees lining the river glowed golden in the early morning sunlight. The crispness in the air told her autumn had arrived, in spite of the warmth during the day, and winter would soon follow.

They moved slowly. The overgrown horse trail they followed looked like few wagons, if any, had ever crossed it. Several times they had to hew trees or clear brush to get through. As a consequence, they spent another night on the east side of the Big Blue River.

Sinclair, determined to catch a fish for supper, cut a pole and baited a hook with one of the myriad of grasshoppers bounding through the grass stalks. Matilda accompanied him and sat on an old log lying half in and half out of the water, watching the sun as it slanted towards the horizon.

"Best time to catch fish," Sinclair averred. "Sunset's

when they come out to feed." The line bobbed. "Wow! I've got one already." He hauled a large catfish ashore.

Matilda laughed at the fish's wide, comical mouth and long, floppy antennae. "Watch out for the spine on his back," she cautioned. "Looks like he could go right through your hand with it."

While Sinclair proceeded to catch more fish, Matilda watched the sun sink behind the trees on the opposite bank. Light filtered through the branches, making dappled patterns on the clear, swiftly running water. She shivered a little as cold crept over her.

Tomorrow they would cross the Big Blue and start towards her father's newly named Fancy Creek. They had been five weeks on the trail. She thought of Alf and Sam, far away in California, and tried to imagine what it would be like to travel like this for four months, over high mountains and barren deserts. She gave up. She had only a vague concept of such conditions. Maybe some day she would find out.

But for the moment, she contented herself with the thought of sleeping under a roof again. Her thoughts turned to the ferry crossing. She certainly hoped the boat would be a sturdy one.

At high noon the next day they reached the crossing at Juniata. The stone abutments, solid iron rings, and heavy ropes guiding the ferry reassured Matilda a little. At least the railings on the small craft looked secure.

A young man greeted them, green eyes above wide cheek bones glowing with the warmth of his smile. Matilda found herself responding to his open friendliness. "Howdy, folks. I'm Abe Dyer. Me and my Pa run the ferry here for the Government." He looked up and down the row of wagons with a practiced eye. "Where you folks from and where you headed?"

"Illinois." Gardner replied. "Got my eye on a pretty

piece of land just across the river, fourteen, fifteen miles back upstream."

"Good spot," Abe remarked. "No one lives up there except a few Pottawatamies. They've got a village on the east side of the river. Sod's real tough to break around here, but once you get a crop in, it breaks up real fine. And the bottom land is right good for a garden. We've got a batch of turnips you wouldn't believe."

An older man approached, hat in hand. He mopped his brow with a big red handkerchief that looked like it had performed that particular function many times before and ran his hand through his thinning gray locks. Tucking the handkerchief back in his pocket, he replaced the hat on his head and extended a hand to Gardner.

"Welcome, folks," he greeted them, as cordial as Abe. "I'm Sam Dyer. See you've met my son, Abe. This here's my son Jim." He indicated a quiet lad of about sixteen. "The two boys and I came here the first of May last year from Fort Scott. Guv'mint offered me the job of running this here ferry, and you better believe I took it quick."

Abe and Jim, with the help of Britt and George, started to load the first wagon onto the ferry. The loquacious Sam Dyer rambled on. "Yes, sir, me and the boys built our cabin here so's it'd be ready, then Abe went back for the rest of the family. Last November he brought 'em all out." He paused to tamp and light his pipe. "Abe says you folks hail from Illinois. Got up there a bit myself in '32, as a Major in the Black Hawk Wars." With a wry twist to his mouth he added, "That war should never 'a been fought. Black Hawk sent a peace party to meet Stillman's bunch. If Stillman's men hadn't 'a been half drunk, never woulda been a shot fired."

He shook his head. "Hard to believe it all started because one of 'em fell down and his gun went off. Then they all started shootin'. Any one of 'em been sober enough to look, they'd 'a seen Blackhawk's men wa'n't armed." He sighed. "Well, been twenty years ago, now. Water under the bridge." He tapped the ashes from his pipe on the stone abutment and tucked it back into his pocket. "Let's get to work and get you folks across."

As the third wagon rumbled onto the ferry, Sam Dyer doffed his hat to Betsy Ann and said, "My wife and I would be right proud to have you folks for supper. Don't get many womenfolk as visitors, and I know she gets lonesome for another woman to talk to."

"Why, thank you, Mr. Dyer," Betsy Ann replied. "After all those weeks on the road, it'd feel mighty good to set at a table again." She chuckled. "My main memory of the Black Hawk war is one of Stillman's men come by ailin' and asked us to take care of him. Turned out he had the measles, and he gave 'em to everyone in the whole house."

"'Tilda," Minerva called, "come and help us with these wretched hogs. They won't go anywhere Weldon and I try to drive them."

Matilda glanced back and saw Minerva, Weldon, and Sinclair struggling to herd the dozen razorback hogs towards the ferry landing. With a sigh of exasperation, she started towards them when Abe Dyer spoke beside her.

"I'll help," he said. "Believe me, I know how much trouble hogs can be. Wait until my sister Sarah tells you about her experiences bringing our hogs over from Fort Scott last fall." He laughed. "She says she and our sister Martha used to wish every night that the hogs would all die before morning."

"Don't I know it," Minerva chimed in. "And they never sleep at night like the other stock. Someone has to watch 'em all the time."

Abe stopped in his tracks as Minerva approached. She somehow always unconsciously managed to be a vision of loveliness, an ability Matilda had often envied. Minerva's face flushed with exertion, making her cheeks even rosier than usual. The tousled blonde hair caught the sunlight, and the blue of her simple calico dress enhanced the color of her eyes. Matilda, suddenly aware of the change in Abe, watched as Minerva smiled at him.

"I'm Minerva." She shyly offered him her hand. "Most folks call me Min."

A slow smile crept over Abe's face as he took the proffered hand. "And I'm Abe, Miss Minerva. I am delighted to meet you, and will be happy to call you Min."

He held her hand, their eyes locked for several moments. A blush crept up into Minerva's cheeks. Matilda, watching closely, saw her sister's breath quicken. Both seemed to have forgotten her presence.

Weldon, oblivious to the magic moment he interrupted, wailed, "Come on, Min! You've gotta help us! These hogs keep trying to head back for the Missouri line."

The Dyer cabin was actually three log cabins built together. "It's a three story long and one story high," Abe laughed as they stood gaping at it. Hog pens, sheep houses, and stables surrounded the main house. The Dyers owned about one hundred and fifty head of hogs, so, with Abe's help, Weldon and Sinclair herded the Randolph hogs into one of the pens.

Sinclair sighed with relief as he shut the gate behind the grunting pigs. "Boy, 'Tilda, sure is a relief not to have to watch the miserable things for one night, at least."

Sam Dyer grinned in understanding. "They'll do just fine here. Come on up to the house and meet the rest of the family. Settlers have just started coming in around here. When me 'n' the boys came here to Cedar Creek, we was the first white folks around these parts."

"Yes," put in his wife, Permelia, a jolly, buxom woman

whose dark hair showed just a few strands of gray, "and until just the last few months, we were still the only ones. Thought when the Kansas-Nebraska Act passed last May we'd get a lot. Took a while for word to get around, I guess."

"We waited for the creeks to go down," Gardner said. "I 'spect others did the same. South part of Illinois gets real swampy in the spring and summer. Makes travel hard."

"And the miasma causes a lot of the ague," Betsy Ann volunteered. "Better to travel after it dries up some."

The rest of the Dyer family stood waiting to be introduced. Will and Enoch were grown men. Martha, at fourteen, had black hair and large dark eyes set in a lovely oval face with a cream complexion. Matilda smothered a laugh as she saw Tom and John as stunned by Martha's fragile beauty as Abe had been by Minerva's fairness.

"And this is our Sarah," Sam beamed, patting her dark hair. "She's twelve, and she's my madcap. Ain't nothing she won't try or a horse she won't ride." Sarah beamed under his praise. "Mary's our baby." Eight year old Mary, shy and pretty, had eyes as blue as Minerva's.

"And Freddie here is our foster baby," Permelia said with pride, holding the blond, blue-eyed toddler. "His ma died last October when he only had six months, poor little thing. They were coming out from Maine and got as far as Fort Leavenworth when she died. Fred here was the youngest of five. Their pa found homes for all five and headed for Colorado. Never have heard from him since." She chucked the baby under the chin. "Say 'Hello' to the nice people, Freddie." The baby hid his face in her neck. "But come in, come in! Supper is about ready."

When the simple meal of fried fish, cooked turnips, cold venison, and corn bread was served, with parched corn coffee, they gathered around the table.

Sam Dyer seated himself at the head of the table. "Gardner," he said, "as our guest, will you offer Grace?"

"Be proud to," Gardner replied. Everyone bowed their heads while he intoned the ritual thanks for the simple food and hospitality.

"Well, well," Sam beamed when Gardner finished, scanning the gathering. "This your whole family?"

"No," Gardner said. "Got three sons out in California and two daughters back in Illinois. Oldest daughter died, three, four years ago."

"That's a shame," Mr. Dyer murmured in sympathy. "We lost our oldest daughter, too. Elizabeth, her name was. She and her husband, Selkirk Weddle, headed for Oregon back in '50. Both took the fever along the Snake River. Died a week apart, so they ain't even buried together." He shook his head and Permelia's eyes filled with tears. "Not likely we'd ever even be able to find where they was buried."

"Worried us, too," Gardner said, "when our boys went headin' off into that wild country. God be praised, they all made it. Britt here even made it back."

Sam Dyer turned to Britt. "You been to California?" His jaw dropped. "What was it like?"

"Beautiful country. Mild winters, good farm land. No rain all summer."

"Why'd you come back?"

Britt smiled at Sarah and his four children. "Couldn't stay away from the family. My two brothers were single, but I'd left Sarah in Illinois. Didn't want to expose her and the young ones to the dangers until I knew what they were. When my brother Will went out in '52, he took his whole family." He glanced at Gardner. "Still, that country gets into your blood."

"We decided on Kansas because we hope to get it admitted as a slave state," Gardner said. "Hope to get a real plantation, just like all my Randolph cousins in Virginia."

Matilda thought Sam Dyer looked startled, but he recovered himself and said, "Well, good luck to you. I'm a

Southerner myself, born in Tennessee, but I'm not all that sure slavery is good. Never owned any myself. All depends on how a man treats 'em, I guess. Father-in-law had two when I married Permelia, old Uncle Jack and old Uncle Albert. They had good lives, cabins to live in with their families. Pa Catching never sold off any of the young-uns. He treated his slaves same as he treated the two white men as worked for him. They ran his saw mill and corn mill over in Kentucky."

Gardner nodded. "That's how a man should treat his slaves. If everyone did as your father-in-law, those Abolitionists wouldn't be able to get folks so riled."

The scene in Hannibal popped into Matilda's mind again. She looked at John. His little smile told her he knew her thoughts. She also remembered the trip to the slave auction with Sarah Williams. No, Pa, Matilda thought. As long as slavery exists, slaves will be abused. She said nothing.

After supper, Sarah and Martha washed the dishes and Matilda and Minerva offered to help.

"So," Matilda asked, picking up the first plate to dry, "where were you folks living before you came to Juniata?"

"Fort Scott, here in Kansas. Pa had a government job there until they closed down the fort. Then he ran a grist mill until he got this job on the ferry. When he and Abe 'n' Jim came out, they left my brother John to care for Mother and us girls. But John didn't tell anyone he'd got married two months before. So right after Pa and Jim and Abe left, he took off to be with his bride. That left just Enoch to protect us, and he was only nineteen."

"That was scary, too," Martha put in. "We had a lot of sleepless nights, I'll tell you. After the soldiers left, the Indians prowled around a lot looking for stock to steal. Anyway, our brother Will's wife and babies died, so he came back home. Were we glad to see him!"

"I'll say we were!" Sarah chimed in. "The Indians had

stolen a mare and two colts and we were scared they'd come back for more. When Abe arrived to bring us out here to Juniata, he and Will went to get the horses back."

"Alone?" Minerva gasped.

"They had Old Charlie, a half breed Cherokee. He guided them to the Indian camp. They had to go sixty miles to get there. Old Charlie wouldn't go into the camp, so Will and Abe took their rifles and rode in. They untied the mare and drove the horses away."

"Oh, that was so brave of Abe," Minerva said, her face and voice filled with admiration. Matilda noticed, with some amusement, that her sister made no mention of Will's bravery.

"Wasn't it?" Sarah agreed. "That was early November, 'bout a year ago. Then they loaded us up. Will drove the four-horse wagon, Abe the prairie schooner, both crammed with everything we could get in."

"But they wouldn't let us bring our cat and her two kittens," Martha mourned. "They said it was bad luck to move a cat. But I don't see how it could be any worse than moving the dogs. I think they just didn't want to be bothered with the cats."

"And," Sarah added, "since we couldn't fit everything in, we had to leave the cradle Pa made from the old sugar tree, the one mother raised all of us in. We wanted to take it, but Abe said Ma was through raising babies, so it could wait. And one of the boxes we left had Pa's uniform from the Black Hawk Wars. That uniform was our pride and joy. We had to leave it with a neighbor. They said they'd take care of it for us."

"But when Abe went back last spring to get the boxes and cradle and the other things we'd left," Martha said "the people had moved away. No one knew where any of our things went," she added, her indignation still unappeased.

"Did you have any trouble with Indians on your way

across?" Minerva asked.

"Oh, no," Sarah replied with a breezy wave of her hand that sent soap bubbles in every direction. "But it took us ten days where it should have only taken a week. We had to spend two days in camp with a lame horse."

"What a procession we must have made," said Martha, laughing. "That rattley old wagon, a tattered prairie schooner, twenty-five cows, calves and steers, thirty sheep, all the chickens in coops on the back of the wagon, with three mangy, old dogs to guard the sheep from wolves. And," she paused for effect, "the hogs."

"Those wretched hogs!" Sarah shook her head. "Us girls used to hope every night we'd wake up and find every one of those miserable creatures either dead or stolen. The other stock would settle down at night, but not those hogs! They had to be watched all the time."

"And eat!" Martha added. "Pa told us to gather all the nuts we could along the way so we'd have mast for the hogs for the winter. But those greedy hogs ate every one we could gather every day."

Mrs. Dyer joined them. "Complaining about the hogs again? You like the bacon and ham and soap, though." She chuckled in understanding. "They were miserable things to travel with, I have to admit. But if you've finished those dishes, your father wants Abe to play his fiddle to entertain our guests."

Chapter 19

1854 to 1855

TWO WEEKS LATER, Matilda stood in the doorway and surveyed the land her father had chosen, where the beautiful stream Gardner had named Fancy Creek met the Big Blue River.

Matilda and Minerva, with their parents and brothers Tom, John, and Sinclair, and Weldon Crose, settled into the simple two-room cabin. Due to the scarcity of wood, they constructed the cabin with shakes, rough boards split from tree trunks with a broad axe. Britt and his family built their home a little to the north, up Fancy Creek.

"We'll spread out all over the valley and down the Big Blue," Gardner said. "I've staked out an area five miles square. When we get Kansas voted a slave state, we'll get a few slaves and have ourselves a real plantation, like my cousins in Virginia."

Memories of her surreptitious visit to the slave auction raced through Matilda's mind again, as did the death scene at Hannibal she still saw so clearly. She fervently hoped she would never be forced to own slaves.

Matilda and Minerva converted the loft, rough puncheons placed over the rafters, into their own private sanctuary. The straw-filled ticks they used as beds lay on each side. Their brother Tom drilled holes in the logs, inserted wooden pins, and laid shakes across the pins to make them a simple set of shelves. These shelves held their few precious books and other personal items. Their clothes hung on a rope strung along the wall. The low ceiling did not allow them to stand except in the very center, but the colorful quilts on the beds made the whole area quite cheerful. They covered the floor with some of the vibrant Indian blankets purchased in St. Joseph. Tom had shot an antelope, so the loft also boasted an antelope skin rug.

She found Kansas as pretty as Illinois. Oak, hickory, walnut, and cottonwood trees dotted the landscape. Wild blackberries, raspberries and gooseberries grew along the river banks the same as in Illinois. They had arrived too late in the season for berries, but the next year promised a good crop.

They often saw Indians passing by at a distance, but the natives ignored the white settlers. Matilda wanted to meet them, but Gardner, wise in the ways of Indians, advised waiting. "They'll meet us in their own good time," he assured her.

From the doorway, she watched the men clear the fields for planting in the spring. The time was the third week in October, and the trees had changed to a riot of reds and golds. The muggy heat remained during the day, but the evenings had a definite chill. Sam Dyer had said the summer heat had lasted a long time this year, but Matilda was glad. It gave them a chance to get settled before winter arrived in earnest. Matilda knew her father, with his usual foresight, brought enough provisions to tide them over until the crops came in the following year. The ample supply of wild game in the area assured them of meat. The Big Blue teemed with fish, and the Dyer's had sent them off with a winter's supply of turnips. Matilda missed potatoes, but Permelia Dyer informed her there were no potatoes to be had anywhere in Kansas.

Some of their claim was river bottom, sandy and easy to turn with Mr. Deere's new plow with its steel mold board. The tough prairie sod, unbroken since the beginning of time, defied the plow. The men had to use an ax or a shovel to break through it. But the soil beneath held a rich clay.

Gardner crumbled a handful and grunted with satisfaction. Matilda assumed his expression meant it would make good crop land.

Sinclair, with Betsy Ann directing every move, staked out and cleared the garden plot to be ready for planting in the spring. Melons and pumpkins would be sown between the stalks of sweet corn. They would also grow tomatoes, potatoes, beans, and peas. The little fruit trees survived their trip in the washtub. Tom planted them on the side of the cabin where they received the morning sun. Some years would pass before they bore any fruit. The trees were only a foot tall.

Clementine, once she no longer had to walk every day and ford creeks, accepted her leash with her usual aplomb, and her milk production increased. As Matilda predicted, the chickens, happy to be out of their coop, relished the plethora of grasshoppers.

Until a shelter could be built, the hogs and sheep roamed along the river bank under George's watchful eye. Lush grass for the sheep lined the banks of Fancy Creek, and the hogs found plenty to eat among the supply of nuts under the trees. They had to guard the stock, however, for wolf packs roamed across the prairie in abundance. The howling at night made Matilda shiver. She remembered hearing wolves as a child in Illinois, before so many people arrived and drove them away. She had not been sorry to see the wolves go. The sound had bothered her then, too.

Gardner assigned Sinclair the task of chinking the cracks between the planks of the cabin walls to keep out the wind and rain. Most settlers filled the spaces with daubs of mud, but Gardner insisted on using cement. "Mud can wash out in heavy rain. I've had that happen," he declared. "Don't see any reason not to prevent it if we can. Not that hard to mix a little limestone and clay with the sand. Plenty of limestone around here."

The following morning, Matilda took pity on the grumbling Sinclair and went with him in the cart to bring back buckets of sand.

"If it was just getting the sand, it would be easier," he griped when they paused to rest a moment, "but Pa insists I wash it first."

Matilda laughed at him. "Use your head," she said. "It's easier to wash here. Doesn't make sense to carry all that dirt back with the sand. We'd only have to carry water to wash it out with." She reached for the parcel of cookies behind the seat of the cart. "Here, have a cookie. You'll feel better."

Unable to argue with her logic, Sinclair grunted and ate the large sugar cookie she handed him.

"Besides," Matilda continued, "be glad you didn't get the job of helping John powder the limestome and the clay."

Sinclair refused to be appeased. "John only has to pound half a bucket full of the limestone and clay. We have to wash thirty buckets of sand."

Matilda consoled him with another cookie. "Then we'd better get started."

They worked in silence as the sun rose higher in the cloudless October sky. Matilda recalled stories of how cold Kansas got, but so far the weather remained benign. Her dress clung to her back, and she felt rivulets of sweat running down between her breasts in spite of the cold water swirling around her ankles. Barefoot, her skirts tied up around her knees to keep them dry, Matilda had just plunged her hands into another bucket to slosh the water through the sand when she heard a horse whinny. Big Red, still hitched to the cart, lifted his head in response, his ears cocked.

Matilda's eyes followed his gaze. Silhouetted along the riverbank, twelve Indians rode single file. Each horse towed a fully loaded travois, covered with buffalo hides. Apparently the Indians had been hunting.

Paralyzed for a moment, Sinclair and Matilda did not move. The leader saw them and approached, followed by the rest of his retinue.

"Back to the cart," hissed Sinclair, the first to recover from the shock. He seized Matilda's arm and pulled her with him. She winced as the rocks stabbed into her bare feet.

The leader reached them just as their backs pressed against the side of the cart.

Matilda stared at the Indian leader. His chest, bare except for strings of beads and the strip of leather that held the quiver of arrows on his back, gleamed copper in the sun. She had never seen an Indian so close before. His fringed buckskin leggings boasted beaded decorations and the feathers in his straight, black hair suggested a role of some importance. She wondered which tribe he belonged to. Their eyes met. She offered a tentative smile.

He silently appraised her. His eyes, curious but not unfriendly, roved up and down her body, taking in every aspect of her. Her skin prickled. She felt Sinclair's hand trembling as he gripped her arm tighter. What should they do? Tales she had heard of Indians stealing white girls ran unbidden though her mind.

Then Matilda remembered people saying Indians were always hungry and she thought of the parcel of cookies. Reaching into the cart, smiling and hoping he would not think she reached for a weapon, her hand closed on the parcel. Opening it, she took out a large cookie. Approaching the Indian leader with caution, she offered it to him.

His eyes softened. A smile hovered on his lips as he accepted the proffered morsel. He took a bite, paused, grinned with pleasure and shoved the rest into his mouth.

"Cookie," Matilda said as she offered him another.

"Coo-kee," he responded, carefully forming the new word. He ate the second one.

She handed him the rest of the parcel and he accepted it without comment. Turning his pony, he led the group across the river and up the other bank.

Sinclair remained silent until the line of horses passed from sight, then let out his breath with a long sigh. "Quick thinking, Sis," he said, relief patent on his face. "Now," he added, tossing their boots into the cart among the buckets, some full of sand, some still empty, "let's get out of here before they come back with the whole tribe."

Back at the cabin, the still excited Matilda described the Indians to her father. Sinclair, not to be out-done, interjected his comments.

"Why," Gardner said, "you met some Pottawatamies. Remember? Abe Dyer said their home village is not far away, back across the Big Blue."

Three mornings later, a startled Matilda watched three Indians ride up to the cabin. She immediately recognized the leader from their encounter by the river. This time he smiled first. He raised his hand in greeting and presented her with a beautiful buffalo hide.

Unable to speak, Matilda smiled and accepted the gift. She wondered what he wanted. She did not have to wonder long.

"Coo-kee," he announced firmly.

Fortunately, Matilda had baked a big batch not long before, so she gave him a full parcel. With a satisfied grunt, he turned his horse and rode swiftly away, followed by his companions.

Betsy Ann stood behind her. "Guess we'd better keep some cookies on hand all the time." She smiled at Matilda and shook her head. "Looks like you made yourself a friend. Must be your father's blood in you."

* * *

At the end of November, winter finally arrived. Frost struck the fields with regularity, though the weather remained mild. The first snow did not fall until January, and then only came in light flurries that melted quickly in the warmth of the next day. But the cold nights made Matilda thankful for their snug, well-built cabin. She spread her gift buffalo hide on the floor of the loft beside the antelope skin.

"Maybe Kansas winters are not as cold as we've heard," Matilda commented one night to Minerva. "This certainly isn't bad."

Minerva laughed. "Abe says just wait."

George spent more time in the Randolph cabin than in his own. Matilda suspected he liked her mother's cooking. Betsy Ann claimed he did so in hopes he could persuade Matilda to marry him. Whatever his motivation, he had been present when Matilda read a letter from Alf in which Alf barely mentioned his gold claim. Instead, he raved about California's potential for farming.

> "Many miners got discouraged and returned home after all the good claims worked out or got taken, but I think Sam is right. The future is here in California. Businessmen and farmers are doing well. Crops almost grow themselves. The winters are so mild we can grow two crops a year. I'm hoping to make enough money from our claim to get my own farm like Sam and Will. So is Alfred."

George listened and believed. "Come May, I'm gonna head west," he told his astonished audience. "Soon's the grass starts on the prairie. Wagon trains follow the Big Blue up to the Little Blue, just north of here, comin' up from St. Louie. I'll join 'em."

"Matilda," Gardner announced a few days later, "I've been talking to Britt. We should have some way of teaching the young-uns until we get enough folks in the valley to have a proper school. Since George here is heading west," he motioned to the young man standing beside him grinning, "he says we can use his cabin. He'll pitch a tent by our place until he's ready to leave."

George nodded in agreement. "Only be fer another month. Iffen the weather holds mild like it has, I'll be right comfortable in my tent."

Yes, Matilda thought, and right comfortable eating at the Randolph table three times a day. Then, with a start, she realized what her father had in mind. "Now, Pa," she demurred.

"You turn nineteen this summer. Time you got started doing something constructive."

He means since I've turned down three more proposals of marriage, she translated silently.

"Put all that reading you do to good use," he continued, chuckling at the dismay on her face. "Don't worry. You'll probably only have Britt's youngsters and Minerva and Weldon."

Betsy Ann refilled his coffee cup. "Gardner," she interjected, "don't you think you should 'a asked Matilda first?" Betsy Ann, to Matilda's relief and gratitude, had backed her refusals to the marriage proposals when her father pronounced her 'too fussy'.

Matilda looked from her mother to her father and gulped. Teach school? Could she do it? It might be better than washing wool in the creek, or scrubbing clothes, or any of the other myriad tasks she and Minerva shared. It would certainly beat marriage to any of the suitors Kansas had provided so far. She shuddered at the memory of the last one. His teeth were so stained from chewing tobacco she didn't notice anything else except the yellow streak on his beard where the tobacco juice had dribbled down the side of his mouth.

She could not help comparing him to Curtis Stewart. Curtis may have been a trifle dull, but at least he had been clean. Maybe she should have stayed in Illinois after all, if Kansas could offer nothing better than she had seen so far.

Her mind returned to her father's request. Why couldn't he wait until a real school teacher appeared? Among all the thousands of immigrants swarming over Kansas, there would surely be at least one school teacher. Then, with a flash of insight, she understood.

She had discovered several years previously, to her amazement, that her father could neither read nor write. Orphaned at five and raised by an uncle who wanted him to work, not study, he was never allowed to attend school. She remembered her mother telling her Aunt Fanny how life with his Uncle Thomas had been so harsh he ran away from home at fourteen.

Suddenly she realized why he needed to move when civilization came too close, and why he insisted they all learn to read and write. She wondered why it took her so long to see that his own lack of those skills motivated him to see his children well educated.

Of course, she thought, remembering so many things at once. He's afraid he can't compete with educated men, and he sees the day coming when there will be no more frontier where he can run. He wants to prepare us so we will be ready. She smiled, meeting the intense dark eyes above the high cheek bones. She saw him read the understanding in her eyes.

"Of course, Pa," she replied. "I'll be happy to try."

Three weeks later, she looked out at her pupils over the top of the tall box that served as her desk. The one shelf that graced it held a few of her precious books, including the *Dabold's Simple Arithmetic* she had used to teach Sarah

Williams, a fairly new copy of *Conly's Speller*, and a two-year-old copy of *Scientific American*.

Of her ten students, six were Randolphs. They included Britt's children, Owen, six, Gardner, nine, Will, eleven, and Sarah, fifteen. Minerva and Weldon joined them. They sat five to a side on the rough wooden benches lining the sides of the small crude hut.

The remaining four children, the Briggs family, came from a farm farther west. They rode in each morning, all four astride a big, old bay mare. The youngest, Matthew, rode in front of his big brother Andy, his little legs sticking straight out on the mare's wide back.

A small wooden box, a clean paper on top, stood by the doorway. On the box stood a galvanized metal water pail, covered by a clean towel, and the communal drinking cup.

Behind her, on the wall opposite the door, the cabin's one tiny window boasted four small panes of glass. The glass panes let in barely enough light. Had they been oiled skins or paper it would have been worse. She kept the blanket off the front door to let in more light. By this winter, they would need a real door, but then the little room would be a dungeon.

Of course, leaving the doorway open meant she could not keep out Owen's dog. He spent most of the day curled up at the boy's feet.

She glanced around at her pupils, as they concentrated on writing their letters. They used an assortment of slates garnered from trunks and boxes. Owen's had belonged to the grandfather for whom he had been named, Owen Evans. Owen prized it second only to his dog.

Walking down the line, Matilda stopped beside Will. "Hold the chalk like this," she said, demonstrating the hold. "It's not an ax."

Watching her footing, she circled the room. I certainly hope we can get a wooden floor before winter, she thought.

The accumulation of rag rugs over the dirt made walking treacherous. She could envision the mud when the rains started.

George kept his word, and a week later, the end of April in 1855, he folded his tent and headed for California. The grass had started on the prairie early with the mild winter and the first wagon trains of the season crossed the Oregon Trail, following the Big Blue to the north of the Randolph claim.

He left his cabin to them with his blessing. "You needed a school for the young'uns," he said with the lop-sided grin that had become so familiar to her. "My place might be a tad small, but it seems to serve real good."

The whole family saw him off, each giving him letters for Alf, Sam, and Will. He gave Matilda a special smile as he left. "When you get to California, Miss 'Tilda, you be sure and look me up."

Matilda promised, her dream of going to California re-awakened. Of course, if she accepted George's proposal of marriage . . . . She remembered Caroline's comments when she contemplated marrying Curtis Stewart. She shook her head. Somehow, spending the rest of her life with George did not impress her. Not even if it meant she could go to California.

But she would miss his optimism and good humor. She wished him well.

Chapter 20

1855 to 1856

BY THE TIME OF George's departure, Minerva and Abraham Dyer had become an accepted couple, with eyes for no one else. As a consequence, the Randolphs found themselves invited to many functions at the Dyer home. At the Fourth of July festivities, Matilda met Jenny and Charlie Johnson. The young couple had settled a few weeks before on a section of the Big Blue that Gardner considered his. He visited them on their arrival, but formed the opinion that Charlie would not last long, so he did not dispute the claim. "Wife's too delicate," he had reported to Betsy Ann. "She won't last the winter. He'll have to take her back."

Abe, Minerva clinging to his arm, approached. "Matilda, may I present Jenny and Charlie Johnson?"

"Pleased to meet you." Matilda took the girl's hand with a flash of embarrassment. The soft uncalloused hand made Matilda very aware of her own rough one. She recalled her father's comments and felt a pang of sympathy for them. Guilt surged through her as she recalled that her father regarded them as usurpers. Surely this innocuous young couple could never be a threat to anyone. They were only children. She pulled her thoughts back to the girl. Jenny's blue eyes matched her own and the red highlights in the light brown curls caught the morning sun.

"You must visit me," Jenny invited with a shy smile. "I get so lonesome." She hesitated and glanced at her husband. "Of course, our cabin isn't very nice yet, but ... "

"Takes time, takes time. You've been here less than a month. We'll help you. Matter of fact, I should have been over to see you before now. Please, come and sit, out of the heat." The July sun blazed down upon them with relentless fury. "You look tuckered out." She pulled Jenny's hand through her arm. "When's your baby due? You're so brave to travel all the way out here so close to your time."

Sam Dyer clanged the bell to signal the food was ready so they hurried to take their places in line at the big outdoor table.

"Soon," Jenny said. She hesitated, then confessed, "And I'm scared. We don't know anyone, and I feel so alone."

Matilda embraced her for a moment and felt the slight body tremble. "Don't be afraid. My mother knows all about babies and she'll be glad to help you."

Relief washed over Jenny's face. "She'll really help me?"

"Of course. Just send Charlie over when it's time."

Four weeks after the Fourth of July festivities, Charlie Johnson appeared at the door of the Randolph cabin at dawn, turning his hat around and around in his hands. "Miz' Randolph." He stopped, then began again, "Miz Randolph, can you come . . . come quick? Jenny says it's her time, and she says Miss Matilda told her I could come fer you." He mangled his hat some more. "She just lies there a-moanin'. Worries me to death. Everyone tells me you know everything about babies."

"Of course, Charlie. I'll be happy to help Jenny." Betsy Ann gathered her supplies. "Matilda, come and help me. Time you learned to tend to a birthin'."

So six hours later, stifling in the stuffy heat inside the cabin, Matilda witnessed the birth of Jenny's son. Under Betsy Ann's direction, she bathed the tiny squirming body with warm water, then wrapped him snugly in a soft blanket. As she placed the infant at Jenny's breast, their eyes met. The exhaustion in Jenny's eyes faded, replaced by joy as she gently outlined the baby's tiny face with her forefinger and kissed the still moist top of his head.

"There, now, he's a fine boy." Betsy Ann wiped the perspiration from Jenny's face with a damp cloth. "And you did real well." She walked to the doorway and swept aside the blanket that covered it. Matilda welcomed the slight breeze that wafted in and brushed across her flushed and overheated face. "Charlie! Come in and meet your son."

Charlie had spent the six hours pacing in front of the cabin. As soon as Betsy Ann called, he rushed to Jenny's side and kissed her, marveling at the baby. "He's so little! Are they all this little?"

Betsy Ann laughed. "He's a fine baby, and yes, they are all this little." She watched the scene for a few minutes, then, with a smile of satisfaction, said, "Come, Matilda." Gathering her supplies, she headed for the door. Still in a daze, Matilda followed her mother out of the cabin.

Matilda returned the next day. As she watched Jenny holding the infant that sucked lustily at her breast, she remembered the agony Jenny suffered during the birth. She saw in Jenny's eyes that the joy of having her own baby made up for every pain.

Matilda looked around the cabin. The hard-packed dirt floor must be impossible to keep clean. The blanket over the door would never keep out the winter cold. She could even see daylight through the roof, only partly covered by rough bark shingles, not shakes. Mud filled the chinks between the split logs. No wonder Jenny had worried what Matilda might think when she saw it.

"Jenny." Matilda hesitated, not wanting Jenny to think her critical. "Jenny, now that the baby is here, don't you think Charlie should put on a solid door and finish shingling the roof?"

Jenny sighed. "I hate to bother him. He works so hard all day clearing land to plant next spring." She gave a rueful little laugh. "He's so tired when he gets home nights he can barely eat his supper. If he has any energy left, he uses it to sharpen the ax or the saw."

"We have a little of the lime mixture left. I'll send Sinclair over tomorrow to daub in a few of the worst cracks. That'll help. Mud washes out, you know."

Tears rolled down Jenny's cheeks. "We had such a nice house back in New York. I even had a little piano. Used to give me all kinds of pleasure, playin' it." She quickly wiped away the tears and smiled. "But Charlie says we'll have one again. He wanted to come to Kansas and get his own farm." She stopped to blow her nose. "He grew up in town, never had a chance to farm." She gave Matilda a faint smile. "He always read every book he could about farming."

Matilda said nothing, suspecting that all the books he read would never make Charlie Johnson a farmer.

Jenny watched Matilda's face. "He's a good man, 'Tilda. He really is."

Matilda had seen hailstorms in Illinois, but never anything like the one that struck the end of August, a few weeks after the birth of Jenny's baby. The day, hot and sultry, lacked even a breath of wind to give some relief. The leaves of the trees remained motionless in the ominous stillness.

As Matilda washed clothes at the outdoor tubs, she thought she would like to jump in the tub herself to cool off. Suddenly, in late afternoon, clouds gathered in the west. The sky took on an eerie greenish hue. Thunder rumbled in the distance. Within minutes a strong wind flapped the clothes draped over the bushes and fence to dry. One gust caught a shirt and carried it towards the river.

"Min," Matilda called. "Come quick! Help me or the whole wash will be down in Juniata."

Minerva chased down the escaping shirt. Between them, they gathered the remaining damp laundry and retreated to the haven of the porch where they stood arm in arm and watched the cloud line approach. Thunder boomed and lightning streaked across the sky. Minerva clung to Matilda. They gaped as they watched the storm cut a swath through the prairie grass like a giant mower.

As the storm grew nearer, hailstones, some as large as hen eggs, poured from the clouds with a rush and a roar, leveling everything in their path. The chickens scattered, clucking in protest. Later, after the cloud had taken its toll and gone on its way, they found one old rooster lying on the ground amidst the melting hailstones, his neck broken by one of the larger stones.

"Good thing we got that shed built for Clementine," Betsy Ann remarked.

Matilda and Minerva exchanged smiles. Gardner had felt they could postpone building the cow shed until later, feeling other tasks should take precedence, but Betsy Ann insisted her precious cow be sheltered. She assigned Tom and John the task as soon as they finished building the house.

Clementine stood at her half door and looked mildly out at all those white stones making such a noise on her roof. Her newest calf, just three months old, peered out of the door beside her, emitting an occasional frightened bleat.

Almost as fast as it arrived, the cloud departed. The sun shone again and the ice began to melt. Clouds of vapor arose. The sheep, their legs covered by the mist, seemed to float on top.

"That must be what Heaven's like," Matilda mused to Minerva. "Like walking on clouds."

In the third week of September, the first frost struck the fields, catching everyone by surprise. "Last year at this time we were having a heat wave," Matilda said to Minerva.

"Now it's freezing. Kansas weather sure has a mind of its own."

"Better hurry up and get that corn harvested," Gardner said. "Good thing we got it planted early so it's ready. "Sam Dyer says this'll be the first crop of corn raised in Riley County."

Of course, Matilda thought with a smile. The county just formed on August thirtieth.

"Hear they're paying $1.25 a bushel at Fort Riley," her father continued, rubbing his hands together in glee. "That's the best price I've ever got."

The first snow flurry came in mid-October, and Gardner predicted a severe winter. "All those folks still living in tents are going to have a hard time of it," he told the gathered family that evening. "Told 'em they should have listened to Sam Dyer. Man's been living in Kansas long as he has oughta know."

Matilda had continued to see Jenny at least once a week. After the first snowfall, she found Jenny and the baby wrapped in blankets, huddled by the fire. Charlie shivered in bed, suffering from an attack of the ague.

"Planned to get the cabin finished, now I can't work in the fields," he managed to gasp out between chattering teeth. "Got to keep the cold out somehow."

Matilda shuddered as she looked around the room. Rain and snow poured in through the unshingled part of the roof, making the dirt floor a muddy morass. The blanket over the door provided little or no protection from the wind.

"You can't live like this, Jenny. My father and Sam Dyer both say this winter is going to be a hard one. My brothers will be over tomorrow to finish that roof." Matilda stoked up the fire and swung the kettle over to make some hot tea. "And Charlie, I'll bring you some of Mother's quinine to help those chills."

On the first of November, the Steamship Hartford burned to the waterline at St. Mary's, over on the Kaw River. On the same day, winter arrived in Riley County with a vengeance. As prepared as they were, the first blizzard astounded Matilda with its ferocity. Despite Sinclair's hard work caulking the spaces between the logs, the wind managed to get through. The front door, although facing south to avoid the direction of the worst winds, could not keep the cold out.

Matilda thought of poor Jenny and others who still lived in cabins with only a blanket over the entrance, or who still lived in tents, fooled by the mildness of the previous winter. But the Randolphs had heeded the warnings of Sam Dyer. Their cabin boasted a sturdy wooden door. Her father nailed a thin strip of wood around the inside to cover the space between the wall and the door, for further protection against the fierce wind.

"Good thing we have lots of blankets," Matilda said to her mother as the two of them tacked up extra covering around the door.

"Better than our first winter in Randolph's Grove," Betsy Ann commented. Matilda knew her mother referred to the original shelter, the open-faced camp of three walls and a dirt floor. The following spring they built the first cabin, the small one that served as a smokehouse by the time of Matilda's birth. Thank heavens they improved their lot before my arrival, Matilda thought. She had heard that first winter described often enough to understand her mother's insistence on a comfortable cabin.

That night, snuggled under her quilts, Matilda listened to the howling wind, and thought again of Jenny Johnson, whose cabin still had no floor. She fervently hoped the storm had not trapped anyone outside. Her brothers took turns watching the fire, to be sure it never went out. She heard their soft voices as they talked among themselves a couple of times during the night. The swirling wind occasionally blew smoke back down the chimney, filling the room with a fine haze, sometimes strong enough to burn her eyes.

She smiled to herself. How fortunate I am to have so many big brothers to take care of me, she thought. She drifted, at last, into a deep and dreamless sleep.

Before winter set in, her brothers had put a door on the schoolhouse and built a puncheon floor. The little Topsy stove kept the cabin cozy, so they held school all winter. The round-bellied stove stood on three legs and boasted two burners on the top. Matilda kept a teakettle full and hot, ready for a cup of tea.

One January afternoon, just as she dismissed school for the day, Matilda looked at the sky and noticed a dark bank of clouds building rapidly on the horizon. The Briggs children mounted their horse and started for home. Concerned, Matilda stepped from the protection of the building. A sudden gust of wind blasted her. Snow would soon follow.

"Wait, children," she called, having learned the vagaries of Kansas weather. "Snow'll be on us before you can get home. Come back."

"But Miss Randolph," the oldest protested. "I got to milk the cow, and . . . ."

"You won't milk the cow if you get lost on the prairie on the way home," Matilda told him firmly. With some reluctance he obeyed and turned the horse back just as the first snowflakes fell. Within fifteen minutes, swirling snow surrounded the little building and the visibility dropped until they could barely see the outhouse twenty steps from the door, let alone the Randolph cabin a mile to the east.

Matilda entertained the children with games and songs until, one by one, they dropped off to sleep in spite of very little to eat for supper. Pooling the leftovers from their midday meal, Matilda made a pot of hot soup in the water bucket. They ate in turns from the drinking cup.

Andy Briggs offered to keep the fire going all night. "You try and get some sleep, Miss Randolph," he told her. "You look tuckered out."

She sighed. "You're right, Andy. I am exhausted." She leaned against the wall and snuggled into her coat, sharing part of a rug with Sarah and Minerva. The wind howled outside. She wondered how it could be so blazing hot in the summer and so cold in the winter. Someday, she thought as she drifted off to sleep, I'm going to live where it never snows.

A shout from little Matthew Briggs roused her and she opened her eyes to bright sunlight streaming through the window.

"We're saved," he cried. "There's Papa!" The door opened to reveal Charlie Briggs and Tom Randolph. The Briggs children threw themselves into their father's arms. He wept as he held them close.

Matilda rose stiffly to her feet and silently accepted Charlie's praise for saving the children.

"If you hadn't read the weather right, they would've died in the blizzard," he said.

Matilda later realized how close a call it had been, but at the time, the only thing on her mind was her cozy bed at home.

Busy with teaching school and her work at home, Matilda saw Jenny only rarely during the winter. The finished roof and cemented walls improved the little cabin, but Jenny continued to spend her days huddled in a blanket by the fire.

Her depression worried Matilda. "Jenny," she finally asked. "What ails you?"

"My hands," Jenny whispered. "My hands hurt all the time."

Then one blustery morning at the end of April, when the snow finally showed signs of relinquishing its hold on the fields, Charlie appeared on the doorstep of the Randolph cabin with the infant in his arms.

"Matilda," he begged, "can you watch baby Charlie for me today? Jenny's took to her bed and I got to get the fields ready for plantin'." Tears filled his eyes. "She cries all the time. Says it hurts to move, says she can't move her fingers, and she'll never be able to play the piano again." He wiped the tears away with a grimy hand. "Breaks my heart to hear her talk so. Played real pretty, she did."

Guilt washed over Matilda, "Oh, Charlie," she cried. "I'm so sorry. I should have been over to see her more often." She reached for the infant. "Of course I'll tend to little Charlie. I'll be happy to." Holding the infant in her arms, she chucked him under the chin. He cooed in delight and waved his chubby arms. "He's grown so! I can't believe he's eight months old already."

Charlie smiled, a sad little smile that did not touch his eyes. "I'll be back for him afore sundown."

"Comfrey poultices. Hot comfrey poultices," Betsy Ann announced as the door closed on the retreating Charlie. "She got the rheumatics from all that cold and damp. Sinclair, tomorrow you take your sister over in the cart so's she can treat Jenny."

Much to her surprise, Matilda discovered she really enjoyed teaching. The children, eager to learn, listened avidly as she read them their lessons. She seriously considered a lifetime career as a teacher. Remembering some of her marriage proposals, she decided Sarah Williams was right. There were worse fates than remaining single.

Matilda saw Jenny often. The comfrey poultices gave only minimal relief. She tried to cheer the girl up with bouquets of the brightly colored wildflowers that grew in such profusion as soon as the last of the snow had melted, and tried to help her with the active baby as much as she could.

Life drifted into a routine, much as Matilda had felt in Randolph's Grove. Would her life never have more to offer than this? She began thinking more and more of her brothers in California. Rumbles of unrest from the slavery/anti-slavery factions frightened her. She knew the first Kansas legislature had met at Pawnee, with the Territorial Governor, Andrew Reeder, but nothing had been settled, at least as far as she knew. Groups of men the abolitionists called border ruffians crossed the river from Missouri, leading to clashes between free and slave state supporters. Fortunately they were sufficiently isolated that not much affected them directly.

The romance between Abe Dyer and Minerva continued to blossom. It was Minerva who told her an ice jam on February 26 destroyed the new bridge the government had built across the Big Blue at Juniata.

"So now Abe's father is back to running the ferry," Minerva had laughed. "He says that's more fun than collecting tolls anywise."

"That fine new bridge?" Matilda gasped. "Why, it must have been three hundred feet long!"

"At least," Minerva nodded. "Shows how powerful that ice can be."

One Saturday morning in May, Matilda sat on the porch spinning yarn on Betsy Ann's big spinning wheel and watched a rider approach. The head of a nondescript, flop-eared puppy protruded from a saddlepack. The beautiful golden horse had a white mane and tail, with a white star on her forehead. Horses of this quality were rare in Kansas. Filled with admiration for the horse, she looked more closely at the rider. She rose to meet the sandy-haired young man who dismounted and strode forward to greet her. Impressed, she noted his height, his broad shoulders, the sureness to his step. Her breath came a little faster.

"Morning." He extended his hand. "I'm looking for work. Any possibility you folks could use another hand?"

She met his clear eyes, hazel with little flecks of gold, and placed her hand in his. Her knees grew weak as tingles shot up her arm at his touch.

His smile went straight to her heart. "My name," he said, "is Lewis Clark Baldwin."

Chapter 21

Summer of 1856

"*Pleased to meet you,*" Matilda said, when she got her breathing back under control enough to speak. "I'm 'Tilda. Pa just said a couple of days ago we needed another hand if we're going to get any more fields ready to plant."

She took a deep breath, willing her voice to remain steady, embarrassed at his effect on her, vaguely wondering why she reacted so strongly to his presence. To cover her confusion, she turned to the mare standing patiently beside the man. "What a magnificent horse!"

He grinned and his whole face lit up. "She's my pride and joy." He stroked the mare's nose. She responded by rubbing her head against his shoulder. "She's just barely two, but she broke in real easy. Never owned a gentler horse. Call her 'White Star' because of the blaze on her forehead."

"And who are you?" Matilda laughed to the puppy clamoring for her attention, struggling to free himself from the saddlepack. Lewis lifted the brown and white dog out of the pack and set him on the ground. Matilda stroked the soft, floppy ears. He yipped with pleasure and licked her hand, wagging his tail so hard his whole back end waved from side to side.

"That's Jake. Found him along the side of the road. Guess he couldn't keep up and his owners just abandoned him, half starved and footsore." Lewis gathered the dog in his arms and grimaced as Jake's long, pink tongue lavished puppy kisses on his face. "Carried him in the saddle pack for three days while his feet healed and he got his strength back. Guess he got used to it. Now he wants to ride in the pack all the time."

Matilda scratched behind the floppy ears. "He sure looks healthy now. Welcome to the family, Jake!"

Gardner hired the young man the moment he saw him, as impressed by him as Matilda. That evening, everyone gathered outside after supper to get acquainted. They sat on the porch or on upturned kettles, enjoying the pleasant evening. There would not be many more before the heat began. The sound of chirping grasshoppers filled the air.

"My father and I came from Illinois in '55," Lewis said, "right after my mother died. We settled in the town of Baldwin, about thirty miles southeast of Lawrence, not far from the Missouri border.

"Said everything in Illinois reminded him of my mother, and he liked the idea of a town named after him," Lewis grinned, "although I don't think the founder, Milton Baldwin, is any relation. We opened a dry goods store, but I prefer farming. I like the idea being in the open air, so when my father died last spring, I sold out." He shook his head. "Besides, I'm not much of a hand for senseless fighting, and I got tired of the constant problems between the pro-slave bunch and the free-state men. Some of the men are genuinely defending what they feel is right, but some are just mean-spirited folks taking advantage of the unrest to settle old scores." He smiled at Matilda. "So I sold out before I got burned out. Took what money I got and bought White Star. Figured to travel in style."

As Matilda returned his smile, her heart thumped so loudly she feared he would hear it.

"I knew when Pomeroy and Robinson founded Lawrence there would be more killing," he continued. "They brought

all those folks from that Emigrant Aid Society Thayer founded in Massachusetts back in '54." He chuckled. "But the
pro-slavery side wasn't to be out-maneuvered without a
fight. We were overrun a year ago March when they had
the first ballot on the slavery issue."

"And how do you stand?" Gardner queried.

"I'm no rabid abolitionist. I think compromises can be
worked out without killing." Lewis laughed. "Did you hear
what Jim Lane proposed? He's a real talker, that one. Said
they should line up a hundred pro-slave men and a hundred free-staters and let 'em fight it out. Have a dozen U.S.
Senators and a dozen U.S. Representatives act as referees."
He took off his hat and fanned an offending mosquito away
from his face. "Even offered to be one of the hundred himself. And wanted Senator Atchison to be on the slave holder
side."

After the laughter subsided, Gardner said, "And what did
you hear about the voting?"

"The census in February of '55 listed less than 3000 voters," Lewis reported. "One month later, over 6000 ballots
were cast for slavery." He laughed again. "That's why we
were overrun. All those Missourians came across the border
to vote Kansas a slave territory. And that's how we wound
up with two governors and two capitols."

Lewis paused, his face serious. An owl hooted in the
momentary silence. "It's also why Governor Geary threw
out the results of the voting." He sighed. "But it's far from
over. Did you know some hotheads are even talking about
splitting up the Union?"

"Over slavery?" Tom snorted. "They'd never do that."

Gardner's face turned thoughtful. Matilda felt a pang of
fear. Surely the southern states could never be so foolish.
She looked from one solemn face to the next in the fading
light. Could they? Would there be war? What would Kansas
do? She looked at Sinclair. How old is he? Seventeen. She

felt the blood drain from her face at the thought of him going to war.

"Hard to say," was Gardner's only comment. They fell silent, watching the sun set. The shadows grew long. Betsy Ann lighted a candle and put it in the window. In moments, June bugs surrounded the light, hurling themselves to their deaths against the glass.

Gardner rose to his feet. "Time for bed," he announced. "Want to get to work early on that last cornfield, before the sun gets too high."

Two weeks later, Tom arrived home from a trip to Fort Riley with news of a massacre, over by Pottawatamee Creek.

"Some crazy abolitionist named John Brown killed five unarmed men because he thought they were pro-slavery," Gardner reported, suppressed fury in his voice. "Just *thought* they were pro-slavery. No one will be safe with someone like him running around loose. Sam Jones is trying to catch him, or at least run him out of the territory."

It gets closer, Matilda thought. Fear surged through her in a wave.

She tried to ignore the rumbles of unrest she heard. June passed, then July. A mail route had been established between Fort Riley to the south and Marysville to the north, with a stop at Randolph. The Postmaster General named Gardner Postmaster, and Sinclair built a small extension onto the cabin to serve as Post Office.

As the summer progressed, Matilda found herself falling more and more in love with Lewis. He shyly asked to be her escort for several neighborhood events, and she rode behind him on White Star. He took great pride in the young mare and it made Matilda proud to be seen riding with him. Whenever their hands touched, she felt a thrill shoot through her. She found herself wondering what she had ever seen in Curtis Stewart.

However, she could not tell if Lewis felt the same about her. She thought he might. Whenever their eyes met, he gave her a charming, private smile that seemed to be only for her. But Rebecca Briggs found more reasons to come over now, and so did some of the other neighborhood girls. Lewis showed no favorites. He remained courteous and charming to all of them. Matilda's frustration rose. Of course, she thought, he's only known me for three months.

One morning, as Lewis put the finishing touches on a new water trough for Clementine and her newest calf, Rebecca rode in. Sidesaddle, Matilda noted, so she would need help to dismount. Every other time Matilda had seen Becky on a horse she rode astride, as did most Kansas girls. Matilda's suspicions surfaced. Becky also wore her prettiest dress, the one she usually saved for Sunday. As Matilda watched, Becky rode up to Lewis, smiling and chattering. He stood up from his work and politely helped her dismount.

Matilda stood at the window watching Lewis, admiring the muscles that rippled along his broad back. The sight of him made her heart beat fast. As he lifted Rebecca down, Matilda noticed the girl clung to him longer than necessary. Gripping the curtain so hard her knuckles turned white, a wave of an emotion Matilda had never felt before surged through her. She felt an almost uncontrollable urge to run out and pull every hair from Becky's head. She stared at the scene before her so intently she did not hear her mother join her at the window.

"Hussy," Betsy Ann commented. That brought Matilda back to reality with a start.

"Oh, Mother," she tried to say lightly. "He's nice ..." her voice caught. "He's nice to everyone," she whispered. Their eyes met and Matilda knew her mother, with her usual acumen, saw right through her. She burst into tears and

Betsy Ann gathered her in her arms.

"Hush, now," Betsy Ann consoled. "Lewis is a man of sense. No way he'd go for a featherbrain like Becky Briggs."

Matilda dried her tears and laughed. Betsy Ann commented often on Rebecca's flightiness. If he does decide on Rebecca, Matilda thought grimly, I can always teach school.

The Reverend Charles Wisner, an itinerant circuit rider, happened by the Randolph home the last week in July. Gardner invited him in and persuaded him to hold services for the family.

"Been a long time," he opined. "Having one of the family read the Bible just isn't the same as having a real, live preacher." He ushered the Reverend to a seat in his own chair. "And you can tell us some of the latest news, you gettin' around like you do." He settled into a chair opposite his guest. "Is it true President Pierce ordered the Legislature elected under the Topeka Constitution dispersed by Federal troops?"

"Yes," the Reverend responded. "He sent Sumner to suppress what he said was an insurrection. Even had the leaders arrested."

Gardner grinned, but shook his head. "Much as I would like to see that bunch run out of the state, that kind of action can only lead to problems."

Betsy Ann put a large loaf of fresh bread on the table. "Enough politics," she announced. "Let the poor man eat, then he can do his preachin'."

Matilda laughed to herself. Her mother tried to get the men off of politics whenever she could. Also, Betsy Ann took immediately to this young man, as she never had to the stuffy Reverend Cartwright in Illinois. As Reverend Wisner prepared to leave, Betsy Ann plied him with a sack of potatoes, a dozen of her precious eggs, and a small tub of sweet butter.

"Made that butter the new way," she informed the Reverend. "Brought the milk to a boil, then cooled and skimmed it. Butter stays sweet a lot longer that way."

Matilda had read about the new method in an article in the *Scientific American*. When she first tried to show it to her mother, the scornful Betsy Ann pronounced it too much bother, but, to Matilda's amusement, after her mother saw the results she refused to make butter any other way.

"My wife will be very grateful," Reverend Wisner replied. "She always complains the butter turns rancid too quickly." He demurred when Betsy Ann added a freshly baked raspberry pie to the supplies already in the wagon.

"Looks like she wants you to come back, Reverend," Gardner said. "Now you have to bring the pie pan back." They laughed and shook hands in farewell. "When do you think you'll be by this way again?"

"If all goes well, I should be back about the first of September." He shook the reins to start the horse. "God bless you all," he called back.

"Until September," Gardner yelled after him, and all waved as he drove off.

Lewis took Matilda's hand. "Come with me," he said, and walked her around the corner of the house. Mystified, she followed, acutely aware of the firm grasp of his hand.

When they were alone, he stopped and turned her to face him. His eyes sparkled above the high cheek bones. "'Tilda," he smiled down at her, white, even teeth flashing in his tanned face. "When Reverend Wisner returns in September, will you marry me?"

Her heart raced so fast she felt faint. She couldn't speak. She gaped at him, unable to persuade herself she had really heard him say the words she had wanted to hear for so long. Chickens clucked in the background, and she smelled the fresh mown hay in Clementine's byre. She felt acutely conscious of the slight stickiness of her calico dress as it clung to her body in the stifling summer heat, but all these sensations seemed to come from far away.

He misunderstood her reaction and the animation left his face. "I'm sorry, 'Tilda. I've spoken too soon. I thought you knew how I felt. I've come to love you so much . . . ."

He started to release her, but she clasped his hand tighter, finding her voice at last.

"Oh, Lew," she gasped out. "No, it's not . . . not too soon. I . . . I've loved you since I first watched you ride up on White Star." She smiled at him, her face radiant with her love for him. "Of course I'll marry you."

The light came back into the hazel eyes. The grip of his right hand tightened as he pulled her close. His left arm swung around her to press her body against his. Lips crushed down on hers and she felt herself go limp.

Chapter 22

Fall and Winter of 1856

MATILDA opened her eyes and blinked in the brightness of the morning sun. "Wake up, Min," she called across the loft to her sister. "Today is my wedding day!" She sighed with happiness. "September first, 1856. I'll remember it forever."

The month since Lewis proposed had flown by. Matilda's wedding dress hung on a special peg in the loft by her bed. She and Minerva finished it the night before by candlelight.

Matilda hurried to dress. "Tonight the loft will be all yours," she told her yawning sister. The previous day, Tom and John had put up the tent she and Lewis would share until they could get their own cabin.

Lewis said they would build a cabin as soon as he filed a claim. "Right way, of course, is to not get married 'til after we build the cabin," he had grinned. "But I don't want to wait." Her heart had jumped at the glint in his eyes as he said it.

They would sleep in the tent until then. Her cheeks grew red as she remembered her brothers' teasing while she prepared the interior of the tent for the wedding night. Tingles of anticipation ran through her body when she put down the double pallet for their bed. Her blush deepened at the memory of the talk with her mother about what Lewis would expect on their wedding night. Lewis had not kissed her passionately since the day he asked her to marry him, but every time their eyes met or their hands touched, she remembered the sensation with such force it made her knees buckle.

Reverend Wisner, proud to officiate at the first wedding in the newly formed Jackson Township, had spent the previous night stretched out on the floor in front of the fireplace along with Lewis, Tom, John, and Sinclair. Her father grumbled because Reverend Wisner was not a Methodist, but Matilda didn't care. She would have married Lewis if only a Pottawatamee medicine man were available to perform the ceremony.

"Come on, Min, get up," she called a second time, yanking off the light sheet that covered her sister. "We've got a lot of work to do."

A film of sweat clung to Matilda's body, for the loft remained hot all summer. At least it would be cooler in the tent. The loft seldom cooled off even at night during the months of sticky heat.

"It's not going to rain, is it?" Minerva asked. She scrambled into her dress and followed her sister down the ladder.

"I hope not," Matilda replied, casting an anxious glance at the sky. She knew how quickly thunderclouds could build. A cloudburst would spoil everything. She hurried outside to oversee preparations for the wedding feast. The men had set up outdoor tables for the food. Paper bells and flowers decorated the bower of trees she had selected as the altar for the ceremony. Matilda wished some of the wildflowers for which Kansas was renowned had been available, but it was too late in the summer, so they settled for the paper decorations. The leaves had begun to change to red and gold, and made a beautiful background. The sky remained clear, taking on a brassy color as the heat mounted.

By mid-morning, buggies and carts bearing family and neighbors wearing their finest clothes began to arrive. Everyone brought a contribution to the wedding feast. The makeshift tables groaned under the weight of whole hams, beef roasts, and platters of fried chicken; all kinds of breads, both flour and corn; dishes of pumpkin and apple butter; a variety of relishes; mince, apple, pumpkin, and berry pies; dishes of nuts and dried fruits. Matilda savored the aromas as she surveyed the piled tables. It pleased her to think so many people wanted to come to her wedding.

Some, with abolitionist views, would not come because they opposed her father's efforts to make Kansas a slave state, but most of their neighbors loved a social gathering and would not let politics interfere with a chance to have a good time.

Her sister-in-law Sarah's voice interrupted her reverie. "Owen Randolph, you get your hands off those cookies!" Matilda laughed at Sarah's attempts to keep her brood from sampling the food. While Sarah admonished her youngest son, the oldest snatched a piece of chicken and ran off.

The Dyers came up from Juniata. As Matilda watched Abe and Minerva together, she suspected there would be another wedding in the not too distant future. Minerva would be sixteen next summer. Charlie and Jenny, with baby Charlie, waved to her from their spot under a tree. The Briggs family appeared en masse, with a rather petulant Rebecca. Matilda smiled at her own foolishness. Imagine being jealous of Becky! Lewis treated Becky politely simply because he could never be rude to anyone.

Her heart swelling with love and pride, she watched Lewis greeting their guests. Can such a man really want me? she thought. Today is the happiest day of my life.

When the time set for the ceremony neared, people milled about and visited while Matilda donned her wedding dress. The little general store up in Marysville just happened to have some lengths of white satin in stock, so Matilda swapped a length of it in return for a promise to supply the storekeeper with cookies to sell for three months.

Thrilled to have such beautiful material, Matilda and Minerva had fashioned her gown with great care. They trimmed the high collar and the cuffs with lace Betsy Ann produced from a trunk. Matilda's sister-in-law, Sarah, gave her two dozen tiny satin-covered buttons. Tiny pleats at the waist made the skirt stand out, while the bodice fitted like it was pasted on.

As she helped her sister dress, Minerva chattered with excitement. "Sarah Dyer invited me to spend a few days at her house, and Mother agreed. I'm going back with them after the wedding."

When Minerva fastened the last button down the back of the gown, Betsy Ann arranged the veil over Matilda's face. "My, my, don't you make a pretty bride," she murmured. Tears stood in her eyes.

Matilda, astonished to find such a show of emotion in her stoic mother, gave her a quick hug to hide her own tears, then turned to her father.

Gardner stood in the doorway, a big grin on his face, and offered her his arm. "Well," he said, his voice gruff in his efforts to hide his own emotion, "'bout time you women are ready."

Betsy Ann scurried to take her seat, and the guests stood around in small groups, waiting. They left an open pathway from the door to the bower. Minerva, carrying a small spray of colorful leaves, walked to where Lewis, with John standing beside him, waited with Reverend Wisner. Gardner, Matilda clinging to his arm, began her slow march forward.

Dazed, Matilda repeated the vows. Lewis' ringing "I sure do!" echoed in her head. She heard Reverend Wisner pronounce them man and wife, then felt Lewis' arms around her as he kissed her soundly to the cheers of the audience.

It was over. She was Mrs. Lewis Clark Baldwin.

That evening, finally alone together, Lewis took Matilda

in his arms and clasped her to him. "I only heard half of what the preacher said," he whispered into her hair. Tilting back her chin, he smiled into her eyes. "But I love you. You are the only woman I've ever even wanted to love. I only hope I'm worthy of you."

"Oh, Lew, you are, you are!" Her rapid breaths made her dizzy as her heart pounded in her chest. His lips closed on hers, and she gave herself up to a bliss she had never before imagined.

Matilda had thought she loved Lewis before their marriage, but she had no concept of the happiness in store for her. She would lie awake beside him at night, listening to his even breathing, feeling the warmth of his body and the strength in the arm that lay across her. Sometimes in the morning, if she awoke first, she would raise herself on one elbow and watch his sleeping face, her love for him surging through her body in waves.

She refused to let the stories of battles between the free-staters and the border ruffians interfere with her happiness. When Tom reported the Territorial Governor, John Geary, on the order of the President, had dispatched two regiments of the U.S. Cavalry to settle the unrest, she felt grateful some-one at least tried to stop the constant fighting. She chuckled as she remembered the way they stopped it: by threaten-ing to shoot anyone on either side who chose to ignore the order.

By late fall, Matilda wondered how much longer they could continue to sleep in the tent. Although not anxious to move back into the cabin with the rest of the family, treasur-ing the moments she and Lewis were alone, she knew they would have to make a decision soon. The temperatures at night often fell below freezing.

One morning in mid-November, as Matilda straightened the bedding, Minerva entered the tent. Matilda looked up and greeted her sister with a smile.

"Morning, Min honey. I'll be done here in a minute and can help you and Mother with . . ." She broke off as she noticed tears running down Minerva's cheeks. "What's the matter? What's happened?"

"Oh, 'Tilda, I have to talk to you." Minerva gulped back the tears.

Matilda gathered her sister in her arms and held her. "Hush, love, it'll be all right. You know I'll always be here for you. What is it?"

"It's . . . it's . . . Oh, 'Tilda!" Minerva's words ceased in a spate of tears.

What on earth could have happened? Matilda's mind ran over some possibilities as she waited for her weeping sister to compose herself. Has someone been injured, or taken ill? A stab of fright shot through her.

"It's my monthlies," Minerva finally whispered against Matilda's shoulder.

Her monthlies? Matilda's mind, blank for a moment, caught the meaning of her sister's statement. Oh, no, she thought, suddenly remembering Minerva spent the week following Matilda's wedding at the Dyers.

"Have you and Abe . . . er, uh, ever, uh, been together? I mean . . ." Matilda had trouble asking what she thought.

Minerva nodded, raising her head and reaching for her handkerchief. "When I stayed down to Dyer's, right after you and Lew got married. I don't know how it happened, but it felt so good and so right. I never even thought about it at the time, but afterward Abe said . . . Abe said . . ." she gulped. "He said it was his fault, he should have known better, but that if I took my monthlies, it would be all right. But I haven't!" The last words came out in a wail and she burst into another fit of weeping.

"We'll tell Mother," Matilda said. "She'll know what to do. We just won't tell Pa."

Betsy Ann's solution was simple. "You two young-un's been daft over each other since the day you met. Just get married. Babe comes a little early is all. Not to worry. Folks talk they can just talk. It'll be our secret."

Matilda knew, as Minerva did not, the reason Betsy Ann understood Minerva's plight so readily. During the last weeks of Temperance's life, while Matilda took care of her, Temperance had confided to Matilda that their parents had married on February 15, 1818, in Morgan County, Alabama.

"They tell everyone January 5," Temperance had laughed, "because Britt's birthday came a little too soon after. But it's their secret. Don't tell anyone." Matilda never had.

So, on December seventh, 1856, Minerva became Mrs. Abraham Oakes Dyer in a simple ceremony at the home of Abe's parents in Juniata. The Reverend Wisner performed the ceremony, pleased to be asked to officiate at the marriage of another Randolph daughter. The Dyers hosted a big dinner after the ceremony, and people came from miles around. One neighbor, Mrs. Allen, presented them with one of the loveliest quilts Matilda had ever seen.

Minerva's wedding solved the problem of a home for Lewis and Matilda. They moved back into the loft vacated by Minerva's departure.

"This'll be just temporary, though, my love," Lewis assured her. "We'll have our own cabin by spring. Your Pa says we can build on the nine acre section down on the next creek, by Jenny and Charlie's place."

Two weeks after Minerva's wedding, Lewis came in and announced, "Abe says he and Minerva are gonna move northeast, up to Waterville. Can't imagine why he'd want to move any closer to the Missouri line, what with all the fighting and such."

Matilda met her mother's eyes. So Abe planned to protect Minerva from the gossips by taking her away until after the birth of her baby. While Matilda approved of the plan, she feared Minerva would be lonely and frightened, so far from friends and family. She was only fifteen, after all.

Lewis, of course, did not know of Abe's reason, so Matilda only smiled and said, "I'm sure Abe knows what he's doing."

On January 18, the thermometer dropped to twenty-five degrees below zero. Even with the fire and extra blankets, they could not keep warm.

"Good thing we're not trying to live in that tent," Lewis grinned to Matilda. "We'd 'a been frozen solid for sure."

Matilda only shuddered, thinking of poor Jenny.

The following morning, as Matilda started to rise, a wave of nausea threatened to overcome her. Frightened, she took a deep breath and fought it down. She was alone on the pallet. Lewis had already risen and climbed down to the main floor for breakfast.

"Mother," Matilda called. Her mother's head appeared over the side of the loft. "I feel sick."

Betsy Ann's calm, unruffled mien always reassured Matilda. "And when did you last have your monthlies?" she asked.

"My monthlies?" Matilda's face turned blank as she thought back. "Why," she said, "let's see, shortly before Min's wedding, then . . . ." Startled, she stared at her mother, who chuckled at the look on her face. Elated, the nausea forgotten, she hugged her mother. Still in her nightgown, she scrambled down the ladder and threw herself into the arms of the surprised Lewis. "Oh, Darling," she cried, her face radiant. "We're going to have a baby!"

As soon as he learned of her pregnancy, Lewis forbade Matilda to ride over to Jenny's, fearing for her health and the baby's.

"When the weather permits," he said, "I'll take you in the cart."

So Matilda saw Jenny only rarely during the winter. The finished roof and cemented walls improved the little cabin, but Jenny continued to spend her days huddled in a blanket by the fire. Maybe my father is right, Matilda thought, pain stabbing her heart. Maybe Jenny *is* too fragile for this life.

Chapter 23

Spring and Summer of 1857

THE FOLLOWING SPRING, Samuel Dyer came by the Randolph cabin and reported that a teamster had offered to bring him a load of whiskey.

Chuckling, Sam said, "I told him a permanent minister'd be more benefit to the community. So this here teamster, he persuaded the Reverend Charles Blood to move in here." He paused to fill his pipe, then said, with his eyes twinkling, "I told him you bein' a right religious man, Gardner, this is the perfect spot for him to preach."

As a result, the first formal church services on Fancy Creek were held at the Randolph residence. Gardner grumbled because Reverend Blood was not a Methodist, but agreed he preferred any minister to none.

Spring also found Jenny no better. Baby Charlie, a healthy, active toddler, required more attention than his ailing mother could give, so Matilda, though far advanced in pregnancy herself, spent what free time she had at the Johnson cabin. The muddy floor made the place almost uninhabitable.

"Now the crops are in, Charlie," Lewis announced one evening as he arrived to pick up Matilda, "next thing we got to do is get a floor down."

Charlie shook his head. "No, Lew." He dug a piece of paper out of a metal box that stood on the mantle above the small fireplace. "I'm taking Jenny home to New York. She's just not suited to this life. I can't see her hurtin' all the time." He handed the paper to the astonished Lewis.

"Here. I'm givin' you our claim. It's a quarter section, 160 acres, and runs right up to that piece where you're a-buildin' your cabin. The timber is partly cleared, an' I got two fields of corn planted."

Lewis frowned in protest. "But we've got no money. I can't pay you." He paused, stroking his chin. "Maybe I can borrow some from . . ."

"You've paid us over and over, with somethin' that's meant a lot more to us than money." He ran his fingers through his hair and smiled. "Don't think I never knew Mr. Randolph wanted to run us out. You and 'Tilda gave me a chance to try my hand at farmin'." He shook his head with a sad little smile. "If Jenny's health would'a held, we'd 'a made it."

As Lewis and Matilda gaped in astonishment, unable to believe what they heard, Charlie continued. "We're leavin' next week. We'll take the boat from Kansas City."

Charlie stared out the open doorway at the growing fields of corn, the pain in his face so patent it wrenched Matilda's heart. She thought of the many others Kansas had defeated. So many who came full of hopes and dreams returned east, hurt and broken. It grieved her to see Charlie and Jenny join that tragic group.

He turned back to them. "And I want Bossie to have a good home. I just can't bear to sell her." He smiled shyly, as though ashamed to admit his affection for the animal. "Me and that old brindle cow, we're good friends."

As anticipated, Gardner was pleased to learn Charlie had proven his prediction correct. He promptly named the creek that fed into the Big Blue by the Johnson cabin Baldwin Creek.

"Been a part of the Randolph plantation from the beginning," he declared. "Got enough problems with claim jumpers, what with those Sechrest brothers and that Henry Shellenbaum trying to settle on Fancy Creek. Was all right when they built farther up the creek last fall after they followed the Kaw Indians upriver. But now they're getting into our territory."

Lewis and Matilda had no particular interest in Gardner's plantation plans. Lewis had broken ground for a tiny cabin on the nine acres Gardner had given them next to the Johnson property. But this cabin had twice the floor space, with much of the work already done. They plunged into the task of making the cabin their own.

"First, a solid door," Matilda announced. "I don't want any stray pig or dog just walking in." She grinned. "Or Pottawatamee either." Indians often came by the Randolph home begging for a 'coo-kee.' She knew with only a blanket on the door they would walk right in. She remembered her sister Sarah saying their father always insisted on a solid door back in Illinois for the same reason. Although wise in many ways, the Indians never seemed to grasp the concept of privacy.

Once the door hung from its leather hinges and the bar on the inside stood ready to swing into place, they enlisted Sinclair's help in preparing wood for the roof and floor. Tom brought Sinclair in the cart along with a stack of four foot-long sections of saw logs. While Sinclair split logs into shakes for the roof, Lewis hewed out puncheons for the floor with the froe.

"We'll replace the original part of the roof, too," Lewis said. "Bark shingles don't keep out the rain right."

Matilda, meanwhile, sewed long cloth braids into the rag rug she planned to use to cover the rough floor. She found her last month of pregnancy a nuisance, for she could not do half the things she wanted to accomplish to make the cabin into a real home before the baby came.

"Patience," her mother counseled when she complained about the enforced curtailment of her activities. "Won't be more'n another month."

When the shakes and puncheons were ready, Britt, Tom, and Gardner came to help Lewis and Sinclair. They finished the cabin in a day and Lewis and Matilda were alone at last in their own home. Lewis took Matilda in his arms and kissed her. Together, they looked around the cozy cabin. Their bed stood in one corner, covered with bright quilts. The colorful rag rug lay on the finished floor. Their few china dishes stood with the mundane tin plates on shelves resting on pegs above Matilda's sink. She was thrilled to have the wooden sink, even though she still had to carry water in and the waste water outside. So many women had to wash their dishes outside in a washtub or a bucket. They took pride in the snug door, the watertight walls, the sound roof.

"Tomorrow," Lewis promised, "Soon's I get done work in the field, I'm going to start building a bed for our son." He kissed her again, then shook his head in sorrow. "Can't help but think about poor Charlie. If he'd 'a put more effort into making this cabin cozy for Jenny, she might 'a been happy to stay."

The last Sunday in May, Lewis and Matilda joined her parents at the Randolph residence for the Reverend Blood's services, and stayed to spend the afternoon. As Matilda and her mother washed the dishes, Matilda glanced out of the window and saw a wagon pull into the yard. She immediately recognized Abe. Her heart lurched as she realized he sat alone on the seat.

Dishtowel in hand, she raced to meet him as fast as her advanced pregnancy would allow. "Abe," she cried, seizing his hands as he climbed stiffly down from the high seat. "Where's Minerva?"

"Relax." His face broke into a smile. "She's fine, just worn out. Sleepin' in the wagon."

Betsy Ann joined them. "And the babe? Shouldn't 'a

been born yet." She kept her voice low so only Abe and Matilda heard her words.

"Dead. Born too early. Never breathed once." Abe shook his head. "Ague so bad around where we went Min took sick almost as soon as we got there. Spent the whole time in bed, she did. Birthin' woman said the poor little mite never had a chance. After the babe died, Min wanted to come home. Came as soon as I figgered she had the strength to travel."

The men, who had been doing chores, gathered around them, so they said no more about the baby. Matilda climbed into the wagon to see her sister.

Minerva's eyes opened, and she gave Matilda a wan smile. "'Tilda, I've come home."

Matilda fell to her knees beside the bunk and clasped her sister in her arms. "Your secret is safe. Now we just need to get your strength back. No more babies until you are completely well."

Minerva's eyes twinkled. "That's what Abe says. He says I'm too young to have babies."

"Good," Matilda smiled, tears in her eyes. "You can help me take care of mine." She put her hand on her swelling abdomen. "We expect him to be born mid-June."

Minerva sighed, and tears streaked down the side of her face. "That's when mine should 'a been born." She shook her head. "You don't suppose God punished me for ... for .... After all, me and Abe shouldn't have .... " Her voice trailed off.

"Don't think like that," Matilda said firmly. "I know Pa says everything is God's will, but I think sometimes things just happen. Don't you go blaming yourself."

A smile broke through the tears. "That's what Abe says."

"Good. Listen to him. He's a wise young man. Now, do you feel able to get up and come into the house for some supper?"

Soon after Minerva's return, a letter arrived from Caroline, announcing the birth of her second daughter.

> "We've named her Sarah, but we're calling her
> Sally. Too many Sarah's in this family already.
> "Tommy still has a bad cough, and sometimes
> coughs up blood. He's also losing weight, although
> he denies it. I worry about him."

Matilda's heart sank as she read her sister's words.

With a frown, Lewis asked, "Does Tommy have consumption?"

Matilda sighed. "I hope not, but I'm afraid he might. Remember I told you his first wife, Susan, died of it." Matilda's heart ached for her sister. So happy in her own marriage, Matilda understood Caroline's behavior. Would her sister and Tommy have only a few years together after waiting for so long? It didn't seem fair.

The buzzing of a mosquito diverted her attention. "Is it my imagination," Matilda asked, "or are the mosquitoes worse here than at my folks' place?" She looked up from the letter to swat at the offending insect and surveyed several welts on her arm.

"We're on lower ground, closer to the river. Does seem to be more of them here, and this is the time of year when they're the worst." He rose from the little table and hugged her overly ample waistline. The baby kicked in protest.

Lewis laughed and put his hand on her abdomen. His face lighted as he felt the baby moving. "Jealous already. Gonna be a lively one." He pulled his suspender straps over his shoulders and reached for his battered hat on its peg by the door. "Did I tell you John killed a buffalo in his cornfield? Must've been the last straggler from that bunch that came through last week. Guess it heard John got himself elected representative to that convention on the state constitution over at LeCompton. Must 'a come by to congratulate him." He kissed the tip of her nose and headed for the door. "Along with the one Tom shot, ought to give us buffalo enough for the whole winter. Ed Sechrest says that big, old bull Tom got is the one like to took the corner off his cabin." He grinned. "I'm off. See you at dinner."

The threat to Gardner's claims turned out to be more real than they had thought. The Sechrest brothers said he did not have enough family to settle all the quarters he claimed. Henry Shellenbaum disputed Sinclair's quarter, saying Sinclair, at eighteen, was a minor and too young to file.

"Your Pa's going to lay out some cities," Lewis announced at noon when he returned for dinner. "Says he's made a plat for Randolph, at the mouth of Fancy Creek close to the house, plus two others he's calling Timber City and Blue City." He grinned and hugged Matilda. "I told him that's a lot of work. He says he's hired young Pease to do the building of a blacksmith shop, a church, and a home for himself at the new City of Randolph. He's got Tom and Sinclair busy laying out the other two."

Matilda sighed, half in exasperation, half in sympathy. She felt heavy and uncomfortable, and had little patience with the constant bickering. "I just wish he'd get this plantation notion out of his head. This slavery business has caused enough grief already, and it's only going to get worse."

"I tried to suggest that, love," Lewis said. "He almost bit my head off."

"Don't I know it!" Matilda laughed and shook her head. "I just hope he doesn't get in too much trouble over it. We sure don't need to attract the attention of anyone like that John Brown." She dismissed the whole subject. "Come and eat before your food gets cold. I've put it on the table for you."

* * *

Two weeks later, Matilda woke in the night. Lewis lay beside her, his whole body shaking so violently the bed rocked. "Lewis!" she cried. "You've got the ague." She remembered how near Minerva had come to dying, and Betsy Ann's tales of the death of her father. Grandfather John Stringfield had died of the ague in January of 1822, long before Matilda's birth, but the tale had been told and retold. She knew other settlers suffered from it. In fact, Dr. Stillman, down Manhattan way, had treated a number of cases. But, except for Minerva, their family had been spared. Until now.

"C . . . c . . . can't . . . stop . . . shakin'." He clenched his teeth to stop them from chattering.

Frantic, Matilda ordered herself to think. Warm him, that's what Mother would say. And vapor baths. She threw on another quilt and hurried, as quickly as her advanced pregnancy would allow, to the fireplace, wondering how in the world she could make a vapor bath. The fire, just a few embers to keep the heat down, flared to life as she added some shredded bark. She moved the teakettle over the flame.

"Quinine," she said. "That's what Mother uses. Quinine with a little laudanum in port wine. I'll have to get some in the morning. Mother always has a supply made up. I'm fixing you a cup of hot tea, and warming some bricks."

"You . . . you . . . c . . . c . . . can't ride!" Lewis managed to gasp out.

"Don't worry, my darling," she soothed. "Maybe I won't have to. One of my brothers may come by." She knew she would have to ride, but saw no need to make him worry. Through the window, faint light glowed pink in the east. Dawn would come soon.

She helped him drink a cup of the hot tea, and tucked the heated bricks around him. She covered him with another quilt and lay down beside him, trying to transfer some of her body heat to him.

"Hush, love," she murmured softly. Stroking his fore-head, she comforted him as she would a child until he finally fell into a restless sleep.

Matilda woke with a start. Dawn had broken, filling the room with light. Lewis still slept. Sweat beaded his fore-head. He's in the fever stage, she thought. He needs the quinine. She rose with care, trying not to wake him. Maybe she could get over to her mother's and back before he woke. She dressed as quietly as possible, then saw his eyes on her, bright with fever.

"Got to finish hoeing that last field of corn," he gasped. "Got to get . . ."

"Hush," she interrupted. "I'll ask Sinclair or Tom to do it for you. You just think about getting well." She finished dressing. "I'll be back soon's I can."

"Be careful," he muttered.

She smiled. "Don't worry your fever any higher. I'll be fine."

But as she tightened the strap under White Star's belly, her apprehension increased. White Star seemed to sense this would be no ordinary trip. She snorted, but stood per-fectly still.

"Come on, White Star," Matilda urged. "You've got to help me." She led the mare over to the mounting block.

As she settled on the horse's back and urged her toward the Randolph residence, visible to the eye on the top of the rise about a mile away, her heart sank. She had not been on a horse since last March, and felt as though she were breaking in two. A surge of pain started in her lower back and swept around to the front.

"Not now, Baby, not now," she whispered, holding her abdomen with her left hand. "Please, not now." The pain passed and she sighed in relief. She had to go very slowly, and the ride seemed endless. She thanked heaven White Star knew the route and needed little direction.

When Matilda reached the front porch of her mother's home at last, she dared not dismount, for she knew she would never be able to mount again. Twice more on the ride over the pain had swept through her, forcing her to cling to the horse's mane, glad she rode White Star instead of one of her father's half-wild horses.

"Mother," she cried.

Betsy Ann appeared so quickly she seemed to materialize. "Matilda? Is it your time? What on earth are you doing riding? I told you . . ."

"It's Lew," Matilda interrupted. "He's got the ague. He had chills last night, now he's got the fever. He needs quinine." She did not mention her pains, though it took all of her control to hide the next one from her all too observant mother. I have to get back to Lew, she thought wildly. If I let Mother know I'm having the pains, she'll never let me ride back.

Weldon stood wide-eyed on the porch as Betsy Ann went for the medicine. "Is he going to die?" he asked.

"Of course he's not going to die," Betsy Ann snapped as she returned to the porch, bag in hand. "Stop trying to scare your sister to death. Look how white she is."

Matilda smiled with no humor, only a tight little movement of her lips. Her hand gripped White Star's mane so tightly her fingers ached. Good, she thought. Let Mother think it's because I'm afraid for Lew.

"Weldon," Betsy Ann ordered, "I may be gone all day. Have Tom and Sinclair come over to Matilda's as soon as they come in. They'll have to finish Lew's hoeing for him." Moving the horse to the mounting block, she swung up behind Matilda. "He'll never get better if he's lyin' there fretting about the crop not getting proper care."

Matilda had to laugh in spite of the pain of another contraction washing over her. Her mother knew Lew pretty well.

The ride back took less than twenty minutes, but they were the longest twenty minutes of Matilda's life. The pains swept through her every few minutes, and grew stronger. When they arrived at the cabin, Betsy Ann swung down from the horse and watched Matilda with a professional eye. At that moment, Matilda felt a warm rush of fluid on her leg. Startled, she gasped aloud.

With a soft laugh, her mother said, "I knew it was your time. That's why I came back with you. By rights, you shouldn't have come back, but I knew you'd fret over Lew. Come on, let's see if we can get you into the house."

Lewis, his eyes bright with fever, gasped, "'Tilda! Are you all right? I've been so worried. You shouldn't 'a been riding."

"Hush, love, I'm fine." She touched his forehead, relieved to find it cooler to her touch. She doubled up as another spasm of pain struck her. More warm fluid ran down her leg.

Her mother took charge. She stirred the fire into life and swung the teakettle over the flame, then tossed a quilt on the floor. "We're going to need the bed," she told Lewis, helping him up. "By rights, you should wait outside, but since you're ailin', you'll have to lie here." She tucked an extra quilt around him as he lay on the floor and moved the table to make a barrier between him and the bed.

"All right, young lady. Get over here and lie down while I get Lew his dose of quinine and get his towel baths started." Betsy Ann covered the bed with a piece of India rubber sheeting and took Matilda's arm. With her mother's help, Matilda managed to lie down just as another spasm washed over her. She bit hard on a corner of the quilt to keep from crying out, fearing worry for her would make Lewis' fever worse.

As the sun reached its zenith, the baby arrived. Lewis, feeling better with the quinine and the towel baths, watched as Betsy Ann propped Matilda up and put the baby to her breast. Matilda's eyes met her husband's. She saw the love and pride in his face and she smiled. Looking down at the infant, she murmured, "Say 'Hello' to your father, John Baldwin."

Chapter 24

Summer of 1857

"*BID'S FAIR* to be a rainy summer." Lewis shook the water off his hat on his return from the barn. A week had passed since John's birth. Almost every afternoon after the end of April a thunderstorm had roared overhead, drowning the growing shoots of corn and flooding Matilda's vegetable garden.

The spring close to the house, their source of drinking water, flooded with muddy water from Baldwin Creek as the Big Blue backed up the creek. That forced Lewis to ride to the Randolph residence every day to get drinking water from the Randolph well.

Matilda, carrying Baby John, went with him on the days her father was due back from his weekly trip between Riley and Marysville with the mail, unless the rain prevented him from going. The new road from Manhattan to Marysville made the mail route much easier.

Gardner reported meeting the Dahlberg family on one of these trips. "From Sweden," he said. "Look to be real fine folks. Crossed over that new pontoon bridge the government put up for Sam to run down at Juniata and come up the west side. Quite a trick with a wagon, even worse than when we came." He grinned. "Were looking for Randolph, they said, so I told 'em, 'You've found him. That's me!' " He laughed at his own joke. "And I hear tell Winkler has built a grist mill seven, eight miles up Fancy Creek. Means I won't have to go all the way to Table Rock any more to get our flour ground."

"Didn't know Fancy Creek ran fast enough to turn a mill," Tom commented in response to the news.

"It'll grind slow," Gardner grinned, "but I'll bet, like the mills of the gods, it will grind exceedingly fine."

The first week in September the sun came out. The constant heat sucked the moisture from the land. By the end of September the corn, ripe and ready to harvest, rustled in the hot wind. The prairie grass that flourished with the summer's rain turned a listless brown.

"All that grass is gonna cause problems," Lewis reported with a scowl. "It's dry as paper. Won't take much to set it to burning. We're harvesting as fast as we can, but if it goes, we can lose the whole field."

Matilda, nursing John, sat across the table from Lewis, a contented smile wreathing her face as she stroked the baby fuzz on John's head. The past three months had been the happiest of her life. She had never dreamed having her own baby would be so wonderful. She looked up and smiled at Lewis, her heart full of love for him. They had celebrated their first anniversary two weeks before. Could it be a whole year already? *We have our own home, our own baby.* Though her heart gave a jump at the thought of going through another prairie fire, nothing could spoil her contentment.

"And all that rain kept the corn from filling right," he continued in a doleful tone. "Lot of the ears are less than half full. Even your pumpkins haven't set well. Hardly enough for the Pottawatamees to steal."

She laughed. "At least the tomatoes and beans liked all the rain," she soothed him. "We still have Priscilla. Those two baby pigs Pa gave us from his last batch are growing like weeds, and the chickens seem to thrive on all the grasshoppers."

"Wish they could eat the grasshoppers in the cornfield

as well," Lewis continued, not responding to her attempts to cheer him. "You should see the big holes in the leaves from those blasted grasshoppers."

"We don't eat the leaves." Matilda tucked the sleeping baby into the little bed Lewis built for him and smiled down on him. "Let the grasshoppers enjoy them."

As she rose from beside the crib, she smelled the air. Smoke! Startled, she turned as Lewis jumped to his feet. They ran to the door, appalled to see the sky to the north almost obscured by a rolling cloud of smoke billowing high into the air.

"Prairie fire," Lewis muttered. "Knew all that dry grass would spell trouble." Behind him, Matilda gave a little cry of fright. "Get the baby," he ordered.

Stunned, she stood numb.

"Move!" His voice rose. "I'll get the cart."

The second order reached her and she dashed for the sleeping infant. Clutching him to her breast, she ran to the barn where Lewis hitched White Star to the cart. He threw buckets and some burlap sacks in the back while Matilda clambered onto the seat.

"We'll head for your folks' place. From there we can see where the fire's headed." Lewis jumped up beside her. "Gee up!" White Star lunged forward so fast Matilda's head jerked backwards.

During the wild ride, Matilda clung to the baby with her left arm. Her right hand clutched the metal rail on the side of the seat, her feet braced against the floor. The buckets rattled about in the back.

They arrived in a remarkably short space of time, Matilda gasping and bruised from the jolting ride. Her father and brothers worked on a backfire, sacrificing one field of corn to save the rest. Lewis ran to help them.

Matilda climbed stiffly down from the cart. Joining her mother on the porch, she saw the fire line. With the wind direction she realized with relief that the fire would probably miss the house, but still threatened her parents' fields.

"Will the backfire be in time?" she asked her mother. Concern for the infant in her arms brought a worried frown to her forehead. Smoke completely covered the sun. Her eyes smarted, the acrid fumes irritated her nose. She held John close to her breast to protect him.

"Bring the babe in the house and go help Minerva," her mother directed, as unperturbed as ever. "The backfire should hold."

Tucking John into her parents' bed, she returned to the porch. The sun glowed dimly through an eerie halo created by the cloud of smoke. Fire flared to the west as another tinder-dry field of corn went up in flames. A flickering line of crimson crept back from the fire line along the sparse grass. Matilda remembered her father's insistence on a good firebreak around the buildings and blessed his wisdom. Tying up her skirt, she grabbed a bucket and a burlap sack. Filling the bucket from the barrel beside the house, Matilda ran to where Minerva beat the low line of fire. Water from the bucket sloshed over the sides as she ran, filling her right shoe and soaking her stocking.

Minerva looked up as Matilda arrived, her grimy face revealing her fatigue. "Heavens," she panted, "did I ever pick the wrong time to visit Mother."

Matilda laughed, a grim, humorless chuckle, at the expression on her sister's sooty face. Dipping the sack into the bucket, she began to swat the low line of flames with the wet burlap. With both of them working, they developed a rhythm and soon extinguished the line of fire. By then, both were grimy.

"Hi, dirty-face," Matilda gasped to Minerva as they collapsed on their up-ended buckets, the fire safely past the Randolph property. Matilda wiped her sweaty face on her sleeve. "I'm sure glad we don't have to do this every day."

She unbuttoned the high-topped shoe and emptied it of water. Squeezing more water out of her stocking, she pushed her wet foot back into the soggy shoe with a grimace.

The men returned on a run. "It cost us one field of corn," Gardner said. "Fire's headed for the Collins place. We've got to help them." He and Tom mounted their horses. "It took Britt's fields, but looks like it missed John's. Lew, bring the cart with the buckets and sacks. Sinclair, help him." He turned his horse and rode off. Tom followed.

Minerva and Matilda helped Lewis and Sinclair load the cart. White Star whinnied and stamped nervously.

"Let me come with you, Lew," Minerva begged. "Patty Collins is a friend of mine." She gulped back tears.

Matilda hugged her sister. "We'll both go. Mother, please take care of John." Betsy Ann agreed and the two girls climbed into the cart for another wild ride. From the top of the far rise, they watched the fire for a moment.

"It's going to burn Ben and Patty's place!" Minerva cried. As she and Matilda watched, the flames slowed a little as they passed through a low swale with short grass, then flared anew as they caught another dry cornfield.

"Told Ben he should cut that grass a ways back from the buildings," Lewis muttered. He pulled White Star to a halt on a little rise behind and to one side of the fire's path. "I'll walk her in," he said. "Don't want her spooking."

Sinclair jumped down to help him. "Don't get her too close, Lew."

Lewis agreed and tied the reins to a cottonwood tree, a hundred yards from the fire. As they watched, the thatched roof of the cowshed burst into flames. A man hurried from the building, leading a cow by the halter.

"House'll go next," Lewis muttered. No sooner were the words out of his mouth than a gust of wind picked up a sheaf of burning grass from the shed and dropped it on the roof of the cabin. He and Sinclair, buckets and sacks in hand, ran toward the fire.

Matilda heard Patience scream and saw her run toward the burning building.

"Patty! No!" Minerva cried, running forward. Matilda followed. Behind them, White Star whinnied in fear and jerked against the restraining reins. Matilda and Minerva stopped, watching in horror as Patience's slender figure raced into the cabin. Ben, without a moment's hesitation, followed her in.

"They're dead, they're both dead!" Minerva, near hysteria, hid her face against Matilda's shoulder. Stunned, Matilda stared as frantic men threw buckets of water on the flames that fully engulfed the cabin.

"Please, God," Matilda whispered. She held the sobbing Minerva and gazed, transfixed, at the scene before her. "Please, no. Don't let them burn."

A cheer went up as the couple emerged, Patience clinging to a lamp with roses painted on the glass shade. Matilda started to laugh and cry at the same time. "Min, look, that silly Patty ran back in the house for that lamp the Dyers gave her!" She shook Minerva gently. "It's all right. They're out. They're safe." She did not mention that the men were throwing buckets of water on their smouldering clothing. "Go back to White Star and keep her calm." Matilda gathered up her skirts and started on a run for the house.

Lewis and Ben, Ben carrying Patience, met her. "She's badly burned, 'Tilda." Lewis said. "We have to get her back to your mother. Come on."

Matilda recoiled in horror when she saw the fire had burned off Patience's eyebrows. Her swollen eyelids covered her eyes.

"My lamp," Patience murmured, half conscious now, "My lamp." Her voice rose, and she gave a hoarse cry. "I have to save my lamp!"

"Hush, Patty." Matilda smoothed back the fire-singed

blond curls, sick to think of the risk the girl took to save the bauble. "Your lamp is safe. Now we have to take care of you."

Ben sat in the back of the cart, holding his young bride. Matilda rode in the back with them, trying to comfort her. Folds of blackened skin surrounded red patches on the girl's face. The smell of burned flesh and singed hair nauseated Matilda. She kept taking deep breaths to keep the sensation from overcoming her. The ride seemed endless, but they finally arrived back at the Randolph residence.

Betsy Ann met them as they drove up. Taking one look at Patience, she said, "Comfrey poultices. Cool comfrey poultices. Come, Ben. Carry the child into the house."

The burns were not as severe as first feared. Patience healed well, with only minor scarring. Even her eyebrows grew back, though not as full as before. Gardner said it was God's will. Betsy Ann credited the comfrey poultices.

Chapter 25

Fall and Winter, 1857 to 1858

A FEW DAYS after the prairie fire, three young Pottawatamie squaws visited Matilda for the first of what would become regular visits. Matilda enjoyed their company more than she could ever explain to Lewis. Previous Pottawatamie visitors had always been men looking for cookies. These were the first women of the tribe ever to come to her home. They wore the tribe's typical full skirts, which reached almost to their ankles, long sleeved blouses, and full leggings and moccasins laced with leather thongs that crossed and re-crossed around their legs. Each wore a large, intricately beaded necklace. Matilda decided the neckpiece must be symbolic, as all of the Pottawatamie women wore them, even the little girls.

"Hello," Matilda greeted the young women. They smiled, but did not speak, and presented her with a pair of moccasins and leggings like they wore. Maybe to repay me for all the cookies I've fed their men, Matilda thought with amusement. Chattering among themselves in a language unintelligible to Matilda, they investigated the room, pointing out oddities to each other. Fascinated by the embroidered towel she kept tacked up over the dish shelves to keep the dust from settling on the clean plates, they kept lifting the towel to look and laugh.

Matilda's skirt puzzled them. She had recently added a stylish hoop to her petticoat. They walked around and around her, as if unable to decide why the skirt stood out from her feet. Finally, curiosity overcame the tallest one and she tentatively raised the skirt. When they saw the hoop, all three burst into giggles. Matilda, infected by their contagious laughter, joined in. "These things really are silly, aren't they?" Matilda gasped between fits of the giggles. It took the amusement of these unsophisticated young women to show her how ridiculous hoops really were, and how unsuited to frontier life. She resolved never to wear one again, fashion or no fashion.

The voices woke Baby John, and she gathered him in her arms. The squaws circled around, laughing and saying, "Petite papoose." Most Pottawatamie spoke a little French, the result of years of dealing with French traders. Each held him in turn, marveling over his fair hair and blue eyes. He bore the ordeal with his usual aplomb. Matilda thanked heaven he was so good natured.

Matilda showed them the daguerreotype of herself, Lewis, and John, taken when the traveling photographer's wagon passed through on its way to Marysville from Manhattan. He repaid them for a night's lodging and his supper with the picture, and Matilda treasured it. The young women seemed a little frightened by the image at first, turning the card over to look at the back, then accepted it as readily as all the other marvels in the house. The quilts seemed to intrigue them, so she gave them a small one from John's bed. They chattered and stroked the quilt, laughing the whole while. Matilda recalled hearing someone say the Indians had no sense of humor. Whoever said that, she thought with a chuckle, never met a Pottawatamie.

When they rode off, she stood in the doorway with John in her arms and waved until they vanished from her sight.

They returned three days later with a beautiful cradleboard made of deerskin and decorated with intricate bead designs. They taught her how to use it, giggling among themselves. Probably at my ignorance, Matilda thought with amusement. After they left, John waved his chubby arms and cooed as she carried him on her back while she did her chores. Her work was so much easier with both hands free she wondered why more women didn't use these practical carriers. She knew most women rejected anything Indian, but she felt that notion foolish. She certainly found the pair of Indian moccasins they gave her far more practical than shoes. They enabled her to save her shoes for special occasions.

Lewis returned that evening to find her digging potatoes in her garden with John riding contentedly on her back. He ruffled John's hair, kissed Matilda, and laughed.

"Kansas is turning you into a regular Pottawatamie squaw."

The next day, the first blizzard struck. Lewis, staggering under his second load of firewood, entered the cabin. He shook his head. "Going to be a cold night. We'll need a lot of wood to keep the fire up." He brushed the dirt and leaves off his jacket. "Reckon this'll be a hard winter. Last year, first snow didn't come 'til the end of November."

Matilda helped him remove his coat. "Glad I got the rest of the potatoes gathered yesterday," she said. "From the looks of this, the garden is going to be under snow until spring."

By early November, the Dahlbergs had their cabin built, settling on a claim just three miles from the Randolph residence. "Going to make right fine neighbors," Gardner reported. Matilda wondered if the Dahlberg acceptance of Gardner's claim to Timber City had something to do with his opinion of them as neighbors, but kept the thought to herself.

"They've got a new baby girl name of Clara Josephine," Betsy Ann told Matilda. "Young Carl came for me last night to help deliver her." She chuckled. "Poor little rabbit is only eight years old. He ran all the way, in the dark and the cold, scared to death the whole time. I gave him a ride back on my horse."

"And Mrs. Dahlberg?" Matilda asked.

"Doing fine. Matter of fact, Carl could 'a saved himself the trouble. Babe was born before we got back."

Lewis' prediction of the weather held true. By Christmas, the snow reached the eaves of the cabins, blowing into ten foot drifts. Every cabin kept a lantern burning in a window to guide anyone caught in a storm. When the family gathered for Christmas, weather formed the main topic of conversation.

They also discussed the vote of December 21 on the LeCompton State Constitution. John had returned home from the convention just the day before Christmas.

"Can't believe the fools voted against slavery," Gardner grumbled. "What'd you say the vote was?"

"Seven for, fourteen against," John repeated, shaking his head. "Me and Will talked until we were purple. Just no way to sway the abolitionists. They've all read that Stowe woman's books and are determined all owners treat their slaves that way. Can you believe Beecher and his bunch are even holding contests? They're offering prizes to whoever can come up with the best anti-slavery stories, essays, and poems."

Matilda kept silent, but in her heart she rejoiced. The scene she witnessed at the slave auction back in '44 had never left her mind. The sad eyes of the little boy taken from his mother still haunted her. She held John close and kissed the top of his head. The thought of John being torn from her as that child had been torn from his mother wrenched her heart. She could not see how any mother would ever approve of such cruel actions.

She looked at the men, discussing the subject with their usual convictions, and wondered how different the world would be if women made the laws. I hope Mrs. Stanton and Mrs. Mott are successful in their fight to get more rights for women, she thought, although hesitant to voice such an opinion out loud. And I'm glad to see Mrs. Stowe standing up for her beliefs. She sighed with envy for such courage. I can't even tell my own father I'm for abolition, she castigated herself.

She was glad when the conversation swung back to the weather.

January's blizzard proved the worst. Without warning, after almost a week of sunny skies and blustery, cold north winds, dark billowing clouds roared across the skies. Blinding blasts of snow raged over the prairie with cyclone fury. For three days, Matilda and John huddled by the fire. Snug as they made the cabin, the frigid air still found its way in. Lewis struggled as far as the barn to feed White Star and the chickens and pigs, and milk and feed Priscilla. A rope strung between the barn and the house acted as a guide.

"Whoosh," he said, shaking the snow from his coat. "This is the worst storm I've ever seen. Hope it doesn't last too much longer." He took off his gloves and held his hands before the fire. "Good thing we strung that rope. I couldn't even see the lantern, let alone the house. Man could get lost and die out there."

Matilda poured him a cup of tea, the rising steam thick in the frosty air of the cabin. "And Pa's cattle?"

Lewis shook his head. "Soon as the blizzard stops, I'll ride over and help him."

The next morning dawned clear and cold. The rising sun sent little diamonds dancing across the mounds of new snow. The porch, facing away from the storm, held only about a foot of snow, but it took Lewis half an hour to battle his way to the barn.

"Be careful," she begged when he returned, mounted on White Star. "Don't overtire yourself. You can bring on another attack of the ague."

Reaching down, he stroked Matilda's cheek and smiled, the gentle smile of affection he had just for her. The smile that always melted her heart and still made her knees go weak. "You take care of yourself and John. I'll be back as soon as I can." He turned the horse, and Matilda watched White Star struggle through the drifts.

Matilda turned back to the house. She certainly had enough to do. Bundling John against the cold, she tucked him in the invaluable cradleboard and fought her way to the barn to milk the cow and feed the chickens and pigs. They heard her approach and started to squeal.

"No grasshoppers for the chickens now," she told John. "Have to feed them some of our corn. The table scraps aren't even enough for the pigs." She dumped the parings from last night's supper into their trough, laughing at their antics as each scrambled to eat all of the food before the other could get any. Her breath formed a cloud in front of her as she continued her monologue to the baby. She swung him off her back and leaned the carrier against the cow's stall. Jake licked John's face then flopped down beside him with a little groan.

"Stand still, Priscilla," she told the patient animal as she tied the halter to the post. Setting down her bucket, she pulled off her mittens and blew on her hands to warm them before sending the steaming streams of white milk into the pail. Lewis had laughed at her choice when she re-named the cow, but Matilda proclaimed, "Priscilla is much more dignified than Bossy." The gentle old cow amiably accepted the change.

Back in the cabin, the milk boiled and set in a snow bank to chill, beef simmering in the big pot in the fireplace, the potatoes, turnips and onions ready to add, Matilda waited for Lewis to return with growing anxiety. She wished she could communicate with her parents' house, but without White Star to carry her, she knew it was impossible. She looked out of the window, reassured to see smoke rising from the chimney at the Randolph residence.

As the sun dipped low on the horizon, and the red rays of sunset across the white snow mingled with the black of growing shadows, she saw Lewis on White Star working his way back through the snow. Quickly pulling on her boots and coat, she left John asleep in his little bed and rushed out.

They met at the barn. Tears poured down Lewis' cold-reddened cheeks as he wearily dismounted and lifted down the half-grown heifer White Star carried slung across the pommel.

Matilda gasped, "Lew, what happened to the poor thing?"

"The same as happened to the rest of them." His tears continued unchecked. "Broke my heart to see them suffer so. Some had their mouths frozen shut. The steam from their breath froze and they suffocated behind the ice, waiting for us to come and help them." He pulled out his well-used handkerchief and wiped his nose. "Those were the lucky ones," he continued. "Others had their feet frozen off, and," his voice broke, "they stood on bloody stumps," he whispered, sinking to his knees beside the surviving calf. He took a deep breath. "The pain in their eyes will haunt me the rest of my life."

Matilda knelt beside him. Pulling his head to her breast, she stroked his hair as he wept, comforting him as she would a child. She could find no words to ease the pain.

He did suffer another attack of the ague that night, as Matilda predicted. She spent the next week nursing him and the calf he rescued. She feared John would take sick in the cold and damp, but he thrived. At seven months of age, he crawled all over the floor. He pulled himself to his feet by the bed where Lewis lay. Laughing in delight to find his father's face so close, he slapped at him with his chubby hands.

Matilda watched them, smiling at John's attempts to speak. "I do believe 'Daddy' is going to be his first word, my love."

Chapter 26

Spring of 1858

THE MONTHS PASSED. In March, the government hired a young down-easter to carry the mail, so Gardner no longer made the weekly ride. The young man traversed the route by foot, spending one week for the trip from Riley to Marysville, then the following week to return.

"Guess growing up in Maine, he doesn't think a thing about a little snow," Sinclair laughed. On one of his visits to the Baldwin residence, Sinclair told Matilda of the experiences the young man reported. He spent the night at the Randolph cabin on his trip up as well as on his return.

In April, a brief warm spell gave Matilda a chance to visit her parents, so she was present when the mail carrier came through. Among the letters was one from her sister Caroline. Her sister reported the successful birth of another daughter, but also bore bad news.

> "Tommy is worse. I had so hoped this child would be a son, for I fear she will be his last. Even he has finally admitted he has consumption, and nothing seems to help. He grows weaker each day, and coughs blood more often now. I have named the baby Anna Thomas, after her father, even though she is a girl, for I wanted him to have a child that carried his name."

Gardner had some good news to report. "Got a Methodist minister on Fancy Creek now," he said, satisfaction ringing in his voice. "Name's Hartford. Gave his first sermon last Sunday, over at Mitchell's house. It's about time."

Matilda glanced at her mother, and their eyes met. Was there finally someplace where the meetings could be held other than the Randolph residence?

The sound of horses approaching attracted their attention. The men walked outside to greet the riders. Matilda and her mother watched from the doorway. Matilda kept watch on John, who played on the floor by the fireplace, reluctant to leave the warmth of the cabin. The sun might be warm, but the air off the snow carried a biting chill.

"You Randolph?" the elder of the two riders asked.

"That's me," Gardner replied. "What can I do for you?"

"I'm J.K. Whitson," the man replied. "This here's my partner, Jonas Kress. We just come by to tell you we're abolitionists, and we're challengin' your claim to this part of Kansas."

Matilda's heart pounded and she felt the blood drain from her face. Her father's face flushed with anger. Her brothers went rigid.

"And what makes you think you can do that?" Gardner's icy voice carried rage in every word. It's finally here, Matilda thought in despair. We thought it was so far away, but I knew we would not be able to escape much longer. Too much controversy, too many people coming in.

"Been checkin' with the Land Office over to Ogden," Whitson proclaimed. "They don't show no papers sayin' this here town belongs to you."

"I filed papers proper, and a copy of the plat as well. Got a church, a blacksmith shop, and a private home. Even sent fliers back east lookin' for settlers. Qualifies it as a town, and it belongs to the Randolph Town Company."

Whitson turned his horse and Kress followed. "Just warnin' you. We've started building two cabins in the town, and mean to take it over. Kansas is going to be a free state, and free men should own her land."

With that, they galloped off, leaving Gardner shouting

after them, "You ding-danged Black Republicans, I'll see you in hell before I let you take my town!" He shook his fist at the departing horsemen.

Matilda watched her father, her knees shaking so badly she could barely stand. Lewis returned and took her in his arms.

"Don't worry, love," he murmured in reassurance. "I'll see it doesn't come to fighting. At heart your father is a peaceful man."

Matilda tried to convince herself, but the rage on her father's face frightened her.

Betsy Ann, in her serene way, called, "Now Gardner, calm yourself, or you'll bring on an attack of apoplexy."

The dispute went back and forth, with Whitson and Kress building their cabins in Randolph, and each side riding back and forth to Ogden, filing papers to defend their claims. When it seemed neither side planned to start shooting, Matilda breathed a little easier and got back to the business of day-to-day living.

An unseasonably late blizzard struck on the first of May, then the sun came out to stay. The weather warmed with alarming speed.

"Going to be a problem," Lewis muttered one day towards the end of the month as the sun rose on another cloudless day. "Meltin' that snow too fast. River's highest I've ever seen it."

Matilda looked towards her parents' home, at the top of the rise. "Should we move over there for a week or so, just in case?" she asked as she followed him to the barn and watched him saddle White Star.

"Might not be a bad idea." He paused, his face thoughtful, then shook his head. "Well, I got to go down to Min and Abe's. Promised Abe I'd help him get his plow mended. We'll see what it looks like when I get back." Mounting the horse, he rode off. Jake trailed along behind him at White Star's heels, and Matilda returned to the cabin.

The day passed quickly, between caring for John, skimming the milk, churning another batch of butter, and piecing a new quilt. About three in the afternoon, a strange noise caught her attention. She stopped her work and listened, recognizing the sound of rushing water, a sound she had only heard before when close to the river.

Alarmed, she ran to the porch and stared aghast as the Big Blue took the barn, carrying it downstream like a child's toy boat. "Priscilla!" Matilda cried, running towards the barn. The pigs squealed in terror and she heard the doomed cow's despairing bellows as she beat against the boards with her hooves in a vain effort to free herself from the debris. In seconds, every sign of the building vanished. Priscilla, the poor yearling heifer Lewis had rescued from the blizzard, the chickens, the two pigs, the sacks of seed, the new plow, all swept away by the raging water.

Matilda stood frozen with horror for several seconds, then realized the water continued to rise. Baldwin Creek, by then a roaring torrent, had divided in two. It filled the swale beside the house, forming an island of the slight rise on which the cabin stood. Hypnotized, she watched it creep closer. Galvanized into action when she realized she and John were in danger, she ran back to the house. She stuffed the sleeping John into the invaluable cradleboard and, ignoring his loud protests at being so rudely awakened, strapped him on her back. Glancing about the cabin at her possessions, she remembered Patience's foolishness in risking her life for the lamp. She hesitated a moment for her books. Should she try to save them? They were stored in the loft, which would require several moments. She glanced out of the window at the water and realized the folly of such an action.

"We've got to get out now, Baby," she muttered to John, wishing Lewis would return. "Thank God your father has

White Star." She shuddered to think how close they had come to losing the horse, too.

Running out of the door, she jumped from the porch into the ankle deep icy water. Had she waited too long? Were they to be swept away like poor old Priscilla? No! Her fear of water surged through her and she ran towards her parents' home on the hill. As she splashed through the water, she tried to remember how deep the swale was. She looked about wildly. Rushing water surrounded her. She had no way to gauge the depth.

But she had to cross the swale. Baldwin Creek would be even deeper. The slight rise on which she stood would not give her refuge for long.

"Please, God," she sobbed. "Help me save my baby." She struggled on. The water rose to her knees, and it became harder for her to keep her footing. She walked carefully, knowing only too well that if she slipped, even for a moment, the torrent would sweep them both away.

She screamed when a rock rolled beneath her left foot, but did not hear her own voice. Her mind riveted on only one thing, keeping her footing. She could not remember how wide the swale was before the ground would start to rise on the other side. Her eyes remained transfixed on the swirling water, which reached nearly to her hips. Debris raced past her. Sticks knocked against her legs. She barely evaded a large branch threatening to take her with it by pushing it with both hands, thankful she had John secure in his cradleboard, leaving her hands free. The bodies of three chickens whirled by, blobs of red feathers. She shuddered in horror to think John could be swept away from her just as easily, were he not securely tied in the cradleboard.

As she stood staring at the swirling water, wondering how high the water would rise, a familiar voice reached her from far away. "'Tilda, 'Tilda! Hold on, we're coming."

Wiping her eyes, trying to clear her blurred vision as the

sound penetrated her consciousness, she saw safety twenty feet in front of her. The water raced past her, her legs numb from the cold. She braced herself against the current, afraid to move lest she lose her precarious footing. Tom and Sinclair waded towards her as fast as the water allowed.

She sobbed with relief as Tom grabbed one of her arms and Sinclair the other. They half dragged, half carried her to safety.

"How . . . how . . . did you know?" she gasped, trying to catch her breath.

"Saw the water rising," Sinclair said with a grin, "and figured we'd better check on you since Lew was over to Dyer's."

"Then we heard you scream," Tom added, "and started to run. You sure can make a noise when you've a mind to. That scream raised the hair on our heads." He walked behind her and chucked John under his chubby chin.

John gave Tom's beard a tug. "'om, 'om," he gurgled, unaware of their narrow escape.

Tom chuckled. "Little guy doesn't seem any the worse for wear. A true frontiersman. But we'd better get you back to the house and out of those wet clothes."

An hour later Matilda sat in front of the Randolph fireplace, wrapped in warm quilts and sipping one of her mother's viler concoctions guaranteed to ward off a chill. John, all smiles, sat in his grandmother's lap eating spoonful after spoonful of porridge.

As Matilda finished recounting her adventures for the fourth time, Lewis burst into the room. "'Tilda, oh, 'Tilda, my love," he gasped. He fell to his knees beside her and threw his arms around her, nearly upsetting the cup she held. "Can you ever forgive me for leaving you? When I saw the water almost to the roof of the house, I nearly died." Unable to continue, he buried his face in her neck.

Tom leaned against the door jamb, grinning. "Good

thing you told me to go watch for him, 'Tilda. Otherwise he'd 'a plunged headlong into that water lookin' for you."

She laughed softly and stroked Lewis' hair. "Why, Darling, we managed just fine. Didn't we, John?"

John banged his spoon against the table. "Wadder, Daddy," he burbled, bouncing with glee. "Lotta wadder."

It took two days for the water to recede. On the third morning, Matilda left the baby with Betsy Ann and rode with Lewis to see what remained of their home. Sinclair and Tom rode with them.

Not a trace of the barn remained. The water had totally ruined everything in the root cellar. The outhouse lodged drunkenly on its side next to a tree some forty yards from the house. Jake nosed around, trying to identify some of his familiar smells.

The porch had vanished, but by some miracle the house still stood, although it teetered at a precarious angle. The east side sagged into a two foot deep gap, washed out by the raging water. The tilting had wrenched the siding, so some boards stuck out, while others twisted inward. Inside they found a scene of total destruction. Marks on the wall told them the water had reached the base of the loft. Matilda shuddered, thinking how close she and John came to not escaping in time.

She stooped and picked up a shattered plate. The twisting of the walls had torn the dish shelf from its pegs, and the shattered crockery lay under a coating of silt. Here and there, a few shards poked above the mess. "At least the tin plates survived," she said with a rueful little laugh.

Mud covered the bed, the table, the chest with their clothes, everything. She thought, with an aching heart, of her precious satin wedding dress, realizing it also would be ruined. A plank from the wall lay across the bed, breaking down the legs. John's little bed, covered with the slimy mud, seemed undamaged. She stood shaking her head. She knew she would never get the mud out of the quilts. "We can't rebuild here, Lew. It's too close to the river. If this happened once, it will happen again." Her heart ached at the devastation in front of her, her throat tight with unshed tears.

Lewis understood. He took her in his arms. "You're right, Sweetheart. We'll finish the other cabin on our original claim. It's on higher ground. We can farm this land from there. Land office rules be damned."

Sinclair, risking his neck on the damaged ladder, climbed down from the loft carrying an armload of books, apparently undamaged. "At least your books survived, 'Tilda."

"Thank heavens." She took the books and held them lovingly. She glanced at the top one and read the title, *Two Years Before The Mast*. It was her favorite because it told so much about California.

Her dream of California, never far from her mind, resurfaced.

"Lew," she asked. "do you suppose they have floods like this in California?"

Chapter 27

Summer of 1858 to January of 1859

AFTER THE FLOOD waters cleared, Kansas smiled on them for a while. The weather remained pleasant and they got their crops planted. A letter arrived from Alf in which he told them he had moved from Placerville down to Hicksville. Sinclair brought it over for her to read.

> "Got myself 150 acres of prime farm land, not far from Sam's and Will's. Alfred is still trying to get some more gold out of our claim, but I like it better in the valley. Never any snow and doesn't get as cold.
> "Is your free-stater Charles Robinson the same man as got himself thrown in jail in Sacramento for taking a shot at Mayor Bigelow during the squatter's riots back in '50? We heard he moved to Kansas in '54."

Matilda chuckled. She could just imagine her father's reaction to *that* comment. She looked up from the letter. "Lew," she said, "ever think of moving to California?"

He looked up from the three-week-old copy of *Harper's Weekly* that he read and smiled. "Aren't you happy here? We're close to your folks and have a good piece of land. We'll have a comfortable cabin again."

She did not know how to explain her dream of California, so she just returned his smile. "Of course I'm happy. Alf's descriptions just make me curious to see it is all."

Summer progressed. In July, one month after his first birthday, John cried out in the night, a shrill cry of pain that brought Matilda awake in an instant. In the semi-dark, she crept to the side of his little bed. "Hush, love," she murmured. "What ails you?" She patted him on the back. "We don't want to wake up your father."

The baby quieted for a moment, then let out another sharp cry. "Have you a touch of the colic?"

Picking him up, she laid his head on her shoulder and patted his back. The cries subsided to a whimper and Matilda sighed with relief, but too soon. Another spasm of pain evoked a shriller cry and woke Lewis.

"What is it?" he asked.

"I don't know. He seems to have a touch of colic." Suddenly, the smell from his diaper left no room for question. "He's got the flux," Matilda said. She kept her voice soft, but it revealed her sudden fright. "Pray it's not second summer complaint."

Twenty four hours later, Matilda could no longer deny it. Her healthy, lively son lay seriously ill. For several days he hovered between life and death. Matilda and her mother took turns tending him, urging him to drink the comfrey and peppermint teas.

A week passed before he turned the corner. The bloody diarrhea stopped and day by day he slowly began to mend. Matilda, dry-eyed all the time he was ill, shed copious tears of relief when it seemed he would survive.

But a month later, John, though over his illness, had still not recovered his strength. He ate listlessly, and would take only a few steps before sitting down again. Even his smile lost its luster. Matilda's heart sank as she thought of the coming winter. Would he be strong enough to survive?

In October of 1858, a letter arrived from Caroline with the sad news they had been expecting for several months.

"Tommy died on September 24. He left $255.00 with Elijah Scott so Eli can bring me to Kansas.

Tommy knew I would not be happy alone here in Lexington. His last thoughts were to provide for my care.

"We will leave October 1, to arrive before the weather turns cold. Eli says we take the steamer from Pekin to St. Louis, then up the Missouri to Kansas City. Should take about two weeks. Eli says he'll hire a buggy to bring us to Randolph, since he has to go right back, so no one has to meet us.

"I was sorry to hear Uncle James Stringfield died, though he certainly lived his 'three score and ten!'

"Please tell Britt to take care telling Sarah of Tommy's death. He was her favorite brother.

"It will be good to see everyone again, even though my heart is heavy."

She finished reading the letter to Lewis and sighed as she folded it up. Poor Caroline. Matilda looked across at Lewis and her heart twisted. If she ever lost him .... She ordered herself not to think about it.

Two weeks later, Sinclair rode up to the cabin in the cart. "Caroline's here," he grinned to Matilda, "and real anxious to see you. I told her I'd fetch you right over. She brought enough boxes of stuff to open a dry goods store. Told her I'm going to have to build an extension on the cabin just to store it all."

While Matilda loaded herself and John into the cart, he added, "And she sure has got three of the prettiest little girls I've ever laid eyes on."

They celebrated Christmas of 1858 at the Randolph residence, as usual. Britt and Sarah, with their brood, Minerva and Abe, Caroline and her girls, Tom, John, Sinclair, Lew and Matilda with Baby John, and several single neighbors crowded into the cabin for the gala affair.

The smell of gingerbread and spiced cider filled the room and mingled with the smoke and the aroma of numerous bodies, some of whom bathed only sporadically in the winter cold. Matilda, holding John, greeted the guests as they arrived. Small parcels lay heaped beneath the pungent little pine tree standing in the corner.

"Treat that tree with respect," Tom grinned. "It's come a long way to get here." Tom, determined to have a pine tree for Christmas, rode miles to get it. Little tallow candles stood in holders, ready to be lighted. Strings of the popped Indian corn were draped around cut pieces of tin. The dangling bits of tin caught the light from the morning sun. The children hung cut out stars and bells on the lower limbs of the little tree.

"Don't put your paper doo-dads too close to where we'll be lightin' the candles," Betsy Ann cautioned, as nine-year-old Owen hung his bell. "We don't want to celebrate Christmas by settin' the whole place afire."

By the time the gifts were distributed, the aroma from the wild turkey Sinclair turned on a spit in the fireplace told them dinner would soon be ready. Sinclair had shot the turkey himself and took great interest in seeing it properly prepared. The table already groaned under the weight of pumpkin and mince pies, bowls of beans and potatoes, and dishes of nuts, dried fruits, jams, and relishes. Matilda's stomach jumped in anticipation, her mouth watering. She hoped the smells would be as tempting to John.

He seemed to be slowly improving. She could get him to eat a little better, and he walked more. If the winter held mild .... She brushed the melancholy thoughts aside, forcing herself to join in the gaiety.

That evening, everyone sated by the huge meal, the candles lighted on the tree, they sang Christmas songs. The strains of Silent Night and The First Noel echoed through the little cabin, often off-key. As bedtime approached, with the younger children nodding and John asleep in Matilda's arms, Gardner rose to his feet.

"I've great news to share. Jonas Kress gave up his claim in Randolph. He's moved over Mill Creek way, so now we only have to contend with Whitson. We'll close the evening with a prayer to thank the Lord for all our blessings."

The next morning, Caroline's daughter Rebecca woke coughing and felt feverish.

"Better bundle her up good," Betsy Ann advised. "Sounds to me like she might be taking the croup."

Terror surged through Matilda's body as she watched Becky coughing. Strong and healthy, three-year-old Becky would probably recover from the croup.

Would John?

She tried to convince herself John would not take the croup, but two weeks later, as she fed him his breakfast porridge, she noticed his flushed face. She put her hand on his forehead. He definitely had a fever. While she prayed it was not the croup, he began struggling to get his breath.

Betsy Ann looked up from the dishes she washed. Their eyes met. "Good thing we got plenty of comfrey for poultices." She said nothing more, and returned to her dishes.

John died on January 27, 1859, and they buried him in the new cemetery at the little town of Randolph. Matilda, exhausted from over two weeks of tending to him with little or no sleep, went through the ceremony in a trance. Lewis, his face set, stood beside her with his arm around her as the men lowered the tiny coffin into the ground. Without Lewis' arm to support her, she would not have been able to stand.

"Blessed is the Lord, who giveth and taketh away," intoned Reverend Hartford. "We are grateful to have been blessed with this child, even though for so short a time. We take comfort in knowing he is with You in Heaven."

Matilda tried to find comfort in that knowledge, but could not keep herself from thinking, if you are so powerful, God, why couldn't You save him? If You are so merciful, how could You take him from me? Frightened to find herself questioning God, she forced the thoughts from her mind.

The following weeks passed in a haze of grief. Her arms felt empty all the time. Lewis tried to cheer her.

"We've still got each other, my love," he soothed one night several weeks after John's death as they lay together on the bed. "We'll have more babies."

"Another baby won't be John," she whispered, her eyes dark with pain. But she realized the wisdom of his words. She had to put it behind her. Other women had lost children. Some had lost several. Tomorrow, she told herself, determined to rise above her grief for his sake if for no other reason, from tomorrow I will look only forward.

The next morning, when she tried to carry out her resolution, a wave of nausea struck her. For three days she lay on the bed, fighting the queasiness that threatened to overcome her every time she rose to use the chamber pot, or tried to eat any of the food the solicitous Lewis brought to her.

On the morning of the fourth day, she heard her mother's heavy step on the porch of the little cabin. Lewis, looking anxious, followed her though the door.

"All right, young lady," Betsy Ann announced. "Enough of this. I'm surprised at you. How many babies do you have to bear before you recognize the signs yourself, without me a-tellin' you?"

Chapter 28

Spring of 1859 to September of 1860

THREE MONTHS LATER, the problems with Whitson reached a climax.

"We'll have this out once and for all," Gardner declared at the family gathering after Easter services, held, to Betsy Ann and Matilda's relief, at the Mitchell residence. It was the first time Easter services were held anywhere but the Randolph home.

Matilda, discussing with her mother the news that Minerva again expected a child, due a month after Matilda, stopped in mid-sentence and turned to her father. Now what, she thought, her heart jumping. Fear the dispute would escalate into violence never completely left her mind. So many violent acts had racked the land over the last few years.

"We'll take this to the Land Office in Ogden for settlement." Gardner looked around the assembled family members. "Britt," he said, "you're the oldest. You can represent the Randolph Town Company."

The following morning, Britt, with several neighbors as witnesses, rode to Ogden. Matilda and Lew joined her parents and brothers at the home of Mr. Pease in Randolph Tuesday morning to be on hand when Britt returned. The day dragged by.

"What's taking so long? It's only twenty-seven miles to Ogden," Gardner finally exclaimed in exasperation.

"Hearing probably took all day. You know how long these things can take, once they get to arguing," Tom said. "They'll have to wait for daybreak to head back. No moon.

Not safe to ride at night with all the prairie dog holes."

Wednesday morning at dawn, Betsy Ann prepared a hasty breakfast. Matilda had no appetite. She no longer suffered from morning sickness, but nervousnous deprived her of any desire for food. The second day dragged on with still no sign of Britt. Matilda's uneasiness increased with each passing hour.

As the sun reached its zenith on the third day, they heard the hoofbeats of a horse being ridden hard and rushed out of the house. Whitson pulled his spent steed to a halt. Jumping to the ground, he grabbed an ax and drove it into the nearest tree.

Gardner strode to where Whitson worked. Matilda watched, her heart pounding, her mouth dry. What would happen? Whitson's three friends stepped up beside him and Gardner stopped.

"You ding-dang Dutch abolitionist," he shouted, "what's going on? Why you building another cabin? What'd the Land Agent say? Where's Britt?"

Whitson did not reply, only continued to chop, sweat beading on his forehead from his exertions. His friends stood by him, arms folded, silent, their faces grim.

Within thirty minutes, Britt rode up, panting and exhausted, his horse also spent. Gardner gripped Britt's arms as he climbed down from the horse.

"The agent said . . . ," Britt paused to take a deep breath, "that neither claim's in order. Declared it open land again, belongs to the first one to build." He sank to the ground, his head in his hands, his arms braced against his knees. "Came as fast as I could. Left at first light. Kept to the divide west of Mill Creek, figgering that'd be the fastest route." He looked up at Lewis with a rueful grin. "Should have accepted your offer of White Star. Would've made it ridin' her. Just never thought they would dispute our claim. Argued for two whole days. Told 'em we've been here since

'54, and that when we got here, it was all open land for miles and . . . ."

He stopped and stared at the foam-flecked horse Whitson had ridden. "That's not the same horse you left Ogden on," he accused.

Whitson grinned. "Course not. Stopped by my old friend Jonas Kress's place on Mill Creek and got a fresh horse."

"You cheated!" Britt shouted. He jumped to his feet and started forward. One of Whitson's friends put his hand on his gun and Britt stopped. Matilda's heart lurched. Please, Britt, she begged silently, don't fight. It's not worth anyone dying for. Let him have the town.

"Ain't cheatin'. Just smart. Yore sore 'cause you weren't smart enough to do the same thing." Whitson smirked. "Or because you ain't got no friends would trust you with a horse."

Britt started for Whitson in spite of his armed friends, but Gardner intervened. "Come on, Son. Let him have it. He wanted it bad enough to cheat, he probably wants it bad enough to kill. Not worth it."

Lewis assisted Matilda and Betsy Ann into the cart. "Right, Father Gardner. Let's get out of here. We've still got plenty of good land to farm. Let him have the town." He urged White Star into motion.

As the Randolph procession rode away, Whitson shouted, "And as of now, the name of the town is Waterville. Won't have my town named after any slavery man."

Matilda watched her father. He did not turn his head at the taunt, but the back of his neck turned a bright red. She sighed, knowing the effort it took for him to hold that calm.

Pease moved out of Randolph, Whitson married Tamar Condray and moved into the Pease home, and Gardner abandoned his plans to own a town.

"Man should stick to what he knows," he declared.

"Born a farmer, I'll die a farmer."

Britt, less forgiving, grunted, "And I'll bet he married Tamar to get himself a rich father-in-law."

They soon had far greater concerns than ownership of the town. The crops and prairie grass sprouted green and lush after the rains in May and June, then the rains stopped and the land dried up. Strong, hot, sand-laden winds covered everything with a layer of fine silt. It made the food gritty and irritated Matilda's eyes. Dust settled on the dishes in spite of the protective cloth. Somehow it even managed to work its way into the folds of clothes stored in trunks.

Water became more precious with each passing day. By September of 1859 all of the springs and creeks were dry. The only water they had came from the Big Blue. It still flowed, but sluggishly, frequently fouled by animals seeking water.

Lewis came in day after day and sat at the table with his head in his hands. "Don't know what we're gonna do," he muttered one night shortly before Matilda's baby was due. "Got to have water or we can't grow a crop. Cattle have eaten all the grass already. They'll be lookin' for food soon." He looked up at Matilda and smiled. "Maybe we ought to see if that gold discovery out west on Cherry Creek is real or just tall tales."

Matilda felt her heart drop. Leave this nice home and live in a tent? When I'm eight months pregnant?

He laughed at the fear in her face. "Don't worry, Sweetheart. I'm not going to chase off west. I talked to Britt and he says with all of these fools dashing off shouting 'Pike's Peak or bust' all the good claims will be gone. That's what happened in California. A few made it big, but most just barely made a living, if that." He rose and took her in his arms, patting her abdomen as the infant within her moved against him. "We'll make it. The rains will come again."

Matilda carried water to her garden in buckets. Lewis filled a barrel at the river every day, but even with the water the plants wilted and their leaves turned brown around the edges as the hot, dry wind sucked the life from them.

They celebrated a very solemn Christmas in 1859, with no pine tree like the year before. Worry over the political situation and concerns about the drought took away any enthusiasm for the festivities. The meager feast showed their awareness of the critical food supply. Even the news that Minerva successfully delivered a baby girl she named Laura, and the birth of Matilda's daughter, Mary Jane, did not dispel the sense of doom.

Gardner had one cause for jubilation. "Hear they caught that John Brown over in Virginia, near Harper's Ferry." He nodded his head for emphasis. "Also heard they hung him. About time. Dangerous man."

Matilda heard the news with mixed feelings. She knew Brown had felt justified in his actions, but, remembering what everyone called the Pottawatamee Creek Massacre, she had to agree with her father.

In January of 1860, on a freezing cold day with still no snow on the ground, they received another letter from Alf. "I've added to my place. Got 250 acres of prime farm land with a little house and a good well." Tom looked up from his reading. "Hear that?" he told his listeners. "A good well. No snow, no drought, no freezing cold, no grasshoppers, no bickering, no ... "

"You've made your point, Son," Gardner interrupted. "Get on with it."

"There's a store at Hicksville now," Tom read. "And even a blacksmith shop." The rest of the letter raved on about the quality of the farm land and the mild climate. Alf closed with, "When you going to stop fighting with Kansas and join me?"

Matilda sat beside the fire as she listened to Tom's voice. She held sleeping three-month-old Mary Jane. The baby boasted her grandmother's red hair and her mother's striking blue eyes. Already a flirt at three months, she had the whole family enamored of her.

At first, Matilda could not mask her disappointment at not having another boy, but soon took great joy in her daughter. She still felt the loss of John very deeply. She found it hard to believe almost a whole year had passed since he died, and often found tears coursing down her cheeks and dripping on the tiny warm baby in her arms. But Mary's birth did help pull her out of the depression she suffered after John's death.

Lewis, delighted with his beautiful daughter, had tried to cheer her. "As easy as you take," he often said, his voice filled with pride, "you'll have as many as your mother. There'll be more sons."

Matilda looked across at Lewis where he sat listening to Tom. He turned towards her. Their eyes met, and they shared a private smile. She felt he read her thoughts, for he mimed her a little kiss across the room. She blushed. He was right, of course. She couldn't let her loss come between them, or interfere with the care needed by the precious baby she held. She thrust the thoughts of John aside and returned her attention to the conversation in the room.

". . . be a good idea," Britt was saying. "Going to be war soon, especially if that lawyer feller from Springfield gets elected President. There's talk that new Republican Party is goin' to nominate him when their convention comes up in May. He keeps spoutin' about how important it is that the Union be preserved at any cost. And I hear his wife's an abolitionist."

Gardner growled, "Don't see why they don't let the South do what it wants, peaceable-like." He frowned. "If they want to form their own union, let 'em. And it's nobody's business if a man wants to own slaves, long's he treats 'em right. My cousin John in Virginia freed his slaves in his will when he died, back in '33. They couldn't take care of themselves. That dang Stowe woman and that Faneuil Hall bunch has got all those abolitionists stirred up."

"Well," Tom announced, "they can have their war without me. Alf is right. California is the place to be. Come spring and the wagons start again, I'm heading west. I'll get myself hired on as an outrider if no one else wants to go. I'm sick and tired of plantin' a crop only to have it die in the heat, or helpin' a cow birth a calf only to have it freeze to death." He rose to his feet. "Anyone wants to come along is welcome."

Silence greeted his challenge. After a long pause, Gardner spoke.

"We'll talk about it later," he said.

In March, a young man arrived to help the Reverend Hartford minister to his small flock of Methodists on Fancy Creek. They held services at the home of Henry Condray in the little town of Waterville, nee Randolph. The Randolphs sat on one side of the room, J.K. Whitson and his wife on the other, the truce holding only for church services. The first Sunday that Ely Robertson spoke, Matilda and Caroline sat in the congregation. After the services, he introduced himself.

"You have such lovely girls," he told Caroline, taking her hand. "And so well behaved." Their eyes met and a slow smile spread across his face. "You must be very proud of them. Reverend Hartford has told me of the loss of your husband. Please accept my sympathies."

Matilda, watching closely, saw the light in Caroline's eyes and chuckled softly.

As Tom's departure time approached, Abe Dyer decided he, too, had tired of Kansas weather and political bickering. On April 30, 1860, Jack Keetley of Marysville, Kansas became the first rider to head west for Sacramento on the newly formed Pony Express. In the shiny, new leather mantilla he flung across the pommel rode a letter to the Randolph brothers in Hicksville, California. The letter said that Tom, with Minerva, Abe, and baby Laura, were on their way west.

"It's sure lucky George and Lydia wanted to buy your land," Matilda said to Minerva as she helped her sister with some last minute packing. "Folks are having a tough time selling now, what with the drought and all the fighting. Some have just up and left, abandoning their claims altogether."

Minerva smiled. "We sold it pretty cheap, seeing as they're family, but it should be enough to get us to California and get us started there. They wanted it because with Papa Sam's 160 acres, it makes a parcel of five hundred." She smiled at Matilda. "Maybe next year you'll follow us, if the rains don't come."

Matilda sighed. "I'd love to come with you. You're so brave, setting out a such a long trip with Laura only six months old."

Minerva nodded. "I don't feel brave. I'm scared. I don't put much faith in Alf's glowing reports. I think it's a lot harder than he says."

"I'm glad you came through your confinement with Laura so well. You were so frail for so long after . . . after you came back from Waterville."

"You can say it, 'Tilda. I nearly died having the poor mite. No wonder he died. I was so sick with the ague." Tears welled in Minerva's eyes.

Matilda's own eyes filled as she thought of Baby John. Why did God give women babies only to take them back? It seemed so cruel. She took Minerva in her arms. They did not cry, but stood holding each other, each deep in her own pain, until Abe appeared in the doorway.

"You women done packin' those boxes? I got to get 'em loaded if we're gonna get out of here at dawn."

The following morning, May 1, 1860, Matilda and Minerva parted with tears as the little party bid farewell to family and friends and headed north, crossing the Little Blue River to meet the westward bound wagons. The Dyer and Randolph wagons did not go alone. A number of other families left Kansas about the same time, a few to follow the call of gold to western Kansas, some discouraged by fighting the elements, others frightened by rumors of war. Dozens of wagons creaked and groaned their way across the trail.

But the settlers on the Big Blue had other worries besides war. "Bids fair to be another dry summer," Lewis told Matilda after Tom, Abe, and Minerva left, shaking his head in despair. "If the rains don't come this summer, going to be a lot of folks going hungry. Most used up what extra stores they had this past winter, last year's crop doin' so poorly and all." He shook his head. "Another year of drought will see a lot more giving up."

The well by the Randolph home dried up. Water had to be hauled in barrels from the Big Blue. The side creeks and springs had long since vanished. The Big Blue fell to the lowest level they had ever seen. Despair settled on the farmers along with the dust. More families ceded the land back to nature and departed.

Towards the end of May, Sinclair arrived home from a trip to Marysville eager to report what he had seen.

"A sailing wagon," he declared. "Right up the trail it went, following alongside the Little Blue. Feller name of Peppard, Samuel Peppard, outta Oskaloosa, over in Jefferson County. Never saw anythin' like it before, this contraption, with four men and all their gear, flying over the prairie pulled by two big sails."

"Humph," Gardner grunted. "I heard some feller name of Thomas tried it back in '46. Got only a couple of miles before the whole thing broke apart."

Sinclair laughed. "They say this one's had a couple of crack-ups already, but they've patched it back together. Say they're heading for Pike's Peak to find some gold."

"They might make it fine across the prairie, but I'd sure like to see 'em try and take a sail wagon over the Sierras."

Sinclair grinned. "Right now, the fellers around Marysville are taking odds on whether or not he makes it as far as Fort Kearny."

On June 26, 1860, to nobody's surprise, Caroline married Ely Robertson in a simple ceremony held at the Randolph residence. Gardner consented, pleased Caroline had found such a fine young man. Matilda thought the idea of being married to a preacher might just be overdoing religion a little, but, seeing the glow on her sister's face, she said nothing.

She did, however, question the haste with which Caroline had rushed to wed. "Carrie," she asked her sister when they were alone. "You've only known him three months!"

"And how long did it take you to fall in love with Lew?" Caroline countered.

Matilda grinned, a little abashed. "About three minutes," she admitted. "But you and Tommy were so in love, and Tommy's been dead only . . . ." She paused.

"Since '58, 'Tilda dear," Caroline said with a smile. "It's been almost two years."

Matilda did not reply. She remembered how she felt when Josh married again just a year after Temperance's death. She thought of Lewis with the flood of love that still washed over her even after four years of marriage and two babies. Can someone you love so much be so easily replaced?

Caroline, watching Matilda's face, added, "I have to think of the girls, 'Tilda. He loves the girls. What if something happened to me? What if I take the consumption, too?"

At the end of June, Gardner burst into the house waving a sheaf of papers. Matilda looked up from the quilt she and her mother blocked. She had taken advantage of the balmy weather to ride over and her mother immediately got out the quilt. With Caroline married and moved into her own home, Betsy Ann confessed she got lonely.

Betsy Ann looked up as well. "Land sakes, Gardner, what is it?"

"The survey done last month, of Randolph."

Matilda turned away to hide a smile. Her father consistently refused to use the new name of Waterville.

"What about it?" Betsy Ann asked.

"Whitson says right here . . . ," Gardner unfolded the papers and held them for Matilda to read. "Britt read it to me. It says 'lots in the town of Waterville, formerly known as Randolph.' "

Matilda read the paper. "Yes," she acknowledged. "So?"

"Don't you see?" Gardner crowed. "He admits everyone called the town Randolph. That ding-dang Black Republican actually says they called my town Randolph." He started to chuckle, and laughed until Matilda became alarmed, fearing he neared hysteria.

He stopped and wiped his eyes. "I maybe can't get my property back," he said, "but I have the satisfaction of getting him to confess on paper that he stole my town."

Summer dragged on, day after day of unrelenting heat and hot, dry, gritty wind. The dispute with Henry Shellenbaum, a continuous, ongoing squabble for the past three years, finally demanded a solution.

Sinclair brought it up. "Pa," he said, "Henry Shellenbaum is getting more persistent in claiming that section you
put in my name. He insists since I'm a minor I can't claim
it."

Gardner sighed. "I suppose we'll have to do the same as
we did for Randolph. The Land Office moved from Ogden
to Junction City last fall, so it's a little farther."

Sinclair grinned and glanced over at Lewis. "I'll take
White Star, Lew. Won't make the same mistake Britt made."

Three days later, Sinclair, with his witnesses, and Shellenbaum with his, headed for Junction City. Matilda and
Lewis joined the family to await the outcome.

Early the following morning, they arrived at Sinclair's
claim, astonished to see Mr. Shellenbaum already building
his cabin with Sinclair nowhere in sight.

Henry stopped to mop his brow with a big, blue handkerchief and grinned. "Was almost dark when they declared
it open land, open to the first one to build. Sinclair had
that fine fancy horse of Baldwin's, so he decided to wait for
mornin'. I took off shank's mare 'cross country."

Sinclair rode up a short time later, White Star's mane
flashing in the morning sun.

Lewis watched their approach. "She sure runs pretty,"
he murmured in admiration of the horse.

Sinclair pulled White Star to a halt and jumped off. He
looked abashed. "Sure thought we could beat him, riding
White Star, so I slept overnight. Guess I slept a little too
long."

Gardner started to laugh. He strode up to Henry and
held out his hand. "Welcome, neighbor. You won it fair
and square."

Matilda laughed at the expression on Henry's face when
Gardner took the loss so well. He shook Gardner's hand
with enthusiasm. "Never wanted to quarrel with you, Gardner. Just wanted this little piece of land. Been courting Eliz-

abeth Siebecker and need a home to offer her. Never was greedy like some of the rest." He grinned with a lop-sided twist of his mouth. "And I never take no interest in politics."

He reached into his pack and pulled out a bottle of whiskey. "I know you don't hold with liquor, being a Methodist and all, but our buryin' the hatchet deserves a little celebration drink."

Gardner's hearty laugh brought smiles from the whole group. "Haven't been a Methodist all of my life, Henry. You're right. I think this is one such occasion."

One day, toward the end of September of 1860, with no rain in over a year, Lewis returned with a barrel of muddy water. He looked a little green.

"What's the matter?" Matilda asked.

"Dead calf in the hole where I been filling the barrel. Had to go upstream." He shook his head. "Makes me wonder how many more dead animals died in it farther up. Drought is real bad. Saw smoke from another prairie fire down across the Big Blue."

Matilda looked across the dry fields, dingy under their film of dust, and wiped her hand across her sweaty face. She made no reply.

Chapter 29

September of 1860 to Summer of 1863

FOR YEARS people talked about the drought of 1860, remembering it as a harsh and terrible time. Gardner sold the cattle they could not eat, for no grass grew on the prairie. They managed to scramble enough feed for the milk cows by milling the seed corn. The chickens lived on what they could scavenge.

"No point in planting," Lewis griped. "Might as well feed the corn to the cows. Get something out of it anyways."

Matilda wrote to her sister Sarah back in Illinois, explaining the plight of the settlers. Barrels and boxes of food came from relatives and well-wishers to help the beleaguered pioneers. They traded with Indians for dried buffalo meat, hunted for what game they could find, and combed the countryside for anything edible. Many left, either returning east or going on to California or Oregon. Those who remained struggled to stay alive on land so parched it opened in great cracks.

At the end of September, as another hot, dry summer day drew to a close with still no rain in sight, Matilda stood at the doorway and looked out over the barren landscape. She thought with sympathy of those who lived farther west, away from the major rivers. Water must be impossible for them to find. As muddy as the Big Blue was, it at least continued to flow.

With a smile, she looked down at Mary who, at almost a year old, had just mastered the art of walking. Mary's red hair sparkled under its film of dust, and her blue eyes shone with mischief. Whenever Matilda felt discouraged, Mary always cheered her. She could not help comparing the lively Mary with placid John. With a laugh, she swept the child up in her arms.

"I'm so glad we have you, my precious little one. But whoever said girls are easier to raise than boys certainly never met you!"

The drought had one positive effect. A neighbor to the west, farther up Baldwin Creek from Lewis and Matilda's claim, pulled up stakes and returned to the East, owing money to the storekeeper in Waterville. The day after Mary's first birthday, the man rode up to the Baldwin cabin and asked to see Lewis.

"Got a proposition to make to ye, Mr. Baldwin," the storekeeper said in greeting. "Seems as how John Sullivan, to the west of you folks, has headed back East." The man shifted his wad to his left cheek and spat a stream of tobacco juice. It raised a puff of dust as it landed in the dirt beside the washtub. Matilda shuddered inwardly, again thanking her lucky stars Lew did not chew tobacco.

"He, er, he, um, owed me several hundred dollars," the man continued, "so he give me the papers to his land, all 169 acres plus the house. Thought you folks might want it, seein' as how it's almost part 'o yer land, so to speak."

He cleared his throat and again spat. Lewis and Matilda waited.

"Anyways," he repeated, "I got a proposition to make. I ain't no farmer, and all I want out of the propitty is what's owed me, so . . ."

"I have no cash money," Lewis told him. "If that's what you're drivin' at."

"No, no," he hastened to assure them. "What I really want is goods to sell at my store. Hear your wife makes butter what don't turn rancid quick. I c'n sell all of it I can get. That and eggs. Alluz need eggs to sell."

Lewis glanced over at Matilda. Their eyes met. They knew the Sullivan home. It had twice the space of their tiny cabin. Concealing his excitement, Lewis said casually, "Well, that bein' the case, I suspect we can come to some sort of terms."

When they took possession of the Sullivan cabin, they discovered it boasted a fancy stove, rust-coated, covered with grease, and clogged with ashes.

"What a mess!" Lewis shook his head in disgust.

"But look," Matilda exclaimed. "It's a roaster stove!"

"A what?"

"See here?" She lifted the cover of the rounded projection on the right side of the stove to expose a spit. "You turn the handle like this," she demonstrated, "and the chicken or roast turns and cooks even on all sides. And the fat drips down into this pan." She pulled out the grease pan and wrinkled her nose. "Oh, my."

Lewis grinned. "Looks like there's been a lot of roasting done, but not much cleaning."

Matilda shook her head "I don't see how anyone could let something so precious get to be such a mess. But look at the size of this hot water reservoir! I remember when this model came out last year. The ads were all over the paper. It's made by R.P. Myers of Cleveland." She indicated the name on the ash box. "It's supposed to have a baking cover as well. It must be around here somewhere."

"He probably used it as a water dish for the chickens," Lewis commented. "It's a pretty fancy stove for a man as couldn't pay the storekeeper his due. If you're going to get this cleaned up, you've got a big job ahead of you."

Matilda spent a week scrubbing on the stove, with Lewis laughing at her sooty face and grimy hands, but her persistence paid off, and the clean stove became her pride and joy. The baking cover, as Lewis predicted, had served as a water dish for the chickens, but fortunately sustained no serious damage by the experience.

Twice a week after they moved in, Matilda, with Mary in the cradleboard on her back, rode White Star into Waterville, nee Randolph, with several pounds of butter and two dozen eggs in her saddlebags. One of Clementine's daughters supplied the milk, although between the drought and poor feed, she gave only half as much milk as she should have. Every time she milked this cow, Matilda remembered poor Priscilla's death in the flood of the Big Blue, and the young heifer who died with her.

She called the cow Clarissa. Lewis laughed and wanted to know how she dreamed up such outlandish names. Matilda had actually read it as the name of the heroine in a cheap novel she had kept hidden from her father years before. "Oh," she replied loftily, "I like fancy names."

In mid-October, a shipment of corn and flour and, to Matilda's delight, a barrel of apples, arrived from her sister Sarah back in Illinois. "Apple pie again!" she exclaimed, grinning at her mother across the top of the barrel. Mary, in Matilda's arms, leaned down, seized one of the bright red fruits with both hands, and promptly sank all four of her teeth into it.

Matilda rescued the apple and opened the letter that accompanied the barrel. In it, Sarah wrote,

> "Sarah Evans died on September 29. Poor woman.
> I think she was ready to go. She'd outlived Owen by
> fifteen years. When Tommy died, it seemed to take
> all the heart out of her. Tommy meant so much to
> her. I think Jane has written to Sarah."

A week later, a brief note arrived from Minerva by way of the Pony Express.

"Can only afford one sheet, but wanted you to know we arrived safe. Alf may have enjoyed the trek when he came in '50, but I sure didn't. Laura survived the trip better than I, and is even starting to walk. The heat didn't seem to bother her at all. Abe says it proves she's a true pioneer. But as for me, I never want to see another desert."

In November, the rains returned at last. Matilda stood out in the downpour, catching the cool drops with her hands. She had forgotten how good rain in her face could feel. How long had it been? Over a year, she knew. She counted the months on her fingers. It had rained in June of '59. And this was November of '60? Almost a year and a half. How could it not rain for so long?

Lewis came up behind her and circled her with his arms. Burying his face in her neck, he murmured, "Now maybe we can get a decent crop."

They stood in the rain, letting it soak their hair and their clothes until Matilda began to shiver and Lewis insisted she come inside and warm herself.

"You can stand in the rain again if this drought really is over."

On January 29, 1861, Kansas was admitted to the Union as a free state, forcing Gardner to admit his hopes for a plantation with slaves were lost. Governor Robert Walker had ended Southern control of the legislature and the bickering was finally quelled enough to settle on a constitution.

In April, Lewis planted the fields with more hope than they dared to have in a long time. A brief letter arrived from Tom by the Pony Express. In it, Tom told them he bought his own farm, one hundred acres, less than a mile from Hicksville.

"Have my own house, all to myself. Plenty of

room for anyone who would like to join me. Abe's got a place, too. Sorry to write so little, but Pony Express costs dearly. I had to pay five dollars for just this one sheet."

On April 24, 1861, Henry Shellenbaum married Elizabeth Siebecker and the Randolph clan attended the wedding festivities en masse. After the ceremony, the main topic of conversation was war.

"Hear both sides have traded shots at Fort Sumter. That's in South Carolina," Matilda overheard Charlie Briggs tell Sinclair and John.

Sarah Dyer stood beside Matilda, her mouth agape. "Do you think we'll have a war?" she whispered. Matilda shushed her, for she wanted to listen.

"Bound to happen," John said, his voice solemn, "after South Carolina seceded like she did."

"That was last December," Sinclair interposed. "Why'd they wait so long?"

John shrugged. "Some folks are sayin' let 'em go ahead and secede, but President Lincoln thinks it's vital the Union be preserved."

Sam Dyer entered the conversation. "Vital enough to kill for?"

"Not right," Gardner growled. "South wants to form their own union, they oughta be allowed."

Several other men joined them and the argument went back and forth. Matilda took Sarah Dyer by the arm and led her away.

"Let's help set out the food. If I listen to much more of this I won't have any appetite."

Sarah gave a shaky little laugh. "Agreed. The thought of my brothers going to war frightens me to death."

"Lew has assured me he won't go," Matilda said with a sigh of relief. Especially since her monthlies had not come at the end of March and she suspected she was in a family way again, although it was still too soon to tell Lew. "Says he's got all the responsibilities he can handle right here. I'm so glad! But I'm afraid Sinclair might take it into his head that he ought to go. He says since Kansas joined the Union as a free state, she ought to send troops to defend it."

Sarah shook her head and silently began arranging biscuits on a plate.

The political news frightened Matilda. She wished she and Lewis could join the rest of the family in California. California sounded so far away, far from rumors of war.

She forced the dismal thoughts from her mind and changed the subject. "Didn't Elizabeth make a lovely bride? I'm so happy the feud with Henry is settled. He's such a nice man."

Matilda's fears resurfaced one morning the following July when Sinclair stamped into the cabin. One look at his face told her he and their father had quarreled again. Four months pregnant with her third child, she found her emotions more easily aroused. She stared at him, her heart sinking.

"Pa still won't let me join the Union army," he stormed. "News just came down that the Union troops were routed at Bull Run. The Reb's are just outside of Washington! The Union needs all the help she can get."

"More men or better generals?" Matilda asked, a comment from John popping into her head. "You know Pa is from the South. So is Mother. Their sympathies are bound to lie there."

"They don't have to. A lot of Southern men have gone North to join the Union army because they think the Union should be preserved." He paused and met her eyes. "And because they feel the same way about slavery as you and I do."

Matilda started.

Sinclair grinned. "You've never said it, but you were just as pleased as me when Kansas came in as a free state. Will and Abe are right. Slavery is wrong."

She nodded slowly, the image of the little boy at the slave auction so many years before forming in her mind. She often wondered what ever became of him. "Yes, I admit it, though I'd never have said anything to upset Pa." She put her arms around Sinclair and held him close, unable to keep the tears from running down her cheeks. To her, he would always be the baby brother she had adored since that long ago icy January morning when the tiny fingers coiled around her thumb. "But I don't want to lose you. Please, please, don't leave me."

He returned her embrace and patted her back. "I'll think about it."

He would promise no more. She had to be content with that.

In November of 1861, to everyone's surprise, John returned home from a trip to Nebraska with a bride on his arm. He introduced her as the former Mary Ann Tate of Peru, Nebraska.

"The wedding was last week, November 6," he announced. Mary Ann smiled shyly from his side. "Been courting her for over a year now, so when she finally said yes, I didn't want to leave without her." He grinned and pulled her hand through his arm. "Didn't want to give her a chance to change her mind."

"Well, I declare," Betsy Ann said. "I was beginnin' to think you were a confirmed bachelor like Sam and Tom."

By the time Elizabeth Anne Baldwin joined them on December 7, 1861, the North and the South were locked in mortal combat. More young men left to join the Union

Army. Some, it was said, left to join the Confederacy. Border skirmishes increased. Neighbors quarreled over which side was right and which was wrong. Jefferson Davis' inauguration as President of the Confederacy in February of 1862 made the split of the Union more official.

At the end of March, they received a letter from Minerva.

"It's March, and already spring wildflowers are starting to bud. I couldn't believe it when they told me winter was over. But did we have rain! All the rain that didn't fall in Kansas during the drought fell here this winter, I do declare.

"They had a lot of flooding in Sacramento. The Cosumnes River went over its banks and threatened to take Mr. Hicks' fine bridge with it. All that water racing down the river scared me, but we were never in any danger. Only the low-lying areas flooded.

"They say Governor Stanford had to go to his inauguration in a rowboat. That would have been a sight to see, him in his fancy clothes climbing into a rowboat.

"I worry about you. The war seems so far away, but the news we get frightens me. I wouldn't wish that trip across the desert on anyone, but I'd feel so much better if you were all out here where I would know you are safe.

"But here's my great news. We're going to have another baby in September. I hope this one is a boy. Laura has become quite the young lady, and Anna is starting to walk, but I do so want a son for Abe."

In June, a letter from Sarah told them Josh Tovrea, Temperance's widower, had been killed fighting with the Union Army. It gets closer, Matilda thought, with a stab of fright. It saddened her to think of Josh's bright smile dimmed, his hearty laugh silenced forever.

On September 11, Sinclair rode up, waving a paper.

"A telegram," he cried. "A real telegram! Just picked it up in Marysville this morning." He handed the paper to Matilda and she read,

"James William Dyer born Sept.9 stop Minerva recovering well stop Abe."

Matilda held the telegram in her hand. "Imagine," she marveled. "Just imagine. News from two thousand miles away in only two days."

The Monitor defeated the Merrimac, Stonewall Jackson captured Harper's Ferry, and two days later, Lee was checked at the Battle of Antietam and driven back to Virginia. Sinclair, once the Union seemed assured of winning, stopped talking about going to war, much to everyone's relief.

Matilda closed her mind to it. She tended her garden, cared for the girls and Lewis, and carried her butter into the little store in Waterville twice a week. Elizabeth rode in the papoose carrier, and Mary sat proudly in front of Matilda holding the reins and pretending it was she who directed White Star. Slowly, time passed, and the war dragged on. Even Lincoln's proclamation freeing the slaves did not touch her, nor did Stonewall Jackson's death at Chancellorville.

"Shot by his own men," Sinclair told her as he reported the sad news, shaking his head in disbelief. "Can you imagine getting shot by your own troops?"

Matilda nodded and gazed out over the fields. In her mind, she saw waves of young men in blue and gray uniforms shooting at each other and falling. She closed her eyes. How long, she wondered, could she continue to live in her little island of isolation? How long would it be before the war touched her directly? The thought frightened her, and she forced it from her mind.

Chapter 30

August of 1863

AUGUST 19, 1863, began like many other days. A sleepy cry from Elizabeth woke Matilda. Dust motes danced in the beam of early morning sunlight that crossed the bed. The sticky August heat already made the room stuffy, even with the window open.

Sitting up, she looked at Lewis asleep beside her. Gently brushing back the lock of hair that always tumbled across his forehead, she smiled. She loved him so much.

Tossing aside the light sheet that covered her, her primary thought was to get to Elizabeth before she woke Mary. Mary would be four in October, and demanded constant attention. Elizabeth, already calm and matronly at twenty months, had her father's blond hair, hazel eyes, and serene disposition. She reminded Matilda of John in many ways.

Easing off the bed, trying not to disturb Lewis, Matilda gathered Elizabeth in her arms. If she could get her fed and tended before Mary woke up, the whole day started easier.

"Mama!" The cry from Mary shattered her hopes and woke Lewis. He caught her look of exasperation and laughed.

"Wait 'til October when the next one comes," he told her. "Then you'll really have your hands full." Flinging back the cover, he sprang from the bed. "Good thing she woke us up. Wanta get into that well before it gets too hot."

"It's pretty deep now. Shouldn't you be hitting water soon?" Matilda, heartily tired of relying on the barrel of water her brother Sinclair brought twice each week from the well at her parents' house, eagerly awaited the new well.

The spring they had relied upon dried earlier each year, so Lewis determined he would dig their own well. She did not share Lewis' faith in the water-witch. The old dowser's stick bent obligingly at a spot conveniently near the house. Matilda suspected the old man bent the stick himself, but Lewis had believed and started to dig.

"Should be almost there," Lewis replied with a cheerful grin. He tucked in his shirt and gave her a hug and kiss, ignoring Elizabeth's protests at being squeezed between them. Mary tugged at the hem of Matilda's nightgown, demanding her share of the attention. Lewis scooped her into his arms to entertain her while Matilda tended to Elizabeth.

Later, busy at the stove, the aroma of freshly ground parched corn coffee filling the room, Matilda remarked, "Sinclair said yesterday Mother's coming with him today." She laughed. "He said she's coming to help me, but I think she just misses her granddaughters."

Mary banged her spoon on the table, demanding breakfast. As Matilda set Mary's bowl of porridge on the table in front of her, the coffee boiled over. She hastened to move the pot to protect the beautiful stove she had labored so hard to clean.

"Ho, Lew, 'Tilda! You lazy lug-a-beds up yet?" Sinclair's voice hailed them through the open door. "Where're my girls?"

Lewis went outside to greet the wagon, Mary and Elizabeth at his heels. While the two girls threw themselves on their adored Uncle Sinclair, Lew helped his mother-in-law down and gave her a warm hug. "Good morning, Mother Betsy. Appreciate you coming to give 'Tilda a hand. Between tending the girls and supplying all of Riley County with butter, she has her hands full."

As Betsy Ann entered the house, Lewis turned to help Sinclair with the water barrel. "Today's the day, Sinclair. I can feel it in my bones. Should hit water soon. Then we won't have to do this any more."

"It's hot already, Lew," Sinclair commented. "I have to take this other barrel over to John's. Why don't you wait 'til I get back to start? Be safer, two of us workin'." He climbed onto the wagon seat and gathered the reins. "I'll leave the wagon and ride the horse. I can be back here in an hour."

Lewis laughed off Sinclair's concerns. "Don't worry. I'll be fine. You'll be back before it gets too hot."

"Okay, just be careful. If you start to feel dizzy, get out."

Lewis reassured him and Sinclair prodded the horse into motion. The wagon creaked in protest, the water in the remaining barrel sloshing from side to side.

Matilda, listening, said, "It worries me, too, Lew. Can't you wait for Sinclair?"

Lewis laughed at her fears. "I'll be fine." Anxious to get started, he added, "Sinclair'll be back in an hour." He hugged her close for a few moments, his beard scratching her cheek.

"I love you," she whispered, returning his hug.

"Love you, too." He ruffled her hair and kissed the tip of her nose. Tossing the pick, a shovel, and a couple of buckets attached to ropes into the well, he grinned at her and started down the ladder.

As Matilda returned to the house, the baby gave her a kick. "Easy, Son," she laughed, patting her abdomen. "You've already got me bruised and battered." She always thought of this baby as a boy. She wanted another boy, to have a son for Lewis, even though he said he didn't care, as long as she and the baby were healthy. Tears stung her eyes as she thought of Baby John. I wonder if I'll ever get over losing him, she thought. Her mother said it would get easier with time, but it had been over four years. Having another boy might help.

Matilda's mother brought a new quilt to tie. So much for

wanting to come over and help me, Matilda thought with a smile. She just likes to have company while she ties her quilt. With her daughters married and only Matilda and Caroline still in Kansas, Betsy Ann spent a lot of time alone. After years of being surrounded by a large family, she admitted she found the house empty.

They set up the quilt rack in the shade of the big hickory tree beside the house. The breeze outside cooled them a little. Jake flopped down in the shade the quilt provided. Betsy Ann settled into the rhythm of tying. Matilda, watching her mother's face, knew she had something on her mind.

"That Mrs. Andrews!" Betsy Ann burst out at last. "Do you know what she's been saying?"

Matilda confessed she hadn't the slightest idea.

"She's been saying around that Gardner's been sendin' money to the South all during this wretched war." Indignation made Betsy Ann short of breath. She yanked the yarn so hard it broke. "Gardner told her he tried to get Kansas voted a slave state, yes, but when it was admitted to the Union as a free state, he accepted it. He told her in no uncertain terms he opposed this war from the beginning."

Matilda wondered vaguely where Mrs. Andrews thought her father might have gotten money to send. She never remembered any extra money.

Betsy Ann paused for breath and started again, but Matilda only half listened. She glanced down at the two girls playing beside her. She couldn't help thinking of all the young men who were being killed. Kansas had sent twenty thousand soldiers to fight for the Union. She did not know how many had died, or would die. Matilda felt a pang of sympathy for the wives and sweethearts of those men. She certainly hoped the war ended before Sinclair took a notion to go over his father's objections.

She thrust the thought aside and returned her attention to her mother.

Betsy Ann had moved on to another subject, having dismissed the offending Mrs. Andrews from her mind. "The Briggs' youngest has second summer complaint," she announced, her face solemn. "He's had the flux for three days now, and nothing seems to help. The comfrey and peppermint haven't stopped it, and he started passin' blood yesterday. I've even tried ginger syrup." She sighed. "Poor little mite. Only eleven months old."

How sad for Mother, thought Matilda. She always takes it so hard when she is unable to cure all of her charges. In her mind, Matilda crossed her fingers as she glanced at Mary and Elizabeth, both strong and healthy. Pain stabbed her as she recalled how second summer complaint had so weakened John he succumbed to the croup.

Betsy Ann saw the tears start in Matilda's eyes. "Oh, dear," she said, furrowing her brow. "I didn't mean to remind you of John." She reached over and patted Matilda's hand. "It'll be easier with time, love. And you got the new baby coming. Bound to be another boy, as high as you're carryin'."

Matilda smiled through her tears, remembering her mother had said the same thing for both Mary and Elizabeth. "You're right, Mother. I just seem to cry so easy now."

"Of course you do," her mother explained, in her best medical voice. "Normal thing, you bein' pregnant."

Matilda laughed. Getting up, she ran to check on Lewis. She could not see the well from where they worked, for the house stood between them. She arrived just as he finished pulling up two buckets of dirt to empty and he assured her he was fine.

"Ground's damper now. Should be hittin' water any time." He emptied the second bucket and tossed it back into the well. "Stop fussing over me like an old mother hen." He grinned. "Just have one stubborn rock to get around. Hope it's not so big I have to move the whole well over a few feet!"

With a quick hug, he kissed her and started back down the ladder.

Feeling better, she returned to the quilt. "I do hope Minerva having another baby so soon after Will won't do her any harm," Matilda commented to her mother. She referred to the news received in the last letter from California.

Betsy Ann sighed. "She's such a frail little thing. She shouldn't 'a took so quick, her takin' so long to get her strength back after losin' the first one. Hope she's drinking the lobelia tea like I told her."

"I miss her so much," said Matilda with a wistful smile. "I wish I could see her again. It's a shame Abe lost his land in that squabble, but he'll make a good living building wagons. He's so talented." She tied another knot and cut the yarn. "Has Pa said anything more about joining them in California? I know Lew would go if he did."

"No, but Britt's kind'a pushing for it. He says once the war's over it's gonna be hard on folks like us who were for slavery. But are you sure you'd want to go with all these babies?"

Matilda shook her head slowly. "I want to go, but the idea of crossing that desert with the children . . . ." Her words trailed off. What do I want? she pondered. She heard talk of a railroad, but everyone said it would be impossible to build one across those mountains. The thought of seeing Minerva and her brothers again pulled hard at her. And the dream of seeing the magical land of California was never far from her mind. Her only hesitation came from fear for the safety of the children.

Betsy Ann spoke again. "Shame about that young man from over on Swede Creek."

Matilda, her mind still on California, asked absently, "What young man?"

"You didn't hear? Name of Charlie Meyer, drowned in Fancy Creek, two, three miles up from Henry Shellenbaum's place. Guess they brought his body in to Henry's and Lizzie like to fainted." Betsy Ann's voice showed her scorn for such a sign of feminine weakness. Matilda laughed to herself. She could never imagine her mother suffering from such a malady.

"Did we know him?" The name sounded familiar, but Matilda could not put a face to it.

"Sinclair says we met him down to Dyer's last June, when Sarah Dyer married that Union soldier. Don't think he ever came by the house." She sighed in sympathy. "Hear he just got back from the War. Shame to live through battles only to drown in your own neighborhood."

"How on earth could anyone drown in Fancy Creek this time of year?" Matilda wanted to know. One could wade across in most places.

"Guess he stepped in a hole. Panicked when he felt the water go over his head is all anyone can figure. Never will know for sure." Betsy Ann lifted her head from her work at the sound of hoofbeats. "That Sinclair coming back already? How time flies!"

Looking up, Matilda saw Sinclair returning on horseback. Waves of shimmering heat rising from the ground gave him a ghostly appearance, like the horse had no legs and floated across the prairie. She smiled at the fantasy, remembering crossing the Kansas plain, and how intrigued she had been by the strange images. Good, she thought. He will keep an eye on Lewis for me.

Then she heard a faint cry from the direction of the well. "Lew!" she cried. She jumped to her feet with a start, dropping her scissors. The ball of yarn fell from her lap as she ran to the well. Kneeling over the side of the pit, Matilda looked into Lewis' pale face. Almost up the ladder, he clung to the rung with both hands, swaying back and forth.

"Lew!" she cried, her eyes wide. "Hold on, don't let go!"

"Dizzy," she heard him mutter.

Lying as flat as possible for a woman seven months pregnant, Matilda stretched her hand down to him. He put his head against the rung of the ladder. She could just reach the top of his head. "Come on, give me your hand." She wriggled a little farther and grasped a handful of his hair. "One more step," she urged. Beside her, Jake whined his encouragement. "Sinclair will be here in a moment."

Then Lewis' head fell back, tugging against the hair she held. In horror, she watched as his grip failed and he fell. The handful of hair slid through her desperate fingers. He seemed to fall in slow motion. She heard her mother gasp behind her as his body slid down the ladder. His head hit the side of the well, wrenching his neck to a horrible angle.

"No!" Stunned, Matilda lay staring at his body, then started to scream. Her voice echoed and re-echoed in the deep well. Her mind reeled. She felt Sinclair lift her from the ground. He carried her into the house and laid her on the bed. Sinclair's frightened voice and her mother's soothing one reached her, but she could not respond. Jake's mournful howl echoed through her heart as she drifted into unconsciousness.

Matilda went through Lewis' funeral in a daze. The sight of his dead face, the sickening thuds of clods landing on the coffin, the smell of the newly dug earth, all had a sense of unreality. She kept telling herself this couldn't be happening. Her father and her brothers all looked so solemn as they performed the ritual. Ely Robertson conducted the services and paused twice to regain his composure. Ely and Lewis had become like brothers.

God, she thought, how could You let this happen? We were so happy. I loved him so much. The well. Oh, God, the well. She tried not to dwell on it. In her mind, she would see Lewis fall, feel his hair slipping through her fingers. She would wake in the night and relive the horror of watching him fall, smelling again the musty dampness rising from the well. She prayed he had not lain injured at the bottom of the well until Sinclair could get help to get him out. No, her mother assured her, again and again. His neck had been broken in the fall. He died the instant he landed. Guilt washed over her in waves. She should have checked him more often. She should have insisted he wait for Sinclair. She should have warned him not to spend too much time on that stubborn rock.

Two days after Lewis' funeral, while she stilled reeled from that blow, Quantrill's raiders invaded Lawrence and massacred one hundred and fifty unarmed men and boys. Though Lawrence was nearly one hundred miles away, shock waves from the incident echoed across Kansas.

Matilda wept when she heard the tale. "When will this senseless killing stop?"

Three days later, while Betsy Ann and the girls napped, Matilda sat in the shade of the tree and watched the mirages dance in the heat. The baby seemed as tired as she, for he moved listlessly. She put her hand on her abdomen. She felt so desolate. To think she would never see Lew again!

As though reading her mind, Jake laid his chin on her lap, his limpid brown eyes meeting hers. He whined and she stroked the silken ears.

"You miss him, too, don't you, Jake," she whispered. Even White Star was off her feed. Matilda sighed and closed her eyes. Two drops squeezed out from behind her closed lids and streamed down cheeks still stained from prior tears.

As she sat immersed in her loneliness, Jake raised his head and let out a sharp bark. Matilda's eyes flew open and she saw a horse approaching at a slow walk. It took her a moment to see the rider, for he slumped over the pommel, his head on the horse's neck.

"He's hurt, Jake, or he's ill." She jumped to her feet and ran to meet the approaching rider. When she reached him, she saw caked blood on his shirt and down his right trouser leg.

When she touched his hand, he opened his eyes. "Please, help me," he whispered, his voice hoarse through cracked lips. "Water."

Betsy Ann appeared in the doorway as Matilda led the horse, with its inanimate burden, up to the stoop. Between them, they managed to get the young man off the horse and onto the bed.

"Water," he begged again, and he drained the cup Matilda held to his lips. When he sagged back on the bed, they washed the grime from his face and saw how young he was.

Fortunately, the wounds were superficial, and a week later the stranger felt well enough to join them at the table. Betsy Ann took pride in her young patient's quick recovery. He had given his name as Wes Overton, but they knew nothing else about him.

As he savored his coffee and, for the first time, did full justice to the ham, eggs, and cornbread Matilda placed in front of him, he met her eyes. She said nothing. Even Mary and Elizabeth were strangely silent as they watched the young man.

He shifted in his chair. They saw him wage his internal war. Finally he spoke.

"You ladies been right good to me." He took a sip of coffee. "You ain't asked no questions. But you got a right to know." He paused. "I got shot in the fighting at Lawrence. I been ridin' with Quantrill for two years."

Silence greeted his announcement. He went on. "But I never shot no one lessen they shot at me first, I swear. I know some kilt unarmed men, but never me." He met Betsy

Ann's eyes. "I got no family. If you folks will consider takin' me in . . . ."

"How old are you, Son?" Betsy Ann interrupted in a gentle voice.

"Eighteen. I joined Quantrill when the Union soldiers burned out my home in Missouri. They shot my brother, and might just as well have shot Pa. He died soon after. Lucky Ma died ten years ago. Would 'a killed her to see her home burned to the ground thataway."

Matilda's tears slipped out again at the grief in young Wes' voice. When would this dreadful war end? So much hard feelings on both sides.

Betsy Ann spoke. "I think we can probably use another hand, Wes. Put the war behind you. Soon's you're able, we'll move you over to the main house."

From then on, Matilda shut herself off from stories of the war. She spent her time caring for the girls and preparing for her baby's birth. Time, she thought, time, the ache a constant dullness in her breast. Betsy Ann warned her the baby was not due for two months.

"If your grieving makes him come early, you can lose him, too," she cautioned.

In the weeks that followed, Matilda made every effort to pull herself together. She knew she should not blame herself for Lew's death. Baby Lewis remained lively and active. She must think of him. She forced herself to eat, though she had no appetite.

Finally, one morning just before her baby's birth, she took out Lewis' picture for the hundredth time, remembering again when the traveling photographer came through. Lewis, so tall and handsome, looking so proud, baby John just a month old. Now she had lost both of them. More tears flowed down her cheeks.

She should stop staring at the picture and give herself a chance to heal. The baby gave her a kick. "You're right, Son," she told him. "Hundreds of men like your father are dying every day in this dreadful war." She put the picture away at the bottom of the drawer. "I'm alive and well with three children to take care of. I'd better get on with it."

She set her jaw and strode from the room.

Chapter 31

October of 1863 to May of 1864

"*HE'S SO BEAUTIFUL,* Mother. Lew would have been so proud of him." Matilda's tears dripped from her cheeks onto the soft blond fuzz on the head of the infant at her breast. Lewis Gardner Baldwin had been born five days earlier. Matilda sat by the stove nursing the infant while her mother washed the breakfast dishes.

Her mother had delivered the baby and stayed on at the cabin with her, brushing off Matilda's attempts to thank her. "Shoo, now," she said. "That's what mothers are for. He's a fine baby and will be a proud namesake for his father, poor, dear man to be taken so young." She shook her head. "Now, you try not to cry. It'll stop your milk and little Lewis here needs it."

Matilda nodded. She knew she should not cry so much. In the two months since Lewis' death, she kept herself busy, fighting to keep back the tears, but everything she touched, everywhere she looked, reminded her of Lewis. Jake lay at her feet. He refused to leave her side since Lew died, as though fearing she, too, would disappear.

The morning had dawned clear and beautiful, but the frost on the dried grass outside the window and the chill in the morning air told her winter approached. She shivered. Soon that horrible north wind would howl down off the northern prairies and no amount of warmth from the stove could keep the cold at bay.

Hoofbeats sounded in the distance. Betsy Ann had left Gardner, Sinclair and Weldon to fend for themselves, but Sinclair's coffee never suited his father. Gardner made it a habit to appear on Matilda's doorstep each morning for a cup of his wife's coffee.

Sinclair, bless him, had come every day since Lewis' death to chop wood and pull water from the well. The well. Tears filled her eyes again. The well Lewis gave his life for. Sinclair and her father finished it for her.

Gardner burst into the room, Sinclair behind him, a broad grin on his face. Matilda glanced up. Betsy Ann paused in her dish washing. Both stared at him, at first afraid his haste indicated bad news, but one look at the excitement in his face told them otherwise.

"It's done, Mother," he blurted before he was fully inside the door. "Henry Condray will buy our property in Randolph. He's got plenty of money. Look at that fine stone house he just built there. He's going to own half the town."

Matilda smiled. Her father still refused to recognize the name change even though it had been four years since Mr. Whitson took over the town and renamed it Waterville.

"That will give us enough cash for the trip," he continued.

"Trip?" Betsy Ann stared at him. "What trip?"

Betsy Ann's shock did not dampen her husband's enthusiasm. "The last letter from Alf convinced me. John will stay here and sell the rest of the property for us. He says once this war is over land will be more valuable, so best we wait a while 'fore selling more'n we have to."

He grinned and gave Matilda a hearty kiss on the forehead. "Alf especially wants you, 'Tilda," he said, beaming down on her. "Just think. No more Kansas blizzards."

Matilda laughed. "He wants me to keep house for him. He's been doing his own cooking for a long time now." He's thinking of me, she thought. He knows if I get away from here it will help me stop grieving for Lew. He also knows if I'm with him, he can take care of me. Bless you, Alf. I love you.

Gardner continued, grumbling more to himself than to them, "And no more bickering over slavery, and no more accusations of supporting the South in this curst war." He shrugged out of his coat and tossed it over a chair. "And no more pressure on me to send Sinclair."

Betsy Ann's usual aplomb reasserted itself. She finished the dishes and calmly dried her hands. "Be good to see everyone again," she nodded.

Matilda did not have her mother's ability to accept everything life dealt her with such serenity. The idea of no more Kansas blizzards had its appeal, as did the thought of seeing Minerva and her brothers again. But when she looked down at the sleeping baby, Lewis' only surviving son, her heart quailed. The prospect of that long trek across the wide open prairie with a young baby frightened her. And the girls were still so young. Could they survive the rigors of such a trip? She remembered Minerva's reports. They varied with the glowing reports from Alf's letters. "But, Pa, what about Indian attacks, and cholera, and . . . ."

"The stage road has outposts every twelve to fifteen miles, and soldiers are stationed at forts and garrisons along the way. It's not near as hard as when Alf and Sam and Britt went in '50. Remember Tom said it wasn't bad at all when they crossed in '60. And Injuns won't attack a big, well-armed train." Gardner pulled a cup from its peg and poured himself some coffee, ladling in three heaping teaspoons of the sorghum sugar. "We'll pick up the trail where it crosses the Big Blue at the junction with the Little Blue." He stirred vigorously to dissolve the massive pile of sugar. "Tom and Alf both warn about snowstorms in the Sierra mountains. We have to get through the pass and into the valley of the Sacramento before the end of September."

Matilda's mind raced around the room. How much could she take? How much would she have to leave? Perhaps in California, the memories of Lewis would be less acute.

Maybe being far away from everything that reminded her of him would ease some of the constant pain she felt. At least, she thought, taking some comfort from the knowledge, she would finally realize her dream of seeing California.

Gardner talked on, full of plans. "We'll cover four carts. That'll make us four wagons. Should be enough. We'll have to see how many join us. Britt's been talking it up since the drought in '60. He wants to go back." He grinned. "Young Wes Overton heard us talking last night and asked Britt if he can come along. We told him come and welcome. Sure have taken a liking to that lad. He's a fine young man."

Matilda smiled. "You sure Ely will let him go? With that voice of his, Ely has come to depend on him to lead the singing." Then she sighed, remembering some of the jibes Wes endured. "Poor Wes. Bothers him, knowing the South's losing the war." She sighed again. Could the whole country ever forget all of this animosity? She hoped so, but, deep inside, she feared it would take a long time. She dismissed the war and returned her mind to the conversation.

Gardner hugged Betsy Ann's waist with enthusiasm and gave her a rousing kiss. He looked young again. The continual disappointments in Kansas had aged him, Matilda thought with an ache in her heart. His dream of building a plantation like his cousins in Virginia shattered when Kansas entered the Union as a free state, his once vast holdings dwindled to only 342 acres. The loss of the land plus the constant criticism he endured from the abolitionists had taken their toll.

But today, his eyes held the old fire as he outlined his plans. He crossed to the sleeping Lewis, lying across Matilda's shoulder, and stroked the fine baby hair at the nape of his neck. "And you, young man, will start your life in a fine, new land where a man can breathe."

* * *

Matilda's parents refused to allow her and the children to live alone through the winter, and insisted she move in with them, so she was present on the frosty December morning when Ely Robertson drove his buggy up to the Randolph home looking for Betsy Ann. The buggy wheels broke through the light crust of snow remaining on the ground from the previous week's snowstorm.

"Anna is running a fever," he said, his brow furrowed with concern, "and has been for two days. Doesn't seem to get any better, only worse. Got so now we can't wake her up. Caroline wants you to come."

"Of course, at once." Betsy Ann scurried about gathering her supplies.

Matilda, torn between love for her sister and concern for her own children, stood hesitant.

Betsy Ann glanced at the indecision in Matilda's face. "Stay here," she ordered. "Carrie will understand. Take care of the men folk. I may be gone a few days."

Relieved to have the decision made for her, Matilda stood in the doorway and watched the buggy drive away.

Betsy Ann did not return that night, so the next morning Matilda sent Sinclair to find out how Anna fared. He returned at noon, his face grim.

"Mother says it's brain fever," he reported. "Anna's in a stupor, no one can rouse her." He shook his head. "Looks bad. Mother doesn't hold out much hope."

Matilda's heart sank. Poor Carrie. Poor little Anna, only five years old. Poor star-crossed Tommy. Would even his namesake die young?

It seemed so. Anna Thomas Evans died on December 15, 1863. They buried her on the east side of Lewis in the little cemetery outside of Waterville. John's grave lay to the west, on Lewis' right. The bright autumn leaves Matilda placed on both graves when the flowers faded glistened with a sprinkling of snow.

Matilda longed to comfort her sister. She knew only too well the agony Caroline experienced with the loss of a child and a husband, but, standing beside Lew's grave, her own grief was still too fresh, the pain too great. She walked away from the graveside, the snow crunching beneath her feet, to a little rise that overlooked the river.

She stood very still for a long time, staring across the placid waters of the Big Blue, her throat tight with unshed tears. Would it ever get easier to bear?

The following spring, when it came time to pack for the journey to California, she returned alone to the cabin where she and Lewis had spent so many happy hours. Standing in the middle of the room, waves of pain washed over her. She could almost see his face.

"Lew, my love," she whispered to the empty room, "I'll never, never forget you." Tears streamed down her cheeks as she picked up his favorite tin coffee mug, still on the peg where she had hung it the morning he died. The sight of him sitting at the table in his favorite chair sipping the parched corn coffee from the battered cup flashed into her mind. She closed her eyes, seeing again the special smile he had only for her. It took her several minutes to get her emotions under control. Sinclair would be coming soon to gather her belongings. She had to get busy.

As she packed, each item brought its own special heartache. She stood for several moments hugging Lewis' worn, woolen jacket, made from wool she had spun herself. She buried her face in it and inhaled deeply, savoring the dear, familiar smell. "I'm never going to finish," she told the silent room. In despair, she started to shove things into boxes and trunks with scarcely a glance at each item.

She had been working for perhaps half an hour when the sound of hoofbeats reached her ears. She looked up from the picture she rolled, the one of herself and Baby John, and saw the three young Pottawatamee squaws who had become such frequent visitors. She regarded them as her friends, though she spoke not a word in their language and they very few in hers. Today their usually cheerful faces were solemn as they approached her. The oldest produced a little box which she opened to reveal a small gold ring. Taking Matilda's hand, she placed the ring on her finger.

"Good squaw," the Pottawatamee woman intoned. The other two nodded their agreement. "Good travel to far place." They turned as one, mounted their horses, and rode away.

Matilda, speechless, stared at the plain, gold band. "Good travel to you, too," she whispered to the departing young women. "You'll never know what your friendship has meant to me." She knew she would never see them again.

The time had come for final decisions. Britt and Sarah looked forward to the move. Britt had spoken of California often enough to convince Sarah. John and Mary Ann would stay and take care of the sale of the remaining Randolph property. John, currently active in Kansas politics, felt he could do better by staying behind. He had been re-elected County Commissioner the previous fall. Besides, their second child, Joshua, was less than a month old. After losing Will, her first, at just eight months last spring, Mary Anne feared losing this one as well. Matilda certainly understood her concerns.

Caroline and Ely elected to stay. "Ely's parish is here. I know he could get another in California, but how can I leave Anna's grave?"

"The same way I am leaving Lew's and John's," Matilda replied. "To make a better life for my three living ones."

The packing continued. Gardner heard of a book on

the trail by Captain Randolph Marcy of the U.S. Army and managed to obtain a copy. He kept Sinclair busy reading it to him. He ignored Betsy Ann's scorn and had her boiling then skimming the butter which he soldered closed in what she termed "those new-fangled tin cans."

Following his orders, Matilda cut vegetables into thin slices for Sinclair to press between two blocks of wood in the vise. They slowly dried the pieces on racks beside the fireplace.

"Do you really think we'll be able to eat these little rocks?" Sinclair asked, holding up a bit of carrot for scrutiny.

Matilda laughed. "I certainly hope so, after all this work!"

They ground bags of parched corn for johnny cake and pinole. A neighbor who had fought in the Mexican War taught Matilda how to make pinole.

"Mexicans use it all the time, Miss Matilda," he told her, his weathered face beaming in earnest. "Little sugar and cinnamon and some hot water and it's food fit for a king. Lasts forever." He nodded his grizzled head for emphasis. "Good even if you can't get fuel for a fire. Just mix it with cold water."

Matilda's Pottawatamee friends had taught her to make pemmican, so she pounded a good enough supply of dried buffalo meat to fill a dozen parfleches, the rawhide bags used by the Indians. She knew the Indians ate pemmican raw, but she preferred it boiled with a little flour. Cold raw lard had never tempted her palate.

Tin plates and cups, frying and baking pans, a big camp kettle, Betsy Ann's favorite Dutch oven, the one with the missing leg she had carried to Illinois so many years before, knives, forks, two tin buckets, all were stowed in the big camp trunk. Marcy cautioned against wooden buckets, warning that they shrank in the dry climate.

"Imagine, dry enough to shrink wood," Betsy Ann marveled. "Main thing I remember of the trip from Randolph's

Grove to here is bein' wet all the time."

The matches were corked in bottles to protect them, and Betsy Ann brought her supply of herbs; comfrey, lobelia, elecampane, quinine, and a big bottle of laudanum, sealed with a glass stopper. She packed a big bottle of citric acid "in case we can't find enough wild onions to stave off the scurvy."

By the time they added extra parts for the wagons, additional supplies of lariats and buckskin, the water barrels, the plow, their weapons, and all the tents and bedding, the wagons were as full as they dared load them. Alf had warned them of the foolhardiness of trying to pull overweight wagons across the desert and up the Sierra mountains.

At dawn on Monday, May 1, 1864, all preparations for departure completed, Gardner tied his favorite chair to the back and climbed up on the seat of the lead wagon. With her usual calm resignation, Betsy Ann clambered up beside him. Dozens of friends and family gathered to see them off and wish them a safe journey.

Matilda and Caroline separated with tears. Caroline presented Matilda with a large packet of blank paper.

Matilda laughed through her tears as she accepted it. "I can take a hint, Carrie," she said. "I'll write you every chance I get. Send letters to me in Fort Laramie and Salt Lake City. I know I can get mail there."

Matilda hugged her sister one more time and climbed into the wagon behind her parents. She joined an excited Mary and Elizabeth, and tucked the still sleeping Lewis into the little bed prepared especially for him.

"Gee-up!" Gardner cracked the whip over the oxen, stirring them into motion. The wagon creaked in protest and the long journey began. Gardner and Britt had held long and heated discussions over oxen versus mules. Gardner, who detested mules, selected oxen, while Britt insisted on mules. As a result, oxen pulled two of the four wagons and mules drew the other two.

Weldon drove the first supply wagon, Wes Overton the second. Britt brought up the rear with his family's wagon. Sinclair, on White Star, and Britt's oldest sons, Will and Gardner II, herded the stock. They brought Clarissa and her calf, four of Britt's prize milk cows, two colts, four extra oxen, including Bert, Matilda's ox who had pulled the plow for Lewis for so many years she could not bear to leave him behind, and four extra mules. Jake trotted along beside Clarissa. The dog was over eight years old, but Matilda could not bring herself to part with him.

"If he can't keep up," she announced when her father suggested leaving him with Carrie and Ely, "he can ride in the wagon with the children. He adores Mary and Elizabeth, and it would break his heart to be left behind." She didn't add that it would break her heart as well.

One of the wagons carried a crate on the back with six hens and the old red rooster. They decided against trying to bring the sheep and hogs.

"Too hard to get sheep and hogs over those mountains," Britt had declared, so they sold the sheep and killed the hogs, curing the meat to take along.

Matilda waved to Caroline as long as she could see her, then settled back into her space for the long day's drive. She did not know if she felt happy or sad. It saddened her to leave friends and loved ones, but she looked forward to seeing her brothers and Minerva again. Also, her heart beat rapidly in anticipation of the adventure and the prospect of seeing California at last.

Mary turned to her mother, her eyes wide with excitement. "Mama!" she gasped. "Are we really going to California?"

Matilda laughed and hugged her. "Yes, Darling, we are really going to California."

As Matilda watched the familiar Kansas prairie pass slowly

by the wagon, she thought of the jubilation of Mr. Whitson and Mr. Sechrest when her father conceded defeat and announced his plans to move. We are leaving Sechrest and Whitson to tell the story, she thought. They won't be fair. Sechrest will make my father look bad in the eyes of history.

She turned her mind from it. Look forward, she thought. The past is behind us. Let Sechrest and Whitson have it. A new life awaits in the fabled land of California.

The rising sun cleared the tops of the trees and glistened on the two tears of acceptance that furrowed a path down her dusty cheeks. "Good-bye, Lew," she whispered. "Good-bye, Baby John."

BOOK III: THE TRAIL

1864

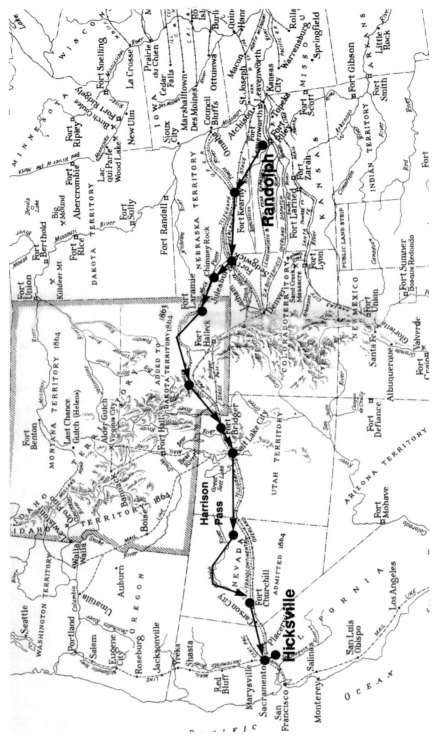

Randolph, Kansas to Hicksville, California 1864

Chapter 32

Randolph, Kansas to Fort Kearny

FORT KEARNY
Wednesday, May 12, 1864

Dear Carrie,

What a routine! Up at dawn, a quick breakfast, on the trail before the sun is above the horizon, stop at noon for two or three hours to rest the animals, then travel again until about an hour before sunset. I feel I have been traveling like this my whole life. I had planned to write some each day, but by the time I get the children fed and asleep, I am too tired to do anything except sleep myself. I hope I get into better habits soon.

We arrived here at Fort Kearny yesterday, and this is the first chance I have had to write. Pa says we leave tomorrow at dawn, so I just have to get this letter off to you today.

The day we left Fancy Creek, we got as far as the junction of the Big and Little Blue. We camped west of the Little Blue just above Blue Rapids, crossed Tuesday morning, and intercepted the main Independence to Fort Kearny road. Pa took one look and said, "Man would have to be blind to miss this." Several wagons can travel abreast on it, it's that wide.

Mother and I were relieved to find such a well-beaten track. It's still rough from all the ruts, but at least there are no ravines to cross. You weren't with us when we came out in '54, so you missed the ravines.

Some of the wagons we've met are California bound, but most are going to Oregon. Tuesday night we camped on the ranch of Mr. Gerat Hollenberg. Sinclair, curious as *always, asked around and found Mr. Hollenberg built the place about '57 to take advantage of all the traffic along the trail. It was a Pony Express stop until the telegraph came through. Judging from the magnificence of the house, he has done right well by himself.*

Wednesday found us at Rock Creek Station. This, they tell us, is where Mr. Hickok killed Mr. McCanless and his two friends back in 1861. Remember everyone talking about it? Seems Mr. McCanless sold the house to the stage company and only wanted to get his money. Poor man. They even say Hickok killed him with his own rifle.

Sinclair hauled me over to one of the sandstone bluffs on the east side of Rock Creek to show me where Fremont carved his name. Fremont has become his hero. He even carries a copy of Fremont's book in his saddlebag all the time.

Over the next several days we passed a number of farms and small settlements. Some used to be Pony Express stations. One was named Lone Tree for a magnificent oak. It's the largest one I have ever seen. I forget most of the other names. I suppose I should have written them down. At one ranch, we met a lovely family named Eubanks (at least that's what it sounded like). Mrs. Eubanks sent her nephew out to offer us a drink of cold water. It tasted so good! Seems they have a deep well with very good water.

We hear rumors all the time of problems with the Sioux and Cheyenne farther north, but so far we haven't seen any Indians at all. We reached what they call Thirty-Two Mile Creek on Saturday night. I don't know what it's thirty-two miles from or why they call it that. Even Sinclair couldn't find out. All along this part of the road the Little Blue is about fifty feet wide and lined with oaks, cottonwoods, and willows. Sinclair and Weldon caught some fish so we could have something different for supper. I saw plovers in the creek. Jays, bluebirds, and red-winged blackbirds filled the trees. I walked along the side, away from the wagons when I could, listening to the sounds of the birds and showing them to Mary when she feels like walking instead of riding.

Once, when I was alone, I saw an antelope. I almost called Sinclair, for the thought of antelope meat made my mouth water, but when my eyes met the creature's, I couldn't bring myself to do it. We watched each other for a while, then he turned and marched off, with a dignified nonchalance that fascinated me. Almost like he knew I would not harm him. Don't tell anyone. You know what Sinclair would say. He always teases me when I ask him to kill a chicken for me.

We spent Sunday resting. You know Pa and his notions about Sunday being a day of rest. It was our first lay-over day and it did feel good to stop for a while. I needed to spend a day catching up with laundry and baking anyway. Mother and I spent the whole afternoon rearranging the wagon. Nothing like traveling for a while to teach you how to pack a wagon. Some day of rest.

Since the station looked reasonably clean (as opposed to the rest of them), I decided to spend fifty cents to treat the children and myself to a real Sunday dinner of fried chicken and peach pie. Pa scoffed at my extravagance, but it was worth every cent. The family that runs Thirty-Two Mile Station is from Vermont, and I soon learned why the soldiers go over there from Fort Kearny. I'm sure they don't get pie like that here at the Fort.

On Monday, we headed across the desert area between the Little Blue and the Platte. I suppose the sand hills were not really very high, but they looked high to me. All sand. Not a tree or a bush, not even a blade of grass. I had never seen anything like it before. It was a barren twenty miles, let me tell you. Britt laughed at me and said I haven't seen anything yet. We saw mirages all along this stretch. It made the men walking ahead look fifteen feet tall. I also saw squiggly areas that looked like ponds in the distance, but were only more sand.

But when we crested the last hill! I stopped in my tracks to gaze in awe, for there before us lay the mighty Platte River. Even from the distance it looked at least a mile wide. It's in a broad, flat valley. If it ever overflowed, it would in-undate an area ten miles wide. As we grew closer, we saw the water rolling within three feet of the banks. It looked totally impassable, but it's only three or four feet deep, yet so muddy it's a wonder it flows. I immediately thought of what one man wrote: 'too thin to plow, too thick to drink'. Just a moving mass of sand.

In fact, since sand is piled up all along the sides, I guess it is sand and not mud. The only trees around grow on the islands, so when we camped that night, Sinclair and Weldon had to cross the river to get wood for the campfire. The current is very swift in the channel, and I held my breath as I watched them.

The next morning, we intercepted the main road from the East. From this point on, all the roads west follow the Platte, on either the north or the south side. Pa says we will follow the south side, at least until he gets the latest infor-mation here at Fort Kearny. That's fine with me. The fewer times we have to cross rivers the better I like it.

Anyway, the road was so wide and so well beaten that we reached Fort Kearny by mid-afternoon. We went through a place everyone calls Dogtown, the first town west of Marysville. They call it Dogtown because a large commu-nity of prairie dogs lives nearby. It's a pretty little spot. They have a stage stable, a store, and the attractive home of Mr. Hook, the station keeper. He is also the Postmaster, and the Post Office is in his house. While we were there, the mail arrived. It had been slung under the stagecoach in a leaky mailbag, as usual, according to Mrs. Hook. I helped her lay the letters out to dry, but I fear the water soaked many of them beyond reclamation.

We saw a chimney and a flag pole of the Fort as soon as we left Dogtown, though we were still eight miles away. When Mary saw the flag, she exclaimed, "Mama, look! There's California!" I tried hard not to laugh as I explained we were still many miles from California. Poor Mary. She has no concept of the distance we have to travel.

The road passes between the Fort and the river. They want the wagons to camp at least two miles past the Fort, so we are camped just east of the town of Kearney City, about three miles from the Fort. Quite a title for a very unprepossessing little town. Most people call it Dobytown, because most of the buildings are made of the unfired adobe bricks. I hear they do have some stores in between the gambling halls and saloons, so I plan to go into the town as soon as I get back from mailing this letter.

I tried to persuade Sinclair to take me to one of the gambling houses, as I'd never seen one. He says Pa told him not to go in one under any circumstances, so I guess I'll have to contain my curiosity.

When Mary saw us going past the Fort without stopping, she started to cry. I had to promise we would ride White Star back to see the Fort. The soldiers in their uniforms looked so handsome on their fine horses that she wanted to meet them. I fear I have a flirt on my hands at the tender age of four and a half.

The Fort is a very fine collection of buildings. As well as the usual barracks, officers quarters, and stables, they have a sutler's store for the use of travelers, a tiny church, a fine blacksmith shop, even a post hospital that holds up to thirty patients. Some of the buildings have been whitewashed and have shingle roofs and glass windows. They have planted a lot of trees, so it is green and shady. Quite an improvement over Alf's description when he went out in '50.

But most important of all, they have a Post Office so I can mail my letter to you. It's managed by a very gracious gentleman named Moses Sydenham. He told me he has run the Post Office here since autumn of '56. It's not only a Post Office, he also sells books, stationery, and newspapers. Some of the papers are several weeks old but since everyone is so eager for news of the war he sells all he can get. They are read and re-read and passed around. I suspect he may not be above selling a newspaper twice, should it return to his possession.

One man asked for papers he ordered sent to him here and Mr. Sydenham told him nothing had arrived. When the man saw the same paper in the rack for sale, he accused Mr. Sydenham of selling his paper, but could not prove it. Some people cross from the north side of the river just to see if they have any mail. One gentleman, a Mr. Roberts, came in while I browsed though the books. When Mr. Sydenham could find no letters for him, he looked very downcast. I think he would have cursed, but he saw me standing nearby, so he only muttered something about getting "nothing for his pains but a view of the town." Poor man. I felt sorry for him.

The stage, a magnificent Concord Coach, came through from Omaha about three in the afternoon. It will arrive in San Francisco in less than three weeks. Just imagine! Only three weeks! They speed along between five and six miles an hour while we are fortunate to average two. Of course, they travel often at night, especially if the moon is full, and seldom even let their passengers get so much as a few hours of sleep. Four mules pulled the coach, and it carried ten passengers. Baggage and mail bags were piled so high on top it's a wonder it did not topple over. Everything strapped to the underside got sopping wet crossing the river. Mr. Sydenham grumbles, just like Mr. Hook, that he usually has to dry the mail before he can distribute it.

I thought how much pleasanter it would be to travel by

stagecoach. Unfortunately, it costs about five hundred dollars per person, well beyond our means.

I get more excited about the trek every day, now that we are on the way. The soldiers here say the rumors about the Sioux and Cheyenne attacks are real, so they want everyone to go in groups of thirty or more. We have joined with some others who also plan to leave in the morning. One family, name of Andrews, has two little girls the same age as Mary and Elizabeth. Mary and little Susan Andrews are already fast friends. The Andrews' are traveling very light, with just one wagon. Mr. Andrews plans to buy supplies at outposts along the way. Britt says he could regret that decision. Prices at the outposts are pretty high, and they don't always have what you need.

Britt also says this is the real beginning of the trail. All the other roads from the East merge here and follow pretty much the same route all the way to South Pass.

I will close now, dear sister, and get this in the mail. Mary is getting restless, and I have promised to take her with me to the little store in Dobytown. I find travel is very hard on clothes, and I want to buy some more cloth while I have a chance.

Give my love to Ely, and hug and kiss Becky and Sally for me. We are all in good health and Pa is good spirits. Getting away from all that conflict has been good for him.

I will write again when I get a chance. They say there are some mail stations between here and Fort Laramie, but the stage company charges a dollar to transport each letter back to the States. That may limit the number of letters you receive, but I will write you from Laramie for sure, because they have a Post Office there.

Your loving sister,

'Tilda

Chapter 33

Dobytown

HER LETTER to Caroline safely tucked into Mr. Sydenham's mail bag, Matilda mounted White Star. Wes Overton, who had accompanied her to the Fort, lifted Mary into her mother's lap.

"Can we go to the store now, Mama?" Mary asked. "Can we? Can we?"

"Yes, now," Matilda assured her. She laughed at Mary's eagerness and urged White Star forward.

They covered the few miles from Fort Kearny to Kearney City in under an hour and walked the horses along the dusty path that traversed what seemed to be the main street. The houses had been built here and there with no apparent order or pattern.

Matilda shook her head at the disorganization. "It looks like the owners just built the houses wherever they took a notion."

Wes nodded in agreement.

The noises coming from the open doorways told them patrons were getting an early start on the evening's festivities. Matilda wrinkled her nose in disgust at the odor of alcohol and stale tobacco. She turned to Wes with a laugh.

"Kearney City indeed! There can't be more than fifteen or twenty buildings altogether. And most of them are saloons and gambling houses. No wonder everyone calls it Dobytown. And look at those men. Don't they have anything better to do?"

Wes grinned. "Sure are a scurvy looking lot," he agreed. "Still want to go to the store? That is, if we can find which one of these rag-tag buildings is a store."

Matilda's eyes fell on a weathered sign leaning drunkenly against a whiskey barrel. "Dry goods," she read. "There it is." She looked at the loafers idling in doorways and ambling up and down the dusty street. As Wes lifted Mary down and turned to help her, Matilda said, "Wes, you stay with the horses." She had no intention of letting one of those men get their hands on White Star.

"Yes'm, Miz 'Tilda," Wes replied. "I'll watch her real close. Don't want to have to buy her back."

"Buy her back?"

"I hear some of these loafers make a livin' stealin' stock. Blame it on Injuns, then wait to see if the owner offers a reward." He grinned down at her. "If he does, the thief 'finds' the missin' critter and collects the reward."

Matilda shook her head. "Of all things! You keep your eyes open." Taking Mary's hand, she stepped over the worn sill of the little sod house. It took a few moments before her eyes adjusted to the dimness inside, but the cool air felt wonderful. Looking about, she concluded tobacco and gunpowder were the principal items stocked. She also saw barrels of flour, sugar, and coffee. Some tins of sardines and jars of ginger snaps and crackers lined the dusty wooden counter. Spider webs, also laden with dust, festooned the corners. One had anchored a web to a side of the flour barrel.

The proprietor was nowhere to be found. Matilda looked around the barrels and stacks of boxes, her eyes seeking the yard goods. She circled a pile of loosely coiled rope, carefully holding her skirts so they did not brush against anything, not wanting to dislodge any more dust into the air. A well-dressed young woman stood by the back wall of the building.

The woman greeted her with a friendly smile. "Come on in. If you're looking for yard goods, they're over here. What a beautiful little girl you have!" The bright smile beamed down on Mary as the stranger stroked the red curls. "And what lovely hair."

Matilda warmed to the young woman. "Her name is Mary," she volunteered. "And I'm Matilda Baldwin."

"Just call me Cora, Mrs. Baldwin. Everyone does. Are you staying long?"

"We're leaving in the morning, headed for California," Matilda replied. "And please, call me 'Tilda."

"Thank you. I will. And you're going all the way to California! You must be very brave. I hear the Sioux and Cheyenne are on the war path."

Matilda had heard the same rumors, but preferred not to give them credence. She shrugged. "Tales get started. Sometimes I think folks just like to make the story a little better. Do you know how much the proprietor wants for this cloth?" She fingered a light blue calico decorated with sprigs of white flowers. The blue would bring out the color in Mary's eyes.

"Twenty cents a yard."

"Twenty cents!" Matilda gasped.

Cora chuckled. "This is your last chance until you reach the City of the Saints on the Great Salt Lake. He always gets whatever he thinks the traffic will bear. Especially on things they don't sell at the sutler's store at the Fort, like cloth."

They visited for over half an hour, Cora's easy friendliness leading Matilda to tell about her family, the trip, even Lewis' death. The time flew by. Just as Matilda began to feel a little sorry for making poor Wes wait so long, an unkempt, bearded man dressed in the dusty overalls and red flannel shirt of a freighter reeled though the door, stumbling a little on the raised sill. He slapped his hand on the counter. Matilda started at the sound, as loud as a thunderclap in the small room. With a little squeal of fright, Mary scurried behind her mother's skirts.

"Hey, old man," the stranger shouted. "Where you at? I need me some t'baccy." He looked around and spotted Matilda. "Well, well, what have we here?" He leered at her. "One of them scurvy Southern sympathizers as is runnin' now the South is gettin' licked? If so, yore shore a pretty one. Most of 'em ...." He drifted off into a long string of invectives, most of which Matilda had never heard before, but she certainly understood their meaning.

Her heart thumped with sudden fright. Should she call Wes? She rejected the thought at its inception. Wes would take offense at the man's remarks, and his quick temper could lead to a fight, even to shooting. No, she dared not call Wes. But what should she do? Her throat tightened on her vocal cords. She tried to speak, but no sound came. She clutched the bolt of blue calico to her breast. Mary's arms clung to her knees, immobilizing her.

The man started towards her, but Cora stepped between them. "You've been on the prairie too long, Jeb. Can't you recognize a lady when you see one?" She took his arm and steered him towards the counter. "George has stepped out for a moment, but he won't appreciate you bullying his customers. Give me your sack. I'll get you some tobacco." She lifted the lid on one of the kegs and measured out a scoop of the pungent flakes.

Matilda's fright vanished. She watched with amusement as Cora deftly filtered the tobacco into the little cloth sack and pulled the string. She weighed the full sack and scribbled in one of the books the proprietor kept lined up on a shelf behind the counter.

"About time you paid something on your bill, too," she told him. "Now, get out."

To Matilda's astonishment, the man obeyed, grumbling and muttering under his breath. Cora turned to Matilda with a smile.

"We get a few like him. Most of the men are basically

pretty decent." She took the bolt of cloth from Matilda's arms. "Is this what you've selected?"

"Yes, but I can only afford a couple of yards. My money has to last until I get to California."

Cora smiled and returned the bolt to Matilda. "Here, take the whole bolt. No charge. You deserve it after the fright Jeb gave you."

Guilt and desire fought a battle in Matilda's mind. Desire won, so she simply thanked Cora for her kindness and accepted the gift. Then a new concern assailed her. "Won't the store owner be angry with you?" she asked.

Cora shook her head. "Don't worry, it'll be fine. He owes me."

"Thank you again. I really must be going. If you ever do get to California, please look me up." The wistful look in Cora's face startled her. "Mary," she told her daughter, "tell Miss Cora good-bye."

Mary held up her arms and Cora dropped to her knees to give her a warm hug. As Cora clung to Mary, tears welled in her eyes. The sight touched Matilda's heart. She wondered if perhaps Cora, also, had lost a child. She thought back to their conversation. Cora had said very little about herself.

Matilda shrugged. They needed to go. The sun already dipped toward the horizon. Her father would worry, even though Wes accompanied her.

They rejoined Wes on the decrepit porch. He helped her mount White Star, then lifted Mary up to her. Cora stood in the doorway of the shabby little store, waving good-bye. Just before Cora turned away, Matilda thought she saw the cheerful mask fall and a glimpse of sadness show. She rejected the thought as her imagination.

The next morning, as Matilda filled Wes' coffee cup from the big pot, he grinned at her.

"Saw your friend Cora again last night. She looked different from when you saw her, if you get my meaning."

Matilda almost dropped the pot. "You mean," she stammered, "Cora is . . . is . . . a fallen woman?" It was the only expression that came to her mind.

Wes tried to smother his smile with partial success. "I guess that's one way to put it. She sure is pretty."

Gardner overhead them and scowled. "Matilda, what were you doing striking acquaintance with a strumpet? You stay away from that kind of woman, you hear?" He strode away, shouting, "Sinclair! Get those oxen into the traces."

Matilda said nothing. She had never seen a fallen woman before, but she remembered Cora's easy friendliness, her bright smile, her readiness to assist them when the rude teamster entered the store. She had always been told such women were evil. The sight of the tears in Cora's eyes as she hugged Mary flashed into Matilda's mind.

No, Matilda thought, standing stock still, the coffee pot still in her hands. Cora is far from evil. She is kind and gentle and lonely. She may be a strumpet who entertains men for a living, but she's one of the nicest people I've ever met.

Her mother's voice broke into her thoughts. "You going to put that pot back on the fire, or you going to hold it until the coffee's cold?"

Chapter 34

Fort Kearny to Fort Cottonwood

MATILDA LOOKED BACK and watched as the buildings of Fort Kearny slowly faded from her sight. She turned and hugged Mary. "Now we really are on our way."

They approached the next landmark in mid-afternoon, the stage stop at Seventeen Mile Station. There they observed the hostlers change the mules on the stage, swearing roundly the whole time. Matilda tried to ignore the words as she admired the skill and speed with which the men accomplished the task.

"Why do they call it Seventeen Mile Station?" she asked Sinclair. "Pa says we're ten miles from Fort Kearny. It should be Ten Mile Station."

"Who knows?" Sinclair shrugged.

Her curiosity unsatisfied, she watched in silence as the stage, fresh mules in the harness, jerked forward. With a crack of the whip and a loud "Gee-up" from the teamster in the box, the mules took off at a sturdy trot. She watched the passengers jolting around inside as the stage passed in a cloud of dust and turned to Sinclair with a laugh.

"I thought it might be easier to ride the stage, but I'm not sure I'd want to be bounced around like that for three weeks."

They camped that night close to the Platte River, about twenty miles from Fort Kearny. Matilda took the children for a stroll along the river bank and Mary picked a bouquet from the masses of wild flowers covering the prairie. Farther up the river they saw a log cabin that appeared abandoned.

"Probably one of the Pony Express stations," Sinclair said when Matilda pointed it out to him. "Some of the stations were taken over by the stage companies when the telegraph put the Pony Express out of business, but a lot of them were just abandoned." He carried the two tin buckets. "Mother says there are wells along here someplace. Mary, why don't you help me find one?"

Mary ran to his side, her face bright. Matilda followed them with her eyes as they strolled off, Mary clinging to Sinclair's sleeve with one hand, the other clutching the small bouquet of rapidly wilting wild flowers. Matilda felt a touch of sadness. While glad Sinclair could fill the gap left in Mary's life by the loss of her father, Matilda's heart still ached to see anyone take Lew's place. Lewis, my love, she thought, I promise I will never, ever, let Mary forget you.

She followed Sinclair and Mary, carrying Lewis and matching her steps to Elizabeth's short legs. Sinclair dipped the first bucket into the shallow well, drawing it up full of muddy water.

"Ugh," Mary shuddered. "Look at all the crawly things."

"We'll strain 'em out," he consoled her. "At least it's better water than is in that river."

Back at camp, Betsy Ann boiled the water "to get out all the deleterious properties" as she put it.

"At least it will kill all the critters swimming in it," Sinclair grinned.

Matilda shuddered.

The next evening, they reached Plum Creek Station and Matilda took advantage of the Mail Station there to write back to Caroline.

> "It's now the fourteenth of May, and we have been on the trail for two weeks. The travel so far has been easy. Plum Creek boasts a stage station and a military post. Even a telegraph office! This station

is famous for its buffalo steaks. We thought to try one, but Pa said the station keeper wanted too much money. They do have a trading post, but the main thing they sell is whiskey.

"What sets this place apart is that all the buildings are made from logs. Usually they use sod. We have met several very nice people. The landlady works very hard to keep her establishment clean, even though she suffers from periodic attacks of the ague. The land around here is so swampy it's no surprise. They say the miasma is at its worst in August and September, so we are fortunate to be passing through in June.

"From what I understand, we will continue to follow the Platte until we reach the town of Julesburg on the Denver road. Britt says before the Denver road went through in '58, all the wagons crossed earlier, but that we can avoid some steep hills and some very sandy areas by crossing farther along the South Platte.

"Britt also says we have it easy, with all the stage stops and mail stations along the way. Sinclair says he's going to punch him if he says it one more time."

Four days later, they reached Fort Cottonwood and McDonald's station. The Fort reminded her of Fort Kearny. McDonald's store boasted a cedar log building two stories high, with a large corral. Across the road, a trading post offered canned goods and liquors.

Britt looked at all the signs of civilization around them and grumbled. "Sure didn't look like this when Sam and Alf and I came through in '50."

Matilda laughed at him. "I can't say I'm sorry. I want some water from that famous well they say is 46 feet deep. It will be nice to have water we don't have to strain the bugs out of first."

Sinclair appeared beside her with the two tin pails. "Mother heard about the well too, and ordered me to fetch some."

The well, located in front of McDonald's store, was rigged with a pulley and chain and heavy oaken buckets. Sinclair filled both of his pails with the clear cold water. Matilda could not resist sampling it.

"Oh," she marveled. "It's wonderful! Can we fill the water barrels from it?"

Sinclair grinned. "I'll see. Where you headed?"

"I thought I'd check out the stage stop and see what kind of food they serve."

He laughed. "From what I hear, it's mainly cakes of flour, grease, molasses and dirt. About equal amounts of each."

"Ugh. Then I won't bother. I'll go back and help Mother with supper."

When she reached the campsite, she overheard her father and Britt arguing with two soldiers.

"What's going on?" she asked her mother in a whisper.

"Seems the Commander at the Fort has ordered all wagons searched for contraband weapons. Guess they've had a lot of trouble with folks selling rifles to the Indians." Betsy Ann shrugged. "Told 'em as far as I'm concerned, they can go ahead and look, but your father got all upset."

"Upset? Why?"

"Says he's a citizen of the United States, and didn't the Constitution say no searches and seizures? And if that didn't mean anything, why did Mr. Lincoln want to fight a war to preserve the Union." She chuckled. "Britt's trying to settle the whole thing."

It ended, as Matilda knew it would, with the soldiers searching the wagons while her father stood by, his brow knitted in a fierce scowl.

She watched the young soldier give a cursory glance through her wagon. How young he is, she thought. His carefully clean-shaven face showed only bare traces of a beard.

When he emerged, their eyes met and he smiled. "Thank you for your cooperation, Ma'am." He touched the brim of his hat and walked to the next set of wagons.

The next commotion arose when Matthew Andrews walked back to tell them the Commander said they had only thirty-two armed men in the group, and so must wait here at the Fort until more wagons joined them.

"Rule is no group leaves with less than fifty armed men, since the Injuns been givin' so many problems."

Gardner grumbled. "Gettin' so's a man has no freedom at all, what with the government feelin' they have to take care of us. I remember when we struck off for Randolph's Grove back in '22. Just me and Jim and the women and young-uns. No trouble with Injuns. Guvment had nothing to say in the matter." He shook his head and stomped off.

With all the furor, they did not eat supper until after dark. Matilda finally got the children fed and in bed. Exhausted, she fell asleep herself and woke in the middle of the night to find herself still fully dressed and stiff from her cramped position. She listened for a moment and discovered what had awakened her. The stage had just pulled up to the station, with shouts from the teamster and a lot of rattling of harness and stamping of hooves.

Heavens, she thought. It's the middle of the night. She crawled out of the stuffy tent, careful not to wake the children, and stretched, enjoying the cool breeze that wafted over her, bringing the damp smell of the river along with the dust still settling from the stage. She sneezed from the dust and watched the passengers emerge and stagger into the station.

Sinclair, sleeping in his blanket nearby, also awakened. Sitting up, he chuckled softly. "Make enough racket, don't they?"

"Guess they feel if they're awake the rest of the world should be too." Matilda yawned. Swatting at a mosquito, she retreated to the relative haven of the tent. She debated putting on her nightgown, but fatigue overcame her again. She slipped off her shoes, loosened her dress, and returned to her pallet.

The stage had long since departed when she rose at dawn. "Good heavens," she remarked to Sinclair. "The poor souls on that stage didn't get much chance to rest."

Sinclair pulled out his big watch and consulted it. "Four hours," he nodded. "Probably didn't get much sleep, either. I hear all ten of 'em had to crowd into one small room and sleep three to a mattress."

Matilda grimaced. "The more I learn about traveling by stage, the less attractive it sounds. We may travel slowly, but at least we get to sleep at night." Lewis crawled to her and she stooped to pick him up. "My things are packed. You can take the tent down and stow it."

She walked to where Mary and Elizabeth watched their grandmother and Aunt Sarah preparing breakfast. The aroma of coffee, frying bacon, and stewing apples filled her nostrils.

"Here," her mother ordered. "Set that young'un down and give me a hand with the johnny cake."

"Yes, Mother, I'll be glad to." She thought of Sinclair's description of what the stage passengers were forced to eat and laughed.

Chapter 35

Fort Cottonwood to Julesburg

JULESBURG,
Sunday, May 23, 1864

Dear Caroline,

We reached Julesburg last night and are 205 miles from Fort Kearny. We lost a day at Fort Cottonwood, for we had to wait for more wagons to catch up with us. The Commander insisted on fifty armed men with every train. The next bunch to arrive at the Fort had over forty, so we have nearly seventy with us now. That made the Commander happy and he let us go. Pa is still grumbling about the lost time and the government trying to run his life, but it was a pleasant place to spend another day. I cut out new dresses for Mary and Elizabeth from the calico I got in Dobytown. I have so little time to sew, for it is impossible in the wagon when it is moving. Besides, I walk most of the time anyway.

The soldiers also searched all the wagons for contraband weapons. I guess the army is really worried about Indian uprisings. I hope it is just a precaution. All this talk is beginning to scare me.

Tomorrow we cross the South Platte and head across the plains to intersect the North Platte at Scott's Bluff. They say we can see the Courthouse from forty miles away. It's hard to imagine any rock that would stand so high. Britt says Chimney Rock is even higher. I can hardly wait to see them. There are a lot of tales about the Courthouse, but I think they are just that, tall tales. They tell one about two traders who held off a whole tribe of Sioux from the top. More likely a hunting party of five or ten warriors just having a little fun.

It will seem strange not to be following the river, after so long. We could hardly tell where the two rivers came together, the area is so swampy and the river is so high with the spring run-off. I think it looks like a scary crossing, but the men don't seem to be worried. Britt, of course, says it was worse when they came in '50.

Julesburg is a thriving little town. A man named Jules (naturally) founded it in '59 as a trading post on the newly opened Denver Road. I hear the poor man was killed by the outlaw Jack Slade. I guess Slade still runs the station at Horse Creek. I hope he is still there when we arrive. It will be interesting to meet a real outlaw.

Anyway, they say Julesburg boasts a dozen buildings, with a stage stop, a warehouse, a telegraph office, a stable, a real store, a billiard saloon, and even a blacksmith shop. I wanted to go into town to the store, but Pa wouldn't let me. He says Sinclair can take my letter in, but this town is even tougher than Dobytown. I hear it's a real mecca for gamblers and drunkards.

After we left Cottonwood Springs, we passed a number of small establishments. They call them 'ranches' after the Spanish term, but most are just two or three buildings and a corral. The finest was Jack Morrow's. He's an interesting man, short, very slender, with a light complexion and long hair the color of mine. He keeps several squaws. I could never determine if he was actually married to any of them or not, and I really didn't think I should ask. He certainly has good Indian connections. There were Sioux all over the place.

Morrow's Station is famous for the number of stock thefts by Indians, so we kept a close eye on all of ours, especially White Star. Whenever anyone loses an ox or a horse, Morrow is very sympathetic and offers to sell the injured party a replacement - at a high price, of course. No one can prove that Morrow is actually involved in the thefts, but suspicions of the gentleman run very high. Giles says the army is talking about running him out because of so many incidents folks have reported.

Did I tell you about Giles? I guess not. We met him in Fort Cottonwood while we waited for more wagons to join us. He's been an army scout and has guided wagons across the trail for twenty years. All those years of crossing deserts have taken their toll. His face looks like a dried prune, although I don't believe he's that old. He has twinkling blue eyes and a shy, charming smile. I just wish he didn't chew that vile tobacco. It's so repulsive, spitting all the time. But he is going to be a valuable addition to our party, with all of his knowledge and experience.

Anyway, after we left Morrow's Ranch, we followed the river until O'Fallon's Bluffs started to rise. There the trail left the river and crossed the bluffs. We went up and over because the Bluffs provide an excellent place for ambushes if the wagons stay below on the river bank. From the top of the bluff, we had a magnificent view of the whole Platte River Valley.

I haven't mentioned the weather before, but in the past two weeks we have endured three rainstorms and one hailstorm. You should have seen Mother cooking in the rain holding her umbrella over the fire. It makes me look forward to the desert and a chance to get everything dry. The canvas on the top of the wagon keeps the water out pretty well, but with everyone going in and out and with the air so damp, it's hard to keep things dry.

The days have been very long, and in spite of the easy traveling, I am worn out by the time I get the children tended to of an evening. How I wish I had you to help me! Fuel has been very scarce. We have to look for buffalo chips, but the old-timers say they are not as plentiful as before. Too many white men killing the buffalo just for their hides. Some of the ladies from the East were a little squeamish about using *buffalo chips at first, but now they scurry for a supply along with the rest of us.*

At O'Fallon's Bluffs, we camped by a small stream that feeds into the Platte, with plenty of good water, grass, and, believe it or not, real wood for the fire. Those luxuries will become scarcer as we get farther west.

Jake has managed to keep up so far. He picked up a thorn in one paw just out of Fort Kearny and had to ride in the wagon for a few days, much to Mother's disgust, and the children's delight. Most of the time he just trots along beside Clarissa and her calf. Her stride seems to suit him. It's charming to see the three of them together. Sometimes the calf will butt Jake with his head, and Jake will growl and nip at the calf's heels. The calf thinks that is great fun, and dances around the dog and butts him again. One day I laughed at their antics until my sides ached.

Have to close now so Sinclair can get my letter mailed. Pa says we leave at the crack of dawn tomorrow. I will write again from Scott's Bluff and tell you all about the famous Chimney Rock.

So far everyone's health has remained good. I pray our good fortune holds out for the remainder of the trip.

With much love,

'Tilda

Chapter 36

Julesburg to Chimney Rock

THE RISING SUN touched the canvas of the wagon with orange as Matilda opened the flap of her tent and looked out over the campground. She took a deep breath of the clear, crisp air. A horse whinnied and shied at some small night creature scurrying towards its hole.

Beyond the circle of wagons, to the west of Julesburg and across the South Platte, the road stretched in an unbroken line. So many wagons had crossed that the ruts stood clearly visible as far as Matilda could see. Most of the white settlements were behind them. She knew that from here on, vast stretches would be uninhabited.

The French word for flat made an appropriate name for this river, she thought. Broad and shallow, the muddy river meandered along, so level she sensed no rise at all, but Britt assured her the land rose steadily every day and would continue to do so until they reached South Pass.

At least the going had been easy, and the grass plentiful. Fortunately, the dreaded cholera had not appeared. The danger should be behind them soon. Alf had said cholera seldom struck past Fort Laramie.

Sinclair slept on the ground beside the wagon, only his tousled curls visible above the blanket. She looked down at him. A fond smile touched her lips. No matter how big he grew, he would always be her baby brother, remembering again her feelings as his tiny fingers curled around her thumb on the day of his birth.

Could it really be fourteen years since Sam and Alf left for California? She could still see Alf's eyes sparkle as they conspired before he left. She hoped John and Caroline would follow next season. Then they would all be together again for the first time since Alf and Sam left. Except for Temperance, she thought with a pang.

She tried to picture her sister's face. The memory had faded. Strange, she mused. How can I forget her face, when she meant so much to me? All she remembered clearly was the morning Temperance died. She shuddered as she thought, why can't that image fade? And poor Josh! To die in this dreadful war when he had found happiness again with his second wife. She had felt sympathy for poor Julia when they received word of Josh's untimely death, but now, widowed herself, she really understood Julia's pain.

Matilda's eyes traveled again to the unbroken line of the trail. She wondered what it would have been like to be among the first to see this vast land, and envied those who had seen it before anyone had settled here. She felt out of place in this vast expanse of waving grass. She remembered Alf's descriptions in his letters. The buffalo herds and the Indians seemed a part of this country, the white men did not.

People seemed so small and insignificant in all this space. Out here, the earth could swallow them up and they would vanish forever, with no trace. Well, at least Pa has enough room to breathe, she thought with a smile.

"Mama, I can't find my stockings." Mary's face appeared between the tent flaps. The blue eyes rebuked Matilda for neglect and brought her back to reality. At least the trip had accomplished one thing. Mary no longer asked when her father would return. She seemed at last to accept the explanation that her father was in heaven with her brother John and her cousin Anna.

The camp stirred into life. Men swore as they fought the mules and oxen back into harness. Rustling in the tents and wagons told her the women were preparing for the day's trek.

A rush of exuberance filled her with a sudden zest for life, a life full of adventure and new experiences. Laughing with sheer joy, she gathered Mary in her arms and nudged the sleeping Sinclair gently with her foot.

"Come on, you lazy lug-a-bed. We'll leave you here if you don't get moving."

The thirty-odd wagons continuing towards South Pass and Salt Lake City pulled into a line for crossing with Britt's wagon in the lead. The remainder elected to follow the stage road through the new town of Denver, high in the Rocky Mountains.

While the men conferred, Matilda listened to the debate, her old fear of water making her uneasy.

"River must be six hundred yards wide," Gardner declared. "Reported to have quicksand at the bottom. Also, we can't tell how deep it is."

"Tie a rope on me," Sinclair volunteered. "I'll walk across and check."

Matilda's heart missed a beat. The current looked dreadfully strong to her. If the water swept him away, could the men holding the ropes get him back before he drowned? Not wanting to embarrass him, she remained silent and watched with growing anxiety as Sinclair edged his way across the river. When the water reached his chest, he floundered for a moment. Matilda gasped in fright, but he caught himself and continued on.

When he approached the other shore, and the water dropped to his knees, he turned around and retraced his steps, giving a wide berth to the section where he had nearly fallen.

"Not too deep," he reported, squeezing the water out of his pants and replacing his boots. "One spot of quicksand on the east side. Gotta be real careful there."

The first wagon started across, followed by the second. When half the train had crossed, Matilda began to breathe a little easier. Maybe it would not be a difficult crossing after all.

Then it happened. Matthew Andrews allowed his wagon to drift too far down the river. The right wheels dropped into the quicksand and the wagon tipped to a precarious angle. His wife screamed.

"Get some more mules on that wagon," Gardner roared. Britt, already across with his wagon, quickly unhitched his mules and drove them back into the water.

"Watch for the quicksand, Britt," Sinclair shouted from beside the horrified Matilda. "Don't get too far down the river!"

Men hurried to help. Mrs. Andrews handed the three little girls to them, another assisted her to safety. Matt waded to the head of the team. The mules on the tilting wagon strained to pull it back. The wagon tipped farther. One of the mules lost his footing and fell. Britt tried frantically to hitch his mules to the front of the struggling team, but a second mule fell and the current seized the wagon.

"She's afloat, Matt," Gardner shouted from the shore. "Cut 'er loose. Save the mules."

Matt froze. Britt lunged forward with his big Bowie knife and started slashing traces. The two lead mules scrambled free and Britt struggled to the next span. Two more men reached Britt's side and tried to help. They succeeded in freeing the two center mules before the victorious current seized the wagon, drawing it and the two doomed mules down the river.

Matilda shuddered at the despairing bray of one of the mules as the current dragged it to its death. In minutes, the wagon and the mules vanished from her sight.

"My dollies, my dollies," cried little Susan Andrews as she watched the wagon disappear.

Matilda shook her head sadly at the tragedy. She knew the Andrews family lost all of their possessions, for they only had the one wagon. What would they do now?

Mary, beside her, said, "Don't cry, Mama. I'll give Susan one of my dolls."

On Monday, the group camped at Nine Mile Station, on Tuesday they made it to Pole Creek. On Wednesday, May 26th, they spent the night by a government well, and the next day reached a spot bearing the elegant name of Mud Springs, where clear water ran through a black, miry hollow. Watercress grew in abundance by the creek. As Matilda gathered some to supplement their diet and Mary gathered a handful of morning glory blossoms, she looked up and saw a huge rock mass on the horizon.

"Britt," she asked, "Is that the famous Court House?"

"Yep," he assured her. "Looks a mite different from this angle. We came at it up the North Platte from Ash Hollow. It's weathered some since I saw it in '50, but there's no doubt. That's it."

The next morning, Matilda pointed the landmark out to Sinclair. "It looks so close! Will it really take us two days to get there?" As the sun rose, the shape seemed to change before her eyes.

Britt heard her. "You'll soon learn distances out here are hard to judge."

In spite of her disbelief, it did take them until the next evening to reach the camp close to the massive structure, and she saw not one, but two huge masses of rock. Matilda could not believe her eyes. She had never seen anything like them in her life. She stood and stared in awe. Britt assured her their campsite was over two miles from the two massifs, yet she felt they were so close she could reach out and touch them. She walked away from the camp to get out of the dust stirred up by the hooves of all the animals. Sinclair accompanied her.

"The air is so clear," she exclaimed. "What do they call the smaller one?"

"According to Britt, most folks call it the Jail House. Makes sense, it being right beside the Court House." Sinclair picked up Mary to give her a better view. "Bet you've never seen anything like that before, have you, young lady," he grinned as he hoisted her to his shoulder.

"Want to touch it," Mary declared. "Carry me, Uncle Sinclair."

"It's over two miles, Sweetheart. Your poor old Uncle Sinclair has been riding all day and is ready for supper. Judging from what your Uncle Britt says, I suspect you'll get a chance to touch all the rocks you want."

Matilda, a little disappointed because she, too, wanted to touch it, stood silent and stared. It looked like a huge, dilapidated building. She saw walls, turrets, a dome, even guardhouses in front of the main body of the rock. As she watched, the setting sun turned the monolith to gold. She took a deep breath. What a magnificent country!

The following morning, they crossed the creek that came down from the Court House, a bubbling stream of clear water running over sand and stone. Impressed by its beauty, Matilda asked Britt for its name.

Britt grinned. "Depends on who you ask, 'Tilda. Some call it Punkin, or Pumpkin, or Pumpkinseed. It's even been called Lawrence, or Gonneville, after some trapper or other supposedly killed by Indians. Sure is pretty, though. Joins the North Platte just before Chimney Rock."

On Saturday, they reached the North Platte and saw Chimney Rock. Since they camped there over Sunday, she and Sinclair, with Mary tucked in between them, rode White Star to get a closer look and to read some of the thousands of names inscribed on the base.

"Well, 'Tilda," Sinclair remarked, "it's easy to see where it got its name."

Matilda nodded in agreement, staring in awe at the monolith rising from the prairie like a sentinel, its broad, round base two-thirds of its height. The upper third gradually tapered to a slender spire.

Sinclair consulted his copy of Fremont's report. "According to Preuss," he began.

"Who's he?" Matilda interrupted.

"Fremont's surveyor," he retorted. "If you'd read the book like I told you to, you'd know."

"You're the one with time to read books," she snapped. "I've got three children to tend." She looked at Mary, whose eyes had grown large at the sound of the irritation in her mother's voice. Mary's expression pulled her out of her pique and she laughed. "All right. What does Preuss say?"

Sinclair grinned at the change in tone and read, "'It consists of marl and earthy limestone, and the weather is rapidly diminishing its height, which is now not more than two hundred feet above the river.'"

Matilda wondered what on earth marl was, but did not plan to reveal her ignorance to Sinclair. Instead, she pointed to a date inscribed on the base. "Look. 1845. Nearly twenty years ago."

The masses of gray rocks lining the horizon fascinated Matilda. They reminded her of buildings from medieval times. She pointed them out to Sinclair.

Sinclair glanced in the direction she indicated. "Sure a lot of rock around here," he commented.

Matilda shook her head. Men, she thought. No imagination at all.

That night, rain turned the road into a muddy morass. As Matilda grumbled about the mud, Giles laughed. "You just wait, Miss Matilda," he warned. "You get on that desert, you'll remember this like it was paradise."

Chapter 37

Chimney Rock to Scott's Bluff

SCOTT'S BLUFF
Tuesday, June 1, 1864

Dear Caroline,

We reached Scott's Bluff this afternoon and corralled the wagons at the base of the bluff for protection from the wind. You would not believe the gale that whistles through here. Britt says it's like this every afternoon. Burton, in his book, declared Scott's Bluff the permanent headquarters of hurricanes, and I believe it. The children and I slept in the wagon. Sinclair refused to put up the tent. Said we'd wind up five miles away if we tried to sleep in it.

We have come 285 miles since we left Fort Kearny, and are now 51 miles from Fort Laramie. We had planned to spend a day here, but since this wind makes it impossible to bake or do laundry we might as well continue.

Chimney Rock is even more striking than the drawings indicate. Since the distance from the camp by the Court House was only 12 miles, we arrived early Saturday afternoon. Several springs of good water and fairly abundant grass make the Chimney Rock campground very popular, so Pa decided to stop even though we could easily have gone another six or eight miles. Sinclair and I appreciated the chance to get a close-up view of Chimney Rock Sunday morning after Pa held services. To Pa, the formation didn't look like a chimney, it looked like a church steeple, so it inspired him to go on at an even greater length than usual. Sinclair and I, anxious to get started, thought his sermon would never end.

Since Mary was so disappointed when she didn't get to

touch the Court House, Sinclair and I took her with us. Sinclair had to climb up and add his name to the thousands already inscribed there. I told him he was wasting his time. Some of those from the '40's have already been worn away until they can barely be read, but you know Sinclair. The rock is pretty, mostly a light yellow in color, and cuts easily with a knife. I'm sure that's why so many names are carved in it. If it was harder work not nearly so many would have bothered.

The formation is more impressive from a distance. All around the base are crumbled pieces that have fallen from the top. It probably was higher 30 or 40 years ago as the trappers claim. Guesses as to its height ranged from 200 to 500 feet. The Indian name for it is meapate, which means "the hill that is hard to go around."

Along the river the sand is piled in great drifts, making for hard pulling. I felt so sorry for our poor, struggling oxen. Bert has been favoring his right foreleg and I fear he may have pulled up lame. I suppose I should have let him stay in Kansas, but I couldn't bear to leave him behind. The dear faithful creature works so hard. His feet have gotten so sore I had Sinclair wrap them in gunny sacks.

The ridge line that extends from Scott's Bluffs south of the river appeared first as a blue line, then, as we neared, became the most magnificent view I have ever seen. Court House and Chimney Rock paled in comparison. We saw barren, yellow hills and wind-carved rocks eroded into fantastic shapes, like a magician waved a wand and turned castle, fort, and mansions into stone. I almost expected to see a ghostly knight in full armor riding around the ruined fortress. I wish I could have shared it with you. Sinclair is such a lump. They were just rocks to him. And you know Mother . . . no imagination at all.

They say Scott's Bluff received its name in the memory of a young man left here to die back in the '30s. Some clerk with a fur trading company returning from the mountains became too sick to travel. Two of the company tried to bring him down river in a bullhide boat and got him this far. The sad story has as many variations as it does tellers, but I guess the poor young man really did die here all alone.

An old man at the trading post says some folks digging a well nearby found the skeleton of an elephant, but I think he's been drinking too much whiskey.

Britt says in the '50s the trail went around the east end of the Bluff and was (of course) much more difficult, but that now a pass has been cleared around the west end, between Scott's Bluff and South Bluff. I'm sure glad we don't have to cross the river. There is a lot of water coming down it now, let me tell you.

Sinclair says he talked with a Captain Shuman here who is in charge of building a fort by Mail Station 23, on the other side of the pass (where I will mail this letter to you). He says General Mitchell is determined to set up military posts at Julesburg, Mud Springs, Ficklins Springs, and here at Scott's Bluff. There were a lot of Indian attacks in '63. He says the Sioux are restless all up and down the trail, even as far as South Pass.

I can't help but wonder if a lot of the problems aren't from misunderstandings. Like the Grattan massacre. We'll be passing the place where that happened in a few days. All those soldiers killed because they foolishly shot the Brule chief, Matriya, over one silly old stray cow! Matriya had even signed a treaty with the Government. Then the soldiers massacred the Indians because the Indians killed the soldiers. No wonder the Sioux call the Americans Wasiche, which means 'bad man.' It never seems to end.

Fortunately, we ourselves have not had any Indian problems. We met a number of Sioux at Morrow's Station. The men are very handsome, tall and muscular, with beautiful copper skin. And such intense dark eyes! Mary's red hair fascinated them, and several wanted to touch it. They don't see very many children with such flaming red hair. I kept a close eye to be sure none of them wanted to take any of it for a souvenir, and so did Sinclair, but they just gently stroked it and marveled over it.

Am closing now as I can hardly keep my eyes open. Writing by this flickering candle makes my head ache. I'll finish tomorrow when we get to the mail station.

Mail Station #23
Wed, June 2, 1864

I am sitting on an overturned pail finishing this letter while the rest of the wagons wend their way through that pass. Some call it Devil's Gap, with good reason. It's the roughest, most tortuous route I have ever seen. The big 'S' shape makes the wagons almost double back on themselves. And the gap is barely wide enough for the wagons in some places. The ruts have been cut so deep you can't even see the trail until right on top of it.

The road passes between Scott's Bluff and South Bluff, then curves around in front of Dome Rock. Dome Rock brings to mind a huge mausoleum, which reminds me that one thing I have not mentioned before is the number of graves we pass. I try not to look at them. Pray to God none of us die on this trek. To even think of spending eternity on these lonely, windswept plains makes me shudder.

It's getting colder at night. Britt says that's because we are 4000 feet high already. It doesn't feel like we've been climbing, the slope is so gradual, but we definitely are.

The more I see of that river, the happier I am that we don't have to cross it. It's half a mile across here and although it's only three to four feet deep, there's quicksand.

Those who've crossed say the current is very swift. Men come over from the trail on the north side to the trading post or the mail station, just like they did at Fort Kearney.

Another party of four wagons has joined us. Sinclair objected to taking them with us. He says we're making a big mistake, that their leader is going to get us all in trouble, bragging he is going to kill the first Indian he sees.

Have to close now and get this in the mail bag, for Pa has the wagons moving and I have to go. I will write to you again from Fort Laramie. If all goes well, we should be there in three or four days.

Love,

'Tilda

Chapter 38

Scott's Bluff to Horse Creek

THE LEADER of the party of four ox-drawn wagons Matilda referred to in her letter to Caroline had approached Gardner Randolph upon their arrival at Scott's Bluff.

"Name's Sid Parsons," he said, offering his hand, "and we'd like ta join up with you folks. Group we was with, they left us behind," he whined. "Said we was too slow, said we was makin' them fall behind schedule."

"By all means, join us," Gardner invited. "We've got oxen pulling some of our wagons too. You should keep up easy."

At supper the evening after they left Scott's Bluff, Sinclair repeated his concerns about Parsons to Matilda. "He's going to get himself in trouble." He dropped his voice and muttered, "And us too."

"Why so?" Matilda asked absently, stirring the stew with one hand and trying to keep Mary from sampling the sugar with the other.

"He's still waving his gun around and braggin' about how he's gonna kill the first Injun he sees." Sinclair broke off a big piece of cornbread and picked up one of the tin cups of tea Matilda had poured and set out on the nearby wagon tongue. "Lot of us have tried to tell him we're in Sioux country. Sioux're not as easy goin' as the Pottawatamee and the Kaw."

"Oh, he's just making sounds to hear himself talk," Matilda replied. "He'd never be that foolish." She ladled a scoop of the steaming stew from the pot onto a tin plate. "Stew's ready."

"Smells wonderful, 'Tilda." Sinclair inhaled deeply, savoring the aroma, then grinned. "Makes it worth all the time we spent making those rock carrots." His smile faded. "Parsons is a mean sort, claimin' white folks need to kill all the Injuns. I sure hope he's just talkin'. I don't think the Sioux will take too kindly to being shot at. Been enough trouble already."

Matilda gave Parsons no further thought. Two days later, just after Horse Creek, they passed a Sioux hunting party. She saw the women working near a cluster of wigwams erected on the banks of the North Platte, at a site with plenty of water and wood available. They're probably making pemmican, she thought, while the men are out hunting. Walking beside the slowly moving wagon, watching the women work, she felt a pang of homesickness. The scene reminded her of when her three Pottawatamee friends taught her how to make pemmican. She missed them and the companionship they had shared.

As she watched, a shot rang out and one of the women fell. Horrified, Matilda heard Parsons shout, "I got me one!"

"Damned fool!" Sinclair shouted, galloping White Star to where his father sat on the wagon seat. A cloud of dust enveloped them as White Star slid to an abrupt halt. "Now we're in for it."

Frightened, Matilda ran, coughing and blinking from the dust, to the front of the wagon where the children rode with their grandparents. Mary and Elizabeth stared at her wide-eyed.

"What's happening, Mama?" Mary asked. Her voice quavered and her eyes widened.

Gardner pulled the oxen to a halt. "Stay here, Sinclair," he ordered. Scowling, he growled, "So the fool did it in spite of all of our warnings." Mounting White Star, he rode forward to confer with the other men gathered by the Parsons wagon.

Matilda tried to reassure the girls, but her words sounded hollow. "Grandpa will think of something. He has a way with Indians." She offered a silent prayer he would somehow be able to placate the Sioux. Fright weakened her knees, forcing her to momentarily grasp a wagon wheel for support. She felt light-headed and took a deep breath, willing herself to drive down the rising panic.

Sinclair stood beside the wagon, his face red with fury. "The idiot! Does he think for one minute he's frightened off the Sioux? He'll bring the whole tribe down on us!"

"Please, Sinclair," Matilda tried to quiet him. She put a hand on his arm and led him away from the wagon. "Don't frighten the girls," she told him in a furious whisper.

Leaving their weapons behind, several men from the wagon train rode toward the cluster of wigwams, waving a white shirt as a flag of truce. Gardner rode among them. Betsy Ann gathered her medical supplies.

"In case she's alive," she said, "I may be able to help her."

A band of Sioux warriors rode into the cluster. They had no doubt heard the shot and hastened back to camp to protect their women. Matilda's heart sank when she saw their numbers. The men conferred, then one rider returned to the Randolph wagon for Betsy Ann.

Matilda's heart still pounded in her chest, but she felt her hopes rising. "Is the woman still alive?" she asked. If so, perhaps Betsy Ann's medical skill could ward off a battle.

"Barely," he said, shaking his head. "We told the Sioux we had a healer and would try to save her."

But before they reached the Indian camp, a wail went up from the Indian women.

"Sounds like she died," Sinclair muttered to Matilda.

Matilda's heart sank. "What do you suppose they'll do?" Stories of Indian cruelties had circulated among the settlers for years, losing nothing in the re-telling.

They did not have long to wait. Within half an hour, the men returned. Gardner rode to where Matilda and Sinclair waited. Betsy Ann slid down from White Star's back and Gardner, without a word, left to rejoin the men clustered around the Parsons wagon.

"What's happening?" Matilda demanded. Seeing her normally calm, serene mother so visibly shaken frightened her more than anything else that had happened.

"They've agreed ... they've agreed ...." Betsy Ann covered her face with her hands.

"Tell me!" Matilda cried.

"They'll let us go, unmolested, if ... " she faltered, then her words came in a rush, "if we hand Parsons over to them."

Relief mixed with horror as the information sank in. "But they'll kill him," Matilda gasped.

"Yes," Betsy Ann agreed, "and not quickly." She shuddered. "Praise God he has no wife or children."

"He was a fool," Sinclair declared, not a hint of sympathy in his voice. "He could have gotten us all killed. I tried to warn him and so did a lot of others, but he wouldn't listen."

Matilda watched aghast as three men, their faces set, dragged the struggling Parsons away from the wagons, towards the line of implacable Sioux. Several more men kept their guns pointed at the others in Parsons' party, to keep them from interfering.

"I'm a white man," he shouted. "You can't give me to these savages. You know we've got to kill 'em all ...." He fell silent as two Sioux warriors took his arms. When the men turned their backs and slowly returned to the row of wagons, he began to scream.

Matilda climbed into the wagon with the children. She did not want to see or hear any more. She knew many people agreed with Parsons, that the only way to maintain peace was to kill all of the Indians. Matilda rejected the argument. The idea of killing the Indians because of a few trouble makers on both sides assaulted her basic sense of fairness. She remembered her reaction when she learned the Kickapoo and Delaware had been evicted from their land in Illinois because of the actions of the Sauk and Fox tribes. Actions which, from discussions she recalled, were probably fully justified.

"Please, God," she whispered, "surely there must be some way to reach a compromise without all of this killing."

The line of wagons moved forward. Gardner, his jaw set, returned White Star to Sinclair and, without a word, climbed back onto the wagon seat. He cracked the whip, stirring the oxen forward. Betsy Ann rode beside him, unmoving. Parsons continued to scream. Matilda clutched the three children to her breast. She tried to sing one of their favorite songs to soothe them, but her mouth and throat were so dry no sound came out. She covered their ears to block the cries.

Half an hour later, Sinclair returned, sweat running down his white face. The screams still echoed across the prairie, growing fainter now.

Matilda looked at him. Their eyes met.

"They skinned him alive," he whispered, mopping his face with his big, red handkerchief, leaving streaks in the dust that had settled there.

Matilda closed her eyes. Betsy Ann shook her head in sorrow.

Gardner lashed at the hapless oxen in his frustration. "We had no choice," he cried in a hoarse voice. "They'd have killed more in an attack, even if we could've held 'em off. We're none of us soldiers. They could've killed us all!"

"No, Gardner, you had no choice." Betsy Ann placed a comforting hand on his arm. "You did what you had to do."

Two large tears rolled down Mary's cheeks. Matilda, clasping both girls to her breast, remained silent.

The next morning, the four wagons in Parsons' party turned back towards Scott's Bluffs, vowing revenge on the whole Sioux Nation.

"Injun lover!" the man driving the first wagon shouted, waving his fist at Gardner as they drove by. "We won't travel with no man who'd turn a white man over to savages just to save his own skin."

Gardner did not reply. He watched as the wagons passed, then put a shaking hand on Mary's head. "Not to save my skin," he whispered. Tears filled his eyes as he stroked the red curls. "No, not mine."

As the dust from the departing wagons faded, Matilda turned to her father and sighed. "They'll tell the soldiers about Parsons' death, but will say nothing of the provocation."

"Yes," Gardner said, sadness in his voice, "and the poor Sioux will have the soldiers after them with no one to tell their side. No wonder this war gets worse and worse." He shook his head. "Sure hope we get across before something happens to unite them all against white men."

The train continued on its way. Matilda never heard anyone mention Parsons' name again.

Chapter 39

Horse Creek to Fort Laramie

FORT LARAMIE
Saturday, June 5, 1864

Dear Caroline,

We arrived at Fort Laramie about noon today. This has been a very eventful four days, let me tell you.

First off, Sinclair was right. We made a big mistake in taking in the party I mentioned in my letter from Scott's Bluff. Not two days later, their leader, a fool named Parsons, shot a Sioux woman washing clothes in the river just past the Horse Creek station. Brought the whole tribe down on us. Some fast talking got us out of it, but it sure scared me. The men had to give Parsons to the Sioux, but it was a small price to pay to save our lives. It didn't bother me at all to trade Parsons' life for Mary's, or Elizabeth's.

But before that happened, we camped at Horse Creek, about eighteen miles from Scott's Bluffs. Mr. Reynal, who runs the station there, brags to everyone going through that the Fort Laramie Treaty was signed at his station in September of 1851. Ten thousand braves, representing Oglala and Brule Sioux, Cheyenne, Arapaho, and half a dozen others whose names I forget all met there because it was the closest place to Fort Laramie with enough grass for all the horses. Can you imagine ten thousand horses all in one place?

Mr. Reynal is very proud of the history of his little trading post, although I doubt many people have ever even heard of it. Sinclair says that if Reynal knew what Burton's book says about him and his establishment he wouldn't be such a braggart. Mr. Reynal's wife is a wrinkled up old squaw. His daughter is very pretty, but in twenty years she'll probably *look just like her mother.*

The morning after we left the camp at Horse Creek we had the problem with Parsons. The rest of his group went back to Scott's Bluffs to complain to the soldiers. Since they won't tell the soldiers why the Sioux killed Parsons, the Sioux will have no one to tell their side, and there will be more senseless killing.

We camped at Cold Springs at a lovely campground. The water from the spring tasted better than any we've had in a long time. The next day we got as far as Bordeaux station, then yesterday came the rest of the way to Fort Laramie. Bordeaux station is close to the site of the Grattan Massacre that I mentioned in my last letter. Mr. Bordeaux claims he witnessed the whole battle and loves to talk about it. He tells the story to anyone who will listen. He took Sinclair out to show him where the soldiers are buried. I declined to join them, and would not listen to his descriptions of the battle. Sinclair laughed at my squeamishness. In the uprising that followed the massacre, Mr. Bordeaux claims his Sioux wife saved his scalp. All over one lame cow! It still upsets me to think of all those people dying for so silly a reason.

We crossed the Laramie River on a fine new government bridge built in 1859. Before that people had to ferry across. One look at that raging river would have been enough to convince me to turn around and go back to Kansas. They had a lot of drownings at the ford. The water is only three or four feet deep, but very swift and turbulent from the snow melting in the mountains. Even after they built the bridge people drowned trying to go around it because they didn't want to pay $2.50 a wagon. Can you imagine running the risk of losing your wagon, or even drowning, just to save yourself $2.50? Only men would do that. No woman would risk her life or her children to save a few dollars. Pa grumbled when Britt counted out the ten dollars for our four wagons, but did admit it was better than trying to ferry across.

The barracks here at the Fort are the same dried adobe bricks they used at Fort Kearny, but all have been white-washed. The officers quarters is a magnificent two storey frame building they call 'Old Bedlam.' Several dozen soldiers are garrisoned here and it makes one feel quite safe. Although except for Parsons' stupidity, we've had no Indian problems.

Some folks that caught up with us here say the Sioux murdered two men and burned their wagon outside of Cottonwood a couple of days after we left. We just missed that one, I guess. Apparently the Commander had good reason to insist we travel in a large band.

The soldiers here at the Fort are all from the Eleventh Ohio Volunteer Cavalry under Colonel Collins. Britt says they have been spread very thinly because of the war. All of the regular soldiers are fighting the South. I can't say as I blame them for preferring frontier duty. The closest they come to war is drilling on the parade ground and marching in the flag raising and lowering ceremonies. Mary was quite impressed watching them strut around in their fine uniforms.

The sutler's store is very well stocked. The sutler, Mr. Seth Ward, has made himself a good living. It's no wonder, at the prices he charges. Would you believe $18.00 for a hundred-weight of flour? Fortunately, we have plenty of supplies. Mr. Ward built himself a fine new house last year. He has been here since 1857, and said he felt it high time he built his wife a decent home. It looks so out of place in the middle of all this wilderness that everyone comments on it. One lady from the east says it is a Victorian style cottage, whatever that means.

They also have a fine Post Office. Sergeant Schneyder has been Postmaster here since 1859. They say he just took on the job himself when he got so disgusted with the chaotic system of mail disbursement. He established firm rules for mail delivery, and even 'helped' one officer over the rail *when the man attempted to get his mail out of turn. I wish I could have seen that.*

Of course, the system is only for the soldiers. I found your letter in a bushel basket where all mail for passing travelers is put for anyone to rummage through. Everyone, naturally, delves into the pile on the outside chance they might have mail, so the letters get pretty dirty and tattered by the time the real addressees get them. We were glad to hear everyone is well. I wanted to send you a telegram but Pa said it cost too much.

They have a bakery, a saw-mill, and a blacksmith shop here at the Fort. The blacksmith charges $2.00 to shoe an ox, $4.00 for a horse, and $2.00 a wheel for setting tires. He's a long way from any competition, and can get away with charging those prices.

We have come about a third of the distance to Sacramento. Britt says we are making excellent time because the trail is so much easier now. I think if he tells me once more the trail is 'easy' now, I'm going to scream. Anyway, we should be in Salt Lake City in about a month, and I look forward to your next letter there.

From here we have a magnificent view of Laramie Peak. It stands over 10,000 feet high. We can see snow on the peak, even though it is 40 miles away. It's the highest peak in the Laramie Range. Everyone calls the Laramie Mountains the Black Hills because the trees are such a dark color. Britt says if I think Laramie Peak is high, to wait until I see the peaks around South Pass.

We are now over 4,000 feet high. We have been climbing steadily, and will continue to do so. I understand the trail gets steeper from here on.

We are going to rest two full days, and am I glad. I hope it doesn't rain so we can unpack and dry everything out.

The land around the Fort is no good for farming. The soldiers have tried and tried, but all they have is a few straggly fruit trees and some hay from the meadows by the river. No wonder it is still such a wilderness.

Pa had Britt sign the register for our party. They wanted a count of men, women, children, wagons, horses, oxen, and cows. They also asked about any deaths. Thankfully Parsons was the only one we had to report. The young man writing down the information looked bored with the whole procedure and didn't ask any questions, so Pa just said Parsons died and left it at that.

It seems we have been gone much longer than five weeks. It's hard to explain. Everything is so different out here. It distorts my concept of time. Does that make sense? Maybe not.

Will write again from the Horseshoe Creek station where we get to meet the infamous Jack Slade. I can hardly wait.

Love,
'Tilda

Chapter 40

Fort Laramie to La Prele Creek

ON TUESDAY MORNING, June 8, Britt shouted a loud "Gee-up" and they were underway again. Deep inside, Matilda sensed a strange feeling, a feeling that she wanted to pull her head inside like a turtle and not go any farther. You silly goose, she chided herself. You know you want to go on. She had never felt that way before. But each day the land got a little more rugged, the nights a little colder. Shadows of doubt crept in as her fear of something happening to one of the children again threatened to overwhelm her.

As she watched the first wagon start down Mexican Hill, the feeling swelled within her. She had never seen such a steep hill. The wagons braked heavily, with mules attached to lines at the rear of each wagon to prevent it from running over those mules pulling in front.

"Good heavens," she gasped to Sinclair as he and their father ran lines from the rear of the first Randolph wagon to a span of mules, "isn't this dangerous?"

"Not as bad as going down the hill to Ash Hollow by the old road, according to Britt." He grinned and dodged the blow she swung at him. "I know. I think if I hear once more that it was harder in '50, I'm going to knock him down." He gave her a quick hug. "Don't worry, 'Tilda. The extra mules are just a precaution. The hill is pretty steep, but I don't think anyone's ever been killed here."

"You do relieve my mind," she told him. "And where did you get your information?" As the wagon in which the children rode approached the rim of the hill, she called,

"Mother, give me Lewis. I'll carry him. Mary, Elizabeth, you come with me. Maybe no one has ever been killed here, but I don't want one of my children to be the first."

"Relax," Sinclair assured her. "Britt says just before Ward's Station there's a great campground, and he's got something to show us."

"I can hardly wait. Here, take Elizabeth. Mary, you hold on to my skirt." She stopped talking for she needed all of her strength. Lewis grew heavier every day, and, while thankful for his obvious good health, she found carrying him harder and harder. She struggled to keep her footing on the steep grade. The plants and patches of loose dirt made the path treacherous. When the wagon safely reached the bottom of the hill, she passed the baby back into the wagon to his grandmother with a sigh of relief and dropped her aching arms to her side.

Sinclair boosted Elizabeth, then Mary, back into the wagon. "See? You were worried for nothing. Not one wagon had a problem."

Matilda ignored him. She scooped up a handful of water from the barrel on the back of the wagon and cooled her overheated face. Westward, Laramie Peak raised its majestic head far above the surrounding mountains. She looked back at Mexican Hill, which looked like a small rise in comparison. Suddenly she threw back her head and laughed at her own foolishness. Sinclair looked at her, a questioning look on his face.

"No," she assured him. "I've not gone mad. I just thought, here I worried so about that little hill." She gestured towards the distant mountains. "Look what we will be crossing."

The campground before Ward's Station proved as lovely as Britt promised. A broad meadow, covered with lush grass and dotted with wild flowers, ran up to a line of pale yellow cliffs, reminiscent of Scott's Bluff. While supper cooked over the fire, Britt approached. "Sinclair, 'Tilda, come with me. I want to show you something."

The four of them, for Mary tagged along, strolled towards the base of the cliff where the late afternoon sun glinted on the yellow rock. Matilda again saw where many names were carved in the soft sandstone. Britt, with a broad grin, pointed to one name she immediately recognized, scrawled in big, bold letters:

S. RANDOLPH

"Sam," she cried in delight. "That has to have been our Sam!"

"No one else. We camped here on our way across in '50 and nothing would do but he had to inscribe his name. Spent half an hour doing it. Said he wanted it to be deep enough to last. I promised him I'd check when we came through to see if it was still there. And here it is."

All the hesitation she felt in Fort Laramie vanished. She thought of how she missed her brothers and Minerva and suddenly could hardly wait to be moving. She felt a resurgence of the vitality and curiosity that had driven her before. Her sense of adventure surged through her again. No river would prove too wide for her to cross, no mountain too high to climb. She was going to California.

The next morning, a half mile beyond the campground, they passed Ward's station, heading ever westward, ever higher. Two miles past the campground, they climbed a sandstone hill where the metal tires from thousands of wagon wheels had cut ruts up to six feet deep into the stone, often barely wide enough for a wagon to pass. They rode in among pine trees now, their pungent odor wafting on the morning breeze. The dark-colored needles earned the Black Hills their name. One tree by the trail had apparently been hit by lightning, for only lightning could have left the craggy remains. The gnarled tree fascinated Matilda. She hoped no one ever cut it down. To cut down a tree with such determination to live would be a sacrilege. Nearby, a thistle sprouted a large white flower trimmed with bright yellow. She had never thought of a thistle as lovely before.

Matilda shook her head. This country is getting to me, she thought. I never used to attach such emotions to plants and trees.

The country continued to grow more rugged. The day grew hotter as the sun rose higher. In spite of frequent sips from the water bottle she carried, the dry air made her mouth feel parched all the time. Lewis accepted it all with his usual aplomb, but Mary and Elizabeth grew cranky. When they reached the camp at Cottonwood Creek they found grass and fuel, scarce along the trail, in abundance.

"This is a strange creek," she commented to Sinclair. "It can't be over six inches deep. It doesn`t even look like it's flowing."

They passed another small shop inhabited by a trapper with his Indian squaw and large brood of dirty children. Matilda remarked to Sinclair, "Why would anyone choose to live out here all alone?"

Sinclair grinned. "And how would all the good Christian ladies back in civilization react if he moved in next to them with his squaw and pack of half-breeds?"

Matilda laughed. "You're right. They're better off out here. I hope for their sakes civilization doesn't catch up with them too fast."

Britt came by. "Get to bed early. We're heading out at daybreak."

"No breakfast?" Sinclair traveled on his stomach.

"No breakfast. We have to make twenty five miles tomorrow."

"Twenty-five miles?" Sinclair objected. "We can't make twenty-five miles in one day. Oxen're not mules, you know."

"Got to," Britt replied. "The next place with decent water and grass for the stock is at Horseshoe Creek, and that's a good twenty-five miles. We'll rest up good once we get there."

"Horseshoe Creek!" Matilda marveled. "We'll get to meet the famous Jack Slade."

Britt grunted. "From what I hear, that's a mixed blessing."

But Matilda's expectations were doomed to remain unfulfilled. After a long, arduous day they arrived at Horseshoe Creek after dark. The next morning, the station master in residence advised them the nefarious Mr. Slade no longer resided there.

"Headed up Montana way a year or so ago," he told Matilda when she inquired. "Heard he got himself hung by the Vigilante Committee. Too bad, too. He had many fine qualities, he did, for all his killin' ways. Never knew a gentler man when he weren't drinkin'. His friends and his wife, they tried to save him, but the Committee, they was determined to do their duty."

Matilda, knowing her father would not approve if he thought she had been anxious to meet the infamous outlaw, swallowed her disappointment.

Then her eyes widened at the sight of the lady of the house. She could only have been a follower of Amelia Bloomer. Her hair, cropped short, curled around her face like a duck tail. The woman returned Matilda's startled gaze with a sullen glare. She looked as if she seldom smiled.

"'S'matter, you never seen a lady wearin' Bloomers afore?" she snarled.

"Why . . . why . . . yes . . . no . . . no, I guess not," Matilda stammered. "But they look very . . . very . . . uh, practical. I've often wished for a dress which would make traveling easier."

The creature relented a little. "They sure are that," she

said, holding out a leg clad in glazed brown calico for Matilda's inspection. The large foot protruding from the end of the pantaloons wore a thin-soled patent leather shoe with elastic sides. "Nothin' like 'em fer gettin' around, let me tell you. All them fancy petticoats and gee-gaws may be fine in the East, but they got no place out here."

Matilda agreed, but visions of her father's reaction to a request that she wear Bloomers kept her silent.

They rested the stock the next morning, left at noon, made a dry camp that night, and covered the rest of the twenty five miles to the LaBonte River the following day. The road, broken and jagged, took them out of sight of the river. At noon, they stopped for a very welcome respite to allow the exhausted animals to rest.

"Are we only half way there?" Matilda sighed to Britt. "I'm worn out, climbing up and down all of these creeks and arroyos." She wiped her sweaty face on her sleeve and looked down in dismay at the red streak on the blue cloth. She looked around. Everything bore a coat of the dull, brick-red dust.

"'Fraid so, little sister. We have to keep going, though. Look around you. No water and no feed for the cattle."

Matilda looked at the coarse wiry grass which the cattle ignored, the ragged sage, the small, scrubby plants with which her mother struggled to make enough of a fire to boil a pot of coffee. She smiled thinly. "You're right, of course. We do have to keep going. I don't now why I'm so exhausted. I hope I'm not getting sick." The thought sent a shot of panic through her. What would happen to the children should she contract some malady out here so far from medical help and die?

Britt patted her shoulder in reassurance. "It's the altitude. We're approaching 5000 feet. Everything is more difficult the higher we get. Even the fire doesn't burn as hot.

By the time we got to South Pass in '50, we could barely get a pot to boil."

"Right. I'd better help Mother." She turned away. She looked out over the vast red wasteland once more, then joined her mother at the cooking fire. Lewis woke up and called for her to pick him up. She had been putting him in the cradleboard when they reached camp, to be out of the way and safe while she helped with the cooking, but three weeks out of Fort Kearny, he decided he had outgrown the cradleboard and set up a continual howl whenever she strapped him into it.

She tried again, but he immediately started to yell. "Pottawatamie babies ride in these until they are a year old," she sighed in exasperation as she released him from the confines of the board. "Why can't you?"

"Mama," he burbled as she lifted him out. He wriggled free of her arms. She put him down on a blanket and he promptly crawled off, heading gleefully for a nearby clump of cactus.

She snatched him up in frustration. "Mary," she called to her daughter, "come and entertain the baby for me. I have to help your grandmother."

They barely began the afternoon's trek when a man approached Matilda, hat in hand. "Miz Baldwin," he asked, then paused, turning his hat around and around. "Name's Arthur Ridgeway." He stopped.

"Why, yes, Mr. Ridgeway, I know you," Matilda replied. She had visited Mrs. Ridgeway several times. They had two charming children. "You're Matthew's father. He's such a polite little boy. And Jenny often plays with my girls. What can I do for you?" She knew Mrs. Ridgeway expected a child soon, and suspected the reason for his visit.

"It's my wife," he replied, twisting the hat into a shapeless mass of felt. "She's, she's . . . ," he stopped, then blurted, "I hear your mother knows all about birthin'."

Matilda struggled not to laugh at his discomfiture. After all, she and her mother had already delivered four babies since leaving Fort Kearny. She managed to say politely, "Of course, Mr. Ridgeway. We'll be happy to help."

Thus Matilda spent the afternoon inside of the swaying, jolting Ridgeway wagon helping her mother assist at the birth of Arthur James Ridgeway, Jr. . Matilda could only think, *at least I didn't have to cross this trail pregnant.* It was hard enough in her normal good health. She felt a wave of pity for Mrs. Ridgeway. The wagons could not even stop to let the poor woman deliver her baby in peace.

The desolate drive finally ended. As daylight began to fade, they sighted La Bonte Creek below them. Matilda nearly burst into tears at the beauty of the scene. The clear mountain stream, bordered with trees, bisected a green valley. A labyrinth of paths made selecting the correct route difficult. Twice they had to pull back and choose another, for the first two ended at a sheer drop of four or five feet. They reached a grove of trees by the creek and spent the night amidst cottonwoods, willows, box elders, and wild cherries. Surrounded by the familiar trees, Matilda almost felt herself back home in Kansas.

The next morning, the ordeal began again. The trail crossed a vast red wasteland of rugged hills marked by sandstone precipices up to 200 feet in height. Black-green cedar trees dotted the landscape. Ravines carved across the road with dismaying frequency, bearing witness to the torrents of water heavy rains had sent coursing on their way to the valley of the Platte. Huge boulders littered the path, often requiring a change of route to detour around them.

For six miles the struggle continued, up and down, often over slopes steep enough to force them to lock the wheels. When they stopped for noon, Matilda felt she had walked at least fifty miles. When she voiced this opinion to Sinclair, he advised her they had covered only six.

"Six?" she gasped to Sinclair. "Only six? You must be wrong. How can it be only six miles? We've been going for hours."

Sinclair, mounted on White Star, grinned down at her with sympathy. "It feels like a lot longer because we've been doing so much up and down." He held his hand out to her. "Come on up. I want to show you something."

She swung up behind him and he walked White Star forward along the line of wagons to a point where a huge pile of boulders stood about 200 feet high beside the path.

"Oh, my," she gasped. "We don't have to climb anything like that, do we?"

"Fortunately no," he said, laughing at her dismay, "but I wanted to show it to you. Some folks call it 'Brigham's Peak', saying old Brigham Young himself gave a Fourth of July oration here. Other folks just call it Knob Hill. But it sure is interesting."

She gazed at the mound of boulders, then noticed why they appeared so strange. The entire landscape was red, from dirt and sand to rocks and boulders, but these rocks were gray.

"Well," she demanded of Sinclair, "you're the one who reads all the books. Why is this pile gray when everything else around here is red?"

He laughed. "You've got me there, Sis. All the books say it's limestone, but no one offers any reason for it to be here in the middle of all this red stuff. But they do say the rough part of this stretch is behind us. We'll be back in the valley of the Platte soon. And we've only about eight miles to La Prele Creek, where we'll camp. Should be there by late afternoon."

Matilda sighed with relief. She had never felt so tired before in her life. She thought how good it would feel to soak in a hot bath and just let herself float. With a little shake of her head, she dismissed that dream. She might find a hot bath in Salt Lake City, but chances of one before then were non-existent.

She found the afternoon's journey much easier, the road wide and easily traversed again. The sun still hung high in the sky as they descended into a beautiful red rock canyon. A clear, spring-fed stream bubbled over the rocks. The horse-tail plants which gave the creek its name grew in great abundance along the banks.

Matilda had lain down in the wagon to get the children to nap and the gentle swaying of the wagon lulled her to sleep. Refreshed by the brief rest, she looked about eagerly. Although it could not have been any later than five o'clock, the breeze carried a definite chill and she shivered.

"We're over 5000 feet high," Britt explained. "That's why it gets so cold at night. Today is Saturday, so we'll be laying over here. Tomorrow, if you and Sinclair are up to it, follow the stream down for about a mile, mile and a half. I think you'll find it worth your while." He refused to say any more.

Early the next afternoon, the church services over and the laundry done, she put the children down for a nap. Leaving Betsy Ann to tend the baking of corn bread and watch the children should they awaken, Matilda and Sinclair mounted White Star and headed downstream to investigate.

Heavy brush frequently forced them to enter the water. Finally, they dismounted and led White Star, fearing the horse might slip on a rock in the stream. At one point, the unmistakable whir of a rattlesnake froze them in their tracks.

"There it is." Sinclair pointed out the reptile making his way off to the side of their path. White Star whinnied uneasily.

Matilda gave a shaky little laugh. "She doesn't like rattlesnakes either. Did you see how big that one was?" They continued their slow progress forward. "Whatever this is Britt has sent us off to see had better be . . . Oh!"

She stopped, speechless with awe at the sight before her. The water had worn its way under a red sandstone cliff, forming a natural bridge across the creek. The afternoon sun cast its light over the stream, sending diamonds dancing and racing across the bubbling water. They broke through the last of the brush and found themselves on a small beach. The water sang as it rolled pebbles along. In the clear, sparkling water, she saw the rocks in the bottom of the stream. The smell of sage wafted over her, carried on the light breeze that cooled her forehead. Matilda took a deep breath. Whenever she thought she had seen everything this country had to offer, it handed her another surprise.

"Sinclair!" she finally managed to gasp when she got her breath back. "Isn't this marvelous?"

Sinclair slapped his hat at a mosquito hovering around his ear. "Sure is right pretty, I have to say."

Matilda smiled. His acknowledgment, while faint praise, testified to the beauty of the place. She sat down on the little beach and sifted the sand and tiny pebbles through her fingers. As the shadow from the cliff grew closer, she reluctantly forced herself to accept Sinclair's suggestion that the time to head back to the wagons approached.

"Probably not too good an idea to spend too much time out here, clear away from everyone else," he advised. "Never know what might be lurkin' around."

Matilda started as she heard the shade of anxiety in his tone. So taken with the beauty of the spot, she had completely forgotten they were in Sioux territory and that the Sioux had been restless of late. Still, it seemed impossible to believe anything bad could happen in such an idyllic spot. Tucking a small, perfectly round pink pebble in her skirt band as a souvenir, she mounted White Star. In silence, Sinclair led the horse back up the trail.

Chapter 41

La Prele Creek to Red Buttes

RED BUTTES STATION
Mail Station #28
Wednesday, June 15, 1864

Dear Caroline,

We arrived here late this afternoon. It is nearly nine o'clock at night, but I still have enough daylight to write. I will have to write quickly, for the wind blows through here almost as fiercely as it did at Scott's Bluff. It will be impossible to keep a lantern lighted.

We have crossed some very interesting country since Fort Laramie. A lot more rugged, let me tell you, and a whole lot colder at night. I did not get to meet Jack Slade after all. The present occupant of the stage station told us the Vigilantes hung Slade up in Montana, last year some time, he thought. What a disappointment! Did get to meet a 'Bloomer', though. Very interesting creature. But the outfit she wore is much better suited to this trail than long dresses. I've taken to hoisting my skirts up above my ankles. The hem always dragged in the dust, and every dress I own has burn holes from the campfire. It scandalized Pa at first, until Mother started doing the same thing. Then he just kind of grumbled and muttered something about how it probably *is* more practical.

Britt showed us Sam's name carved in a bluff by a pretty campsite just before Ward's Station. And directed us towards what has to be the most beautiful spot in the world, where La Prele Creek has carved a course through the cliff, making a natural bridge of solid rock some thirty feet wide.

When we left La Prele Creek, we climbed up to the top of the rise and found ourselves on a bare, windswept plateau where nothing grows but a tough plant the men call salt grass, and which the cattle refuse to eat. When the sun comes out, it gets hot at midday, but several times clouds have come over and it felt almost like winter. The clouds fascinate me. The bottom edges are driven by the wind so they look like the mane of a horse streaming out behind. Britt says that's from rain that falls but doesn't reach the ground. I'd never heard of such a thing before.

We stopped for nooning at a pretty campground by the Box Elder Station, but we could not stay. We went on another ten miles until we reached the station of Mssr. Bissonette at Deer Creek. By then, we were following the Platte again. Here it has shrunk to only about 100 yards wide, but is as swift as ever. Deer Creek is a little stream, and the station boasts a Post Office, a blacksmith shop, and a store. The Indian Agency has a representative nearby, but we did not meet him. I'm sure he did not approve of Mssr. Bissonette's store, for the major item he stocks is whisky. The poor Indian agents have a dreadful time trying to keep whiskey away from the Indians.

From Deer Creek, we traversed another ten miles across a vast wasteland with not much growing on it but wild sage. At Muddy Creek we had to build rafts to ferry ourselves across. That's another place where a government bridge would be a good idea. Eight miles farther up the river we crossed Snow Creek, on what Mr. Burton (according to Sinclair) referred to in his book as a 'vile' bridge. It was a rickety affair, to be sure, and I held my breath the whole time we were on it, but everyone crossed safely.

The next landmark was Platte Bridge Station. Soldiers are garrisoned here to protect the immigrants and the telegraph line. I think they are needed more to protect the telegraph lines because Indians constantly cut the lines to take the wires. I'm sure they find many uses for that wire. I saw one squaw using some to tie a load on a travois back at Horse Creek Station.

They used to call this the Mormon Ferry station, for the Mormons made a lot of money ferrying immigrants across until the bridges were built. Guinard's bridge, the bridge everyone calls the 'Upper Crossing', is close to the Station. Of course, the gentleman charging tolls at the bridge gets whatever he thinks the traffic will bear. He stops just short of asking so much his patrons go seven miles back down river to Reshaw's bridge at the Lower Crossing. The prices range from fifty cents a wagon up to five dollars. I hear he charges all the Mormons five dollars. We must have drawn his fancy, for he let us by with fifty cents.

He grumbled that business has been slacking off. Said after last year's reports of Indian attacks more and more folks were afraid to travel. He ridiculed the idea, saying the Indians have never caused any real problems for white men, and that a lot of last year's reports were just rumors that were never verified. I sure hope he's right.

A party of Arapahos came through while we were there. They were a sulky lot. I gather their war party had not been too successful. I didn't ask who they were after. I don't think I even want to know.

Crossing the bridge put us on the north side of the Platte, and we then had to climb a hill seven miles long. It took us most of the day. At these altitudes, just walking on flat ground is exhausting . . . three steps and my chest would start to hurt. We let the animals rest often, and every able bodied soul had to get out and walk to spare them as much as possible. The only ones who rode in the wagons were one real old lady and the very young children. Even Mrs. Ridgeway walked, though her baby is only a few days old. I rode White Star for a while, but even she winded quickly. We had to climb very slowly.

Once we crested the hill, another ten miles brought us here to Red Buttes. From this point we leave the Platte River for good, and go across country until we reach the Sweetwater.

You would not know me, I am getting so strong. The muscles in my arms have made the sleeves so tight they were putting my hands to sleep. I had to sew in a gore to make them larger. Sinclair is as dark as an Indian, but my skin refuses to turn brown. My nose peels continuously. Elizabeth has tanned nicely, but Mary has the same problem I have. We both have to keep sunbonnets on or we pay the price.

Red Buttes is a pretty place. The bluffs are actually about five miles from the station, but are very colorful. Sinclair rode over and brought me back a sample of the rock. It had the shells of some animal embedded in it. I had never seen anything like it before. Sinclair, for all his reading, could not tell me what they were or how they got there. Remember how Sinclair used to hate reading in school? Now he reads all the time, and sometimes drives me crazy quoting from this book or the other. Some of the things he comes up with are interesting, though, so I'm glad he does it.

We are camped beside a clear, cold stream, but we don't dare use the water. The banks are covered with a white powder almost like hoarfrost. We fear the water might be poisonous, for there are alkali streams in this area. For dinner, we had a prairie hen that Sinclair shot. Was it good! We hadn`t had any fresh meat in so long. Mother refuses to allow us to eat any of her chickens, insisting on keeping them for eggs. I know one hen hasn't laid an egg in months, but Mother remains adamant, so the old biddy goes right on eating her ration of corn and not producing anything in return. She always ducks behind one of the other hens when she sees me. I think she knows I'm ready to toss her in the soup pot.

I am running out of daylight, so will close for now. I will write again when I get a chance.

Love,
     'Tilda

Chapter 42

Red Buttes to Independence Rock

THE NEXT MORNING, leaving the Platte River for good, they embarked upon the overland crossing from Red Buttes to the Sweetwater. After eighteen miles, they descended a steep hill and reached Devil's Backbone Station at Willow Springs.

Matilda asked the station master why they called it by such a strange name. He pointed out a jagged, broken ridge of huge boulders, tilted on edge, that curved over the crest of a nearby hill. The rocks resembled the back-bone of some gigantic sea serpent.

"They say it looks like something only the Devil would 'a made," he informed her, his face solemn. "They's a lot of things out here as only the Devil would know about."

"I guess it's because it's so desolate," Matilda mused to her mother when she returned to the cooking fire to help prepare supper. "This barren prairie could make one think only the Devil would live here."

Her mother shrugged her shoulders. "Injuns been livin' out here for years," she replied.

"I know, but I've often wondered how. I remember what Britt said about them, when he came back in '52." She frowned. "But now that I've seen it ...." her voice trailed off. She looked out over the rolling, windswept plains with the strange rock formation crawling across the hill. The trip to the Sweetwater at Independence Rock would take them three days. Three days of dry, dusty road with little or no water. The water they would pass would often be alkali lakes, dangerous to animals, and impossible for humans to use. The lovely, clear spring that fed Willow Creek was something to be treasured and enjoyed.

Sinclair and Britt rode up to the cooking fire. Broad grins creased their weathered faces. Britt's horse bore a small prong-horn antelope slung across the pommel.

"Look at this, 'Tilda," Sinclair exclaimed. "I got me an antelope!"

"Oh, wonderful," she gasped. "Fresh meat! How did you get him? I thought it was very hard to get close enough to one to shoot it."

"Their curiosity is their downfall," Britt explained. "We ran the rattlesnakes out of a little ravine, hunkered down inside, stuck Sinclair's big red handkerchief on the end of a stick and just waved it back and forth, real slow and easy. Pretty soon it catches the eye of one of the little critters, and he has to check it out. We just waited until we figured he was close enough to be an easy shot, and Sinclair nailed him." Britt grinned, a little abashed. "Actually, we both shot at him, but I missed. Sinclair always has been a better shot."

Sinclair tried to look modest, but failed completely. "Young one, too," he explained. "It's the young ones who're the most curious. Should be real good eating."

"It's always the young ones whose curiosity gets 'em in trouble," Betsy Ann commented. "And not just among antelopes, either." She dug into her camp locker and pulled out her favorite skinning knife. "Here, skin him so's we can get him on a spit over the fire. And skin him careful. That's a real nice hide."

The next morning, the memory of the delicious dinner of roast antelope still fresh in everyone's mind, they followed a hogback between two shallow draws to scale Prospect Hill, which rose four hundred feet in about a mile.

Struggling up the hill with Mary's hand in hers, Matilda panted in the thin mountain air. Sweat poured down her back in spite of the chill remaining from the previous night. The wind evaporated the moisture, sending shivers through her body. Just before they reached the summit, Sinclair rode back for her.

"Here, you girls ride for a while," he said, dismounting and lifting Mary onto the pommel. Thankful for the chance to ride, Matilda swung up behind her. "I want to show you something." Leading White Star, he started up the hill.

In a few minutes, they stood at the crest and Sinclair waved his arm westward. "There's your first view of the Sweetwater Mountains."

"They're magnificent," she murmured, awed by the vista before her. "We must be almost on top of the world."

He grinned. "Won't be long now, and we will be."

Nine miles later, they crossed Horse Creek and stopped for a rest. "Have to recruit the stock after drivin' 'em up that steep hill," Gardner said. "Crossing the heavy sand ahead will be hard enough for 'em, even rested."

Matilda leaned against a nearby boulder, glad of the chance to stop. She found it more and more difficult to catch her breath as the trail grew higher and steeper. The only plants she saw growing were rabbit brush, the yellow flowers dotting the landscape in between the rocks, and wild sage. While she liked the smell of sage, she found it overpowered her.

"Come on, girls, let's gather some of this sagebrush for your grandmother's fire." Eager to help, and with an energy Matilda envied, the girls scurried to assist her.

"Watch out for rattlesnakes," her mother cautioned.

"Always," Matilda responded. "I don't want anyone practicing any of those wild cures for snakebite on me."

"Only indigo poultices work," Betsy Ann scowled. "All those other remedies are worse than useless. Can you imagine burning gunpowder in a bite?"

"I don't even want to. Come on, girls. Watch Lewis, Mother. He's still asleep." Thankfully, the swaying of the wagon had lulled Lewis to sleep. He became more difficult to care for each day. He kept trying to pull himself to his feet and required constant watching while awake. She regretted not being able to use the cradleboard any longer.

That afternoon, as Matilda slogged her way through the heavy sand, Sinclair rode up and hailed her. "Leave the girls with Mother. I want to show you something."

Curious, she mounted White Star behind her brother. Mary and Elizabeth immediately voiced loud protests at being left behind. To quell their complaints, she promised to tell them what their Uncle Sinclair showed her when she returned.

They rode about half a mile off the main trail to the top of a little rise. Sinclair pulled White Star to a halt and waved his hand towards the valley below.

"What is it you ... Oh!" Before her lay the remains of a wagon train. Scraps of burned timber, metal tires unmistakably from wagon wheels, and bleached animal bones left no doubt. She felt a stab of fright, her thoughts immediately on the three precious children she had left back at the wagon.

"Relax," Sinclair assured her. "It's several years old, at least. Look how white those bones are."

"But ... but, if they've burned one train, what's to say they won't burn another?"

"Nothing, but stop and think of the number of wagons that come through here every year. These poor souls were just in the wrong place at the wrong time."

Far from reassured, Matilda stared at the grisly scene before her. Thinking suddenly of the people who must have been in the wagons, she asked, "Did you go closer? Is there, I mean, did you ...." She stopped.

"No sign of anyone, if that's what you're trying to say. Only thing left is the burned out wagon remains you see and a few cattle bones. Whoever did this took everything that might have any value."

"Except the wagon wheels."

"I guess if you're used to a travois, wheels are useless. Besides, a lot of the ground the Injuns cover won't handle wheels."

Matilda shuddered. "Let's go back."

The next milestone was Saleratus Lake. It lay to the west of the road, in the midst of an arid wasteland.

"Britt," Matilda queried. "Is that a frozen lake?"

He grinned. "Nope, it's all saleratus. Washes out of the ground, then the water evaporates and leaves the carbonate. I hear the Mormons come out and collect it. They gather it up for free and sell it for twenty-five cents a pound in the city."

"You mean it's edible?"

"They say so, in small quantities anyways. Those who've tried it say it makes the bread kind of greenish. Has to be used in small amounts."

She stared at the masses of white powder, with the reddish-yellow salt grass growing by its edges, and marveled at yet another strange feature of the amazing countryside.

"Can't let the cattle near the grass," Britt continued. "Most of 'em won't eat it, but if they do, they get the alkali and it often kills 'em."

Matilda remembered Alf's descriptions of some of the emigrant treatments for alkali and thought with horror of anyone doing that to her dear Clarissa or poor old Bert or her beloved White Star. "We'll be sure and keep them away from it," she assured him. "And the deserted ranch?"

"Used to be Sweetwater Station, back in the days of the Pony Express. Been abandoned since then."

She took a drink from her canteen. Just looking at all that dust made her thirsty. Britt grinned down on her in sympathy.

"You've been doing just great," he said. "Another four miles will put us at Independence Rock. Just beyond the camp at the rock is Sweetwater Creek. That always has plenty of good water."

When they reached it, all Matilda could think was how out of place Independence Rock appeared, rising sixty to one hundred feet from the treeless, barren plain. Its dome shape, a thousand feet long and four to five hundred wide, made it look like a massive turtle rising out of the valley floor. Another group of wagons had already camped a few hundred yards away.

Matilda sighed with relief. "I'm so glad today is Saturday," she confessed to her mother. "I'm really ready for a day in one place." She nodded towards the other party, a group of about twenty wagons. "I wonder where they're from."

Her mother swung her head in the direction of the wagons and shrugged her shoulders. "Who knows? Will be good to rest a spell. And this looks like a good place for it."

Sweetwater Creek ran a few hundred yards from the Rock. Matilda and her mother approached it as they, accompanied by the two girls, gathered fuel for the evening's fire. When Matilda saw the creek, she cried, "Look, Mother. Imagine being able to wash in water that's cleaner than the clothes! I hope the whole river is like this." Jake, never far from her heels, reached into the creek with his tongue and lapped up some of the crystal-clear water.

Betsy Ann laughed. "They say it is. The Indians call it Pina Pa, Sweet Water. Sure looks mighty sweet to me. It's the only creek out here with no alkali along its banks."

A shot rang out, followed by a woman's scream. Jake barked once, then fell silent, huddled close to Matilda, who stopped in her tracks, clutching the armload of sagebrush tightly to her breast. "That came from those wagons," she gasped, her eyes wide. Mary and Elizabeth ran to her and clung to her skirt.

Several men started on a run towards the sound, Sinclair and Britt among them. The woman continued to scream. The sound echoed across the prairie and through Matilda's head. She felt her skin prickle.

They waited, not knowing what else to do. Soon Sinclair returned, shaking his head.

"What happened, Uncle Sinclair?" Mary asked in a quavery voice, still clinging to Matilda's skirt. "Did a bad man shoot someone? Was it an Indian?"

Sinclair shook his head. "No, Sweetheart. The man shot himself pulling his gun out of the wagon by the barrel."

"By the barrel!" Matilda exclaimed. "How could anyone be so foolish?"

"We'll never know. He killed himself on the spot. Bullet went right through his heart. Leaves a wife and five children."

"Oh, no!"

"Oh, yes, and, judging from the looks of his widow, number six is not far behind."

Matilda only shook her head.

The next morning, out of respect for the grieving widow, their whole contingent attended funeral services for the unfortunate Mr. Ringo, though the man was a stranger to them.

"Only right," Gardner observed. "Man dies, no matter how, rest of us have to see he's buried proper."

Matilda stood at the edge of the group gathered around the graveside. She listened to the voices of several men praising the dead man and the muffled sobs of his widow, Mary. The sight of her own husband dead in his coffin would not leave Matilda's mind. Finally, unable to bear any more, she turned and walked away.

Chapter 43

Independence Rock to South Pass

ON MONDAY, June 20, they left Independence Rock and crossed the Sweetwater, at that point seventy to eighty feet wide but only axle deep. Still, water swirled about the wheels in the swift current.

Shortly after they started, one of the mules on Britt's wagon developed a limp. Sinclair, driving the wagon for his brother, pulled out of line and stopped.

"What's the matter?" Matilda walked up as Sinclair examined the injured hoof. "Did he pick up a rock?"

Sinclair lifted the hoof and shook his head. "Lost a shoe," he reported, "and managed to cut himself on something. We'll swap him for one of the other mules, give the cut a chance to heal. We'll get him re-shod at the next black-smith shop. Supposed to be one just up ahead."

The mule, meanwhile, evidently decided the best way to relieve the pain in his hoof was to lie down. The mule in the trace beside him, in obvious agreement, settled himself comfortably as well. Sinclair, seeing his father's wagon out of earshot, swore as he struggled to get the mules back on their feet so he could unharness them.

"Britt," he roared to his brother, "bring a spare mule. And bring Weldon with you. I need your help."

Matilda, unable to restrain herself any longer, sat down on a convenient boulder, shaking with laughter. It took nearly an hour to get the other mule into harness, the lame mule out of the way, and his partner back on his feet. Half the train had passed before Weldon took up the reins and the wagon resumed its place in line.

A short distance farther on, Sinclair, again mounted on

White Star, rode back for Matilda. "'Tilda," he grinned, "you've got to see this." Handing Lewis to her mother in the wagon, she climbed up behind him and they rode off.

When he pulled White Star to a stop, they dismounted and Matilda stood awestruck at the sight before her. The Sweetwater flowed for at least a quarter of a mile through a chasm of perpendicular black rock that stood over three hundred feet high. From the crest of the hill, Matilda saw the valley where the Sweetwater meandered its way down from what must be South Pass. To the right, as far as she could see, ranged a nearly perpendicular wall of gray, granite rock. To the south, rugged peaks glittered with snow.

Britt strolled up with Mary and his son, Owen.

"Look, Mama," Mary cried. "See how the river goes right through the mountain?"

"They call it 'Devil's Gate'," Sinclair told Matilda. "Good name for it. Those rocks are black as Lucifer himself. Britt says this is the place where Will Hodge almost hit Alf with his boot."

"And Alf was right," Britt commented. "Climbing that rock was sheer foolishness. I hear some young lady died when she got too close to the edge and fell. She's supposed to be buried around here some place."

"The poor thing," Matilda murmured.

"I take it you're not going to try again, Britt," Sinclair said with a smile.

"Not me. Too old fourteen years ago. Not any younger now." He looked up at the massive tower of ebony rock. "Did I ever tell you how the Indians say this formed?"

"No, tell us, Uncle Britt," Mary begged. Matilda smiled. Mary always loved a story.

"The Shoshone and Arapaho say years ago an evil spirit, a powerful beast with enormous tusks, roamed up and down the Sweetwater Valley. The creature would not allow the Indians to hunt. A prophet told the tribes that to get rid of this beast they had to destroy it, so they attacked by launching thousands of arrows. The enraged beast, with a mighty thrust of its tusks, ripped apart the mountain and disappeared through the gap. According to the story, no one ever saw the monster again, and the Indians were free to hunt and camp in the valley. And the mountain has looked like that ever since."

"And why is the rock so black?" Matilda asked.

"Uncle Sinclair says it's from a volcano," Mary pronounced, with all the wisdom of her five years. "He says Colonel Fremont says it in his book."

"Then it must be so," agreed Matilda. "How could we dispute the sainted Fremont?" She shook her head. "No wonder Alf said you have to see this country to believe it."

Half a mile more brought them to the Devil's Gate Station, operated by yet another French-Canadian with a squaw and large brood of children.

Matilda felt a twinge of guilt as they passed the station. She hadn't written a single line to Caroline since leaving Red Buttes. She regretted not keeping up her correspondence to her sister as she had promised, but found it harder and harder to stay awake in the evening, often falling asleep as soon as she got the children settled. The reasonably smooth level road had tempted her to ride in the wagon, at least until the rising sun drove away the morning chill.

Sinclair rode beside them. He gestured to the gray, barren mountains to the north. "They call those the Rattlesnake Hills," he said.

"For good reason, I'm sure," Gardner grunted. "Easy, Bert," he said as the ox who pulled in the left rear trace slipped on a rock. Bert regained his easy stride.

"Supposed to have mountain lions and grizzly bears, too," Sinclair added helpfully.

"Lions and bears?" Elizabeth's voice quavered.

"And they're coming to eat you!" Mary added, pretending to be a bear and growling at her younger sister.

"Sinclair!" Matilda exclaimed in exasperation.

Sinclair laughed and rode off.

When they reached the anticipated location of the blacksmith shop on the Sweetwater, they found only the crumbled remains of several buildings. One of the men, in response to Sinclair's questions, said, "Oh, sure, that was Seminoe's place. Abandoned in '55 or '56, I forget which. Not long after a war party come through and run off all his stock. His wife, now, she were a Snake Injun, but reckon he didn't figger that'd save his scalp. No love lost between a Sioux or a 'rapaho an' a Snake." The man laughed at his own joke and scratched his side with a vigor that told Matilda he probably had good reason to do so. She shuddered, thinking of the number of bugs that probably shared the man's clothing with him.

"Them buildings, now," he continued, "they helped save some of them hand-cart Mormons. Several bunches of 'em got caught out here and took shelter in the buildings." He chuckled. "They 'bout did themselves in, they did. Started takin' down walls for their fires and caved in the roof. Volunteer out of Salt Lake City, name of Jones, he came out and helped rescue 'em an' stayed the winter, lookin' after their stuff. Told me all about it, he did." The man shook his head. "They was all so sure God would protect 'em. No one ever told 'em it takes more'n God to protect you from the winter out here." He strode off, scratching the other side.

Matilda and Sinclair watched him go.

"We-ell," Sinclair remarked, "looks like that mule's going to have a little longer for the cut to heal. I'd hate to have to re-shoe him myself. Marcy's guide book is a little out of date."

"I think it just goes to show not all the answers are in books," Matilda observed.

A few miles farther on, the trail passed another 'pond' filled with powdery alkali. As the sun rose higher, Matilda kept her face hidden with her sunbonnet. The glare from the sun hurt her eyes. Bored with riding in the wagon, and tired of coughing from the dust all the animal hooves stirred up, she persuaded Sinclair to allow her to borrow White Star. She took Elizabeth in front of her and Mary sat behind, clinging to her mother's waist.

They rode ahead of the train, out of the dust, and reached the top of a little rise. "Look, girls," she cried. She pointed west to the high peaks that rose among the fleecy clouds resting upon the horizon. "Those have to be the Rocky Mountains."

"The highest one, that's Fremont's Peak," Sinclair advised, riding up on Britt's horse. Matilda smiled. She should have known Sinclair would not be afoot for long. "Over 13,000 feet high. It's at the apex of the Wind River Range of the Rockies. Got snow on it all year around."

"Just imagine, girls," Matilda told them. "A place where the snow never melts."

"We don't have to live there, do we, Mama?" Mary's voice quavered.

"Don't worry." Matilda patted the little hand at her waist in reassurance. "Your Uncle Alf says it never snows where he lives in Hicksville."

Below them lay the valley of the Sweetwater, a tapestry of green grass and wild flowers. Aspen and beech trees lined the stream, with pine and cedar scattered about in the nooks and crannies of the rocks. Looking down on the beauty before her, Matilda felt a deep pleasure almost like a pain. Thinking of the barren wasteland they had just crossed made her appreciate it all the more.

"I think," she observed to the uncomprehending children, "that when we are surrounded by beauty all the time, we never see it the way we do when we come upon it in the places we least expect it."

They continued up the valley of the Sweetwater, resting for several hours in mid-day to recruit people and animals alike. Matilda found just a short walk made her heart pound and sent sharp pains through her chest. Britt was right. The high elevations were much harder to cross. The deceptive warmth of the day faded by late afternoon and by dark, she shivered in the piercing cold.

They camped for the night at Split Rock Station. Matilda did not know whether to be reassured or frightened by the presence of a garrison of at least fifty soldiers. If the government felt a need for so many soldiers, perhaps the rumors that persisted up and down the trail possessed more merit than she had so far credited to them.

She tucked the children to bed in the tent and wrapped a shawl tightly about her shoulders. The sun, a cold, red ball, hung low in the western sky. Matilda stood watching the shadow of the mountain creep closer as the crimson globe sank lower and lower. She shivered and looked out past the log cabin that filled the role of Stage Station at the number of horses in the large corral. Tents dotted the meadow below the corral. She swatted at a mosquito buzzing past her ear and sympathized with the soldiers. The mosquitoes must be even worse down in the meadow. At least where she stood the wind kept some of them away.

Sinclair came up beside her and wrapped a blanket around her. "You're shaking. Mother says you'll take a chill if you don't stop standing out in the cold this way every night. She's liable to decide to dose you with some of that vile Number Six compound of hers. It's guaranteed to cure any chill." He chuckled. "As well as take the skin off of any mortal throat."

Matilda ignored his observations. "Why are there so many soldiers?" she asked. "Are we in any danger?" The wreckage of the wagons Sinclair showed her remained vivid in her mind. Her fears for her children never completely left her.

"Relax. They're just a precaution. I guess they did have quite a few attacks last year, but only on smaller groups. We've got over thirty wagons."

Somewhat reassured, she stared at the top of the mountain that gave the station its name. The sun still touched it, but at an angle so that shadows made the deep cleft even more pronounced. She smiled. "Look, Sinclair. The mountain looks like a giant split it with a huge ax."

"Knights and castles and now giants with huge axes? This country is affecting your head, Sis." He dodged the blow she aimed at him and grinned. "You're right. It does look like someone hit it with an ax. But come in out of the cold now. They say we can see this for two days, so you'll have plenty of time to exercise your imagination over it."

Shortly after leaving the next morning, less than two miles from the camp at Split Rock, they passed a rectangular mass of gray clay on the left of the trail. Matilda pointed it out to Mary and Elizabeth. "See, girls? That looks like a mansion."

Mary observed it critically. "It's falling down. See all the piles of dirt around it?"

Matilda hugged her. "You're getting as skeptical as your Uncle Sinclair. Come on. Let's pick some of these pretty flowers and surprise your grandmother with a bouquet."

The next landmark they reached was Three Crossings Station.

"An appropriate name," Gardner remarked. "We've crossed the Sweetwater three times in the last mile and a half. It just wanders all over this meadow. Good thing it's not deep."

"I want to see if the Miss Moore Burton refers to in his book is still here," Sinclair told Matilda, out of earshot of their father.

"Why?" she asked.

"She sounds like a real interesting lady. Burton says her husband brought her from England when he converted from the Church of England to the Church of Utah."

"Then why are they clear out here? Why didn't they go on to Salt Lake City?"

Sinclair grinned. "Because the good lady found out that the Abrahams in the Church of Utah are not content with a Sarah. They also feel entitled to an unlimited supply of Hagars."

"What?" Matilda gasped.

"Shhh. Pa will hear you. I guess she just put her foot down and her husband couldn't get her any closer to the City of the Saints. He managed to get himself a job out here running the stage station. Burton raved about the good food, so I guess they've made a success of it. From what he writes, I guess he's real hard to please."

To Matilda's disappointment, they did not even pause as they passed the station, but kept on until they camped at a spot called Ice Springs. She had looked forward to meeting the intrepid Miss Moore.

When they reached Ice Springs, she felt they had to be getting close to the top. "If it gets much harder to breath, I'm going to have to ride in the wagon along with the children and old Mrs. Martin," she panted to Sinclair and Britt as they rode up to her.

"Relax. How would you like some ice in a cup of lemonade?"

"Ice? You mean they really have ice in this place? I thought they called it Ice Springs because the place gets so cold at night."

"Well, that too," Britt grinned. "But it's really because it stays so cold here the part of the bog that's insulated by the marsh never thaws. At least not until late in the summer." He and Sinclair took spades and dug away the top of the marsh. To Matilda's astonishment, they actually found a layer of ice.

They continued the upward struggle over the rocky trail until finally, on Saturday, June 25, they reached Strawberry Creek. There the road left the Sweetwater and headed for South Pass. Excitement mounted in Matilda. Soon they would cross the Continental Divide, and in another two weeks they would be in Great Salt Lake City. But dismay stirred in her breast as she stood beside Sinclair and looked at the hill they had to climb to reach the summit.

"Oh, my!" Her eyes widened in horror. "Do we really have to go up that steep hill?"

Sinclair did not reply. He did not need to. The marks of thousands of wagon wheels scarring the barren, rocky slope gave her the answer.

"Good thing tomorrow's Sabbath," Gardner remarked. "Gives the animals a chance to recruit." He shook his head. "Going to be a tough climb."

But the knowledge that two more days would see them at the Pass buoyed everyone's spirits. After supper, Matt Andrews pulled out the fiddle he bought from another traveler, his own lost in the disaster at Julesburg, and began to play. Another fiddler joined him. Most of the troop gathered in the long summer twilight for a hoe-down.

Gardner, whose Methodism frowned upon dancing, scowled as Matilda took the Ridgeway baby from his mother so Mr. and Mrs. Ridgeway could dance.

"Dancin' is the Devil's tool," he muttered.

"Now, Gardner," Betsy Ann reproached him, "they been havin' a tough time the last few weeks. Good for 'em to get out and kick up their heels a bit."

Matilda, tapping her toes surreptitiously to the beat,

wished she could dance as well. She contented herself with rocking tiny Arthur Ridgeway, Jr.. He slept in her arms, his rosy cheeks chapped from the sun. She smiled down on him. He had grown in the short time since his birth, she mused. She could not even remember the date, but he couldn't be over a couple of weeks old.

He roused in his sleep and yawned, stretching his chubby arms above his head. She laughed and nuzzled her nose in the folds of baby fat at his neck. He was an adorable baby. She felt a fondness for him she had never developed for the other four babies she and her mother had delivered. When the dancing stopped and his mother reclaimed him, she almost regretted having to hand him back.

Mrs. Ridgeway's eyes met Matilda's. "You're young and pretty," she said. "You'll marry again and have more babies."

Matilda's eyes filled with tears as she watched them walk away. Her love for Lewis surged through her. Marry again? How could she ever marry again? Surely she would never find another man she could love with the depth of feeling she had felt for Lewis.

The tears overflowed and spilled down her cheeks, glistening in the last rays of sunlight as the sun slid behind the mountain. Her sharp-eyed mother spotted them, but said nothing. Instead, she took Matilda in her arms and the two stood silent until the gathering gloom enfolded them in darkness.

The next morning, they started the final assault on the rocky road.

"This is the roughest so far," Gardner commented to Betsy Ann as they struggled across yet another ravine. The oxen's hooves slipped on the loose rock. "Shouldn't have listened to Marcy. Should have used horses. Oxen too slow, mules too stubborn," he grumbled. "When we get to that city of the Saints, I'm gonna buy me some horses."

Matilda walked beside the wagon with Mary. "Walking sure is easier than riding," she told the child beside her. "Being tossed around inside that wagon has left me bruised and battered." She laughed. "Little Lewis is the lucky one. He can sleep anywhere."

The sun rose higher, and so did the temperature. She wondered how it could be so hot in the day and so cold at night.

"Mama, carry me," Mary begged.

"I can't, Darling," Matilda panted. "It's all I can do to carry myself." She waved Sinclair over. "Let White Star carry you."

"White Star's beginning to feel the strain too," Sinclair grinned as he dismounted and lifted Mary into the saddle. "Marcy may have been wrong about the blacksmith shop at Devil's Station, but he sure knew what he was talking about when he said the animals need to rest more often in the high mountains."

Matilda stroked White Star's muzzle and hugged her neck. "You're a good girl, my darling," she told the horse. "Please try to carry both of us for a while." Matilda swung up behind Mary, wishing she had a pair of the Bloomers a few of the women sported, to the strong disapproval of Gardner Randolph. When Matilda brought the subject up, he announced they were immodest in the extreme. He firmly disapproved of Amelia Bloomer, and anything connected with her. Remembering the woman at Horse Shoe Creek, Matilda had to admit her father had a point.

Sinclair pointed to the crest of the next ridge. "That should be the top," he said. "Want to ride up and stand on top of the world? Come on, White Star. We'll take it slow." Sinclair walked up the incline, leading the horse.

From the crest, they continued for another half-mile, then gazed down on the other side to Pacific Springs.

"Look, Darling," Matilda told Mary. "See the creek running down into the valley? That's the first river we have ever seen that runs to the Pacific Ocean." Mary's eyes widened and Matilda continued. "We're right on top of the whole continent of North America. This is the Great Divide."

"Yep," Sinclair pronounced, quoting from the battered copy of Fremont's report he carried in White Star's saddlebag. "It feeds into the Green River, then to the Colorado, to the Gulf of California, and out into the Pacific. Everything on the other side finds its way to the Mississippi."

"Mama," the ever practical Mary suggested, "why don't we just take a boat?"

Chapter 44

South Pass to Fort Bridger

July 5, 1864
FORT BRIDGER

Dear Caroline,

We arrived here at Fort Bridger late yesterday. It's located on Black's Fork of the Green River and is an oasis of civilization in the middle of the wilderness. The trail follows Black's Fork across a barren, windswept plateau, and although the elevation has been dropping since crossing South Pass, I understand we are still over 6600 feet high. At least it's a little easier to breathe.

The post sutler, William Carter, came with General Johnston's army in 1857. He liked the country and stayed. Most folks call him 'Judge Carter.' Some even call the fort 'Carter's Fort,' but the official name is Bridger after the famous mountain man Jim Bridger who built the place. In 1853, Mr. Bridger sold it to the Mormons and they burned all the buildings when they abandoned it as the army approached in 1857. (Remember the Mormon War?) Everything here has been rebuilt since then.

Judge Carter's wife's name is Mary. She invited Mother and Sarah and Mrs. Ridgeway and me to tea. She has a lovely board-and-batten home. All the other buildings at the Fort are log cabins. She says they started building the house in 1858, and laughs when she tells how it has grown. Every time she had another child her husband added a room. It's a big house, so goodness knows how many children she has. She never said and I never thought to ask, I was just so overwhelmed with the whole place. It seemed so strange to be in a real house after all these weeks of camping.

Judge Carter's store carries all kinds of canned goods and dry goods, and every piece of wagon and harness gear you can imagine. The prices were a little more than we cared to pay, so fortunately we didn't need anything. They say things cost a little less in the City of the Saints. I, for one, will certainly be glad of the chance to buy some fresh vegetables.

The scenery continues to surprise me. We will cross miles of nothing but alkali and sage, then come upon a lovely little meadow filled with flowers. At one point, we even had ice for our lemonade.

Nothing however, can compare with standing on the top of South Pass and looking down into the meadows around Pacific Springs. We stood, literally, on the top of the world, at the Continental Divide. We spent the whole day climbing up that last rocky hill to reach the summit. Mary and I rode White Star for the last mile. All of us were sweaty and dusty. When we reached the top, I looked around in awe at the vast, tumbled mountains, at the snow-clad peaks, (yes, snow in July), and let the cool wind blow across my face.

When Sinclair pointed out to Mary how all the rivers flowed west from Pacific Springs, and lead to the Pacific Ocean, she suggested we take a boat. I let Sinclair get himself out of that one.

On the way up, the Ridgeway wagon lost a wheel. That wheel went bounding and leaping back down the hill we had struggled so hard all day to climb. Fortunately it didn't hit anyone, or they would have been killed on the spot. It barely missed one man. You should have heard what he said! I didn't understand half the words, but I sure knew what he meant. Pa lectured all of us after supper that night on why we should never use such words.

No one wanted to go back to the bottom of the hill to retrieve the wheel, let alone try to remount it while we were on that steep slope, so Sinclair borrowed an idea from Marcy's book and the men made a travois for the axle. It worked pretty well. They attached two poles to the front axle and strung them out behind and lashed them to the back axle. The wagon kind of tilted, and needed two extra mules to help pull, but they made it to the top.

We spent Tuesday, the 28th, at Pacific Springs to let animals and people alike rest after that hard pull. Everyone needed a chance to make repairs anyway. The boys had to drive the cattle about a mile away from camp to find grass, but we had plenty of water. Mr. Ridgeway replaced his wheel with a spare he bought from one of the other wagons. The men say they're going to remember that trick with the poles, though, because it sure came in handy. Sinclair just looked smug, especially when Britt had to concede maybe reading wasn't always a waste of time.

On Wednesday we reached Dry Sandy Creek. We had only covered fifteen miles, but traveling at this altitude so exhausted us we stayed the night. Twelve miles beyond the Dry Sandy we reached what is now called Sublette's cutoff. Britt says he and Sam and Alf took it in '50, only everyone called it Greenwood cutoff then. Just goes to show how fleeting fame can be. Everyone's forgotten poor old Caleb Greenwood. From what Britt says, I guess he was quite a character.

Eight wagons left us at the cutoff, bound for Oregon. The Andrews family left with them. They had planned all along to go to Oregon. Their group thought about taking the new Lander's Road to Fort Hall that the government paid seventy thousand dollars to build. It cuts about a hundred miles off of the trip for the emigrants headed for Oregon. They decided to stay with the larger group until we crossed South Pass. I don't know why. I sure wouldn't mind making the trip a hundred miles shorter.

Matt bought another wagon at Fort Laramie. Remember,

I told you they lost their wagon at Julesburg. He also bought some more dolls for his girls, so before they left, Susan Andrews returned Mary's doll. Good thing. Mary shared happily as long as she and Susan played together every day, but I don't think Mary ever really considered Dolly's change of ownership permanent. Mrs. Andrews has promised to write and tell us how they fared. I gave her Alf's address in Hicksville.

I miss them. It's surprising how quickly close friendships form out here. It's hard to explain, but there's something about the shared struggle that binds together people who might not even be casual friends at home.

On Thursday, we drove fifteen miles to the little Sandy, then on Friday, eighteen miles to the Big Sandy. The Big Sandy is a major feeder of the Green River. The local Indians call it Wagahongopa, which means 'Glistening Gravel Water'. It's a good name for it. The water is clear and the current very swift. Flowers filled the surrounding meadow. Blue lupine, purple daisies, white mountain heath. Mary and Elizabeth picked a bouquet for their grandmother. One field had enough milkweed to stuff a dozen bed ticks, and you should have seen the butterflies.

You'd think they could come up with better names for three creeks so close to together, but 'Sandy' is a good description. They are mostly sand bars. Shallow crossings, but the deep sand made it necessary to add extra mules or oxen to each wagon. Sometimes the wheels sank almost to the axle. I felt so sorry for the animals. Poor old Bert has been working so faithfully. Sometimes at night I go out to where the cattle are corralled and scratch behind his ears. He does so love that little bit of attention. The trip has been very hard on him. He is ten years old, after all.

Big green-headed flies have been a major problem, especially for the animals. Those wretched flies sting like wasps, and we have to protect the cattle with a coating of grease or the flies drive them mad. Then dust sticks to the grease and makes them look like ghost cattle.

Pa is talking of selling the oxen when we get to the Great Salt Lake. He wants to buy horses. Says oxen are too slow. It breaks my heart to think of selling Bert, but I can't think of any practical reason not to. At least it would spare him the hard trip across the coming desert. It's just that he seems like a member of the family. Pa, of course, ridicules any such notions. Affection for horses he can understand. Mules and oxen, never. Especially mules. He hates mules even worse now than when we left.

At the Big Sandy is Simpson's Gulch or Simpson's Hollow. In '57, during the Mormon War, Mormon riders under a man named Lot Smith captured and burned a group of supply wagons destined for General Johnston's army at Camp Scott. Without the supplies, the army could not reach Salt Lake City, so he saved the city from attack. Britt says that was the Mormons' first act of open rebellion against the Federal Government. Pa grumbled that if the position of President had been held by a firmer hand than that of poor old Mr. Buchanan, the scenes of Nauvoo would have been repeated at Great Salt Lake City. Mother hushed him, like she always does when he gets started on politics.

But Mr. Burton spoke very highly of Mr. Smith. He took great care not to kill anyone, and even gave the wagoneers two wagons and enough supplies to return home. I guess the story is true enough. Two black semicircles still char the ground. The grass is growing up, but you can still see where it happened.

On Saturday, July 2, we reached the Upper Ford of the Green River after travailing for 21 miles. We pushed on, knowing we would lay over on Sunday to recruit, but it made a very long day. We didn't get supper over until nine o'clock. Thank Heavens the days are so long. The Green River must have filled a larger channel at one time. Sinclair

*says that's the reason the whole valley is filled with flat table-
land and elevated terraces. Mother tells him he's going to
ruin his eyes, reading by the flickery light of the fire like he
does.*

*The next morning, we decided to go down river the seven
miles to Lombard's Ferry at the Lower Ford. Many wagons
cross at the Upper Ford, but the water looked so deep and
swift Pa and Britt and the other men decided to use the ferry.
We had to pay $1.50 a wagon, but Mother and I were both
glad. The Indians around here call the Green River the Piya
Ogwe, or 'Great Water'. It's about 300 feet wide now, and
about three feet deep, but they say at flood stage it reaches
up to 800 feet wide and six feet deep. Then everyone has
to use the ferry.*

*The little grocery store at the crossing didn't have much
to sell. They had some jelly they make from the buffalo
berries that grow around here, and some whiskey they call
Valley Tan made in Great Salt Lake City. I must tell you
why they call it 'Valley Tan' whiskey. Seems the first industry
in the Salt Lake Valley was leather tanning, so they call all
home industry products 'Valley Tan'.*

*We crossed Ham's Fork on a fine government bridge
about 500 feet above the mouth of the fork. They didn't
even charge toll. I wish you could have seen the station
at Ham's Fork. It's just two tiny rooms of dry stone built up
against a cliff, I guess to save them the work of making a back
wall. I have never seen so many flies. Flies darkened the
table and swarmed over everything on it. The stage came
by while we were there. The poor stage passengers had a
choice of eating in that filthy place or going hungry. I suspect many of them choose to go hungry. I assume the station
master was Mormon, for he had two wives (or two women,
anyway. I didn't ask). They had a large brood of the dirtiest
children I have ever seen in my life.*

We crossed Smith's Fork before we started following

Black's Fork. We forded Black's Fork three times before we reached Fort Bridger, but fortunately accomplished the crossings without incident. We have had pretty good camps along the way. Sometimes we have had to move the cattle several miles from camp to get grass, but otherwise no problems.

We lost one of the babies Mother and I delivered. Poor little mite got diarrhea, and it turned into the bloody flux. Nothing helped. We were all so sad for the poor mother. A lot of people have suffered from the flux, but luckily cholera has not made an appearance, and usually a few days clears up the problem.

At least we are going mostly downhill, and it isn't quite as cold at night. The days are starting to get fiercely hot again, with a dry heat that I can feel sucking the moisture out of my body. During the day, the temperature inside the wagon reaches 95 degrees. Poor Jake can't decide which is worse, so he gets in and out of the wagon until Pa has threatened to leave him at the next station. He'd never do it, of course. He's as fond of Jake as everyone else.

The air is like a blast from a stove, and the sun is a blaze of fire in the sky. There are no trees to speak of around the stations, for all have been cut down. You would think they would have sense enough to leave a few by the buildings to provide a little shade, but they seem compelled to hew every tree in easy reach.

The air is so dry I drink all the time and still feel thirsty. When the wind blows, it blows dust all over. When the air is still, mirages surround us, even more so than on the trip from Illinois to Kansas. Some people are even fooled by them, thinking it is real water. When I tell Britt how parched my mouth gets he just laughs and tells me to wait until we get down along the Humboldt. He also says that on the Humboldt Sink, the mirages are more dangerous. Sometimes people in need of water ignore a real pool, thinking it is just *another mirage.*

We spent the Fourth of July traveling. It seemed so strange. No fireworks, not even a special picnic. Remember the Fourth of July picnic I went to with Curtis Stewart? That seems so long ago. Sarah says he hasn't married yet. If I had married Curtis, my life would have been much different, but I have no regrets. What Lewis and I had together was very special.

We did have another hoe-down to celebrate, though without Matt we had only one fiddle. Mr. Ridgeway played his mouth harp, and Mr. Martin beat time on a kettle. One wagon had a few fire-crackers, but we did not dare set them off. Giles says we're in Paiute country and, as he put it, 'don't pay to raise too much ruckus'. We took him at his word and kept a low profile. We even kept the cooking fires down. He says the river is named for a trapper named Black killed by a band of fifty Blackfoot Indians in 1832.

We are leaving Fort Bridger in the morning, and should be in Salt Lake City within a week. Then we will be half-way there. Some of the men are saying we should go a little faster, maybe not rest on Sundays, but Pa refuses to travel on the Sabbath, even if it means staying the winter at a settlement of the eastern side of the Sierras. I'm inclined to agree. Mother and I really like the day we have to catch up on laundry and baking. I'm glad there are enough settlements along the way so we could winter east of the Sierras should it get too late in the season to cross in safety.

I look forward to your letter in Salt Lake City.

Love,

'Tilda

Chapter 45

Fort Bridger to Salt Lake City

THEY LEFT Fort Bridger at dawn and an hour later again crossed Black's Fork.

"I don't think this is Black's Fork at all," Matilda grumbled to Sinclair. "How can we keep crossing the same river? I'll bet they don't even know if this is the same one."

Sinclair grinned. "Giles says in another hour we'll pass Sugarloaf Butte. Says it's a famous landmark. We follow a bench around the north end of Bridger Butte. He also says, if you want, we can ride to the top and see for miles, all the way back to Fort Bridger."

"I decline. I've seen enough scenery to hold me for a long time."

Britt heard her and chuckled. "I said you'd see all you wanted by the time we got to the Great Salt Lake. Old timers on this road say folks get so sick of scenery they'd pay a thousand dollars just to look at a blank wall."

Matilda gave him a faint smile. "Well, I wouldn't go that far." She turned to the child beside her. "Come, Mary. The wagon is getting ahead of us."

Two days later they passed the remains of the Needle Rock Pony Express Station and, as jaded by the scenery as she was, Matilda had to marvel at the jagged rock formation on Yellow Creek that everyone called The Needles. From there, they entered Echo Canyon, where red rock walls rose hundreds of feet straight up.

"Used to call this Red Fork Canyon when I first came through, back in '47," Giles told her. "They say Jim Bridger renamed it Echo Canyon." He grinned down at Mary, who stood beside her mother. "Claimed 'fore he'd go to bed, he'd shout 'time to get up, Jim,' then go to sleep. The echo would bounce back down the canyon at dawn and wake him up."

Mary's eyes grew wide. "He can't do that!" she protested in disbelief.

"Probably not. But a shot fired in this canyon will echo up to twenty times." Giles chuckled. "I remember once a Paiute took a shot at the stock. By the time that one shot stopped echoing, we thought we were surrounded."

At the Canyon Stage Station, Sinclair pointed out Castle Rock. Mary looked at it in disappointment. "It doesn't look like a castle to me," she declared.

"Use your imagination, Darling," Matilda said. "You're as bad as your grandmother."

The next morning, while they strolled along the canyon following the creek, Giles pointed out the fortifications put up by the Mormons during the brief Mormon War in 1857.

"How in the world did they get up there?" Matilda wanted to know.

Giles laughed. "Ain't too hard from t'other side. But they never had to use 'em. Lot Smith burnin' all the army's supplies meant the soldiers had to hole up for the winter at Fort Bridger. By the next spring, things had cooled off considerable. So's instead of a battle with guns, they had one with words. Old Brigham ain't never lost a battle of words yet, and he persuaded Johnston to take his army and settle down to Camp Floyd. We go past there after we leave the city."

As they progressed, the canyon narrowed until it reached the Weber River. There they turned south along the Weber to Silver Creek thence to Silver Creek Station. They did not stop, but continued on to the mouth of Parley's Canyon. When they reached the Parley Canyon Station, Matilda wiped her overheated brow with a handkerchief she dipped in the cool water trickling down into the trough built against the cliff behind the rude building. The lengthening shadows warned her night would soon be upon them.

Sinclair joined her and laughed at the expression on her face. "Be glad it's cooled off," he said. "They say it got to over 100 degrees here today."

She sighed as she looked ruefully at the thick coating of red dust on the once clean piece of cloth in her hand. "The walls in Echo Canyon were lovely, but this dust is turning everything we own the color of an old brick."

"Cheer up," he grinned. "Giles says it's only ten, twelve miles more to Great Salt Lake City. You can have a real bath in the bathhouse, and even get all of the clothes washed at a real laundry if you want."

"Marvelous. Simply marvelous. I haven't soaked in a tub for so long I've almost forgotten how it feels. I think even Mary is ready for a bath."

Sinclair hugged her and stepped back. Putting his hands on her shoulders, their eyes met. "You know, Sis," he said, his usually teasing voice solemn, "you've been a real trooper."

The warmth of his praise flooded through her, sweeping away the fatigue.

Sinclair gave her another hug and released her with a grin. "Giles also says you can meet Mr. Eph Hanks here. He's one of the triumvirate of Mormon desperadoes, along with Hickman and the late Mr. Rockwell, who all those anti-Mormon writers call 'vile villains'. He's a Destroying Angel."

"Destroying Angel? What on earth is that?"

"Men set apart by the Church to arrange for the permanent disappearance of obnoxious citizens."

"What!" Matilda recoiled in horror.

"You're the one as wanted to meet Jack Slade. You should meet Mr. Hanks. He's actually a very pleasant fellow."

Matilda scooped another handful of the cool water and

splashed it on her face. "Thanks," she grimaced. "I think I can survive without the honor."

Finally, on Sunday, July 10th, the wagons struggled over the last ten miles to the crest of the hill. Before them lay the valley of the Great Salt Lake. Gardner had yielded to pressure from his fellow travelers to continue over Sunday to save time, as they planned to spend several days in Salt Lake City. At the summit, he stood beside Matilda and they stared out over the valley. A broken wall of light blue mountains limned the western horizon. To the south, bluffs buttressed the southern end of the lake. The eastern ends of the bluffs sank in steps and terraces into the basin of the Jordan River, green and yellow with ripening corn. The sun, sinking behind the far mountains, bathed the whole valley with a crepuscular golden light.

Before them, a semicircular sweep of hilltops shut out all but a a few spans of the valley. The hills bore the remains of a shaggy forest. Axes rang in the distance. The sound told Matilda these trees were destined to suffer the same fate as others along the path of the stage stations. Threads of snow clung to the highest mountains.

Gardner took off his hat and held it over his heart. "Daughter," he said to Matilda, "I thought it unholy to travel on Sunday, but I see now God meant us to spend the Sabbath on this spot. Surely no place shows His hand more clearly."

Matilda, gazing across the magnificent sight which had even the unimaginative Sinclair gaping in awe, panted to regain her breath after the climb. Then she looked down at the steep incline they would have to descend.

After their father strode back towards the line of wagons, she turned to Sinclair and said, "I hope he feels the same way after we get down that slope and up the next rise."

The next morning, they struggled to the top of the last

ridge and before them lay Great Salt Lake City. Matilda stared in awe. After weeks of crossing barren plains and gaunt mountains, broken only by a few rude settlements and traders' shacks, there, in the middle of the vast wasteland, stood a magnificent city.

Betsy Ann chuckled at Matilda's expression. "Well," she commented, "they may be heathen, but they sure look to be hard-working heathen."

Sinclair rode up. "Look, 'Tilda. Strawberries! They have whole fields of 'em." He offered her his hat, filled with large, red berries.

Matilda inhaled. "Oh, Sinclair, they smell wonderful." She selected a choice berry, popped it in her mouth, and sighed with pleasure. After weeks of boiled beef, dried vegetables, beans, and cornbread, with an occasional bowl of stewed dried apples or peaches, the tang of fresh fruit sent spasms of ecstasy through her taste buds.

Gardner joined them and helped himself to one of the plump berries. "Goin' to town tomorrow and get myself a shave. Been a long time since I had a shave in a real barber shop."

"Don't eat too many," Betsy Ann cautioned. "Too much fresh fruit after all these weeks without can cause griping of the bowels."

Giles heard her and agreed. "Seen it happen. Happened to me once. After a long time of boiled buffalo, beans, and bread, I ate a whole hatful of fresh peaches when I hit this place." He chuckled at the memory of his own discomfiture. "Sure tasted good, but I paid the price."

Matilda grimaced. "Okay. Just one more."

They camped two miles outside of town, in the area designated for passing wagon trains. Britt and Andrew had returned with the information after conferring with the Mormon leaders.

"Where we won't contaminate them," Sinclair muttered.

"They quarantine all the wagons," Britt reported. "Don't want anyone bringing in diseases from the States. Guess they've had some real problems in the past. Can't blame 'em too much. And they don't stop anyone from riding in to buy goods." He chuckled. "That would be bad for business."

The next morning, Matilda and Sinclair volunteered to go for the mail. They wanted to visit to the bath house as well. Leaving Lewis with their mother, Matilda took Mary on White Star. Sinclair borrowed Britt's horse and carried Elizabeth.

They sought out the stage station which served as the Post Office. "Feels strange to be among buildings again," Sinclair commented as they rode through the streets.

"But such wide streets," Matilda exclaimed. "They've room enough to turn a team and wagon. I've never seen streets so wide."

"Smart," Sinclair commented. "I've always wondered why towns make the streets so narrow. Got plenty of space. Why not use it?"

The broad, level streets fanned out around them, bordered by block after block of trim dwellings of sun-dried brick or wood frame. Each house boasted an orchard and a garden. Channels carried water along the streets and into every yard. Clear, clean water, instead of the filthy gutters that usually plagued most cities of any size.

Sounds of activity surrounded them. No idlers hung about the store fronts or on the corners. Instead, Matilda saw factories and workshops, manufacturing everything from plows and corn planters to shoes and kitchen knives. The whole city teemed with activity. Matilda gazed about her and started to laugh.

"What's the joke," Sinclair demanded.

"Look around you. Their symbol is the beehive. And

when I saw all these people scurrying about, all so intent on their activities, the first thing that came to mind was a swarm of bees."

Sinclair glanced about and nodded. "Good point. Quite a contrast to Dobytown and Julesburg."

They finally located the stage station, a fine, two-story wooden frame building, across the street from a pharmacy and a paint store. A letter from Caroline, dated June 15, awaited Matilda. Caroline wrote neatly, without flourishes, her letter filled with neighborhood news and family activities. But, although eager to hear from home, Matilda felt remote and detached from everything her sister told her. Caroline's last comment, however, made her heart lurch. "The Sioux and the Cheyenne have been attacking farms and stations all over Nebraska Territory," Caroline wrote. "We are all hoping they don't move farther south."

Matilda blinked back tears. Poor, poor, bleeding Kansas! After all the killing between the Border Ruffians and the Jayhawkers, after all of her men who went, and would go, to fight and die in this dreadful War, would she now fall victim to Indian depredations? It seemed so unfair, so futile. What was it that made men think they had to kill each other to settle differences? She quickly brushed away the tears to hide them from Sinclair and handed him the letter.

He read it, shook his head, and muttered, "Glad we're out of there."

The bath house stood next to the Post Office. Matilda had anticipated a bath for a long time. When she saw the sign on the building, she giggled.

"Look, Sinclair. The City Bath House and Bakery are in the same building. Do you suppose they serve hot biscuits in the bath?"

"I don't know, but I'm sure going to find out. I've got my last clean shirt right here." He patted the bundle tied behind his saddle.

"We're ready, too." Matilda dismounted and tied White Star to the hitching post by the front door of the bath house. The smell of baking bread wafted out the open door. "Come on, girls." She lifted Mary down. Elizabeth and Sinclair joined them on the wooden porch.

Matilda and the girls stepped across the sill, Sinclair at their heels, and found themselves surrounded by shelves filled with delicious looking pastries. Tantalizing aromas filled the air.

"Mama," Mary cried, pointing to a tray of strawberry tarts. "Look! Can we have one? Please? Please, please, please?"

Matilda laughed. She understood Mary's entreaties, for she felt the same way herself. "Later, Darling," she told the little girl. "First, a bath."

"Uncle Sinclair?" Mary turned her pleading face to the young man beside her.

"Later, minx," he responded. "Go get clean first."

A plump woman, her round, ruddy face reflecting the heat from the oven, overheard them. She came around the counter wiping her face with a corner of her apron and greeted them with a warm smile.

"Come in, come in. The bath rooms are back here." Matilda and the girls obediently followed. Sinclair tagged along behind them, with reluctant glances back at the tempting morsels on the shelves. Matilda had to smile. He was as bad as the girls when it came to sweets.

"You folks must be on your way to California," their amiable hostess chattered on. "Get lots of folks from wagons goin' through. Came out ourselves in '59. Know how good a hot bath feels after all those weeks of tryin' to get clean in a bucket of cold water."

She led them to a hallway with a row of closed doors. On some of these, signs reading 'occupied' hung from a nail on the outside. Their hostess opened the door of one room without a sign and motioned Matilda and the girls inside.

A large, galvanized bath tub stood at the far end of the little room. A wooden bench lined one wall, and large nails for clothing had been driven into the opposite wall.

"A bakery and a bath house seem a strange combination," Matilda said to the woman. "Why did you decide to put in a bath house?"

"Husband was a baker back in New York," she said, "so we started this bakery here, soon's we got ourselves a place. Then all them folks in the wagons kept comin' through, and every one as come through my shop sure looked like they could use a good bath. And we got all that heat from the oven, so I tells my George, why don't we put a water tank on top o' the oven, use some of that heat to make hot water?" She chuckled and tucked a wisp of her sparse gray hair back into the bun at the nape of her neck. "Worked like a charm. Got all the hot water we need, and make as much money on the baths as we do from the bakery." She grinned. "'Course, George denies that. Won't have nothin' to do with the bath house part. Says he's a baker, he is. So me and Bridget takes care o' this side o' the business."

She set a stack of clean, white towels on one end of the bench, placed a bowl of liquid soap beside them and said, "Your hot water will be along directly. You just get comfy." She took the 'occupied' sign from the inside of the door, hung it on the outside nail, and strode off shouting, "Bridget! Bridget! Water for the ladies in Number Three!"

Matilda hugged the girls. "Now for a real soak!" She sighed in ecstasy and began peeling Mary's dress over her head.

An hour later, scrubbed cleaner that she had felt in weeks, skin wrinkled from the long soak, she emerged from the bath room with two equally clean little girls and returned to the bakery. Sinclair, admiring the baker's wares, awaited them there, his still damp blond hair carefully combed. His face had a two-tone look, tanned above and white where the beard had protected his skin from the fierce rays of the sun.

The girls, having grown accustomed to his beard, stared at him. Elizabeth's eyes grew wide. "Uncle Sinclair looks funny," she finally declared, her voice solemn. "He looks like two faces put together."

Mary's interest in her uncle's face waned as she recalled his promise. "Now can we have a strawberry tart, Uncle Sinclair?"

He looked over at Matilda for approval and she laughed. "I believe," she declared, "that we can celebrate the occasion with one strawberry tart apiece."

Matilda wanted to see the Great Salt Lake close up, so the following morning she and Sinclair took the two girls and a picnic lunch and rode seventeen miles out of the city. They reached the lake just before noon, and dismounted to walk closer, across the fine, soft sand, crunching through crusty salt flakes that varied in color from white to tan to dark green. Sinclair carried Elizabeth. Matilda walked beside him.

Mary, trotting along after them, suddenly wrinkled her nose. "Mama," she cried. "What is that horrid smell?"

Matilda laughed. "That's the water, Darling. They say it's so briny you can't even sink in it. Bathers just float."

"And look at all the islands!" Matilda had begun instructing Mary in the use of numbers, and the child counted proudly, "One, two, three, four, five, uh, seven . . . no, six, seven! I see seven islands, Mama," she cried in triumph. "Can we go out on the islands?"

"Not this time. I'm not going to walk in this water. They say there's quicksand in places."

Sinclair set Elizabeth on her feet and she ran to join Mary at the water's edge. "Do you suppose," he mused, "that the bathers smell like the water afterwards?" He looked along the edge of the water at the remains of thousands of worms, gnats, and mosquitoes cast up by the current. "Actually, I believe these are the source of the smell."

On the afternoon of their third day, Betsy Ann offered to keep Lewis so Matilda and the girls could ride into the city and stroll up and down peering in the windows of the shops. Though Matilda's finances did not include money to buy hats, the display in one shop so intrigued her she entered to look more closely.

A young girl approached them and introduced herself as Annie. Matilda mentioned their names, saying she was part of a wagon train bound for California. "I'm afraid I don't have a lot of money, but your bonnets are so lovely."

"Thank you, Miz Baldwin," the girl responded with a shy smile.

Matilda wound up buying small sunbonnets for the girls. While she paid for them from her meager purse, Annie burst out, "Oh, Miz Baldwin, I do envy you so, gettin' to go on to California." Her eyes filled with tears. "My father wants me to become a plural wife." The tears spilled over and ran down her cheeks. She quickly brushed them away. "Of course, it is a great honor, and Ma and Pa are very pleased he has accepted me, but . . . ."

Heavy footsteps approached the shop from the back of the building. The girl fell silent. After a pause, she said, "I do hope your little girls enjoy their bonnets, Miz Baldwin."

Matilda's questions froze on her lips. She caught the anxious glance Annie cast her as a grim-faced woman entered the room. Must be Annie's mother, Matilda thought. And Annie's afraid of her. She replied, as calmly as she could force her voice to be, "I'm sure they will, Annie. Thank you so much for your time. Perhaps you can come out to the wagons and visit a spell before we leave in the morning."

Plural wife? What in the world is a plural wife? She

thought back to what she had heard of Mormons and realized how little she really knew. And from what she saw of Annie, she felt certain the girl was pregnant. The loose clothing hid it fairly well, but would not do so for much longer. And why did her mother instill so much fear in her?

But Annie made it plain their visit had ended. After all, Matilda thought, it's none of my business. She gathered the girls, each clutching a new sunbonnet, and departed.

Restlessness stirred through the train. Everyone had been busy with repairs and washing and replenishing supplies, but impatience to be under way again affected more and more people. Gardner had made good his threat and sold the oxen. With the money, he purchased eight sturdy draft horses for his two wagons.

"Should 'a bought horses in the first place," he grumbled.

It had hurt Matilda to sell Bert. Patient, loyal, old Bert, who had pulled the plow in Kansas for so long, then crossed all those weary miles only to be sold to a stranger. She hoped Bert's new owner would be kind. As her father prepared to lead Bert away, she hugged the faithful animal's neck then turned away quickly so no one would see the tears in her eyes. She had resisted the impulse to ask her father to be sure and tell whoever bought Bert how the beast liked to have that spot behind his ears scratched.

As she had retreated to the wagon and watched her father lead the oxen away, Mary spoke up beside her.

"Cheer up, Mama. Now Bert won't have to pull the wagon anymore."

She smiled and brushed away the tears. "You're right, Darling. He will be happier here." And so another tie is cut, Lewis, my darling, she thought. Well, we still have White Star and Jake.

* * *

"Be good to get going again. Tired of paying these Saints to pasture the livestock," Gardner declared to Betsy Ann at supper that evening. He had just returned from another meeting.

"I hear the roughest part of the trail is ahead of us," Betsy Ann said, absently stirring her coffee.

"Yes," Gardner nodded. "Got to cross some bad deserts, starting with the Wendover, just south of here. Also got to get through the pass before September is over, and here it is the middle of July. Wagons ahead of us will be using the grass, and the waterholes will be drying up."

Betsy Ann refilled his coffee cup. "We'll be headin' out tomorrow," she soothed. "Only been here three days. Feels good to light for a spell."

Gardner grinned.   "Some thought of settling here. There's a Gentile settlement out east of the city, by Camp Douglas, where Captain Connor's got his California Volunteers camped. Guess he's been encouraging Gentiles to settle there." He chuckled. "President Lincoln won't let him fight the Mormons, so he's tryin' to dilute 'em."

Matilda started gathering up the supper dishes, her mind on the young girl from the hat shop. Mary proudly wore her new sunbonnet to supper, refusing to remove it.

But Matilda's mind was not on the bonnets. She recalled the strange conversation with Annie. "Pa," she asked suddenly, "what is a plural wife?"

Startled, her father stared at her. "Where'd you hear that? That's something young girls shouldn't know about."

"Land sakes, Gardner," Betsy Ann interjected. "Matilda's a widow with three children. She's old enough to know."

Grumbling, Gardner muttered that he supposed so. Matilda waited.

"It's a heathen practice," he finally said. "Bishops eye a young girl and marry her. She's supposed to spend the rest of her life waiting on him and raising children for him."

"And young girls have to marry old men?" Matilda gasped.

"Lecherous old men if you ask me," Betsy Ann murmured, half under her breath. "Some Saints they are."

"Forget it, Matilda," her father advised. "We'll be out of here tomorrow."

Annie's face loomed in Matilda's mind. She saw again the tears welling up in the blue eyes. And no wonder, Matilda thought, if that's what's in store for her. Forget it? How can I forget it? But what can I do about it?

She sighed in resignation and went to get a kettle of hot water from the fire to wash the dishes.

Chapter 46

Salt Lake City to Willow Creek Camp

THAT NIGHT, after she finally got the children to sleep, Matilda stepped out of the stuffy tent for a breath of the cool, fresh evening air. A faint breeze brushed her forehead, drying the beads of perspiration. She could not get Annie's stricken face out of her mind. The camp lay still under the light of a huge harvest moon, silent except for the occasional stamp of a restless animal, or a cough from one of the tents. A lone sentry patrolled the outer rim. In a nearby tent, a baby cried.

As Matilda watched, a shadowy figure circled the end of Britt's wagon. The figure, too slight for Sarah, approached Matilda's tent. Jake raised his head and a low rumble sounded in his throat.

"Hush, Jake," she murmured to the dog. Who could be coming to see her so late at night?

She did not have long to wait for the answer. "Annie!" Matilda gasped in surprise as she recognized her nocturnal visitor. She lowered her voice. "What are you doing here at this hour?"

"Shh." Annie seized Matilda's arm and urged her into the tent. "Let's get out of sight," she whispered hoarsely.

A sense of foreboding swept through Matilda. She suspected what Annie had in mind, but allowed the girl to draw her inside the tent where they sat in the semi-darkness and spoke softly. The moon cast an eerie glow. Through the open tent flap, it carved a bayonet of light across the blanket she used to protect their bedding from the soil.

"Take me with you," Annie begged, coming straight to

the point. "Please don't leave me to marry that horrid old man." She began to cry softly. "My father beats me when I tell him I don't want to marry Bishop Bensen."

Matilda could only gasp at the girl's words. "But your mother! Surely your mother will help you."

"Yes, she'll help me. She held me while my father beat me." Annie laughed without humor. "My father says Bishop Bensen insists I agree, so I'd better convince him I want to marry him." She burst into a fresh spate of tears. "But I don't. I don't!"

"Of course you don't," Matilda murmured, distressed to think the girl's parents could force her into such unhappiness. I have to help her, Matilda thought, but how? Surely the wagons will be checked if Annie disappears at the same time we leave. Of course, there are a lot of wagons, and there are even two other groups planning to leave soon, but . . . .

Annie's voice interrupted her thoughts. "I'll work, Miz Baldwin. I'll help with the children and the washing and anything I can. I'll try not to eat very much, and when I get to California, I'll get work and pay you back for every cent you . . . ."

"Hush, child," Matilda reassured her. "We've surely food enough for you. My concern is that your father will come after us looking for you."

"Oh, he will," she whispered with certainty. "He's positive marrying me to Bishop Bensen will guarantee his passage into Heaven." She added bitterly, "He won't give that up easy." Her voice caught and she broke into sobs again.

Matilda wondered what kind of man would trade his daughter's happiness for his own benefit. Deciding she would never understand such a person, plans for possible places Annie could hide raced through her mind.

"We'll probably have to tell my mother and father," she said, taking the weeping girl in her arms. Annie's unborn child moved against her. Matilda wondered if the girl would confide in her, but determined to say nothing until she did. "I'm sure they will help. No one we know approves of a man having more than one wife." She gently stroked the shaking girl's silken hair. "Now, come with me. We've got to get you hidden in one of the wagons before anyone sees you. You can't walk out in front of the whole company tomorrow. Did you see anyone? How did you find me?"

"I told the sentry I had a hat to deliver before you left in the morning. He pointed out your tent."

Matilda knew Giles stood sentry duty, and he never missed anything. He would not have survived twenty years as a scout otherwise. But he would feel no particular loyalty to the Mormons, and Matilda suspected he was a little sweet on her, Matilda. It seemed unlikely he would betray Annie.

"We'll just have to hope he doesn't remember you," she told the girl. "Come on."

On their way to the wagon, she found Sinclair sound asleep rolled up in his blanket beside the rear wheels. "Wake up," she murmured, nudging him gently with her foot. "And keep your voice down. I need your help." In quick whispers, she explained the situation. Under Matilda's direction, he rearranged boxes and sacks in the wagon to create a hiding place.

"Now, Miss Annie, we'll get you outa here safe for sure." Sinclair awkwardly patted her shoulder in reassurance and crawled back into his blanket.

Once Matilda had seen to Annie's needs, she returned to her own tent, shaking with trepidation. What had she done? Could the Mormons send soldiers after her? They were no longer in Kansas. She didn't know anything about Territorial Law. Would this be considered kidnapping? She also knew that beating one's own children, however repulsive the idea seemed to her, was common practice, even legal.

She sighed and forced herself to relax. Whatever comes, she mused as she drifted off to sleep, I'll deal with it tomorrow.

When she saw Annie the next morning, in full light, with bruises on her arms and face, as well as a swollen right eye, all of Matilda's misgivings vanished. "You poor thing," she whispered. "We'll get you away from that brute somehow."

Betsy Ann, when brought into the secret, agreed. She treated the bruises with cool comfrey poultices. "We'll take care of you, child," she reassured the trembling Annie. "Matilda, I think the fewer folk know she's here the better."

They swore Sinclair to secrecy. The wagons left Salt Lake City shortly after dawn, headed south, and followed the Overland Stage route along the left bank of the Jordan River. Annie remained hidden behind trunks of household goods and bags of flour.

They crossed many tributaries that fed into the Jordan. Canyon Creek, Mill Creek, two creeks called Cottonwood, which made no sense at all to Matilda, and Dry Creek. They passed a number of pools along both sides of the road. Matilda asked Giles about them.

"Some are hot, some cold," he replied. "Some reported to be over a hundred feet deep, according to what they say."

"That deep?" Matilda gasped. "Mary," she called, "you and Owen get away from that pond. Right now!" Giles chuckled.

In the late afternoon, they reached Willow Creek and corralled for camp where Willow Creek joined the Jordan River, about twenty miles out of Salt Lake City. As Matilda helped her mother set up the truncheons for the cooking fire, the ever alert Giles reported seven horsemen approached, riding hard.

"Not Injuns," the scout said. "Looks like a bunch of them Saints. All wearin' black coats. Soldier with 'em, an' a buggy carryin' a man 'n' a woman."

He met Matilda's eyes and she read the knowledge there. Giles would not betray her. Her instincts had not failed.

Matilda glanced at her mother. Betsy Ann's face did not change. She turned casually to Matilda and said, "Maybe you and Sinclair should rearrange some of the goods while you bring me that bag of flour."

Matilda understood at once. If Annie's father searched the wagons, Annie would have to be better hidden. She handed Lewis to her mother and hastened into the wagon, Sinclair at her heels. Opening a trunk, she took out an armload of clothing and stuffed it into an empty sack.

"Quick, Annie," she said, motioning to the half empty trunk, "Your father is looking for you. Hide in here until he leaves."

Annie did not argue. She scrambled into the trunk, pulling her skirts in after her, and Matilda closed the lid. Sinclair piled goods around Annie's hiding place and hoisted the flour sack. They returned to Betsy Ann. Matilda took Lewis back and clasped him so close he protested while she tried to get her breathing back under control.

"Here's the flour you wanted for supper, Mother." Sinclair grinned as he set the sack down. Matilda suspected he enjoyed the intrigue, and wished she could feel the same. "The rest of the supplies are well stored."

They acted not a moment too soon. Wes Overton approached with the Mormon delegation. Matilda immediately recognized Annie's mother. She had seen the woman only briefly in the hat shop, but could not mistake the frown line that slashed between the brows over the hawk-like nose, the unsmiling mouth as grim as she remembered. She wondered vaguely if the woman ever smiled. Matilda felt the blood drain from her face. What would they do if Annie were discovered here? Her heart jumped into her throat, pounding so hard she feared they would see it pulsing. For a moment, she regretted her rash decision to bring the girl along.

Visions of the purple bruises on Annie's swollen face loomed in her mind. Her resolve strengthened. She felt more determined than ever to ensure these cruel parents never got her back to abuse again.

"Sorry to bother you, Miz Randolph, 'Tilda," Wes said, "but these folks were askin' for Miz Baldwin. I figgered they must 'a' meant you, 'Tilda. I told 'em they're barkin' up the wrong tree, but they insisted on talkin' to you."

"Of course. Thank you, Wes." She stepped forward. "I'm Mrs. Baldwin," Matilda greeted the newcomers, her new-found resolution pushing her forward with a boldness she did not feel, thankful Wes spoke with complete innocence. Her mother had been right. The fewer people who knew of Annie's presence, the better their chances. "Can I help you?"

"You was in my hat shop," the woman accused. "You was talkin' to my Annie."

"Your daughter? Why, yes, I bought sunbonnets for my girls from her." Shifting Lewis' weight to her left hip, she motioned to Mary and Elizabeth, who stood gaping at the strangers. Mary wore her bonnet, the blue in the printed flowers emphasizing the color of her eyes. Matilda forced her voice to remain steady. She clenched her hands around Lewis so no one would see how badly they shook.

"She's a lovely girl," Matilda continued, looking directly at the woman. "Did she not charge me enough? I felt the price quite reasonable."

"You stole her," the woman accused.

"Stole her? Stole Annie? How could I have stolen her?"

"She's disappeared, and you was the only one from this bunch of wagons she ever spoke to."

"You mean she's run away?" Matilda managed to appear shocked. "Why on earth would she run away? Surely she had no reason to be unhappy at home, did she?"

Matilda sensed Sinclair, beside her, about to explode and prayed he would be able to keep a straight face.

Annie's mother sputtered in rage. Her father, his face grim, remained silent. The young soldier who had accompanied the Mormons tried very hard to suppress a grin and almost succeeded. Fortunately, he held his horse a little behind the Mormons, so only those who faced him noticed.

"Did you wish to look in our wagon?" Matilda asked. "Or any of the other wagons?" she added sweetly. "Two other groups were camped near us. The one that left an hour ahead of us is probably camped about three miles farther on."

Annie's father hesitated. He seemed less sure of himself.

"Perhaps Annie just decided to visit a friend," Matilda suggested. "Have you checked with her friends?"

"She ain't got no friends. We never let her . . . ," Annie's mother began to bluster when her husband held up his hand and stopped her.

"Come, Gertrude," he said. "She was a tramp anyway, always hanging around with Gentiles." He yanked the horse's head around so sharply the bit tore the animal's mouth. Flecks of blood showed at the corner. "Gee-up!" He lashed the horse into a run.

The other Mormons turned and followed. One older man gave them a suspicious stare. Matilda wondered if that was Bishop Bensen. If so, she thought, taking in the thinning hair, the wrinkled face, the paunchy form, it's no wonder Annie objected to marrying him.

The young soldier approached Matilda. Their eyes met, and she could not help smiling at the twinkle in his green eyes.

"Thank you, ma'am," he said in a quiet voice. He pulled off his riding glove and leaned down to shake her hand. Straightening in his saddle, he saluted her. Pulling the glove back on, he turned his mount and hurried after the others, his horse's hooves tossing up small divots of the sandy soil as he rode off.

Stunned, Matilda stood motionless and watched him ride out of sight. In her hand, she clutched the small wad of paper he had transferred as they shook hands.

Wes watched the group's departure. "If the girl did run away from her folks, I sure can't say I blame her." He strode off. Betsy Ann, with a slight smile on her face, said nothing and returned to her cooking fire.

Sinclair grinned down at Matilda once they sat alone again. "Pretty good act, 'Tilda," he said. "You ever think of going on stage?" He whispered in her ear, "We'd better go and get Annie out of that trunk 'fore she suffocates."

Matilda's head still spun. Sinclair repeated his statement before his voice finally penetrated the fog that clouded her mind. "Yes," she replied absently. "Let's get her out. She should be safe now."

Looking down at the folded piece of paper in her hand, Matilda saw 'Annie' written on the outside. The young man knew Annie would be with her. Was he the father of the child she carried? Had they planned her escape together? Matilda smiled, remembering the handsome face and the charming green eyes. No wonder Annie balked at marrying Bishop Bensen!

When Sinclair fished Annie out of the trunk, Matilda gave her the note. The girl took it without comment and Matilda asked no questions.

Chapter 47

Willow Creek to Antelope Valley

THE NEXT MORNING, Saturday, July 16, the line of wagons left the Willow Creek camp and continued along the east bank of the Jordan River. A good, solid road and an abundant supply of grass along the way bolstered Matilda's spirits. They did travel faster with all of the wagons pulled by mules or horses.

A couple of miles after leaving the camp at Willow Creek, they passed the remains of a brewery, used more or less as a stage station.

"This is the halfway point to Camp Floyd, Miss Matilda," Giles told her. "Had to make the camp forty miles outside the city. That were part of the settlement after the Mormon War in '57. Old Brigham got that into the agreement: no army camp any closer than forty miles." He grinned. "Guess he didn't want no soldiers contaminatin' his folks."

As she walked along, Matilda noticed a group of Indian women who industriously swept the bushes with sticks, gathering their quarry in large, conical baskets.

"What are they collecting?" she asked Giles.

"Crickets."

"Crickets!"

"Yep." He grinned at her expression. "They collect crickets, then toss in hot rocks to toast 'em. Do the same with ants. I've seen 'em. They scoop up an anthill, shake the basket round and round 'til the sand is gone, then toss in a couple of hot rocks. When the legs are burned off the ants, they pound what's left into a paste." He took off his hat and wiped his forehead with a not very clean handkerchief. "Pretty tasty. I tried it myself once. You'll see the anthills when we come to the edge of the desert a few days ahead."

"Fascinating," Matilda murmured. "So that's how they manage to survive out here."

"Yep. Collect the seeds from Indian rice grass the same way. Go along with a stick and beat the seeds into the basket. Lots of Indian rice grass grows around here. They make it into flour." He shook his head. "All the cattle going through here must cut into the Injuns' winter supplies."

Matilda watched the women until the wagon rounded a bend and they passed out of sight. She thought of her three Pottawatamie friends, and wondered how they fared. She felt a fleeting pang of sorrow to think how rapidly their way of life was passing. These Indians, being more isolated, would probably suffer from the inroads of civilization a little more slowly, but Giles' comment remained with her as she watched the animals graze along the side of the roadway. She had not thought about it before, but the loss of the grass seeds had to impact the local tribes.

Annie turned out to be a delightful girl, once she felt free and safe. Her smiling face and helpful hands made everyone's day a little brighter. Just one day with Annie's assistance made Matilda realize how much simpler her life would be for the rest of the trip. Mary and Elizabeth had adored Annie when Matilda bought their bonnets, and were delighted she had joined them. Both Wes and Weldon were besotted with her, but she gave them no encouragement.

The wagon full of fresh fruits and vegetables purchased in Salt Lake City, Matilda's fears dissipated and exhilaration swept over her. Maybe the rest of the trip would not be so hard after all.

They crossed the Jordan River, only axle deep at the ford, and ascended the rough divide between Utah Valley and Cedar Valley before reaching Cedar Creek. They passed by the little settlement of Fairfield and camped at the site of the dismantled Camp Floyd.

"Looks like a lot of people lived here at one time," she commented to Giles as he strode up with an armload of sage branches for the cooking fire.

"Largest army encampment of its time, Miss 'Tilda," he said. "Over 2500 soldiers. When the usual hangers-on lived in the town, they called it Frogtown."

Matilda, her curiosity unsatisfied when Giles could not tell her the source of the name, turned to help Betsy Ann set up camp. While supper cooked, Matilda and Annie took Lewis and the two little girls for a walk. Mary tugged at Matilda's skirt, "Come on, Mama, come on!" After riding in the wagon all day, the girls wanted to run.

"Don't go beyond the sentry line," Betsy Ann warned, looking up as they strolled away. She had just placed the Dutch oven with the cornbread next to the fire to bake. The stew pot with beef and beans hung from the cross-pole. "And don't be gone long. Supper'll be ready soon."

They promised and walked back to the little cemetery that had served the camp and its environs. They spent some time reading the inscriptions. Matilda felt a deep sadness as she read the names. Many of them had been very young. Most came from the East.

"Must have been a lot of Irish," Annie commented. "Look. Patrick Goodman. John McKay. John Ryan. They have to be Irish. And here's a Charles O'Brian and there's a Michael O'Brian. Do you suppose they were brothers?"

"I hope not. No mother should have to lose more than one son." Matilda walked farther on. "Here's one that served in the Mexican War." She sighed. "What a shame to survive one war and die in a second."

Finding the graveyard depressing, they continued on, and climbed to the top of a nearby knoll. Matilda looked out at the massive cloud formations. "Look, Annie," she said. "Castles and turrets, straight out of picture books." She pointed and added, "That one even looks like a horse with a rider." She lowered Lewis to the ground. He was almost nine months old and could stand as long as she held his hand. He even took a few tentative steps. He'll be walking soon, she thought. Then I'll really have my hands full.

They spent the next day at Fairfield and decided to celebrate Sunday dinner at the Stagecoach Inn. There they met John Carson.

"Settled here in '55," he told them, ushering them to a table, "but had so many Injun problems we moved back closer to the City. When the army camped here, figgered it'd be safe enough, so we come back and reclaimed the land. That's when I founded the town. Harnessed a spring, started a grist mill. Plenty of business, with all them soldiers livin' here."

"You've certainly done well," Gardner congratulated him. "And are these lovely young ladies your children?" He motioned to three girls who hovered nearby.

"Three of 'em. Girls, come and say howdy to these nice folks. This here's Sarah." He motioned to the oldest. "She's sixteen. That's Susan. She's eight. And my baby here," he swung the littlest one into his arms, "is Verina." The girl cooed with delight and hugged his neck.

He returned the child to her feet and she offered a shy smile to the strangers, clinging to her father's leg and peeking around at them. "Come," he offered. "Sit and visit a spell while the women folks bring the vittles." He waved them to seats.

"Heard anything about how the war is going?" he continued. "Don't get much news out here." Gardner frowned. For him, the war remained a sore subject, but Mr. Carson did not seem to notice.

"Not many folks know it," he rambled on, "but this Utah War were a trick on the part of Secretary of War Floyd.

That's how it got to be called Camp Floyd, after him. He wanted to get Buchanan's mind off the South and slavery by gettin' folks riled agin the Mormons and polygamy instead. Worked pretty good for a while. Got most of the regular army clear out here, miles from Washington, and got all kinds of money out of the US Treasury for Southern contractors to supply 'em." He chuckled. "Then the South seceded, Floyd defected and so did the commander here. Feller named Johnston, Albert Sidney Johnston. New commander, he come out and changed the name of the fort to Crittendon. Said he wa'n't gonna have his fort named after no traitor. They moved the army to Fort Leavenwoth in '61 and everyone started calling it Camp Floyd again."

Matilda watched her father's face. Mr. Carson seemed to be take no sides, merely reciting the facts as he knew them.

As though he felt it time to change the subject, Britt interceded. "Weren't you a little concerned having the army so close to your family, Mr. Carson? Especially with daughters as pretty as these?"

Carson frowned. "Did have to watch 'em close. There was a whole passel of hangers-on whose looks I never liked. They called my town Frogtown." He still looked incensed at the insult. "But when the army left, so did they. Been right peaceful ever since. Close enough to the city to not have Injun problems, and the stage comes through every day."

Steaming platters of food arrived, and the conversation paused. Mr. Carson spoke to Gardner. "Be right honored if you would say Grace, Mr. Randolph."

On Monday, July 17, they broke camp at dawn, and seven miles later crossed the divide between Cedar Valley and Rush Valley. Sunflowers and morning glory vines lined the roadway. Eleven more miles brought them to Meadow Creek, where they found a good supply of grass and water. About four in the afternoon, a furious dust storm had broken over the plain, blasting the whole party with gritty, burning alkali sand. Matilda huddled in the wagon with the children to escape the storm's fury, feeling sorry for the men and animals who had no choice but to endure the torture of the howling sands. She took pity on Jake and brought him into the wagon with them.

"Rush Valley mail station just ahead," Giles reported when they reached Meadow Creek at last. Thankfully the wind had died down. "Grass and water better here. Got to recruit good. Next water for sure is at Simpson Springs, and we can't make that in one day. Only one spring along the way, and it's dry more often than not. Road's bad crossing Skull Valley, too."

They had just circled the wagons for camp that evening when Annie's eyes rested on the bank of clouds boiling over the mountains to the southwest. "Unless I miss my guess," she remarked, "we're due for a thunderstorm."

They barely finished supper before the first drops hit. Matilda, who feared another hailstorm like those they had endured along the Platte, felt relief to find the clouds contained only rain. The wind that accompanied the downpour whipped around them with such ferocity that Sinclair declined to even try putting up her tent.

"Into the wagon with you," he told Mary, bundling her inside. "You'll be better off."

So Matilda shared Annie's cubicle in the wagon. It did make a cozy nest, and the wagon cover had been waterproofed. Hopefully it would hold. At least they were protected from the wind.

Cramped in the tiny space, it took her a long time to fall asleep. Lewis lay across her abdomen, Mary on one side, Elizabeth the other. She felt an almost uncontrollable urge to shift her weight, but could not move for fear of waking the children.

As she lay there, she heard a plop on one of the boxes.

Oh, no, she thought, immediately recognizing the sound. More plops followed. She fervently wished they had been able to buy more lengths of the India rubber sheeting. They had passed through a number of rainstorms on their way up to South Pass. Why did this rain soak through when the others had not? She knew the answer almost before her mind formed the question. This rain had fallen steadily for several hours. The saturated canvas, weakened from months of exposure to the sun, could hold no more. She could not move, and only hoped the rain would do no damage.

The deluge ceased sometime in the night. Matilda, half asleep, numb from the cold and damp, and stiff from lying so still, sighed with relief. She marveled at how the children slept through it all. She gritted her teeth and prayed dawn would come soon. At least it should get no worse.

Then she heard another rumble of thunder. Lighting streaked across the sky, and large drops again pelted the canvas above her. An icy drop landed on her forehead.

She grimaced. Yes, she thought, it can get worse.

Lewis wakened her with a cry of discomfort, soaking wet. The rain had finally stopped. She lifted the canvas flap on the back of the wagon and looked out at a clear sky, the blue night fast fading in the pink of the coming dawn. Only a few stars still shone, the rest paling in deference to the rising sun. She closed the flap quickly as the morning chill swept in, amazed at how it could be over 90 degrees during the day yet turn so cold at night. She had never experienced anything like it in Kansas or Illinois. There, when it was hot, it stayed hot.

Mary shivered in her wet clothing. "Mama, I'm cold."

"Me, too," echoed Elizabeth.

Lewis shook in Matilda's arms. She felt an icy fear run through her as she remembered how she lost John to the croup. What if they took a chill? She needed to get them warm.

"Come," she said to the children. "You, too, Annie. We have to get out of these wet clothes." Digging in a trunk, she found a dry blanket and some clean clothing. Dry, anyway, she thought wryly as she shook out the dust. Quickly stripping the children, she dressed them and wrapped them in the blanket. Ordering them to lie still and get warm, she climbed out of the wagon.

Sinclair had started the fire. A kettle of boiling water hung on the pole. The damp wood made a smoky fire, but at least it burned.

"Bless you, Sinclair," she sighed, holding her chilled hands before the warming blaze.

"Tea?" he grinned, holding out a steaming cup. "I snuck some real tea out of Mother's hoard." He took a sip from his own cup. "Just hope the road dries quick."

They reached Faust Station by noon, and rested during the heat of the day. They had crossed several washes still muddy from the storm, but the road remained intact. Thankfully, the one gully had a bridge, courtesy, Matilda was sure, of the Overland Stage Company. The hot sun burned relentlessly down on their heads. By mid-afternoon, a cloud cover massed over the mountains to the west. She saw thunderheads to the north-east. A welcome breeze wafted over her, cooling her overheated skin.

As they walked along, Annie eyed the clouds. "Sure hope we don't get another thunderstorm," she said, as lightning streaked from the cloudbank to the north towards the ground.

Matilda looked out over the mass of sagebrush, greasewood, and rabbit brush. Snake weed and Indian rice grass grew in between. As she watched, an eagle swooped down and rose with a rabbit in its talons. Mary saw it too. "Oh, Mama," she cried. "The poor bunny!"

Matilda felt a twinge of pity for the rabbit as well, but told

Mary, "The eagle has to eat too, my sweet. I'm sure life is pretty tough out here."

As they started up the next range of hills, they felt a few sprinkles of rain, but fortunately, the deluge they feared did not materialize. When they reached the crest of Lookout Pass, Matilda felt dismay stir in her breast. She could see for miles, but saw only a long line of more sand and sagebrush, with another range of mountains in the distance.

"Them's the Onaqui Mountains," Giles advised her in response to her query. "Pretty, ain't they?"

Britt's eyes were closer to the ground. "Bad news," he groaned. "They've had a fire go through here." Matilda inspected the area he indicated. "All the feed for the cattle is gone. Going to have to spend some time gathering fodder for the animals before we go on. Nothing left out there but sagebrush. Only things that eat that stuff is rabbits and antelope."

"And unless I miss my guess, it's raining cats and dogs in those mountains," Giles added.

"So?" Matilda asked. "That's a long ways from here."

"Comes down and washes out the road. Got some real bad washes to cross." Giles shook his head. "Better camp on the side of the hill. Dangerous to camp on the flat. Liable to get flooded."

Matilda returned to her mother and Annie. "First we don't have any water," she grumbled, "then we have too much. And never any for drinking or washing!"

Betsy Ann paid no attention. "Get a basket and help me pick some of these juniper berries. Let the menfolk worry about the rain."

Matilda laughed and joined Annie and the children in helping gather the berries.

They reached Simpson's Springs late the following day, after struggling over the fifteen miles across Skull Valley. As

Giles had predicted, the rain waters had flooded out sections of the road, and they had to cross some areas very slowly.

"Here's one of the most dependable watering spots in the desert," Giles advised them. "Overland Stage folks built a dam here to improve the supply."

The station keeper advised them to spend a little extra time. "Grass not good past here," he warned. "And the next water is 48 miles. You'd be right smart to fill all your barrels and canteens. Cut some grass to use as fodder to get you past Dugway Station. No grass or water there. You'll find some grass along the sloughs, but no more water 'til you get to Fish Spring. And the water there is bad. Don't dare let your cattle drink too much of it."

Taking his advice, the men filled the water barrels and jugs. Sinclair rounded up all the children to carry grass for the stock as he cut it with the scythe.

Matilda used the time to mend clothes. While she sat sewing, the east-bound stage came by. Matilda admired the four magnificent bays pulling the Concord Coach. She knew the stage had come all the way from California, making the journey in weeks instead of months. She wished once again they could have traveled by stage, but knew they could never afford the $500.00 per passenger.

Besides, she told herself, then we couldn't have brought as many things. She had to leave a lot as it was. Tears stung her eyes as she remembered how it hurt her to leave the table and chairs Lewis had carved by hand with such loving care.

The guard from the stagecoach approached. "Word to the wise, folks. Got to watch out for both the Utes and the Bannocks around these parts. We seen a Ute war party back close to Antelope Canyon. That's a popular raiding spot. Injuns burned the station to the ground in June of '60. They're looking for horses, and you got some fine 'uns.

Keep a wary eye. Egan's Canyon is another likely raiding spot. They burned that station in '60 as well."

Matilda's heart jumped into her throat. She immediately thought of White Star. She had thought this threat behind her since they no longer traveled in Sioux territory. She shuddered, remembering the screams of the ill-fated Parsons. He had been a fool, and could have brought the whole Sioux Nation down on them, but no one deserved to die like he had. She forced the memory from her mind.

Sinclair, beside her, saw the look of dismay on her face. "Cheer up, 'Tilda," he smiled, putting his arm around her shoulder for an encouraging squeeze. "We're well able to handle a small party of Indians. No Ute brave is going to ride White Star if I have anything to say about it."

Matilda only sighed. She stood on the edge of the bench and watched the road they would follow until it vanished in the desert that surrounded it. Only sage and greasewood grew in the fine silt. Sand heaps mounded up here and there across the vast expanse, and bald patches of salt soil scarred the landscape. Crystals of salt, glittering like little diamonds, covered tracts of dried mud. The next range of mountains rose blue in the distant haze. Her heart contracted. If these short sections of desert were so difficult, what would it be like when they got into the valley of the Humboldt? Think about California, she told herself, and forced her fears from her mind.

The next three days seemed the longest Matilda had ever known. For her, and, she knew, for others as well, they were days filled with dread. She watched anxiously as the level in the water barrels sank lower each day. She felt thirsty all the time. They passed thousands of ant hills, many several feet high. The ants had cleared the vegetation around the mounds for several feet in all directions.

"Them's the ants the Injuns eat," Giles advised her when she pointed out the ant hills. "And don't get too close. Some of these desert ants, they get right testy when they suspect someone's a threat to the home place."

Matilda laughed. "I promise to leave their title uncontested."

"I can't really be this thirsty," she told Sinclair as she gulped another cupful of water from the barrel attached to the back of the wagon. "This is my fourth drink in the last hour, and it's only about nine o'clock. It must be because I think we may run short."

Sinclair patted her shoulder in sympathy. "You're right. Giles says old timers on the desert call it phantom thirst. Your mind says you're liable to run out of water, and makes you drink all you can get."

She poured half of the cupful back into the barrel. "Then I'm going to tell my mind to stop playing tricks on me."

They struggled across the desert between Simpson's Springs and the station aptly called Riverbed Station, located by a wide, dry river bed. With no grass and no water, the trek felt much longer than eight miles. Wheels sank in the sand, and the animals lowed for water. The glare hurt Matilda's eyes, and they smarted from the dust. The hot sand burned Jake's paws, and he howled until Matilda took pity on him and put him in the wagon with the children.

"It's the alkali," Giles advised when he overheard her complaint to her mother. "And the glare of the sun reflecting off the white sand don't help none either."

"I hope it won't damage our eyes," she said, immediately concerned for the children. "What can we do?"

Britt walked up with a charred stick. "Do what the old timers do on the desert. Smear soot on your cheeks under your eyes. Stops some of the glare."

Matilda sighed. "I'll try anything." She allowed Britt to rub the soot on her face. "Do I look like an Indian now?" she asked with a shaky laugh. "What about the alkali dust?"

"Drop of laudanum goes into everyone's eyes tonight, soon's we make camp," Betsy Ann announced.

"Thank Heaven we don't have the oxen to slow us down," Matilda sighed to her mother. After struggling across more salt flats and passing piles of black, volcanic rock, they had finally reached Fish Springs Station. They skirted the mountains, passing Black Rock Stage Station, and crossed a marshy area where the road showed signs of damage from the flooding waters.

And I am so glad I didn't put poor old Bert through this, she thought. The number of bleached bones along the way horrified her. She hated to think of Bert's bones added to the grisly collection. She did not tell her ever practical mother what she thought, instead saying, "We barely have any water left as it is. Another day and we would have run out."

On Saturday, they stopped for the nooning by Desert Station, a single room of a partially dug out rock wall. The windows had no glass, and the bunks were built into the wall. Boxes and benches served as furniture. Matilda sympathized with the station keeper.

"The poor man," she murmured to Sinclair. "What a lonely, isolated place to live! His whole life revolves around the stage coming through. He has absolutely nothing else to do."

From Desert Station, they crossed more salt flats, and headed straight west towards yet another range of hills. As they neared Willow Springs, Matilda watched the sun disappearing behind the mountains against a beautiful azure sky. The sun lined the scattered clouds with silver. The clouds themselves reminded her of a flock of geese. To the northeast, the sky turned a lovely pink, and it appeared as though it might rain.

They reached Willow Creek, on the west end of the

desert, on Saturday evening, July 23. Matilda sighed with relief when she saw water in the pools. The water tasted brackish, and gave everyone the flux, but at least there was enough. And grass and hay were plentiful. Several farms lay scattered along the creek, and log cabins had been built for the owners of those farms.

There they met George Boyd. "Everyone calls me Bid," he declared. "Come through here in '58. Was a member of the Mormon Batallion, but when I saw this valley, I told myself, this is the place for me. Been here ever since. Make a good living, between the farm and what the Overland pays me. I built this station for 'em. Also built the last one you passed."

Matilda remembered the dismal quarters the last station keeper occupied, and noticed the one here seemed considerably more comfortable, but she remained silent.

"Dozen Gosiutes tried to run us out last year," he continued, "but we drove 'em off. Gosiute Jack tried it too, back in '61. Guess they've finally got the word now that we don't run easy."

"There's more to the story," Sinclair told Matilda later, after they returned to the wagons. "Troops of those California Volunteers wiped out a camp of Gosiute women, children, and old folks. Chief White Horse set out for revenge."

"So innocent people die because of the soldiers' misguided attacks."

"Seems so. And it got worse. When General Connor sent out reinforcements after the attack on Canyon Station last year, he told the troops to kill any Indian they saw, on sight, no questions asked."

"Oh, no!"

"Oh, yes. And it cost the Overland Mail Company thousands of dollars to buy food to placate the Indians all along the road after that little misunderstanding."

Matilda just shook her head.

After spending Sunday at Willow Creek, washing clothes and resting, they broke camp on Monday, July 25. In two hours, they reached Mountain Springs. There, clear, cold water poured from a pipe tapped into a spring in the side of the hill and emptied into a trough behind the station. Matilda, delighted to have a drink of good water at last, emptied her canteen of the brackish water from Willow Creek and refilled it.

As they followed the left side of a long mesa, they encountered a herd of antelope. Sinclair managed to shoot one. The rest of the herd vanished over the next ridge, the white fur on their rumps flashing in the morning sun. Matilda watched and admired their graceful departure. She felt a strange sadness at the thought of killing such a beautiful creature, though the prospect of antelope for dinner cheered everyone, including Matilda. She sternly reminded herself not to be foolishly sentimental. They were still in a wild land, in spite of the tranquil farms they had passed.

At the mouth of Overland Canyon, they stopped for the midday rest and meal at Round Station. There they found a stone lookout on the top of a hill beside the out post where a man remained on duty all the time, they were told, to watch for Indians.

"Had a lot of problems with the Gosiutes last year," the stationmaster told them. "First station were built in the canyon and the Gosiutes overran it. Murdered five men, they did. You'll see the graves two, maybe three miles down the trail, beside the burned out ruins of Canyon Station."

Leaving Round Station, they entered Overland Canyon. Matilda could only gasp at the narrow, rock-strewn canyon. High bluffs surrounded them on both sides..

"Giles!" She turned to the scout. "Do we have to cross here?"

"'Fraid so, Miss Matilda," he responded. 'But don't you fret none. We'll be right careful, and the ravine is only seven miles long."

"Sinclair!" she called to her brother, "walk White Star through this part. Don't let her stumble."

"Your wish is my command." He grinned at her and saluted, then dismounted. "You're right. This would be a bad place to risk her falling."

As they walked along, Matilda glanced about with apprehension. Shortly after they entered the canyon, she noticed a rock shelter on the left. The blackened overhang told her it had provided shelter to someone, probably Ute. She checked the bluffs across the ravine and shivered. Her imagination pictured a Ute in every bush.

An hour after they entered the canyon, they found the burial ground. Matilda and Annie gathered an armload of some lovely yellow blooms they picked alongside the trail and placed them on the graves. "Seems only fitting to remember them," Matilda said to Annie. "The reason for their killing was so senseless, so unnecessary." Tears filled her eyes as she arranged the flowers. In her imagination, she heard the despairing screams of the doomed men and looked again at the surrounding cliffs with horror.

It took them six hours to cover the seven miles of the rugged canyon, the longest six hours of Matilda's life. At first, she carefully watched the rims of the canyon for hostile Indians, but, as the trek wore on, she found herself struggling just to keep going. She forgot all about Indians. As the sun sank towards the western horizon, they made camp at the end of the ravine where it widened out to a level valley. They dared not camp in the ravine itself.

"Bad place for an Indian ambush," Giles announced, quite unnecessarily.

The next day, they reached Deep Creek Mail Station and found more active farming operations.

"Began as an experiment by some of the church leaders," the young Mormon at the station advised Matilda. "Was going to be a model, it was. They was gonna make farmers out of the Utes, but Utes was born Diggers and they'll die Diggers. Lot of us who been around Injuns told 'em it weren't no use, but they jest wouldn't listen. The Injun's answer was to burn down the house, so they give it up and went back to Salt Lake." He grinned. "So the Egan family settled here in '58 and we made our own farms. Got it set up to irrigate the fields, and we have our own store, a smithy, a sawmill, even a telegraph station."

"This is such a pretty spot," Matilda observed. Three streams fed the creek that passed through the farms. Fields not yet under cultivation, covered with wire grass and wheat grass, lay on both sides of the stream. "Should make good farmland."

"Injuns call the place *Ibapah,* the clay colored water. Ain't caused us no trouble, to speak of. Guess it's 'cause they's so many of us here." He grinned. "Could also be because the Overland pays Egan several thousand dollars a year to give 'em beef to eat."

From Deep Creek, they crossed to the springs at Eight Mile Station, a small stone building with a dirt roof and rifle ports on all sides. Matilda shivered at the sight. While they refilled the water barrels at the spring, the station keeper regaled them with the tale of an attack the previous year by a Snake war party under chief Pocatello.

"Killed the cook and hostler, they did," he declared. "Then hid out in the buildings 'til the eastbound stage come through. Hank Harper, the driver, took a mortal wound right off, but lashed the horses and got the stage away from the station 'fore he collapsed. Judge Mott, Nevada's delegate to Congress, showed he had real grit. He climbed into the box, gathered the reins, and got the coach to Deep Creek. After the stage got away, the chief and his bunch burned and looted the station."

"So who is the problem?" Matilda asked Britt after the

station keeper left. "Snake, Ute, or Gosiute?"

"Or Bannock," Britt grinned. "Who knows?"

From Eight Mile Springs, they continued on through the canyon to camp at the mouth of Antelope Valley. On Wednesday, July 27, they traveled the 19 miles through the valley to the Antelope Valley Station.

When they reached the station, they pulled the wagons in the circle, and herded the horses, cattle, and mules inside. But the usual circle of tents outside the wagons did not appear. Instead, everyone not on guard duty slept in the wagons.

"Do you really think we'll be attacked?" Matilda asked Sinclair as he tethered White Star to one of the wagon wheels.

"No way to tell, but I don't want you sleepin' out in the open, just in case."

Matilda shivered.

"Relax," he reassured her. "We've put on a double guard. Go to sleep."

As Matilda tucked the children in, Mary's eyes grew wide. "Are we gonna be attacked by Indians, Mama?" Her voice quavered. "Will they do to us what they did to that man?" Elizabeth's face paled at Mary's words.

Matilda forced a laugh. "Your grandfather and Uncle Sinclair will take good care of us," she soothed.

When the children finally slept, Matilda lay down, certain her fears would keep her awake, but the exhaustion of the last three days quickly caught up with her. She fell asleep almost as soon as her head touched the pillow and her sleep was like black velvet.

As dawn broke in the east, she heard the first shot.

Chapter 48

Antelope Valley

A VOLLEY of shots rang out in response. Jake started an excited barking from underneath the wagon. Mary cried out in fear. Matilda heard a yelp of pain from somewhere in the circle of wagons. Pushing the child behind her, Matilda scrambled to her knees and pulled aside the heavy tarp. Looking out, she saw at least eight mounted Indians. Their painted bodies glistened in the pre-dawn light. My God, she thought. The raid I've been dreading for so long I'd stopped expecting it! Only two of the riders carried rifles. The rest brandished bows and arrows. As Matilda stared in horror, an arrow thudded into the tailboard of the wagon.

Realizing her stupidity in exposing herself, Matilda ducked behind the heavy wooden barrier, grateful Sinclair's foresight had them sleeping inside the wagon. Startled, Annie sat up and stared at her.

"Keep down, Annie," she ordered. Shoving Annie to the floor of the wagon, she gathered Lewis in her arms and pushed Elizabeth and Mary to relative safety against one of the heavy boxes. The wagon shook on its wheels, buffeted by panicked animals desperately attempting to escape. From under the wagon Jake set up a continuous howl.

"Oh, Miz Baldwin," Annie gasped, "what will we do if the wagon upsets?"

"It won't, Annie. Try not to frighten the children." Matilda knew the terror-stricken animals could knock over the wagon, but tried to reassure Annie and the children. She listened to the whoops and shouts of Utes and defenders, occasionally punctuated by a scream that stabbed through her body like a physical pain. She often found it hard to distinguish between animals and humans in the cacophony of sound.

She secured the children against the heavy box, shielding them with her body. She heard a crash that could only mean a wagon had overturned. "Please, White Star," she whispered, "please don't run. Don't leave me. Stay in the circle."

Matilda heard a woman's anguished scream, and huddled closer over the children, her only thought now to protect them. She waited, her heart pounding against her ribs, beating so rapidly it made her short of breath. Every time she heard an arrow strike she flinched, expecting any moment to feel the pain of one of the missiles tearing through her flesh.

She tried to tell herself what she knew about these raids: that the Indians sought only the animals, especially the horses, and would quickly retreat if they encountered stiff resistance. During a momentary lull, she carefully inched her way to the outer side of the wagon and lifted the canvas enough to peep out. She watched, mesmerized, as a shot echoed and a hole appeared in the coppery chest of a warrior riding towards her, his bow poised to launch an arrow. Blood gushed from the wound and his face changed from fierce intent to surprise. He faltered for a moment, then toppled from the horse. The animal rushed past Matilda's wagon so close she could have touched it.

The Indian's body fell not ten feet away from her peephole. The dull thud of his body hitting the ground echoed in her head. When the dust cleared, she saw his bleeding body clearly and shuddered. The incident passed in seconds. She scrambled back to cover the cowering children again.

It seemed to her she cringed in terror for hours, but less than twenty minutes actually elapsed from the time she heard the first shot until Sinclair's voice penetrated her consciousness.

"'Tilda! Annie! It's over. Were you and or any of the little ones hit?" His anxious face appeared before them as he yanked back the canvas from the rear of the wagon.

"No, no, we're fine, I think." Matilda sat up, taking deep breaths, trying to get her heart rate back under control. She felt dizzy from breathing so fast, and swayed slightly as she rose to her knees.

Annie lay curled in a ball against the rear corner of the wagon, her hands over her ears, her eyes squeezed shut.

"Come on, Annie. Didn't you hear me? It's over." Sinclair gently shook her arm.

Annie cautiously opened her eyes. "Are you sure they've gone?" she whispered.

Sinclair patted her shoulder and nodded. "Yes, they're gone."

The children popped up beside Matilda. Tears stained Mary's cheeks. Elizabeth's wide eyes stared out of her pale face, but Lewis' cheerful smile returned as soon as the noise stopped.

"Sarah? Britt? Mother? White Star?" Matilda questioned.

Sinclair nodded. "Okay so far. All of our wagons stayed upright. Britt got a scratch from an arrow, but it only made him so mad he got two of the Utes in return." He shook his head, his face grim as he added, "Upset the Ridgeway wagon. Killed Miz Ridgeway and the babe. If you're all right, I've got to get a fire goin'."

"Yes, yes, I'm fine. Tell Mother I'll be there to help her as soon as I get the children settled."

After Matilda calmed the girls and Lewis, she climbed down from the wagon to find White Star cowering beside the wagon, as close to her as possible. "Oh, White Star, White Star," she choked. Throwing her arms around the horse's neck, she wept with relief at finding her unharmed. Controlling herself with an effort, she calmed the shivering mare, then said, "Stay with the children, Annie. I have to help Mother." She patted Jake's head and he followed her, huddled close to her skirts.

She saw where the crush of the terrified animals had overturned the Ridgeway wagon. Matilda shuddered at the two blanketed forms, one so tiny. Mr. Ridgeway knelt beside them, twisting his hat. Tears ran down his cheeks and into his beard. Matilda remembered Mrs. Ridgeway sewing the little rabbits on the quilt before the infant's birth. The special quilt lay over the baby's body. Poor little thing, she thought. Her heart aching as she remembered the many times she had held and cuddled little Arthur James, Junior.

She walked to where her mother checked the injuries of Matthew and Jenny Ridgeway. Matthew lay on the ground, his leg obviously broken. Betsy Ann knelt beside him. She looked up as Matilda approached.

"Wheel fell on him. Leg's broke," she reported. "Sinclair's gettin' the fire started. Make me a cup of catnip tea so's I can get some laudanum into this poor mite. We'll set it later, after he's asleep."

"Am I gonna die, Miz Randolph?" Matthew asked, his eyes wide in his tear-streaked face.

"Shoo' now, of course not," she reassured him. "We'll fix that leg and you'll be up and goin' in no time." Matilda noted with relief that the bone, while bulging against the outer edge of his thigh, had not broken the skin. She remembered a neighbor back in Illinois who had not been so fortunate. The man's agony as he died still haunted her.

Jenny sat beside her older brother and held his hand. Her only visible injury was a large lump on her right temple.

One of the single men, one Matilda knew only slightly, had been killed. Another lay dying. Two, including Britt, had suffered minor wounds. Sinclair already had the fire going for tea and for his mother's comfrey poultices. Two iron rods heated in the coals. Newer methods of preventing suppuration had been proposed, Matilda thought with a smile, but Betsy Ann stayed firmly with her method of hot iron cautery.

"Never heard of it failin' yet," she declared.

Britt sat beside the fire sipping a cup of the opium-laden lukewarm tea. His wife, Sarah stood beside him holding a cloth against his wounded arm to stop the bleeding.

"Hello, little sister," Britt grinned at Matilda. "I almost dodged the arrow. Didn't get quite low enough."

Matilda lifted the bandage. The arrow, she saw to her relief, had not cut deeply, and the bleeding had stopped. The burning should keep it from festering. She had to hope the tip of the arrow had not been poisoned by being dipped in an antelope liver filled with rattlesnake venom. She could not remember who told her about that Indian trick, but she tried to forget it.

While waiting for Britt to become groggy, Matilda walked over to where the severely injured man lay. She had spoken to him often, and knew him only as Andrew, a quiet, polite young man, always shaved and neat and clean, in a contrast to most of the single men on the trail. He had a ready smile that always lighted his whole face, revealing clean white teeth without the usual tobacco stains. She felt a pang of loss to think she would never see that smile again.

The shaft of an arrow protruded from the side of his chest. The pink froth bubbling from his lips with each labored breath told her the projectile had pierced his lungs. Nothing could be done to save him, so no purpose would be served by putting him through the agony of removing the arrow. His eyes, open but unseeing, stared into space. She shook her head in sorrow.

Wes Overton sat on the ground beside the dying man, holding his hand. He made no attempt to hide the tears coursing down his cheeks. Matilda knew Andrew and Wes had become friends, as both traveled with no other family members. Weldon stood behind Wes, his face set.

"He looks to be unconscious," Weldon said, his voice gruff with the effort of trying to hold his own tears in check. "We just didn't think it right for him to die alone. He's got no kin with him."

Matilda's eyes filled. She sank to her knees on the opposite side of the wounded man and took his other hand. A slight pressure in return told her he knew she was with him.

"Have you family back home, Andrew?" Matilda choked. "Someone we can notify?"

He tried to speak, but could not. He pulled her hand toward his pocket, then his arm fell back limply. The labored breathing stopped. "He's gone," Matilda whispered, meeting Wes's eyes across the still form. Weldon squeezed Matilda's shoulder and walked away.

Matilda took a small notebook from Andrew's pocket and opened it. Several letters fell out. She opened one.

"My darling Andrew," Matilda read through eyes blurred by tears, "I am addressing this to you in Fort Laramie. I hope it reaches you. I so look forward to your letter telling me you have found a home for us and we can join you in California. It sounds like such a wonderful land. The children ... " A flood of tears blinded Matilda and she read no further. Looking through the notebook, she found a photograph of a smiling young woman with a boy about five and a girl about three.

Matilda took the little notebook and tucked it inside her waistband. "I'll write back and tell his wife what happened, tell her we gave him Christian burial," she told Wes. "It's the least we can do for him." Later, she thought. I'll do it later. Right now, I can't. It's been less than a year since ... since ... She could not complete the thought even to herself. Her loss of Lewis struck her like a blow and her heart went out to Andrew's young widow.

Lifting Andrew's head, as she instinctively felt his wife would have done, she pressed his face close to her breast and sat, gently stroking his hair, with tears running down her cheeks. Unseeing and unhearing, she sat immobile, filled with her own pain, until her mother touched her shoulder.

"Come, Matilda," Betsy Ann said gently. "I need your help."

Numbly, Matilda rose to her feet. She wiped her eyes as Sinclair approached to help Wes. The two men picked up Andrew's body and walked away. Matilda's eyes followed the direction they took. She saw her father and a couple of other men digging graves.

Drawing a deep breath, she forced herself to speak calmly. "Yes, Mother, just tell me what to do."

So Matilda held Britt's hand while her mother seared the slight cut on his arm, frightened to think it could have been her brother instead of Andrew who took the arrow through the chest. Two men held the wounded arm to keep Britt from jerking during the procedure and getting an extra burn. Sarah, too squeamish to watch, retreated to their wagon.

"Ready?" Betsy Ann asked.

"Ready." Britt, groggy from the laudanum, gritted his teeth. He gripped Matilda's hand.

Matilda, her eyes squeezed shut, heard the sizzle as the iron touched the cut. The smell of burning flesh sent a wave of nausea flowing through her. His hand slippery with sweat, Britt tightened his grip and Matilda feared he would break the bones in her hand. Fortunately, the operation lasted only a few seconds before she felt his hand relax.

"Here." Betsy Ann handed Matilda a strip of clean cloth. "Bandage it for him."

Matilda's hands shook as she carefully bandaged her brother's arm. The odor of seared flesh surrounded her. It took all her control not to gag. "Thanks, little sister," Britt whispered, his eyes losing their focus as he relaxed and permitted the laudanum to take effect.

Sarah returned with an armload of bedding. "Let him lie down right here," she said. "He can sleep it off while we finish putting the wagons back together."

The other wounded man refused to allow Betsy Ann to burn the gash on his shoulder, preferring to treat it himself.

"Good whiskey's the best there is to keep a wound from festering, Miz' Matilda," he declared as she prepared to dress his shoulder for him. The smell told her he had already applied his cure liberally, both inside and out.

"As you wish," she smiled, averting her head to avoid the odor from his breath as he spoke. "Just let me cover it with a clean cloth to keep the dust out." She applied the bandage deftly and as quickly as she could, trying to hold her breath until she could get away.

"Ready, Matilda?" Betsy Ann called from beside the Ridgeway's overturned wagon. "Matthew's sound asleep. Let's get this leg set."

"Ready," Matilda replied, hurrying to her mother's side. Little Jenny could not have been over four or five years old, but she sat bravely by her brother's side, still holding his hand. Her other hand held a cool, comfrey poultice to the purple swelling on her temple. Tears stained her pale cheeks, but she made no sound.

She's trying to take her mother's place already, thought Matilda. Her heart ached for the poor, motherless children. Remembering her own foolishness when she looked out over the end of the wagon, she could not help thinking that her children could have been left motherless just as easily.

"Sinclair," Betsy Ann turned to her youngest son, "got those boards ready?"

"Ready." Sinclair held two splints cut to the length of Matthew's leg. He positioned them on either side of the wounded limb, strips of cloth in place to tie as soon as the bone was set correctly.

"Get a good hold of his leg, Matilda." Betsy Ann directed Matilda to Matthew's thigh, above the break. She herself gripped the lower part of the limb. "Now," she ordered, "hold steady." She pulled gently. Matilda strained to keep Matthew's body in place as the boy groaned in his opium-induced sleep.

Matilda felt rather than heard the ends of the bone grate as they slid past each other and popped into place. The sound vibrated up her arms and through her body. She shivered. As the ends settled together, Matthew cried out.

"Hold him, Matilda. Don't let him jerk and pull the bone out of place," Betsy Ann cautioned. "Sinclair, get those boards tied on." Both strained to obey. In moments it was over. The cloth strips secured the splints in place, holding the limb straight. Matthew relaxed into a deep sleep again. More tears streaked the face of faithful little Jenny.

Sinclair helped Betsy Ann as she struggled to regain her feet. "Hoo-ee," she panted. "Gettin' too old for this." She rubbed her knees. "Must be gettin' a touch of the rheumatics."

Arthur Ridgeway hovered nearby, his eyes rimmed with red, still mangling the hat he held in his hands. "Will he . . . will he . . . ?" He seemed unable to bring himself to ask the question.

"He should be fine, Arthur," Betsy Ann assured the distraught man. "Just keep the boards in place at least a month. Children heal up fast." She smiled in sympathy. "Doubt he'll have more than a limp, if that. Keep those cool comfrey poultices on, half-hour out of ev'ry hour 'til the swelling's gone." She walked away, back towards the sleeping Britt.

Matilda smiled gently at Mr. Ridgeway as he knelt beside his sleeping son, and patted his hand in sympathy.

* * *

The men spent the rest of the day repairing the damage to the wagons. They recovered most of the scattered animals. Several dozen had escaped through the breach in the barrier made when the Ridgeway wagon overturned but fortunately, since the defenders drove off the Utes quickly, only a few were stolen. The raiders wounded three mules and one horse so badly they had to be destroyed.

The Indians also shot one of Britt's cows. Muttering deprecations against Indians in general and the Utes in particular, he butchered her to salvage the meat. The fact that she was a prize milker made the task even less palatable.

They were forced to leave the bodies of the three mules and the horse, even though it bothered everyone to know the Indians would return later to eat the carcasses. "They do that, Miz Matilda," Giles explained. "If they can't run 'em off, they shoot 'em. They know we've gotta leave, then they can come back and get the meat. They're always real hungry for meat." He paused. "Any kind of meat, even mules."

Matilda shuddered.

The owner of the horse wanted to bury it, but the magnitude of the labor involved deterred him. "Breaks my heart to think of them savages eatin' ol' Ben, Miss Matilda," he said with tears in his eyes.

Matilda laid a comforting hand on his arm. Knowing how she would feel if White Star lay there, she could think of no words of sympathy.

One young man, anxious to get his horse back, urged the others to join him in pursuit of the Utes, but saner heads prevailed.

"Not worth it," Gardner told him. "May take three, four days. Remember, they know this country. You don't. Besides, you might get yourself killed in the process. Sorry, son, I know how you feel about your horse." He smiled wistfully and Matilda knew he thought of his favorite horse, old Alice, the pie-bald mare he rode for years. "Felt that way about one myself once."

The death of his wife and baby took the heart out of Arthur Ridgeway. With two injured children to care for and his wagon destroyed, he elected to return to Salt Lake City.

"It's only ten, twelve days back," he told Gardner. "The other wagons in my bunch will come with me. We'll wait there, let Matt 'n' Jenny get well. Maybe come across next spring."

They left Antelope Canyon in mid-morning on Wednesday, July 27. Ridgeway's small party turned east, back across the desert they had struggled so hard to cross. The remainder continued west.

.

Chapter 49

Antelope Valley to Ruby Valley

BECAUSE THEY did not leave Antelope Valley until mid-morning, they only covered fifteen miles and camped by the Spring Valley Station. Matilda, tears in her eyes at the thought of poor Andrew's death, managed with some difficulty to write a letter to his widow. "He was a fine young man," she wrote, after telling how he died, "and very brave. His last thoughts were for you and the children, and he wanted me to tell you." The tears blurred her vision, forcing her to blink them away before she could continue. "I understand your grief, for I am recently widowed myself. If you ever come to California, please look for me through my brother, Alfred Randolph of Hicksville. I would like very much to meet you."

Her letter finished, she walked to the small stone building that served as the mail station. Inside, an unmade cot took up most of the back wall. A small table and a Topsy stove stood on one side. In the opposite corner, two large canvas bags, one marked "East," the other marked "West," leaned tipsily against the wall.

The station keeper rose to greet her. The plate of greasy food congealing on the plate made her stomach churn.

"Evenin', Miss," he grinned, revealing gaps between his tobacco-stained teeth. His beard bore evidence of at least the previous three meals, perhaps more. He scratched his side vigorously, like he had a real purpose for the activity.

Matilda repressed a shudder and involuntarily stepped back. She knew instinctively the man's bedding crawled with vermin. Her skin prickled.

"I would like to mail this letter, please," she said, trying not to notice the odor that permeated the small room. She passed the letter to him and watched him stamp the date and the name of the station, then carefully counted out the dollar for the stage company and the three cents for the postage. I should start sending fewer letters, she thought since the cost is so prohibitive. The stage company does provide the service, so I suppose I should be thankful, but a dollar still sounds like a lot of money.

When he tossed the letter into the "East" bag, Matilda hastened from the room, knowing at least the letter got into the right bag. When she got into the fresh air again, she took a deep breath, and realized she had held her breath while inside the cabin.

Matilda's heart ached for Andrew's widow. She thought of the poor woman waiting for word from her husband, praying for his safety. Matilda knew for a certainty that his letters had been regular, for she had seen him mail them at every station.

A tent for the hostler stood a short distance from the station. A rough corral behind the tent held six horses and as many mules. The whole area, dirty and dust covered, bore an aura of hopelessness. She thought of the station keeper and wondered why anyone would choose to live in such a miserable, desolate place.

The next morning, they crossed to Schell Station, and Matilda could only gape.

"What a difference from the last stop," she marveled to Sinclair. Before them lay a whole community. "Makes me feel like we're almost back in civilization."

"Yep," he agreed. "Guess the Overland decided this would be the jewel of the stations. They must grow tons of hay. And look at the size of that garden! Four or five acres at least. Ready for some fresh vegetables?"

"Am I ever! And how lucky today is Saturday. What a

great place to spend Sunday."

"Just finished that new shop building," the station keeper boasted. "Company brought in stone masons from Utah. Got twenty skilled workers here all the time: carpenters, painters, wheelwrights, even a coach builder. Whitewash the buildings twice a year." He shifted the wad to the other cheek and spat. "Yep, this here is the Overland's biggest facility between Salt Lake and Carson City."

Matilda cringed as a line of tobacco juice dribbled down into his beard. She thought chewing tobacco had to be the filthiest habit men had ever developed.

The man rambled on. "Had a few problems with Injuns last year when the California Volunteers was out stirring up trouble, but it's been right peaceful since the Company's been supplying the tribes with food and such. Still an occasional raid, like happened to you folks, but, in general, they've not bothered the stage line. Most of the raiders are looking for horses." He eyed White Star, who stood with her chin resting lightly on Sinclair's shoulder. "Many a brave would risk his life to ride a horse like that one you got there."

Sinclair wrapped his arm around White Star's neck. "Then he'll have to get past me," he declared. "Come on, 'Tilda. Let's get some supper."

Matilda shivered as she followed Sinclair back to the camp. Was White Star the draw? Did Mrs. Ridgeway and her baby die, she thought, because I brought White Star?

Sinclair, studying Matilda's face, grinned down at her. "Now, don't go blaming yourself. White Star's a fine horse, but she's not the only one those Ute's were after."

Her common sense exerted itself and she sighed. "I suppose you're right. Let's go eat."

The next morning, they left Schell station at daybreak, wanting to get as far as possible before the heat of the day forced them to stop and rest the animals.

Betsy Ann announced her intention to walk for a while. "Need to move the old bones," she declared. "Settin' on that hard bench all day makes a body stiff." She tied her sunbonnet firmly under her chin. "Long's it's nice and cool, I'm going to walk."

"Want to ride next to Grandpa," Mary announced, climbing onto the seat beside Gardner.

"Me, too!" Elizabeth chimed in, climbing up beside her.

"There's no room for you," Mary argued. "This is my seat." The squabble continued, beginning to heat up.

Gardner chuckled. "Settle it between you. Just be sure and hold on."

As the dispute showed no signs of abating, Matilda felt it time to intervene. "Now, girls, there's plenty of room for both of you." She stepped onto the wagon tongue and arranged the children side by side on the bench beside their grandfather.

"There's not enough room," Mary grumbled. "She's pushing against me."

"Am not!" Elizabeth pronounced in a loud voice.

"If you don't get along, Grandpa won't let either one of you ride up here." Gardner's growl ended the vocal exchange. He grinned and shook the reins. "Gee-up!"

They traveled in silence for nearly an hour, down the hillside from Schell Station and started across a wide valley. The scent of sage almost overpowered Matilda's senses. She looked out across the expanse before them towards the next range of hills.

This certainly is strange country, she thought. We just cross one line of hills after another, with wide valleys in between. So different from the areas along the Mississippi Valley. And sage has to be the toughest . . . .

A scream from Mary interrupted her thoughts and she whirled to see Elizabeth tumble from her seat on the lumbering wagon, falling directly in front of the left front wheel.

Everything happened at once. Gardner pulled back on the reins, yelling a frantic "Whoa!" at the horses. Mary continued to scream. Matilda, her only thought to reach Elizabeth before the huge wheel crushed her, lunged forward. As she gathered the fallen child, she felt strong arms grab her and pull the two of them back, out of danger.

The threat passed in seconds. Matilda found herself, with Elizabeth clutched to her breast, held firmly in Sinclair's arms. She felt his heart pounding in his chest. Her own pulse throbbed in her temples. Matilda shuddered in horror. What a narrow escape! Tales of children killed by falling under wagon wheels abounded on the trail. She struggled to get her breathing back under control as Sinclair released her. Their eyes met.

"Thank you," she murmured inanely, her thoughts still jumbled.

He grinned down at her. "You're welcome. I just hope the next time you decide to throw yourself under a wagon wheel I am as close by."

Matilda gave a shaky little laugh. "So do I." She turned to calm the child in her arms. Elizabeth buried her face against her mother's neck and sobbed hysterically.

Matilda looked up at Mary. Guilt spread all over the little face. "I didn't mean for her to fall, Mama," she explained, earnestness in every word. "She pushed me and I just gave her a little shove back." Tears welled up in the blue eyes and overflowed, making streaks in the dust on the freckled cheeks.

Betsy Ann strolled up, wiping her forehead. "I'll settle this. Into the wagon with both of you. Sinclair, give me a hand. I think it's time I rode again."

The girls settled down in the wagon and Gardner stirred the team into motion.

Matilda just shook her head.

Chapter 50

Ruby Valley

RUBY Valley Mail Station
Thursday, August 4, 1864

Dear Caroline,

Sorry for neglecting you. We are now 150 miles from Camp Floyd, roughly halfway between Salt Lake City and Carson City. Another two weeks should see us in Carson City, with the desert finally behind us. Will I be glad! I have seen enough desert to last me a lifetime, and they tell me we haven't even come to the worst part.

We got into the Ruby Valley Station late this afternoon, traveling on Sunday because no one wanted to stay in Ute territory any longer than necessary. Pa says he is sure God will understand. But we are going to stay at least part of tomorrow to rest and recruit the animals. This desert is one rugged canyon after another, with dry, alkali desert in between. The wind blows the grit into everyone's eyes. Between that and the glare from the sun it's a wonder we're not all blind.

A small party of Utes attacked us in Antelope Valley. We lost only a few head of stock, but unfortunately four people were killed. One was that nice young man from New York who joined us in Fort Kearny, the one Wes befriended, and we also lost Mrs. Ridgeway and her adorable baby. Poor Mr. Ridgeway! He and his party returned to Salt Lake City, as his two other children were injured when the wagon overturned. Losing his wife and baby seemed to take all of the heart out of him. Britt lost one of his best milk cows in addition to getting a slight wound from an arrow. I don't know which made him madder.

After we left Antelope Valley we were all on edge, watching for Utes at every turn, but thank heavens nothing happened.

We are in the country of the pinon pine now. It's a dwarfish tree that looks almost like a shrub, the way the needles are feathered all the way to the ground. Giles says the seed from the cone of the pinon pine provides the Indians around here with the principal part of their diet. He seems to know a lot about Indians. He's real interesting to listen to, but I don't like to encourage him too much. I fear he's becoming a little too fond of me.

Anyway, we finally reached Egan's Canyon after struggling through heavy sand, crossing a rough road hedged in by thickets and dotted with boulders. I swear, I thought I saw an Indian behind every boulder. Giles did find Indian sign, so we were cautious. The children and I slept in the wagon. Giles pointed out where the Indians had walked, then covered their tracks by brushing them with a sprig of brush. I don't know how he knew. It just looked like sand to me. I'm glad he's with us.

Not wanting a repeat of the Ridgeway tragedy, when the stampeding animals upset the wagon, the men decided to herd the stock outside of the wagons with several men on guard. I refused to let them put White Star out, however, and kept her tethered to the side of the wagon.

During the night, an Indian brave (probably Ute, though no one ever saw him) snuck into the middle of the herd and let out a war whoop. Cattle and horses and mules and men went in every direction, and the enterprising brave got away with two mules in the resulting melee.

All the men looked upon it as a huge joke. They are still laughing at the guards. Losing two mules to one lone Indian. That brave is probably still laughing too. But it was kind of scary, to think he could get so close with no one noticing him. Britt especially felt foolish, because an Indian played a similar trick on them when they came out in '50. Remember? From Alf's letter?

In Egan Canyon, we camped on a bench above the station. It was a lovely site, but there were enough mosquitoes to carry off a small horse. I don't think I slept a wink. I'd pull the blanket over my head until I couldn't breathe, then take it off until the whine of the mosquitoes drove me back under. I did this back and forth all night. Fortunately, the children can sleep though anything, so I just covered their heads with an apron and they slept all night. Even the ruckus when the Ute scattered the stock didn't wake them up.

While we were at the station in Egan Canyon, we talked to the station keeper, a Mr. Salisbury. He told us he gets fifty dollars a month and his keep. I guess that's pretty good, but I wouldn't live clear out here for any amount of money. Especially since the accommodations are a cook stove and two bunks built into the wall of a one room cabin. The food they supply is flour and bacon. He does have a hostler to care for the stock and an Indian handyman who lives nearby in a brush shelter, but I don't think they give him much company.

Silver has been mined near there since 1861. Mr. Salisbury told us one story about a miner who killed his partner then rode all the way into Austin to turn himself in to the sheriff. He got himself acquitted because he claimed he hit the man in a fight, then shot him to keep him from suffering when he couldn't nurse him back to health. And the sheriff believed him! Honestly, men will believe anything. I sure never would have accepted that story.

The next day we crossed the divide and the north end of Butte Valley. Halfway up the hill was Butte Station. It had a very small spring, but the water was good. That's one thing I have really come to appreciate — good water. I must describe the station to you, as it was so typical of these western 'homes'. A simple cabin of sandstone compacted with mud, and roofed with split cedar trunks. Behind the *house is a corral of rails with a small shed in one corner to give the poor beasts shelter from the cold in winter or the hot sun in summer. But it's so small not very many can get in at any one time. I guess the poor things have to take turns.*

They made the door to the cabin from the backboard of a wagon, with no hinges and no lock. I guess there's no need of locks in this godforsaken country. They probably don't have anything worth stealing anyway. A slab of metal that looks like it came from a locomotive (though how in the world it got clear out here I can only guess) served as a stepping stone. They just throw the slops out the front door, and the metal step lays in a mass of soppy black soil strewed with ashes and other garbage that I shuddered to look at too closely. A load of wood stood to one side. On the other side they formed a tank of sorts by damming up a dirty pool which flowed through the corral behind the cabin.

They separated the inside into living and sleeping quarters with a canvas partition. The bunks were standing bedsteads of poles planted in the ground and covered with piles of filthy ragged blankets. I swear the blankets swarmed with vermin. Beneath the framework they piled everything from saddles to bags of potatoes, and the dogs slept in amongst the lot, wherever they could find room. The dirt floor had one corner perpetually soaked by water from the spring. You would think they would have sense enough not to build the cabin right over the spring, but apparently not.

The fireplace, a magnificent piece of architecture almost out of place with the rest of the furnishings, covered half a wall. They had two rough-dressed plank tables, and some posts that served as chairs and stools. Pegs on the walls supported spurs, pistols, whips, gloves, leggings, and all kinds of tools. They provided a tin skillet of water and a dipper for diners wishing to wash, but a handful of gravel served as the soap and evaporation as a towel. I only looked in and shuddered, thankful I could return to our own clean campfire for a decent supper.

Some call this station the Robbers Roost, and for good reason, I'm sure. I know we kept a close eye on White Star. In fact, we didn't camp close to the station. We went on a couple of miles past before we stopped.

The next day we ascended a long divide, with two steep hills and falls, to cross the north end of Long Valley. Crossing the creek was tricky, for the banks are very steep. The barren landscape got depressing after a while, but as we ascended the divide to the station at Mountain Springs, it improved. We spent the night there to rest after the climb.

The next morning we began the descent into Ruby Valley and the road became excellent. Ruby Valley is such a pretty place. From the top of the pass after we left Mountain Springs, we had a magnificent view of the whole valley. It must be a hundred miles long and three or four miles wide. Since the springs are scattered all along the base of the western mountains, water is plentiful. Because of all the water, the grass is lush and green, in spite of the heat in the day. The cattle, after all those miles of desert, are enjoying the bounty.

Farmers have settled a large portion of the valley. Springs come down from the mountain all along the west side of the valley. In one place I saw four, only a few yards apart. Sunflowers and a lovely white flower I didn't recognize pop up all along the way. Mary and I went walking through a small stand of willows and saw two fawns. We didn't tell anyone, because the sight so entranced me I couldn't bear the thought of anyone killing them.

The Ruby Valley Mail Station is supposed to be one of the best on the road, so I am determined to get this letter off to you.

They named the valley for the rubies they say can be found in the crevices of the rocks. Sinclair, Wes and Weldon, along with Britt's boys, went looking to see if they could find any, but, needless to say, without success.

I stood at the station and looked across the valley. Those black cedar trees cover the hills, and the mountain peaks tower above it all. I thought I could see Pilot Peak, but Sinclair says it's my imagination. We did see it coming across, and I couldn't help thinking of those poor people who struggled across that salt desert.

We met a young (at least I think he's young. It's so hard to tell) Shoshone chief with an unpronounceable name. Everyone shortens it to Chokop. He assures us we will have no problems in his lands. He says the Utes are bad people, and that his tribe fights them at every opportunity. I suppose I should find that comforting, except that we are quickly passing from his land and back into Ute territory.

Here at the station we also met a George Stuart Douglass. Quite an imposing name, don't you think? His wife fell ill on their way across, so they stayed here to see if she would recover. The rest of his party went on. Mrs. Douglass died last week, and Mr. Douglass wants to join us to continue on to California. It's just him and his boy, George Edward. They had only the one child. Young George is about ten years old, and has fair hair and the biggest batch of freckles I ever saw. I think we will see a lot of him, for he is quite taken with Mary, and follows her everywhere. She, of course, has quickly turned it to her advantage and has him running and fetching all the time.

There is a pass near here that the Biddleston-Bartwell Party used, but that Hastings says is too steep for wagons. Since he is the one who sent the Donners to their fate, I don't know how much credence to put in his advice. The stage goes about twenty miles south to Overland Pass. The men are arguing about it as I write. Claim is we'll be on the Humboldt in two days, three at most if we cross Harrison Pass, even if it takes all day, whereas it will take at least five and maybe six days to go around. Britt says there'll be plenty of grass on the Humboldt, and it's getting sparser as we follow the stage road.

Whatever they decide, we should be on the Humboldt within two to five days. Britt knows the area around the Humboldt and is anxious to get back to it.

Once we reach the river, I will really feel like we are getting closer, even though we still have a long ways to go. I look forward to Carson City. Pa says he hears it is the wickedest city this side of Sodom and Gomorrah. I can hardly wait.

Will try and write oftener from now on.

Love,
'Tilda

Chapter 51

Ruby Valley over Harrison Pass to the Humboldt Sink

BRITT AND SINCLAIR RODE UP to the summit of Harrison Pass and returned to report the climb would be a tough one, but it could be done. The argument between the men lasted well into the evening.

"Got to have grass for the stock," Britt said. "We'll find it on the Humboldt. It's less than four miles from here to the summit. From the top, we saw the Humboldt Valley. Can't be over two days. One day to get over the top, two days or less to the South Fork. River bottom all the way."

"Compare that to four days to go around by Overland Pass, plus two days more to come back up," Sinclair chimed in. "And water for the stock is harder to find."

"And if we lose a wagon?" Weldon asked.

"Shouldn't happen if we're careful," Britt assured him. "No one rides in the wagons. We lead the horses up, hitch up double teams. Have a man ready by the traces. Wagon goes, cut it loose, save the horses. Won't be any worse than crossing the Sierras."

"What about goin' down? Kin lose a wagon jest as easy going down." George Douglass remained unconvinced.

"Chain the wheels, drag a log behind. C'n also tie a mule or two behind to help keep 'em steady."

Matilda and Annie stood a little apart from the speakers, but they heard every word. Matilda glanced over at Annie. The girl looked frightened. She still had not mentioned her pregnancy, but Matilda knew she was far advanced. They dared not let her ride in one of the wagons on such a dangerous slope.

"Don't worry, Annie," she murmured. "We'll walk slow, take our time. It'll take them all day to get those wagons up and over." She grinned. "And we'll stay clear away from 'em!"

The next morning, the four Randolph wagons, the Douglass wagon, and two others began the climb up Harrison Pass. The remainder of the group elected to continue to Overland Pass and headed south.

"Will we be safe from Indians with only seven wagons?" Matilda asked. Her voice trembled as she spoke, in spite of her effort to keep it steady. "Isn't that too small a group?" She remembered how the commanders at both Fort Kearney and Fort Cottonwood refused to allow anyone to leave with less than thirty wagons.

"We're well-armed, and have a number of outriders," Britt reassured her. "Giles is sticking with us. Him being sweet on you is an advantage." Matilda blushed and Britt chuckled. "He's real good at spotting Injun sign. We'll just be extra cautious. Not usually much problem with Indians along here, anyway. Too many settlements close by."

Matilda sighed. She watched as Weldon led the first wagon, with eight horses, and started up the hill. Britt attached all eight of his mules to the first of his wagons and fell into line behind, leaving a safe distance between them.

Gardner, with Wes Overton and Giles, stayed to guard the remaining wagons until the teams could return. When the dust from the first group settled, the women and children started their upward struggle.

They had barely begun when Betsy Ann chortled with glee and scurried to a row of bushes growing by the side of the trail. "Chokecherries!" she cried, gathering the sides of her apron to form a basket. "We'll have chokecherry syrup for the johnny cake tomorrow. Maybe even make some flap-jacks to put it over." She began industriously filling her apron. "Come on, Mary, Lizzie. Give me a hand."

When Matilda hesitated, she added. "They'll be all day getting those wagons over. We've got plenty of time."

Matilda laughed. Her mother always put things in proper perspective. After all, what good would it do to worry about the wagons? She couldn't do anything anyway. If they lost one, they lost one. Might as well look forward to flapjacks with chokecherry syrup. She gathered the edges of her apron into a basket and threw herself into the task of picking the ripe berries.

By noon, everyone stood at the summit, ready for dinner and a rest before they tackled the descent on the other side. The last quarter of a mile, up to the head of the canyon, had been the steepest part of the climb. There the source of the spring that fed back down into Ruby Valley widened into a bowl. Tall aspen trees lined the creekbed.

Betsy Ann not only had an apron full of chokecherries, which she promptly gave to Sinclair to stow in the wagon for her, she had also gathered a mass of watercress from the creek.

"Helps stave off the scurvy," she declared. "Good to have fresh greens."

"They's a plant as grows along the Humboldt the Injuns eat all the time," Giles advised. "Call it two-leaf orach. It's pretty tasty. I'll show you some, soon's we get there."

Matilda stood for a moment at the crest of the hill and looked out over the valley below. The hot desert wind blew over her. The descent looked even steeper than the climb.

"How high are we?" she asked Giles, who strode up and began filling his bowl with some of the steaming stew in the pot.

"Over seven thousand feet, I believe. High enough the water doesn't get hot enough to cook beans proper. You can see why this pass is not popular, but it does cut off about four days if a body is heading for the Humboldt. The stage, now, it goes farther south, cuts across so it don't have to cross the Forty Mile Desert. But they don't need grass for as many cattle."

It took the rest of the day to get everyone down the other side. On the trip down, the canyon widened into small meadows. Beaver dams frequently blocked the creek, making pretty little ponds of still water. At the foot of the canyon, they camped in a lovely meadow surrounded by lush grass and meadow flowers — and innumerable mosquitoes. Giles built a smoky fire upwind so the breeze carried the smoke over Matilda's tent. The smoke burned her eyes, but, to her relief, the tactic really helped cut down the number of the pesky creatures.

She laughed ruefully to Annie, "It would be so nice to have enough water sometime without mosquitoes along with it!"

Annie swatted at one buzzing around her ear and agreed.

But the next morning, when they left the meadow, and reached the river bed, Matilda's heart sank.

"Isn't there water in the river at all?" she asked Giles, trying to keep the fear from her voice.

Giles hastened to reassure her. "These are side washes, Miz Baldwin. Only run when it rains or with the snow melt in the spring. There'll be water when we get to the South Fork of the Humboldt, I promise. Always find water there."

Later, as Matilda related to her mother what Giles had said, she lamented the lack of water. "If I could just wash the dust off my face I would feel so much better."

"Don't you even think about dipping into that water barrel, young lady," her mother said sternly. "That water's far too precious to waste on washing." She smiled in sympathy. "Won't be too much longer. Soon's we get to the river, we'll have all the water we want."

Matilda only sighed.

* * *

At mid-day, on Sunday, August 7, after crossing twenty miles of dry river bottom, they reached the South Fork of the Humboldt. They traveled on Sunday, not daring to stop until they reached water. The river, about ten feet wide at the crossing, was shallow, but the water, though slow moving, sang and rippled over the rocky bottom. Little rainbows danced in the sunlight where the water rose over the larger rocks.

People and animals alike fell into the cool wetness. With a sigh of relief, Matilda scooped the water up in her hands and poured it over her face. Jake splashed along beside her, lapping as though he could not believe he had found water at last.

"See, 'Tilda," Britt said, "I told you we'd have water along the Humboldt."

She gave him a wry smile. "Did I ever doubt you?"

They spent the afternoon enjoying the river. Matilda washed clothes and the men soaked the wagon wheels to tighten them on their rims and refilled all the barrels and jugs.

At dawn on Monday, August 8, they started along the south fork of the Humboldt. They followed the river to its intersection with the Humboldt. Shortly afterwards, the river entered a narrow canyon, forcing them to again leave the river and cross over the hills. They followed a hogback, a curving swale between rolling hills.

The dust impressed Matilda the most. Kicked up by dozens of hooves, it rose above them in a cloud so thick she could not see the whole length of the line of wagons. She stood almost knee deep in dust in some places. It sifted through the handkerchief she wore over her nose and mouth. The dun colored dust caked on their sweaty bodies. They dared not waste water on washing. Food tasted like the dust, and it made everything gritty.

A brief stop at Emigrant Springs revived their spirits and they continued, descending a long hill to meet the river once more at Gravelly Ford.

"This is supposed to be where Reed and Snyder quarreled and Snyder was killed," Britt reported.

"And driving Reed out sealed their fate," Sinclair commented.

Britt shrugged. "We'll never know. Put on a double guard tonight. This is also a famous spot for trouble with the Utes."

They had no Indian trouble, and three days later reached Iron Point and a great bend in the river. In the coolness of the morning, Giles pointed out great plumes of steam rising from hot springs a mile or so to the south. The desert lay before them, a wavering mass of dancing heat waves.

"Big battle in the mountains just north of here, back in the fifties, between emigrants and Injuns," Giles reported. "Utes run off a bunch of stock and the emigrants gathered about a hundred men and went after 'em." He grinned. "Got 'em back, too. Cattle real important then. Man get stranded with no animals to pull his wagons or carry his supplies, he'd be in real danger. Nowadays, they's so much traffic runnin' back and forth, and so many tradin' posts along the way, it's not as bad."

Matilda looked at the barren, tumbled hills and shivered. "Do you suppose we'll be attacked again?"

Giles shrugged. "Not likely. Hard to say."

Matilda somehow found little comfort in his words.

From Iron Point, they crossed to Lassen Meadows. Once they left the tule beds at the loop where the river turned south, they faced a seventy mile stretch of desolate emptiness. Seventy miles of heat and dust. The hot sand burned Matilda's feet. The very ground looked like it had been consumed by fire, leaving piles of tumbled cinders and ashes in its wake. Even the river lost its clarity and ran thick and dark and sluggish. Keeping the animals from drinking out of the alkali ponds around the river presented a constant problem.

Some of the cures for alkali poisoning she remembered from Alf's letters persisted in the minds of some of her fellow travelers. "Would you believe," she told Sinclair, shaking her head in despair, "that one of these poor fools actually chopped off the end of his poor beast's tail, swearing that would cure him?" The memory of the abused creature bellowing in pain as his owner smeared hot tar on the stump to stop the bleeding bothered her still. "And another cut off the tips of his cow's horns, as if that could possibly help."

"I'll believe anything," Sinclair said. "Martin claims the others are wrong, that the only cure is raw bacon." He chuckled. "You should have seen him trying to get bacon down the mule's throat. Pa's probably right. He says the best cure for alkali poisoning is to make sure your cattle don't drink the wretched water in the first place. He has us watching our animals like hawks."

When they finally reached Lassen Meadows, Matilda joined her mother and Annie at the cooking fire. "What a relief not to have to travel tomorrow." She sighed with ecstasy. "We'll have time to bake some proper bread and get everything in the boxes aired out. And this will be our only chance to wash clothes. From here on, we'll be rationing water again."

"Stuff'll dry quick in this weather. Look at Mary's hair." Annie, seated on a stump by the wagon, brushed Mary's beautiful red-gold tresses, which flew around her head in a halo. The Douglass boy stood just back from the group. Mary's hair seemed to fascinate him. Matilda noticed he always appeared whenever she or Annie combed Mary's hair. The pinafore Annie wore hid most of the evidence of her pregnancy, but Matilda knew the day fast approached when Annie would be giving birth. She saw Betsy Ann's eyes on the girl and knew her mother shared similar concerns, but Betsy Ann only made a face and remarked, "This country sure gets hot as the inside of a cow. George," she said to the boy, "want a piece of johnny cake?"

Gardner joined them. "I've set Sinclair to getting the youngsters to gather grass for fodder. George, go help 'em," he ordered. "Don't just stand there a-gape." George, the chunk of cornbread in his hand, took off on a run. "That boy is like sticking plaster. Always under foot." Gardner grinned and turned back to Betsy Ann. "We'll fill everything that'll hold water. Britt says we got to go thirty miles before the next reliable supply."

Matilda shook her head. We're still in the middle of the wilderness after all, she thought. As she watched, Lewis let go of his hold on Annie's skirt and tottered towards his mother. Matilda held her breath, then cried out, "Look, everyone, he's walking!"

Lewis laughed in triumph as she scooped him up in her arms and wriggled free to try again. He tottered to his grandfather, who grinned and tossed the baby aloft. "Won't be any flies on this one from now on," he bragged. "A true Randolph."

Matilda, watching them, had to agree, although she felt it a mixed blessing.

That night, moments after Matilda drifted off to sleep, Annie woke her.

"I'm so sorry, Miz Baldwin," she gasped, keeping her voice low so she did not waken the children. "But I'm scared. There's somethin' I got to tell you. I . . . I need your help." She started to cry.

Matilda tossed her light blanket aside and scrambled to her knees. Knowing immediately why Annie had come, she gathered the trembling girl into her arms.

"Hush," she whispered. "It's nothing to be scared of. It's wonderful, you'll see. Come on." She led Annie back toward the wagon, shadowy in the fading moonlight. As she helped Annie lie down on her makeshift bed on the floor of the wagon, she said, "I'll get my mother."

"Don't leave me," Annie cried, grabbing Matilda's arm with both hands.

"I won't be but a moment," Matilda reassured the frightened girl. She put a hand on the swollen abdomen and felt the intensity of the contraction that rippled across it. "My mother knows all about birthing babies."

"You know? I mean, you knew I'm having a baby? How did you know? I never told no one."

The darkness hid Matilda's smile. "I've known since the day I saw you in the hat shop."

"And you never said a word?"

"I knew you'd come to me when you were ready."

"And your mother?"

"She knows, too," Matilda soothed. "Why do you think she was always fussing about what you ate, and insisting you ride in the wagon more?"

"I . . . I guess I thought she was . . . just being, being . . . Oh!" The clutching fingers tightened on Matilda's arm as another contraction swelled across Annie's abdomen. "Oh! Oh, Miz Baldwin. I think . . . I think I wet on myself."

"Relax. It's only your waters. How long have you been having the pains?"

"Since early this morning. At first, just a twinge, but now . . . Oh!"

"Lie back and try to relax. I'll get Mother."

As the first rays of the sun rose over the mountains in the east, Annie's baby entered the world.

"You have a fine little girl," Betsy Ann soothed the exhausted girl as Matilda put the infant in her arms.

Joy suffused Annie's face as she kissed the still damp head. "Annie," the girl said simply. "I'm going to name her Annie, after me. She's the start of a whole new family in a whole new land. What's the date? I have to remember her birthday."

"It's August 19, Annie," Matilda told her. "Now, you get some rest. It's dawn already. Wagons'll soon be moving."

So, she thought, watching Annie stroke the baby's cheek, she's still not ready to say who the father is. Matilda's mind flashed to the young soldier who handed her the note. She smiled slightly. No matter, she told herself. Annie will tell me. In her own good time.

Later that morning, they left Lassen Meadows, headed for the Sink of the Humboldt.

"It seems so strange," Matilda commented to Annie as they jolted along in the back of the wagon where Annie and her new baby lay, "to think that a river has no mouth. Britt says it just disappears at the bottom of the valley."

"I'm sure glad the road is better now," Annie replied, "since we're out of the boggy areas. I swear, bouncing along in the back of this wagon is harder than walking."

Matilda laughed. "I learned that a long time ago. Don't worry. In a couple of days, Mother will let you walk again. She's always had nothing but scorn for women who think they have to lie abed for two weeks after they bear a child."

But walking did not improve things much. As Matilda strolled along beside the wagon the next day, she remembered Britt saying to her on the Wendover, when she complained of her mouth being dry, to wait until she got along the Humboldt. Now I know what he meant, she chuckled softly to herself. The sand made everything gritty. The mules kicked up little clouds of dust and it settled on her sweat-soaked skin and stayed there. Lewis, my darling, she thought, her deceased husband never far from her mind, you wouldn't know me, I'm so grimy. My hair is the same gray color as the alkali. When I get to California, I'm going to soak in a tub until my skin wrinkles. With a sigh of pleasure, she remembered soaking in the tub in Salt Lake City. That seemed so long ago. She tried to recall the feeling to ease the discomfort of the present circumstances.

Two days later, just before they arrived at Big Meadows, they encountered a shallow slough with good water and some feed. From the slough, they traveled the short distance to the meadows proper. The meadows extended for eight miles.

"Got to be a mite careful here," Giles warned. "Cattle get in that meadow, they get lost. Reeds are so high you can't see over 'em."

"Better water 'em with buckets, then," Gardner ordered. Sinclair started to protest, but Gardner silenced him. "Unless you want to spend two days slogging through that muck looking for a cow."

Sinclair sighed in resignation and picked up a couple of buckets. "Come on, then," he grumbled to Weldon. "Get yourself a couple of buckets. This is going to take a while."

Matilda smiled at Sinclair's complaints. "How big is the lake?" she asked Giles.

"Take a day to get around," he replied.

So, on August 22, Matilda stood on the ridge at the upper end of the Humboldt Sink and stared in amazement. "Look, Annie," she exclaimed "The river really does just vanish!"

From the Humboldt Sink, they entered the Forty Mile Desert and began their struggle across the sandy, alkali wastelands. The wagon wheels sank in the soft, sandy soil, and a dust cloud covered the whole train all of the time. When they stopped for the nooning, Matilda looked across the harsh and desolate land where only the coarsest grass grew in the alkali.

She turned to Sinclair with a rueful laugh. "I suppose it's fortunate there is no water for the animals to drink. At least they can't get poisoned."

"In a way," he replied, "but we're passing out water by the cupful. We're liable to run short if we're not careful. It's two more days to the Carson River."

"I know. White Star licks the bucket after she drinks her share and looks at me so expectantly, just like she knows I'm really going to give her more." Matilda sighed. "It hurts me to see her suffer so. I give her as much as I dare. I am so afraid of losing her. All these bones along the way frighten me."

Then she laughed. "Giles gave me a smooth pebble to suck like a candy drop. He says it keeps your mouth moist and helps you swallow oftener. It did help." She smiled, remembering the reaction of Mary and Elizabeth to the pebbles. It took some convincing to persuade Elizabeth not to swallow hers. Lewis, of course, did not understand, so she gave him sips of water from her own share.

"We've decided to travel at night," Sinclair said. "Cooler, traveling at night. Easier on everyone. They say the heat during the day out here can reach a hundred and ten." He turned away and began to unharness the horses. "We'll start at dusk. Moon should be up early tonight."

That evening, after the hot afternoon finally ended, Matilda nursed Lewis, thankful her milk had not dried up from the dreadful heat. She smiled and stroked the blond head nuzzling at her breast. He is growing so fast, she thought. And now that he is walking, he seems to grow even faster.

When he finished nursing, she tucked him into his little bed in the wagon. At least the children could sleep through the long night ahead of them. All the adults would have to walk to spare the animals. She thought of Annie, but the girl strapped her sleeping infant into the cradleboard with a nonchalance that made Matilda envious.

As the light faded, Matilda finished work for the evening on her next letter to Caroline. She replaced the glass stopper in the ink bottle and wiped off the nib of the pen. The children already slept. Jake, curled on the floor of the wagon beside them, whined and kicked in his sleep. Restless, she ignored the preparations to begin the night trek across the desolate wasteland and walked forward to the head of the row of wagons.

Matilda stood and stared across the flat endless miles at the lines of the trail as they vanished into the horizon. The hot desert wind whipped her skirts around her. A stronger gust blasted her face with the fine alkali sand. She shut her eyes for a moment to protect them.

As she watched, the sun slowly disappeared behind the line of distant mountains, forming purple silhouettes against the reddening sky.

A hundred and ten. She licked her thirst-parched lips and sighed.

Chapter 52

Humboldt Sink to Carson City

Saturday, August 27, '64
Carson City

Dear Caroline,

We reached this famous city (or infamous city, depending on who's telling the story) about noon today after a trek across the desert I hope never to repeat. Everyone assures me that the desert and the Indian dangers are behind us. All we have to do now (Britt says) is cross the Sierra Nevada mountains.

That's all? I stood by the wagon and stared. I thought the Rockies were high, but the Sierras go straight up. You have to see these peaks to believe them. I can't imagine how anyone ever managed to get the first wagon across. It's impossible to keep the Donners out of my head, no matter how many people tell me the road is much better now.

Words cannot describe crossing the forty miles between the sinks. Forty miles of bottomless sand with no water. Bones of animals littered every step of the way, and the remains of wagons told a terrible, terrible story. Giles says that after the animals died, the people had no way to pull the wagons, and had to abandon them.

When we reached the edge of the desert, we came to Ragtown on the Carson River. They say Carson Lake is a shallow sheet of water that spreads out for eighty or so miles and just disappears. The Carson River keeps pouring water in, but the water never resurfaces. It just vanishes into that vast expanse of sand.

I remember what Uncle Thomas always said Hell was like, but I'm sure no Devil could ever devise a worse Hell than that desert.

I'm afraid I have to confess I shared my portion of water with White Star. Mother would be furious if she knew, because if my milk dries up, Lewis will suffer. Sinclair kept offering to water White Star for me, so I think he suspected. I had to sneak the extra water to her when he wasn't looking.

Foolish, yes, I know, but I so feared I would lose her. And when she finished her share, she always looked at me like she knew I would give her more. Which, of course, I did.

The children managed fairly well. Mary complained all the time, and Elizabeth, with her usual stoicism, said nothing. She just looked at me so I would know she suffered in silence. Only Lewis seemed completely unaffected by the whole experience, except for a few episodes of prickly heat. Poor old Jake rode in the wagon with the children most of the time, although I don't think he minded. He seem perfectly happy just to be with them, no matter how miserable the conditions.

We halted briefly at Ragtown, an unprepossessing little spot on the edge of the desert, just a couple of non-descript log huts. They say it got its name because of all the clothes hung out on the bushes by people who just came off the desert. The stationmaster here is a jolly scalawag who (they say) works with the local Indians to steal stock from travelers, so we once again kept a very close watch on our animals, especially White Star.

For the last ten miles before we reached the river, the sand was very thick, which made it hard even to walk. We plowed through acres of powdery alkali, with the poor horses struggling along sinking knee deep at every step. The dust rose around the wagons in a thick cloud and covered everything — people, wagons, animals — with a thick, gray coating. Poor White Star turned a dingy gray.

*I think the solitude affected me the most. Although sur-
rounded by people, I felt so alone in the midst of that desolate wasteland. The desert went on for miles in all directions,
with the greasewood waving in those strange mirages. Even
though we could see the line of trees along the river for miles
in that flat land, I got so used to ignoring all the fake water I
almost didn't realize we had reached the Carson River until
the animals caught the smell of water.*

*We crossed the Carson River at Ragtown and followed
the south side for a day and a half until we reached Fort
Churchill. There we crossed to the north side and visited
the Fort. It's a very fine establishment, set up to protect the
mail from Indian depredations. They say its purpose is to
protect travelers as well, but I suspect we take second place
to the mail.*

*The Buckland family has been farming here since '59,
and they built the Fort in '60 on the Buckland Ranch. The
Fort has a whole lot of buildings, even a separate building for
the laundress, if you can imagine. And the officers quarters
all have indoor privies. Sinclair told me. What luxury!*

*We followed the river, crossing one pretty meadow after
another. At one spot we saw a flock of chukars and Sinclair
managed to shoot one. We had a very tasty dinner that
night, let me tell you. There is a lot of good farm land here,
and some of it is already settled. But once you get away from
the river, it goes right back to desert. We passed a lot of real
black volcanic rock. At one spot, the cliffs went straight up,
and huge blocks of rock had fallen off. I wouldn't let Mary
and Elizabeth go near them. Giles said the rocks only fall
in the winter when freezing and thawing makes the chunks
break off, but I wasn't taking any chances.*

*After we left the bluffs, we had sand dunes on the north
for a long time. River meadows on the left and sand dunes
on the right. What a country!*

Just before we reached the crest of the hill overlooking

Carson City, we passed the turnoff to Virginia City. I wish we could have seen it. I guess it's even more wicked than Carson City. Two of our seven wagons left us, so all that's with us now is our four plus Mr. Douglass.

I, for one, was very glad when we crested the hill and I could see the buildings of Carson City on the horizon, in the midst of a barren expanse of sagebrush and greasewood. The thought of being in a civilized town again really appealed to me. We got our first glimpse from several miles away because the plain is so flat. It looked like a bunch of white dots overshadowed by the towering mountains on the other side. And what mountains they are!

We drove right down the main street, which consists of block after block of little white frame stores, packed side by side, as if they designed each building to hold up the one next to it. I couldn't help making the comparison to Salt Lake City and the spacious streets there. Wooden sidewalks cross the fronts of the buildings, I suppose to protect against mud if it ever does rain in this benighted country. The middle of the town boasts a spacious plaza for (they say) public auctions, horse trades, and town meetings.

Shortly after we arrived this afternoon, the 'Washoe Zephyr' struck. That's what they call the wind some claim blows every day from two in the afternoon until two in the morning. It's a fierce wind that blows away everything not tied or nailed down, and sometimes things that are. Hats, chickens, and sagebrush all whirl by in the billows of flying sand. I quickly learned why they built the houses so close together.

I guess everything needs to be done between daybreak and two PM, before the wind comes up, for I don't see how anyone could do anything outdoors in that blowing sand. The children and I are huddled in the wagon now, listening to the wind howl as it buffets the wagon about. Even Mary is content to stay inside. The dust manages to sift through the canvas and everything is covered with a fine layer of sand.

Wes and Sinclair plan to spend the night at a local boarding house. They struck up an acquaintance with a couple of surveyors. It seems the Governor is very interested in a possible route for the railroad. Just imagine crossing all those weary miles in a comfortable train instead of plodding along beside a mule!

I'm so sleepy I can barely keep my eyes open, so I will finish this tomorrow and get it off to you before we leave. Since tomorrow is Sunday, we are going to spend all day here, so I will have time.

August 28th

Wes and Sinclair came back this morning just after daybreak. They explained why they returned so early (they'd planned to sleep late, since we're not traveling today) and why they look like they didn't sleep at all.

Seems a couple of the boarders had captured ten or twelve tarantulas, big hairy spiders that roam all over the desert, and had a row of them in glass jars on a shelf along the wall of their dormitory. During the night, the wind blew something (turned out to be the roof of the stable next door) against the wall and knocked over the shelf. Sinclair said the thump on the wall woke him, Wes said all he heard was breaking glass and someone shouting that the tarantulas were loose. They spent the next ten minutes or so climbing up on boxes and trunks, in momentary terror of feeling the fangs of the tarantulas. Wes says they were as big as saucers. Sinclair swears they would cover a dinner plate, but I suspect their fright increased the size of the spiders a little. The ones I've seen are only three or four inches across.

Anyway, when the landlady finally came with a lantern to check the damage done to her wall, she saw all these brave men clinging to bed posts, boxes, and trunks. Not a

single spider could be found. I told Sinclair probably all the
yelling and jumping around sent the poor spiders scurrying
for cover, cursing the day they ever met these strange two-
legged creatures.

Needless to say, nobody wanted to return to a bed which
might still harbor one of the crawly things, so they sat up and
played cribbage until dawn, then came back to the wagon.

I'll close now, as Weldon promised to mail my letters only
if he can do it before the wind comes up.

My next letter to you will probably be from Sacramento.
Can you believe we are almost there? Another two weeks
and the trek will be over at last.

Believe me, I have seen the elephant.

Love,

'Tilda

Chapter 53

Carson City to Lake Tahoe

GARDNER'S SERMON SUNDAY morning voiced thanks to God for bringing them safely across the desert and saving them from hostile Indians. As she listened to her father's words, Matilda's mind flew to those who had died on the trip, especially Mrs. Ridgeway and Baby Jamie, and poor Andrew. She wondered if Mr. Ridgeway and Andrew's widow would feel the same gratitude, then cast a quick look around to see if anyone suspected her blasphemous thoughts. She dared not look at Sinclair.

On Monday, August 29, 1864, the five wagons left Carson City and headed south along the base of the mountains, bound for the entrance to the new Kingsbury Grade Road. They camped that night just outside of Genoa. After supper, Matilda walked a short distance from the camp and climbed up on a rock to look at the mountains. The tall, snow-tipped peaks appeared both majestic and foreboding. She knew the road would go through a pass, bypassing the tallest of the peaks, but still their height intimidated her. Almost hypnotized by the majesty of the scene before her, she fancied herself soaring up to touch the snow-clad tops, floating through air so clear it almost sparkled. How could something so lovely turn so deadly?

She shook her head and, with an effort, tore herself away from the view and returned to the camp to wash the evening dishes. Thankfully she had enough water at last. Scrubbing the dishes with dry sand always left everything feeling gritty, no matter how hard she tried to get off all the sand.

Britt and Gardner, meanwhile, had ridden to the home of the toll-keeper, located just behind the Cary grist mill. When they returned, they still wrangled.

"$17.50 a wagon!" Gardner fumed. "Outrageous. He said it's for the round trip. But we aren't coming back! Why do we want to pay for a round trip?"

"They have to get their money back for building and maintaining the road," Britt explained patiently. "Believe me, it will be worth the money. Remember, I came across before we had the luxury of a well-maintained road."

"Cost Kingsbury and McDonald $580,000 to build the road," Giles interposed, his voice solemn. "I hear they took in about $190,000 last year in tolls. Lotsa folks use it. Saves a whole day over the previous road. To freight companies, a day means money."

"And they keep the dust down by sending horse-carts to sprinkle the road every day," Britt added. "Be worth the money not to have to eat all that dust."

Gardner strode off, still muttering under his breath. With a smile, Matilda returned to her dishwashing.

The next morning, shortly after breaking camp, they passed through the tiny settlement of Mottsville. Matilda, enchanted by the little schoolhouse, could not resist a brief visit. A dozen children enthusiastically cheered two small boys who raced along a pathway rolling hoops. When the smaller of the two won the race, everyone ran to congratulate him.

The teacher stood by watching with a smile. She looked friendly, so Matilda introduced herself.

"Good morning," the woman responded to Matilda's greeting. "Pleased to meet you. I'm Eliza Mott. My husband George's family settled here in '51. Three years later I opened this school. Need a school for the young ones if you're going to build a community, I told my George. He agreed, and has been very supportive. Even," she laughed, "when it has meant his supper is late!" She pointed out a little girl of about ten. "That's my second daughter, Louisa. She's the first white girl born in these parts." Her face tightened. "My third baby became the first to be buried in our cemetery."

Matilda sympathized. "I know how hard it is. I lost a child too." She noticed the children watching Mrs. Mott and realized it was time they returned to class. "I won't keep you. I just want to say I admire you for what you're doing."

"Thank you." Mrs. Mott offered her hand. "Good luck on your journey. Believe me, it's much easier now, with the Kingsbury Road."

Matilda laughed. "So I understand, but you should have heard my father when he learned how much he had to pay!"

One mile later, they turned west and started up the grade. Except for the last quarter mile of Harrison Pass, Matilda found the road steeper than anything else she had ever tried to climb. And they kept on climbing. And climbing. At one point, she turned to look back out over the Carson Valley. Farms and ranches spread up and down the valley. She knew the discovery of the Comstock Lode had led to the settlement. The farmers provided livestock, hay, and vegetables to the miners. She tried to imagine what it must have been like prior to the arrival of so many people. Probably sagebrush and greasewood, she thought, like we passed all along the way. She turned her efforts to the uphill struggle again.

"Don't tell me we've made only four miles!" Annie gasped. They stopped to allow a freight wagon to pass, grateful for the chance to catch their breath. The girl took the cradleboard holding her baby off her back and collapsed beside the wagon.

"Only four miles." Matilda pulled off her boots and rubbed her aching feet. "Pa reassured me," she added with a wry grin. "He said we are still five miles from the first summit. I hear the climb to the second is the roughest." All the adults and older children walked to make the wagons lighter. They even used double teams over some of the steeper inclines.

"I pity the poor mules," Matilda continued. "Some got so tired they lay down and refused to get up. The men had to beat them to get them to move."

"Yes, I saw that," Annie responded. "Dreadful!"

"I thought they should just let them rest a while, but Sinclair said if they didn't get them up and moving, they would just lie there and die. Can you imagine any animal that stubborn? No wonder my father refuses to use mules."

They stopped at the summit to rest and eat. Before putting the children down for a much-needed nap, Matilda took them for a stroll among the tall pines. They stood in awe at the size of the trees.

"How old are these trees, Mama?" Mary asked. "They must be real old, to get so big."

"I don't know, Darling. They look like they have been here since the beginning of time." The sound of axes rang about them. Matilda felt a surge of pity for the destruction of such beautiful creations, then chided herself. If the men didn't cut wood, how would they cook?

After the noon rest, they started down the other side, surrounded by the susurration of the wind in the pine trees, the scent wafting over them. Pine needles made a soft carpet all along the sides of the road. They crackled under Matilda's feet as she walked, preferring the side of the road whenever possible to the mud and dust in the center.

A mile later, Sinclair rode back for her. "Come on, 'Tilda. You have to see this." He dismounted and led her to a break in the trees. "Look at that."

She caught her breath at the beauty of the scene that lay before her. A large lake glinted in the sunlight, amidst miles and miles of evergreens. The deep blue color of the lake's water made her think of a brilliant gem stone.

"Lake Tahoe," he grinned. "We'll be camping there tonight. Britt says you think it's pretty from here, wait 'til you get next to it."

Matilda could only stare. She thought of Kansas and all those people who spent their whole lives there. They never got a chance to see anything of this magnificence. Sechrest and Whitson wanted Kansas? They could have Kansas!

That evening, they passed Friday Station by the edge of the lake and camped about a mile beyond. Giles strode beside her as she walked away from camp down to the edge of the lake to admire the view. The deep blue water of the lake mirrored the soaring mountains on the other side. Matilda could not help thinking she stood in the most beautiful spot on earth.

"Look," she said, pointing across the lake. "The snow makes a cross on that mountain."

Giles nodded. "Mount Tallac," he said. "Most times there's snow in that crevass all year round."

"Wait 'til my father sees that," she laughed. "He'll make up a whole sermon on it."

Giles grinned. "He won't be the first. When Fremont come through here, he named the lake after Governor Bigler, but I guess Bigler fell out of favor, so they changed the name to Tahoe after some Injun chief from these parts. Half the folks still call it Bigler. Trail used to go around by Donner Lake 'til the Mormons made the trail up around Carson Pass. We'll take Johnson's cutoff. Follows the American River, down through Placerville. Best way to get to Sacramento." He offered his hand to help her over a fallen tree.

"Used to call Donner Lake the Truckee Lake," he continued, "after the Indian as helped 'em find the trail, back in '41 or '42. But after so many of the Donners' party died there, the folks in the guv'mint decided to name the lake in memory of 'em. It's a right pretty lake, too, though not as big as this one. They say this one ain't got no bottom. I don't reckon that's so, but it is mighty deep. Water's cold, too."

Matilda remembered the many tales of the ill-fated Donner expedition. Trees rustled in the slight evening breeze. She took a deep breath, savoring the scent of the pine needles. It seemed impossible such a lovely setting could be the scene of so much tragedy. But as the sun sank behind the mountains and the air turned chilly, she realized how cold the winter would be.

Giles noticed her shivering. "Gets right cold at night in these mountains, Miz Matilda, just like it did in the Rockies. Desert is so hot we forget how cold them nights was. You want to bundle them young'uns up good."

"That snow," she asked, pointing to the distant peaks, her mind not on his words. "It hasn't started to snow yet, has it?" She had visions of being trapped like the Donners.

"Oh, no, ma'am," he assured her. "That's from last winter. Some of these mountains are so high the snow never melts all summer long."

She remembered Alf saying the same thing about the Sierras, and some of the high peaks she had seen in the Rockies. While she gazed at the beauty before her, the scout spoke again.

"They tell some pretty grim stories, 'bout the folks with the Donners. Some of their bunch drove Jim Reed out for killin' a man as hit Miz Reed. Just give him his horse and his rifle. Had to leave his family behind. That happened at Gravelly Ford, back along the Humboldt." He shook his head and picked up a pine cone at his feet. Absently pulling it to pieces, he said, "Funny how things work out sometimes. Reed was one of the men who helped save the survivors. Saved his whole family, he did. Lives down by San Jose now. Fine man."

He chuckled. "They tell one story about the Reeds. Seems afore he left the train, Mr. Reed give his wife his watch and his silver Masonic medal." He stood staring out over the water. Pine trees cast long shadows across the lake as the sun sank lower in the reddening sky.

"Miz Reed, now," he continued, "she traded the watch and medal to a man name of Dolan for beef to feed her children. Then Dolan himself died trying to get to Sutter's Fort on foot." He shook his head. "Couple of Sutter's Miwoks found Dolan's body and took it to the fort. Mr. Sutter himself returned the watch and medal to Mr. Reed."

"That's amazing." Matilda's mind remained on what she had heard about the Donner party, tales told and re-told among the travelers. Knowing the fondness of the storytellers for a good yarn, she wondered if perhaps many of the tales were exaggerated. Still, she felt she had to know if they were true.

"Are the stories of ... of ...." She hesitated, avoiding the word. Then she spoke in a rush, "I hear they ate dead bodies."

"Reckon some of 'em are true, all right. The rescuers found bodies in the cabins, and some had flesh cut off 'em." He mangled the pine cone some more. "Don't think the stories of killin' folks for food is true, though. Most believe they just ate those as died from starvation and cold."

Matilda grimaced. Brushing the accumulation of pine needles off a nearby boulder, she absently sat down, her mind on her own children. If they were starving, could she use flesh from a dead body to save them? Yes, she told herself in all honesty, she probably could, but she certainly hoped she never had to make such a decision.

As though reading her mind, the scout said, "Them as had whole families, like the Reeds, more of them survived than them as was single. One young man, traveling alone, laid down aside the fire and died. Them as was with him say his arm fell into the fire three times and they pulled it out. On the fourth time, they just left it." He shook his head. "Never did say why they didn't just pull him farther from the fire.

"First rescue party," he continued, "started at Johnson's rancho, down by Sly Park. They stopped at the snow line to make snowshoes and left the mules. Took only what they could carry and hiked seventy miles through the snow." He grinned at her. "Guess you've never spent much time on snowshoes, Miz Matilda, but let me tell you, that was some hike."

"How brave they must have been."

"One of 'em, name of Stanton, did it twice." Giles shook his head and swallowed, turning his head a moment too late to keep her from seeing the tears spring into his eyes. "Died himself on the second trip. Those as knew him say he were one of the best. Heart o' gold."

"The poor man," Matilda murmured in sympathy. She wondered if the scout had known Stanton. He seemed so moved by the tale.

He stood silent for a moment. Matilda, anxious to hear more, motioned for him to sit beside her on the boulder.

"Ye-ah," he said, accepting the seat with such alacrity she wondered if she had made a mistake in offering it. She certainly had no desire to encourage him in any amorous overtures.

"They say," he continued, "the survivors was just skeletons. Saw a few of 'em myself, but they'd been fattened up a bit. That first bunch of rescuers took about twenty of the strongest, mostly women and children, and got 'em safe to Sutter's Fort."

Giles offered Matilda a shy smile. "Cap'n Sutter, he was real generous. Gave supplies out of his own pocket to save a lot of emigrants. Like to broke him, it did. That and everyone settlin' on his land and refusin' to pay for it. Said he had no claim since it were a Mexican land grant. He left Sacramento in '49 to settle on Hock Farm, his place up on the Feather River. Said he wanted to be a farmer anyway, not a merchant and administrator.

"Anyhow, he tells of one batch as was so hungry they ate not only the mules, but the two Injun boys he sent with the supplies. Took that straight to heart, he did."

"How dreadful!"

"Yep, Cap'n Sutter, he was allus real fond of his Miwoks. They come to him right after he founded the fort and camped outside and asked to work for him. Guess they's a real good bunch 'a Injuns. But them as ate the Injuns, they weren't the folks in the Donner party. That come later, during the gold rush, when every fool and his brother was dashin' to California to get rich. Half of 'em didn't have no notion of what they was gettin' into."

Matilda eyed the cloudless sky. A flash of anxiety crossed her features. "We're not in any danger of being trapped here are we?"

"Probably not. Usually the snows don't start 'til end of September, early October. Besides, not much danger any more. Them as runs the road, they tamp down the snow in the winter so's it's open all year 'less it's actually stormin'. They's so much traffic over these mountains now, what with the stage coaches and the freight wagons and all. Especially since the strike at the Comstock Lode." He grinned and edged a little closer on the boulder. Matilda edged away the same distance. "I hear tell they've even opened another road up over Donner Pass, too.

"Folks tried to tell the Donner brothers they was gettin' started too late in the season," he continued, "but I guess nobody could tell George or Peter Donner nuthin'. They just wouldn't listen. Felt they knew it all. Even late as they was, if they'd 'a' stuck with Harlan's party, helped Harlan get through Weber Canyon, they'd 'a' all made it."

" 'Thus do we cast invisible dice with death'," she quoted softly.

"What?" The scout appeared puzzled.

"Nothing," she laughed. "Just a line I remember from a book. How deep does the snow get here, anyway?"

"They say it got up to twenty feet deep in '46, the winter the Donners got trapped."

"Twenty feet!"

The scout laughed at the expression on her face. "Yes, ma'am. Come winter time, this place looks a lot different." He reached for her hand, which she hastily moved beyond his reach. "I'd be right happy to take good care of you and your young-uns, Miz Matilda," he said, his voice earnest.

She jumped to her feet. "Thank you so much, Mr. Giles, but I'm sure my brothers can manage." She knew she should terminate this conversation before it went any further along those lines, not wanting to hurt his feelings. "Come on. I suspect supper's about ready."

He followed her, a little forlorn. As they walked back to the campsite, he added, "Folks as know their way around, now, they can survive up here. In '44, young Moses Schallenberg lived the whole winter in a cabin he and two others built at the lake. The other two made it on over, but Moses, he were too weak." Giles chuckled. "He says wolf makes mighty poor eatin', but when that's all there is, that's what you eat. And that cabin helped save some of the Donner bunch. They moved right in."

When they reached Matilda's wagon, he tipped his hat with a shy smile. "Sure nice talkin' to you, Miz Matilda."

She watched him walk away and shook her head sadly. A kind, gentle man in his own crude way. Shuddering at the memory of the poor grammar, the tobacco stained teeth, and the food stuck in his beard, Matilda could not help contrasting him with Lewis. Someday perhaps there will be another, but not yet. And certainly not the eager Mr. Giles.

Matilda awoke the next morning before the camp stirred and lay on her bedroll, thinking. Had it really been a whole year since Lewis' death? Yes, a year ago last Friday. And tomorrow would be September 1. Their anniversary. Tears stung her eyes as she thought, eight years. Eight years since our wedding day, my love. Sometimes it felt so long ago, other times it seemed just like yesterday, and she could clearly see the glint in Lewis' eyes as they met hers when he had lifted her veil. The children still slept, so she lay quietly, thinking of Lewis and the happiness they had shared. In the year since his death, she did find herself crying less often. As she thought of Lewis, the tears trickled from her eyes and dripped onto the folded blanket beneath her head.

"Lewis, my darling," she whispered, "I wish you could see our son. He's going to be just like you. You would be so proud of him."

Mary sat up. "Mama, you're talking to yourself," she accused. Wrapping her blanket around her shoulders, she said, "Brr. How come it's so cold in the morning and so hot in the day? Is it 'cause high up in the mountains we're closer to the sun?"

"That's part of it, darling," Matilda laughed, brushing away the tears before Mary could see them. "Hurry and dress. Uncle Sinclair will have the fire started."

From their campsite, they traversed eight miles and crossed the Upper and Lower Truckee Rivers before they stood at the base of the mountains. Matilda looked at the granite wall in front of them. The incline seemed to rise straight up.

"Sinclair!" she said, staring in horror. "Don't tell me we have to scale that!"

"Sure do," Sinclair grinned. "It's two miles to the top, and it's going to take the rest of the day to get the wagons up. Look."

Her eyes followed the direction of his arm. A freight wagon loaded with ore, pulled by eight straining mules, struggled upwards. The profanity of the mule skinners blistered her ears. She smothered a laugh as she saw her father overhear the blustery banter and scowl.

Her father, assisted by Wes, Weldon, and Britt, attached double teams to the first of the Randolph wagons.

"I see why Alf warned us about overloading," Matilda commented.

Sinclair, watching the men work, turned back to her. "Yes. Some folks have had to make two or three trips or leave some of their stuff behind." He grinned down at her. The tallest of her brothers, he stood just over six feet. "And everyone walks up this one, 'Tilda, even the small children. Too steep to risk anyone except the driver. And too steep to ride a horse. If the horse slips and falls . . . ."

"You don't have to draw me a picture!" Matilda understood only too well. She watched the first wagon start up the steep trail. She knew all the men would be needed to help with the wagons. "And Elizabeth and Lewis?" she asked. "Do I have to carry them?"

Her nephews Owen and Gardner approached. "We'll help you, Aunt 'Tilda." Owen took Elizabeth's hand while young Gardner picked up Lewis. George Douglass appeared beside Mary and took her hand. "I'll help Mary, Miz Baldwin," he said, proudly leading her away.

Matilda laughed and followed, with Gardner and Owen behind her with Elizabeth and Lewis. Annie strapped baby Annie into the invaluable cradleboard and slung the board onto her back with a practiced fluid movement.

Sinclair mounted White Star and called after her, "Stay to the side. Don't let any of 'em get close to the trail in case one of the wagons gets loose."

Matilda waved back to him. "I'll take care of the children. You take care of White Star."

An hour later, exhausted, she collapsed onto a boulder. "Heavens, don't tell me we're not even half way there yet," she gasped to her mother and Annie, who rested nearby. She drank deeply from her canteen as she panted for breath, attempting to slow her pounding heart and ease the pain in her chest. The day grew hotter as the sun climbed higher in the brassy sky. A slight breeze rustled the pine trees and cooled her perspiring face.

She rubbed her aching calves and inspected the bruise on her right forearm. She had slipped climbing up a particularly steep spot and struck her arm on a rock. Her knees still stung from the impact. She wiped her face and looked ruefully at the reddish-brown stain on the handkerchief. In spite of the efforts of the sprinkler carts, dust stirred up by dozens of hooves and feet made a cloud that hung over the whole train.

"Mama, I'm tired and thirsty. Are we almost there?" Mary dropped to the ground beside Matilda. The faithful George offered her his canteen. She took a drink and made a face. "Your water tastes funny," she complained, handing the canteen back to him.

"Now, darling," Matilda laughed, "be grateful to George for pulling you up the hill. I wish I had someone to pull me up."

"Look, Mama," Mary pointed down the hillside. "Someone threw away a clock."

Matilda looked and saw what had been a large, beautiful Grandfather clock, the wood now weathered and cracked. She felt a pang of sympathy for the woman forced to discard such a treasure.

At that moment, young Gardner reached her, carrying Lewis. Lewis, his face flushed from the heat, remained as cheerful as ever as he held out his arms to her. The golden ringlets clung to his damp forehead. She took him in her arms and sat him down on her lap. He nuzzled at her breast.

"Looks like the babe's hungry," Betsy Ann stated.

Matilda blushed. She had never managed to be as matter-of-fact about nursing a baby as her mother. His demands persisted, so she turned her back on the others and opened the front of her dress.

While he suckled, she stroked the damp curls, thanking God she had him. He looked more like his father every day. A wave of desolation washed over her. One year of widowhood had not yet eased the pain.

Gratitude to her family swept through her. How in the world, she thought, would I have ever managed to care for three children without them, especially Sinclair. But, she added, with a pang of guilt, I'm going to have to do something. I can't expect them to take care of me for the rest of my life.

"Look out!" The sound of her brother Britt's voice jerked Matilda from her reverie, even startled Lewis and he released her breast. She closed the front of her dress and scrambled towards the line of wagons with Lewis in her arms, stumbling over fallen pine cones and scattered branches that lay on the mat of pine needles covering the forest floor. Britt clung to his tilting seat. She immediately saw the reason. One wheel rode high up on a rock.

"Jump, Pa. Jump!" young Gardner shouted at his father as the wagon seemed about to overturn. Several men scurried for the uphill side, grabbing lines, using their weight to help keep the wagon from tipping.

"Sinclair!" she heard herself scream. "Don't get on the downhill side!" As she watched in helpless horror, Sinclair put his shoulder against the left rear wheel and shoved. "Please, God," she prayed aloud, frantic at the thought of losing her favorite brother, "don't let anything happen to

Sinclair."

Matilda, her heart pounding, held Lewis so tightly he squirmed in protest as she watched Sinclair in danger. Terrified, she relived the scene of Lewis falling to his death as she saw her beloved brother in peril, as helpless to save Sinclair as she had been to save her husband. As quickly as the trouble began, it ended. The wagon crossed the rock and settled down to a normal pitch. The mules, persuaded by the crack of Britt's whip, pulled forward and the danger passed.

Mary approached, her face even dirtier from a sticky sweet the faithful George had given her, and said, "What's the matter, Mama? Why did you scream?"

Still shaken, Matilda fought hard to get her voice under control. She suppressed the urge to run to Sinclair and throw her arms around him. She knew he would never forgive her if she embarrassed him in front of the other men with such a display of affection. She took a deep breath and met Mary's trusting blue eyes. "Nothing, darling. It's all over."

Chapter 54

Lake Tahoe to Sacramento

THE SUN dipped low in the sky before the last wagon reached the summit and took its place in camp. Sinclair, again mounted on White Star, rode to where Matilda helped her mother prepare the evening meal.

"We did it, 'Tilda," he grinned at her in triumph. "Every wagon made it."

Matilda thought of the piles of wreckage they had passed on the hike up, how close Britt's wagon had come to joining them, and sighed with relief. "Are we over the worst?"

"Downhill all the way," he assured her. "Be in Sacramento in five or six days." He reached down for her hand. "Climb up. I want to show you something." He kicked his left foot out of the stirrup so she could hoist herself up.

With a quick glance to be sure her father would not see her riding astride, she adjusted the skirts beneath her and hugged Sinclair's waist. "Let's go."

They rode to the crest of the next hill. From the treeless, rocky ridge, the valley of Lake Tahoe spread out before them. "Oh," she gasped. "It's magnificent!" In her mind, she had run out of superlatives to describe the beauty. She stood watching the shadow of the mountains creep across the lake until she started to shiver from the cold.

"They say the stage stops here just to let folks off to admire the view," Sinclair said, "but I think you'd better come back now, before you take a chill."

She stood there, entranced. Sinclair had to repeat his words before she realized he had spoken. "Magnificent," she repeated, still awe-struck at the scene before her. A sense of pride filled her. She had brought her three children safely across the Hades behind them to this beautiful land. During the long, arduous journey, she had traversed harsh deserts, climbed gaunt, barren mountains and faced hostile Indians. She laughed to herself when she remembered her misgivings about leaving Kansas. Soon she would see Minerva and the rest of the family again. She had at last fulfilled her dream of seeing California.

Mid-morning of the next day, the road traveled beside a waterfall that plunged hundreds of feet down the face of a bare, granite mountain to join the sparkling river at the base. A rainbow danced in the spray cast up by the cascading water. Matilda had never seen a waterfall before. She showed the spectacle to the children, pleased when they found it as enchanting as she did. What would this country show her next!

They continued down, following the river, passing sheer rocky cliffs on both sides of the road. Matilda wondered vaguely how anyone had ever managed to carve a road out of these cliffs. When they reached Strawberry Lodge, and camped just beyond it, Matilda took the children and gathered a large quantity of the wild strawberries that grew in abundance close to the lodge.

As they proceeded the next day, the elevation dropped and activity along the road increased. Several times they had to make room for freight wagons, and twice for the stage. As the day wore on, and Matilda began to think in terms of camping for the night, Sinclair rode up beside her.

"Come with me." He offered her his hand to help her mount. He took her to a break in the trees where they gazed out over the valley.

"There it is 'Tilda," he grinned. "The Valley of the Sacramento."

"Oh," she gasped. "It's beautiful. But why is it so hazy? Is it fog?"

"Smoke. The Indians call it the Valley of Ten Thousand Smokes. According to Fremont, it's a huge valley, two hundred miles wide and seven hundred long, completely ringed by mountains. The only outlet is through San Francisco Bay. All the rivers from the whole valley feed into the bay.

"Look back at the snow, 'Tilda," he told her, with a quick hug, knowing how she hated snow. "It's the closest you will ever be to it again."

She stared out across the valley for several moments longer, relishing the feeling of conquest. Never again would she doubt herself. If I can conquer this trail, she thought, I can conquer anything.

Three days later, they reached the outskirts of Sacramento. For several days they had passed ranchos, a word Matilda finally learned to say instead of farms, and fields of recently harvested grain. Orchards and scattered settlements dotted the landscape.

"Look, Mama," Mary cried when she saw the first one. "A real house!"

Matilda laughed and hugged her. "Yes, darling, a real house. We are almost there at last. Just think, you will meet your Uncle Alf and your Uncle Sam. And see your Uncle Tom and Aunt Minerva again. You don't even remember them. You were less than a year old when they left Kansas." And I, she thought, sighing in contentment, will get a real bath with hot water. She hugged herself in anticipation of the luxury.

After getting the children bedded down that night, Matilda and Annie sat alone, enjoying the cool evening breeze. As the elevation fell, the temperature rose dramatically. In the quiet of the sleeping camp, they watched the cooking fire slowly die to embers.

"We'll be in Sacramento tomorrow, Annie," Matilda said at last, after some moments of watching the fire. "Don't you think it's time you told me your plans?"

Matilda waited. A long silence followed before Annie spoke. Then the girl took a deep breath and said, "You're right, Miz Baldwin. You're entitled to know. You ran a big risk for me." She paused, tossing small slivers of wood into the fire, where they flared with a moment's brightness. "I guess you figured all along me an' Ben planned it. Ben's the soldier as gave you the note for me. He's been stationed at Camp Douglas, just outside o' Salt Lake City. Me and him courted for over a year." She drew a long, tremulous breath, and the words tumbled out, as though she had kept silent for so long she could not stop the torrent once it started.

"We never meant to deceive you. What I told you is God's honest truth. My father refused to let me marry Ben, 'cause Ben's a Gentile. As if I cared," she spat. "Anyhow, he arranged for me to become one of Bishop Bensen's plural wives 'for the sake of my soul'," she quoted. "He beat me every time he found out I'd seen Ben. The Bishop would never accept me if I was pregnant, so when my father found out about the baby, he twisted my arm so hard it broke. Look." She held out her left arm to the light of the fire. "It healed crooked 'cause he wouldn't take me to the doctor."

Matilda did not need to look. She had noticed the crooked arm long before.

"Wouldn't take me to a doctor," she repeated, the bitterness of the memory and her mistreatment still evident, "because Brother Brigham always tells everyone to treat their children gentle, never held with hittin' on 'em, so my father didn't want anyone to know how he treated me. Sometimes he kept me locked up for days until the bruises healed. So no one would see 'em. But we fooled him. Soon's we found out the baby was coming, we got the chaplain at Camp Douglas to marry us. I'm Mrs. Benjamin Hurd and I got the paper to prove it."

She smiled at Matilda. Tears in her eyes reflected the firelight. "But we had to get away from my father, or he might 'a got our marriage annulled. And he would 'a taken my baby and give her to someone else to raise, so she'd be raised Mormon. I told Ben how kindly you seemed, and we decided to risk it. Can you forgive me?"

Matilda's own eyes filled. She rose and crossed to Annie. Taking the trembling girl in her arms, she stroked the soft hair. "Hush, child, there is nothing to forgive. I think you are a very brave girl, and Ben is a fortunate young man. Besides," she gave a soft laugh, "I think Sinclair really enjoyed outwitting your father." She stepped back, put her hands on Annie's shoulders and met her eyes. "I assume you and Ben have made plans for meeting? Have you written him? Does he know he has a daughter?"

"Oh, yes, Miz Baldwin." Annie brushed the tears from her cheeks. "I been sendin' him letters regular, 'cause he said he'd worry if he didn't hear. He's to write me, General Delivery, in Sacramento. He gets out of the army in April, then he's coming out and we can be together forever and never have to worry about my father again." She smiled, her love for Ben shining in her face. "He gave me some money when I left to open a hat shop in Sacramento, to keep myself and the babe until he can come and take care of us himself. I make real good hats, Miz Baldwin, and the first hat I make in my new shop will be for you, to repay you for your kindness."

Matilda smiled. "I'm sure it will be the best hat shop in all of Sacramento." She again wondered what she was going to do herself. Keep house for her brother Alf? That's what he wants now, she thought, but what if he gets married?

"Annie," she said with a little laugh, "maybe you should

teach me how to make hats. We could go into business together." She stretched her arms over her head and yawned.
"Come on. Let's get some sleep. Tomorrow is going to be
a busy day."

As she walked away, leaving Annie staring into the fire,
Matilda felt a sudden stab of fear. Somehow she had a
strange premonition that the news awaiting Annie in Sacramento would not be good.

BOOK IV: CALIFORNIA

1864 to 1867

Chapter 55

September of 1864

MATILDA WOKE the next morning at daylight. Her heart jumped in anticipation. We're here, she thought. We've made it. She hurried to dress, eager to see her new home and excited to think she would soon see her brothers and Minerva again.

Mary popped out of the tent and ran to the fire where her mother and grandmother prepared breakfast. "Mama, are we there? Do we have to go in the wagon some more?"

Matilda hugged her. "Just a little ways, my darling. Today we're going to stay in a nice hotel in Sacramento and have a real bath." Alf's letter they received in Carson City told them to go to the Pioneer Hotel at Second and 'M' Streets and send a message out to him at Hicksville.

Annie, the baby on her arm, emerged from the back of the wagon. Her eyes sparkled. "And we have to go to the Post Office. My letter from Ben will be waiting for me."

Sinclair walked up, tucking his shirt into his pants. He ran his fingers through his tousled blond curls and yawned. Betsy Ann handed him a cup of coffee and began heaping a plate of bacon and beans for him.

"Ah," he sighed in ecstasy, savoring the aroma. "Real coffee. Must mean we're getting close to civilization."

"Go on with you." Betsy Ann, accustomed to being teased for her habit of hoarding the coffee, smiled fondly at her youngest son. "Eat your breakfast. You're going to have a long day today."

"You women have my day all planned, I suppose." He cast a teasing glance at Matilda.

Ignoring the barb, Betsy Ann said, "Soon's we get to the hotel, your father wants you to ride down to Hicksville and locate your brothers. Alf gave directions to the Hicksville Store on the Upper Stockton Road. Mr. Patterson will send someone to guide you to Alf's place. It's close by. Wes and Weldon will stay here with the supply wagons and the cattle."

"And tonight," Matilda told him, "we are going to have a real bath and sleep in a real bed."

At noon, they pulled two of their four wagons up in front of the Pioneer Hotel. Hostlers ran to lead the wagons around to the stables behind the hotel.

"I could get used to this," Sinclair grinned, watching the two men lead the first team away.

Matilda handed the children to Sinclair and climbed down after them. She gazed in awe at the size and magnificence of the two-story hotel. The weathered brick building, half hidden under a mass of ivy, even boasted a port-cochere so carriages could discharge their passengers protected from the rain. Massive carved wooden doors stood open. Matilda knew that was for ventilation in the stifling heat, but they reminded her of open arms, welcoming her to the hotel. She shook her head at the fancy when she realized the probable cost of a room in such an expensive appearing establishment.

"Sinclair," she murmured in a low voice. "Can we afford to stay here?"

Sinclair grinned and helped his mother down off her elevated perch on the seat of the wagon. "This is where Alf told us to come, so this is where we'll stay." He picked up the small satchel she had packed for the hotel visit. "Come on."

Matilda, her feet sinking in the plush red carpet, approached the desk and asked the clerk about a room for herself and Annie and the children.

"Your room is ready, Mrs. Baldwin. Number Four, upstairs and to your left. The boy will bring up your bag." He brushed aside Matilda's attempts to pay. "It's been seen to."

Puzzled, she turned from the counter. A tall, well-dressed man stood smiling down on her. It took her a moment to recognize him. He had matured in the fourteen years since he left Illinois. Laugh lines creased his face, and a touch of gray showed against the black hair at his temples.

"Hello, Matilda," said the soft voice she remembered so well.

"Oh, Alf!" she cried, throwing herself into his arms. "It's so wonderful to see you. Let me look at you. You're so dressed up." In her astonishment, her words came out in a jumble.

"You've turned into a mighty handsome woman yourself, from that skinny girl I remember. And who are these lovely young ladies?" He bowed to Annie and the girls, endearing himself to Mary and Elizabeth forever.

Matilda introduced Annie and the children, then asked, "How did you know we'd get here today?"

He laughed. "I didn't. I've been here for three days. Guessed by your letter from Carson City about when you might arrive. In case you're interested, Nevada is about to become our thirty-sixth state. Anyway, Tom and Sam are taking care of my stock so I could be here to greet you."

He put his hands on her shoulders, then gave her another hug. "Do you like the hotel? Been here since forty-nine, first brick building built in Sacramento. Even survived the fire of '52." He grinned. "There are fancier hotels, but I've always been partial to this one."

Betsy Ann walked up at that moment and he turned to greet her.

"Sinclair," Matilda directed above the confusion, "find the Post Office and bring Annie's letter to us in Room Four." Gathering Annie and the children, she climbed the stairs to their room. There, she collapsed into the big easy chair in the corner. A lamp, its porcelain shade painted with red roses, stood on a small ornately carved table. The washstand bore a pitcher of water and a basin. Snowy white towels hung on a towel rack above it. The embroidered counterpane also displayed red roses. She looked around at the luxurious room and sighed in contentment. All she needed now was a bath!

"Imagine, a real chair!" Matilda marveled to Annie. "I'd almost forgotten what it feels like to sit in one. Find the chambermaid and tell her to bring hot water for the tub." Forcing herself to rise from the enticing comfort of the chair, Matilda gathered the children and headed down the hallway towards the bath room.

An hour later, luxuriating in cleanliness, Matilda carefully combed Mary's red-gold hair into ringlets, while Annie did the same for Elizabeth's dark locks. Baby Annie, scrubbed clean and garbed in a lacy, white dress, slept in the middle of the big bed.

Lewis wandered about the room, chattering in delight at all the new things to see and touch. Matilda watched him, a fond smile on her lips, and said to Annie, "See how well he walks now that he has a level floor!"

A knock sounded at the door. "'Tilda, Annie, it's me," came Sinclair's voice from the other side. "Are you dressed? Open up."

Annie jumped to her feet and ran to the door. "Oh, you have Ben's letter!" she exclaimed, snatching the packet from his hand.

The expression on Sinclair's face made Matilda's heart contract. Something's wrong, she thought. Poor brave little Annie, who has been through so much and come so far.

Annie's face paled as she looked at the packet. "It's not from Ben," she whispered. "It's from Henry." She looked at Matilda, her eyes dark with pain. "Somethin's happened to Ben."

"Now, Annie," Matilda soothed, "maybe he had his friend write for some reason. Sinclair," she told her brother, "take the children for a walk to look at the store fronts for a while."

"But 'Tilda, Alf wants me to ride with him out . . . ." He caught the look in her eyes and stopped. "Sure, be glad to." He scooped Lewis up in his arms. "Come on, girls, let's see what kind of excitement we can stir up in this town."

Mary and Elizabeth eagerly followed their Uncle Sinclair out of the room. Once the door closed on the departing children, Matilda turned to Annie. The girl stood rigid, holding the missive with her fingertips, as though the paper burned her. She made no move.

In a gentle voice, Matilda asked, "Do you want me to open it, Annie?"

"Please," the girl whispered numbly, handing the letter to Matilda.

Matilda's hands shook as she broke the seal. The letter contained a single sheet of writing, and a small folded paper. As Matilda quickly scanned the contents of the page, pain surged through her.

"Read it!" Annie commanded in a hoarse voice. "I've got to know."

"Dear Miss Annie," Matilda read, forcing the words around the lump in her throat. "I'm real sorry to tell you, but Ben took an arrow in a fight we was in with some Ute raiders. He died from it two days later." Matilda's eyes filled as she remembered Ben's handsome young face and twinkling green eyes. She blinked away her tears before reading on. "Afore he died," the letter continued, "he axed me to write to you in Sacramento City and tell you what happened. He was real worrit you might think he had changed his mind about coming." Matilda glanced at Annie, frightened by the set look on the girl's face.

Steadying her voice with an effort, Matilda read on, "He said to tell you he loves you and the babe. He said he was right sorry he never got to see her, but he's sure she's as purty a gal as her ma. He says you go ahead and use the money he give you to make yourself the finest hat shop Sacramento City ever seen."

Matilda looked up. "He signs it, 'Henry'," she said softly. "Oh, Annie, I am so sorry." She unfolded the other paper and found a lock of light brown hair. "Look, Annie. He sent you . . . " Her throat tightened and she could not go on. She held out the little packet wordlessly.

"A lock of Ben's hair," Annie finished for her. "Bless you, Henry. You've always been a true friend to Ben and me." She folded the lock of hair into its paper and tucked it inside the front of her dress. She looked up and met Matilda's eyes. "Henry used to help cover for me 'n' Ben so's we could meet." Her face crumpled and she broke into sobs.

Matilda gathered the weeping girl in her arms. "Poor, poor child," she murmured, stroking the soft hair. Why, God, why? she asked silently. How could You allow this to happen?

She held Annie closer and their tears mingled.

That evening, after they put the children to bed, they talked for a while.

"You give me courage, Miz' Baldwin," Annie told her. "You went on after your man got killed, and you with three little ones. I only got myself and little Annie to take care of."

"But I had my whole family," Matilda demurred. "You're all alone. Are you sure you wouldn't rather stay with me? You're more than welcome."

"No," Annie said firmly, "I'll not be beholden to you forever. My Ben wanted me to open a hat shop and that's what I'm gonna do."

Looking at the set of Annie's chin, Matilda smiled. "And I'm sure it will be the best hat shop the city of Sacramento has ever seen."

That evening, after Annie cried herself to sleep, Matilda, still restless after all the excitement of the day, stood staring out the window at the activity that continued on the street below. After dark, she marveled at the miracle of light from the gas lamps. She had heard of such wonders, but had never seen them before.

As she stared out of the window, she thought about her feelings when she finally looked out over Sacramento Valley. She thought she knew how Hannibal must have felt when he realized he had finally made it across the Alps and looked out over the plains of Rome.

She recalled her sense of triumph as she stood beside Sinclair high above the valley. She smiled faintly. Heroes are not brave, handsome soldiers on magnificent horses, she thought. Heroes are ordinary people who just keep struggling, dirty, sweaty, tired and thirsty, until they get where they want to go. She had not thought of herself as heroic until she stood on the top of that mountain. Matilda, the girl, stayed behind in Kansas. The Matilda who crossed those mountains and conquered those deserts was a woman.

She looked over at the sleeping children. How wonderful to see Alf again after all those years. And tomorrow she would see Tom and Sam and Minerva. She suddenly thought of Alf's partner, Alfred Wheelock. She remembered Alf's references to Mr. Wheelock in his letters home, and how she, as a young, romance-stricken, girl, had thought he seemed so nice. She wondered if she would meet him, then blushed. Silly, she told herself. He's probably ugly and chews tobacco.

Matilda blew out the lamp and crawled into bed, careful not to awaken Annie.

The next morning, Matilda awoke to the clatter of boot heels on the wooden walkway beneath her second story window, the creak of cart wheels in the dusty streets, and the shouts of drivers as they urged their animals along. She shook her head.

"Heavens, what a racket," she commented to Annie, who stood beside the window looking out at the scene. "How in the world does anyone ever get any sleep?"

Annie smiled, a movement of her lips that did not reach her eyes. "Guess I'll have to get used to it, Miz Baldwin." She took off her bonnet. "I been out walkin'. I think I've found a good spot for my shop. It's just a few blocks away, on 'K' Street, close to Fourth. There's a little room in the back where Annie and I can live. That way, I'll be able to tend to her and the shop at the same time, least until I get enough money to hire a girl to help me." She paused, then added bravely, "As soon as I get my customers built up."

By mid-morning, Matilda had settled Annie in her small room, fed and dressed the children, and packed all of their belongings, ready for the final trek to their new home. She watched the street from her window, waiting for Sinclair and Alf to return with Tom and Sam. The three children crowded around her. The amount of activity amazed her. Sacramento certainly was a busy place. Foot passengers threaded their way between riders on horses, dodging small carts pulled by mules or horses. She even watched a huge Conestoga wagon lumber by, taking up half the street as it did. Dust swirled around the horses' hooves. Little clouds merged into larger ones before settling again, in a never ending wave. She could imagine how it would be when it rained.

"There they are," she cried, spying Sinclair on White Star behind a cart loaded with rattling wooden kegs. Tom rode between Sam and Alf. Sam's blond hair, so like Sinclair's, contrasted with that of his brothers, who had dark hair like their father. Alf rode a magnificent stallion, almost the same color as White Star, with the same snow white mane and tail. She so seldom saw a horse like White Star. Most of the horses she had seen were sorrels or roans.

"Come, children," she said. "Come and meet your other uncles." She gathered Lewis in her arms and headed for the door.

Finally the horses were rehitched to the wagons, and everything stowed, ready to depart on the last leg of their long journey. Tom headed for the outskirts, accompanied by Britt's boys, to lead Wes and Weldon with the stock. Sinclair strode to where White Star waited patiently at the hitching post. As he untied her and prepared to mount, three idlers seated on the hotel porch rose and ambled over to him.

One of them, the tallest and ugliest, spat a stream of tobacco juice in front of Sinclair and demanded, "And how'd a poor farm boy like you ever git hisself a horse like this 'un?"

Matilda looked for Alf and Sam. Alf was nowhere in sight. Sam rode beside Britt's wagon in the lead, out of earshot. The second idler jeered, "Mebbe you jest oughta give 'er to us, farm boy."

Gardner, on the seat of the wagon, gave an angry growl, and Matilda saw Sinclair's ears and neck turn red, a sure sign of his temper rising. She quickly climbed down and approached the group.

"The horse is mine, young man," she said, icicles dripping from her voice. "Do you have a quarrel with that?"

Startled, the idler turned to face her. She stared at him, barbs shooting from her eyes. "I asked," she repeated, "if you have a quarrel with that?" She continued to glare at him, then added, "Or do you prefer I call the sheriff?"

The three backed down. "Uh, no, ma'am, whatever you say." They hastened on down the street.

Sinclair turned to Matilda with a grin. "Thanks, 'Tilda.

Thought for a minute I was gonna hafta fight all three of 'em."

A glimmer of a smile crossed Matilda's lips, impressed by her own courage herself. "My pleasure." She climbed back into the wagon, suddenly very pleased with the way she handled the bullies. She smiled again, more broadly. I think, she thought, I am beginning to like the new Matilda.

Chapter 56

September of 1864

"*OH, ALF,* your home is beautiful." Matilda looked out over the fields and outbuildings as the wagon turned into the lane. She saw a pump house with a large windmill, a corn crib, a tool shed, even a barn with a spacious corral for the horses.

"I'm afraid the house is a tad small," he replied. "Bachelor like me doesn't need a lot of room, just a space for a bed and a place for my books." Then he grinned. "But we're all family. We'll fit in somehow. Welcome to California."

"So far, it's everything I imagined it would be." She could not resist teasing him, "But you have this lovely home and all those nice clothes. Why haven't you married?"

He laughed. "Waiting until I find a woman like you, I guess. Bring any with you?" Dismounting from King's back, he took her arm and helped her down from the wagon seat. "Come in and get settled. There's letters for you. The one from Carrie is just burning a hole in the table, waiting for you to read it." He lifted the children down and the girls started toward the house. Lewis toddled along behind them.

When they entered, Alf pointed to the packet of letters on the table. "There they are. Enjoy. I'll ride over to Abe and Minerva's and tell them you're here. Min promised to skin me alive if I didn't tell her the moment you arrived."

She looked at the packet of letters, eager to read them, but Lewis had started to fuss. He needed a nap. Gardner, Sinclair and the little girls set off to explore their new home and Alf rode off, King's hooves kicking up little clouds of dust as they headed down the lane.

Betsy Ann promptly kicked off her shoes and settled down for a brief rest. "Been pushing these old bones pretty hard for a long time," she declared. "Feels good to just rest a mite."

As soon as Matilda settled Lewis for his nap, she scooped up her letters and sat down to read. Sarah Williams had written, as had her sister Sarah, her brother John's wife Mary Anne, and Caroline. She opened the one from Caroline first. The letter talked of newsy items, neighbors, crops, and, as always, the weather, since weather played such a major role in the life of any Kansas farmer. Matilda sighed. It all seemed so remote. Kansas seemed so far away, several lifetimes ago. Caroline also wrote about the progress of the war.

"I guess it should be over pretty soon, thank goodness. That General Sherman has boasted he is going to march from the Mississippi to the sea and cut the South in half. Don't tell Pa. It would just upset him."

The next lines made Matilda's heart miss a beat.

"I was so glad to receive your letter from Salt Lake City. What a relief to know you had passed safely through Sioux territory. Shortly after you left, the problems with Indians spread south along the Little Blue. They burned the Oak Grove station, killing all the folks there. Then in August, Indians (they say Cheyenne, I'm not sure) destroyed a wagon train and the stage station at Liberty Farm. They killed and scalped Mr. Eubank and eight or nine of the family, including the girl, Dora, and a twelve-year-old boy.

Young Mrs. Eubank, her little girl Isabelle, her baby, William, along with a girl named Laura Roper who was on a visit from a neighboring farm were kidnapped. I guess the soldiers went looking for them. I haven't heard whether they found them or not."

Matilda's mind went to the Eubanks family she had met, and the boy who gave her the drink of water from their well, the boy with the charming smile. He had to be the twelve-year-old Caroline referred to. Her heart ached to think of what had befallen them. She hoped the soldiers were successful in their rescue attempts.

But Caroline had more bad news to impart. The next paragraph told an even more vivid story.

"The Indians destroyed another train of wagons at Plum Creek Station. Which tribe I never heard, but probably Sioux. They didn't burn the station, but they killed everyone there. Why they didn't burn the building no one can figure. It's probably the only one left standing west of Fort Kearny. They've burned all the rest.

"I'm just glad they decided to move west and not come any farther down the Little Blue. I suspect the proximity of Fort Kearny had something to do with their decision. The volunteers manning the fort are just as good as the regular soldiers when it comes to Indian fighting, and the Indians must know it. At least so far, the fort has never been attacked."

Matilda had to laugh at her sister's next words:

"For weeks after you left, the Pottawatamies came by asking for a 'coo-kee'. I tried to tell them you had left for California. They just shook their heads and said, 'no coo-kee?' I felt sorry for them and offered them some of mine. The chief, the one you befriended at the beginning, took a bite and put the cookie back on the plate. He just shook his head and said, 'No good coo-kee. Want good coo-kee from red hair lady.' I didn't know whether to laugh or be insulted."

Matilda smiled as she recalled the image of the Pottawatamie chief. She pulled the gold ring on its chain from beneath her bodice and held it in her hand, remembering the day the three young squaws came to bid her farewell and gave her the little ring as a token of what her friendship had meant to them. It seemed hard to connect the Indians she knew with the incidents Caroline described. She shivered to think how close they had come to being included in the attacks. She remembered the Sioux who stroked Mary's hair with such gentleness. It seemed hard to believe those same men could be capable of such savagery.

Then the ill-fated Parsons sprang into her mind. Yes, beneath that gentle veneer dwelt a fierceness she could not even imagine. She thought of the poor lady at Plum Creek Station who always worked so hard and always complained of the ague. Well, at least the poor soul can rest now, Matilda thought. She could do nothing, so she refused to dwell on it. She folded up Caroline's letter and turned to the others. When she finished, she tucked them in a drawer to read again later.

She could hardly wait to see Minerva again. They should be here soon, she thought. Lewis stirred in his sleep and she rose to check on him. Alf had given up his bedroom so she and the children could use it. Her parents had been given the other bedroom.

She glanced around when she returned to the main room. The two bedrooms opened off the big parlor. A cozy kitchen ran across the back of the house, and opened onto a small covered porch.

Yes, she smiled to herself, settling into the big easy chair to await Minerva's arrival, we will be very comfortable here. She yawned. The chair tempted her to lie back and rest, and the soft velvet lured her into dreamland.

* * *

Two days later they had settled in. Britt parked his wagons on Tom's land until he could buy property or decide what to do. He talked of going on to Santa Barbara, where Sevier Stringfield had settled. Sevier swore Santa Barbara was the most beautiful place on earth.

White Star shared a small corral behind the barn with Alf's horse, King. Matilda walked out to stroke White Star and treat her to a lump of sugar. Alf strode along beside her, slowing his pace to match Matilda's shorter legs.

"She's a beautiful horse," he commented when they stood by the rail of the corral.

"I love her," Matilda said simply. "We've been through a lot together, haven't we, White Star?" The horse whinnied in response. Matilda stroked the soft muzzle while the horse daintily nibbled the morsel of sugar in her hand. When the animal laid her head over Matilda's shoulder, Matilda hugged her neck. "I was so afraid I'd lose her crossing that terrible desert." Tears sprang into Matilda's eyes as she confessed, "I even gave her part of my water rations. She got so skinny I could see her ribs." Then she laughed and scratched the favorite spot behind the mare's ears. "But she fattened right back up again, soon's we got off that horrid desert, didn't you, my darling?"

"How old is she?" Alf asked. "Have you ever thought of getting a colt out of her?"

Somehow Matilda had never thought of White Star as an ordinary horse, but she calculated her age. White Star was a two-year-old when Lewis rode up on her that long ago day in Kansas. "Ten," she told Alf. "And I've never seen a horse worthy of her." She paused. "Before King, that is." She looked over at the stallion who watched them closely. "He's a real fine horse."

Alf grinned down at her. "He's the nugget you told me to find. I'd never part with him, either."

Matilda stepped back from White Star and smiled. "And what do you think, my beauty? Do you think King is worthy of you?"

White Star whickered and stamped her foot. Matilda laughed. "See, Alf? She agrees."

Chapter 57

October of 1864

October 1, 1864
Hicksville, California

Dear Caroline,

At last I have time to sit down and write to you. Forgive the brevity of the note I sent from Sacramento. I wanted to let you know of our safe arrival, but with so much going on I could not do justice to a letter.

We are settled in at last. Alf has a lovely home. He says it's small, and I suppose it is by California standards, but compared to what we had in Kansas, it's a mansion. The children and I have a room to ourselves, and Mother and Pa have a room as well.

When we arrived, your letter, as Alf put it, was burning a hole in the table waiting for me to read it. I also had letters from our sister Sarah and Mary Anne and Sarah Williams.

The news from the war is sad. I think it preys on Pa's mind all the time. He never discusses anything to do with the war, and always walks away or changes the subject whenever someone else brings it up. All I can think of is poor Josh and all the other young men who have died so senselessly. My heart aches for the wives and mothers of those men. I, for one, will be so glad when this dreadful fighting is over at last. It should never, ever have happened.

You're not the only one glad we got through Sioux and Cheyenne territory before they started to burn all the stations. We did hear of one attack shortly after we left, but on one wagon travelling alone. Had I known they were burning the stations, I would have been frightened to death. Pa said he

hoped we would get through before something happened to
unite all of the Indians. He fears they will one day decide
to forget their tribal differences and see the white man as a
common threat.

I suppose it could happen, but it's hard to imagine. Can
you picture a Sioux and a Pawnee sharing a calumet? Or an
Arapaho and a Snake sitting around the same fire? It would
take something big, like a major massacre.

I do hope the soldiers were able to rescue Mrs. Eubanks
and her children. I felt so sad to hear about their kidnapping.
And poor Mr. Eubanks and the others murdered! The whole
area seemed so peaceful when we passed through. It's hard
to believe it could be the scene of such a tragedy. They had
just finished building their lovely home and were so happy.
Just goes to show, I guess, that nothing is certain in this world.

That climb over the Sierras took everything I had, let me
tell you. The eastern slope is very steep. But when we reached
the other side and I finally looked out over the Sacramento
Valley, I felt I had conquered the world. And the scenery!
Miles and miles of pine trees, and magnificent granite peaks
towering above the timberline, like islands in a dark green sea.
Snow still clung to the highest ones. Along the top, scrubby,
wind-blown pines and scraggly chaparral clung to cracks in
boulders scraped smooth by glaciers (according to Sinclair
who quoted Fremont who quoted somebody, I forget who),
grinding across the mountains. I find it hard to believe. Can
you imagine such a wall of ice moving south along a mountain
top? Sinclair swears it's true.

Once we got over the top, it was downhill all the way, and
took us five days to get to Sacramento where Alf met us. He
had spent three days at the hotel waiting for us, he was that
anxious to see us. Words cannot describe how wonderful it
felt to see him. Sam and Tom joined us the next day.

Seeing Minerva and Abe again was the crowning event.
Laura will be five in November, Annie is three, little Will just

turned two, and Charlie is six months old. *Minerva worries me. I think four children in five years has worn her out. She's lost weight since she left Kansas, and admitted, when I pressed her, that she feels tired all the time. I told her I hope she doesn't have any more children until she gets her strength back.*

The neighborhood girls have discovered Sinclair. Alf laughs and says if he had known Sinclair would attract so much feminine attention he would have persuaded him to come out sooner. Sam and Alf gave a welcome party and everyone came from miles around. Now all the young girls keep coming over to bring all kinds of things — pies, fresh corn, crochet works, even toys for the children. They always arrive around noon so the men will be in from the fields for dinner. If Sinclair happens to be gone, they always look around, watching for him to appear, although, of course, they never say a word. It's so funny.

Will and Polly have a ranch (they don't call them 'farms' here) right next to Sam's place. They have 250 acres, and just finished harvesting the second crop of corn. The land is by a small stream called Laguna Creek, and the water level is so close to the surface their well is only six feet deep. They can grow crops in the summer even though it never rains. Will Jr. is almost grown, and Michael will be fourteen in December. He is turning into a very handsome young man. Mary adores him, and follows him everywhere. His patience with her is amazing. Not many fourteen-year-old boys will put up with a five-year-old girl tagging along after them.

Their other children are all hale and hearty. Alf is right. The air in California is very healthy. I suspect it's because it doesn't get so cold. Little Maggie is two, and into everything. Baby Sam is still in arms. That makes eight for them so far, and they've not lost a one. Compare that to Kansas. I can't help feeling I'd not have lost baby John if we hadn't been living in that dreadful climate.

Tom, Alf and Sam are well, and so strong and tanned you wouldn't know them. Wes and Weldon got to be such good friends on the trek out that they have decided to form a freight company. The two wagons we drove out here in will be their start. I think they will do quite well. Giles is talking about joining them. He says it's getting so there's not much need for scouts anymore, between the stage road and the train coming.

Poor little Annie had bad news waiting for her in Sacramento. Her Ben was killed in an Indian fight. Her baby, a beautiful little girl, was born in August while we were along the Humboldt. She's opened a hat shop in Sacramento. I admire her courage. I still have no idea what I want to do with my life. Alf is delighted to have me keep house for him, but if he marries, his wife won't want me and my three under foot all the time.

California is so different from Kansas. We are in this huge valley, flat for miles in every direction. To the west, the Coast Range mountains stand against the skyline, especially the one they call Mount Diablo. It's an extinct volcano, of all things. I've never seen a volcano before. At least, Alf says it's extinct, and I hope he's right.

To the east, the Sierras range as far as the eye can see. Snow clings to the highest peaks. They have had some flurries already. I'm sure glad we got across when we did.

Here in the valley, the rains haven't started yet, but the days have begun to get cooler. Everything is dry and dusty. Magnificent oak trees spread out over the whole valley except where they've been cleared for farming. The leaves are covered with dust, making the whole landscape look like it should be sent to the laundry.

But even on the hottest days, a breeze springs up from the west in the evening and cools everything down. They say we are due inland from the gap in the mountains into San Francisco Bay, and that the ocean breeze comes right up the delta. Just imagine being so close to an ocean! I do hope some day we can take a boat trip down the river to San Francisco, although I guess it can be dangerous. *Alf says that shortly before we arrived, the boiler on the steamer 'Washoe' blew up by Steamboat Slough and killed a lot of people. I would love to stand on the edge of the Pacific Ocean and smell the sea. Britt says the next land going west is Japan, clear on the other side of the world. I can't even conjure up a picture in my mind of so much water.*

Britt also says the smell of that ocean gets in your blood. That's why he's thinking of relocating to Santa Barbara, where Uncle Sevier settled. They are close to the coast there. But Britt says he just wants to stand on the beach and watch the water move. After his trip from San Francisco to New York, he says he will never get on another boat as long as he lives.

Give my love to Ely. I was so glad to hear the good news. It's about time you and Ely got a family started. Are Becky and Sally glad they will have a little brother or sister?

Anytime you get tired of Kansas blizzards and that muggy Kansas heat, we would love to have you join us.

Love,

Tilda

Chapter 58

April to August, 1865

ALF ran his hand across White Star's belly and grunted with satisfaction. "No doubt about it," he told Matilda, who stood beside him waiting anxiously for his decision. "She's carrying King's foal. Should be born about mid-summer, way I figure it."

Matilda hugged White Star's neck. "I'm so proud of you, my darling," she murmured into the horse's soft skin.

The April morning dawned bright and clear. The cold north winds of March had finally ended several weeks before. Matilda thoroughly enjoyed her first winter with no snow. Towards the east stood the snow-laden Sierra Nevada mountains. While she admired their majestic beauty, she preferred the mountains just where they were with their load of snow, many miles away.

She looked out over the fields and smiled at the beauty of the scene. Alf's hired man already plowed for the spring wheat. Areas yet untilled burst with the color of yellow mustard, orange poppies, and lavender and white wild radish. In the afternoon, the purple four o'clocks added to the tapestry.

The winter had passed pleasantly. Matilda found everything new and fascinating. This young country seemed so alive, so bustling with activity. She ignored her mother's predictions that she would contract all sorts of fatal illnesses from the chill and went for long walks in the mist that Alf called tule fog. The dampness penetrated her clothing, and droplets of fog clung to her hair and festooned the spider webs with silver beads. Sounds drifted in the mist, making them seem almost there, like sounds of a piano played in a room with damp walls. She walked across the fields in the late evenings, intrigued by the ghostly mist rising from the ground.

The ever practical Alf explained the phenomena to five-year-old Mary, whose inquisitive mind wanted an answer to everything. "The ground warms up from the sun," he explained patiently, "then the cold night air comes in. When the cold air meets the warm air rising from the ground, it makes fog."

"But Uncle Sinclair told me the Valkyries make the mist so no one can see them ride through the fields," Mary protested. "I want to see the Valkyries."

Matilda came to Alf's rescue as he looked at her helplessly. "Uncle Alf is right, Mary," she laughed. "Your Uncle Sinclair just likes making up fancy stories."

At the end of April, the Cosumnes River overflowed its banks, filling the low-lying land with rushing water. Matilda remembered the flood on the Big Blue and her narrow escape with John on her back. Frightened, she asked Alf if they were in any danger.

"Floods like this every spring," he reassured her. "When the snow melts in the Sierra. No one ever builds on the low areas. Every once in a while the Sacramento and the American get high enough to flood Sacramento City. That's why they built the levees, and why all the houses have second stories. But the Cosumnes never makes any trouble for us."

When Matilda mentioned her concerns about the floods to Minerva, her sister told her Alf's information was accurate. "Never been any problems in the four years we've been here."

Matilda sighed. "I feel better. I was afraid Alf just didn't want me to worry."

Minerva still looked tired. As Matilda watched, concern

for her sister's health never far from her mind, Minerva picked up a letter from the table.

"We got another letter from Abe's sister Sarah, the one that married that nice young Union soldier. They've moved to Oregon and want us to join them."

"You're not going are you?" Matilda asked. She feared another journey would be very hard on Minerva. Besides, after finally getting her back, she wanted her close.

"No, Abe says as long as the wagon-building business holds good, there's no need to move. We both like it here." She sighed. "I'm glad. I sure don't like the idea of another long journey, though at least there isn't any desert between here and Oregon."

Matilda laughed. They had compared their desert experiences, and agreed they never wanted to see another desert.

"Sarah also reports lots of problems with Indians since that horrid Chivington killed all those Cheyenne at Sand Creek last November. Since the village he attacked had signed a peace treaty with the United States Government and was flying an American flag, the Indians are now fully convinced the white man can't be trusted. A number of outlying settlements have had folks murdered."

"Pa predicted something would happen to unite them," Matilda said, shaking her head. "He said they would eventually see the white man as a threat to all of them. So it finally happened. Now what?"

Minerva shrugged her shoulders. "I'm just glad we're here. Our Miwoks would never be a threat to any of us." She pulled the kettle forward over the heat of the stove. "Want a cup of tea? Sarah also says they just heard the news that General Lee surrendered. And that Mr. Quantrill was shot and killed in Tennessee on his way to join General Lee. It's kind of sad, in a way. The poor man was only 28 years old. I know he had his detractors, but he only did what he thought he should."

"Wes must be told," Matilda said. "I'm sure he'll want to know. He still kind of admires Quantrill, though I've never understood why."

Minerva laughed. "Sarah also said, according to rumor, that Quantrill left $800 to his mistress, Kate King, and that she plans to use the money to open a bawdy house in St. Louis."

As Matilda laughed with her sister, her mind returned to her reaction to Quantrill's raid on Lawrence. Perhaps Quantrill had thought he was right, and he certainly had those who felt he had cause, but she still thought of him as a murderer.

"Mama," Mary's voice interrupted her, "Lewis has waked up from his nap and he is all wet." She wrinkled her freckled nose in disgust. "He wants me to pick him up, but I won't touch him."

Matilda pulled herself together. "I'm coming, my love."

By July, the dry grass crackled beneath Matilda's feet as she walked. The temperature often reached the nineties, on occasion topping a hundred, but in the dry air she scarcely noticed the heat. Every evening a breeze rose in the west, cooled the air, and made sleeping comfortable. She thought of the sleepless nights in Kansas, tossing and turning in the muggy heat. She wondered why they had stayed back there so long, fighting the weather and the political harassment of men like Whitson and Sechrest.

"You look like you're about to burst," Matilda laughed at White Star as she watched the horse greedily drink the cool water from the wooden trough. White Star's time approached and Matilda watched her closer than ever.

In response, White Star turned her dripping muzzle to Matilda and nuzzled her ear. Matilda squealed as the cold water ran down her neck. "You're all wet!"

Sinclair joined them and eyed White Star. "Wouldn't be surprised but what she foals in the next day or two. Look at the size of her. Looks like she's got two of 'em in there."

"Oh, my!" Matilda's eyes sparkled. "Imagine getting two."

Sinclair smiled at her enthusiasm, then changed the subject. "Did you hear about that ruckus in the Assembly chambers last night? Disgraceful. Some gentlemen they are." He shook his head. "Wouldn't it serve 'em right if the voters rejected Low and Barton both and elected someone else entirely?"

Matilda, her mind only on White Star, did not hear a word he said. "You don't suppose she'll have any problems, do you?" she asked, a tinge of anxiety in her voice.

Sinclair chuckled. "She is ten years old, and this is her first time. If the foal's too big ..." He paused at the panic on Matilda's face. "I'm sure she'll do just fine," he hastened to reassure her.

But that night, Matilda could not get White Star out of her mind . After putting the children to bed, she started for bed herself, then felt an uncontrollable urge to check her beloved horse. She knew she would never sleep if she did not. Taking a lantern and shaking her head at her foolishness, Matilda returned to the barn. There she found White Star pacing back and forth in her stall, in obvious discomfort.

"Oh, White Star," she gasped. "It's your time! What shall I do?" She stroked the sweat-matted neck and matched her pace to the horse's stride around the stall. Then White Star stopped abruptly and lay down on the bed of straw, grunting and straining, her eyes rolling.

Matilda had never attended a horse before, and a flash of fright ran through her. "Come on, White Star," she murmured in encouragement to the horse, continuing to stroke the mare's sweaty neck. After what seemed hours to Matilda, White Star whinnied and a foal appeared on the straw behind her.

Both Matilda and White Star hastened to clean the foal's tiny muzzle. The ungainly colt snorted and shook his head. Matilda laughed and hugged the newborn, tears of joy and relief running down her cheeks. "Oh, White Star, he's just beautiful. I'm so proud of you, my darling. He's so little! I was afraid he'd be too big, and . . . ."

Matilda looked up as she heard a low chuckle and saw Sinclair standing by the stall door observing her. "You should see yourself," he laughed. "You're a mess. But you're right. He's a beautiful colt. And if you can take your eyes off of him for a moment and look back at White Star, you'll see why this one's so small."

Matilda turned back to White Star in time to see the second colt born. "Two! Oh, White Star, you're wonderful. Wait until Mary sees your babies."

Brother and sister spent the next hour cleaning the two little colts while White Star looked on with interest. "Oh, Sinclair," Matilda marveled, "aren't they marvelous?"

"Yes," Sinclair agreed, "but don't you think we should go back to bed? I'm sure White Star can manage without our help."

But dawn broke over the distant Sierra before Matilda finally allowed Sinclair to persuade her to leave the barn and return to the house.

Mary, as enchanted as Matilda predicted, immediately claimed the colt with four white ankles. "I'm going to call him 'Four Stockings', " she announced.

Elizabeth promptly dubbed the second one with the inelegant sobriquet of 'Long Legs'.

"As you wish, girls." Matilda laughed. "We will call them Four Stockings and Long Legs."

Chapter 59

August of 1865

TWO WEEKS later, Gardner came in from the fields for dinner and said to Betsy Ann, "Billy Bandeen is willing to part with that colt he got out of his black mare." At the wash basin on the porch outside of the kitchen door, he scrubbed his hands. "Got real good lines to him. Sinclair has been wanting a horse of his own so he won't have to borrow White Star from Matilda when he doesn't want to ride that broken down old bay."

Matilda demurred. "I don't mind him riding White Star, Pa, and her colts are growing well. In two years he can have one of them." She glanced at Mary who had opened her mouth to protest and added hastily, "Of course, if he wants Four Stockings, he'll have to ask Mary." She turned back to her father. "Besides, are you sure that colt of Billy's is broken well enough? I saw Billy riding him last week and he looked real frisky."

Gardner brushed off her fears. "Sinclair is an experienced rider, Matilda. I don't think he wants to wait two years for your colts to grow up. Besides, White Star is too gentle for him. He'll welcome a horse that'll give him a real challenge."

"If Uncle Sinclair wants Four Stockings," Mary announced, not to be outdone, "he can ride him, but only until I get grown up."

The following Sunday, the family gathered at Alf's house for dinner after church as usual. When they finished the meal, Gardner rose to his feet.

"Everyone out to the barn," he announced. "I have a surprise for Sinclair."

"Pa! Did you really ...? I mean ... do you mean it?" Sinclair stammered with excitement then dashed for the door, followed by the rest of the family.

Matilda matched her pace to Lewis' short legs, and so arrived at the barn a few moments behind everyone else. When they reached the group, Sinclair stood stroking the sleek, black neck of the young horse. Gardner, on the other side of the horse's head, proudly held the bridle.

White Star looked out across the door of her stall at all the excitement. When Matilda stopped to pet her as she always did, White Star whinnied a soft greeting. The two colts slept in the stall beside her.

Sinclair's face glowed with happiness, his hazel eyes catching the light of the sun.

"Devil Wind," he babbled. "I'm going to call him Devil Wind, because he's black as the devil and will run like the wind."

Matilda felt a stir of anxiety, but she ignored it. Sinclair is an experienced rider, she told herself. If anyone can handle Devil Wind, it will be Sinclair.

"Tomorrow," Sinclair went on. "Tomorrow, I'm going to see what he can do!"

The next morning, as soon as he finished his breakfast, Sinclair headed for the barn. "I'll be back by noon with the mail, Mother," he promised. "Just want to swing by Davis' on the way back, and show them my new horse."

From the kitchen window, Betsy Ann and Matilda, washing the breakfast dishes, watched him ride off. Matilda felt a return of the anxiety she had felt the day before while she watched Sinclair saddle the prancing black horse.

"The horse seems pretty frisky," she commented to her mother.

"He's a man grown, Matilda," Betsy Ann said. "You'll learn when your children are older that sometimes we just have to watch and pray."

Matilda nodded. "I suppose you're right. Sinclair is good with horses. It's just ..." She shook off the feeling. They finished the dishes in silence.

But Matilda and her mother waited in vain for Sinclair to return. Gardner and Alf rode up to the porch as the sun settled into the cloud bank to the west. Sam accompanied them. Since their arrival last fall, Sam made it a habit of appearing regularly for supper. Betsy Ann and Matilda both teased him.

"You got along just fine on your own cookin' all those years," Betsy Ann had told him. "Now how come all of a sudden you got to have someone cook for you?" Sam had just hugged her and flattered her until she finally shooed him from the kitchen.

The early evening sky glowed with the golden orange and reddish purple of sunset. Matilda, setting the table for supper, heard Betsy Ann greet the returning men.

"Where's Sinclair, Gardner?" she asked. "He didn't come back with the mail. Isn't he with you?"

"He's not back yet? Must have gotten involved talking to the Davis girls and forgot to watch the time." Matilda had to laugh. She knew Sinclair's clear hazel eyes, blond curls, and handsome face had caught the eye of many in the neighborhood. That, combined with his gentle good nature, made Sinclair one of the area's most eligible bachelors, and he thoroughly enjoyed his status with the unmarried young ladies.

Gardner frowned. "Maybe I'd better ride around and check. Just let me get a lantern. Probably be dark before I can get back." Taking the lantern Betsy Ann handed him, he rode away.

Matilda paused, holding the stack of plates. Fear gave her heart a squeeze. Surely nothing could happen to Sinclair. Sam and Alf joked as they cleaned up. They weren't worried. She laughed. Silly, she told herself. Don't borrow trouble.

The meal passed in silence. When Alf offered grace, he included a plea for Sinclair's safety, the only hint he gave that he, too, felt uneasy. Each seemed lost in thought. Even the light-hearted Mary seemed to sense the tension in the room. Little Lewis watched the faces of the silent adults around him, his eyes wide. Matilda's attempts to reassure the children sounded hollow, for she felt a cold lump in her chest. She pushed the food around on her plate, but could not bring herself to eat.

Matilda finally rose, unable to sit still any longer, and began clearing the table. One plate slipped from her nerveless fingers. She burst into tears as it shattered on the floor.

Betsy Ann took her in her arms. As they clung to each other, Matilda trying to control her sobs, the sound of approaching hoofbeats reached their ears.

Matilda's tears instantly dried and she began to laugh, almost hysterically. "Oh, how foolish of me. Here they are now." She ran to the door, Betsy Ann at her heels.

They tried to see the rider through the gathering gloom. A lantern glowed, bobbing with the motion. The horseman was Billy Bandeen, not Gardner Randolph. As he neared the porch, they recognized the black horse he led and Matilda gave a faint cry.

Devil Wind bore an empty saddle.

Billy, his Scottish burr more pronounced in his excitement, tried to reassure them. "Sure, and he only come back to me as he's not been with ye long enough yet. Must have got loose from young Sinclair, mayhap while he were showing him off to the Davis girls."

"Pa left for Davis' not half an hour ago to look for him."

Matilda grasped at the straw. "Maybe that is what happened. See, Mother? The horse got away and Sinclair had no way to get back. When Pa returns, he'll bring him."

"Sure and that's it," Billy agreed. "I'll just put his horse in the barn and be on my way, then."

They thanked him for returning Devil Wind, but he did not leave. He came back from the barn and stood on the porch. Fidgeting with his hat, he mumbled, "Since it was my horse . . . sold him . . . feel kind of, er, uh . . . ."

Matilda took pity on him. "Please, Mr. Bandeen, do sit down and have a bite of supper." She filled a cup with steaming coffee and placed it in front of him.

They waited in silence as the long summer twilight slowly ceded the day to night.

Gardner returned alone. They heard him put the horse in the barn and walk back to the house. No one spoke as he entered the room.

He looked around expectantly, and his voice boomed, "So he got home okay. I see Devil Wind in the . . . ." He stopped, noticing the silence and the absence of the one face he sought. The color drained from his face as he met Betsy Ann's eyes and saw the fear in them. "Oh, no," he whispered.

Sam spoke first. "We must search. He's probably injured, or he'd have walked home by now. Come, Pa, Billy. Get Will and the hands from his place. Alf, get Tom. I'll swing by Britt's and meet you at Davis'. We should start there, since that's where he was last seen."

"Right, Son." Gardner pulled himself together. "Come on," he gruffly told the other men. "If he's hurt, there's no time to lose."

After the men departed, Matilda and Betsy Ann washed the supper dishes, feeling the need to do something. Lewis fell asleep on the floor, so Matilda stirred herself to put the children to bed. Mary looked at her mother, her blue eyes anxious. "Is Uncle Sinclair going to be all right?" she asked. "He is my favorite uncle, you know."

"Yes, darling, I know," Matilda soothed.

Elizabeth piped up, "Mine, too."

Matilda's heart sank. If something happened to Sinclair, who had been almost a father to them since Lewis died .... She could not bring herself to complete the thought. "Please, go to sleep. I'll have him come in and kiss you good night just as soon as he gets home."

"Promise?" they chorused.

"No matter how late?" Mary insisted.

"Promise," she vowed, her heart like a lump of lead in her chest. "No matter how late."

As they waited alone, Betsy Ann tried to ease Matilda's fears. "Try not to worry. They'll find him. He can't have gone far."

Shortly after the clock struck twelve, Sam and Tom strode through the door bearing Sinclair in their arms. Gardner, Britt, Alf and Will, accompanied by several neighbors, followed. With a little cry, Betsy Ann ran forward. Matilda stood frozen, her limbs refusing to move.

"He's alive, Mother," Alf said. "He's breathing. He took a bad blow to the side. You can see where the hoof struck." The marks showed plainly on his shirt. "Pray God he will recover."

During the endless night, Gardner told Matilda and Betsy Ann what had happened. "He was still conscious when we found him. He had ridden over to see the Davis girls, as we thought, but instead of coming directly home, he swung by Wahl's. That's where we found him, not far from Wahl's." Gardner's voice faltered. "He said Devil Wind seemed to be favoring his left hind foot. Thinking maybe he picked up a stone, Sinclair dismounted to check." He drew a deep breath to steady his voice. "I guess the horse was not as well broken as we thought. When Sinclair lifted the hoof, Devil Wind kicked him and took off."

Gardner paused to stroke the hair back from Sinclair's clammy forehead. The gray pall settling over the loved face of his youngest son brought tears to his eyes.

"The pain was too great for him to move, and calling out just increased it." Gardner's calm broke and he paced the room. "God help us," he cried, "he lay there for hours waiting for us to find him." He pounded the wall in his frustration. "If only we had found him sooner!"

Betsy Ann's voice interrupted his anguished wail. "Don't blame yourself. It would have changed nothing."

Britt sat at the foot of the bed. Sam, Tom, Alf, and Will stood leaning against the wall, staring at the still body of their youngest brother. They neither spoke nor moved.

The endless night passed slowly, each tick of the big clock counting down the seconds of Sinclair's life. Matilda sat at the bedside holding his hand, Betsy Ann across the bed from her. Unfortunately, little could be done except put cold, wet cloths on his head and comfrey poultices on his abdomen.

"He's bleeding inside," Betsy Ann reported, motioning to the swelling on his bruised and distended abdomen. "We can do nothing but pray the comfrey poultices stop the bleeding."

As the first light of dawn shone through the open window, promising still another day of stifling heat, Sinclair's respiration grew shallower, more ragged. The skin on his face took on a bluish hue.

Matilda's face paled as she matched her breaths to Sinclair's. Tears furrowed her cheeks as they poured unchecked, dripping on her shirtwaist. Instinctively she knew death approached. Sinclair's breathing became more and more labored.

As the sun reached the tops of the trees, the gasping breaths stopped. Betsy Ann's face remained the frozen mask it had been all night. Tears rolled down Gardner's cheeks.

Matilda could restrain her sobs no longer.

Chapter 60

August to December, 1865

THEY buried Sinclair in Hicksville Cemetery, the large number of people present silent testimony to his popularity. Tears poured down many cheeks. One of the Davis girls wept openly, her face buried against her father's shoulder.

Matilda's mind returned to the agony of telling Mary and Elizabeth their adored Uncle Sinclair was dead. Dead! How could he be dead? His easy laughter echoed in her mind. If he opened his eyes, they would still have the sparkle she remembered so clearly. How could he seem so alive to her yet be lying in that coffin?

She did not even hear the service, only realizing it had ended when people began moving about, offering their condolences. Matilda murmured automatic responses. Later, she could not remember anything she said, or even to whom she spoke.

A bearded, dark-haired man she did not recognize stood close to her brother Alf, hat in hand. She wondered fleetingly if this was Alf's partner from Placerville. Alf had mentioned the man might be coming.

Alf approached her, accompanied by the stranger. "'Tilda," he smiled, "allow me to present my friend and partner, Alfred Wheelock."

"I am so pleased to meet you at last, Mrs. Baldwin." The stranger's deep, resonant voice vibrated through her body. "Alf has spoken of you often. I am only sorry it had to be under such sad circumstances."

He took her hand in his. Matilda raised her head and saw his face through a haze of pain. Their eyes met and she read the sympathy there. The kindness in his face broke her carefully controlled reserve. Turning to her brother, she buried her face in his chest and wept.

Two weeks later, as Matilda washed clothes at the wash-tub stand in the shade of the big oak tree beside the house, thoughts of Sinclair consumed her. As her hands dunked the clothes up and down in the soapy water, she remembered the fun times together. She tried to think of him as alive, only somewhere else, someplace where she could not see him, or ever visit him. It made the pain a little easier to bear.

The hot afternoon sun began its descent in the west. "This has to have been the hottest day so far this summer, Jake," she sighed to the dog lying in the shade beside her. He had dug a spot in the cool earth where the water spilled from the tubs.

The dog lazily thumped his tail a few times, not even exerting enough energy to raise his head. Under the sun's glare in the white-hot sky, the parched air sucked the moisture from her mouth. It reminded her of the desert heat, and she thought of the ordeal she had endured crossing the Humboldt Sink.

Reaching into her bodice, Matilda pulled out a handkerchief and wiped the sweat from her face. Even in the dry heat, the hot water from the tub made her perspire. Her thoughts returned to Sinclair. Why, God? Why Sinclair, with so much to live for, and so many who loved him so dearly? She thought of Lewis and, in her mind, again saw his body crumpled at the foot of the well.

She lifted another pair of overalls from the tub of soapy water. What was the purpose of it all? We wash, we clean, we cook, we work hard to get crops planted, and then life is snuffed out in a flash. Why do we struggle so hard?

Mary trotted up to her, towing little Lewis by the hand.

"Mama," she reported, "Lew says he's hungry and I can't reach the cookie jar."

Lewis looked up at his mother, love shining in his blue eyes. "Cookie, Mama," he said, nodding his head vigorously.

With a laugh, Matilda scooped him up in her arms. This is why we do it, she decided. She hugged him to her and nuzzled the blond curls, her love for him surging through her. This is why.

September faded into October, and the days turned cool. Again the leaves on the trees changed from green to golden and, one by one, drifted to the ground. Matilda, finding it hard to believe they had been in California for a whole year, helped the children gather the walnuts from the tree by the barn. A windstorm had blown many of the nuts from the branches. Using a long pole, Alf knocked down the remainder that clung tenaciously to the limbs.

Every morning, after breakfast, Matilda headed for the barn to feed a ration of grain to White Star and her colts. She also took them a treat, usually a carrot or a lump of sugar. Alf complained she pampered the horse.

"You'll spoil those colts, too," he accused.

Matilda laughed. "White Star is not just a horse. She's my friend."

Alf shook his head.

Matilda had enrolled Mary in the nearby Hicksville School when the term started at the end of August. The school boasted forty-nine students, including one Negro girl and two Indian boys from the local Mi-Wok tribe.

But Gardner had changed. Matilda watched him with concern. Instead of taking an active role with the chores, as he always had, he would sit in front of the stove and watch the flicker of the flames through the mica window. He no longer offered to ride for the mail. Even the antics of the neighborhood boys at Halloween failed to rouse him, though he had always before been as enthusiastic for the games as everyone else. He even deferred the task of saying grace before the Thanksgiving feast in favor of Alf. Never in Matilda's memory had her father not given the blessing at any family gathering.

As they cleared the table after the Thanksgiving festivities, Minerva set a load of plates on the counter, then clung to the sink, swaying.

Matilda, startled, put an arm around her sister and eased her into a nearby chair. "Min," she exclaimed with concern. "Aren't you feeling well?"

Minerva smiled and shook her head slightly. "'Tilda, I don't like to complain, but do you mind if I don't help with the dishes? I just feel . . . tuckered out."

"Oh, Min!" Matilda hugged her sister. Dismay surged through her. "Of course I don't mind. What's the matter? You're not in a family way again, are you?"

She shook her head. "No, that's not it. I don't know. Somehow I just don't feel right. I haven't gotten my strength back since Charlie. I'm tired all the time."

"You probably need some of Mother's comfrey tea. She says that cures everything, even the dismals."

Minerva shook her head. "Maybe you're right. I . . . I don't know what it is." She smiled at the worry in Matilda's eyes. "Forget it. I'll be fine."

One evening, not long before Christmas, Matilda found herself alone with her father. Alf had gone to Sacramento and Betsy Ann decided to spend the night with Minerva. Matilda felt this would be a good opportunity to try and talk with her father to see if she could help him regain his spirits.

She worked for a while at the table with Mary, helping her with her numbers. Elizabeth watched with interest. When Mary tired of writing the numbers, and Lewis nodded by the fire, Matilda announced bedtime for the children. After tucking them in, she returned to the parlor. Her father still sat in front of the fire where he had not moved since supper.

She eased herself to the floor beside his chair and asked gently, "Pa, what's wrong?"

He shook his head. "There's no more frontier, 'Tilda. This is as far as I can go."

"But Pa, we've a good home here with Alf. He's happy to have you, and he's also happy to have your help. It's got to be something else."

He did not speak for a long time. Matilda leaned her head against his knee and waited. The fire crackled in the silence of the room. His hand rested lightly on her hair.

"It's Sinclair," he said at last. "My joy in my old age, my youngest son." His eyes filled with tears. "I killed him."

"Pa, don't say that," Matilda cried, seizing the hand he dangled by her head.

"I killed him," he repeated. "I gave him that horse. I should never have done that. Devil Wind! A good name for him. He's a devil, all right. It's been preying on my mind ever since Sinclair's death."

"Pa," Matilda told him, "you're the one that tells me these things are God's will. You can't blame yourself. You could never have foreseen it. Sinclair is a good rider ... ," she paused and her voice dropped to a whisper, "was a good rider." The words echoed in her mind. Her heart broke at the sound of her voice speaking of Sinclair in the past tense.

She forced back the tears. Mother would say he was with us, she thought. He was with us, we loved him, and he is gone. We have to accept it. She hoped some day to develop her mother's calm acceptance of whatever blows life dealt.

But Gardner would have none of it. "I should never

have bought that colt. I should have taken your advice and
let him wait, ride White Star until her colts were grown. He
would have been happy with one of them. He loved White
Star."

"I know, Pa," Matilda said gently, "but you can't blame
yourself."

"My life is over," he said. "I can't take any more."

"Your life is not over," Matilda protested. "You're not
even seventy yet." She smiled. "Remember? The Bible
says three score and ten."

He returned her smile with a glimmer of the twinkle she
remembered. Responding to her attempts to cheer him, he
rose and picked up the Bible lying on the table beside the
lamp. "You win," he said. "How about reading some to me
before we go to bed?"

The family gathered at Christmas, all of them crowding
into Alf's little house. It reminded Matilda of the Christmases
they had shared in Kansas. They sang their favorite Yule-
tide carols. The table sagged under the weight of the food.
Strings of popped Indian corn and red cranberries festooned
the tree, as did bits of tin cut to reflect the candle light. Mary
had come home from school and proudly presented Matilda
with the three crudely made angels that hung on the tree in
a place of honor.

Minerva and Abe came, with all four children in tow.
Matilda watched Minerva closely. She seemed, to Matilda's
watchful eye, to be deliberately trying to look like her normal, healthy self.　A pang went through Matilda as she
watched Abe tenderly escort her to a chair. She's not well
yet, Matilda thought, and Charlie will be two in March.
Plenty of time for her to recover from his birth. There had
to be something else.

She knew Abe had taken Minerva to a doctor in Sacramento, but he failed to diagnose any illness. Matilda shook

her head. Maybe it's just the strain of caring for four young children, she thought. Laura just turned six in November. Or maybe giving birth to four children in under five years. She recalled how long it had taken Minerva to get her strength back after the first babe died, and how long she had been sick with the ague.

She brushed aside her concerns. If Minerva could put on a bold front, so could Matilda. Rain had threatened all morning, but the leaden skies did little to dampen anyone's spirits. Everyone seemed determined to make the first Christmas without Sinclair a joyous one.

Alfred Wheelock came down to spend the holiday with them. He brought the small pine tree from the forests around Placerville. The scent of its fresh needles filled the room and mingled with the smells of roasting turkey, mashed sweet potatoes, cranberry sauce, and mincemeat pies.

Mary and Elizabeth greeted Alfred with enthusiasm. They remembered the candy he gave them on his brief visit after Sinclair's funeral. For Christmas he again thought of them, this time with bags of peppermints and a gaily wrapped parcel for each.

Mary opened hers at once, but Elizabeth scolded her sister for her impatience and solemnly placed her own box beneath the tree with the other gifts.

"Presents are s'posed to go under the tree," Elizabeth advised, with all of the wisdom of her four years.

"Oh, look, a doll with a real china head!" Mary gasped, ignoring Elizabeth's comment. "Oh, thank you, Mr. Wheelock." Mary threw her arms around his neck and kissed him soundly on the cheek.

Elizabeth forgot her remonstrances to her sister and tore open her parcel as well. "Oh," she exclaimed, "I got one, too!" With the precious doll cradled in her arms, she sedately kissed Alfred's other cheek.

He chuckled, one little girl in each arm.

Matilda laughed. "Well, Mr. Wheelock, you certainly have made the day a success for the girls. Come, sit here." She indicated the chair between her own and Alf's. "Just let me get the children settled. I'll be right back."

Gardner passed the carving knife to Alf, as he had at Thanksgiving. Matilda felt a sharp pain in her heart. But she only smiled and said, "Pa, you're shirking your responsibility."

Gardner smiled back at her and replied, with a hint of his old joviality, "I've earned my rest."

Everyone did justice to the food, and when all had eaten their fill, the thunderous roar of a cloudburst poured rain onto the roof. Alfred laughed. "You know, this reminds me of my first winter in California."

"Tell everyone about it," Alf ordered. "I've told them you've some great stories to tell."

"Okay, Partner, if you insist." Alfred looked around at his audience, silent and ready to listen. He smiled and began. "After spending almost two weeks smothering in steamy Panama City, I managed to get deck space on the *Capitol,* out of Boston. She arrived in San Francisco towards the end of July. I wanted to go immediately to the gold fields, but I had about come to the end of my funds. That canoe up the Chagres River, the extra fare above my 'through paid ticket', then living expenses in Panama while I tried to get passage to San Francisco took nearly every cent I owned."

"Everyone has to get their share from the folks going through," Tom commented. "On the trip out from Kansas, the prices doubled at every outpost as soon as a wagon appeared on the horizon."

"Yankee enterprise," Alfred nodded. "We anchored just off the end of Montgomery Street. San Francisco had only two docks at the time, and they were too crowded to be approached, even had the captain tried. Several of us tried to get a crewman to row us ashore, but the captain refused to allow them to leave the ship for fear they'd not return." He chuckled. "Too many ships were left stranded in the harbor by crews heading for the gold fields.

"We finally got a boat from shore to come out and get us, but it cost us a dollar apiece. When we reached shore, men stood around offering to carry baggage for another few dollars. Fortunately, I had brought only what I could carry myself. I learned the wisdom of that early.

"The shoreline where we landed was a garbage dump. Broken boxes, old clothes, rotting food, and dead animals mingled with thousands of empty bottles. The miasma rising from the lot stank so bad the wonder is we did not all take the cholera.

"Fortunately, we arrived in the dry season. The streets had no planking, and we walked ankle deep in dust. I could imagine the muddy morass the place would be once the rains began. I finally managed to find a room, of sorts, which I shared with one of my shipmates for $25.00 a week. It cost us another $20.00 a week for meals. We had two cots, two chairs, a plain table, and a small mirror, in a garret so low we were unable to stand upright. No sheets or pillows. Just one blanket, too, and San Francisco gets surprisingly cold in July." He gave one of the soft laughs that Matilda found so endearing. "Mark Twain was right when he said the coldest winter he ever spent was one summer in San Francisco. That cold fog rolls in off the ocean and soaks into a body's very marrow.

"One week's room and board took all of my money, so I got a job as a carpenter making benches, tables, and bedsteads for the manager of the Portsmouth House." He restocked his plate with turkey, mashed potatoes and stuffing, and ladled the rich gravy over the pile. He inhaled deeply in appreciation of the delicious aroma. "The food I got sure wasn't anywhere near as good as this.

"Best hotel in town was the St. Francis, at Dupont and Clay, but the inside walls were so thin it soon became famous as a source of stories of comical incidents, and even some scandals. Anyway, what with one thing and another, I didn't arrive in Sacramento City 'til mid-October. Hadn't rained since the end of May and everything was all dried up and dusty." He grinned. "I loved it. I had seen enough rain in Panama to last me, I'll tell you. I bought supplies from General Sutter's store and dickered for two mules, one to carry me, the other to carry my supplies. I did learn to respect the hardy little creatures on the trip across Panama. Stubborn, but level headed.

"But," he added ruefully, "that left me at about the end of my money again, so I knew I had to get where I could find some gold pretty quick or I'd have to find another job. There were plenty of laboring jobs available around Sacramento City, especially if one had a turn for carpentering. The city was being built up around me. But I had come to find gold. That dream of picking up your fortune off the ground dies hard."

"It sure does," Sam exclaimed. Everyone laughed, remembering the expectations when Sam, Alf, and Britt left Illinois.

"I heard tales of good prospecting sites around the settlement of Placerville, so I set off. They called it Hangtown then. Legislature changed it to Placerville in February of '50. Said it was more dignified."

"Alf told us how the settlement got named Hangtown," Matilda interposed. "Disgraceful."

Alfred smiled. "Anyway, the morning I left Sacramento, the air sparkled crisp and clear, and the leaves had turned to red and orange. Even the mules seemed to enjoy the trip. But by mid-afternoon of my second day out, a stiff breeze sprang up out of the south and clouds began gathering. The air held a promise of rain if, as I had been told, it ever did rain in California. Did I learn!"

"Yes," Sam laughed. "It does rain in California." As if to emphasize Sam's remark, an even louder downpour began, bringing more laughter from the assembled group. Matilda glanced at Alfred. She admired the sound of his soft voice, the glow in his hazel eyes, the animation on his handsome face as he spoke. Happiness swept through her. Could she ever really expect to find love again? Surely no one could ever replace Lewis in her heart.

Or could this gentle man? The girls seemed taken with him. Of course, Mary was the only one who had really known Lewis. Elizabeth had only been two when he died. Tears sprang unbidden into her eyes as she remembered that dreadful day, watching Lewis fall to his death in the well. She quickly blinked them away and shook her head to clear it. She returned her attention to Alfred's words.

". . . reached a little settlement named Mud Springs," he continued, "when huge raindrops began to pelt me. At the time, the ground was dry and dusty, but in the morning I learned the settlement's name was quite appropriate.

"Mud Springs boasted a hotel, if you could call it that. But at the rate the rain poured down, I decided anything would be better than spending the night under some tree. I paid a dollar for the privilege of sharing a cot with two other men. I took the middle, so at least I had the blanket over me all the time. My bed partners kept pulling it back and forth between them so one or the other spent half the night uncovered.

"The so-called 'hotel' was just a huge canvas tent, with one thirty-foot pole in the center. During the night, the wind built up, and the racket from the flapping canvas made sleep impossible."

Alfred paused and smiled at the memory. "I must have dozed off," he continued, "when a blast of wind stronger than its fellows broke loose the tent pegs and carried away the whole canvas. Then the rain fell on us with a vengeance."

The men laughed. "You poor man," Polly murmured in sympathy. Matilda shivered.

"My bed-mates and I crawled under the bed, but it was only a piece of canvas stretched between two poles. My advantage at being in the center of the blanket was soon negated by the disadvantage of being in the center of the bed." He chuckled. "It sagged and collected rain in the middle, then the rain seeped through the canvas and dripped down on me. The wooden floor also collected the rain, which ran underneath us. Before long, all three of us were sopping wet, and we huddled together to keep from freezing.

"It was without question the most miserable night of my life. I'd 'a been better off had I saved my dollar and slept out under a tree between my mules." He shook his head. "That storm began the wettest season they've ever measured in Sacramento City. They got thirty-six inches between then and the end of March." He grinned at Matilda and took a sip of his coffee. "Lucky me. I land in California just in time to get in on its wettest winter."

He laughed. "I remember one of my bed-mates, a Jewish peddler. A number of them made the rounds of the camps in the summer and fall of '49. He had shirts and socks and all kinds of cheap jewelry to sell to the Indians. I met him again later, after I'd found a little gold, and he charged me half an ounce for one shirt."

"But you should've seen the shirt, 'Tilda," Alf chuckled. "Brightest blue you ever saw. You could see Alfred coming for miles, even through the trees." Laughter swept the room again.

"I liked that shirt," Alfred grinned, "even if I did pay three times what it was worth." He paused to finish the last portion of turkey on his plate. "The dinner was delicious, Mrs.

Randolph," he told Betsy Ann. "And Mrs. Baldwin and Mrs. Dyer." He smiled at Matilda and Minerva. "Is that mince pie I smell? Bachelor like me doesn't usually eat this well."

Matilda met his eyes and returned his smile, happiness welling within her. "You will just have to come back, Mr. Wheelock. Please, go on with your story."

"Land sakes, 'Tilda, let the poor man eat," Betsy Ann admonished, handing Alfred a large slab of the warm, succulent pie.

Alfred only laughed. He picked up his fork and continued. "In the morning, I discovered the rain had turned the dust on the road into a quagmire. The mules sank to their ankles in the mud." He flashed Matilda a wry grin. "But I learned well from my experience. My first purchase in Hangtown was a comfortable tent. I had to swap one of my axes and some food supplies for it, since I had spent my last dollar on my ill-fated night in Mud Springs. Never again did I rely on someone else to protect me from the rain."

Alf chuckled. "When Sam and Britt and I arrived in Placerville the following September, we gave no thought to a tent either. We didn't really believe those tales of California rain."

"But we learned fast," Sam interposed. "Lucky for us we shared Alfred's tent while we learned. And we arrived in a drought year!"

"Floods terrify me," Matilda shuddered, remembering her experience in the flood of the Big Blue. "I was afraid last spring when the Cosumnes went over its banks, but Alf assures me we are in no danger here. He did say they have had floods in Sacramento, though."

"Yes," Alfred said, finishing off his mince pie with evident relish, "the floods in Sacramento that first California winter were terrible." "I rode down shortly after the first one. January of 1850 will be long remembered. The water had begun to recede by the time I arrived, but it had reached the tops of the first floor. All of the businesses without a second floor saw their merchandise ruined by water. Or watched it float off down the river."

Polly gasped. "Didn't a lot of people drown?"

Alfred shrugged his shoulders. "I heard the patients at the city hospital were abandoned to die. The poor wretches floated about on their cots until a passing boat heard their cries for help and transported them to higher ground." He shook his head. "Dr. White was out of town at the time, from what I heard. I'm sure he never would have left them. Most of the ones who didn't drown died anyway, from the cold and the damp."

"The poor souls," Matilda cried. "It couldn't have been a very sturdy hospital."

"Oh, no. Just frame and canvas. Like my hotel in Mud Springs."

Matilda shivered and Alfred continued his story. "Dead animals littered the place. Did they stink! Kept my handkerchief over my face the whole time to keep from gagging."

Betsy Ann grimaced in distaste. "Would 'a thought they'd 'a had a lot of sickness."

"They did, and many died," he responded. "Made coffins for the dead and ferried them out to Mormon Island for burial." He chuckled. "One story went the rounds about a Dutchman hired to ferry coffins across the river. Seems this Dutchman never trusted anyone, so he carried all his gold in a belt around his waist. Had about two thousand dollars worth, which is pretty dratted heavy."

"I should think it would be," agreed Sam.

"Anyway, in the middle of the river, the boat got to careening and sank. The Dutchman told his partner to hold on while he swam ashore for another boat."

"With all that weight around his waist?" Abe asked in disbelief.

Alfred nodded. "With all that weight around his waist.

Gold kept pulling him under 'til he finally drowned." He shook his head. "Ironically, his partner floated ashore on the coffin."

Matilda rose to check on the children. She returned to the table in time to hear Tom ask, "When did they build the first levees?"

"Shortly afterwards. After a lot of arguing."

"Did they work?" Minerva wanted to know.

"Well, they got Bigelow elected mayor," Alfred grinned. "I remember at the next flood, a couple of winters later, the water just went around the levees into the city. Then the levees held the water in so it couldn't get out."

"Did you have any Indian trouble?" Tom queried. "I heard some of the miners got killed by Indians."

"No, most of the Indian troubles were caused by white men. They seemed to feel they had a right to insult the Indian women, excuse me, ladies," he nodded to Betsy Ann, "and when their men protested, one thing led to another."

"Remember Bill Rogers' War?" Alf laughed to Alfred.

"Never heard of him," Gardner stated.

Alfred shook his head. "Not many have. A Colonel William Rogers took it upon himself to 'teach them Injuns a lesson', as he put it. Took eighty men and raided a small rancheria just outside Kelsey. No one home but one old blind squaw and four half starved dogs. Our brave hero killed all of them, then came back into town with the old woman's scalp. Folks hooted him out of town."

"Had more problems with ruffians from Texas and Missouri than we ever did with Indians," Alf grunted. "Remember that one mean 'un as used to accost strangers in the saloon? He'd pull a Bowie knife and tell the man to say his prayers and get ready to die. If the stranger offered to buy him a drink of whiskey, that usually settled it. Never did know if he'd have actually killed anyone or not."

"What happened?" Matilda gasped.

Alfred chuckled softly. "He pulled the trick one time too many. Came up against an old Kentuckian who said he'd done enough praying in his younger days to last him a lifetime. Old man pulled his gun and shot the bully dead."

"Coroner ruled self defense," Alf said, "and that was the end of it. Law not too complicated in those days."

Alf, Sam, and Britt started reminiscing about their mining days together. Matilda listened with fascination. How she wished she could have joined her brothers when they came west in '50, as she had wanted to. Of course, she would never have met Lewis, and her life would have been much different. A loud guffaw from Sam interrupted her musings.

"Remember that greenhorn as came by when we were workin' Emigrant Ravine?"

"I'll say," Alf laughed. "The joke was on us."

Tom grinned. "I think I remember this story."

"I don't. Tell us, Sam," Matilda demanded.

Sam nodded. "We were working a cradle in the creek. Three other men worked nearby. A stranger came by with a pick and pan and asked them where he could work. One of 'em, as a joke, pointed to an oak tree and said that was the finest place he knew of. The stranger, not knowing any better, dug for two days until he reached bedrock eight or ten feet below the surface."

"The poor man," Matilda cried. "That was cruel."

"Cruel my foot," Britt interposed. "That 'poor man' cradled out more gold in a week than us and the jokesters did in a season."

Gardner chuckled. "So the joke was on the jokester."

"Yes," Sam shook his head ruefully. "And on us, too. We'd walked right past that tree." He rose to his feet. "Let's let the women-folk get at these dishes."

* * *

At the conclusion of the day's festivities, Matilda walked Alfred to the door.

"I have to be getting back to Placerville soon, Mrs. Baldwin," he said with a shy smile, "but could I come by and visit with you tomorrow evening before I leave?"

She met his eyes and felt her knees go weak. "I will be very pleased to see you, Mr. Wheelock."

Chapter 61

December of 1865 to April of 1866

"MAMA, WHY do we have to go to bed so early?" Mary's blue eyes rebuked Matilda the following evening. "You usually read to us longer."

"Because, Little Miss Nosy, Mother is expecting company."

"Is it that nice Mr. Wheelock?" Elizabeth chimed in, carefully cradling the china doll he had given her for Christmas.

"Can we stay up and see him?" Mary asked, eagerly bouncing up and down on the bed. Mary's doll lay on the counterpane where she had tossed it, one kidskin leg askew. Mary did not share Elizabeth's maternal instincts.

"You can say hello, but then I want you both in bed. Agreed?"

The girls promised. Donning their robes, they ran into the parlor where their Uncle Alf sat reading. Gardner and Betsy Ann had retired to their room.

Matilda carefully tucked the blankets around the sleeping Lewis. He had turned two the previous October. Again she thought how much he looked like his father, but this time the memory did not bring as much pain. Her heart lifted. Could she be falling in love again? She blushed, thinking of her reaction to Alf's first letter when he described his new partner, so many years ago.

She rose from the side of the small trundle bed. Her first feelings were right. Mr. Wheelock had turned out to be a charming gentleman. Did he feel the same about her? True, until yesterday at the Christmas festivities, she had only seen him for the one brief visit after Sinclair's funeral last August.

But that short visit had been enough to charm the girls, she thought, amused at Mary and Elizabeth's fondness for the man. She smiled to herself. Maybe he is coming to see the girls instead of me. She heard the sound of hoofbeats in the lane, and hurried back to the parlor.

When she ushered him into the house, Alfred spent a few minutes distributing his little gifts to the girls. She met his eyes above Mary's red hair and he smiled. The smile wrapped itself around Matilda and made her feel warm and cozy inside.

She pulled herself from her trance and turned to the girls. "All right, Mary, Elizabeth. Give Mr. Wheelock a nice kiss, then it's time for bed."

They threw themselves on him. He hugged one girl in each arm as they kissed his cheeks. Matilda saw the tears in his eyes as he held the children. His loneliness touched her. She remembered her brother telling how Alfred had left his family in Vermont and never communicated with them. She found herself longing to comfort him. Instinct told her this kind, gentle man would fill the emptiness in her own life.

Later, after the children slept and Alf had made his excuses and retired, Matilda and Alfred settled on the sofa, a plate of cookies and a pot of coffee on the table in front of them. Matilda secretly suspected Alf of setting the meeting up, but found no fault with the arrangement.

"These cookies are delicious, Mrs. Baldwin," he said, biting into his third.

Matilda laughed. "The Pottawatamies liked them."

"Who?"

She explained. ". . . and they refused Caroline's. They told her 'want good coo-kee from red hair lady.' Poor Carrie said she didn't know whether to laugh or be insulted."

He smiled into her eyes. "They showed excellent taste."

Matilda blushed, not quite knowing how to take that remark, so she said, "Now, Mr. Wheelock, it's your turn. Please, tell me some stories of your journey from the East to California. My brother says you had all kinds of adventures."

"Please, Mrs. Baldwin, call me Alfred." Their eyes met. "May I call you Matilda?"

Embarrassed to feel herself tongue-tied like a school girl, she said, "Of course, Mr. er, uh, Alfred. And call me 'Tilda. I feel I know you already, after reading all of Alf's letters describing your experiences. We all laughed our heads off when he told the story about the mule and the featherbed."

Alfred chuckled. "That dratted mule!" he exclaimed. "He gave us no end of trouble. But if you want mule stories, you should have seen me plodding across the Isthmus of Panama. Those mules were so set in their ways they wouldn't budge a step to one side of the trail or the other. They made deep holes because they stepped into the same place each time. With every step, they sank up to their bellies in rain water."

"Do they have a lot of rain there?" Matilda asked.

"Do they ever," he sighed. "It rains all summer in Panama. Every single day, for at least two hours or more. And whenever the mules stepped in the holes, the muddy water splashed back up over the riders. We were caked with mud when we arrived in Panama City." He smiled at her, and again she felt her knees grow weak. "The natives were wiser. They rode nearly naked, and carried their clothes in a bundle until just before we reached the city. They had clean clothes to put on when we arrived."

He took a sip of coffee and helped himself to another cookie. "I remember another experience of the trip across." His eyes twinkled. "We landed at Chagres, on the Atlantic side, at the mouth of the Chagres River. It's a village of sorts. Filthy place. I hear Mr. Aspinwall has moved the landing around to Navy Bay, away from the mouth of the river. The fellow who made the first contract for the railroad, guy named Paredes, wanted to call the new town Aspinwall, but the government of New Granada wanted to call it Colón, after Christopher Columbus. So the official name is Colón, but everyone calls it Aspinwall. They say it's a regular American town, but I'd have to see that to believe it.

"Anyway," he continued, "to get to the head of the Chagres River, I had to get a seat in a canoe. It took some doing, with so many men in a hurry to get to the gold fields. Every man feared the others would get all the gold first. The boatmen sold the seats to the highest bidder." He chuckled. "And the scoundrels were not above selling a seat twice. I paid for mine and stayed right beside it until the canoe left the beach. Many men lost their money by making the mistake of leaving to get their belongings. They came back to find the canoe gone with another passenger. It was every man for himself."

He smiled. "I'm sure the trip is much less eventful since they finished the tracks in '55 and one can now make the trip by train. I, unfortunately, arrived before that luxury, so I spent the first night at Gatun, in what they called a hotel. We slept in hammocks to be away from the bugs and snakes."

"Snakes!"

"Yes. Poisonous ones." With a rueful smile, he added, "I took the lower hammock, because the roof leaked, and the man above me soaked up most of the water."

"Clever."

"It seemed so when I went to bed, but I soon discovered that the owner's dog used the occupant of the lower hammock as a back scratcher. The hammock stood just high enough. I suspect the innkeeper adjusted it to that height on purpose."

Matilda giggled. In her mind, she saw the dog rubbing the under side of the hammock.

"And, yes, the dog had fleas. Unfortunately for me, the critters quickly discovered I was tastier than the dog."

They dissolved into laughter and Matilda felt her nervousness vanish. The companionship of the shared humor brushed aside the last of her reservations. Their eyes met and he clasped her hand. Had the months of loneliness ended at last?

The winter had been a mild one. The March storms seemed less ferocious than the previous year. Maybe because I'm getting used to them, Matilda thought, or maybe because I'm falling in love again. She blushed. Alfred visited frequently, every chance he had to get down from Placerville She knew he came to see her.

He appeared one afternoon in early April. It had rained the day before and the air sparkled fresh and clear. Billows of clouds rose high over the mountains to the east. Clouds to the north and a breeze from the south promised more rain, but at the moment, the sun shone brightly in a brilliant blue sky. It seemed to Matilda the grass grew an inch overnight after a spring rain. The wild flowers had started to appear. In another week or so, the fields would be a riot of color.

"Please, Matilda, would you take a walk with me?" Alfred asked in a shy voice.

"I'd be delighted," she smiled. Her heart pounded in anticipation. Did he plan to propose? Would he feel it too soon to speak? No, a man of action like Alfred would not wait for any polite timetable. If he loved her, as she hoped, he would say so.

They walked for several minutes in companionable silence. Matilda felt no need to talk. She just enjoyed the quiet comfort of his presence. Her hand rested lightly on his arm. She noted the strength of his muscles developed by years of hard work, yet the touch of his hand, as it occasionally covered hers, was gentle. Yes, she thought, happiness welling up within her, he is fond of me.

A cloud blocked the sun with surprising suddenness, and large drops of rain began to fall.

"Uh-oh," Alfred said, pulling her hand more securely through his arm. "We'd better find some cover and fast." They headed for the barn, the nearest structure, and barely took shelter inside when a cloudburst poured torrents of rain upon them.

White Star whinnied a welcome from her stall. Her two long-legged colts, by then half grown, rose to greet them as well.

"I'm so sorry, my darlings." Matilda stroked White Star's querying muzzle. "I have nothing for you. I didn't realize I would be coming here."

Four Stockings snorted and returned to his bed in the back of the stall.

"See," Matilda laughed. "He's punishing me for not bringing him any sugar."

"They're beautiful colts," he said. "White Star must be valuable."

"Yes, the tax assessor valued the three of them at $175.00 last fall. I had to pay Sheriff McClatchy $4.69 in taxes."

"The Sheriff?"

"Yes. He serves as our ex officio tax collector. I guess that's so if anyone doesn't want to pay he can arrest them. Or shoot back, if someone really objects."

Alfred laughed. "If they are worth that much, it's no wonder you're so proud of them."

"And grateful to White Star for giving them to me."

"Alf said you think of that horse as a person. You really do, don't you?"

"Oh, yes," Matilda said. "She'll be with me all of her life. I will never, never sell her. No matter how bad her teeth get." She laughed, remembering Sarah Williams and Old Buck. "I'll cut up grass for her just like my friend Sarah did for Buck."

"What?"

She explained. ". . . and Sarah absolutely refused to let her father shoot Old Buck. She swore she would cut grass for him as long as he lived."

"And how long was that?" Alfred smiled.

She laughed. "I'm not sure. In her last letter she did not mention him, so he may finally have joined his ancestors. But he was a nice old horse."

The rain pelted the roof with renewed force and a clap of thunder startled Matilda. She gasped in fright. Alfred put his arm around her and held her close to him.

"Don't be afraid," he murmured into her hair in reassurance. "It's harmless. Very seldom does lightning strike anything here in the valley."

She lifted her head and their eyes met. He kissed her gently on the lips. Her heart pounded as tingles ran through her whole body.

He smiled. "I find myself growing very fond of you, Mrs. Baldwin," he said.

She smiled back. "I think I could say the same of you, Mr. Wheelock."

"I don't have a great deal to offer you, 'Tilda, my love, but I would be proud if you would consent to marry me."

It took her a moment to get her breathing back under control, then she said, formally, "I am honored, and will be glad to accept your offer." Then she laughed and confessed, "I think I have loved you since the first letter from Alf, way back in Illinois."

A gleam came into Alfred's eyes as his arms tightened around her.

From her stall, White Star whickered.

Later, their love and future plans established, they found themselves still pinned in the barn by the storm. Alfred found a convenient box which he dusted off and moved so they could sit in the doorway side by side and watch the rain. They sat with his arm around her, her head snuggled comfortably against his shoulder. She nestled there, very conscious of his faint masculine scent. The smell of wet earth and damp hay wafted over them. Matilda loved the smell of rain.

An even louder downpour began and they both laughed. Happiness in her new-found love swept over Matilda. She had never expected to feel such joy again. She pushed aside a twinge of guilt. Surely Lewis would be happy she had, once more, found someone to love. Tears stung her eyes. Lewis, my darling, I will never forget you, she thought, and I promise never to let the children forget you either. But I have been so lonely, and Alfred is such a good man.

He shifted his weight to turn her more towards him and gently kissed the tip of her nose. "I can't believe you really do love me," he murmured, gently stroking her face, as though entranced to think she was his.

"Yes, I really do love you," she said. Could this be true? Could it be possible for her to find another love as deep as the love she had felt for Lewis?

The rain lessened, so Matilda added, with a touch of regret, "I really should be getting back to the house. Mother is over at Minerva's, and Alf is watching the children. Being a bachelor, he doesn't quite know how to handle them. Mary's constant questions drive him to distraction."

Chapter 62

May of 1866

As APRIL progressed into May, Matilda's concern for her father deepened. Alfred returned to Placerville, so she did not have his support. She felt the coming of spring, with the re-blossoming of the earth, would bring Gardner out of his depression. He loved the wild flowers and the smell of new mown hay and freshly turned earth as much as Matilda herself did.

But Gardner continued to spend all of his time sitting in front of the fire, staring into the flames, even when the days turned warm. He grew thinner, and she knew he did not eat enough. She wondered if perhaps he might be ill with some wasting disease.

One evening in May, Matilda put the children to bed early and tried to persuade her father to talk to her. She urged him to take a walk with her in the cool evening air.

He smiled, refusing to rise to her attempts to cheer him, but finally spoke. "There's no place for me in this world any more, 'Tilda. This is a world of educated men, of lawyers and politicians, of bankers and shopkeepers. I'm just a simple farmer."

"Don't say that!" Matilda cried. "We love you. You're very precious to us. Mary and Elizabeth adore their grandfather, you know that. So do Laura and Annie. They never tire of hearing your stories, about when you were young, about your adventures, even about your fight with the Creek Indians."

He smiled sadly. "That seems so long ago. I often think, now, about the young warrior I killed. He never had a chance to have sons. I took that away from him." He paused. Matilda waited in silence, watching her father's face.

"He never knew the joy of seeing his sons grow, or the agony of watching his sons die. Never had the pleasure of holding a granddaughter on his knee, and telling her how bravely he fought to defend the tribe."

"Pa," Matilda said gently, "that was years ago. You did what you had to do. He would have killed you."

"Yes, in the heat of battle, he would have. But we had no right to attack them. Peacock wanted to kill all of the Creeks, and that was wrong. I knew then it was wrong. I should never have taken part in it." His voice rose. "We killed over seven hundred warriors that day. We destroyed a whole generation of young men. And for what?" His voice dropped so low Matilda had to strain to hear his next words. "So one egotistical army major could brag about winning a battle. Peacock hated the Creeks. So did Jackson. They wanted to kill them all." He stared off into space, his eyes fixed on a point beyond her head.

Matilda knew he saw that long ago battlefield and the young man dead, his own tomahawk buried in his skull, his life blood pouring out upon the ground. She remained silent.

He spoke again, softly, "No, 'Tilda. That's wrong. I should never, ever, have been a part of that battle."

Matilda did not answer. She looked into his face and noticed the gray hair, the sunken cheeks, the wrinkles around the corners of his eyes. His mouth drooped downward now, where before it had always been smiling and positive.

Although it tugged at her heart, she thought, perhaps he is right. Perhaps his day is really over.

Two days after her conversation with her father, as Matilda and her mother picked ears of sweet corn in the garden, she asked Betsy Ann if she had noticed how Gardner had lost his interest in the world around him.

"Yes," Betsy Ann replied, "I've noticed. I've noticed it a lot. His failure in Kansas just preys on him." She smiled in reminiscence. "You know, when he was a young man, nothing could stop him. The world was his to conquer. In Illinois, everything he touched succeeded. Everybody admired him and looked up to him as a leader." She shook her head.

"Then the world changed, and he couldn't change with it. The educated folks came and began to edge him out. He saw it coming. That's why he decided to go to Kansas. In Kansas he thought he could start over. New land, new people. 'We'll start at the beginning again, Betsy,' I remember him saying. 'It'll be like it was when we went into Illinois.' " She sighed. "But it's never like it was before. The laws had changed. All those squabbles over the land, with Sechrest and Kress and Whitson. And to lose! He had never lost before. That bothered him. Really bothered him." She stopped and moved away to the next row of corn.

Matilda said nothing.

Betsy Ann returned and dumped another armload of the plump ears of corn into the basket. She stood and stared out across the field for several moments, not moving. Matilda waited in silence. Finally, her mother spoke again.

"He was so sure he could get Kansas admitted to the Union as a slave state. He always wanted to be a big land-owner like his cousins in Virginia. I think he wanted to show that uncle of his he could be somebody. That's why he sent John to that convention in '57." She wrenched an ear from the stalk so hard the stalk itself came out of the ground. "But it was not to be. The time for big plantations and slavery had passed. He thought if he came to California, he could try again. But when he got here, there was no free land. He found he needed book learning, which he never got."

She stared, unseeing, at the ear of corn in her hand. A long moment passed before she continued. "And then he lost Sinclair."

Matilda remembered her father's words of despair with a sinking heart. "But what can we do?"

"Nothing," Betsy Ann sighed. "He has to face it himself. He'll either pull out of it or he won't."

"But how can you just accept it?" Matilda cried.

Betsy Ann smiled grimly. "Someday, Matilda my love, you'll learn that in this world there are some things we just have to accept. Like ...." She stopped and grunted a little as she stooped to pick up an ear of corn that had fallen from the basket. Matilda waited. A meadowlark trilled in the background, but Matilda did not hear it.

Betsy Ann met Matilda's eyes. "Minerva hasn't got her strength back after Charlie's birth. If she takes again too soon ...." Her voice trailed off.

"Oh!" Matilda gasped. Worries about her father had driven away all thought of the concerns Minerva had expressed. "I ... I thought perhaps she was not, but...." She stopped a moment, then rushed on, "you don't think, you don't really suspect ...."

Betsy Ann shook her head slowly. "I'm afraid for her, that's all." She hoisted her basket to her shoulder. "I think we've got about all the corn we're going to get today, Matilda. Let's get to working on it."

After that, Matilda spent more time with Minerva, almost afraid to leave her for fear she might not see her again.

"I'm going to be fine, 'Tilda," Minerva assured her anxious sister.

"Are you drinking the herb teas Mother gives you?"

"Of course I am," Minerva replied. "As vile as some of them are. I don't know if they are helping or not."

"Are you as tired as ever?"

"Yes, I'm still tired. I don't know what it is. I just feel. . . worn out. I rest, I don't do anything." She smiled and shook her head ruefully. "Abe, bless his heart, has to help me all the time. You should see the poor dear trying to dress little Charlie." She paused. "I don't know what it is."

Matilda felt a cold lump of fear deep inside of her. Her baby sister? Surely she could never lose her baby sister. She thought of Temperance, of Lewis, of Baby John, of the agony of losing Sinclair the previous summer.

No, God, no, she thought, you can't do this to me again.

Chapter 63

May to July, 1866

THE MAY MORNING SPARKLED crisp and clear, promising a lovely spring day. Wild flowers, mingled with shoots of growing wheat, covered the fields with a riot of color. Matilda admired the view from the kitchen window as she washed the breakfast dishes. Just as she immersed the last plate in the pan of soapy water, Abe burst onto the scene, driving his sorrel into a lather.

"Minerva!" Matilda gasped. She rushed to the door to meet Abe, drying her hands on her apron as she ran. He had come the day before for Betsy Ann, saying Minerva had been suffering severe abdominal pains.

"'Tilda!" Abe caught his breath, but did not dismount. "Your ma says to come quick."

Matilda's heart thudded against her ribs at the sight of his grief-ravaged face. Alf appeared beside her in a instant.

"I'll get Pa and the young-uns and come over in the buggy," he urged. "Go." He boosted her up behind Abe. Matilda barely had time to get firmly seated when Abe spurred the horse. She clung to Abe's waist to keep from falling as the animal, seeming to sense the need for haste, lunged forward.

During the wild ride back, coughing in the dust raised by the horse's hooves, Matilda's heart pounded so hard it made her dizzy. Please, God, she prayed, You can't take Minerva away from me.

When they reached the house, Matilda saw Laura and Annie sitting very still on the steps of the porch, clinging to each other, their eyes wide and frightened. Charlie, too young to be aware of the unfolding tragedy, clung to Will's hand and looked from one face to another. Matilda rushed into the bedroom just as Betsy Ann tucked the light blanket over Minerva's chest. She placed the limp arms outside of the cover, and gently smoothed back Minerva's hair, her face a mask as she looked down at her dying youngest daughter.

A basin filled with blood-soaked cloths stood in one corner. Matilda shuddered and looked away from the grisly contents. Minerva lay white and still against the pillow.

"Is she gone?" Matilda whispered to her mother.

Betsy Ann's face remained set. "Not yet. I told Abe to get you so's you'd have a chance to say good-bye."

"What happened?"

"Baby came real early. She hadn't even told anyone she was in a family way again. None of the herbs I've tried stopped the bleeding. That's when I sent Abe for you."

Matilda knelt by the bed and stroked the tendrils of sweat-soaked hair back from Minerva's pale, damp forehead. "Minerva, darling," she murmured. "Hold on. Don't leave us. Please don't leave us. We need you." The tears in Matilda's eyes poured down her cheeks and left streaks in the dust from the ride. "I need you."

Minerva tried to answer. Her lips moved. Matilda held her ear close. "'Tilda," the quavery voice whispered. A ghost of a smile hovered about the ashen lips. "I'll ... tell ... Sinclair ... you love him." She exhaled the last three words in a rush.

Abe sat still as stone on the other side of the bed, clutching Minerva's limp hand, tears running down his cheeks and disappearing into his dark beard.

In the silent room, blood dripping from the rubber sheeting beneath Minerva's body made the only sound. Drop after drop added to the growing pool in the basin beneath the bed, slowly growing larger, draining the last of Minerva's life.

When Minerva drew her last breath, Betsy Ann pulled the sheet over her face. Abe walked to the window and stood staring out, his eyes unseeing. Matilda rose and crossed the room to stand beside him, her hand resting lightly on his arm

He covered her hand with his, and whispered, "She meant everything to me, 'Tilda. Everything. You know that. I keep seeing her as she was when I first saw her, when you first came to Kansas, a pretty little girl of just thirteen." His voice caught, but he set his jaw and continued. "She had the bluest eyes and the loveliest golden hair in all the world." He paused. "She was ... she was ...."

His reserve broke. Tears spilled from his eyes. Matilda took him in her arms and held him as he sobbed out his grief.

When he regained his composure, they walked slowly out of the room to the porch where the children waited. Will looked at his father's face, and Matilda saw from the fear in his eyes that he knew his mother had died. Abe clasped the children to him and held them close. They made no sound.

As they sat together, Alf and Gardner arrived with Mary, Elizabeth and Lewis. Mary scrambled down and ran to Matilda.

"I'll take care of Charlie, Mama," Mary offered. Showing wisdom beyond her years, she took the little boy's hand. "Come, Charlie, let's go see if we can find some eggs."

Alfred Wheelock came down for Minerva's funeral. Matilda wondered how she would have gotten through the ceremony had his strong arm not supported her. As he prepared to return to Placerville, she said, "Thank you for being here. I needed you."

"I will always be here for you," he told her, kissing her hand. "I have the property in Placerville up for sale. As

soon as it sells, I'll have some money to set us up in farming. Gold mining has spoiled the area anyway." His eyes
clouded. "The huge hoses from the hydraulic mining wash
down the mountains and leave a pile of rubble. When I
came out in '49, the mountains were beautiful, the streams
clear and full of fish." He slowly shook his head. "Now it's
changed. I hate to see it.

"So," he said, smiling down on her, "I will marry Matilda
Baldwin and become a farmer."

She smiled up at him in spite of her leaden heart. "And
I'm sure you will be very successful." He held her closely
and kissed the top of her head. How fortunate she was that
God sent her such a fine man for the second time! Could
she banish the ghost of Lewis enough to be worthy of him?
She hoped so. She shook off her hesitation and said, "I'll
count the days."

Alfred returned to Placerville, Abe hired a housekeeper
to take over the care of Minerva's motherless children, and
Matilda set about trying to get her life back to normal.

Two weeks later, during the first summer heat spell, Matilda awoke with a start, bathed in sweat. What had awakened her? Probably the heat, she thought, tossing aside
the light sheet that covered her. Usually the evening breeze
coming through the open windows cooled the room, but
tonight, not a breath of air stirred. Even the night insects
made no sounds.

A whimper reached her ears. Realizing what had roused
her, she rose quietly and crossed to Mary's bed.

"What is it, my darling?" she whispered, keeping her
voice low so as not to disturb Elizabeth and Lewis. "Do
you hurt?" The fear that Mary might be ill cut through her
like a knife.

"I'm too hot," Mary complained, tossing from one side
to the other. "I can't sleep."

Matilda felt the moist forehead. Relieved to find Mary's face cool to her touch, she smiled. "It's warm in here. Let's go outside for a while. Maybe the breeze will come up."

She helped Mary into her robe and slippers. Hand in hand they crept from the room and out the door.

"Oh, look, Mary." Matilda pointed to the rising moon. "The man in the moon is just getting up." The full moon loomed larger and larger on the horizon as they strolled down the lane.

"Mama." Mary stopped and gulped, tears in her voice. Matilda waited, thinking that now she would hear the real reason Mary could not sleep. "Mama," she repeated, "you're not going to leave me, are you?"

"Of course not, darling. Mama would never leave you."

"Auntie Min left Laura and Annie, and Papa left me. And Uncle Sinclair left me." Her voice caught. "And Grandpa says that's God's will, that we have to a - sept . . . ac - cept God's will, that . . . that," she gulped down a sob, "that God knows best, and . . . and . . . oh, Mama!" Mary burst into tears and threw her arms around Matilda's waist.

Tears stung Matilda's eyes as she gathered the weeping girl into her arms. She sat down on a convenient log and held her, stroking the red-gold curls. As she soothed Mary, Matilda's mind reverted to her first husband.

Lewis, my love, she thought, now do you see why I must marry again? If something happens to me, they will be alone. My mother and father are old, Minerva is gone. Caroline and Sarah are so far away. Alfred adores the children and they are fond of him. He will be a good father, and will always see they are cared for. And, she smiled, I do love him. You do understand, don't you Lew? she pleaded in her mind. Please understand. I will always love you, but I have been so alone since you left me.

She sat, lost in her thoughts, for a long time. She brought herself back to reality and looked down at the sleeping child.

Matilda smiled to herself. Heat may have been part of the problem, but fear was the real reason Mary had not slept.

She sighed. Struggling to her feet with Mary in her arms, she returned to the house. Thankfully, the evening breeze had sprung up and the house would soon be cool.

As she laid Mary on her bed and pulled up the sheet, she thought of Lewis again. I will marry Alfred, Lew, my love, but I promise to never, ever, let Mary forget you.

Three weeks later, Alfred arrived to help them celebrate the Fourth of July. On his arrival, the girls ran to greet him and threw themselves into his arms. He walked towards the house carrying a girl in each arm, his face glowing. The girls clung to his neck, showering his face with kisses.

"Did you bring us some candy?" Mary demanded, between kisses.

"Are you going to stay with us this time?" Elizabeth queried.

"You've been gone for ever so long," Mary accused, clinging tighter to his neck and knocking off his hat, which the dog promptly grabbed. "We thought you were never coming back."

"Girls, girls," Matilda laughed, coming to Alfred's rescue and snatching his hat away from Jake, who had headed toward the barn with his prize. "You're strangling him." Their eyes met. She saw his love for her shining in his eyes. Lewis will understand, she told herself. I know he will be glad to see me happy again.

She tucked her hand through Alfred's arm and smiled at him as they walked toward the house. "Yesterday's Sacramento Union carried a notice from Mr. Crocker that his railroad is offering an excursion from Dutch Flat to Sacramento and back for two dollars a person. Get to see the fireworks in Sacramento and all the Fourth of July festivities. I thought it would be fun." They entered the back door of the house into the kitchen where she drew a glass of cool water from the hand pump at the sink. "Here, you must be thirsty after your long ride."

He accepted the tin cup of water she offered. "Thank you. I am. And I assume we are not taking the excursion?"

She laughed ruefully. "My ever practical mother informed me that by the time I paid for a room at the Dutch Flat Hotel the night before, and the train fare, it would be too expensive." Matilda sighed. "She's right, of course. I just thought it would be fun. I've never ridden on a train."

He took her in his arms and kissed her. "The experience is vastly over-rated, let me assure you. But I promise I will see you get a train ride after we're married."

Her heart beat faster at the thought of being married to such a man, but she only said, "I'll hold you to that promise!"

That evening, Alf returned home with a copy of the Sacramento Union from the previous day.

"Be careful when you read this to Pa," he warned Matilda. "Says Jim Lane committed suicide."

"Lane? The Senator? Oh, my. Why would he do that?"

Alf shrugged. "Paper says he voted against the Civil Rights Bill. Lot of folks in Kansas were for it, especially the radical Union men."

Matilda sighed. "The poor man. After all the criticism he's taken it seems sad. You're right. Don't let Pa hear."

The next morning bade fair to be a hot Fourth of July, as usual. Anticipating the weather, they had scheduled the family picnic in a grove of trees close to a section of the Cosumnes River that boasted a swimming hole. The water in the river ran low, but enough passed through to keep the pool fresh.

"Careful where you set that basket of chicken," Betsy Ann admonished Alf as he picked it up. "Last year you set it down beside the buggy and the dog got into it." Jake watched Alf carefully, with a look of total innocence.

"I remember, I remember," Alf grumbled. "You don't have to keep reminding me."

"Take the biscuits, Mary," Betsy Ann directed.

"Want to help too," Elizabeth announced, and received a jar of pickles which she delivered to the buggy, handling them as though they were fine crystal.

Matilda put the potatoes and ears of corn for roasting in the basket with the boiled eggs and carried them out. Little Lewis carefully carried the jar of jam entrusted to him.

Alfred picked up the jug of lemonade and smiled into Matilda's eyes. "This will be the first of many Fourth of July picnics, my love." He leaned forward and kissed her on the cheek. "And a train ride!"

Happiness flowed over Matilda in a wave. She returned his kiss and nodded. "And a train ride." With a mischievous smile she added, "And Mr. Batchelder is offering one of Mr. Shakespeare's plays at the Metropolitan Theater. Galley seats are only fifty cents. Can we do that, too?"

Alfred burst into laughter. "I just hope I can afford you!" He hugged her. "Yes, we can do that, too. In fact, we can do that before I go back to Placerville this week, if you'd like."

Her eyes sparkled. "I'd like that very much."

As Matilda helped her mother clear the dishes after the picnic and the men prepared the fireworks for the evening's festivities, she heard a splash.

Mary called out, panic in her voice, "Mama, come quick! It's Lew."

Matilda dropped the plates in her hands. Gathering her skirts to her knees, she ran to the pond. Her inability to swim never entered her head. She reached the edge of the muddy water and saw Lewis' blond hair floating on the surface. The water roiled about him as he struggled. Without a moment's hesitation she plunged into the waist-deep water. Just as she gathered him into her arms, the bottom went out from under her feet. Panic struck as she felt the water go over her head, then strong arms encircled her and her head cleared the surface.

Gasping for breath, she opened her eyes and looked into Alfred's concerned face. Lewis coughed and let out a squawk.

In two strokes, Alfred reached shallow water and stood with them both in his arms. "Really, 'Tilda," he said solemnly. "You should remember you can't swim."

She laughed with relief as they waded ashore. She pulled her soggy handkerchief from her bodice and wiped the muddy water from Lewis' face.

"I told him not to go so close," Mary announced, "but he wouldn't listen."

Lewis started to cry. "Not wanna fall in, Mama," he proclaimed between sobs.

Matilda half sighed, half laughed. "Mary, take him to your grandmother for some dry clothes." As Mary led off the protesting little boy, Matilda turned to Alfred. "Still think you're ready for fatherhood?"

"I can hardly wait." The gentle smile she had come to love so much slowly spread across his features. He stroked the wet hair back from her forehead. She knew she must look like a scarecrow, for she had lost every pin in her hair. But she also knew that to him, she looked beautiful. In that moment, all of her doubts vanished. No longer would she be alone. No longer would she need to fear for her children. She returned his smile, her love for him glowing in her eyes.

"'Tilda!" Alf's voice roared across the distance between them, "Where did you put the matches?"

Matilda shook her head.

Alfred eyes danced as he took her hand and kissed it. "I somehow get the feeling that my life will never be dull again."

Chapter 64

July to September, 1866

On SUNDAY, July 8, Alfred returned to Placerville. As Matilda watched him ride off, she hoped she could pretend to be patient until she saw him again. She wondered if he would remember her birthday. Embarrassed to remind him, she had said nothing, but felt sure Mary and Elizabeth had chattered about it.

On Tuesday, Alf brought the Monday edition of the Sacramento Union with a grin. "So much for newspapers," he said. "This one says Lane's expected to recover from his wound."

"And a week ago they said he was dead?" Matilda put down the spoon she used to stir the beans and shoved the pot to the back of the stove where it would stay warm but not burn. She wiped her hands and reached for the paper. "That's a quick recovery. Or do we call it a resurrection?"

Alf nodded. "Sure glad we never told Pa. He'd a' been all upset for nothing."

Matilda sat down at the kitchen table and read the article he placed in front of her, then glanced across the rest of the page. "Oh, look, they arrested Dr. Major Walker for wearing a Bloomer dress on the street in New York."

"Serves her right," Alf growled. "Bloomers're not fit for a lady to wear."

They had been through that argument before. "But she's a heroine for her work in the Civil War! How can they treat her like that?" She read on. "She says a woman has the right to wear what she wants and she's right. After all, men wear whatever they want."

"Next you'll be sayin' women should have the right to vote!"

She bit back her reply, for she did feel exactly that. "The charges were dismissed," she announced loftily.

"Humpf," Alf grunted. He turned on his heel and stalked out of the door, slamming it behind him.

"Is Uncle Alf mad, Mama?" Mary stood in the doorway, Elizabeth wide-eyed beside her.

Matilda laughed. "Not really. He just hates to admit he's wrong. Run and tell Grandpa supper's about ready. He's out by the barn fixing one of the wheels on the new wagon Uncle Abe brought over."

Two weeks later, as the family gathered to celebrate Matilda's thirtieth birthday, they heard a horse coming up the driveway.

"That's Alfred!" Matilda exclaimed.

"Don't know how you know it's him," Alf teased. "Sounds just like any horse to me."

Matilda ignored him and ran to the door. "He said he would try to come, but it's so far, and he has to go right back." Proof he really does love me, Matilda thought with a blush. Her love for him swelled in her heart. And she had thought she would never have these feelings again! A little embarrassed at running to him like a school girl, she threw herself into his arms, Mary and Elizabeth right behind her.

"My," Alfred grinned. His face beamed as he gathered a child in each arm and tried to embrace all three at once. "I'm glad all of my girls are so happy to see me."

Later, the candles blown out, the cake eaten, and the children in bed, Alfred and Matilda sat alone at last.

"The gold in my claim is almost gone. The only way I could get more would be to wash the hillside away with those hydraulic hoses. But my five acres is only about a mile out of Placerville. Land's bound to go up in value. Only paid Taylor four hundred dollars back in '64. Has to be worth more now. Anyway, I'll ask around and see what I can get." He grinned and hugged her. "We'll see what happens. As soon as it sells, we can get married."

Matilda's mind was not on land sales. During the evening's festivities, with her loved ones gathered about her, she could not help thinking about Alfred's family back in Vermont. They must have wondered what ever became of him. Or at least wanted to know if he still lived.

She hesitated, not knowing what he would say. His family remained the one thing Alfred never talked about. But surely he would feel she had a right to know.

Finally, taking a deep breath, she broached the subject. "Alfred, my darling, have you ever thought of writing to your folks? Letting them know you are well and happy?" She tried to make light of it, and added. "At least let them know you are going to have a ready-made family!" She fell silent, and watched his face.

"My father disowned me," he said at last, his voice grim. "Said if I insisted on leaving Salisbury to go to 'that outlandish country' as he called it, I was no longer a son of his." The hazel eyes flashed. "But I had to come. Something inside of me drove me to come." He kissed her gently. "And I'm glad I did. If I had stayed in Vermont, I never would have met you."

She refused to let him distract her from the subject. "But he must have relented by now. And it's not just your father. What about your mother? And your brothers and sisters?"

"My mother died in '48." He set his jaw.

Matilda said no more. She knew the discussion was over.

But the subject would not leave her mind. For several weeks, she wavered back and forth, then decided to write his family herself, without telling him. But how? What should she say? She sat staring at the blank piece of paper in front of her. Did she really want to do this? Maybe she should leave it alone. Maybe Alfred would be angry with her. What if he never forgave her for interfering? She picked up the pen and dipped it in the inkwell, then hesitated for several moments. Finally, gritting her teeth in resolution, she lifted the pen and began to write.

> "Hicksville, California
> August 15, 1866

"Dear Mr. Wheelock,

"You don't know me, but I am engaged to be married to your son Alfred. He is living and well, here in California.

"I know he has never written to you, and I understand the reasons, for he has told me of your quarrel. But I know you must be concerned about him, and I felt you had a right to know how he is faring.

"If you wish to contact him, send him a letter in my care, addressed to me at Hicksville, Sacramento County, California, and I will see he receives it.

"If you choose not to write, I will understand. He knows nothing of this letter, and I will never tell him, if that is your wish.

"Hoping to hear favorably from you, I remain,

> Your future daughter-in-law,
> Mrs. Matilda Baldwin"

She posted her letter at the Hicksville Post Office. Her heart pounded as she bought the stamp and her hand trembled as she licked and sealed it in place. She handed the packet to Mr. Patterson, and he read the address.

"Vermont?" he queried. "That where young Wheelock is from?" He chuckled. "Tellin' his folks the good news, I take it."

"In a way," Matilda returned, non-commitally. She watched him toss the letter into the bag for outgoing mail and felt a sudden urge to ask him to give it back, but stifled the impulse. For a moment, she had a strange feeling she would faint. She pulled herself together and took a deep breath. "Thank you, Mr. Patterson."

She walked back out to the buggy. Alf had not yet returned. What had she done? Would Alfred be angry with her? Should she tell him? No, she had promised to wait, to say nothing. She climbed into the buggy and sat quietly until Alf returned.

She waited for three weeks. Then, on September 9, as the sun blazed from the blistering hot sky of a windless day, while everyone baked in the heat, Alf returned from his daily trip to the Post Office. He flourished an envelope in front of Matilda.

"'Tilda," he said with a frown, "you've got a letter here from Vermont." He looked at her. "Do we know anyone .... Wait a minute. Alfred's from Vermont." He scowled. "You been writing his folks behind his back?"

Matilda flushed. "Just thought I'd see how they felt. I told them they didn't need to answer if they didn't want to hear from him." She raised her chin in defiance. "And I didn't tell him because if they never answered, no old wound would be re-opened." Her eyes sparkled. "But they did answer!"

Alf grunted. "Don't get too excited until you read what they say. Go on, open it," he ordered when she hesitated. "You started this. You gotta finish it."

With some difficulty, Matilda forced herself to open the packet in her hand. The first words brought the smile back to her face and tears to her eyes.

"Must be good news," Alf said.

"Very good news. Listen:"

"My Dear Mrs. Baldwin,

"Words cannot express my delight when I read your words and learned my beloved son Alfred still lives. I was so sure he had died I told his mother's people he had been killed by Indians. They were preparing a book on the descendants of Aquila Chase, and my wife, Sarah, was a Chase.

"Many harsh words passed between us before he left, and I have regretted them ever since. I have prayed every night he would write to me and tell me where he is so I can beg his forgiveness. I so feared something would happen to him, going out to that wild country.

"Please ask him to forgive a foolish old man whose life has been lightened a thousand fold by the knowledge that he still lives.

"Also, please offer him my congratulations on such a wise choice for a bride. I wish you every happiness. I will be proud to have you as a daughter-in-law.

"Again my gratitude to you for caring enough to write.

"Very sincerely yours,
Jonathan Wheelock"

Matilda looked up, her eyes bright with unshed tears. "Oh, Alf," she said. "What a beautiful letter! What a surprise I will have for Alfred when he comes down from Placerville. He's coming tomorrow. He's promised to take me to the State Fair"

"He'll be surprised, all right," Alf grunted.

As promised, Alfred arrived on the evening of the tenth.

"Ready to go to the Fair, Mrs. Baldwin?" he asked as he released her from a bear hug. "And are my girls ready too?" He turned to hug them as well.

"Oh, yes," Mary cried. "Uncle Alf has put in his biggest ears of corn, and Aunt Polly is entering her mince pie."

"And Mama put in one of Aunt Minerva's best table-cloths," added Elizabeth, her voice solemn.

Alfred looked at Matilda. Her eyes filled.

"She did such beautiful work," she murmured. "She was always too shy to enter it herself, but I felt I had to. I wanted the world to know how talented she was."

"And I'll bet it wins a blue ribbon," Alfred declared stoutly.

Matilda banished her sad thoughts. "But come in! You must be famished, riding all day. Supper is about ready."

After the meal, she put the children to bed and brought out the letter. Not knowing quite how to say what she had done, she simply put it in his hands and waited.

By the time he finished the brief note, his hands shook. He stared at her.

Finally, unable to stand the silence any longer, she said, "I'm so sorry. I took it upon myself to write him. I knew how I would feel, not knowing. If he had not answered, I would have said nothing." She stopped as tears welled in Alfred's eyes. She pulled his head to her breast and held him while he wept. In her heart she rejoiced, glad she had taken the chance. She had made the right decision.

In a few moments, he pulled himself together. He raised his head and blew his nose. "Sorry," he said, abashed. "Never realized it would hit me like that."

She smiled. "It makes me love you all the more."

He grinned. "Besides, I always wanted to write, but was too proud to beg him to take me back. Since you made the first move, my pride is still intact!"

Chapter 65

October to December, 1866

MINERVA'S death sent Gardner Randolph deeper into his depression. Since the day of Minerva's funeral he denied having any appetite. Every day Matilda and her mother coaxed him to eat. Matilda sensed him drifting away. He wanted her to read to him from his Bible all the time, so she read until her throat turned raw. It seemed the only thing that comforted him.

"This is part of God's plan," he murmured one afternoon late in October. "He knew how dearly I loved Sinclair and Minerva. He took them so they'll be in Heaven waiting for me."

Matilda and her father sat alone in the parlor. Matilda could think of nothing to say, but he seemed to expect no response. Lewis napped while Betsy Ann and the girls gathered the fall crop of walnuts. Alf, muttering deprecations against all manufacturers of windmills, had gone to the Hicksville store to get another replacement part for the windlass.

"You're a good daughter, Matilda," Gardner told her. Rousing himself for a moment, he patted her cheek. "Young Wheelock is a fine man. I'm glad he will be here to take care of you." He leaned back in his chair and closed his eyes. "Tell your mother . . . tell her . . . "

He gave a little gasp and his body jerked. Matilda jumped to her feet. "Pa!" she cried. "What's wrong?" Frantic, she felt for a heartbeat. Yes, he still lived, but she could not get him to respond. What shall I do? she wondered. Shall I go for Mother? Do I dare leave him alone? A cold band tightened around her chest.

Undecided, she picked up his limp, work-worn hand and held it to her cheek. Her eyes dry, she stared at his silent face, the pain in her heart a dull ache as she wondered how she could bear another loss.

When Alf returned an hour later, he found them sitting together, Matilda with her father's hand still pressed to her cheek.

"What happened?" Alf asked, kneeling beside her.

"I don't know," she whispered. "He just stopped talking. I haven't been able to wake him up since."

With Matilda's help, Alf carried his father to the bed. Gardner opened unseeing eyes and swallowed convulsively. His heart still beat, strong and regular. Rasping breathing assured them he lived, but they could get no other response.

"Apoplexy," Betsy Ann reported in a grim voice when she saw him. She shook her head. "Knew his constant fretting would bring on the apoplexy. Tried to tell him." With a sigh that broke Matilda's heart, Betsy Ann caressed the forehead of the man she had wed nearly half a century before. As Matilda watched, the first tears she had ever seen her mother shed slowly slid down the withered cheeks.

Caring for her bed-ridden father, in addition to her other work, drained Matilda's strength more than she dared admit even to herself. She knew she had lost weight, for her dresses hung loosely about her waist and her face had lost its fullness. For the first time in her life, unsightly bags showed under her eyes.

Alfred came down from Placerville at the end of November. She had not seen him since he had taken her to the State Fair. He apologized for not joining her sooner.

"I wanted to come in October, for I know you would have enjoyed that lecture by Mr. Twain at the Metropolitan Theater. He's an interesting speaker, and I know you are curious about the Sandwich Islands. But I had a man as wanted to see my property," he said, "and he kept putting off our meeting date. He looked like a good prospect, though, so . . . ." He broke off and looked at Matilda closely. He frowned, and concern showed in his eyes. "'Tilda, my love, have you been ailing?"

"No," she replied. She hesitated a moment. "My father had a stroke of apoplexy the end of October. He needs a lot of care and I've been tending to him."

"All by yourself? As well as taking care of three children?"

"Mother does what she can . . . ," Matilda began.

"You're killing yourself! Are you getting any rest at night?"

When she did not answer, he continued. "And you're not eating. You've lost weight." He took her in his arms and murmured into her hair, "Now that I've found you, I don't want to lose you."

"My father needs the care . . . ."

"Does your mother know how hard it has been on you? Don't you realize they are taking advantage of you? Alf can help you at night. Do you ever call him?"

"He needs his rest, and . . . "

"So do you!" Alfred exploded. "Marry me now. We don't have to wait. I'll take you back to Placerville with me. Let's just go find the preacher tomorrow and let me take you away before you make yourself ill."

Her eyes flashed. "Leave my father when he needs me so? How can you even suggest such a thing? Go back to Placerville and leave me alone!" She stalked into the room where her father lay and slammed the door.

Gardner opened his eyes at the sound.

"Pa," she cried. "You're awake! Speak to me." Her heart rose whenever his eyes opened, thinking each time perhaps he would answer her, that he would finally start to recover. "Please," she whispered, "say something. Anything."

But the dark eyes only stared, unresponsive to her pleas. Propping him up, she fed him some broth from the bowl on the bedside stand. As she lifted the spoon, she noticed her hand shaking with fatigue. Alfred is right, she thought. She suddenly realized how hard she had been driving herself. With a start, she recalled her harsh words to him. Oh, no, she thought, what came over me? He'll think I don't love him. Don't let him think that, God. Please don't let him think that. I have to tell him he's right.

As she rose quickly from her father's bedside, the sound of a horse galloping away reached her ears. She ran for the door, but Alfred had ridden down the lane and was nearly out of sight when she reached the porch. "No," she cried, her hoarse voice carrying only a few feet. She stood numb, staring after him, mutely willing him to return. Don't go. Please don't go. Come back. I didn't mean it when I told you to leave.

Her brother Alf strode up as she stood watching Alfred's vanishing figure. "Alfred gone already?" he asked in total innocence. "Thought he planned to stay for supper."

"Oh, shut up!" Matilda ran into the house and slammed the door behind her, leaving her brother gaping after her.

Gardner Randolph lived another week, until Wednesday, December 2, with Matilda and Betsy Ann feeding and caring for him. The weeks of tending her father had left their mark. The day before his funeral, Matilda stood by the mirror in her room, noticing deep wrinkles around her eyes. Her heart ached as she thought of Alfred smoothing them back, and gently kissing her eyelids. She remembered every endearment he had murmured against her hair. She picked up the small photograph she kept on the dresser beside the mirror.

"Alfred, my love," she whispered, meeting the smiling eyes in the photograph, "you must know I spoke in anger only because of my exhaustion. You do still love me, don't you?" she asked the picture. "You must still love me."

"Mama," Mary's voice spoke behind her, "why are you talking to yourself?"

As they prepared to leave for the cemetery the following Friday, Betsy Ann remarked, "Haven't seen young Wheelock yet. I know Alf wired him about Gardner. Something happen between you two?"

Matilda tried to appear casual, "I guess he's just been busy up in Placerville. You know he's trying to sell the mine, so he has a lot to do . . . ." She turned quickly so her mother would not see the tears in her eyes. "Oh, Mother," she whispered. "I told him to go away. But I didn't mean it!"

Her mother gathered her in a warm embrace. "Shoo, now, child, you go on and cry. You been through a lot these last few months." Betsy Ann patted Matilda's back and stroked her hair. "Young Wheelock's a smart man. He knows you'll make him a good wife. He'll be back."

Matilda tried to persuade herself that her usually sagacious mother was right. She stepped back, ashamed of her display of weakness. "Of course he will. I'm just being foolish."

But as she remembered her last words to him, and the speed of his horse as he departed, her heart sank.

After the funeral, Matilda stood by her father's grave and looked across to where Sinclair and Minerva had so recently been laid to rest. She shivered in the cold December air and looked at the loved ones who surrounded her. Will and Polly stood with their whole brood, from tall, sturdy Will, Jr., and handsome Michael, down to baby Sammy; Britt and Sarah with their four, including young Gardner II.

Somehow, Matilda thought, it seemed appropriate for there to be another Gardner Randolph.

Her bachelor brothers, Tom, Sam, and Alf, shoveled dirt into the grave. Matilda tried not to hear the sounds of the clods striking the top of the wooden coffin. The hollow thuds made her shudder. Surely, she thought, that has to be the most dismal sound in the whole world.

One face remained painfully absent, a face she missed more and more each day. She tried to dismiss Alfred from her mind, telling herself she did not need him. She had managed without him before and could do so again, but the ache in her heart never quit. Everything reminded her of him. The sound of rain on the roof brought to mind the day the storm had trapped them in the barn, when he declared his love for her. At the hoofbeats of every approaching horse, she imagined Alfred returned to her, and she remembered the feel of his arms around her, the touch of his lips on hers. A neighbor brought a mincemeat pie and she remembered Alfred's fondness for her own mincemeat pie. Had it only been a week since she told him to leave? It seemed the longest week of her life.

Her heart aching, she turned her face from the sight of her brothers filling in the grave. The cold sun finally broke dimly through the heavy fog still gripping the countryside, hiding the tops of the trees and blowing in wisps across the fields. The icy cold crept upwards from her freezing feet through her whole body, until it reached her heart.

Only then did she recognize the lone figure standing apart from the family. "Alfred," she gasped, her heart leaping. "Oh, Alfred!"

Holding out his arms, he smiled the gentle smile she had missed so much the past, lonely week.

She ran to him, throwing herself into his embrace. "Oh, Alfred," she managed to choke. She buried her face in his neck and clung to him.

He clasped her closely and murmured, his lips against her cheek, "I'm such a wretch. I should never have left you in anger like that. I should have understood the strain you were under. Before I was a mile away I wanted to come back, but I feared you wouldn't want me."

"Oh, Alfred. Not want you!" Matilda's voice caught with a little sob. She raised her head and met his eyes. "I've been so lonely thinking I drove you away from me."

"Never again. You're stuck with me for the rest of your life, Mrs. Baldwin. Even if you tell me to go away, I will refuse."

Chapter 66

December of 1866

THE SUNDAY evening following Gardner Randolph's funeral, the first real winter storm struck with a vengeance. Dark clouds vanquished the sun. When Matilda rose on Monday morning, she lighted a lamp to dispel some of the gloom while she prepared breakfast.

Mary, at the table eating her porridge, looked hopeful. "Is it raining too hard to go to school, Mama? The roof leaked the last time it rained. Soaked some of Teacher's books. Was she mad! She said next time it rained, she was going to stay home."

"Your cousin Michael is coming with the buggy. He said whenever it rains, he'll bring his brothers and sisters and swing by here for you. If Teacher doesn't come, he'll bring you home again."

Mary's face brightened. "Oh, I love Cousin Michael. Do you suppose he'll let me sit beside him?"

"I want to go to school too," Elizabeth wailed. "Why can't I go with Mary?"

Lewis banged his spoon on the table and nodded. "Wanna go too," he announced.

"Next August, my sweet," Matilda soothed Elizabeth, ignoring Lewis. "You have to be six."

The wail deepened. "I'm almost six," she protested. "Gramma says I'm five today." Her face brightened. "You do remember today is my birthday, don't you, Mama?"

"Of course Mama remembers." Actually, with all of the activity over the last few days, Matilda had forgotten until she recalled it with a start the previous evening. She glanced out of the window. "Hurry, Mary. Michael is just turning in the driveway. I'll get the umbrella."

Mary swallowed the last of her milk with a loud slurping, wiped her mouth with the back of her hand, and ran for her school-bag.

"Use your napkin, Mary," Matilda sighed in futility to the child's vanishing back.

Elizabeth daintily dabbed at her lips with the square of embroidered cloth. She refolded it with care and replaced it in the pewter napkin holder, then, with a smug look, said, "I know how, Mama. See? I'm old enough to go to school."

Mary returned, school-bag in one hand, her hat in the other. Matilda escorted her to the waiting buggy and settled the squabble over who would get to sit on the seat next to Michael. As she stood watching the buggy retrace its route back down the lane, Jake greeted her with his usual enthusiasm, placing both forepaws on her apron. He left two large, muddy prints on the white cloth.

"Jake," she exclaimed in exasperation. "Look what you've done! I put this apron on clean this morning."

The unrepentant Jake wagged his tail, also muddy, slapping it against her skirt, then happily followed her back to the porch. She sighed. "I suppose you're looking for your breakfast as well. I think I have a bone from last night's supper that has a little meat left. I planned to use it for soup, but . . . "

"Woof," Jake barked.

She laughed. She knew she pampered him. Alf had told her often enough. "You win. But you have to stay out here. I don't want my floor as muddy as you've made me." She dug the bone out of the cool-box standing on the corner of the porch and handed it to him.

The old dog obliged. Taking the bone, he retreated to a relatively dry corner and started to gnaw.

Shivering, Matilda retreated to the warmth of the kitchen

and consoled the still weeping Elizabeth. "Come on, Lizzie. We have to get started on your birthday cake. And we have to work on some Christmas ornaments, too, so we can surprise Grandma and Uncle Alf."

School forgotten, the tears vanished as Elizabeth's cheerful smile returned.

As time for the mid-day meal approached, Elizabeth proudly helped her mother place the birthday cake in the oven to bake. Matilda fed the children to the continuing sound of rain on the roof, then put them down for a nap. She overrode Elizabeth's protests, telling her she wanted her to be bright and cheerful for her birthday party. A small affair, Matilda thought sadly, for it would just be the six of them, so soon after Gardner's death. Fortunately, Elizabeth was young enough to be happy with a modest celebration.

Betsy Ann also retired for a brief nap. "Too dark to do much, might as well catch up on my rest. Carin' for your pa all the time took more out of me than I thought. Must be a-gettin' old."

So when Alf arrived, the brother and sister were alone. He waved a letter in his hand. "Went by the Post Office. Wasn't much else I could do, rainin' like it is, so I sat a spell with some of the fellers while we waited for the mail to come in. Some of 'em tried to get me into a card game, but they play too slick for me. So I told 'em I had to get this letter here to you. It's from your friend Sarah Williams."

"Sarah! I haven't heard from her in ever so long. Do you suppose she's writing to tell me she's finally decided to get married?"

Alf grinned. "I doubt it, knowing her. Wouldn't surprise me if she was one of those blasted suffragettes."

"Go on with you. Sit down and eat your dinner while it's hot. Mother's lying down. She hardly ate a bite. Says she's not really hungry." Matilda shook her head. "She never says much, but losing Pa hit her real hard. I'm so worried she may go into a decline. He was so much a part of her life."

Alf nodded as Matilda placed a large helping of the fragrant beef stew in front of him. "I know," he murmured, "but don't worry. She's a tough old gal. She'll weather this storm the way she has all the rest. Why don't you read the letter? Let's see what Sarah has to say."

The vision of Sarah's lovely face and sparkling green eyes popped into Matilda's mind. It had been so long! She hadn't seen Sarah since the summer before the move to Kansas. A lot of things had happened in Matilda's life since that carefree summer in 1853. Could it be thirteen years already? Why, it seemed like . . . .

"Gonna read it or aren't you," Alf interrupted her reverie.

With a start, for her mind had been miles away, she broke the seal on the letter.

"My Dearest 'Tilda," the letter began. Matilda could see Sarah writing the words. She always called Matilda her dearest 'Tilda.

> "You'll never believe this, but I have moved into St. Louis and opened a dress shop. Me, who has always hated to sew. I still hate to sew, but I have two girls working for me who do all the actual work. Pa died last summer, and my brothers decided they were tired of running the ferry. They wanted to try farming, so they moved to western Kansas."

"They're sure welcome to all the Kansas they want to farm as far as I'm concerned," Alf interposed. "From all I hear of droughts and blizzards and locusts, I can't imagine anyone wanting to farm there."

Matilda laughed. "You left out the ague. There are some very pretty parts of Kansas, but you're right. It's a tough place to make a living." She returned to the letter.

"They offered to take me and Ma with them, but I had stashed away a little money and decided I wanted to be independent.

"My shop carries only the most stylish material, and both girls are very good seamstresses, so I get business from all of the society ladies. Believe me, that's where the money is. The wives of all of these rich businessmen spend money like water. When I think of all the time I spent grubbing that little bit of money out of travelers on that ferry, makes me wonder why I didn't do this sooner.

"Pa's death was actually a relief for everyone, including him. He got so swollen he could hardly move, and his skin turned an orangish yellow. Doctor said his liver gave out. Said he noticed that real often in men that drank a lot of whiskey like Pa did. He figures the whiskey destroys the liver. I don't know. I'd never touch the stuff myself."

Alf's laughter interrupted her. "Jim Williams always liked his whiskey."

"Yes," Matilda nodded. "I remember very well. I guess we're lucky Pa never drank." She thought for a moment of Jim Williams, remembering many incidents when he had whiskey on his breath, then shook her head and continued Sarah's letter.

"I know you're wondering if I'm ever getting married. Well, I haven't met the man yet that I'd be willing to give up my freedom for. Get them coming around all the time, now that I'm a success. I suspect they just want to get their hands on my property. Terrible the way the law says your property becomes your husband's as soon as you marry.

"I've joined a group here in St. Louis that's working to change some of those laws, so you may hear of me being arrested one of these days. The movement has gained a lot of followers since Mrs. Stanton and Mrs. Mott held that Women's Rights Convention in Seneca Falls back in '48 and a lot of men want to stop it. They arrested Dr. Major Walker in New York last July for wearing one of Amelia Bloomer's pants and tunic outfits on the street. Disgraceful. That outfit is so much more practical that these wretched skirts that drag on the floor."

Alf's laughter interrupted her again. "I knew she'd wind up in this crazy women's movement."

"Oh, hush. She's sure right about one thing. These skirts that drag in the mud all the time are a curst nuisance. I'll have to tell her Major Walker's arrest even made the Sacramento paper. And why should she have to give up a nice store she built with her own money to a man just because she marries him? That doesn't seem right."

Alf continued to laugh. "You're beginning to sound just like her. Better not tell Alfred."

"Alfred agrees. He thinks women should have more rights. He even...." She stopped, knowing how her brother felt about women voting. She figured she had better not say Alfred felt women were just as smart as men, and deserved the right to vote.

"He even what?"

"Nothing. Do you want to hear the rest of the letter or not?"

Alf grinned. "Go on."

"Did I tell you Old Buck finally died? Bless his heart. He must have been over thirty. Died peacefully in his sleep. I just went out one morning and found him. My brothers refused to dig a hole to bury him. Said I was crazy, wanting to bury a horse. But Buck had been my friend for so long I felt he earned the right to be buried, so I asked Josh to do it.

"Josh, bless him, was happy to oblige, even though a hole that big was a major undertaking. He even promised to keep putting flowers on the grave after we left. He seemed to understand how much I loved that old horse.

"When we sold the ferry, the new owner hired Josh, so he is still there. He bought his wife her freedom in '60, and after the war, two of their sons joined them. They have a little cabin not far from ours. I don't know how I'd have ever run the ferry without Josh."

"You never knew Josh," Matilda said to Alf. "I met him when I visited Sarah the summer after you left. He had escaped from Mississippi by the underground railroad." She had not known he had been forced to leave his family so he could earn the money to buy his wife's freedom. She thought of Josh singing in his deep, rich voice. At last she understood the tinge of sadness she always felt whenever she listened to his songs. "I'm so glad slavery is finally gone forever." She shook her head and finished the rest of the letter.

"You should see Ma. Now that Pa is gone, she looks ten years younger. She keeps house for me and the two girls, even goes around singing while she works. I don't think I ever heard her sing once while Pa was alive. Neighbor offered to marry her even before we left the river, but she refused. Don't blame her. After all she went through with Pa, no wonder she wants to stay single. Especially now, with us making a good living in the shop.

"Ma's only 52. She always looked old because she was so worn down with worry, Pa never being able to stay with anything for very long. Wouldn't have stayed with the ferry if Hank and Jim and I

hadn't been running it for him. He talked about selling out and moving on, but we refused to go. We'd
been through that enough when we were young. Ma
married Pa when she was only 14, so she never really
had a chance. No wonder she's so happy now.

"So write to me at the address here in St. Louis,
and tell me what you are doing, now that you have
finally achieved your dream of moving to California."

"She closes with love to everyone." Matilda re-folded
the letter with a chuckle. "Same old Sarah," she told Alf.
"Highly unlikely she'll ever marry now."

"Especially if she's going to be one of those suffragette
females," Alf growled. "Would 'a thought she'd have better
sense."

Matilda only smiled. She would never say so to Alf,
but she agreed with many of the ideas that Mrs. Stanton
and Mrs. Mott proposed. Especially the one about property
ownership. She could not blame Sarah for not wanting to
let a husband own the shop she bought and built up to a
success all by herself. Sarah was right. The ferry succeeded
due to Sarah's determination. Having Jim Williams for a
father and watching what her mother went through also put
Sarah off of the idea of marriage. She thought of her own
happiness in the years she spent with Lew, of her present
love for Alfred, of the long years of companionship her parents had shared. She sighed.

"Maybe," Matilda suggested, tears welling in her eyes at
the thought of her father, "if Sarah's father had been more
like ours, she might have a better view of marriage."

Rain continued for the rest of the afternoon. Alf stayed
in the house until time to feed the stock. When he grumbled
about having to go out in the rain, Matilda laughed at his
complaints.

"If you were in Kansas," she quipped, "you could be struggling through a snow bank. You don't know what you missed, not moving to Kansas."

Alf only grunted. He pulled his hat over his head and splashed his way to the barn.

When he returned, Matilda and Betsy Ann put supper on the table, then brought out the birthday cake.

As Elizabeth blew out the five candles on her cake, the clip-clop of hoofbeats reached their ears.

"Who in the world is crazy enough to be riding on a night like this?" Betsy Ann asked.

Alf strode to the door, Matilda behind him, in time to see the rider dismount.

"Alfred," Matilda cried, the joy she always felt when she saw him suffusing through her. "You've come for Elizabeth's birthday! I can't believe you remembered."

He strode through the door and swept his free arm around her, his broad smile lighting the whole room. The lantern glow caught the gleam in his hazel eyes. He swung his saddlepack on the other arm. "If I'm going to be a father, I'd better start practicing," he grinned. "Where's the birthday girl?"

With a squeal of delight, the usually sedate Elizabeth launched herself into his arms. Matilda noticed that Mary hung back. Probably remembering that he did not come for her birthday. Oh, dear, she thought. Jealousy already. She wondered how she could tactfully bring the subject up to Alfred.

Elizabeth opened the gaily wrapped parcel. "Oh, Mama, Grandma, look! A tea set for my dolls!"

Matilda picked up one of the dainty tea cups. "Real china! Oh, Alfred. How extravagant!"

Alfred smoothed Elizabeth's hair. "Nothing but the best for my girls," he said. His eyes sparkled. "And, since I did not get down in October," he handed a parcel to Lewis and another to Mary, "here are some belated birthday gifts for my other two!"

Chapter 67

December, 1866

MICHAEL Randolph's birthday came only eight days after Elizabeth's, on the fifteenth of December. Matilda and Polly debated the propriety of a party.

"It's so soon after Father Gardner's death," Polly demurred. "What will folks say?"

"The sixteenth birthday is so important to a boy, " Matilda returned. "Let's leave it up to Mother."

When they conferred with Betsy Ann, she agreed to a small family party. "Just do the same as we did for Lizzie last week. Can't anyone fault us if it's just family. Sure would be a shame not to have some kind of a celebration."

Early in the morning on the day of the party, Matilda hitched White Star to the buggy, loaded up the eager children, and drove over to Polly's to help with the preparations. By noon, the cake baked, the presents in a pile in the parlor, the family gathered at the table. Delicious aromas filled the air.

Matilda looked around, a little sadly. Without Sinclair and Minerva, it had been hard enough. She thought of the table back at Alf's, where her father's favorite chair stood empty, the chair they had so carefully packed in the wagon and brought across the prairie. It had remained in its place at the head of the table during the long, dreary weeks while he lingered between life and death. After he died, no one had the heart to remove it or to sit in it.

But children never remained downcast for long. Mary, her red-gold curls bobbing, insisted on helping her Aunt Polly ice the cake, squabbling with her cousin Maggie over the privilege. Will and Polly's youngest son, Sammy, tried unsuccessfully to persuade his father to allow him to light the candles. The children's happy laughter helped remove some of the pall, and Matilda found herself joining in.

After the games were played and the cake had disappeared, Michael opened his gifts. With great pride, Mary handed him her present. When he tore the wrapper from the box, he found a raggedly hemmed handkerchief with a crude 'M' embroidered on one corner.

"Mary! You made this yourself? It's beautiful." Matilda silently thanked Michael for his tact. Household arts did not come easily to Mary, and she had spent so much effort making the gift.

Mary's blue eyes sparkled as Michael gave her a hug and a kiss. She adored her big cousin Michael. She tagged along after him at every opportunity, and his patience with her never ceased. Very few young men his age would have any time for a seven-year-old girl. Michael's brothers certainly would not. Michael Randolph was indeed a very special young man.

"Attention, everyone!" Will's eyes glowed as he clapped his hands. "Now for Michael's special present." He turned to the chest and pulled out a carefully wrapped Winchester shotgun.

"Pa! Did you really ...? I mean ... is this really mine?" Michael stammered with excitement as he carefully unwrapped the gun, holding it with reverence.

Michael's face glowed with happiness, his hazel eyes reflecting bits of light from the lamp on the table. Shadows built in the gathering darkness as the sun slid beyond the horizon in the short winter day. Night would be upon them soon.

"Tomorrow," Michael went on. "Tomorrow, I'll see how this shoots. Johnnie Wahl and I are gonna go goose hunting. The field down by the Cosumnes is full of geese. Johnnie and I have been wanting to go all week. Mother, Grandmother, Aunt 'Tilda, get ready for a goose dinner tomorrow."

Betsy Ann said, "A goose dinner would be lovely, Michael. We look forward to it. Just be sure you shoot a fat one."

Everyone laughed. The last goose Michael had brought home had been so scrawny and tough no one could eat it.

"I promise to shoot a young juicy one," Michael said, joining in the laughter.

The next morning Matilda woke to fog so thick she could barely see the barn. Polly and Matilda, washing the breakfast dishes, watched Michael through the window over the sink as he headed for the barn to saddle his horse. He placed the beloved new gun in the saddle holster with tender pride and rode off to meet his friend.

His mother smiled, an indulgent look on her face. "He's a man grown already, 'Tilda. Time goes so fast. Seems only yesterday he and Will, Jr. were babies." Polly rinsed another cup and placed it in the rack for Matilda to dry, then shook her head with a rueful laugh. "Kind of hate to see them grow up. Would you believe Will is already courting one of the Davis girls?"

Matilda nodded in agreement. "They do grow fast. Thank goodness Lewis won't be courting for a while anyway. But I'm afraid Mary is going to attract the boys soon. She's a flirt already and she's only seven."

The morning dragged on and Michael did not return with the promised goose. Matilda saw Polly glance at the clock on the mantel over the fireplace several times as the hours passed.

"Do you suppose the geese have gone from the field?" Polly asked. "If he doesn't get that goose here soon, it won't have time to cook."

Matilda shrugged. "Guess we'll just have to wait and

see."

As the sun broke through the morning fog, Will, accompanied by his brothers Tom and Alf, rode up to the porch.

"Where's Michael, Will? Isn't he with you?" Polly's voice carried just an edge of anxiety. "I expected him back here two hours ago."

"He's not back yet? Maybe they decided to ride over to Matt Davis' and show off Michael's new gun. Must have got to talking and forgot to watch the time." Will's hearty laugh did not reassure Matilda, nor, she thought, will it reassure Polly. Michael had promised to bring the goose for dinner. Jack or Will, Jr. might lose track of time, but Michael always kept his promises.

Evidently Will felt the same. He hugged Polly and added, "If it makes you feel better, I'll ride out and check. Come on Tom, Alf." Turning his horse, Will rode off into the lingering mist. Tom and Alf followed. Will, Jr. decided to follow and hurried to saddle his horse.

Matilda joined Polly on the porch. Looking into Polly's face, she saw the fear in her eyes. Arm in arm, they watched the horses disappear from sight.

Time dragged. They put dinner, minus the goose, on the table and fed the children. Betsy Ann saved the extra food on the back of the stove to keep warm until the men returned.

They ate in silence. Even light-hearted little Mary seemed to sense the uneasiness in the room. Her cousins, from fourteen-year-old Jack to baby Sammy, ate quietly. Lewis' eyes widened as he watched the faces of the adults and older children. Matilda's attempts to reassure the children sounded hollow, for she felt fear's icy fingers touch her heart.

Polly's face grew paler as they waited. She pushed food around on her plate, but ate nothing. Finally, unable to sit still any longer, she rose to her feet and began carrying plates to the sink.

Matilda washed the dinner dishes, feeling the need to do something to keep her mind busy. Polly helped her until the second dish dropped from her nerveless fingers. With a gentle smile, Betsy Ann took the towel from Polly's hand.

"Please, Polly, allow me while you still have some dishes left." She held her for a moment in a brief hug. "They'll find him. Try not to borrow trouble."

They did find him. Shortly after two o'clock, just as the sun burned away the last of the fog, Will strode through the door, Michael in his arms.

With a little cry, Polly ran to his side.

"He's alive, Polly," Will said hastily. "He's breathing, but he's lost a lot of blood. Pray God he will recover. Tom's riding to Sacramento to see if he can get one of the doctors to come."

The stricken Johnnie Wahl followed, sobbing to Polly, "I'm so sorry, Miz Randolph," he managed to get out between sobs. "I don't know how it happened. He was right along side of me while we snuck up on the geese and . . . and somehow . . . somehow my gun just went off." He wiped his muddied, blood-stained face with a grimy hand. "I couldn't leave him to come for help," he stammered helplessly. "I had to keep holding my hand against the hole in his side. So . . . so much blood." Unable to continue, he stumbled to a chair and buried his face in his hands.

Matilda had to escape from the room, from the smell of blood, from the sight of that still, pale face. She stepped out on the porch as Will, Jr. led the horses to the corral by the barn. She watched him take his brother's prized new shotgun out of the gun boot on the saddle. Poor Michael, Matilda thought, her heart aching. He never even got to fire the treasured gun. The tears in her eyes spilled down her cheeks. She wiped the drops away quickly so the children would not see them.

The anguished cry from her daughter Mary pulled her from her trance. She hastened to pull the stricken child into her arms.

"Hush, my darling," she murmured into the red curls. "He is still alive. We must not lose hope." But, remembering the size of the wound, her heart sank.

The long winter night passed slowly, each tick of the big clock on the mantel counting down the seconds of Michael's life. His mother sat by his side, holding his hand. Will stood grimly silent behind her. Betsy Ann's medical knowledge was tapped, but little could be done. She bandaged the boy's injured side as tightly as she could, but the blood oozed through the cloth, telling them the bleeding continued inside of Michael's body.

Tom found Dr. Caswell at home and persuaded him to come, but he could add nothing to what Betsy Ann had already done. With a few words of sympathy he climbed back into his buggy and returned to Sacramento.

They could do nothing more but pray the comfrey poultices would stop the bleeding. Matilda, filled with bleak despair, remembered how ineffective the comfrey had proven to stop the bleeding for Sinclair.

Dawn broke bright and golden through the window, and the day promised to be clear and cold. Michael's breathing grew more shallow, more ragged. His body twitched. Polly's face took on a bluish hue as she matched her breathing to Michael's. Tears poured down her cheeks at the signs of pending death. No one spoke. The room remained silent except for Michael's labored breaths.

The sun rose higher in the sky, the beams through the window approaching Michael's motionless body. When the sun bathed his face, the breathing stopped.

* * *

They buried him in the Hicksville Cemetery the following day, next to Sinclair and Minerva. All of our young ones together, Matilda thought as she stood by the graveside. Her mind reverted to how she held the sobbing Mary the night before. Mary had refused to be consoled when she learned she would never again see her favorite cousin. She cried over and over, "God hates me. He must hate me. Why does God hate me, Mama? First He took Papa, then Uncle Sinclair and Aunt Minerva and Grandpa, and now He has taken Michael away from me."

Yes, God, Matilda said to herself. If You are supposed to be a merciful God, how can You be so cruel? Michael, so young, so handsome, so kind, so full of life and promise. To cut him down so senselessly!

The sight of Lewis' body lying at the bottom of the well loomed before her eyes. The pain she thought her new love for Alfred had banished forever surged through her again, as fresh as the day it happened. Unable to bear any more, she turned and walked away.

Chapter 68

April, 1867

ALF strode into the room and waved a letter in front of Matilda. "If I give this to you, does it mean I won't get my dinner until after you read it?" His eyes gleamed with humor as he held the letter beyond her reach.

"You wretch. If you want to eat at all, you'll give it to me right now!"

He laughed. "You win. It's from Carrie. Read it while I wash up."

"She's probably writing to tell us she's had her baby." Matilda hurried to tear off the protective covering and eagerly scanned the page.

> "We have another girl. Seems Ely is not destined to have sons. We have named her Minerva, which seems only right."

Tears blurred Matilda's vision. How thoughtful of Carrie to name her daughter after their lost sister. Especially, she mused with a little chuckle, since Carrie really didn't like the name, especially the nickname 'Minnie' that seemed to be attached to anyone named Minerva. She blinked her eyes to clear them and read on.

> "John is doing well in local politics. Would you believe he has begun a campaign to get Waterville's name changed back to Randolph? Now that all this war business is settling down, he thinks the chances are good. After all, Pa founded the town in the first place.

"The Post Office has never really recognized the name change anyway, since there is another town of Waterville up river, towards Marysville.

"Mary Anne and I weren't sure which baby would be first. Hers should be born any day now. She and John send their love. Their family is growing like weeds. Little Alf turns three this month, and your namesake will be two in September."

Alf interrupted her. "You finished that letter yet? I got to get back to the fields. If I'd known I wouldn't get fed, I'd 'a hidden it until after dinner."

She aimed a blow at his head with the dish towel and laughed. "Dinner coming up. Mother," she called into the bedroom where Betsy Ann busily folded clean laundry, "come and eat. Elizabeth, wash your hands." She lifted Lewis onto the two books she added to the chair to elevate him so he could reach the table. "Isn't the fact that you have another niece worth waiting for?"

"Carrie out to populate the State of Kansas with females? How many's that make for her, anyway?"

"Only four, since she lost Anna. I sometimes think we need three or four more females around here just to take care of you! Here." She handed him the platter containing the roast. "Start carving while I dish up the potatoes."

As Alf sank his fork into his second slab of apple pie, they heard a horse approaching. A few moments later, their brother Will's oldest, Will, Junior, entered the room. He eyed the table.

"Is that apple pie I smell, Aunt 'Tilda?" His eyes shone. "I sure could use a piece."

Matilda laughed and returned to the sideboard to cut another large slab of the fresh apple pie. She added a slice of cheese and placed it in front of him. "You always seem to know when I have apple pie. The aroma must carry over to your place. What brings you here in midday? Shouldn't you be helping in the fields?"

"Came by with the big news," he grinned, attacking the pie with relish.

"Polly's had her baby!" Matilda exclaimed. "I thought she wasn't due for another two weeks."

"Guess the little guy got tired of waiting," Will chuckled.

"Another boy," Betsy Ann chortled. "Knew it would be a boy, high as she was a-carryin'."

"Is your mother doing well?" Matilda asked. "And have they decided on a name?"

"Oh, yes, she's fine." Will frowned. "She wants to name him Michael."

"Michael! Oh, my."

"Yeah. Pa's kind of against it. Says he already has a son named Michael." His eyes misted at the thought of his dead brother. Matilda felt her own eyes sting.

"Oh," she said, "but we can call him something else. Bud, or Jim, or something. It would be nice to name him after Michael."

"She wants Michael Brittain, after Uncle Britt as well." He grinned. "So that's what she'll get. You know she always gets her way with Pa."

Matilda nodded. And so, she thought, remembering Michael's handsome face and charming ways, another Michael Randolph is born. She met Will's clear brown eyes and smiled. "After we eat, we'll go over and visit the newest member of the family."

The next morning dawned clear and sunny. With no rain for over a week, the roads had dried. On an impulse, Matilda decided to go to Sacramento for some shopping.

"Alf," she said as he sat at the table finishing off his third slice of ham, "I'm going to Sacramento today."

"Today? I got too many things to see to. Got to get that last . . . ."

"I can go alone. Hitch White Star to the buggy for me. She's docile enough I won't need anyone to drive. Jake likes to go with me. He's all the protection I need. Mother can keep the children."

"Why today?"

Matilda smiled. "Alfred and I are getting married as soon as he sells that land in Placerville. I don't have a shred of material for a wedding dress, and I need to get started. Can't get married in a half-finished dress, can I? And I want to get Annie started on my wedding hat."

"You just want an excuse to see Annie."

"I haven't seen her in an age. And little Annie will be three this August. Doesn't seem possible. I'm so glad she has made such a success of her little shop."

Alf grunted. "If she'd get married, she wouldn't need to run a hat shop."

Matilda ignored the comment. They had discussed the subject often, especially since the last letter from Sarah Williams.

Alf did not seem to expect a reply. He drained his coffee cup and stalked to the barn to hitch White Star to the small, light, single seat buggy. Matilda refused to have White Star pull anything heavier.

As she urged the horse forward, she recalled how Alf once started to hitch White Star to the buckboard and Matilda had intervened. "After all," Matilda had explained. "She's not a cart horse."

Alf had sulked for days, accusing her again of pampering White Star. "King's not above pulling the buckboard," he grumbled.

The morning, clear and cold, promised midday warmth as the sun rose higher in the cloudless sky. Wild flowers blossomed, covering the fields with a maze of color. As she drove across the Cosumnes River, the force of the water going beneath the bridge frightened her. The water reached almost to the underside. She heaved a sigh of relief when she had crossed safely. The spring runoff had been light, but she still suffered a resurgence of her fear of water whenever she crossed the river at flood stage. Alf teased her.

"If you want to see water, Sis," he often said, "you should have been here in the winter of '61 to '62. One big lake from here to Liberty."

She always admired the oak trees that studded the land on both sides of the river between the still overflowing flood channels. She loved the oak trees, with their gnarled shapes and wide shade. The new spring leaves made them more beautiful than ever.

She drove on, with White Star at an easy walk, enjoying the glorious day. Jake lay on the seat beside her, content as always just to be near her. Her spirits rose. She thought of the new baby in Polly's arms yesterday, then looked at the signs of spring all around her.

Yes, she thought, plants die and new plants grow. Leaves fall, and new leaves come. People die and babies are born. She thought of Minerva, of Sinclair, of Michael. We grieve for those we lose, but we go on living. That's God's plan.

Kansas seemed so far away, so many lifetimes ago, even a different world. Alfred's face now rose in place of Lew's. Could she really ever again find the happiness she had shared with Lew?

A hawk soared over the field by the side of the road, where young shoots of wheat grew. She watched him, admiring the grace with which he rode the air currents. As he swooped and rose with a rabbit in his talons, she thought again how nature, with all of its beauty, still showed streaks of cruelty. The rabbit, of course, she smiled to herself, had been attracted to the tender stalks of the newly sprouted wheat, and the hawk seemed to know he would find a rabbit there. So the hawk saved the wheat for the farmer, but hawks, in turn, also ate chickens and young lambs, so farmers often shot the hawks as pests. She shook her head at the paradox. She hated to see anyone shoot hawks. They were such magnificent birds.

She always relished the trip to Sacramento, seeing the fields and orchards, the homes of farmers with their neatly tended gardens. The sun rose higher, warming the air, sparkling like diamonds on the water standing in low spots along the way.

As she reached the city, she started White Star down 'J' Street towards Annie's hat shop. Each time she came, it seemed to her the buildings reached closer and closer to Brighton. She chuckled as the thought of Brighton reminded her of Alf's accounts of the fight between the bull and the bear.

Sacramento had certainly changed since that long ago day in 1850. She could just hear the uproar if any of the present day city fathers and custodians of the morality of the citizens heard of any such enterprises!

"Look, Jake," she told the dog half asleep on the seat beside her as they passed between Ninth and Tenth Streets. "They've almost rebuilt the whole block. Remember when we visited last fall? The only thing left after the fire was Dr. Bowman's Drug Store and Mr. Bollman's Grocery." Jake opened one eye and stretched.

As she watched the builders, she wondered why they did not rebuild with brick. The brick construction had saved the drug store and the grocery when the entire remainder of the block burned. Sacramento boasted several fine brickyards. Annie had told her all about the fire. Since her own shop stood only six or seven streets away, Annie had feared the fire would spread. Fortunately, Sacramento's fine Fire Department, with its modern engines, had restricted the fire to just the one block.

She turned left on Fourth Street, then left again onto 'K'. Dismounting from the buggy, she looped the reins over the small bronze horse head, green with age, that stood on the hitching post in front of the neatly painted shop. The sign read 'A. Hurd, Milliner - Fine Hats and Accessories'.

Two well dressed ladies emerged as Matilda approached the door. With a pleasant nod and smile to the departing customers, Matilda entered the building. A bell tinkled as she crossed the portal.

"'Tilda!" Annie exclaimed, rushing forward to embrace her friend in a warm hug. "It's been so long!"

"October 14," Matilda smiled. "I remember the date because it was only two days after the *Yosemite* blew her boiler at Rio Vista, and you were still all atwitter over it."

Annie laughed. "Because I took that very same steamer to San Francisco on her previous trip. Suppose I had been on her when she blew?"

"Yes, scary thought, isn't it? I've wanted to make that trip myself, but this is the second one to blow in two years. Maybe I'll wait until they find out what's causing the problems." She looked around the small room, piled high with finished hats, hats in various stages of construction, and hat accessories. Another counter held a selection of gloves and shoes. "I see you've expanded your line. Business must be good."

"Oh, yes." Annie's eyes sparkled. "Ever since Governor Low's wife ordered a hat from me last year I've gotten business from a number of society ladies. Did you see the two ladies who just left? One of them was Mrs. Bernard. Her husband owns the Eureka Carriage Factory, and she is one of the leading lights of society. Annie!" she called to the shy child peeping around the corner. "Come and give your Aunt Matilda a kiss."

As Matilda lifted the little girl into her arms and hugged her, she saw the tears in her mother's eyes.

"When you're done shopping, 'Tilda, come back and see me. I want to talk to you about little Annie."

"Of course I'll be back. I want you to make my wedding hat!"

"Does this mean you've set the date?"

Matilda shook her head. "Not yet. Alfred's still trying to sell his mining claim in Placerville. But when it sells, I have to be ready!"

Annie laughed. "And with the best hat I've ever made."

Matilda spent a pleasant two hours looking at yard goods, finally selecting a length of finely woven blue cotton. She would have preferred satin, but it cost too dearly. She settled on blue, for that was Alfred's favorite color. He told her it was because her eyes were so blue. She blushed as she held the material under her chin. Alfred always said such pretty things. But the color in the cloth did bring out the blue in her eyes, so she bought it.

When she returned to Annie's shop, they spent some time selecting a hat to match the material. Another customer came in, so Matilda entertained little Annie while the child's mother waited on the newcomer.

After the young woman left, Annie chuckled softly. "I do get all kinds of customers. That was Bridgette. She works the steamers between San Francisco and Sacramento."

Works the steamers? Matilda knew she must have looked blank, for Annie laughed at her expression.

"I forgot how sheltered you are. She's one of the women that travel back and forth on the boats. Some men like to be entertained on the trip, if you get my meaning, and are willing to pay for companionship."

Matilda gasped in shock. "And it's allowed?"

"Oh, yes, even encouraged . Some of the captains take a percentage. Others just charge for the cabin. Some pretend the women don't exist and ignore them." She grinned wryly. "The women prefer those kind. Then they can keep all the money for themselves." Annie met Matilda's eyes. "I've learned not to judge these women too harshly. If I hadn't been so good makin' hats . . . ." She shrugged. Matilda's mind flew to Cora, that long ago day in Dobytown. "Yes," she said, nodding her head slowly. "We should never rush to judge."

They sat in silence for a moment, then Annie, her voice serious, said, "And that's why I wanted to talk to you."

"Me? About Bridgette?"

Annie laughed at the puzzled look on Matilda's face. "No, not about Bridgette. About little Annie. You see, I've thought long and hard. If I was to take bad sick, or die, especially while she's so little . . . ." Her voice trailed off. "You see, I've got no kin out here." Her eyes narrowed. "And I'd never let my father get his hands on her," she spat. "Ben was an orphan, so he never knew any of his kin. I'd hate to see her wind up in an orphan's home, or worse.

"I been to see a lawyer," the girl continued. "Got a will all drawn up proper. All I need is for you to agree." Tears filled Annie's eyes as she fondled the soft curls of the child at her side. "You're the closest to family I've got."

Matilda gathered Annie in her arms and whispered. "I hope you live to be as old as my mother. But if you don't, I'll see little Annie is cared for. I promise." She stepped back and smiled into Annie's eyes. "Besides, you may get married again."

Annie shook her head. "My Ben's waitin' for me in Heaven, 'Tilda. He's the only man I'll ever love."

Back in the wagon, on the way home, with the afternoon sun slanting into the buggy, Matilda thought long and hard about Annie's response to her suggestion of a second marriage.

"Am I being disloyal to Lew by marrying Alfred, Jake?" she asked. The old dog lay on the seat beside her, soaking up the sun. He opened one eye, slapped the seat with his tail, and closed the eye again with a long sigh. She laughed and stroked his head. "You loved Lew, too, Jake. I think you understand."

Suddenly, the memory of Alfred's kisses washed over her, sending a thrill surging through her body. She longed to feel his arms around her, to feel his body pressed against hers. She shook her head and tried to dispel the feeling, but it would not dissipate.

"Sorry, Annie," she muttered. "Sorry, Lew. Life is for the living and living is what I want to do right now."

With a sudden zest for life, she jiggled the reins. "Come on, White Star," she cried. "Hold on, Jake. Let's live! Let's run!"

White Star threw back her head and took off. Matilda shook her hair loose and let it fly in the wind. Let the neighbors say what they wanted. She, Matilda Randolph Baldwin, planned to live life to its fullest.

She was still laughing when she pulled White Star to a halt in front of her horrified brother and mother.

Chapter 69

June, 1867

ON THE MORNING of June 15, Matilda stepped out onto the porch. Jake did not greet her as usual and she felt a twinge of fear. "Jake," she called. "Where are you? It's breakfast time."

No response. She took a deep breath. Face reality, Matilda Baldwin, she told herself. He's eleven years old. How long do dogs live? If the dog had died in the night, she needed to find him. Mary would be devastated if she found him dead. Matilda tried not to think of her own emotions. After all, she tried to tell herself as she searched, he is just a dog.

Right, she thought, tears springing into her eyes. Just the dearest, most faithful . . . . She stopped herself and blinked to clear her vision.

A thorough search around the house and windmill revealed nothing, so she headed for the barn. White Star whickered a restless greeting and stamped her foot. Four Stockings and Long Legs paced nervously around their stalls.

"What's the matter, White Star?" She stopped for a few moments to calm the horses. The two colts continued to shiver, but did cease their pacing. All three stared toward the back of the barn.

Circling the pile of hay, she came upon the cause of their unease. A coyote stood there, in a menacing pose. Jake faced the intruder, low growls sounding deep in his throat. Matilda grabbed the first implement at hand, a three pronged pitchfork, and, with a yell of defiance, headed for the coyote. When he saw her charging at him, he turned and ran.

She dropped the pitchfork and gathered Jake into her arms. "My brave Jake," she murmured against his silken ears. "I'm so glad you're all right. I was so worried." Tears of relief streamed down her face and Jake whined as he licked them off. She closed her eyes to protect them from his ministrations and continued to hug and pet him.

Only after he calmed down did she see what he protected so staunchly.

Against the pile of hay nestled a calico cat, secure under his fierce protection. Sixteen tiny paws massaged the mother cat's belly as her eight new kittens, in variegated colors, nursed and purred in contentment.

"Oh, Jake," she sighed. "Look at all the babies! And you stood guard. You're wonderful." She hugged the old dog until he grunted in protest, trying all the while to lick her face. She heard laughter and looked up to see Alf standing over her.

"Telegram from Placerville," he teased, holding it over his head, out of her reach. "That is, if you can stop hugging Jake long enough to read it."

"You wretch! Give it to me at once." She scrambled to her feet and jumped for the envelope. Grabbing his arm, she pulled it down.

"Easy, easy," he laughed. "Here, take the blasted thing."

She tore it open, trying to get her breathing back under control, and scanned the two lines on the page:

"PropertysoldtodayJune14stopHowdoesJune19
wedding date soundstopLoveAlfred"

Happiness surged through her. "Send my reply at once," she ordered the grinning Alf. "One word: Wonderful."

Matilda floated into the house. Opening the armoire where the blue dress hung, ready and waiting, she held it up in front of herself and looked in the mirror. Her cheeks flushed with excitement, her blue eyes enhanced by the color in the dress, she hardly recognized the image in the mirror. She had never thought of herself as particularly attractive, but had to admit the glow on her face did make her seem almost beautiful.

Little Lewis stood in the doorway watching, his eyes wide with awe. "Pretty, Mama," he nodded, his voice solemn. "Real pretty."

The next few days flew by in a flurry of preparations. Alf, dispatched to make the rounds of the neighborhood, invited everyone to the wedding. Polly and Sarah, with the help of several neighbors, started cooking food for the expected crowd.

"Sure you don't want to use the church?" Betsy Ann asked as Matilda started decorating the area around the huge oak that stood beside the house.

"With this magnificent tree right here? This is more God's creation than any stuffy building. I married Lew under a tree, remember?" Matilda hung another ribbon from the stack in her basket, humming a little tune.

Betsy Ann just shook her head and returned to the house.

Alfred arrived on the 17th. His hazel eyes danced as he swung Matilda off her feet in a bear hug and gave her a rousing kiss. The three children also clamored for their hugs. As he tried to hold all three at once, he said, "Mr. Short is willing to rent eighty acres to us until we can buy our own place. It's just up the road a piece from here. I spoke to Haskell Swain. He and Amanda have that two hundred acres by the school and they want to sell it as soon as they get the title clear. Right now, it's all tied up in the court fight between McCauley and Harvey and all the rest of that bunch."

"We don't want to lose our land like Abe did in that squabble between the Chabolla heirs."

"We won't. We aren't buying anything until it's settled. We'll just farm this eighty acres I've rented and save our money. I got $1150 dollars from Charlie Brewster for the property in Placerville. That should give us a good start."

The morning of the nineteenth finally arrived, and Matilda rose at dawn. A light, westerly breeze from the delta promised a cooler day, a blessed relief from the heat of the past few days. She walked around the outdoor tables, securing the linen coverings. She smiled with tears in her eyes as she touched the one her sister Minerva had given her as a wedding present so many lifetimes ago in Kansas. She fingered the delicate embroidered flowers in the intricate pattern. Minerva always had such a knack with her needle. She thought of Abe, who showed no interest in marrying again, despite the effort of raising four children by himself. Over a year had passed since Minerva's death, and a number of single women showed a willingness to become the second Mrs. Dyer, but he remained politely aloof.

Jake ambled along beside her while she made her rounds of the tables. "California has been good to us, Jake," she said, "even though we have lost Minerva, Sinclair, and Michael. Remember how we hated Kansas winters? Here we've had good crops, we've had a good life, and we'll soon have our own home again." She stroked the dog's ears. "Let's go see White Star and the kittens you rescued from that coyote."

In the barn, White Star whinnied a welcome. Matilda pulled a lump of sugar from her pocket and White Star daintily nibbled it. Matilda wrapped her arms around the horse's neck. Jake flopped down beside her feet. Her mind went back to the day Lew rode up, White Star just a filly and Jake a puppy with his head poking out over the rim of the saddle pack. She still remembered the thrill she felt when Lewis took her hand.

The good times and the bad times rolled through her mind. The birth of the children, the loss of Baby John, the joyful times with her Pottawatamie friends, the chief who always begged for her cookies. The prairie fires, the floods, the blizzards, then the beauty of a Kansas spring, with the wild flowers in bloom. Walking along the Big Blue, fluffy white clouds reflected in the clear blue water, with throngs of birds singing in the trees.

Her eyes softened as she looked down at Jake, recalling how he had struggled at her side, footsore and weary, over mile after mile of endless desert. She remembered White Star so thin her bones protruded, her coat gray under the layer of dust from the trail.

And when they stood on the top of the mountain and looked out over Lake Tahoe! Realizing the desert was behind them, that the road went downhill from there, through beautiful pine trees, until they reached their goal: the Sacramento Valley.

She dropped to her knees and hugged the dog. White Star nuzzled the back of her neck.

"I'm so glad I have both of you with me. We'll start a new life together, just like we did in Kansas."

"Mama." Mary stood in the doorway. "Are you talking to the dog again? Grandma said I'd find you here. She says we've got a lot of work to do."

Matilda laughed and stood up. She patted White Star and kissed the soft muzzle.

"Right, Darling, we do have a lot to do if we're going to get married this afternoon." She took Mary's hand and they turned towards the house. Jake trailed along behind. As they stepped from the barn, the sun rose above the trees behind the house, driving away the last of the shadows, bathing the whole scene with a golden light.

She smiled. It was going to be a beautiful day.

Enjoy AAA discounts and these value added offers.

Up to $15 off weekend
All car classes
PC# 119766

$20 off weekly
All car classes
PC# 107520

$35 off weekly
Collections vehicles
PC# 113691

Important Rental Information: **Your AAA CDP# and the applicable PC# (above) must be included in the reservation.** Only one PC code may be used per rental transaction. Subject to availability, these offers are redeemable at participating Hertz locations in the U.S, Canada and Puerto Rico. Hertz Green, Fun and Prestige Collection vehicles are available at select locations. Not all vehicles, vehicle equipment and services are available at all locations. These offers have no cash value, may not be used with Pre-pay Rates, Tour Rates or Insurance Replacement Rates and may only be used with a AAA CDP#. No other CDP#, certificate, voucher, offer or promotion applies. Hertz age, driver, credit and rate qualifications for the renting location apply and the car must be returned to that location. Taxes, tax reimbursement, age differential charges, fees and optional service charges, such as refueling, are not included. Discounts apply to time and mileage charges only. Discounts in local currency on redemption. At the time of rental, present your AAA membership card or Hertz/AAA Discount Card for identification. Offers are valid for vehicle pick-up on or before 12-31-2009. Hertz rents Fords and other fine cars.

Visit hertz.com, or AAA.com/hertz for low web rates,
call your AAA travel office or
call the Hertz/AAA Desk at 1-800-654-3080.

BIBLIOGRAPHY
for Matilda's Story

A Collection from **Harper's Magazine** *The Midwest* (Reed International, 1991) Kansas, pp 146-162

Barton, O.S. *Three Years With Quantrill* (University of Oklahoma Press, 1992)

Bird, Roy *The Land and The People, The Settlement of Riley County* (Riley County Historical Museum)

Bowles, Samuel *Across the Continent* (Samuel Bowles & Company, 1865)

Burland, Rebecca, Burland, Edward A *True Picture of Immigration* (R.R. Donnelly & Sons, 1936)

Burnett, Peter *Recollections and Opinions of an Old Pioneer* (D. Appleton & Co., 1880)

Burton, Richard F. *The City of the Saints* (Harper & Brothers, 1862)

Childers, Roberta *Magee Station and the Churchill Chronicles* (Jamison Station Press, 1985)

Colt, Mrs. Marian Davis *Went to Kansas* (L. Ingalls & Co., 1862)

Crawford, Charles Howard *Scenes of Earlier Days* (Quadrangle Books, 1898)

Crome, Alice *Tour Guide to the Old West* (Quadrangle, The New York Times Book Co., 1977)

Curran, Harold *Fearful Crossing* (Great Basin Press, 1982)

Custer, Milo *The Original Town of Bloomington, Illinois and its First Proprietors* (Bloomington, 1843)

Custer, Milo *Old Family Records, Number Five* (Compiled and printed by Milo Custer, 1919)

Dahlberg, C.V. *Settlement of the Blue Valley in the Vicinity of Randolph* (March, 1923)

Dana, Julian *River of Gold* (J.J. Little & Ives, 1919)

Dary, David True *Tales of Old Time Kansas* (University Press of Kansas, 1984) pp 39-56, 139-147

Delano, Alonzo *Life on the Plains and Among the Diggings* (Miller, Orton & Milligan, 1854)

Dick, William B. *Encyclopedia of Practical Receipts and Processes* (H. Keller & Co., 1872)

Eckerson, Katie "Babe" *Only Yesterday* (Grape Press Printing, 1981)

Fehrenbacher, Don E. *A Basic History of California* (D. Van Nostrand Co., 1964)

Fehrenbacher, Don and Tuturow, Norman, *California An Illustrated History* (D. Van Nostrand Company, 1968)

Foster-Harris *The Look of the Old West* (Bonanza Books, 1954)

Gerson, Noel B. *Harriet Beecher Stowe* (Popular Library, 1976)

Haines, Aubrey *Historic Sites Along the Oregon Trail* (The Patrice Press, 1981) pp 1-231

Harlan, Jacob Wright *California '46 to '88* (The Bancroft Company, 1888)

Hastings, Lansford W. *The Immigrants Guide to Oregon and California* (Applewood Books, 1845)

Holiday, J.S. *The World Rushed In* (Simon and Schuster , 1981)

Hutchinson, W.H. *California* (American West Publishing Co., 1967)

Ise, John *Sod and Stubble* (University of Nebraska Press, 1936)

Kemble, John Haskell *The Panama Route, 1848-1869* University of South Carolina Press, 1990

Kloss, Jethro *Back to Eden* (Back to Eden Publishing Company, 1988)

Langdon, William Chauncy *Everyday Things in American Life 1776-1876* (Charles Scribner & Son, 1941)

Lockwood, Charles, *Tourists in Gold Rush California* (California History Magazine, Winter 80/81) pp 315-333

Log Cabin Days (**Riley County Historical Society,** 1929) pp 24-26

Marcy, Randolph B. *The Prairie Traveler* (Applewood Books, 1859)

Mattes, Merrill J. *The Great Platte River Road* (University of Nebraska Press, 1969)

Old Settlers of McLean County (Published **Bloomington,** Illinois, June 1, 1874)

Paden, Irene D. *The Wake of the Prairie Schooner* (Southern Illinois University Press, 1943)

Panati, Charles *Extraordinary Origins of Everyday Things* (Harper & Row, 1987)

Potter, David Morris *Trail to California, The Overland Journal of Vincent Geiger and Wakeman Bryarly* (Yale University Press, 1945)

Reed, G. Walter *History of Sacramento County* (Historic Record Company, 1923)

Rolle, Andrew F. *California, A History* (Thomas Crowell Company, 1969)

Royce, Sarah *A Frontier Lady* (Yale University Press, 1932)

Ryder, Lyn *Tragedy at the Little Blue* (Prairie Lark Publications, 1993)

Schlissel, Lillian *Women's Diaries of the Westward Journey* (Schocken Books, 1982)

Slagg, Winifred *Riley County, Kansas* (Winifred Slagg, 1968)

Snow, Horace *"Dear Charlie" Letters* (Mariposa County Historical Society, 1979)

Stewart A.A. *Riley County: Some Interesting Facts About its Early History* (Manhattan Homestead, March 1897)

Stewart, A.E. *Some Pioneers of Randolph, Illinois, John Gardner Randolph* (McLean County History, Sketches of Old Settlers. Handwritten copy, undated)

Stewart, Clark Emerson *On Randolph Hills* (Heyworth Star, 1843)

Stewart, Elinore Pruitt *Letters of a Woman Homesteader* (University of Nebraska Press, 1961)

Stewart, George R. *The California Trail* (McGraw Hill, 1962)

Stone, Irving *Men to Match my Mountains* (Doubleday, 1956)

Stratton, Joanna *Pioneer Women* (Simon and Schuster, 1981)

Taylor, Bayard, *El Dorado, or Adventure in the Path of Empire* (The Rio Grande Press, 1967)

The History of McLean County ((William LeBaron Jr. Co., Chicago, 1879)

Thompson & West *History of Sacramento County* (Thompson & West, 1880)

Todd, Edgeley Woodman, *A Doctor on the California Trail, The Diary of Dr. John Hudson Wayman, 1852* (Old West Publishing Company, 1971)

Townley, John M. *The Overland Stage* (Jamison Station Press, 1994)

True, Charles Frederick *The Overland Memoir of Charles Frederick True, A Teenager on the California Trail* (McNaughton & Gunn, 1966)

Twain, Mark *Roughing It* (Penguin Books, 1962)

Upton, Charles Elmer *Pioneers of El Dorado* (Charles Elmer Upton, Placerville, 1906)

Visscher, William Lightfoot *The Pony Express* (Outbooks, 1980)

Warp, Harold *A History of Man's Progress* (Harold Warp Pioneer Village, 1978)

Warp, Harold *500 Fascinating Facts* (Harold Warp Pioneer Village, 1992)

Webb, Michelle R. *My Folks Came in a Covered Wagon* (Capper Press, 1956)

Werner, Emmy E. *Pioneer Children on the Journey West* (Westview Press, 1995)

White, Stewart Edward   *The Story of California* (Doubleday, Doran & Company, 1932)

White, Stewart Edward   *The Forty-Niners* (Yale University Press, 1918)

Williams, Jacqueline   *Wagon Wheel Kitchens* (University of Kansas Press, 1993)

Williams, R.H.   *With the Border Ruffians* (John Murray, London, 1907) pp 73-226

Winther, Oscar Osburn   *Via Western Express & Stagecoach* (Stanford University Press, 1945)

Woodward, Sarah,   Personal Account written for her family

APPENDIX I

Randolph Genealogy

Children of John Gardner Randolph, son of Thomas and Hannah Randolph, and Elizabeth Ann Stringfield, daughter of John and Sarah Boydston Stringfield.

1. James Brittian (**Britt**), born 10-15-1818
   Married Sarah Evans, born 1817, on 7-23-1838
   Children: Sarah, born 1840
   Minerva, died 10-8-184?,
   age 1 yr, 1 mo, 11 days, b. Stewart Cem.
   William, born 1844
   Gardner, born 1846
   Owen, born 1849

2. **Temperance**, born 2-14-1820, died 6-4-1851,
   buried in Stewart Cemetery
   Married Josh Tovrea 11-18-1838
   He remarried, to Julia Moore,
   and died in 1862 in Civil War
   Children: Sarah, born 1842
   Henry R., born 1848

3. **William**, born 12-10-1822
   Married Mary (Polly) Cottrell (born 2-9-1829)
   in August 1846,
   Children: William, Jr., born 1848
   Michael, born 12-15-1850,
   died 12-17-1866 b. Hicksville Cmty
   John Sinclair (Jack), born 1855
   Frank
   Susan, born 1859
   Mary, born 1858
   Margaret Ann (Maggie), born 2-11-1862
   Samuel, born 1864
   Bud, (Michael Brittan), born 4-29-67

4. **Sarah Boydston**, born 10-11-1824
     Married Albert Welch 10-22-1846
     Children: Lawson D. Welch, born 12-2-1847
                         Married Arabella Lernen
               Elizabeth, born 1849 (died young? No records)
               John
               Matilda
               Rachel

5. **Thomas C.**, born 7-28-1826

6. **Samuel Thomson**, born 3-22-1828
     Never married

7. **Alfred**, born 7-15-1830

8. **John Sevier**, born 6-15-1832
     Married Mary Anne Tate (b. 11-7-1841) on 11-6-1861
     Children: William, born 9-1-1862, died 5-26-1863
               Joshua Alfred, born 4-15-1864
               Matilda Bell, born 9-24-1865
               George Thomas, born 5-2-1867

9. **Caroline**, born 5-3-1834
     Married (1) Tommy Evans 8-22-1854,
                                 who died 9-24-1858
               (His first wife, Susan, died 8-5-1853. They had
               two sons, John 2-1-1847, and Eli)
     Children: Rebecca, born 1855
               Sarah (Sally), born 1857
               Anna Thomas, born 1858, died age 5,
                                 12-15-1863 in Kansas
     Married (2) Ely Robertson, born 1832, on 6-26-1860
     Children: Belle, born 1865
               Minnie, born 1867

10. **Matilda Virginia**, born July 21, 1836
    Married (1) Lewis Clark Baldwin 9-1-1856
         died 8-19-1863, bur. Randolph KS
    Children: John O., born 6-27-1857, died 1-27-1859
       Mary Jane, born 10-6-1859
       Elizabeth Ann, born 12-7-1861
       Lewis Gardner, born 10-28-1863
    Married (2) Alfred Wheelock 6-19-1867

11. **Sinclair**, born 1-27-1839, died 8-9-1865,
         buried Hicksville Cemetery
    Never married

12. **Minerva Elizabeth**, born 8-23-1841, died 5-27-1866,
         bur. Hicksville Cmty
    Married Abraham Oakes Dyer, (b. 11-18-1833)
         on 12-7-1856
    Children: Laura, born Nov. 1859
       Anna
       James William, born 9-16-1862
       Charles H. ("Too Tall Charlie") 3-13-1864
       One baby died in infancy

13. **Andrew**, born 1843, died in infancy

APPENDIX II
Chronology
1796 to 1836

1796.   Gardner Randolph born March 16, in the hills of Randolph County, in North Carolina. Son of Thomas and Hannah Randolph, second cousin of John Randolph of Roanoke

1801.   Gardner orphaned at age 5. His father, Thomas Randolph, reported killed by an Indian in the Battle of Tippecanoe. Taken in by uncle named Wilson who moved the family from North Carolina to Tennessee.

1810.   Age 14. Forced to work, not allowed to go to school, ran away from home because of the uncle's harsh treatment.

1814.   Age 18. Gardner in battle of Horseshoe Bend under Major Peacock in Gen. Andrew Jackson's campaign to exterminate the Creek Indians. 750 of 900 Creeks slain. Gardner grappled with one, and killed the Creek with his own tomahawk. After the battle, Gardner found 16 bullet holes in the shirt wrapped in his knapsack.

1818.   Gardner marries Elizabeth Ann (Betsy Ann) Stringfield, daughter of John and Sarah (Boydston) Stringfield 2-15-1818, Morgan Co., Alabama
        James Brittain (Britt) Randolph born 10-15-1818

1819.   Stringfield clan decides to move to Illinois with sons James, Sevier, Alfred Moore (A.M.), daughters Fanny, Betsy Ann, with husband Gardner, and Delilah, with husband James Burleson.

1820.   Temperance Randolph born 2-14-1820

1822.   January 5. Betsy Ann's father, John Stringfield dies of malaria (ague)
        Betsy Ann & Gardner, with her sister Delilah and husband, James Burleson, leave the Sangamon, looking for less swampy land, just before John Stringfield dies. Settle in Randolph's Grove on the Kickapoo River
        William Randolph born, 12-10-1822. First white child born in McLean County

1823.   Sevier, age 22, and Arthur Moore (called A.M.), age 15, Stringfield, bros of Betsy Ann, follow with her mother and sister Fanny, age 16, who later marries Jesse Funk. Settle in Blooming Grove James Stringfield, uncle of Betsy Ann, Methodist minister, leads first religious services in Randolph's Grove.

1824.   Sarah Randolph born, 10-11-1824

1825.   Young stranger named Sattlefield killed by lightning, becoming the first adult white to die in the new settlement. Buried in Stewart cemetery.
         Built larger cabin with two rooms. First home to have board window and door frames, plus a cupboard and a free-standing bed.
         Gardner borrowed a whip saw from Springfield to make them.
         Gardner buys cow in return for $20 in labor, splitting 4000 rails. Cow dies one week later.
         Built a barn for his horses. Moved it when manure got too high.
         Jesse Funk marries Betsy Ann's sister, Fanny Stringfield

1826.   Thomas Randolph born, 7-24-1826

1827.   Alfred Wheelock born in Salisbury, Vermont

1828.   Samuel Randolph born, 3-22-1828
         Fall: Betsy Ann's mother, Sarah Boydston Stringfield dies in Galena

1829.   William Curtis Stewart born 2-8-29. Son of Samuel & Jane

1830.   Alfred Randolph born, 7-15-1830

1830 - 1831.
         Winter of the 'Deep Snow'. Snow reached depth of 15 feet.
         Gardner spent winter in bed with fever. Neighbor John Moore cut wood, pounded hominy for the family.

1831.   Spring. Snow melted, causing extensive flooding, followed by severe epidemic of fever and ague, thought due to turning over rich soil for the first time.
         Blackhawk Wars begin. Sauk and Fox Indians led by Chief Blackhawk of the Sauks
         Gardner sent with Ebenezer Rhodes and a Dawson to find intentions of Delaware and Kickapoo, determined settlers were in no danger.
         Gardner made road supervisor of Townships 22 and 23.

1831. September: Methodists hold first camp meeting in Randolph's Grove. Rev. Peter Cartwright and Rev Mr. Latta, among others, were speakers.

Inhabitants of Randolph's Grove: Gardner Randolph & family, A.M. Stringfield & family members, James Burleson & family, Jesse Funk, M. Dickson, W. Gaines.

Sevier Stringfield builds a grist mill with stones hand-hewn from prairie boulders

Gardner named to school commission

1832. Family took in fugitive from fatal 'Stillman's Run' who gave everyone measles

1832. John Randolph born 6-15-1832

Gardner member of first Grand Jury in McLean County, with Isaac Funk, Asahel Gridley, and Aaron Foster.

1833. All of Indian land taken by state at the end of the Blackhawk War

Randolph's Grove Post Office established 7-26-1833

1834. Caroline Randolph born 5-15-1834

Gardner, with Jesse Sutton and F. Barnard appointed to lay out a road through Randolph's Grove

Samuel Stewart builds first brick house in Randolph's Grove. (Still standing).

1835. Albert Welch arrives in Randolph's Grove

James & Delilah Burleson return to Alabama, then move on to Texas where he becomes a Colonel in a regiment of Texas Rangers.

1836. Matilda's Story begins

ILLINOIS

1836 to 1854

1836. Matilda born 7-21-1836
       James Burleson participates in Texas War of Independence

1837. United States Bank suspended.

1838. Britt Randolph marries Sarah Evans, 7-23-1838
       Temperance Randolph marries Joshua Tovrea, 11-18-1838
       John Hanley Stewart marries Jane Evans, sister of Tommy Evans
       and Sarah Evans Randolph

1839. Sinclair born 1-24-1839

1840. Census shows Josh & Temperance childless, Britt and Sarah have
       one girl under 5 (Sarah)

1841: Minerva born 8-3-1841
       Samuel Stewart dies, Jan 8, 1841

1842. Failures all over, prices very low

1843. Andrew born, dies in infancy

1844. Slave auction in Missouri
       Longest winter. Lasts from November until May

1846. William Randolph marries Mary (Polly) Cottrell, August
       Sarah Randolph marries Albert Welch, a grocer in Bloomington,
       on 10-22-1846
       Owen Evans dies 8-20-1846, father of Tommy Evans, Sarah Evans
       Randolph, and Jane Evans Stewart. Gardner & Britt witness will

1849. Alfred Wheelock goes from Vermont to California via Isthmus of
       Panama. Arrives in San Francisco in July of 1849 on *'Capitol'* out
       of Boston.

1850. Alf, Sam, and Britt Randolph migrate to California. Listed in 1850
       El Dorado Co. census
       William Hendrix also goes to Placerville. With Randolph brothers
       (?) Probably.
       Sam carves his name in Register Cliff, near present day Guernsey,
       Wyoming, enroute.
       Britt leaves Sarah and four children in Randolph's Grove.
       William & Mary's son Michael born 12-15-1850.

1850. October: Illinois census values Gardner Randolph property at $4000, occupation farmer.

Lists Weldon Cross, (or Crose) age 6, living with Gardner's family.

Also lists Thomas Evans living with first wife, Susan, age 19, and children John, age 4, and Eli, age 2.

December: Asahel Gridley elected to Illinois State Senate.

1851. Temperance dies, 6-4-1851.

State of Illinois grants charter to Alton-Sangamon (later named Illinois Central) Railroad in return for 7% of gross earnings.

Alfred Randolph forms partnership with Alfred Wheelock in mine claim in Placerville.

1852. Sam Randolph buys ranch in Hicksville, raises wheat and cattle.

Britt apparently returned to Illinois about the same time. (?)

Sevier Stringfield left Illinois, settled in Santa Barbara. Son Daniel Kidder an infant.

Will Randolph and family emigrate to Hicksville, California

Temperance's widower, Joshua Tovrea, marries Julia Moore, dau of John Moore.

1853. Tommy Evans' first wife, Susan, dies August 5, age 23.

Spring: Samuel Dyer, with sons Abraham and James, moves to Juniata KS to run the Government ferry across the Big Blue River. Brings the rest of his family in the fall.

1854. Caroline marries Tommy Evans, 8-22-1854, and they move to Lexington, Illinois, NE of Randolph's Grove.

Family migrates to Kansas, probably late in year.

Sells Randolph property in Illinois (500 acres), some to Houser, some to Bell.

Will Randolph owns property in Sacramento County, in San Jon de los Mokelumnes Grant.

KANSAS

1854 to 1864

1854. Settle at junction of Fancy Creek (Gardner names it) and Big Blue River

1855. First corn crop grown in Riley County. Sold for $1.25 a bushel at Fort Riley.

1856. Gardner named Postmaster of Randolph, Kansas.
Mail route established from Fort Riley to Marysville with stop at Randolph. Post Office is in Randolph residence.
Matilda marries Lewis Clark Baldwin, 9-1-1856, in Randolph, the first marriage in Jackson Township. They settle on part of Gardner's claim on the Big Blue south of Fancy Creek. Gardner names the creek 'Baldwin Creek' for them.
November. Edward and Solomon Secrest and Henry Shellenbaum arrive at Fancy Creek. Build cabin up Fancy Creek from Randolph claim.
Minerva marries Abraham Oates Dyer 12-7-1856, at the Dyer home in Juniata. Move northeast to area around present day Waterville

1857. First religious meeting in the area held in Randolph house.
Spring. Secrests and Shellenbaum move onto Randolph Territory on Fancy Creek, creating conflict with Randolphs.
Gardner lays out town plat for Randolph to defend claims, plus two more, Timber City and Blue City. Hires Mr. Pease to live in cabin built in Randolph. Constructed three other buildings as well.
Abe & Minerva return to Potawattamie County. Get land patent for 340 acres from President Buchanan 5 miles from Randolph, abutting 160 acres of his father, Samuel Dyer
Matilda's first baby, John, born 6-27-1857, the first white child born in Jackson Township
Henry Shellenbaum disputes claim Gardner made in Sinclair's name.
Matilda's brother John elected member of pro-slavery convention which adopts LeCompton Constitution, June 15, 1857.
June: John Randolph kills a buffalo in his corn field
Caroline's daughter Sarah Evans (Sally) born in Lexington, Ill.
John named to County Commissioner's office 10-23-1857.
November: Dahlberg family settles three miles north of Randolph cabin.

1857.   Betsy Ann delivers sister of eight-year-old Carl V. Dahlberg after he
        gets her in the middle of the night. Baby named Clara Josephine.
        December: Vote on LeCompton Constitution held 12-21-57. For
        slavery, 7, against, 14.

1858.   J.K. Whitson and John Kress arrive at Randolph. Oppose Ran-
        dolph plan to make Kansas a slave state. Say they are abolitionists
        and announce it is their plan to drive the Randolphs out. Try to
        'jump' Gardner's claim to town of Randolph. Gardner calls them
        'Black Republicans' and 'Ding Dang Dutch Abolitionists'.

        Severe blizzards in Kansas

        Floods in spring after heavy snowfall

        Alfred Randolph buys first 160 acres on Chabolla Land Grant, near
        Hicksville, moves from Placerville.

        Betsy Ann's uncle James Stringfield, the minister, dies 6-12-1858
        in Illinois.

        Anna Thomas Evans born.

        Caroline's husband, Tommy Evans, dies 9-24-1858. In his will, he
        leaves $255 with his friend Elijah Scott to enable Eli to take Car-
        oline and her three daughters to join her family in Kansas, coming
        by stage to Pekin, by boat on the Illinois River to the Mississippi,
        to St. Louis, then up the Missouri River to Kansas City.

1859.   Quarrel over claim to town of Randolph settled by U.S. Land Office
        in Ogden.

        Britt Randolph loses race to become first to build in Randolph

        Whitson renames Randolph, calls it Waterville, marries Tamar Con-
        dray

        January 27, Matilda's baby John dies of croup

        November. Minerva's daughter Laura born

        October 6, Mary Jane Baldwin born

1860.   Brother Tom migrates to California, buys 100 acres.

        Abe & Minerva Dyer accompany him. Abe sells his 340 acres to
        his sister Lydia and her husband, George Jamison

        Abe buys part of Chabolla land grant in Hicksville

        Alf expands ranch to 250 acres at Hicksville

        1860 census of Dry Creek Twp lists Samuel Randolph, William
        Randolph, and Sevier Stringfield. El Dorado Co. lists A. Wheelock.

        Severe drought and famine in Kansas. No rain from June 1859 to
        November 1860.

        Henry Shellenbaum wins claim dispute with Sinclair.

        Census in Riley county shows Weldon Cross (Crose) age 16 still
        with Gardner and Betsy Ann, as is Emaline Johnson, age 12.

1860.   Caroline marries Ely Robertson, Methodist minister, 6-26-1860, at the home of Gardner Randolph.

Sarah Evans, widow of Owen, mother-in-law of Britt and former mother-in-law of Caroline dies 9-29-1860.

1861.   John Randolph marries Mary Anne Tate, 11-6-1861 in Peru, Nebraska.

Elizabeth Anne Baldwin born December 7, 1861.

1862.   John & Mary Anne's first child, William Gardner, born 9-1-1862

Minerva's son James William (Will) born 9-16-1862 in Hicksville

Joshua Tovrea, widower of Temperance, killed in Civil War in Union Army

John Randolph again appointed County Commissioner in Kansas

1863.   Tax records show Lewis Baldwin owning 200 acres, valued at $855, taxes $16.78, and 169 acres valued at $340, taxes $23.07.

Lewis Baldwin dies in well accident 8-19-1863, age 27, buried in Randolph Cemetery.

Lewis Gardner Baldwin born 10-28-1863.

Anna Thomas Evans, Caroline's third daughter, dies 12-15-1863, age 5, of "brain fever".

Sarah Dyer marries Joseph Woodard, a Union soldier, 6-7-1863.

Abe loses his land when title to Chabolla grant is disputed. Becomes a wagon maker.

1864.   Gardner decides to follow the rest of the family to California

Sells his interests in Town of Waterville (Randolph) to Henry Condray

Start trek with oxen pulling wagons. Sell oxen in Salt Lake City and buy horses.

From Salt Lake, cross Jordan River, south around the Wendover desert, cross Ruby Valley, over Harrison Pass to the Humboldt River Valley, to the Humboldt sink, and down the Forty Mile Desert to the Carson Sink.

Minerva's second son Charles H. born 3-13-1864

John's son Joshua Alfred born 4-15-1864

Annie Hurd born.

CALIFORNIA

1864 to 1867

1864.   Arrive Hicksville, probably sometime in September
Lewis has learned to walk on trip across the prairie
Matilda and her children move in with her brother, Alf, at Hicksville
Parents and Sinclair move in with him also.
Alfred Wheelock buys five acres in the city of Placerville from O.M.
Taylor, on Sept. 28 for $400.

1865.   August 9. Sinclair killed when kicked by horse, ruptured liver
Meets Alfred Wheelock, her brother's partner in the mine
Tax rolls show Matilda owns 1 horse, 2 colts, valued at $175, on
which she pays $4.69 in taxes.

1866.   May 28. Minerva dies, age 24 yrs 9 mo, 12 days
Obituary in San Francisco Daily Evening Bulletin, May 31, 1866
December 2. Gardner Randolph dies
December 17, Monday, Michael, son of William and Polly, dies in
hunting accident. Age 16. Obituary in San Francisco Daily Evening
Bulletin Dec. 20, 1866 and Sacramento Union
Shotgun of neighbor boy, Jonnie Wahl goes off as they are sneaking
up on some geese.

1867.   Matilda marries Alfred Wheelock 6-19-1867, rent 80 acres near
present intersection of Riley and Arno Roads, where they owned 2
wagons, 16 cattle, 2 horses, hogs, fowl, and 1 male dog.
Alfred sells five acres in Placerville to Charles Brewster on June 14
for $1150.

Matilda's Story

About the Author

"The more I re-traced her steps, the more I realized her story should be told." And so *Matilda's Story* was born.

The author, great-granddaughter of Matilda Randolph, grew up in the house where Matilda spent the last thirty years of her life. As a child, she heard many stories. Of a brother hit by a scythe, of uncles killed by horses, of fires and floods, of the death of a child.

In an attempt to preserve these stories for future generations, she began her research into Matilda's life. She unearthed stories about how Matilda baked cookies for the Indians, how she lost two sisters, how, as a widow with three young children, she accompanied her parents on the long trek by wagon across the Oregon-California Trail. Through it all shone the courage of a woman who would not allow the world to defeat her.

Researching for the book led the author back to the place of Matilda's birth in Randolph, Illinois, where a monument erected in 1922 marks the original homesite where her parents founded the first white settlement in McLean County. From there she crossed to Randolph, Kansas, the town her great-great-grandfather, Gardner Randolph, founded on the Big Blue River. Fancy Creek and Baldwin Creek still bear the names he gave them.

Accompanied by her brother, the author followed Matilda's covered wagon trek from Kansas over South Pass to Salt Lake City, across the Jordan River, through Ruby Valley, over Harrison Pass, and into the Valley of the Humboldt. From the sink of the Humboldt, they crossed the Forty Mile Desert to Ragtown, on to Fort Churchill and Carson City, over the Kingsbury Grade to Lake Tahoe, up Johnson's Cutoff, and down the American River to Sacramento.

"The more I grew to know her," Ms Hanson says, "the more I admired her. She must have been a remarkable woman. After all the hardships she suffered, with the loss of so many loved ones, she still wrote, in 1886, 'What matters most is not how long we live, but how well we live our lives for others.' "

The author, a graduate of Stanford University School of Nursing, lives in Southern California with her youngest son, and is in business there with her oldest son. She has been published in professional journals, and several of her short stories have been published or won awards. This is her first novel.

Her second novel, *Susan's Quest*, a historical romance based on some of the research done for *Matilda's Story*, will be published soon.

"Then," the author reports, "by demand of the Hicksville Historical Society, I have to complete *Matilda's Story: The Later Years*."